# THE SIEGE

A NOVEL BY ILLÉS KACZÉR

# THE SIEGE

Translated from the Hungarian by
LAWRENCE WOLFE

THE DIAL PRESS    1953    NEW YORK, N. Y.

COPYRIGHT, 1953, BY ILLÉS KACZÉR
LIBRARY OF CONGRESS CATALOG CARD NO.: 53-5727

DESIGNED BY WILLIAM R. MEINHARDT
PRINTED IN THE UNITED STATES OF AMERICA
BY THE HADDON CRAFTSMEN, SCRANTON, PENNA.

# Contents

## Book One

### FEAR NOT, MY SERVANT JACOB

# Book Two

## THE YELLOW HOUSE

# CONTENTS

# Book One

*"A star has risen from Jacob,*
*Fear not, my servant Jacob."*
                    *Old Jewish Song*

THE LITTLE COVERED wagon went creaking along the road. It came from the north, from the direction of the main Carpathian passes. On Sunday night it was tumbling down dark precipitous inclines. On Monday it travelled in a gale, on Tuesday in pouring rain. On Wednesday the urgency was still upon it. By Thursday it was down in the foothills at last. Farther on, a herd of bison came lumbering up the road, followed by flock after flock of sheep, while a herd of swine came tearing along from behind, with the long whips of the cattle drovers and swine-herds cracking like thunder above the clouds of dust. The little wagon trundled along the edge of the road, was held up, set off again. On the low hills forests of vine-stakes stood sentinel in peaceful array. And down the plain one could already catch in the morning haze of late autumn, between puddles, meadows, willow groves, reed banks, and white and yellow cottages, the gleam of the broad, meandering Tisza. Thank God the worst was over. This was a friendlier world for the traveller.

Now it was Friday, a chilly dawn. The wagon was in a hurry again. It went rattling along in the dust and the low eddying mist

3

which had a gentle upward luminosity. The pony did not look to
see what sort of a road this was, whether a highway, a county
road, or just a serf-trodden local mud-track. The straps were not
so taut as they had been up in the mountain road, and the pony's
hoof fell on soft soil, without a trace of stones or paving. It pulled
and jerked the vehicle over deep clay ruts, across rivulets, through
mire, and over rickety wooden bridges. The cart would tumble
forward, slide back, or sway like a boat in the water.

The Jew Sholem did not look at the road either. Yet he ought to
have looked. But what was there to look at about a ribbon of road
that faded into the mist and seemed endless, whereas it was not
endless? Nothing earthly was endless. The Jew Sholem sat on the
driving-seat like a lay-figure. He shook and swayed, but otherwise
he was immobile. Even the whip in his hand was at rest. Was he
asleep? Perhaps he was only sunk in contemplation. He had much
food for contemplation. Things that were, things to come. And
things that were happening by the will of the Most High beyond
the boundaries of what was and will be.

Suddenly, as though yanked up by the shoulder, he stood up.
Raising his ear-curled, bearded face high, he looked to the right
and left, then behind him over the rush-mat hood, scanning the
sky. He shook his head and sat down again. It was half an hour
or more since the ferry had brought him and his sleeping family
across the river, and he had not yet succeeded in discovering
whether the sun was up, and if not, in what direction it was going
to rise. When he started there were still stars reflected in the Tisza.
Now there were clouds in the sky and the stars were invisible.
Most probably, it was already morning. But Sholem knew nothing
for certain. A pity he did not ask them at the ferry what time it
was and which way was east. If it was morning it was time for
the *Shemah* . . . "Hear, O Israel!" But which way was he to turn
as he gave the cry?

All the ferryman had said was that he had better wait till morning; the roads were uncertain and it was not safe to travel at night.
But he had also directed him to drive as far as the Kallo-Karoly
crossroads and turn left for Karoly. Where was the crossroads?
Perhaps he had already passed it. He simply must reach Karoly
before sunset.

Rabbi Jonah, the Saint of Batyu, had also warned him: The sons of Jacob ought not to travel after dark, for then they are followed by the shadow of Esau. But was it not on account of the Saint that he had wasted most of yesterday? Was it not due to his honeyed wisdom that Sholem and his family had been obliged to travel post-haste through the night? Sholem had intended to spend no more than a brief hour with the Saint, not longer than it would take his wife to water the pony and feed the babies.

"Malkah, dear heart," he had said, "you can harness the pony as soon as you like. I'll be back in an hour, then we can go on."

Malkah duly watered the pony and took him to a meadow to graze. She also gave the babies a wash in the Tisza and fed them. Then she harnessed the pony, greased the wheels, removed a faulty axle-pin and hammered it straight on a stone. Next, she tightened the chains on the backboard to prevent the packing-case that held most of the family's belongings from slipping off. All this must have taken her more than an hour. She waited another hour, then another. She waited till dusk, till dark. But Sholem did not return. The two children got hungry again. Malkah gave them what she could: a small slice of dry bread each, a mouthful of cheese and a squashy apple. She also had to tell a fairy tale to soothe Mailech, who was scared of everything: the vast stretch of glittering water, the homing herds, the "bear-headed" herdsman with his strident horn, the yodelling soldiers in the tavern by the ferry, and also the shooting stars. Above all, he was scared of wolves coming over from Poland and slinking into the villages.

"They don't come here, silly," said his sister, Yiteleh. "You don't have to worry about wolves or pandours or pogroms here. They've got post-chaises here and the Emperor looks after everybody."

Her mother had a lump in her throat. She kept looking out from under the hood of the wagon for her husband—in vain. The sounds of the vesper bell had long died away and they were lighting the flares by the ferry. From the distance came the long-drawn chant of serf women returning from the fields. Now the last cart was being ferried across the river. The tavern had quieted down. The dogs were barking savagely in the dark-

ness. The ferrymen had extinguished the flares, but still no
Sholem. Fortunately, both children had gone to sleep in the
wagon. The watchman could be heard crying: "Ten o'clock and
all is well." Then eleven o'clock, then midnight. It was not until
then that the waiting woman heard the approaching sound of her
husband's heavy knee-boots.

"So this was what you meant by an hour?" she said quietly.
"We'll never get to Karoly."

"Don't you worry, dear heart," said Sholem. "We'll be there
by noon to-morrow. It was important for me to have a word
with the Saint."

Now, as he sat there waiting for the hour of prayer, Sholem
recalled those words. It was important indeed, he thought. Rabbi
Jonah had made him recount the story of the two years that he
and his family had spent in the Polish-Ruthenian mountain village.
How the peasants, those savage sons of the north, despoiled him
and how, unable to forgive him the wrong they had done to
him, they tried to murder him. When Sholem had finished the
Saint closed his eyes and was silent for a long while. Then, in a
voice that sounded deep and remote, as though it came from
another, yet familiar world, he said:

" 'What dost thou see, Jeremiah?' "

" 'I see a seething pot, O Lord, and the mouth thereof is to the
North.' "

The words struck terror into Sholem's heart. What did the
prophet's vision mean? Why, it meant that "peril comes from
the north upon all the inhabitants of the earth."

How often had he himself read and re-read those sentences of
grief-stricken reproof. Yet it was only now, through the intonation of Rabbi Jonah, and through their reference to his own
life, that he really understood them. *The peril comes from the
north.* Sholem felt compensated by that right intonation for
everything, even for the torment of the lost years. With amazement in his heart he realized how simple the truth was and how
close it was to every one, though the ordinary mortal could see
it only by the light kindled by a man of God. True, Rabbi
Jonah was not a great Seer like the blind Rabbi Kunitz of blessed
memory, nor did he even approach the mystery-piercing vision

of Rabbi Phineas Luria. Indeed, he was only a sort of local Saint, to whom people passing through on their way to market brought their minor domestic and business troubles. But when he spoke of the destiny of Israel, Rabbi Jonah would grow in stature and his starry gaze would penetrate the fog of the ages.

"Abraham went south, first to Canaan, and thence to Egypt. Jacob went east. Joshua, with sword and trumpet, marched west. Assur and Kain lived in the north; so did Haman. And Babylon was in the north, Babylon, where we sat by the waters and wept. And it was from the north that Jerusalem was attacked by the abominable Antioch, King of Yawan."

He had been reminded of all this by Rabbi Jonah now—now, two years too late. Had he been reminded two years before, when he fled north, he would have turned back in time and travelled east, settling down in the County of Maramaros, which was so lovely and so full of singing birds. Or he might have moved south, to settle in a village near Kallo—or why not in the town itself? That was where they sang, at the third Sabbath meal, the nostalgic song of the Grand Old Man about the coming dawn of Israel:

> "*Wait, o bird, wait . . .*
> *Won't it be too late? . . .*"

Kallo was to the right, Karoly to the left. Sholem wondered whether the pony had taken the left turn at the crossroads, for he simply had to go to Karoly this time.

It was his wife's idea that they should move there, and she had wanted to do so two years before. Malkah was in pursuit of peace and prosperity. But peace and prosperity usually evaded those in pursuit of them. The Rabbinate of Karoly was held by that learned and holy man, Mosheh Aryeh Oesterreicher. Malkah's brother, Mordechai Nikolsburger, also lived there, and he would be sure to help them to their feet. In any case, where there was a living for ninety Jewish families, there would be bread for the ninety-first. Sholem himself thought of teaching, but Malkah had severely enjoined him to forget about any such hungry career and, instead, get himself a bag and a whistle and go peddling round the villages. However, seeing that he was no business man, peddling might turn out to be a no less hungry career for him than teaching. In any case, after their latest disaster up north, Sholem would not have relished going round the villages. Also, he had an instinctive aversion to his brother-in-law. The Nikols-burgers went with their noses in the air and were intolerably condescending. Proud of their ancestry as well as of their superior social status and their business ability, they seemed to be wanting to stare him right out of the family—him, the descendant of cattle drovers, navvies, and "moles" from Marmaros. To go begging to strangers, to hold out your palm for coppers and now and then to be sent away empty-handed, if not with words of abuse, was no humiliation as compared with having to eat your festive meals at the table of a Nikolsburger.

The mud-track now ran through marshland and there was something sinister and startling about the eerie noises and shadows of the reeds swaying in the dawn. This still held something of the perilous north . . . Gee-up, Kese! It was round here that the highwayman Imre Madar had been rounded up the previous summer. Sholem had been told so by the Saint's other visitors. And it was here too that, eight years before, the Emperor's men had hunted down the three French grenadiers who had turned bandits. They had strayed there from the frozen wastes of Russia and were starved for bread and warmth as well as for female flesh. "That," said Rabbi Jonah with a glint of irony in his wise old eyes, "was one of the rare cases when Austrian arms defeated the Corsican's men without foreign assistance. . . . But you'd better not talk about such things, Sholem, nor even think of them."

"Nor even think of them . . ." Well, he would not have thought of them but for that very warning, and but for that other warn-ing that the seed of Jacob is followed by the shadow of Esau after dark. Was it never going to be light? What if a highwayman did come along! "Your money or your life," he'd bawl. Money! How could a poor hunted Jew have any? Now, there was Kranz-tor, the wealthiest Jew of the Tokay vine country. He had plenty of money. Only Kranztor did not care a fig about highwaymen, be they French grenadiers or plain bandits with cudgels. He did not hesitate to travel even on the stormiest night—to him money

served as a sort of pillar of light. He was guarded by the mus-
keteers of the Emperor himself, with muskets and flares, both
when taking his wine to Breslau or Wallachia and when returning with his casks empty and his pouch bursting with
gold. Sholem's pouch, your honor, is quite empty, though on
Monday it still contained two florins and ten kreuzers. What
have I done with all that money? Wait a moment. There was
three kreuzers for axle-grease, to prevent the axles and the brake
getting hot. Then five kreuzers for plum whisky—not too much
for three days and there is still a drop left in the wooden bottle.
Then milk for the children four times, no, five, that's another
twelve. Tobacco, three. The toll-bridge was twice three and
four, that's ten. Eighteen eggs, that's eight kreuzers. A pound and
a half of tallow candles for the wagon, and also for Friday evening, in case we are late getting into Karoly and Mordechai
hasn't enough—that's another eight kreuzers. The ferry was
twelve kreuzers—ought to have been only six by rights, but you
pay double at night. That's sixty-two kreuzers altogether. Then
I still have one florin and nine kreuzers left. Oh, no, I haven't.
I gave a florin to the Saint's wife, so she can give him a proper
Sabbath. That leaves me nine kreuzers altogether. Of course,
nine kreuzers is nine kreuzers, but it's not worth your honour's
while to hold me up for it, is it? As to the wagon, well, you can
see for yourself how rickety it is, while as to the horse, Master
Highwayman, if I were out to steal a horse, I'd steal a young
fiery colt and not look twice at such a skinny hag.

"At last!" cried Sholem suddenly, breaking off the argument
with the imaginary highwayman. He had caught sight of a streak
of red breaking through the grey cloud on the left at the end of
the horizon. The sun! The streak grew and rose rapidly, flooding
the land with light and colour. Sholem's ear-curls were like
tongues of flame, his red beard like a burning hawthorn bush.
His low forehead, fleshy nostrils and full lips, his whole head
became illuminated. Anxiety and doubt had suddenly dissolved.
Sholem flung the reins over the wheel-stake, stuck the whip next
to them, then extracted from under the seat a threadbare prayer-
bag. The gestures with which he unfolded his old black-bordered
prayer-shawl and draped it over his head and round his body

belonged to the ages. That was how the Greek citizen donned his chlamys, how the dying Roman adjusted his toga over his head. And that was how the nomadic Arab donned his burnous in the desert. However, before Sholem draws the prayer-shawl over his head, and before reciting the appropriate benediction in Hebrew, he announces the impending act in more ordinary language, in Aramaic. He announces it to Him for whom it is meant; to the Name who shall be blest. Alone on the empty road, alone between heaven and earth, and away from the smallest canonical congregation, Sholem is now about to don the holy garment, into which are woven with everlasting threads the six hundred and thirteen laws given to Israel from Mount Sinai. He who wore this garment could be sure that the gates of heaven would open to him on the day of his death.

The month of Cheswan was past and the keen winds of Kislev were whistling their frigid song. The crow and the raven flew blackly over the scene, cawing and croaking a funeral oration over the dead summer. Yet Sholem sat on the wooden driving seat as though it were a cosy ingle-nook. He was warmed by the garment of the spirit. His body swayed rhythmically, while his head kept nodding rapid affirmation, as though emulating the pony. But Sholem's head was not harnessed with the harness of earthly servitude. Over his brow and on his arm next to his heart were the phylacteries, showing that his thoughts and desires were now regulated by contact with the All-Highest.

His fears too, of course. A huge dark figure was emerging from the mist in the distance; all black but for his white linen skirts. Was it a highwayman? As he approached Sholem could see something gleaming over the man's shoulder. Was it a musket? Or a scythe? Or perhaps a hatchet? Kese, the pony, was curious and suspicious, now putting on a spurt of speed, now slowing down. Sholem was neither curious nor suspicious. In his daily colloquy with the Almighty he had just reached the point where he was praying to be spared that day and all other days from meetings with brazen and evil men, false friends, bad neighbors, and unjust judges. Nothing untoward could befall now. In fact, the black fellow was only a hefty young serf on his way to work, with an axe on his shoulder. Raising his tall, tapering sheepskin hat, he bade Sholem a right good morning. Sholem smiled back at him, but went on swaying his body and nodding his head. Of course, the smile alone was for the serf, and perhaps the momentarily rising pitch of the mumbled prayer, the rest was for the Father who has thus brought a sign of encouragement in the person of this harmless peasant.

Unfortunately, the next greeting could not be acknowledged either with a smile or a nod, or a rising inflection or even a wink. This time it was a peasant driving a bullock team. "Lord with ye, Jew," he said kindly, "where are the goods for?" But Sholem did not even look at him. He was standing erect, with feet together and eyes closed, reciting under his breath the Eighteen Benedictions, the summary of all his supplications. And amidst this most private audience with the Almighty, his senses told him that the bullock cart was laden with warm manure. So Sholem had to concentrate on shutting out his awareness of the sacrilegious odor. He had considerable experience in this. Whenever, during prayers, his tactless pony happened to raise its long, flowing tail, Sholem, if in the middle of a loud prayer, would instantly interrupt himself, linking up with an inarticulate mumbling in which the pony might have sensed a mild annoyance. But of course a silent prayer was different. There Sholem could not even mumble.

So the peasant thought that the Jew was too proud to respond to his greeting. But Sholem could not help that. Face to face with the Almighty, he could not pause to explain that the wagon contained no goods, only his family. Indeed, he did not answer even when his wife, from the interior of the wagon, sleepily inquired:

"Sholem, where are we?"

Malkah did not ask again.

Looking out from under the hood, and seeing her man standing erect in his prayer-shawl, she knew at once that he was in the midst of the silent Benedictions, and that she must wait until he "backed away." On the wagon, this was only symbolical, because there was no room to "back away," but in a room or in a field Sholem would back away three paces, bowing at each pace, then shuffle forward again and bow reverently for the last time to mark the conclusion of the prayer and of the "audience."

Malkah withdrew into the dim interior of the wagon, where her

children lay asleep, tucking them up and listening to their breathing. Then she moved right back, near the packing-case, crouched
down in the narrow space and drew her shawl round her shoulders. Yiteleh's elbow dug sharply into her neck, while Mailech
was kicking her in the back. She took no notice. The important
thing was that her abdomen was protected from such unconscious
assaults. They would be dangerous just now.

Her back ached and she had shooting pains in her side and her
very bones felt crushed. The wagon rolled on and on, shaking
and bumping, but it seemed as though it were journeying not on
an earthly road that had a terminus somewhere, but over the
convolutions of her brain, to which there was no end. How long
had they been on the road? Four days? Or was it four years? Or
perhaps a hundred? Malkah had a dazed, nightmarish feeling as
though the wagon had been rattling along just like this since the
beginning of time, and as though she herself had been wandering
like this since the beginning of time, together with all her ancestors, all her family, all her children, living, dead, and yet to be
born. Where from and where to? No one knew. She belonged
to a tribe that was forever on the go. Even in her narrower family,
that of the Nikolsburgers, they always used to talk about flight,
exile, and a precarious, hunted existence on the face of the globe.
Listening to her elders as they discussed the past—not the great
past of thirty centuries, but the shorter one of three centuries—
she had known the terror of a hundred flights, had trudged wearily
over roads that led nowhere, had journeyed in scared vehicles
and storm-tossed sailing-boats. Her ancestors had fled from
Toledo, Seville, Cordoba, Tudela, carrying a cross that had been
forced into their hands. They had fled over secret paths, travelling
at night, always in fear of their lives. They had fled to Portugal
and to the Netherlands and when the cross and the stake had
caught up with them they fled again, across the sea and across
the African desert, over French highways, Flemish and German
highways, over Polish marshes and Turkish, Russian, Moravian,
and Hungarian mud-tracks.

The Moravian and Hungarian mud-tracks were known to
Malkah herself. The first flight from Moravia into Hungary had
been, to her, a jolly affair. Her elder brother, Mordechai, was

upset, and so were her four elder sisters. But she, Malkah, and her sister Channeleh, who was barely a year older, just laughed and laughed. They laughed if the weather was fine and they laughed if it rained. They even laughed when a packing-case tumbled off the wagon, and some old piece of furniture or a utensil got broken. They were also amused to see troops of hussars galloping past on the road, and when a company of Galician lancers in tall busbies, with their little flags flying, came roaring along frightening the horses. Mamma moaned, papa reprimanded, and Mordechai called them names. Ah, how good it had been to be nothing but a silly child! It was the same with Mailech and Yiteleh now. To them the scramble and confusion was amusing. To them it was fun to travel, fun not to have to sleep in a proper bed and to be allowed to sleep in the cramped and uncomfortable wagon. May the Lord God preserve the laughter in their hearts!

In those days she, Malkah, was called Gina, short for Regina. Her grandfather, David Levi, wanted her to be so named, in memory of the Empress Maria Theresa whom the old man had met and who had been so gracious to the Nikolsburgers. Gina was the seventh and youngest daughter, and her father, Manasseh Nikolsburger, said that she must be called Malkah—Queen—not only because that was the Hebrew equivalent of Regina, but also because she was the "Sabbath" of the family and the Sabbath figured as the "Queen" in the liturgy. At all events, Malkah had been the pet of the family, the little princess.

The Nikolsburgers were so called because for a long time they were the favourites of the Duke of Nikolsburg. More important still, they were the "domestic Jews" of the Kaunitzes. Joshua Nikolsburger acted as steward on the Kaunitz estate at Austerlitz and it was said that he kept the powerful Chancellor not only in money, but also in brains. David Levi, called "the Great" by the family, was the son of Joshua. He supplied both goods and counsel to the Imperial Court—both *prima primissimo.*

But what was the use of brains and money or of being purveyors of brilliant ideas to the highest quarters if in the end they had to run? Manasseh was driven out of Nikolsburg not by war or pestilence, but by the callousness of those same "highest quarters." Manasseh's wife bore him eight children in Nikolsburg, two sons

and six daughters. But according to an Imperial Decree, which
was ruthlessly enforced, only the first-born son, Ariel, could be
married in Moravia. The object of the Decree, of course, was
to keep the Jewish population as low as possible. So when Ariel
had settled down, Manasseh, just like any other less influential
Jewish father, had to take his family and possessions out of the
country. He moved to Pressburg, in Hungary, where life for a
Jew was in some respects more difficult than under the wings of
the Dukes in Nikolsburg, but at least there was no restriction on
marriage.

Still, life in Pressburg was quite happy. The Ephraim Palace in
the ghetto, at the foot of the fortress, was a veritable dovecot.
But the cellars in the damp depths of the courtyard, running
three floors down into the bowels of the earth, and inhabited by
rabbinical students, peddlers, cobblers, market women, and
copyists of sacred texts, with their numerous families, were
wretched beyond description. The Nikolsburgers occupied the
top floor in the front of the building. There was a clear view of
the fortress, with the green-roofed turrets on the battlements.
Often, soldiers in their bright red-and-white uniforms would
march past the house, swinging their arms and singing:

*"O Pressburg, O Pressburg, city of the brave,*
*A palace for the king, for soldiers a grave."*

At bedtime the trumpeter in the fortress would turn his face
towards Vienna and sound the Last Post. After that there was
silence, broken only by the footsteps of a belated soldier advancing over the cobbles to face his punishment. The sound of the
Last Post was said to carry as far as Vienna. "Francis," Manasseh
used to say, "never goes to bed until he has heard it three times.
But when he knows that this part of his Empire also has retired
to rest, he gets under his silken quilt at last and goes to sleep."

But the peaceful days of Pressburg were soon swept away by
the gale of history. In the evening Pressburg heard the Last Post
as usual, and so did Francis, perhaps murmuring a kindly, "Sleep
well, my peoples," before closing his eyes. But in the morning
the frosty air was rent and torn by the sound of trumpets, the
roll of drums, galloping horses and tramping feet. "The French

are coming!" The French were nowhere near yet. But there were soldiers pouring in from all directions, grenadiers, lancers, light infantry, and all the rest. They marched to the roll of drums, but did not sing. There was cavalry racing through the town, artillery and service corps vehicles rumbling over the stones. They were of all nations, Magyars, Russians, Moravians, Piedmontese, and Tyrolese. And three or four days later they came pouring back, a disorganized rabble, ragged and dirty, many of them with blood-soaked bandages round their heads. Manasseh arrived with them. He came into the house with the furrows of care on his brow and a febrile light in his eyes and collapsed into a chair. All he said was:

"All's lost. We were beaten at Austerlitz."

The rest of the family understood at once, but she, Malkah, did not understand till later. To the two defeated Emperors— Francis of Austria and the Tsar of Russia—the defeat did not mean irretrievable ruin. The one dropped one or two provinces and set about preparing for another war, while the other took the remnants of his army back to Russia and did the same. But to the Nikolsburgers Austerlitz meant the end. The French guns had set fire to the granaries on the Kaunitz estate and what corn was not burnt was taken away by the enemy. And all the Nikolsburger family owned, including even loans to the Duke, had been in those granaries.

At Christmas, 1805, Napoleon's generals and ministers arrived in Pressburg to dictate terms to the generals and ministers of Francis. Manasseh and his family were feverishly packing their possessions. The Austrian Emperor hated the Corsican to the day of his death, even when he was embracing him in public, and still more so when he was giving his daughter in marriage to him. But that was only mild resentment as compared with what Manasseh Nikolsburger felt. Years later he once observed: "If Nebuchadnezzar lived like an animal for seven years, eating grass, the Corsican might graze for seventy-seven years in Europe, whose fields he has soaked with human blood."

By then they were already living in the Hungarian townlet of Szentmiklos, and Manasseh was no longer interested in riches. In fact, he was glad he had lost his money, regarding this as a kind of atonement on his own behalf, as well as on behalf of his people. He already knew something of the mystic significance of earthly migration in relation to the migration of the soul—Galgal and Gilgul—and he knew that not only this life, but also the life to come had its vicissitudes. He spoke with anger and horror of the Satanic men who trampled over everything, pillaging and burning, deaf to cries of pain. At the same time, he expressed, in Isaiah's phrase, his faith in the advent of eternal peace. He used to cite the cabbalistic words of Rabbi Jehuda Kunitz:

"It will come in ages, and an age times ages."

Malkah remembered the rattle of the wagon and the tinkle of the sleigh-bells as though it had happened but yesterday. She remembered how and where they changed horses and vehicles on that journey through the valley of the river Vag, right up to the snow-covered Lipto region; how her fevered body shivered in the blankets, how terrified she was of the war that they had left behind, but which might yet catch up with them; and how she wished she could have seen the paunchy little Corsican riding into Pressburg on his grey steed, with the Emperor Francis riding beside him, his head bowed, on a pitch-black horse. "You could never have seen that," her mother told her, "because the French Emperor never left Schonbrunn at all." Malkah's mother—her name was Helen—had been sorry to leave Pressburg, where the family had already begun to take root. But what could she do? Manasseh said Szentmiklos, so who was she to gainsay him? It was Manasseh who had lost the Battle of Austerlitz, so it was for him to decide the escape route.

They had distant relations in the northern townlet, a prosperous family named Holischauer, who had moved there from Moravia earlier. They did all that Manasseh expected of them, helping them financially as well as with merchandise, advice, and credit. It seemed that a ruination or two was not sufficient to ruin a Nikolsburger. They were born to business and soon recovered. Within a few weeks after his arrival in Lipto, Manasseh observed that that allegedly poor region was rich in many things and, in particular, that the ewes not only provided better milk and a tastier cheese than elsewhere, but also grew a firmer coat. On this observation he built up a business in raw hides which was later

brought to prosperity by a son-in-law under the name of Nikolsburger and Fuerth.

However, up north Manasseh underwent a fundamental change.
His interest in business soon began to flag and the new *élan* following upon the collapse rapidly evaporated. Manasseh was in the
early fifties and therefore—being a Nikolsburger—still in his
prime. But he had probably seen at Austerlitz more terrible things
than the conflagration in the granaries and the destruction of his
fortune. He rarely talked about these matters, and even then only
briefly, so the family attributed the change in him not to the
shocks—material and spiritual—of war, but to his new environment and, in particular, Rabbi Jehuda Leib Kunitz, the blind
cabbalist.

Rabbi Jehuda had begun to live on this forbidden fruit of the
spirit as a young man, delving into the sacred mysteries in the
depths of the night. His flock in the sober, dour Moravia had him
watched, then banished him from their midst as a baneful presence.
Here in the small Hungarian town his flock were more tolerant.
In his old age Rabbi Jehuda went completely blind, perhaps from
the shadows cast by the grudging candlelight over the ancient
texts, or perhaps from the even deeper shadows and more tremulous lights that came to his eyes from other worlds. For thirteen
years he went on probing the sacred mysteries with dead yet
seeing eyes. It was those blind eyes that lighted the path of
Manasseh Nikolsburger during the latter part of his life. Instead
of paying the necessary calls on his suppliers, the landowners and
peasants, he spent his time with the blind sage. With unquenchable thirst he sought knowledge, knowledge of the significance of
texts and numbers, of the mysteries of Creation, of the trinity of
the spirit, of the peregrinations of the soul this side and beyond
the boundaries of life, of the infinity of infinity, the radiances of
forces and causes, of the first volition and the ultimate cause, and
of Him from whom the cosmos emanates and into Whom it
merges, and Whose name is *Ensof*—the Infinite. Even at his home
it was not his ledgers that occupied Manasseh's attention, nor even
the Talmud and the Commentators; his hand, increasingly shaky,
was now turning the pages of the Secret Books, of the *Zohar* and
the *Sepher Yezira*. And, poring over them, he failed to notice that

time, earthly time, was passing, and that his daughters were getting
older. Rachel was "getting on." She was already twenty-one and
she had no dowry yet and no wooer. And even if a dowry could
have been scraped together somehow, it simply did not occur to
Manasseh that Rachel must be married off quickly because the
other two girls, Hannah and Gina, were fast growing up.

The girls used to cry a great deal in those days, while their
mother complained and scolded, but Manasseh refused to be
pushed out of his dream life. It was not until three and a half years
after Austerlitz that he was shaken into awareness by an unexpected report. It was brought by Mordechai one sultry summer
day from Vienna, where he had taken some hides. He returned
without any money. And his report was that the Corsican was
here again! He had been rapped over the knuckles at Aspern,
but had hit back at Wagram. Having routed the Hungarian nobles
at Györ, he was now bombarding Pressburg across the Danube.
The fortress was on fire, the ghetto was again in flight. The news
was kept from Mother Helen, so as not to frighten her. Soon
after Mordechai's return she was again quarrelling with her husband.

"If you meant your daughters to become old maids, Manasseh,
it was a pity to leave Nikolsburg."

This time, under the shock of the news, Manasseh was thinking
not with Rabbi Jehuda's head, but with his own.

"Nonsense, my dear," he said. "Three of them were married
off in Pressburg, weren't they?"

"What difference does that make to the other three?" returned
Mrs. Manasseh. "You might as well take them back to Moravia.
And why did you leave Pressburg? Others didn't, not even your
own sons-in-law."

"How do they know that there won't be another war, a blood-
ier one than the last? So long as the Corsican is alive, it's not safe
to live anywhere near the Emperors. I wouldn't take my daughters nearer to the great butcher. I'd bring the others up here as
well if I could. It's safer here in the mountains."

Mrs. Manasseh shrugged her shoulders. Manasseh's tone became
reproachful:

"You didn't say then you wanted to stay, did you? Would
you have liked to stand among the gaping crowd, the noisy,

guffawing mob, staring, staring? Would you have witnessed and
could I have witnessed the humiliation of Austria?"

"You Nikolsburgers!" snapped the woman. "You and your
pride! You and the House of Lorraine! Joshua was the chapman
of the great Kaunitz . . . But this is *lèse-majesté* . . . According
to you, he was Chancellor of the Granaries. Very well. The
famous Chancellor of the Granaries and his son, the still more
famous David Levi, taught Emperors and Empresses how to rule
but they failed in their entreaties to their exalted masters to let
the daughters of the family marry where they were born."

"A Nikolsburger doesn't entreat," said Manasseh. "And he
doesn't revolt, either. A Nikolsburger obeys."

"You didn't obey, did you? You ran away, to get the better
of your Emperor."

"I ran away from the Imperial Decree," said Manasseh in a low
voice, as though trying to justify himself before some higher
forum, "but only to observe the decrees of a mightier ruler.
Could we ask for exemption," he went on, raising his old eyes
to his wife's face, "when all the poorer Jews were obliged to
flee? They all fled when they were overtaken by the years.

"If you look through the family archives, my dear," he went
on in a dignified tone, of a sudden seeming to lose his stoop,
"you'll come upon a copy of a certain petition, whose original
lies in the archives of the Imperial Court. Its argument is reminiscent of the great Maimonides, while the distinction of its style
recalls another ancestor of ours, Don Isaac Abarbanel. 'If Adam
and Eve and their descendants,' says the petition, 'had not carried
out the divine decree given on the sixth day of the Creation, and
beginning with the words, "prosper and multiply," then Your
Majesty's glorious ancestor, the Emperor Charles, could not have
issued his decree which, being contrary to the first divine decree
in this matter, was beyond all doubt invalid.' And if you want
to know, my dear Chayah, these remarkable words were addressed by our David Levi, yes, the great David Levi, to the
Emperor Joseph. Joseph realized that David Levi was right. But
Joseph died and the new régime would not hear of Joseph. Leopold did not understand anything and stayed on the throne for
scarcely more than two years."

The Nikolsburgers talked about Emperors as other people talk about their relations, referring to them by their Christian names: Joseph, Francis, Leopold. Of course, during the years the family lived in Northern Hungary the Emperors were less frequently mentioned, and Manasseh's colloquies with them became rare. The conversation recorded above brought him back for a time to his paternal obligations. He also began to devote attention to business, concluding a partnership with one Gedalyeh Fuerth, a wool and cloth merchant who dealt with a Frankfurt merchant named Mayer Amsel Rothschild, and who, before the Napoleonic wars, used to export wool to England to Mayer Amsel's son Nathan. The partner's son, Azriel, eventually married Rachel Nikolsburger. Soon after this, another daughter, Hannah, married Shmayeh Kahn, head student of the local *yeshiba*, who had had his Sabbath board at the Nikolsburgers' for two years.

When Shmayeh became engaged to Hannah, Manasseh brought along a new "Sabbath boy" from the Rabbi's court. The family exchanged significant glances. The newcomer, Sholem by name, was a big, gawky, ruddy-faced fellow, and looked so shabby and forlorn that he seemed out of place at the festive board. Everybody thought that Sholem would only be a temporary Sabbath guest and would vanish as soon as a more presentable young man was found. But Manasseh thought otherwise. Sholem had one tremendous advantage: he was liked by Rabbi Jehudah. It began after Sholem's first term at the *yeshiba*, on his return from his summer holidays. Sholem, with some fifty other students, stood facing the pulpit. The blind Rabbi pointed at him with his finger, saying:
"Is that you, Sholem? Come up here."
Sholem obeyed with terror in his heart. The Rabbi, though completely blind, had seen him! Of course, the Rabbi had not seen him, but had merely caught the smell of water, soil, and stable manure that Sholem had brought back with him from his native village, and had evidently sensed something behind the smell. Sholem was badly embarrassed when the aged cabbalist asked him how he had spent his holidays. Unlike other students, he was not in a position to say that he had rehearsed the past term's material. His father was a poverty-stricken peasant, and

there were no books in his house at all. But the Rabbi was not
concerned with that. He was interested in the soil, in spades and
rakes, in the worms turned up in the furrow, and in horses with
festering sores in their flanks, and the like. The blind man wanted
to visualize life, the simple life that was linked with God's earth.
When he inquired whether Sholem had scratched the back of his
father's cow and Sholem answered in the affirmative, the other
students roared with laughter. But the Rabbi only smiled—and
not with amusement.

"You were caressing a mother of life," he said gently. Then,
after an instant's reflection: "And perhaps also a dead great-
grandmother."

The latter sentence might have had a cabbalistic significance,
which only a man of deep learning like Manasseh could completely grasp. To Sholem and his colleagues the *Cabbala* was forbidden learning, forbidden by Rabbi Jehudah himself with the
explanation that until the latter part of his life man was not ripe
for this mystic knowledge.

Manasseh retired within himself more and more, demanding
more and more renunciation and discipline of his family. His
former habits of mind he now regarded as sinful. He gave up his
favorite newspaper, the *Frankfurter Journal*, and also banished
all German books from his shelves—even *Nathan the Wise* and
Mendelssohn's *Phaedon*, which he used to love. He further dis-
carded all his western habits, ceasing to have his beard trimmed
and growing a pair of ear-curls. He no longer parted his hair, no
longer looked into a mirror. From then on he always addressed
his wife by her Hebrew name—Chayeleh—and his children were
no longer Marcus, Anna, and Gina, but Mordechai, Channeleh,
and Malkah. In the eyes of the family all this represented a very
big backward step, but they dared not say so in his presence.

Rachel, like her elder sisters, was given in marriage to the scion
of a business family, though even here Manasseh was careful to
see that he should be at home in *pilpul*—learned debate based on
the penetrating subtleties of Talmudic interpretation. In the case
of Channeleh he was stricter. Her fiancé had to be a Cohanite—
a hereditary priest in Israel—and not only a pious Jew, but also,

despite his extreme youth, an acknowledged *lamdan*, a great Talmudic scholar.

As regards Sholem, his claims were of a different kind. Sholem,
with his thick rust-colored ear-curls, his heavy knee-boots smelling of fish oil, and his threadbare caftan, had come from darkest
Maramaros. Not direct, for in between he had already studied
at three other famous *yeshibas*, but he was never able to divest
himself of the external marks of that county of Jewish small
holders and casual laborers. Though not exactly a blockhead, he
scarcely looked like a future *lamdan*. He had certain attractive
qualities and laudable virtues: he was patient and unassuming, a
respecter of authority and an unremitting student of the Law.
His ambition did not soar as high as the title of *lamdan*. He would
be satisfied if after another ten or twelve years, in the prime of
life, his contemporaries would deem him worthy of the more
modest title of *talmid hacham*—wise disciple.

At the Sabbath board he behaved humbly, always refusing a
second helping, and blushing to the roots of his ear-curls whenever he was obliged to ask for anything. But if he happened to
be held up over the meaning of a too concise sentence from the
Mishna or become bogged in the intracies of the Law, he would
appeal to the more learned without embarrassment. Whether he
was studying the Talmud in company or alone, he endeavoured
to analyse and elucidate its difficult arguments with practical
examples, which he recited in a loud sing-song. When he needed
an example for a point in the marriage law or the law of inheritance, he would take the names of the mothers of Israel, and
when it was necessary to illustrate the law on holy days, on
canonical matters, or on civil or criminal cases, he would revert
to the institutions of the ancient Fatherland and cite the sons of
Jacob.

On Saturday morning, while the dining-room resounded to the
preparatory chink of plates and cutlery, the men would be engaged in vocal debate in the bay of the window or in the next
room. Azriel, the business man, and the swarthy Shmayeh, the
*lamdan*, would be putting a poser to Sholem.

"Reuben lent a camel to Simon, Simon lent it to Levi, and
while with Levi, the camel died. . . ."

The two brothers-in-law, more learned than Sholem, often succeeded in pulling his leg.

"The High Priest," they said on one occasion, "had four daughters, Sarah, Rebecca, Rachel, and Leah, and two step-daughters, Bilha and Zilpa. Question: Into how many portions must they divide the food received in tithes from the Temple, of which every legitimate member of the High Priest's household is permitted to eat?"

"If," replied Sholem readily, "if permission to eat this food extends to the step-daughters, then the answer is: six portions."

Azriel, whose right eyelid was narrower than the left, gave him a mocking look from that eye, then burst into a guffaw that seemed to shake the whole house. Shmayeh, like the temperamental Cohanite he was, turned on him with sudden anger.

"*Am-haarez!*" he cried. "Clodhopping fool! Dost not know that the High Priest could not possibly have had any step-daughters. The High Priest of Jerusalem could not marry either a widow or a divorced woman."

Sholem felt terribly ashamed of his ignorance, but tried to suppress any resentment against the two leg-pullers. For a wise disciple will learn even from those that mock at him, just as the teacher often learns from his pupil.

Sholem also had one or two other virtues for which he was liked by old Manasseh. There was his willingness. The aged Rabbi had two older students as his permanent personal attendants, but when the work became too burdensome or even daunting, they sent for Sholem. Sholem went gladly, leaving his bed in the middle of the night if necessary. He would carry the chamberpot without complaint or a trace of finickiness, and if the invalid had to be transferred from one bed to another, Sholem would never call for help, but would lift him up gently and carry him in his strong, reverent arms as if he were a sick child.

As a result Sholem had grown in Manasseh's eyes, for it had been granted to him to hold the Saint in his arms more than once at a time when his spirit was enthralled by a sacred vision. And so, one Sabbath morning, before Sholem had arrived for dinner, Manasseh addressed his wife as follows:

"Chayeleh, dear heart, we've had enough of being court Jews

and counsellors of statesmen, enough of business men, drapers,
and hide merchants. Let there be a godly man in the family at last."

Chayeleh knew at once to whom he was referring, but acted
as if she didn't.

"If he is otherwise suitable," she said, "why shouldn't he be
godly as well?"

Manasseh was too impatient to enter into a game of verbal
hide-and-seek and spoke his mind at once.

"It'll be Sholem. Sholem (peace) in the house and Sholem in
the heart."

"Manasseh!" cried Chayeleh in sudden distress.

The "peace" began with a quarrel in which the whole house,
including the sons-in-law, turned against Manasseh. In vain they
tried to make him understand that the proposed marriage would
not only damage the family's prestige, but would also affect its
business; in vain they tried to appeal to an even more sensitive
side of his nature: Manasseh, with the mute Sholem and the
dying Rabbi behind him, remained adamant. What did it signify
that Malkah was the favorite and that she herself, though only
mutely, was opposed to the marriage? She was then seventeen and
still had memories and dreams of Nikolsburg and Pressburg and
even of the Imperial City. Brother-in-law Azriel, who took the
hides to Vienna, once brought back with him a young button-
maker from the Leopoldstadt. The young man played the violin
very nicely, could talk about Mozart, Gluck and Haydn and
was, according to himself, in the habit of visiting the Kärntnerthor
Theatre at least once a month. "Would you like to go to Vienna?"
her mother had once asked her. "This young man would take
you." "I wouldn't go with this one," she had replied without a
thought. But no other young man appeared. And now it would
have been too late, for Sholem was barring the way. Her father,
in turn, was so fixed in his determination that he even bought
some new clothes for the young man, and the shabbily dressed,
despised Sholem suddenly appeared at the festive board in fine
raiment. In his morocco leather knee-boots, wide-brimmed beaver
hat, and shimmery silk caftan he looked festive indeed. At that
moment the girl was as yet unaware of her father's intention and
she gave Sholem an innocent smile, glad to see him so clean and

"new." Sholem responded with a look from under his rust-colored eyebrows that somehow made her shudder. There was destiny in that look.

Malkah always remembered that fateful Sabbath very vividly. Sholem had been engaged in debate with her two brothers-in-law, defending a point of view of his own modestly but firmly. It was about some medieval codification. Azriel regarded him with provoking irony from beneath his abbreviated eyelid, while Shmayeh simply called him names. Sholem folded his arms on his silk-covered chest.

"What I claim," he said with an assurance amounting to challenge, "is not that I am right, only that the Marshah is right."

"The Marshah," shouted Shmayeh, "never said anything of the kind." He was angry that this nonentity should dare to say "I."

"You don't know anything about the Marshah, my friend," added Azriel.

"It's no use arguing over it," broke in Manasseh. "Why not look it up?" And reaching into a bookcase he lifted down a leather-bound volume and handed it to Sholem. Sholem turned up the disputed passage and proved to his opponents that he had been entirely right.

That was Sholem's first scholarly triumph.

After this he ceased to be dumb at table and began to follow up the learned witticisms of Azriel and the *lamdan* with his own pious construction of some sacred text. And although Azriel kept smiling to himself, while Shmayeh listened with pursed lips, Sholem saw only the encouragement in Manasseh's eyes, and went on. On the first occasion he was expounding the idea that there was no such thing as a first and a last, because the first might become last and the last first. Everything that was big had been small to begin with, except the Universe, which had never been small, because Elohim had created it out of nothing, out of the void. How big any small thing was to grow, was determined by the Above One. A cherry pip would grow into a fine, big tree with lovely pink-and-white blossoms, whereas the rape seed, which was no smaller, became nothing but a blade of grass.

"May your strength increase!" cried Manasseh with gratified

approval, raising his twinkling eyes to Chayeleh and the other women at the table, as though to say: "What did I tell you?"

The women were impressed not so much by Sholem's learned argument as by his subsequent solo performance of one of the hymns. He had now been Sabbath guest for nearly two years, yet he had never joined aloud in the *z'miroth*, the hymn-singing between dishes, humming the text under his breath while the others sang with pious abandon. Now he sang the Psalm of the Pilgrims—*Shir Hamaaloth*—alone.

> *"When Adonai returned*
> *the captives to Zion*
> *we were like dreamers,*
> *our mouths filled with laughter,*
> *our tongues with jubilation."*

Even Azriel's mocking eyes seemed to smile now, while Shmayeh Kahn kept nodding his head, as though to say: "The fellow can sing; I must give him that." Rachel was thrilled, while Hannah regretted that Sholem had kept silent for so long. Those chassidic (mystic) tunes were after all more attractive than the monotonous tunes of the German-Yiddish songs. But their mother only shook her head, as though she had suffered a mild shock. And Malkeleh's heart was filled with a vague foreboding. For some reason she thought of the Viennese button-maker and of the Mozart songs that had died away in the distance. She felt like bursting into tears. But she did not burst into tears until later in the day, when her father came up to her and passing a hand lightly over her hair, said:

"Mazeltov, Malkeleh, you're engaged."

But she cried in vain, both then and during the weeks that followed. Even under the marriage canopy they saw only her tear-stained face, not her broken heart. For every daughter of Israel sheds tears under the marriage canopy, weeping for the widowed bride—Jerusalem. But she had made no protest, no complaint. The Nikolsburgers did not rebel—especially the women.

Yet she felt that mute submission was humiliating. How often since that day had not her mind rebelled against the fate imposed

upon her, without rebellion rising to her lips. For ten long years
her whole being had been saying No, yet she had been living
with Sholem as if she had said Yes from the outset. She, the
proud, pretty Regina Nikolsburger, the spoiled darling of the
family, whom her mother used to beautify with oil of aloes and
perfumed Viennese ointments, had been sharing the existence
of Sholem, a clodhopper with a bushy beard who smelled of
axle-grease.

He was a rock of fortitude, cheerfully bearing disaster upon
disaster for the sake of the small pleasures that life had to offer
him. And so unassuming was he that he did not hanker even
after a surname, being content with the name attached to him by
his native village: Leah's Sholem, and in the synagogue with his
proper Hebrew name: Sholem ben Yoirish. When the Emperor
Joseph had decreed that all Jews must assume German names,
Sholem's father, Yoirish, had been out of reach of the Emperor's
officials, floating timber down the Tisza in the company of
Ruthenian peasants, or ploughing the plot of stony maize land
he was renting from the peasants in the shadow of the chill, dark
mountains. His wife Leah, a delicate little woman, was then pregnant with Sholem, yet she was helping him to draw the wooden
plough. It was a good thing the Emperor's servants never found
him. Yoirish did not need a surname, and the dispensers thereof
probably demanded all sorts of things for it: head tax, smoke
tax, tithe, villenage, Jew tax, and blood tax.

Sholem attached even less importance to a surname than did
his father. At the age of thirteen he had exchanged the burdens of
the barren plot of land for the even heavier burdens of the Talmud. And though sometimes, when his brain grew weary of the
heavy tomes, he experienced a transient nostalgia for the pebbled
banks of the Tisza, the wooded mountains and the constant
struggle with nature, he was never disturbed by any other worldly
desires.

When he became engaged, Malkeleh still had a dowry, but by
the time of the wedding it had all gone. Contrary to the advice
of his clever sons-in-law, Manasseh failed to convert his money
into objects of silver or silver coin, though that precaution was
clearly indicated by the uncertainty of that warring age. In con-

sequence of this Manasseh's business was engulfed in the bank-
ruptcy of the State in 1811, the year of "black banknotes". The
family was badly upset, but Sholem took no notice. Indeed, he
may have been secretly glad that he would now be relieved of
petty financial worries and of the responsibility of the small
fortune he was to receive from his father-in-law. All would be
well, God helping. It so happened that the will of the Almighty
was to make matters even worse. The inflation of 1811 was
followed by a whole series of economic crises and disasters and
when, after the Congress of Vienna, a hundred paper florins were
offered for eight silver florins, Sholem did not own even eight
florins.

Sholem did not know anything about his remoter ancestry or
about their flights. One of his grandfathers had been a cobbler
in Kolomea, in Russian Poland, the other a cattle drover at the
junction of the frontiers of three Empires, Russia, Austria, and
Turkey. These two he had known, and that was enough. Beyond
them, his nearest ancestor was Jacob the son of Isaac the son of
Abraham of Ur in Chaldea. No one could have a more distinguished ancestry than that. He was a big, lumbering fellow, this
Jew Sholem, only thirty-two years old, but so hirsute and shaggy
that he looked fifty. And he was an exasperating fellow, with an
innocent gaze in his brown eyes, the gentle, blushful expression of
a bearded boy, and a constitutional incapacity to realize, even
after the trials and tribulations of the past ten years, that life was
hard. How often had he himself quoted the words of the
Preacher: "*Dor holech v'dor baa.* One generation passeth away
and another generation cometh . . . and behold, all is vanity and
vexation of spirit." But he only saw the beauty of the words, never
the vexation of spirit. And through the beauty of the words he
derived happiness even from the miseries of life.

Since Manasseh's death (a year after that of Rabbi Jehudah)
Sholem and Malkeleh had made a fresh start—and a new flight—
no fewer than six times. Sholem had crashed each time, but
being the offspring of a toiling mother, had rapidly jumped to
his feet each time, without surprise or complaint, and without
expecting succor or aid from anyone. He had been, in turn,
teacher, copyist of sacred texts, yeast maker, wine merchant,

rabbit-skin dealer and flax and hemp buyer. How humiliating it had been to Malkeleh when she had to approach her sisters and brothers-in-law who were so proud that fate was treating them more graciously. Sholem himself did not even know about those approaches. And how much hope Malkeleh had left behind on the highways, and how many valuable pieces of the remnant of the Nikolsburger inheritance! There was little more than anxiety and sorrow to load into the wagon as they left the pitiable ruins of another and yet another meagre living. They left one small mound of earth at the foot of a gigantic mountain in County Szepes, and another on the bank of the river Bodrog. These were the human sacrifices exacted by dire poverty and enforced wanderings.

All this had failed to leave a mark on Sholem. He could carry his trials—were they not manifestations of God's will? Sholem could weep only over the destruction of the Temple, the calamity that had happened more than seventeen centuries before. And he was roused to fist-shaking anger only by the thought of those two vain, litigious Jews of Jerusalem, Kamzeh and Bar Kamzeh, through whose treachery the Holy City and its people were delivered into the hands of Titus. Of his own defeats Sholem took no notice, and the betrayals of himself and his family he readily forgot and forgave. After all, there had to be some bad people in the world, otherwise there would be no virtue in resisting temptation.

Sholem was not a stupid man, and sometimes his reasoning was quite clever. Two years before, he had moved north, near the mountain passes, because life in the mountains was healthier and cheaper and transport (and, if the worst came to the worst, flight) was quicker through the passes. He worked it out that if he did his hemp buying on foot, and if he attended to the retting and scrutching himself, the price he would get from the Silesian ropemaker would be sufficient to enable him to stay immersed in the ageless arguments of the Babylonian Talmud until the next crop. The trouble was that in the second year he retired to his books too early. True, he was only doing it while the hemp was retting in the stream and getting soft, but during that week or two his peasant suppliers had stolen the hemp and carried it back to their own barns. And when Sholem tried to point out to them that their action was improper and contrary to the Ten Commandments and perhaps also to the Emperor's law, the peasants interpreted this as a threat.

So they started a whispering campaign against Sholem; and what they whispered was that the Jew Sholem had hidden the body of a Christian boy beneath the retting hemp, and that that was what they had been looking for. Some heard the bloodcurdling story of the murder from people who had seen Sholem luring away the baby son of a farm servant on a nearby estate, having in his pocket the knife he used for the ritual slaughter of chickens. The *pandours* had heard similar stories before, but this time they did not believe it for one moment. On the estate Sholem was known as a quiet, well-spoken Jew, and in any case, all the children there were alive and well. Yet the *pandours* made a search, not for the hemp that was missing, but for the child that was not. And when, on the Sunday, the peasants came out of the tavern and marched to Sholem's house, smashing his windows and flourishing their knives, it was not them that the *pandours* warned to keep the peace, but the Jew, whom they accused of inciting the populace. Fortunately, the exciting day was followed by a stormy night, and Sholem and Malkeleh were able to snatch up their most indispensable possessions, snatch their children out of bed, pillows, quilts and all, and get away in their rickety wagon without being seen by anyone.

"It's all for the best," thought Sholem, as the wagon was rattling down the valley and the sense of being hunted grew less acute. "God punishes only those that He loves. He does not bother about the others. He does not care for them enough not to let their undertakings prosper."

ON THE WRONG ROAD

MALKELEH FELT she could not bear it any longer. Neither the ceaseless rattling of the wagon, nor the one-sided debate with Sholem and Fate. She must explode, must quarrel with God himself—God, who had made Sholem so intolerably placid. And if God did not answer, Sholem must. He was now smoking his short clay-pipe, occasionally clicking his tongue at the pony and inspecting the fields on both sides of the road. Malkeleh was now sitting beside him on the driving seat.

"They grow pumpkins and melons over there," Sholem observed. "I'd grow roots on this land. You know what sort, Malkeleh?"

But Malkeleh was not listening. An observation Sholem had made some days earlier still remained to be thrashed out.

"You said God didn't love those that were well off," she began.

"He loves best those that are badly off," replied Sholem.

"Then he loves people only so long as He can torment them. Because after all it depends on His will whether we do well or badly."

"Don't blaspheme, Malkeleh. The Good God does not torment anyone."

"Except those He has cursed with poverty and wretchedness."

"If I ever became prosperous," said Sholem, drawing his head down between his shoulders, "I'd have to pray and study twice as much to make up for everything."

"You've been praying and studying too much as it is—that's why we're so poor. Looking after your family comes before the service of God."

The clay-pipe dropped from the man's mouth.

"What are you saying, *Yiddene*! God comes before everything. To love and fear the Lord is the beginning of all wisdom."

Malkeleh drew her checkered shawl closer about her shoulders as a chill gust of wind made her shiver. She glanced down at the convexity of her body and felt a great perturbation.

"The beginning of wisdom," she said in a thick voice, "is to feed our children. Yes, and to have enough money to get a doctor from the town when they're taken ill. You've already lost two children on the road. Do you want to lose the other two as well?"

"They're not ill?" asked the man in a scared voice.

"No," said the woman, "only hungry. And if you go on as you have been doing, they'll stay hungry. Don't tell me that prayer comes before work. I heard our Rabbi himself say in his

Sabbath sermon that work was as pleasing in the eyes of God as prayer."

"That's what our Sages say," observed Sholem approvingly.

"Yet you're afraid of work."

"I never was, dear heart, never."

"You do work, of course, but you're careless lest, God forbid, you get rid of your poverty. You're afraid lest your family should get prosperous."

"I'm not afraid of prosperity."

"You hate the towns, where so many other men get on."

Sholem knew that she was alluding to Karoly, where he refused to go two years earlier. But he was going there now. Malkeleh had been right. Sholem had realized this even as he heard the warning of Rabbi Jonah. "The peril comes from the north." But to some extent he too must have been in the right in refusing to be persuaded and obstinately keeping north, towards the perils of the north. It must have been the divine will to test his faith. But he ceased arguing with his wife, swallowing his opinion of Malkeleh's rich brother who could still not forgive the *mésalliance* and who, no doubt, would make him, Sholem, feel it. Mordechai was going to be agape with surprise when they burst in upon him unexpectedly, on a Friday afternoon too, when it was too late to prepare for guests. Time had mellowed Sholem and he was now prepared to submit to the humiliation. Nor did he say that the reason God had not granted him any "business luck" was that he was not made for business. He knew what Malkeleh would say to that: that when he saw how cleverly Mordechai managed things and how other business men were creating something out of nothing, he too would come to feel like business. Very well, Malkeleh. Sholem gave a flick at the tired pony with his whip, grunting a mild "gee-up!" Then he looked up at the sky.

"It's not going to rain—the wind has risen."

Malkeleh remained silent.

"At least we shan't get wet. But you'll catch cold, Malkeleh."

Malkeleh sat with compressed lips. A peasant cart was rattling past. Sholem might now have inquired whether he was on the right road for Karoly and how far it was. But because Malkeleh

was looking so gloomy he forgot. Turning his head to look inside
the hood, he said:

"They're still asleep. Hadn't we better wake them up? They
can run about a bit on the road."

"Let them sleep on," said the woman. "What'll you give them
to eat when they wake up? If they run about they'll be all the
hungrier."

"Isn't there anything left?" inquired the man mildly.

"What do you expect? A piece of dry bread and a bit of
cheese—hard as rock. I don't know what we'll do if we don't
get there to-day."

Sholem gazed into the distance, at the last eddies of mist over
the stubble-fields, which were now rapidly dissipating as the sun
rose higher. He gazed at the big see-saw swapes over the wells,
designed blackly into the greyness of the morning, at the villages
nestling in hollows beyond the fields, at tall barns with rows of
golden corn-cobs hung under the eaves. It struck him as strange
that there was no village along the road and for an instant he
was seized with the suspicion that the right road was over there.
But with Malkeleh's doubts ringing in his ears he felt he must
reassure her.

"We'll get there, Malkeleh," he said with the confidence of
faith. "The Above One cannot want us not to arrive in time. We
can't travel on the Sabbath."

"The only thing the Above One doesn't want," said Malkeleh
bitterly, "are the things that you don't want."

"If I don't want to get there," murmured the man into his
beard, "then why am I on my way there?"

He might have posed the question to himself. Why was he on
his way to the town where his brother-in-law lived? Was he
really keen to go there, or was he merely yielding to fate, and the
pressure of his hungry family? Malkeleh, watching him from
the obscurity of the interior of the wagon awhile ago, must have
read his thoughts. Had she insisted on learning what was in his
mind while he was alone on the driving seat, he would have
been obliged to confess that he had an idea that Kese, the pony,
with its special, stupid horsy cunning, was taking them to Kallo
instead of Karoly, the former town being somewhat nearer and

the oats there being tastier and cheaper. Well, let the animal take them to Kallo if it liked. He, Sholem, had not told it where to go and where not to go. Perhaps Kese was guided by the guardian angel of horses. After all, Kese had also suffered a great deal during the past few years and he deserved a little peace and prosperity: plenty of hay and oats and perhaps a piece of sun-flower cake on the Sabbath. The Jews of Kallo, as soon as they learned where and what Kese had fled from and how bravely he had hoofed it over those countless miles, would instantly hang a full bag of oats over his head. How did this funny idea enter his head? He did not know himself. After prayers he was feeling very hungry, and having drunk the last of the plum whiskey out of the wooden bottle, he searched his pockets. Right down inside the lining of his coat, his hand touched something that conveyed momentary promise to his palate. But it was only a clove-studded quince, which his wife had taken with her to synagogue on the Day of Atonement, to smell when she became faint from fasting. It was not much good as food, anyhow. How did he come to bring it away? That Sunday night, while engaged in snatching up his most necessary possessions, he had hesitated for a moment whether to take the sack of potatoes or the half-sack of meal. The wind was howling, the pony was neighing and there was no time to lose, and Sholem found himself dashing out of the house without either sack, but carrying the walking-stick he had in-herited from his sainted master, Rabbi Jehudah, and this clove-studded quince. And he felt that he had the most essential posses-sions with him. The yellow, wrinkly fruit reminded him of his mother Leah and of the lovely maize patties she used to make. He glanced at the beheaded sunflower stalks along the road and thought how hungry the pony must be and how it would enjoy a piece of sunflower cake. That was all he had been thinking about. Should he tell Malkeleh?

No, better not. She was in a rather accusing mood just then.

"Sholem," she said, after a silence, "if we'd started at noon yesterday we'd have been in Karoly long ago. But you said you were going away for an hour and you stayed away till after midnight. What were you doing all that time?"

"You know very well. . . ."

"But couldn't you have waited with that Talmudic debate until you failed in Karoly as well, and were returning here on your way to Galicia?"

Sholem looked sideways at his wife's strained, sorrowful features and remained silent for awhile. Then:

"Rabbi Jonah told me some very important things," he said in the tone of one bringing glad tidings.

"I know all about those very important things."

The man glanced at the pale little fist that held the shawl together and suddenly decided not to go on, not to quote the sentence from Jeremiah about the peril from the north, not to tell her about Jacob being followed by the shadow of Esau. In her present mood she might, Heaven forbid, mock at these things.

"You know, Malkeleh," he said instead, "what new wonders there are in the world. Now they're making sugar out of beets and it's just as white and sweet as cane sugar."

"Is that so wonderful?"

"If I could get a lease of some of this land here I'd grow sugar beet, and in a little while you'd be a rich woman."

Malkeleh sensed the warmth and the desire to please in his voice, and though still feeling sulky she could not wholly resist his advance.

"Was that what the Saint was talking about from noon till midnight?" she asked, but there was curiosity rather than sarcasm in her tone.

"It wasn't he, but his visitors who talked about it. You know, people come to see him from all over the country. They said something else as well."

He paused, anticipating a prompting inquiry. But as Malkeleh remained silent, he went on.

"A big ship has come across the sea without any sails or oars. It took four weeks from America to England."

"That ship," pouted the woman, "came over years ago. It was driven by steam."

"You knew?"

"Of course I did."

"You never mentioned it to me."

"You're not interested in such things."

Now it was his turn to be sulky.

"I'm very interested in such things," he said with mild annoyance. Then he added: "But you don't know who died in the spring, do you?"

"Who?"

"The Corsican."

"I knew that too," said Malkeleh.

"You did?" cried Sholem, taken aback.

"Yes, I heard it in the summer. The steward of the big estate was talking about it to the Catholic priest."

"You overheard him? What did he say?"

"He said he was entering the date in the family Bible—fifth of May, eighteen twenty-one."

"How did he know the exact date?"

"He had read it in the paper. He also said the Corsican had died in English captivity on an island called St. Helena."

"And you remembered it all?"

"It was quite easy. Mother's German name is Helena."

"And it never occurred to you to tell me about it?"

"I didn't know that you wanted to know."

"You didn't know! Was it not this Corsican who set fire to the granaries at Austerlitz?"

"Yes."

"And it was he who bombarded the ghetto at Pressburg?"

"Yes."

"And who left his sick and hungry soldiers to lie in the snow in Russia?"

"Well?"

"And who made war so many times?"

"Well?"

"And you say you didn't know I wanted to know that he was dead. Of course I did. Why, now there's going to be peace in the world."

Malkeleh gazed at him and, for the first time in months, felt drawn to him. His indignation, his interest in worldly affairs, was something new and attractive. Perhaps it was just as well that he did visit the Saint and spent a dozen hours mixing with other men. This was a good omen for their future life.

"Peace there may be," she said, "but is there going to be bread for us?" However, she was no longer disputing with him, only expressing aloud her own inner anxiety.

"Where there's peace there's bread," said Sholem with deep conviction, "because the many swords are beaten into ploughshares. Nothing is more important than that the world should settle down at last. You know what Rabbi Simon ben Gamaliel says? The world rests on three pillars: the Law, Justice, and Peace. We read it with Yiteleh a few weeks ago. Yiteleh, are you up yet?"


Sholem did not like going to Karoly. He had a childish terror of the town of the Counts Karolyi, though he had never heard anything to its detriment. But there was one thing there that he looked forward to: the synagogue. After two years of religious solitude, he was at last to become a member of a proper congregation, for they had a *minyan*—ten males over the age of thirteen—twice a day at the synagogue even on market days. Two Jews praying together are still only individual worshippers. Three Jewish men can say grace after a meal as a small community. But ten men is the smallest real community for communal worship according to the laws of Moses and Israel.

Once or twice, as he sat on the driving seat, he caught himself thinking that he would be quite content to be one of a company of three—at table. His nostrils were already sniffing certain odors from Karoly, from the festive board of his sister-in-law, Blimeleh. The odor of gefilte fish, plaited fancy bread, chicken broth seasoned with saffron, pepper and parsley, and other good things. He forgot about the indignity of being a poor relation in his anticipatory enjoyment both of the fine supper and the cordiality that was his rightful due, at least for the first day or two, as a guest arriving from a great distance. Mordechai would be sure to offer him the honour of reciting the *Kiddush*—the introductory blessing over a cup of wine—and it would be his privilege to take the first sip from the silver cup. And what a wonderful wine it was! And upon the conclusion of the meal it would be his privilege to call, again with a cup of wine in his hand, "My masters,

let us say grace." To which the other two men would respond
with the words: "Let us say grace to Him for it is by His
bounty that we have eaten." Yes, of course—God's bounty, not
the rich Mordechai's; he, Sholem, must never forget that.

However, Sholem's spiritual hunger, his longing for community life, was even greater than the physical. There was a
happy twinkle in his mind's eye as he visualized the scene at
Synagogue. On the Sabbath morning Mordechai would be called
aside by Elders, who would make whispered inquiries, and there
would be exclamations of enlightenment and understanding. Then,
the Scrolls of the Law would be taken out of the Ark, the
tinkling coronets, the glittering breastplate and the velvet sheath
would be removed, and the Scrolls would be unrolled on the dais
in the middle of the synagogue; and the Reader would call upon
him in a dramatic sing-song: let Sholem ben Yoirish come up and
read a portion of the Law. And as he made his way to the
Scrolls by the shortest route, all eyes would be upon him. So
this was Mordechai Nikolsburger's brother-in-law, Manasseh
Nikolsburger's son-in-law. Listen to that—he is reciting the
Escape from Peril Benediction! Now he is offering a donation to
the Mishna Society. How much? Eighteen kreuzers? No. Only
nine. Must be a very poor man.

However, none of these scenes were ever enacted. It was no
one's fault. Kese the pony, in its unfathomable animal cunning,
must have taken a wrong turning somewhere while his master
had been dozing, so that the wagon did not go either to Karoly
or to Kallo. Of course Sholem had sensed this, but he had shooed
the sensations away, relying on the pony and fate. The Above
One would be sure to guide them somewhere in the end. It was
only towards noon that it became clear that they had taken the
wrong road and had been moving toward the big Ecsed Marsh.
Now the road was either sticky or boggy, and the wheels either
stuck or sank and rebounded. They met a peasant riding on a
donkey and he said:

"Keep south all the time. It's a bit hard and tricky, but if you're
careful you'll get there just the same."

"Just the same". . . and "if you're careful". . . Of course it did
not occur to the peasant that this was Friday and a short autumn

day, and that a Jew must do all he can not to be caught on the road at the commencement of the Sabbath. Sholem forgot that the children were hungry and would get hungrier still running about, and he let them get off the wagon to lighten the pony's burden. It would be disastrous if dusk found them in the uninhabited parts on the edge of the marsh.

Even Malkeleh realized this. She was again deeply depressed. All afternoon she kept scanning the sky, which was now clear with the sinking sun an angry red, now overcast with grey clouds. Then, far ahead, she espied a church steeple covered with green moss, with little white, blue, and yellow thatch-roofed houses peeping forth from beneath it like chicks from under a brood-hen, and her face reflected weary relief. She urged her husband to make a final effort.

"Let's both push the wagon. We'll be there in a minute."

"In a minute!" said Sholem. "It'd be a very long minute. At least a quarter of an hour." He paused, gazing at the setting sun. Then: "We must stop here," he said. "It is Sabbath already."

Rapidly unharnessing the horse, he tethered it to a knobbly willow-tree in the meadow where they had stopped. A few hundred feet down the road he could see the gypsies of the village lolling outside their mud-huts and ragged tents and it flashed through his mind that they might cast an eye on the animal. But he had no time to worry. The horse had to be removed from between the shafts, not only because it was necessary to let it find its own food over the Sabbath, but above all because this was the only way to make the wagon usable. With the horse harnessed to it it was beyond all doubt a vehicle which a Jew might not even touch on the Sabbath; but in the absence of the horse it was a dwelling, as witness the hood over it.

To confirm the change Sholem sat down for a minute or two in the interior of the "parlor." Then he hastened to the brook that flowed near the gypsy encampment, drank from its crystal-clear water, washed his hands and face, and passed his wet fingers through his beard. He hurried back to the wagon, brushing his clothes with the sleeve of his jacket as he went, and prompting his wife to hurry up and put the children and the home in order for the Sabbath. Then, turning away from his family, with

his back to the setting sun, he raced through the final weekday
prayer before welcoming the Queen.

The earthly "queen" tried to attract his attention to herself
for a moment by inquiring whether she could have some money.
But Sholem had already emptied his pockets of all its mundane
contents. To touch money now, or even to think of money,
would have been a sin. Malkeleh, with the aid of Yiteleh, lifted
the big packing-case from the backboard to the ground and
produced from its depths an earthenware pot wrapped in a piece
of linen, a white silk headkerchief and a cashmere shawl with a
Turkish pattern. The pot and the shawl she handed to Yiteleh.

"Run to the village," she said, "and get some peasant woman
to fill the pot with milk. Say I can't send money because it's
Sabbath and give her the shawl in pledge. See that she gets it fresh
out of the cow, and see that she washes her hands first. And
don't drop the shawl in the mud. It used to belong to my
granny."

Yiteleh hurried off. Mailech tried to run after her, but his
mother caught hold of him.

"You must get washed for the Sabbath," she said.

She took a cake of soap, a homespun towel and a broken
comb from the packing-case, waddled with the boy to the brook
and despite his protests that the water was cold, she gave him a
thorough wash. There, what a handsome boy you are. Then she
herself had a wash. Back at the wagon she tied the silk headkerchief round her head. Her heart was heavy, but for the boy's
sake she tried to smile.

Then she took a number of things from the packing-case: the
linen bag containing all that was left of the family's store of food,
some mugs, a tablecloth, an old baking-tin and four tallow
candles. She halved the candles with a knife, which she then
hastily stuck into the ground, for tallow is unclean and the knife
had to stay in the ground for eight days before it could be
used for food again. Eight days . . . where would they be by
then! But with the Sabbath upon her she could not think of such
things.

SABBATH AT THE GIPSY CAMP

SHE STUCK seven of the half-candles to the bottom of the tin and laid the eighth, which was somewhat larger, in front of them. Then she spread the white tablecloth over the packing-case, placed the few crusts and the lump of cheese at one end, covering it over with a crocheted cloth, and making it look as though the cloth concealed a couple of small festive loaves. The tin with the candles she placed at the other end of the "table," the head of which was next to the shaft, a comfortable seat for the master of the house. She arranged the four earthenware mugs: the cracked one for herself, the two flowered ones, only slightly chipped, for the children, and the best one for her husband. She glanced at him; he was intoning the hymn that introduced the Sabbath: *L'chi n'rannenu* . . . "Come, let us sing . . ." Then she hastened out into the road and stood looking towards the village . . . Wasn't Yiteleh coming yet? It was getting dark. At last!

"I walked slowly," said the child. "A dog ran after me and you know, mummy, if you walk slowly dogs go away. Besides, I had to be careful not to spill the milk."

"All right, darling," said her mother. "Run along and have a wash. Here's the soap and the towel, and there's the brook. Then you'll undo your hair and I'll comb and plait it for you. Hurry up, and don't let your father see you. The Sabbath came in ages ago."

When Yiteleh returned from the brook, her mother had already struck a light with flint, lighting the eight candles. Yiteleh and Mailech stood watching her. They had witnessed this scene so often before, but here under the waking stars everything was new. There was a sort of mother-of-pearly look about their mother's face as she blessed the candles, thrice "embracing" the air above them, then covering her eyes with her small white hands as she whispered the age-old sacred formula. Four of the lights were for the living, two for the dead, one for the budding life in her womb, and one to make the number even, for Sabbath lights could not be odd.

When Sholem returned "home" he found light and a festive air in the "house." He placed his hands on his children's heads and blessed them. All was well. The "house" was somewhat chilly, but there was neither wind nor rain and the candles were not blown out. Sholem was already singing the jolly hymn about peace and the angels of peace, clapping his hands, and the two children were singing and clapping with him. Then he looked across at his wife and intoned the age-old compliment to womanhood. "Who can find a virtuous woman? for her price is far above rubies." There was no wine on the table, only milk, and in other circumstances the ritual would not be valid. But here under the stars it was all right. Yiteleh had her mother's big shawl on her shoulders, while her brother was wrapped in his father's old coat. There they stood, sipping the milk.

"This is better milk than we had at home," said Yiteleh. "The cow must have put some sugar into it."

The little boy was also enjoying it. He asked for more again and again, until his mother told him that they must leave some for to-morrow.

Sholem had meanwhile washed his hands, raising them into the air and reciting a blessing. He removed the cloth from the relics of bread and cheese, broke off a morsel of the bread, and reciting another blessing carried it to his mouth, murmuring "In honor of the Sabbath" as he proceeded to masticate it. Then he quickly replaced the cover. He must not yield to temptation. There were two more sacred banquets to come—at noon and before dusk on the morrow.

Malkeleh gave a sigh and went away to the back of the wagon, to get the children's bed ready. Sholem went on singing hymns. In the darkness beyond the uneasy light cast by the flickering and guttering candles, he could see swarthy faces and glinting eyes as the gypsies came slinking along. Were they after the pony? Or were they simply watching the ritual of a Jewish Sabbath which they had never seen? Whichever it was, Sholem had to dismiss those sinister figures from his mind and concentrate on the ritual.

Having sung a series of hymns, he recited the long grace. Then he sat on, humming further hymns, even when the last of the candles had guttered into darkness. In his pious absorption he

failed to realize that he was already singing the "*Al Tirah*," the
sacred, anxious song that the Jews sing late on Saturday evening
after the departure of the Queen, to give themselves courage on
the threshold of the days of toil and uncertainty. "*Al tira avdi
Jaakov* . . . Fear not, my servant Jacob."


"Good Sabbath!" said Sholem. He had just returned from
"synagogue" which was at the end of the meadow, where there
were nine little trees swaying in the wind, three white birches,
two maple trees, and two squat willows. With Sholem, they
made up a "quorum," a community of ten. There was little difference between them and him, for like him, they kept swaying,
murmuring and whispering, only his voice was at times the more
distinct, he being the "reader." "All living things exalt thy
name . . ." Now he was back home, with his prayer-bag under
his arm, as though he had come a long way.

"Good Sabbath, Tateh," cried little Mailech.

"Good Sabbath," echoed Yiteleh's sweet voice.

Kese the pony was also shaking his head, as though to say "Good
Sabbath, master."

Malkeleh, sitting on the edge of the "table," responded with a
barely perceptible nod. What was the matter with her again?
What was she worrying about? She had been trembling during
the night, shivering with fever. "It's beginning all over again,"
she had said, "the north has caught up with us." "No, no,
Malkeleh," Sholem had said, "the north is still where it was.
We're not going to have any trouble here. The Saint has said so."
"Does the Saint know these gypsies?" "He doesn't. But if the
Saint said it'd be all right, then these gypsies must be good
gypsies."

"Did you notice the way they have been staring at the
children?"

That was during the night. Now she was brooding again.
Sholem went up to her.

"Still worried, Malkeleh? You did enough worrying during the
night."

"I wasn't worried during the night."

"You kept listening and looking out of the wagon till morning. Well, they didn't attack us, did they?"

"No, but now they've taken the last crust we had."

"What? The last crust? What we put aside for dinner and the afternoon meal?"

"Yes."

"In broad daylight?" Sholem was thinking of a daring robbery. Whilst he was at prayers in the company of the nine trees, the gypsies stole to the wagon and . . . So they were not good gypsies after all.

"Mummy is angry," said Yiteleh, with a penitent look on her little face, "because we gave the bread to Duduy."

"Who is Duduy?"

"A gipsy."

"Why did you do it, Yiteleh?"

Yiteleh looked up into her father's hirsute face and saw that there was no anger there.

"You see, Tateh, Mailech and I were walking into the village and Duduy was lying in the ditch, praying."

"Praying?"—Sholem was puzzled.

"He was playing his reed-pipe," cried Mailech.

"Yes," said Yiteleh, "first he was playing, then he started to pray. He said, 'God in heaven, if you were as hungry as Duduy you'd sure send me at least a crust of bread.' So we came back for the bread and gave it to him."

It was all right then, thought Sholem. He could understand Malkeleh's depression, with not even a crust in the "house" on the Sabbath. But glancing at the two children, he felt a sense of elation rising within him. They had been the instruments of God's mercy. God had heard the prayer of Gipsy Duduy, though it had been a crude prayer. Surely, then, he could not fail to hear his, Sholem's, pious and reverent pleadings for bread. It was a reassuring thought, though at the same time the loss of those crusts might have had something to do with his own reflections about bread on his way home from "synagogue," when he feared that he might at last yield to temptation and eat up all the bread—which was too hard for the children—leaving nothing for the Third Meal. That temptation had now been removed.

In any case, there was something more important than food to attend to now. There was the Portion of the Week—the *Sidrah*—to be read, as had been done of a Sabbath morning by all his ancestors since Scribe Ezra.

"Yiteleh, what is the Portion of the Week?"

Yiteleh said she did not know.

"Of course you don't," said her father. "We have been on the road all this week, so we have not read the Portion. It is *Va-yaizeh* . . . 'and Jacob went out from Beersheba and went toward Haran.' Get the rush-mat from the driving seat, Yiteleh, and put it down here, where the grass is dry. That's right. Now let us sit down."

The three of them sat down side by side on the mat and Sholem turned up the Portion of the Week in the book. Yiteleh read the Hebrew text together with her father, while Mailech was content to look and listen. For his benefit rather than Yiteleh's, Sholem's thick, freckled finger ran along the lines of print, from right to left.

" 'And Jacob went out from Beersheba and went toward Haran.' Well, Mailech, what does Rashi say about it? What are you staring at? Why, the blockhead doesn't know what Rashi is. He was our great teacher who explained everything. I wish to God you'd grow up to be like him. But if you don't want to study when you're already a big boy of four, how can you ever become a Rashi?. . . 'And Jacob went out from Beersheba and went toward Haran.' The same as we went out from Latorka toward Karoly. Well, Yiteleh, will you see what Rashi says?"

The little girl bent over the page, then she said:

"Rashi says it would be enough to say, 'Jacob left for Haran.' The rest is not necessary."

"No, no, my daughter," said her father, shaking a finger at her, "there isn't a single word in the Torah that isn't necessary. Every letter is just right. One day I'll tell you about the great competition between the letters of the alphabet. That was before the Torah had been written. The letters came before the throne of God, each wanting to come first somewhere. The *aliph* expected to be right at the beginning of the Torah, but first place was given to the *beth*, for the Bible begins with the word *be-reshith.* The *aliph* was compensated by being put at the beginning of the Ten Commandments: '*Anochi* . . .' So you see every letter is in the right place, with the right meaning. So, Yiteleh. . . ."

"So," broke in Yiteleh, "there's a reason why Beersheba is mentioned. It says here that Beersheba was to be pitied because it is bad for a town when a good man leaves it—the light and the beauty go out of it."

"Very good!" cried Sholem, his eyes a-twinkle with gratification. Then Mailech put in an unexpected question:

"Did Jacob go away from Beersheba because the peasants tried to kill him?"

The smile vanished from Sholem's eyes.

"Esau and his sons were after him," he said thoughtfully. "But I'll tell you about that later."

"Wasn't Jacob afraid?" insisted the little boy.

"He was. That was why he went away."

"Was Jacob always afraid?"

"Often, my son. Then God said to him: 'Fear not, my servant Jacob'—and after that he wasn't afraid any more."

"Did God sing the 'Fear not' hymn?"

"God only said the words. The tune was Jacob's."

"Did Jacob buy hemp from Esau, like you?"

"Not hemp, silly," said Yiteleh, "Jacob bought a birthright."

By now even Malkeleh was watching them. Her eyes were still misty, her heart still heavy, yet it pleased her to see how Sholem was keeping the children quiet, and at the same time cultivating their minds. But she could not forget about the lack of food. In the morning she had still been able to give the children a mug of milk each. But what was she going to do at dinner-time? If she left the shawl with the unknown peasant woman, the latter might let them have another potful of milk and perhaps a few other things as well. But what was the use when lighting a fire and cooking were forbidden. She wished the Sabbath were over.

For Sholem the Sabbath was not too long. Indeed, he would have liked to draw it out by an hour or two. The sun was getting warmer and his inside was also beginning to be pervaded by a feeling of ease and warmth. For five days he had slept in the

driving-seat, and the day before had seen the last of the plum
whisky in his wooden bottle. What was this warmth in his inside,
this sense of lightness in his heart and brain? Was he hungry? Was
he thirsty? No—he was hungry only for the flesh of the Sabbath,
and thirsty only for the truth, and both were provided in para-
disaical abundance by the new *sidrah*. Not for a long time had he
savored those words as he was doing now. Why, even the children
were beginning to light upon the true meaning of things, seeking
to relate their own lives to those of their ancestors. He had often
felt that the Book of Books contained not only the past, but also
the present and the future; now he was certain of it. The destiny
of Abraham, Isaac and Jacob was at the same time his own and
his children's destiny.

He went on reading the Portion of the Week in the age-old
sing-song, savoring the words, lingering over one verse after
another.

" 'And Jacob awaked . . . and Jacob vowed a vow, saying, If
God will be with me, and will keep me in this way that I go,
and will give me bread to eat and raiment to put on . . . and of
all that thou shalt give me I will surely give the tenth unto
thee. . . .' "

"Daddy," said Yiteleh, "why don't you make a vow?"

Mailech was already bored. He put his thumb into his mouth,
fidgeted, and yawned. But Yiteleh was getting more and more
interested. Jacob has reached Haran, and is at the well where the
shepherds water their flocks. Then along comes the lovely Rachel.
Jacob embraces and kisses her and bursts into tears.

"What made Jacob cry?" asked Yiteleh.

"Well—he was upset because he could not bring her any
presents."

"How do you know that that was why he cried?"

Mailech had by now sidled away and was loitering in front
of a gypsy hovel, where Duduy was playing the clarinet,
while his brother, the blacksmith, was hammering away at some
tinplate for baking-tins and smoke-pipes. Sholem turned a blind
eye and did not call him back. In fact he was glad that the boy
had gone away and was not continually interrupting with his
questions. In any case, he was too young to understand the

present discussion, too young to be told why Esau and his son
Eliphaz wanted to murder Jacob. Yiteleh was different. She was
nearly nine, and full of intelligence.

"It was like this, Yiteleh," explained Sholem. "Esau was after
Jacob's blood, saying that Jacob had cheated him of his birthright, whereas Jacob had given him a mess of pottage for it,
which Esau had enjoyed very much. What wouldn't you give for
a mess of pottage or for a plate of nice, hot *tsholent* . . . But that's
neither here nor there . . . Where was I . . .? Oh, yes . . . Esau
got very angry, and he commanded his son, Eliphaz, to go after
Jacob and cut him down. At that time Jacob was a rich man, with
many sheep, cattle, and servants, and much gold and silver. But
when Eliphaz attacked him, Jacob said unto him: 'Don't kill me,
nephew Eliphaz. Take all my possessions instead. For a poor man
is like a dead man, and a dead man has no birthright.' So Jacob
had nothing to bring to Rachel."

"It doesn't say so in the *sidrah*, does it?" observed Yiteleh.

"No," said Sholem, with pride and gratification in his tone
over the child's interest in these sacred matters. "No, it doesn't
say so in so many words, but it's there just the same. Listen
carefully, Yiteleh, and I'll tell you a secret. In our holy Torah it is
not only the words that tell you things but also the letters.
Sometimes each letter in a word is the first letter of another word.
So what I have been telling you is here. Look: 'And he told
Laban *all these things*.' What things? Why, the things you have
just heard. Each letter of 'all these things' stands for a separate
word. And it says: 'Do not be astonished that I bring you no
gifts because . . .' Look here. The Hebrew words for 'all these'
are 'at *Kol*.' The two letters of 'at' mean, '*Al Titameh*—Do not
be astonished . . .' The second word means 'Kih'—that. . . ."

The little girl listened to these revelations with wide-eyed interest. Sholem himself seemed to be overcome with wonderment,
as though this was the first time that he had come upon the
mystery of the Biblical logogriph.

THREE MEN

MALKELEH CAME up behind him and, touching him on the shoulder, said:

"Sholem, there are three gentlemen to see you."

Sholem raised his eyes from the book resentfully. He did not like being disturbed at a moment when he was expounding "all these things." But after an instant he jumped to his feet with the alacrity of alarm. There were three men standing by the wagon. One was a tall, heavy, white-haired man wearing the fur-trimmed cloak of the nobility, though the frogging on it was threadbare, the other a lean fellow with black side-whiskers and a sleeveless dolman, and the third a peasant with a red face and a vast stomach. Scholem bowed to them, involuntarily muttering to himself, still in the sing-song of the Bible reading:

"And lo, three men stood by him."

That was from the Portion of three weeks ago and Sholem wondered just why that phrase had come to his lips now. It flashed through his mind that he was committing a sin by mentally comparing this scene with the appearance of the three angels before Abraham's tent in Mamre, and himself with Abraham. The three strangers stood gazing at him with searching looks, as though to size him up and guess his thoughts. This, together with his scared sensation of sinfulness, made him sorely embarrassed as well as agitated. But now the old man—he must be a great lord, surely—gave a twirl to his untidy white moustache, stroked his stubbly double chin and, leaning on his ivory-handled walking-stick, began to speak:

"Judaeus! Nos nobiles, domini et Lapfalvae et Dengelegis et Bekatavae et Sarosbergiensis, nostram arendam horum pagorum tibi traderemus. . . ."

The rumbling voice of the old man, his dignified intonation and Sholem's utter ignorance of the language he was speaking in, all combined to terrify him. His wife, standing behind him, gave him a gentle dig in the ribs.

"Listen carefully, Sholem," she whispered. "His lordship is speaking in Latin."

Just like a woman, thought Sholem. What was the use of his listening carefully when he did not understand the language? He was somewhat light-headed with fatigue, hunger and Biblical dreams and he knew what he was going to tell his lordship: he was going to tell him "all these things." When the old gentleman had finished his speech, Sholem bowed three times from the waist and replied to his Latin in a still more ancient tongue:

"*Adoni. . . . Al titameh kih loh havathi davar. . . .*"

The old gentleman gave him a startled look. Then he glanced, in turn, at Sholem's family and at his own companions, and there was superstitious bafflement in his old eyes. He had some idea that the Jew was speaking in Hebrew, but he was in doubt whether the Jew might not be cursing him with his queer sing-songed words.

"Quid Judaeus dixit?" he asked the dark, lean fellow with the side-whiskers, who also looked startled.

The dark one turned to Malkeleh.

"Was sagt Ihr Jud?" he asked in German. "What is your Jew saying?"

Malkeleh glanced at her husband, while Sholem passed on the glance to Yiteleh, as though prompting her to show what she had been taught. The little girl turned to the old gentlemen.

"Mein Vater sagte," she began without embarrassment: "My father said: 'My lord, do not be angry with us that we came empty-handed. One time we had a nice fortune, but the sons of Esau have taken it all.'"

Sholem nodded approval, yet made a correction. The sense was right, but the words were not exact. It goes like this, Yiteleh, doesn't it: My lord, do not be astonished . . . Sholem searched the faces of his visitors. Of course, he spoke Hebrew with an Ashkenazi accent, that was why they did not understand him. He had once heard it said that the Bishop of Zips spoke Hebrew with a Sephardi accent. He, Sholem, could not and would not speak like that, for had not his teacher the great Rabbi Moses Teitelbaum banned that accent?

The old gentleman looked less stern. Turning to his companions, he said:

"I like this Jew. We can deal with him."

"A Jew is a Jew," said the lean one off-handedly. "They are all alike."

"That's right," assented the fat peasant. "But at least we don't need to go any further for a new innkeeper. We might walk ourselves bow-legged before we found another. This one has got a beard, a pony, a wife, and children. Why, he's cut out for a Jew."

In the course of further conversation Sholem and his family learned the following: The village Jew, or rather his widow, had died a few days earlier, the Jew himself having departed this life some time before that. The gentry, to whom the lease belonged, were just looking for another Jew, for the village of Lapfalva could not do without a Jew of its own for very long; and a rumor having gone round that morning that there was a Jew encamped near the village, a delegation was sent out to verify the fact. The gentry were represented by Balthazar de Denghelegh and Francis de Sarberek, and the village by its Headman, Mate Bor. The last-named, who was explaining all this, stated that the lease of the tavern would entitle the lessee to sell wine, beer, and all kinds of spirits, including home-distilled gin, and that five chains of land was part of the lease. The inn served three villages besides Lapfalva, to wit, Lapdengeleg, Sarberek, and Gyekenyes. There was a fourth as well, by rights, for there was the hamlet of Bekato, where the fowlers and loach fishers lived. Only Lapfalva had a church and an inn, so this was the only place where you could go to worship and get drunk.

"Well, Jew," said Balthazar de Denghelegh, "what about it? I have got rheumatics in my knee, I can't stand in this damp meadow much longer."

The lean one, Francis de Sarberek, held out his hand.

"Shake on it, Jew," he said, adding the time-honored phrase: "It's a hand, not a pig's foot. The inn's along the road. Come and have a peep. You can move in at once."

The other two visitors nodded approval. But Sholem stood hesitantly, not knowing whether to accept the outstretched hand.

A handshake would mean the sealing of a bargain, whereas it was forbidden even to think of business on this day. Unfortunately, he had already thought of it with keen interest, even delight. He could not help visualizing the peasants of five villages as they poured out of church of a Sunday and made straight for the inn, or the travellers on the road pulling up outside the door. He saw, too, the five chains of land, the picture merging with the sound of the traditional benediction: *Blessed be thou that bringest forth bread from the soil.* He had been dreaming of something like this for years: no trudging from village to village, no pack on his back, no encounters with savage dogs, no dry-throated performance on the reed-pipe, to advertise his presence. All this at a word from a Christian lord. A safe living for ever, and an opportunity to devote most of his time to his Talmudic studies. That had been his dream for ten years, and now it was being translated into reality— if he could only seize that outstretched hand. But could he? He must resist the temptation.

"It's Sabbath," he muttered penitently. "It's Sabbath." Offended by the Jew's seeming rudeness, the three visitors turned on their heels. And the Jew Sholem let them go and, with them, perhaps the chance of a lifetime.

"It's Sabbath," he repeated when they had gone, and his voice sounded even more helpless and humble than when he had said it to the strangers. His look, his bearing, his upturned palms, all expressed apology mingled with penitence. What else could he have done on the Sabbath? Malkeleh's face was calm, without a trace of reproach. Yiteleh gave a pout. As to Mailech, the repetition of the phrase had reminded him of something.

"If it's Sabbath I want some egg-cake."

"You'll get some next Saturday," said his mother.

"Then give me some cheese patties."

"You get that only with your coffee," said Yiteleh.

"Then I want some coffee."

"But there's no fire, so we can't make any," explained his mother.

"I don't care," cried the child, "I want something to eat."

That "something," which meant anything, hurt Sholem, for it

sounded like an accusation made on behalf of his entire family. Malkeleh took the boy into her arms and tried to quiet him.

"If you don't stop crying," she said, "the gypsies'll take you away. See that one with the pock-marked face—he's looking at you."

But Mailech had already made friends with that particular gypsy, so his mother tried something else.

"Listen, Mailech," she said. "In Karoly there is a baker who has such a big oven that it'll take three hundred tins of patties. Next Friday I'll take you to him, you'll carry one baking-tin, Yiteleh two, and me three."

Mailech was now quiet and listening with interest. Sholem called Yiteleh back to the rush-mat and the Portion of the Week. But the little girl had lost interest in study and asked questions that had nothing to do with the story of Jacob, Rachel, and Leah. Did the Christians know all the things forbidden to Jews on the Sabbath? No, said Sholem, even among the Jews only the most learned ones knew all the prohibitions. Yiteleh observed that the Hungarian gentlemen might have thought that it was forbidden for Jews to go into a strange village on the Sabbath. Sholem replied that it was not forbidden, so long as it was less than two thousand yards.

"But, Daddy," objected the child, "the inn is less than two thousand yards from here."

"No matter, I can't go there."

"I'd have liked to go along with you and see the inn."

"You can see it in the morning."

"But in the morning we can only see it from the outside when we drive past," cried the child in a disappointed tone.

"Yiteleh," said Sholem, "do you know who was the R'mah? Of course you don't. He was a great rabbi, like Rashi, though he lived much later, and not in France, but in Poland. His father, who was called Reb Isserl, had a shop and he used to close it at midday sharp on Fridays, so that he could prepare for the Sabbath properly. One Friday morning a great lord came into the shop and started buying a lot of silk and velvet, so many yards of this, and so many yards of that. Noon came and the great lord still kept on ordering. So Reb Isserl said he was sorry but he must

now close the shop. Whereupon the great lord said that if Reb
Isserl did not go on serving him he would leave all the lengths
that had already been cut off. "Very well, my lord," said Reb
Isserl. As the customer turned to go, Reb Isserl saw that it was
Satan disguised as a lord. The cut lengths were a great loss to him,
but God rewarded him for his steadfastness: his son became the
great R'mah."

"Did he have enough left to get food for Sabbath?" asked
Yiteleh.

Her father gave her a startled, searching look, then:

"Go to your mother, Yiteleh," he said with an impatient gesture,
and bending over his book he resumed the sing-song: " 'And
Jacob went out from Beersheba . . . And behold the Lord . . . said:
the land whereon thou liest to thee I will give it. . . .' " Five chains
of land they were giving with the inn. If it was as black and rich
as this meadow, it'd be a joy to work it. His father, Yoirish, had
only three and a half chains and when he was ploughing his children had to follow the plough bent double, picking stones and
roots out of the furrow. Besides, the five chains of land was only
an extra—the inn was in the best possible position, right along the
highway. . . .

Sholem gave a violent start, his face suffused with the purple
of shame. Why, he was thinking not of the holy text, but of the
inn, of wines and spirits, and even wishing he had a piece of egg-
cake to eat! What an abandoned sinner he was to let the craving of
the flesh master him, with the manna of the Book in his very
hands! He was thinking of those three men, no doubt messengers
of the Evil One, come to tempt him. Reb Isserl had realized that
his customer was Satan himself. . . .

Mailech was again cross, bothering his mother about egg-cake,
the traditional tid-bit for Sabbath morning.

"Be quiet, Mailech," said his sister. "Let Mummy tell us what
great-grandfather David Levi said to the Empress."

But Mummy was in no mood to talk now. She closed her eyes,
thinking. Then she looked towards the village. She was trying to
pull herself together, lest her children should sense her despair.
She changed her bearing, forcing a smile, though it was belied by
a soft, sad look in her velvety-brown eyes. She must make Mailech

forget about the egg-cake, and she must not let Yiteleh see that she was troubled.

"Grandma Bereyne," she said, "was very lovely. Her face was like a peach and her hair was red like the copper roof on the turrets at the castle. The Empress once stroked her hair with her own hand, and she said: 'What is your name, my child?' "

"Did she say 'my child?' " asked Yiteleh with wonderment in her tone.

"She said, 'Mein Kind.' "

And Malkeleh proceeded to recapitulate once more the wonderful story she had heard from grandmother Berenice herself. Grandma was by then a very old lady, with scarcely any teeth, but she was still good-looking, and she told with great relish how, when David Levi and she were newly wed, and she was admired for her beauty by every one in Nikolsburg, her young husband decided to let Vienna see her as well. "Wem gehoert dos schoene Weiberl?" (To whom does that pretty little woman belong?) were the very words the Empress had said. Berenice came from a rich family in Troppau in Silesia, where her father dealt in honey and beeswax.

Malkeleh was absorbed in the past, and just talked on, more to herself than to the children.

"I might have gone to live in Vienna myself. Once, a young man came to our house. He was from Vienna and he carried a fiddle. But Father didn't like him because he had side-whiskers and shaved with a razor. Your father's beard and ear-curls have never seen a pair of scissors."

Yiteleh glanced across at her father, who was still swaying his body and sing-songing on the rush-mat. Then she raised her eyes to her mother.

"Mummy, whose daughter would I have been if you'd married the man with the fiddle? Yours or Daddy's?"

The answer took a great deal of reflection, and poor Malkeleh reflected so long that the boy began to bawl about egg-cake again. These stories of the past were no use. The children were starving. It was silly to talk about what might have been. Things were as they were and not otherwise. Those three men had come along and something seemed about to happen. But on the Sabbath nothing must happen. One must not think about such things or make a change of any kind until at least three stars had appeared in the heavens. But she had to do something. Even Sholem, even the stern God of Israel could not possibly want the children to starve and go sick with the pangs of hunger.

"All right, Mailech, all right," she said. "You'll get some egg-cake if you'll only keep quiet. Yiteleh, take the pot and run along to the serf woman and ask her to fill it again. You can go with her, Mailech. Ask the woman for half a dozen eggs as well. I'll bake some egg-cake to-morrow when we get to Karoly. And—and . . . ask her for a bit of bread as well!"

When the children had left, Malkeleh climbed into the wagon to search for Yiteleh's cloth frock and Mailech's woolen waist-coat. The sun was in and out of the clouds and the wind was rising again. It might even rain later. Sholem would have liked Malkeleh to join him, so he could talk with her. Talk about what? Certainly not about the thing he could not help thinking about. He must bear it till evening. If it was bearable at all. Their luck had come and gone. It was still moving away from them, further and further, and by evening it would be so far away that no runner would be able to overtake it. But what could he do? Had he gone along, he would have looked round, and having looked round he would have made mental calculations, would even have mentally made all arrangements, built a new barn, re-paired a fence—all of which God forbid! On the Sabbath the spirit is at rest, but the eye, man's sinful eye, was in search of toil. The Sabbath would turn away and weep.

But Satan would not be conquered so easily. Mate Bor, the Headman, had come back, big stick, paunch and double chins and all, bringing a message.

"Their lordships say they know it's Sabbath in your pouch and it doesn't matter. You don't need to pay any rent for the present. Just come along and settle in."

Sholem looked at his wife, then back at the Headman.

"Not now," he said with a scared gesture, "not now."

"All right, Jew," said the Headman. "But I'll expect you for sure after dusk. The old squire says you got to come, if only for the sake of the three kids."

"Three kids!" said Sholem nonplussed.

Soon after the Headman's departure the children returned, Mailech carrying the bread and Yiteleh the milk and eggs.

"Auntie says it's twenty-three kreuzers altogether," reported Yiteleh, "but if we let her have the shawl we can have two more pots of milk and twenty eggs."

"We can't do that," said her mother.

"That's what I said. I said Great-grandma had it on when the Empress stroked her head. Then Auntie said she must have the money."

"All right. Your daddy has got the money."

"Sabbath!" hissed Sholem with a shocked expression. They were talking about money on the Sabbath! Then more gently: "Malkeleh dear heart, hadn't you better get out your *Tsenerenah* and read to the children. It's Sabbath, you know."

Malkeleh was quite aware that it was Sabbath. But she was not sure where she had put the pious book of Jewish womanhood in the desperate haste of their flight, and in any case the task in hand was more urgent. With a mute shrug towards her husband she proceeded to cut some bread for the children. Then she gave them a mug of milk each and a raw egg with some salt stirred into it. Yiteleh took the egg without a word, but for the boy she had to season it with the assurance that if he ate it he'd be able to sing as beautifully as his father. "You'll be singing at the synagogue in Karoly next Saturday."

"What if we stay here?" asked Yiteleh.

"We shan't," said her mother with a shake of her head. "We're moving into the town."

Sholem buried himself in his book. He did not want to see his children eating food purchased on the Sabbath, nor did he want to hear what Malkeleh was saying. For the third time he was chanting the verse about Leah, who called her newborn son Reuben, "for she said: 'the Lord hath seen my affliction . . . hath seen my affliction . . .' " A vision of the future rose dazzlingly in his mind, and the forbidden thoughts made him feel giddy. Or was it merely hunger? Being hungry was a sin, too. You could starve on a weekday to your heart's content, but not on the Sabbath. On the Sabbath you must live like a lord, in honor of the Queen.

It was now the hour of the second banquet. Sholem went to the table and after reciting the age-old benedictions, he took a bite of the ossified cheese. Then he quickly covered it up again.

"We'll leave this for the Third Meal, dear heart, so we can bless the Father for all the good things He is promising us."

He expected a reply, but Malkeleh responded only with a mute nod.

### THE ORPHANS

TOWARDS EVENING it came on to rain, and Malkeleh and the children sought shelter under the hood of the wagon. Sholem himself got out his greatcoat, which was lined with fox fur and which in dry weather he used to put on the driving seat for Malkeleh or the children to sit on. He now threw it over his shoulders, drew his battered hat down over his eyes, and remained standing about on the damp, soggy meadow. He looked up for three stars, but none were visible now, and he had to wait longer than usual to see the Sabbath out.

The rain did not bother him. Indeed, he was glad. All day it had been fine, and now that the Queen was about to depart it was meet that the heavens should be weeping. Now, on the threshold of the new week he had to pray for "the dew of the heavens, the richness of the earth, and many fishes and much wine." And as he stood there, he was experiencing it all: the dew of heaven above his head, the richness of the earth beneath his feet, and a smell of fresh fish in the wind. This was a good place—would he be able to stay or would he have to continue his flight?

In the afternoon he had dozed off and when he woke up observed to Malkeleh:

"How bracing the air is here—it knocks you over in no time."

"You're starved, Sholem," said Malkeleh sadly, "that's what's sent you to sleep."

Oh, no, it was not hunger, argued Sholem to himself. He always used to doze off on a Saturday afternoon, even after sleeping in

bed, instead of on the driving-seat all the week, and even after a
dinner of *tsholent* with beans and barley and goose giblets cooked
in fat, and goose neck stuffed with stuffing that melted in your
mouth. Beans and rice, or if there were no beans, split peas, were
a good substitute, provided always that the dish was left cooking
in a sealed earthenware pot, and in a sealed oven, from noon on
Friday till noon on Saturday. And the way Malkeleh could prepare that dish was a real joy! You could not smoke after the
dinner, but you could not help dozing off.

When he had come out of his doze this time, there were many
people on the meadow, come to stare at the "wandering Jew" and
his family. The serf kids ventured quite close to Yiteleh and
Mailech, while their mothers got into conversation with Malkeleh.
Sholem was glad. Then a big, hulking peasant with a stern face
came to the rush-mat and began to ask questions.

"Are you the new Jew?"

"Not a new one," said Sholem, smiling into his beard, "I've
been a Jew for a long time."

"I can see that. But are you the new innkeeper?"

"I am just Sholem."

The peasant gave a nod, probably taking the introduction as
a mark of friendliness.

"I am serf Martin Vizhordo," he said, offering his hand.

This hand Sholem was able to accept, for it had nothing to do
with business.

"Well, Jew Sholem," said the peasant, "better hurry up with
the inn."

Sholem made a gesture, as though to say, "We'll talk about that
another time."

"The reason I tell you this," said the peasant, tugging at his
untidy moustache, "is not because to-morrow is Sunday and I like
the inn to be open on Sunday, whatever else is closed. There's a
meaning to what I say. Squire Gyekeny wants to get a Jew from
Varalja, a Jew by the name of Herskovitch, whose father was his
kinsman's Jew there for thirty years."

That was in the afternoon. Now it was evening, with three stars
already peeping forth from behind the clouds, and Sholem was at
last able to think of business, including the disturbing news

brought by the serf. He must hurry, hurry! It was a dark, disquieting evening. The new week with all its anxieties had arrived. Malkeleh and the children were already chorusing the age-old week-day eve verse: "God of Abraham, Isaac and Jacob . . . guard thy people from evil . . . Let a good week come. . . ."

At this point Sholem ought to have marked the division between Sabbath and weekday with wine and a great light. But having no wine, and not even a piece of the traditional multicolored plaited candle, he found a stump of tallow candle, lighted it, and after reciting the appropriate prayers over it, passed his fingers through the flames, and "threw" the blessing towards the four corners of the earth. Then, with a new warmth and a new eagerness in his voice, he cried:

"A good week, Malkeleh. A good week, children! We're off now!"

Then he dashed off to get the pony, greeting it with a hearty cry of: "A good week, Kese!"

"Shall we go, Malkeleh?" he said.

Malkeleh climbed into the driving-seat without replying. What Sholem meant was, shall we go or shall we pause for awhile to talk? But Malkeleh did not understand. "Well," prompted Sholem. But her silence was tighter even than the big shawl that was drawn closely round her shoulders. Sholem cracked the whip in the air and said "Gee-up!" But he was still waiting for an answer. The pony began to pull, slowly, deliberately, the wheels squelching audibly. It took Sholem some time before he could think of an opening.

"So we're going, aren't we?" he said.

"Yes."

"We'll have a look at the inn."

"Yes."

"The two squires want us to."

"I know."

"The lease is theirs."

No reply.

"There is a third squire and he doesn't want to let us have it."

Malkeleh does not seem to be concerned. Does she know about this third man? Why doesn't she say so? And if she doesn't know, why doesn't she ask?

"Gee-up!" A pause, then: "Don't you want to come to the inn?"
"I do."

"It won't hurt to have a look at it."

"No."

"If we don't like it, we can simply go on."

"We're not going on, Sholem."

"No," said Sholem with sudden elation, "we're not going on.
If you want us to stay we will. Are you in pain, Malkeleh?"

"Not yet, but I am very tired. Besides, where can we go on a
cold, rainy night with the children? It's time they had some proper
sleep. At worst, we'll pay for the night."

"Yes, we'll pay," said Sholem, with the elation gone out of his
voice.

"You still have some money left—more than a florin."

"Gee-up!" cried Sholem, laying on the whip for once. "The way
this horse limps along this evening!"

The animal made a spurt. The wagon shook and rattled all
over. The candle in the lantern flared up and went out. The children under the hood were singing the Sabbath evening hymn: "A
star has risen from Jacob, Fear not, my servant Jacob." Sholem
took advantage of the noise to mutter into his beard:

"Less than a florin, Malkeleh." He was hoping that she would
not hear him, or if she did hear, she would not pursue the matter.
But she had heard and was pursuing it.

"I'd like you to pay the serf woman on the way for the milk,
bread, and eggs."

"One doesn't pay out at the beginning of the week," said
Sholem with a show of indignation. "I'll have my hand in my
pocket all the week. How much is it?"

"Twenty-three kreuzer."

"Good heavens! What an expensive Sabbath!"

"We still have a few eggs left."

"Even then."

Sholem liked the week-day eve, when you could resume week-
day talks interrupted on Friday afternoon. On Friday evening in
turn, you reverted to talks on festive matters interrupted on the
previous Saturday evening. But the circle was not complete, for
whereas Sholem was learned, Malkeleh was not interested in the
problems debated by the Sages of various degrees, which consti-

tuted the substance of Sabbath talks. When he "ate days" in the
Nikolsburger home, and, even when he was engaged, he never
talked with Malkeleh. Sholem's passion was the Talmud and its
commentators; while Malkeleh read Schiller, Chamisso, and
Goethe, despite Pa Manasseh's ban, even on the Sabbath. It took
a long time before Malkeleh and Sholem began to converse with
each other, and even then mostly about everyday trifles. Now
Sholem felt that he was considerably behindhand as regards heart-
to-heart talks with his wife. Malkeleh was alternately receding
from and drawing closer to him. Fortunately, the week-days,
when they could talk about everything, were longer than the holy
days, so there was more of the drawing closer. Just now, Sholem
wished she would come closer to him, and quickly. They were
already in the village, fast approaching the tavern, and they had
not yet settled anything between themselves. Of course, he himself had made an intimate talk impossible, first by objecting to the
day's expenditure, then by confessing that he had given some
money to the Saint's wife on the Thursday to "make Sabbath."
That, of course, meant providing festive loaves, fish, chicken, plum
whisky, wine, tsholent, egg-cake, condiments, and fruit. The other
visitors had also left money on Madame Saint's table.

"I only gave her a florin," he said.

"Only," repeated Malkeleh.

If only he had not concealed it from Malkeleh, Sholem thought,
or if at least he had not said "only," the subject would not have
become an unscalable barrier between them and they might now
be discussing the urgent matter on hand—the lease they could get
without money, the wine, beer, and spirits they might sell to the
people of five villages, and five chains of land, the thirsty travellers
of the road, the two kindly lords and the hostile third, who might
perhaps be won over with a little diplomacy. You had to have
the will to be lucky.

Leaning close to his wife, and speaking with a warm, persuasive
urgency, he said:

"You think I wasted my time with the Saint, don't you? You
think we were late, don't you . . . ? Well, that's true, but we were
late only to be in time for this place. And the reason we took the
wrong road was to stray into the right road. The Above One did

not want me to talk to the peasant with the manure, that was why he arranged it so that he should ask where we were going just when I was saying the silent Benedictions. If you go on to Karoly, Malkeleh, you'll be going from certainty into uncertainty. The Lord has promised the land upon which I am lying to me and my seed. And the Lord hath seen thine affliction too, Malkeleh. Why did the Christian lord say we should settle in at once, and why did the other one send a message about three children? Those men were undoubtedly sent by the Above One, that was why they saw into the future. . . What did you say, Malkeleh? It's hard to hear what with the rattling of the cart and the barking of dogs."

"Sholem, I'm against it."

"Against what?"

But at this moment the pony jibbed, jerking the wagon to a halt. The Headman stood in the road swinging a lantern and shouting:

"Whoa, Jew!" Then: "Halt, Jew! This is the inn." He swung the lantern again to show the direction: "This way—turn left— the gate is open—this way to the yard."

When the wagon had stopped, the peasant set about unharnessing the horse, talking the while.

"What's your name?" he asked kindly.

"Sholem."

"Sholem—all right. The other one was called Moshe. He was a good man, only he had a cough. And it took him off in the summer. And now his wife Sarah has gone after him—from grief and the new baby and the hard work. Sroleh is a clever lad, but too young. Doesn't know enough about the business and they cheat him right and left. Besides, who'll pay the rent? What, Sholem?"

Sholem maintained an embarrassed silence. Malkeleh gazed towards a lighted window. She had heard the feeble cry of an infant.

"Is there anyone in there?" she asked, taken aback.

"The three kids," replied the Headman. He went on attending to the pony, while Malkeleh, pulling her children after her, hurried towards the house, followed by her husband.

They all stopped in the doorway. Malkeleh let go of her children's hands. She saw at once what awaited her, and her whole person radiated grief. Sholem had a crushed bearing and a grave face. Yiteleh was about to say "Good evening," but her parent's strange silence kept her silent too.

A sagging candle burned on the table, a wick floating in a cup of oil flickered on the edge of a battered tallboy. Two starved-looking boys, one about fourteen, the other younger, sat at opposite ends of some ragged blankets lying on the floor. Between them was a rounded wooden trough, and in it a moaning baby. The younger boy was rocking the trough, and the baby quieted down for a moment or two, thereby underlining the silence. The older boy, pale, with long ear-curls and burning eyes, emanated hostility. Yiteleh would have liked her mother or father to say something to him to make him friendly, but they did not speak. Slowly advancing into the room, they sat down in front of the three children—still silent. Yiteleh was oppressed by a queer kind of fright, this was her first experience of Jewish grief.

For awhile Sholem sat with his chin resting on his fist. Then, slowly, he raised his eyes to the older boy.

"When did she die?" he asked in a deep, flat voice.

The boy gazed in front of him.

"Tuesday," he snapped resentfully.

"Did she have a Jewish burial?"

"Serf Matthias dug the grave. Aunt Feiga buried her."

"Who is Aunt Feiga?"

"Aunt Feiga is Aunt Feiga," said the boy.

"Do you say *kaddish*?" (prayer for the dead).

"No synagogue here," said the boy, with contempt at Sholem's ignorance.

"How old are you?"

"Fourteen."

"And your brother?"

"Nearly eleven."

"Then he need not sit in mourning yet."

"But he must. Aunt Feiga said so."

The baby began to moan again. The older boy turned on his brother, who sat staring at the visitors:

"Yossef! Don't let it cry!"

Yossef hastily removed his sad, staring gaze from Malkeleh and Yiteleh and resumed rocking the trough mechanically and crooning wearily:

"Ay-yah, ay-yah, baby Chayah . . . ay-yah, ay-yah. . . ."

The baby stopped moaning for a moment, then resumed again. Malkeleh rose to her feet, took the baby out of the trough, pressed it to her bosom and crooned to it. Then she laid it on the table, undid its swaddling clothes and examined the greenish-yellow excrement on its napkin.

"Any clean napkins?" she asked.

"There are some in the kitchen," replied Yossef, trying to rise from the floor to get them. But his brother pulled him back.

"You stay where you are. Aunt Feiga will change his napkin."

But Yiteleh had already gone out, presently returning with some dry napkins. She stood watching as the tiny creature was wrapped up, stroking its puckered face and skinny little hands.

"It's nine or ten days old, isn't it?" said Malkeleh in a somber tone, turning to the boys.

The elder boy gave her a sulky look and did not reply. The look was meant to convey to Yossef also that he should not speak to these strange intruders. But Yossef took no notice. He had a queer feeling that these people were relations. He wanted them to be. Gazing into Malkeleh's velvety dark eyes, he burst into tears:

"It's twelve days old to-day, Auntie."

Malkeleh walked up and down trying to quiet the squalling baby and also trying to suppress her own agitation.

"Is there any milk in the house?" she inquired. "Your little sister is hungry."

This time the elder boy replied.

"Aunt Feiga has gone to the village. She'll be back in a minute." There was now a trace of friendliness in his voice.

The children began to get closer to each other. Mailech went up to the weeping Yossef and stroked his face.

"Don't cry," he said. Then: "Your jacket is torn. And his jacket is torn too. Yiteleh can sew it up for you."

Yiteleh stepped in front of the elder boy.

"What is your name?"

The boy pursed his lips and gave her a defiant look.

"Don't you want to tell me?" said the girl.

"Why shouldn't I? It's no secret." He paused, as if waiting to be prompted. Then he said: "Sroleh Yomtov."

"Sroleh Yomtov," repeated the little girl. Then as though to comfort the wretched boy: "What a nice name."

Aunt Feiga had just arrived. Her shoulders were lopsided and she had a moustache on her wrinkled face.

"At last you've come," she began in a screechy, yet whining voice as soon as she entered the door. "At midday the Headman said you didn't want to come. Was that right, not wanting to come along to these poor orphans? Who shall comfort the mourners if not the other Jews? When the man died Menachem and his wife came over from their village, and so did Mendel the fisherman from Nemeny with his wife. But when Sarah went no one came. They even avoided the inn. A Jew is nothing but a dog, I tell you. The village dogs have a better life than the village Jew. A dog at least has friends in the other dogs, but the Jew is alone."

Pausing for breath, she looked at Malkeleh, then at Sholem and the two children.

"You're a lovely woman, no evil eye," she said, shaking her head contentedly. "And your husband is a fine upstanding Jew. And your children are pretty like a couple of peaches, no evil eye. May you all live to be a hundred and twenty in peace and happiness. And don't forget about poor Feiga, who has been an orphan these seventy years, no father, no mother, no brothers and sisters, no children, no nothing. I brought them up, these boys, I made the rent in the lapel of their jacket twice in less than a year. It was I that buried their father in the summer and their mother last week. All I want now is some one to bury Aunt Feiga, some one who'll light a single candle and say a single *kaddish* in memory of poor old Feiga."

She was now wiping her eyes with the corner of her apron. But a moment later she was bustling about cheerily.

"Sit down, my darlings, I'll lay the table and get the eggs. I boiled them on Friday, I left them in their shells and they're still all right. I expected people to come and comfort these poor

orphans and bring some hard-boiled eggs with them. But they
never came. Only the holy prophet Elijah came. He goes everywhere where there is joy or sorrow in Israel. There's still some
fancy bread left, these children wouldn't eat over the Sabbath.
You can get up from the floor now, Sroleh Yomtov and Yossef,
you don't have to sit more than an hour Saturday evening. Isn't
that right, my fine big Jew-man?" Sholem nodded affirmation,
and the old woman went on: "See? He knows. He must be a very
learned man. You can put on your boots, not to wear holes into
your Sabbath stockings."

She would have chattered on, had not Malkeleh interrupted her.

"Aunt Feiga, the baby is hungry."

"Of course the little mite is hungry," said the old woman, bending over the baby. "It takes Aunt Feiga such a long time to totter
home with the milk. Besides, cow's milk is too strong for her;
she always throws it up. And she won't sleep. Cries day and
night for her mother." A glance at Malkeleh's figure, then: "If
you'd come a little later . . . or if this poor mite had arrived
later . . . you could give her something better. Now, she won't
wait. She's not going to live long enough."

Malkeleh gave a barely perceptible nod. Then:

"Have you any aniseed, Aunt Feiga?" she said urgently. "Or
caraway seed? But we have got something even better. Yiteleh,
there's some dried camilla in a linen bag in the packing-case. All
right, Sholem, bring the case along. We can leave it on the
verandah. We'll boil some camilla and give her the liquor with
milk. She'll live. We'll look after her and she'll live."


THE NEW JEW


SHOLEM TOOK possession of the tavern and meekly suffered the
boys of his predecessor to show him the ropes. This was the big
cask with the "special" rye. The other big cask held potato
whisky or "ordinary." The small cask contained rum. The
wicker-covered pitcher was the plum whisky; the big bottle the

grape brandy, and the small bottle, the liquor. The well-to-do freemen, like Farmer Galagonya, drank "special" while the serfs drank "ordinary." This was the pint measure, this the half-pint. The wine was in the cellar. The beer in summer was kept in the small cellar, beneath the gentry's parlor.

Yossef was eager to help, but Sroleh Yomtov was curt and sometimes even irritable. "This is how it's done," he would say. Sholem felt no resentment. He could well understand, from his experience as a *yeshiba* student, that the person who knew should be irritated with the one who was ignorant. However, Sholem was an apt pupil, and within a week or two he had even become acquainted with his customers. "A pint for Neighbor Bene . . . half for Farmer Ludpal . . . a mugful for Uncle Gazsi. . . Shall I mark it up?"

The fourth week his teachers left him alone in the bar. Sroleh Yomtov muttered something to the effect that he had some business to attend to in the next village, while Yossef spent his time in the kitchen, helping Malkeleh under the instructions of Aunt Feiga.

Sholem sat behind the bar, which was divided from the rest of the room by a lath grille, and when there were no customers, read the Talmud. He felt very happy. There was a twinkle in his eyes, and his full, red lips were like a rude red bloom when he said to his wife:

"It would have been enough to be allowed to settle in this fine village. And it would have been good enough to get the tavern without the land. But we got the tavern *and* the land *and* three fine children."

What pleased him most was the large garden at the back of the tavern and the five chains of black land. The land was on the edge of the marsh and one side was rather soggy and quite near where the peasants cut their peat. But these defects did not damp Sholem's enthusiasm. He found a rusty plough in the barn and took it into his head to polish it to a silvery sheen—in the soil—before winter. Fortunately, that autumn remained mild for a long time and the soil being soft as butter, Kese, the pony, was able to perform what was required. The serfs used to watch the new Jew trudging after the plough and ploughing good and deep. But they were not pleased, for the old Jew used to have this work done by them for good wages. What was the world coming to when the Jew encroached on the peasants' work?

There was no grumbling as yet, because Sholem was greatly in favor with the gentry, though Squire de Gyekeny was still sulking because the inn had not been given to his Jew. When Herskovitch arrived, Sholem was already in possession. He wanted the inn not for himself, but for his son-in-law, and he offered not only a higher rent, but also a bribe for his patron if he could only get rid of Sholem. Herskovitch even approached Sholem himself to accept a lump sum and go. At one time it seemed that Herskovitch was gaining the upper hand and there was consternation in Sholem's home. But in the end the gentry gave the contract to Sholem, and Sholem was confirmed both in his position as innkeeper and in his faith. "You see, Malkeleh, He who brought us here wants us to stay."

In what manner the Jewish God compensated the gentry for the loss of the cash offered by Herskovitch, when they were forever complaining of lack of money, Sholem had no idea, nor did he even speculate on this mystery. All he saw was the final result.

During the negotiations Sholem kept citing the Talmud and the Shulchan Aruch, insisting on harder terms than the gentry wished to impose. When he was told that no rent would be payable for the land, he shook his head, saying that he could not agree to that. Abraham had also been offered the cave of Machpelah free, yet he had insisted on paying four hundred silver shekels. In the end it was agreed that Sholem should pay two florins per annum "in arrear." That expression figured largely in the agreement; the rent of the inn was also payable six months in arrear; the late Mme Moshe having settled up until the summer. Sholem insisted on reserving one half of the net profits for her children, although the two squires said that one-quarter would be ample, the children being minors. Sholem argued that Sroleh Yomtov at least was an "adult," for was he not already praying in phylacteries? Besides, half profits was in this case in accordance with the law of Moses and Israel. In the end, all Sholem's hard stipulations were embodied in the agreement, with the proviso that "no detriment to the gentry shall accrue there-from."

Sholem signed the agreement in Hebrew characters, Malkeleh in Gothic, the gentry in Roman. Squire de Denghelegh made the following declaration.

"From now on, Judaeus, you are under our protection, and none shall so much as touch a hair of your head. You'll be all right here. It has not happened here *post hominem memoriam* that our Jew should have had his ear-curls pulled. Do you pay the Jew tax?"

"I haven't paid it since I have been here, my Lord."

"Well, Jew, don't. The gentry are masters here, not the Emperor."

Malkeleh, who had always intervened in Sholem's business affairs, left everything to him this time. She had a heavy task on her hands: to save the sick infant and win the confidence of the two boys. The moment their wagon was in the yard and she heard the baby crying, she knew that this was the voice of destiny and she would have to stay. And when she had seen the two ragged boys and had hugged the sick baby to her breast, she knew that it was impossible for her to travel on. All her former fears and prejudices vanished. She felt no distaste for the marsh-side, and no longer wanted to join her brother in the town. She forgot about the time Sholem had wasted with the Saint, and about the florin he had given to the Saint's wife. It was good that things had happened as they did. They had to be late and take the wrong road in order to find themselves on the right road. Sholem kept talking about the three angels that appeared to Abraham. Perhaps he was right.

Only once did Malkeleh intervene. That was when Herskovitch set up his headquarters in the next village, close to his patron. She called on Madame Gyekeny and asked for her support in the name of both her own and the orphaned family. The squire's lady was pleased to accept the gift of Grandma Berenice's cashmere shawl, and she had a long talk with Malkeleh on how to make borsht, of which she had had a taste the previous Pass-over. She thought it would do as a "rake soup" against the forth-coming pig-killing banquets. She told Malkeleh to be sure to call in a certain midwife when her time came, because she was very skillful. Malkeleh returned to her two sets of children with an easy mind; and the very next day the gherkin-nosed Hersko- vitch beat a hasty retreat.

Sroleh Yomtov was also said to have a hand in this victory, but he refused to talk about it. In contrast with Yossef, he continued to be unfriendly even towards Malkeleh. Yossef obviously felt at ease when near her and sometimes gazed at her with gratitude in his big, mournful eyes. But Sroleh Yomtov had scarcely changed. He was no less sulky and defiant than on the very first day. Malkeleh did not force matters, but waited patiently for the lad to melt. She wanted to be a mother to the three orphans.

Between Sroleh Yomtov and Sholem a silent struggle was going on. From the boy's sullen expression and resentful gaze Sholem read the charge that he and his family were intruders, a charge that he might one day put into words. In his own mind Sholem vehemently protested that the boy was wrong, that he was not taking the business away from him, but on the contrary preserving it for him. But the boy never gave him an opportunity to say so. Sroleh Yomtov confined himself to constant criticism, and truth to tell, he was better versed in many things than Sholem. Only when he objected to Sholem's eagerness to make the terms of the agreement harder, was Sholem able to reply with a superior smile:

"The only reason we beat Herskovitch was that I made the agreement according to the holy law."

"But why did you throw away two florins for the land, when we always had it for nothing?" said the boy with a sneer.

"What you get for nothing always costs more in the end, my son. Besides, the land is the most valuable part of the whole lease."

"Those paltry five chains," said the boy with contempt.

In the inn their differences of opinion were more serious. Sholem had examined the pint and half-pint measure, and as the sides were dented he had them hammered straight by the gipsy tinsmith.

"Why did you do that, Sholem?" said the boy. "Now we must give the peasants more drink. Isn't it better if they drink less?"

"If they drink less they should pay less," said Sholem.

"And who pays you for the liquor that drips away or evaporates, what?"

"If we are careful it won't drip away, and if we pack the stoppers with rag there'll be scarcely any evaporation. Wait a moment, Sroleh Yomtov, I'll get you the Talmud, so you can see with your own eyes what a great sin it is to give false measure."

"To another Jew," snapped the boy.

"No, my son, our Sages of blessed memory have made it clear that the sin is just as great if it is committed against a Gentile. Do you know that this is a greater sin even than fornication? For why? Because it is done with calm deliberation."

The greenish pallor of Sroleh Yomtov's face changed to purple, and Sholem instantly regretted having spoken to him with such little tact. But after all, he consoled himself, the boy must have discipline and instruction. His parents in Heaven won't take it amiss.

On another occasion Sholem had to be rather severe with the boy. Farmer Galagonya had come in to settle accounts for the previous week or two. Sholem turned up page *gimmel* in his ledger, and handed the ledger to Sroleh Yomtov to call out the items, while he, Sholem, wrote them down in chalk on the table.

"First Sunday after Michaelmas—one pint rye whisky. Right, Farmer Galagonya?"

"Right."

"Monday, another pint, seven kreuzer again."

"Right."

"Wednesday ditto."

"Never had any of that," grunted the peasant. "All I took was another pint."

"That's right, Uncle Galagonya," giggled the boy. "Ditto means a pint . . . Thursday half a pint . . . Friday ditto . . . That makes one pint. Sunday one pint . . . Monday ditto . . . Tuesday ditto . . . Wednesday ditto. . . Thursday, Friday ditto."

"Stop your dittoing, Sroleh," said the peasant, "and let your dirty paw get farther down on the page at last."

"All right, Uncle . . . Sunday ditto."

"Ditto," said Sholem, drawing a line beneath the column of figures he had written on the table. "Sixteen pints altogether . . . Right, Farmer Galagonya? Sixteen sevens. Ten sevens, seventy . . . six sevens forty-two. Seventy and forty-two. Can you get me a sack of wheat for autumn seed—the whiskered kind? I'll pay you as much as the dealers in Karoly. I only want enough for a couple of chains. I'll leave the rest for potatoes and maize. All right, then. You'll have a drop of rum, won't you? It's real Jamaica. Pass the bottle, Sroleh . . . It's distilled by black people, like pitch they are . . . that's why it's so strong . . . Lord be with you, Farmer Galagonya."

When the peasant had left, Sholem went to the ledger to enter the payment. Checking the figures over, he gave a start.

"Sroleh," he said, "go call him back. You made a mistake."

Sroleh made no move. He was not in the habit of making mistakes.

"Look, Sroleh," insisted Sholem, "the book says twelve pints, not sixteen . . . that's twenty-eight kreuzers less."

"What of it?" said the boy. "He's paid it, hasn't he?"

"That's just it, my son, we must pay it back."

"Really?" said the boy angrily. "And who's going to pay us for the sixteen pints that Anton and Paul are never going to pay for?"

"Farmer Galagonya doesn't owe for it, so he is not going to pay."

"One *goy* drinks, the other pays," cried Sroleh, his earcurls trembling with agitation. "I'm not going to call him back!"

"Sroleh Yomtov!" said Sholem severely. "This won't do. It's no use saying your prayers if you aren't honest. Every morning you begin your prayers with '*Mah tovi*' . . . How pleasant are thy tabernacles, O Jacob, thy shelters, O Israel! . . . It was a *goy* that first said that—the High Priest Bileam, whom Balak hired to curse Israel, but who praised us when he saw that there was 'no falsehood or fraud in Israel.'" There was fanatical anger in his tone and a fierce fire in his eyes. The boy dared not meet his gaze.

"Give me the money," he said quietly. "I'll take it to Uncle Galagonya . . . And I'll tell him I tried to cheat him."

"You need not say that, my son," said Sholem gently. "You only made a mistake . . . a mistake."


"All right, Kese," said Sholem to the horse, "we're going to do a bit of ploughing to-day. Sroleh Yomtov is looking after the bar."

When a man has many anxieties and no idea how to get the better of them, it is best for him to revert to the occupation of his fathers. Just now, Sholem favored ploughing. So completely absorbed was he in the work that while engaged on it his mind was relieved of all care. All he was thinking of was that he was now writing a letter to the Almighty himself, the plough being the pen and the soil the sheet of paper. The Almighty was looking down from Heaven to see whether there was substance in the lines thus written, and if so he would compose a reply and write it in green, yellow, blue, red, and gold ink. "To Sholem ben Yoirish. As a reward for thy labors thou shalt receive so many bushels of wheat, so many sacks of oats, maize, and potatoes, and so much sunflower seed for oil." You could have faith in toil and in this sort of correspondence.

But he was not thinking only of the divine hand and the inks of many colors. There were other hands, niggardly earthly hands of which he could not help thinking. He had managed the flight from the north with a balance of nine kreuzers. The lease, by divine favor, he had been granted without payment. Yet things were bad. The outstanding accounts of the inn had come in after the threshing, but had apparently melted away. New money was slow in reaching the till, for most of the peasants were accustomed to long credit, from harvest to harvest. Sholem's stock was diminishing to alarmingly low levels, and unless he wanted to betray the gentry's confidence in him, he must restock soon. On Sunday evening he had heard that Christmas was near, and it was then that he realized his deficiencies. Scarcely any spirits. Even of wine he had but little. He had written a long letter to brother-in-law Mordechai, telling him all about everything. How he had to flee from the north, how on Malkeleh's advice, he was about to move to Karoly and how the Above One had guided

him to settle in this village on the edge of the big marsh. He had
a living here, but had so little on arrival that he might almost
have used the words of Jacob: "With my staff did I cross Jordan."
He was not asking Mordechai for money, tactfully avoiding even
use of the term, but it must have been clear to Mordechai that
he needed money.

Mordechai, on his part, did not beat about the bush. His reply
was mainly about money. The previous year he had invested all
his money in oak-gall, because the crop was good, and according
to the experts the gall-fly only appeared in adequate numbers
every fifth year, so that a good year was usually followed by
four lean years. But he had been misled either by the experts or
by the gall-fly, for this year oak-gall was even more plentiful, and
consequently Mordechai had been obliged to buy up all the oak-
gall thrown on the market to stem the fall in prices, and all his
resources were engaged in the business. The tanners in Galicia,
the Bukovina, and Silesia did not need even half the available
supplies, and it was to be feared that the oak forests might behave
erratically again. A Nikolsburger must make provision against
such things, so he, Mordechai, had started a leather business,
patronizing only those tanners who bought their tanning material
from him. In addition, he had started an ink factory to use up the
surplus of oak-gall. He was now supplying ink to the county
offices, the local municipality, the Customs, and the big landed
estates. The lawyers were also his customers, even Ferenc Kolcsey,
who used a lot of ink writing books. Of course, for much ink
you had to have many jars, and the price of Spanish cork used
for stoppers had also gone up.

Yes, much ink, many complaints, much conceit, and much
blackness. Sroleh Yomtov, who took the letter to Mordechai,
gave him a piece of his mind. On his return he said to Sholem:

"Sholem, your brother-in-law told me to tell you that I am
an impudent fellow."

"You are what?"

"An *azes ponem*—an impudent fellow."

"But why did he say that?"

"Because I refused to apprentice myself to him."

"Did he want you to?"

"Yes. He said, you were a poverty-stricken man and couldn't keep one family, let alone two. But if I went into his service as inkmaker he'd give me board and lodgings and if I behaved myself he'd start paying me wages after four years. So I said: 'Look, Reb Mordechai, if your brother-in-law is such a poor man, why don't you send him some money?' "

"What did he say to that?"

"Nothing. . . But he told me to think it over, and that an industrious, well-behaved boy could go far in his business. Long-legs Naphtali has been working for him for six years. Last summer he gave him money to get married, and now Naphtali's wife is helping to wash ink-bottles in Mordechai's business. When he told me that, I said: 'So after six years Naphtali earns so little that his wife has got to wash ink-bottles?' He got very angry and said he didn't like that sort of talk, and did I want to come to him or didn't I? I answered quite politely that I did not, because ink made you dirty. Then he threw the letter at me and said to be sure to tell you that he had never seen such an impudent boy as me. He said he'd like to put it in the letter, but it'd be a waste of good ink and precious time."

Of course, there was a kind of perky impudence about the boy, and it could not well be otherwise. His father had been an invalid for years, while his mother had not had the time to look after him, so that since the age of ten Sroleh Yomtov spent his life in the bar parlor among drunken peasants. He knew all about the different drinks, and also knew how to handle the peasants, but took no interest in things of the spirit. Sholem determined to educate him. However, Sroleh Yomtov proved a difficult proposition. When Sholem sat down with him to teach him a passage of the *Gemarah*, the boy ceased to attend within a quarter of an hour. He heard only the words, but saw not the profundity thereof. Once they were reading an enchanting discussion in the Talmud, in the tome called "*Boba Meziah.*" The Sages were seeking a solution to a difficult problem. Suddenly, Resh Lakish—Rabbi Simon Ben Lakish—thought he had found the solution and gave a cry like a bird.

"*Zavach Resh Lakish ke-kerikhyeh,*" sing-songed Sholem in Aramaic. Then he looked at the boy, as though to say: Well, what do you say to that?

The boy repeated the sentence in Aramaic and guffawed.

"What are you laughing at?" inquired Sholem in a mildly shocked tone.

"It's the word *ke-kerikhyeh*," said the boy.

"What about it? It only means like a bird."

"Yes, but what bird?"

Sholem was embarrassed. It was unusual for Sroleh Yomtov to be interested enough to ask a question and here he was, unable to enlighten him.

"What does it matter?" he said with a shrug. "The word means like a bird, that's all. This was a hundred years after the destruction of the Temple, so perhaps Resh Lakish gave the cry of the raven, or perhaps the cry of the ostrich of the desert of Judea."

"But it wasn't a raven," said Sroleh Yomtov impishly, "nor an ostrich."

"You know?" said Sholem with surprise. "Have you been taught this passage before?"

"No, I haven't, but I know. *Ke-kerikhyeh* means like a cock. Resh Lakish crowed like a cock—kikereekee . . . ."

"You may be right," said Sholem, his face lighting up. The boy wasn't such a fool, after all. "Yes, the Rabbi crowed like a cock."

"He crowed," laughed the boy, "he crowed—he stood in the college crowing."

His amusement was irreverent, but Sholem tried not to be angry with him. A teacher of young people must have patience.

"What of it?" he said. "The cock crows when he sees the light, and Resh Lakish crowed because *he* had seen the light."

On another occasion Sholem was reading to the boy from the marriage laws. It was early afternoon and the open tome lay on the table in the bar parlor, which was now empty of customers. Sroleh Yomtov was fidgety, longing for the sound of the bell above the door, so that he might go out and serve. But no one came. Sholem's monotonous sing-song began to make the boy drowsy. Then Sholem put a little more liveliness into the sing-song, and a curious rhythm, like that of some ancient folk song, crept into his voice:

> *"Tov lemaytov tandee*
> *Milemaytov armehleh . . ."*

"What it means, my son?" said Sholem in reply to a question. "It means that it is better to live with another than to squat alone. This was a saying that was current among the daughters of Israel, and of course it meant marriage. The Preacher says the same thing in different words: 'Two are better than one, and woe is to him that stands alone, for when he falls who shall raise him.' "

"What if the two always quarrel?" said the boy. "What if the stronger throws the other one down and leaves him there?"

"The sons of Esau do that," said Sholem reflectively. "The Children of Israel must be at peace with each other."

But Sroleh Yomtov was already sick of it all. He thought it was better to be alone—behind the bar—than with another. Above all, it was better to have all the profits than to have to share them with another. At all events, he had had as much of the marriage laws as he could bear just then and he began to talk about business. Karoly, he said, was quite a good place, for the old Count Karolyi liked a Jew with ideas and protected the Jews. Mordechai Nikolsburger had left home with nothing but a whistle and a good idea: he sold a stencil to the Count wherewith it was possible to brush a chessboard pattern on the backs of the horses. The Count, being very fond of the game of chess, in turn sold him his old horses very cheap.

Sholem just kept nodding his head. The boy, he thought, disliked Mordechai, yet respected his ability and his success. He too disliked Mordechai, and he too admitted that Mordechai had a head on him. Of course, he had learned much in his father's business, but his real knowledge he owed to the *yeshibas* he had attended. Sroleh Yomtov ought to be sent to a *yeshiba* too; there, among other boys of the same age, he would no doubt take a deeper interest in the sacred cyclopedia than he did here in the inn. There they would teach him other things than the difference between cherry brandy and between vanilla and kümmel drinks, and how to dilute ninety-three centigrade spirit to make drinkable spirits of various different strengths. A *yeshiba* student might become anything he liked afterwards, from a speculator in oakgall to an ink manufacturer, and from a leather merchant to a grain dealer.

The boy was not in Sholem's way. On the contrary, he was very useful in the bar and Sholem was learning a great deal from him. But he was a bad influence in the family. He tyrannized over Yossef so badly that Yossef dared not tell on him when found in a distressed state. And when Malkeleh asked Sroleh Yomtov himself, the boy replied rudely that it was nobody's business and that Yossef was his brother, not hers. There must be some sort of secret between the two boys, Sholem thought. For they always drew aside for their disputes and when anyone approached they suddenly fell silent.

Sroleh Yomtov's treatment of Sholem's own children was also objectionable. He beat Mailech more than once for being too noisy, saying that it was "not the custom in this house." Yiteleh he nicknamed "The *Rebbets'n*" because she was able to read fluently in the Pentateuch and was able to quote the more pregnant sayings of the Fathers by heart. Of course, Yiteleh could stand up for herself. "It's all right for a girl to be a Rebbetsen," she would say, "but it's all wrong for a boy to want to stay stupid." But this sort of thing only led to a quarrel, because Sroleh Yomtov did not like being bested in an argument.

When Malkeleh complained about this to Sholem, he said:

"Let them quarrel. They're only children. That's how they get to know each other."

"You think Sroleh Yomtov quarrels only with Yiteleh? He quarrels with you and me as well."

Sholem knew that. But that was perhaps why he was so interested in the children's debate. He watched them during the daily lesson, not minding if they strayed from the traditional constructions, and interfering only when the discussion seemed to be degenerating into a squabble. Just now they were reading the passage where Jacob sent his sons to Egypt for provender.

"As there was no grain in Canaan," said Yiteleh, "they had to go to a place where there was some. Joseph gave his brothers everything on credit."

"Not on credit," contradicted Sroleh Yomtov, "he only put the money back into their sacks."

"That's the same thing, isn't it?"

"It isn't. You don't get credit, unless you have money in your pocket."

"But if that's so—" began Yossef.

"Shut up!" snapped his elder brother.

"Why do you tell him to shut up?" said Sholem in consternation. "He has a right to talk."

"Let him talk if he likes," said Sroleh Yomtov, with a threatening look at Yossef.

"I forgot what I was going to say," said Yossef, shrinking into himself.

What one forgets cannot be very important. But the moral of the debate was important to Sholem and it made him think. It filled his mind when he had gone to bed, and even the following morning, as he was sitting in the bar parlor before the *Gemara*, reading his daily portion before morning prayers. As there was no "grain" in his cellar, he ought to go some place where there was some. But having no money, he could not buy anything even on credit. Joseph gave his brothers grain because he had recognized them. But—thought Sholem, this time with Sroleh Yomtov's brain—what would have happened if Joseph had approached his brothers, who had not recognized him?

Sholem would have had to cogitate a little longer but for Mesel, the wine merchant from Batiz. Mesel himself had written to Sholem, not in a friendly way, but to demand the return of the wine casks that he had lent to the previous lessee of the inn, because it seemed to him that Sholem was buying his wine elsewhere. Yet Sholem saw a glimmer of light in that letter. He clutched at the word "lent." If Mesel had lent the casks, he might also be persuaded to let him have some wine on credit.

And on his way to Mesel with the casks, thought Sholem, he would look in on Reb Leizer Lazarovich, who distilled spirits from potatoes, fruit, and grain in the same locality. Reb Leizer also had a large stock of other spirits, and in the summer he even had a special ice-pit in which to keep the products of the brewers of Nagyvarad. Reb Leizer must be a kindlier man than Mesel, for he had not sent Sholem a stern note about his casks. And as he was a wealthy man, it would be easy for him to give Sholem goods to the value of a hundred or two on credit. Lazarovich owned a

big house in the main square of Otvar, but—as Sroleh Yomtov
related—he was very bitter that he could never live in it. For
Otvar had a Royal Charter, which entitled it to forbid Jews
settling in the town. Even Jews like Lazarovich. There was
nothing wrong in that, thought Sholem. After all, even wealthy
Reb Leizer must not forget that he is living in the *galuth*, the
Diaspora, like his poorer brethren. If Reb Leizer remembered that,
and also the word of the Sages that all Israel were brothers, he
would surely not deny Sholem a little stock on credit.

In theory, the question of credit was settled by the simple fact
that Sholem developed a friendly feeling towards the unknown
distiller. He had heard that the distiller served his customers only
on Monday and Thursday and he was very pleased. Monday and
Thursday used to be the traditional buying days even in the
Talmudic age; this was to give village shopkeepers and innkeepers
an opportunity to attend synagogue on the two Torah-reading
week-days. It seemed that Reb Leizer took account of his customers' spiritual needs, and so he could not be a bad man. However, just now there was some difficulty about the time. Sholem
could not leave the inn on Monday and Thursday. But there was
another thing that was more urgent still and that had given him
a headache from the very first day: that *kaddish* that Sroleh
Yomtov had omitted to recite for his dead parents. Sholem himself had been heavily in debt to his progenitors, but as regards
the *kaddish* in this case, the responsibility lay with him. Why did
Jewish parents refer to their sons as "my *kaddish*" if not that
the son should pray for their souls under the only conditions
where such prayer was valid, that is, in a *minyan*?

That was the real reason why Sholem had sent Sroleh Yomtov
to Karoly: so that for at least one day he should attend synagogue
and recite in chorus with other mourners, and amid the Amens
of the rest of the congregation, the *kaddish*. Kese, the pony, was
off with him in the early dawn, on that Monday—one of the
two Torah-reading days—so that Sroleh Yomtov should be in
time for the morning service. The boy also attended the afternoon
and evening services. The whole community learned from him
about the events in Lapfalva, and no doubt they hardly talked
about anything else that day. That must have been why Mordechai

wanted the boy to become his apprentice. Perhaps he meant it
to be a help to his sister, but in the first place he must have
thought of those who were waiting at the gates of the beyond.
For according to the sacred tradition all the children of Israel
share in the after life.

"We are in the wrong," said Sholem to the boy when he had
got thus far in his reasoning. "Mordechai meant well."

"Nevertheless," replied the boy, "I'm not going to be an ink-
mixer. If you want me to leave the house, I'll open an inn in
another village and we'll part company."

"I wasn't talking about separation, my son," said Sholem. "All
I want is that you should live among Jews for a year and say
*kaddish* properly for your father and mother. I'd bring a *minyan*
here if I could, so you shouldn't have to go away."

The boy did not like to be reminded of his bereavement. He
was already thinking of the future. As a makeshift, it was arranged
that Sroleh Yomtov should visit Karoly on the two most important week-days, Monday and Thursday, the Torah-reading
days, and stay there from morning till evening, though this left
five days, including the Sabbath, blank. If he did not like Karoly,
he might go to Csenger, which also had a large congregation.

Sholem received Mesel's letter on Tuesday. By Wednesday
evening he had made friends, in his own mind, with Reb Leizer,
and on Thursday he might have gone over to him for stock, most
of his casks being empty. But Thursday was a *kaddish* day and
Sroleh Yomtov went over to Csenger. On Friday there were
usually few customers, but the principal task was to prepare for
the Sabbath. On the Sabbath it was Sabbath. Saturday evening was
a busy time in the inn. Sholem hummed through the twenty-two
verses of "Fear not, my servant Jacob" and his headache improved. On Sunday morning he left the inn to Sroleh Yomtov
and went out to work in the field, harrowing for most of the
day and sowing the wheat in the late afternoon. The peasants
stood by, laughing, but he did not let that depress him. This seed
was going to come up next year. In the evening he lay in his
bed, tired out, but without any worries over bread. He was reciting, in a whisper, the final verse of the nocturnal *Shemah*, which
is like a lullaby, ". . . and go to rest, Selah." The moon looked
in through the window, its rays moving like a will-o'-the-wisp

all over the room. A voice came from somewhere, a familiar voice. It came from a distance, perhaps from that village in the Jew county of his birth, or even farther. It took some time before it entered his ear.

"Sholem, are you asleep?"

"No, Malkeleh," he said at last, startled awake by his own voice. "Anything up?"

"Not yet."

"Is the baby bad?"

"No. Thank God it's getting on. It hasn't had any diarrhœa for three days."

"Well, then, what is the matter?"

"The business . . . don't you know?"

"Know what?"

"No spirits."

So, thought Sholem, Malkeleh had been in the bar. She must have looked into the pitchers, banged at the casks, examined the big bottles.

"That's right, Malkeleh," he said. "But we'll have some new stock soon."

"Have you any money?"

"Money is not everything. Not if you have a good idea."

The nocturnal dialogue went on across the space between the two beds. At last Sholem could have a good talk with his wife. He was no longer sleepy, not even tired. He spoke quietly, so as not to wake the children. He was going to Batiz on the Tuesday to speak with Reb Leizer Lazarovich. He'd go in the morning, Monday, but he had something else to attend to, something very important. He did not say what, and fortunately Malkeleh did not ask. He merely mentioned that in the morning Sroleh Yomtov was going away to say *kaddish*, and that they could not both be away on the same day. It would be different if Malkeleh's confinement were over. But this time the boy was not going to Csenger. He was going to Batiz, with a message for Reb Leizer to expect Sholem in his store-room on Tuesday for an important talk.

"You think he'll give you some stock?" asked Malkeleh doubtfully.

She was voicing his own doubts.

"Why shouldn't he?" he said, raising his head from the pillow.
"He's got plenty, hasn't he?"

"That's just why—because he has plenty."

"Reb Leizer is a business man. He'll be doing himself a favor,
not me. It's just a matter of business sense."

"I don't know why I am so worried," said the woman. "Up
till now I couldn't sleep on account of the baby. Now. . . ."

"Just go to sleep, dear heart. There's no reason to worry."

"There is, Sholem. We're eating other people's bread. If we
eat up what's left. . . ."

"Then they'll start eating what we've made. I did the sowing
to-day, you know. Next year we'll eat our own bread."

"Next year!" said the woman. "If I were only three weeks older!
I'd go to Karoly myself to speak with Mordechai . . . Hush,
hush, poor dear. . . ."

"That won't be necessary. In any case, Mordechai won't help."

"We must stay here now. I wouldn't like to be on the road
again. It's winter. And with three children. . . ."

"Don't worry, dear heart. It's going to be all right."

Malkeleh did not reply. Perhaps she was reassured. Her "hushaby" also came more sleepily. Sholem would have liked to go on
talking with her, to reassure himself as well. She had stirred up
his own disquiet that there was trouble brewing. He recalled how,
that evening, when he had taken over from Sroleh Yomtov, the
peasants put their heads together, talking in whispers. Ludpal, the
bellringer, gave a sneer, saying that the gin had a fishy smell.
Yet he, Sholem, had not diluted it. Perhaps Sroleh Yomtov had
added some water, because the cask was low. "You must not do
that, Sroleh Yomtov! . . and go to rest . . . and go to rest
. . . Selah."

## A GREAT DAY

MONDAY WAS a great day for Sholem. This was the day on which
he would conclude and recommence his reading of the Babylonian Talmud, with whose sixty tomes he had been struggling

for ten long years, fighting his way laboriously forward by daily study of the debates of the *Tannaim* and the *Rabbanim*, the heavy texts, the brief, enigmatic phrases, the images and dialects of dead ages. By the unflagging endeavor of that decade, he had wormed his way piously through the apparently impenetrable maze of assertions, denials, assumptions, questions, doubts, and arguments, and through jungles of theses and anti-theses, and decisions and counter-decisions. To do all that, he also had to work his way through the thicket of the marginal commentators, the great Rabbi of Troyes on the right, the Frankish-German construers on the left, and often even they could be approached only through sub-commentaries, glossaries, footnotes, and other aids.

At last, however, Sholem had managed to read through it all, from beginning to end, through the *Halacha*, the law, as well as the *Agadah*, the practical, lively, poetic, gay "table talk" of the Sages. And he had done it all by himself, without outside assistance, and he was lucky if, now and then, a peregrinating rabbi helped him over a stiff hurdle of learning. On this Monday Sholem had only the last section of the last paragraph to tackle. He rose at dawn and, with his brain rested, he sing-songed through the passage easily, deciding with a sense of pious elation that he would that very day recommence his reading of the Talmud, perhaps immediately after morning prayers. This time it would not take him ten years, but perhaps only six or seven. That day, on which the end and the beginning were to meet, would be marked with joy in the scroll of Infinity.

But the demon Ashmodai would not have it, and sent his messenger to crash into the quiet atmosphere of this festive day. Sholem, with praying-shawl and phylacteries and his face turned towards the eastern wall of the inn, was in the middle of the silent Eighteen Benedictions, when Squire de Sarberek's footman, Gyuri, burst into the bar parlor carrying a big leather bottle in his hand.

"Hi, Sholem, fill it up! You know what with. Hurry, hurry, his worship is off pig-sticking."

Sholem motioned to the man to wait. But he wouldn't. His worship was in a hurry, the dogs were in a hurry, and he, Gyuri, was in a hurry. For the first time in his life Sholem said the

Benedictions, which ought to be recited in a whisper, with devout concentration, aloud, babbling them at a rapid pace, thereby trying to convey the need for patience. But the peasant lad would not understand and kept pressing him, so Sholem raced through the prayer, conscious of having made mistakes, and of having even omitted important passages. And after all that he found that he had scarcely any plum whisky left, and could only half fill the leather bottle. Would Gyuri humbly apologize for him to his worship: it would never happen again, but just now he was out of plum whisky and had failed to obtain new stock. He started bowing and scraping as if his worship were present. If he had only known that his worship would go pig-sticking that morning!

Later, the Headman, Mate Bor, came in. He had a drink, but kept shaking his head and muttering to himself while he drank it, his full-moon face, otherwise so jolly, now seemed merely bloated. Then he began to talk. It wasn't customary in those parts, he said, for a Jew to till his own land, but that did not matter. Even the fact that he kept a horse of his own and never gave a carting job to anyone else, as Moshe used to do, might be forgiven. But it was a bit too thick his not having in the inn what people asked for, and that what he did have was so weak it made you sick.

"You know, Sholem," said the Headman, as he turned to go, "there's a young man here who could easily get the inn, and without having to offer double rent, like Herskovitch."

The old serf Gore also came in for a tot. At other times he used to toss it off in one, but now he sat sipping it slowly, raising the mug under his greying moustachios, sniffing at its contents, putting it down, then raising it again. His talk was depressed and depressing. He said that the marsh ducks had already withdrawn into the rushes, and that meant that the winter was going to be long and hard. The land was not the same in the low-lying parts as higher up, and people with such low-lying land as Sholem's ought not to sow till spring, because what you sow there in the autumn gets frozen up.

"You people didn't tell me that before," said Sholem reproachfully, his brow furrowing with worry.

"We did and we didn't," replied the serf. "Besides, if you don't ask, why should we tell you? If you'd had the work done by Galagonya, from whom you bought the seeds, he'd have told you a thing or two. Pity to lose all that fine whiskered wheat."

So now Sholem had the wasted seeds on his mind as well. But behind it all lurked a profound disquiet over something else: he felt as though he were no longer so sure of the Almighty. These peasants were so at one with the soil that if you lived among them they dragged you down to it, and away from thoughts of heavenly promises.

However, he had no time to ruminate on that now. There was the thud of horses' hooves approaching the inn and after an instant the door was kicked in, so that the bell above it sounded like a cry of terror. A lieutenant and six soldiers with fixed bayonets came in.

"Hey, Jew," said the lieutenant in snappy German, "where did you put the deserter?"

Sholem gave him a scared look. What deserter? he asked himself. He had seen no deserter. But he did not say so aloud, for experience had taught him that when a Jew makes a negative statement it is regarded as a denial of guilt, and therefore, in a sense, as self-accusation. But to show his willingness to be of help, he said:

"What do you wish me to do, *Herr Lieutenant,* if he happens to come here?"

The lieutenant saw cunning in this and said even more sharply:

"I asked where you put him!"

"How could I have put him anywhere, when I have never seen him?"

"The peasants say he came here to your inn."

This gave Sholem cause for alarm. If the peasants did not see the deserter coming this way, and said they had, there was something preparing against him. But if they did see what he himself had not seen . . . if the man had slipped into the cellar or the barn . . . Well, after all, Benjamin did not know that Joseph's gold cup was in his sack of grain. Could he point this out to the lieutenant?

"I have no knowledge of anyone hiding here, *Herr Lieutenant,*" he said.

"You're a cunning Jew," said the officer. "Well, we'll find out whether he is here or not."

At a sign from him the soldiers searched the room, looking behind the counter at the bar, and tapping the walls with their rifle-butts and stamping on the floor, to discover any secret cavity. Then they went into the next room, which contained only a large table covered with an embroidered cloth, four cross-legged chairs, and a heavy bench along the wall. They looked under the tablecloth and overturned the bench.

"What room is this?" demanded the officer sternly.

"The saloon, *Herr Lieutenant.*"

"What? A saloon for a Jew?"

"It's not for a Jew, *Herr Lieutenant,* but for the gentry."

"So this is where the gentry come to drink?"

"Yes, *Herr Lieutenant.*"

"Who comes here to make merry?"

"I don't know, *Herr Lieutenant.*"

"You don't seem to know anything," snapped the officer.

"I've only been here a few weeks," said Sholem. "They haven't been since then."

"Where did you live before?"

"Up north, in the Carpathians."

"What place?"

"La-tor-ka," replied Sholem uncertainly.

"It seems you don't know even that . . . These Jews roam about like stray dogs. Do you pay taxes?"

"I haven't paid any here yet."

"Well, see that you do. And if any member of the gentry should tell you that there is no Jew tax and no Emperor, you'll come to the Imperial barracks in Otvar and report to me, *Herr Lieutenant* Eberle, the name of the rebellious Magyar. Understand?"

"Yes, sir."

"To whom will you report and where?"

"To *Herr Lieutenant* Eberle at the Imperial barracks in Otvar."

"Correct."

The search went on, in the cellar, the stable, the barn, and the guest-room. They found nothing and the *Herr Lieutenant* was angry. He led his men into the living-rooms. The children gaped.

Aunt Feiga's somber senility became more somber still. Malkeleh
adjusted the headkerchief on her head.

"What can I do for you, *Herr Lieutenant?*" she asked in German, with a polite smile.

Malkeleh could be very charming when there was trouble,
and she could speak German nicely, not like Sholem, who really
spoke in Yiddish, and often irritated a Gentile interlocutor by
mixing Hebrew and Aramaic words from the Talmud into his
conversation. Her smile, too, was attractive and refined, and
there was a striking luminosity in her dark eyes. Her figure now
was not attractive, but the lieutenant saw only her face and
heard only her soft voice. It made him click his heels together
and say very politely:

"I beg your pardon, *gnädige Frau,* I am here on duty. An
infantryman named Bence Darazs has deserted and is hiding
somewhere round the marsh. It seems he is not in this house,
at any rate."

Saluting smartly, he turned to go, ordering his men to leave.
On the way out, through the courtyard, he was accompanied
by Sholem.

"If he comes here," he said, and his tone was harsh again,
"you'll take away his rifle and bayonet and his munition pouch
and bring him to me in Otvar. You'll recognize him by his eyebrows, one being brown, the other blond."

"Very good, *Herr Lieutenant.*"

That day they had bean soup with noodles for dinner, Sholem's
favorite dish. But he did not enjoy it. He was too worried. He
knew how to recognize the deserter, but to take away his—
probably loaded—rifle was another matter. And who was the
young man who was negotiating for the lease? Why should the
gentry stick to him, Sholem, seeing that he was unable to serve
even a bottle of plum whisky when required? Malkeleh, too,
looked less serene; her face was so pale that it seemed almost
grey.

In the afternoon, Zalman, the trough dealer from Gyekenyes,
arrived with five carts laden with fine white willow troughs,
pasteboards, mangles and spoons, and also rush-mats, bread-
baskets, and beehives. The goods were made for him by the

peasants living along the marsh, and Zalman supplied seven counties. He halted at the inn to let the carters water their horses and have a rest. Sholem rarely saw hard cash, yet to-day he would gladly have done without Zalman's big order: he had to keep for his regulars what liquor he still had left."

At the same time, he was pleased to see Zalman. At last, he could talk with another of his own tribe, discussing the outside world and distracting his attention from his troubles. But Zalman only made his heart heavier by taking Mordechai as his subject. Mordechai was a lucky fellow. A big Leipzig tanner had had an order from the Tsar for military knee-boots, and was buying up Hungarian oak-gall at any price. Mordechai Nikolsburger held out against him for a fortnight, until he got a higher bid. He kept sufficient oak-gall only for his ink business, which was a fine business, with several counties buying from him. He had not given up the leather business, either, but he was no longer forcing the tanners to buy his oak-gall; they could go to the woods and pick some if they liked.

"If the money keeps coming to him like this," laughed Zalman, "we'll elect your brother-in-law president. He's only first guardian now." Sholem did not seem to be pleased about the good news.

In the evening Sroleh Yomtov returned from Batiz.

"Reb Leizer says," he reported, with contempt in his expression, "that he is at the distillery on Tuesdays and Wednesdays. I could have told you that myself. On those days he only opens the stock-room if it's very urgent. But if you've nothing better to do, you can try to-morrow. It all depends what business you bring him."

Sholem felt a bad taste in his mouth. He realized that it would be a pity to tire the pony. No use going to Batiz without money. How he had been waiting for the boy's return! He had been waiting for some good news that would lift the burden of worry. What to do now? To whom was he to turn for advice and comfort?

"Get behind the bar, my son," he said, "I've got important work to do."

He would have liked to tell the boy to be sure not to dilute the drinks, and to serve brandy if he had no "ordinary" left, but he was too impatient to get away. He took a candle and the first tome of the Talmud—entitled "Benedictions"—into the empty gentry's room and sat down to re-start the reading of the sixty-odd tomes of the Talmud.

Out in the bar parlor the peasants and day laborers were making a row. The bellringer's high-pitched voice demanded to know where the spirits had got to out of his drink. Serf Vizhordo was spewing oaths.

"Damn your eyes, Sroleh . . . To Gehenna with all the gentry's Jews . . . and the gentry themselves . . ." And so on.

But Sholem heard nothing. He sat swaying his body to and fro before the Talmud. "Toneh Rabbonan . . . Taught Our Sages. . . ."


Before going to bed, Sholem went out into the moonlit yard to load the empty casks and demijohns on the cart, so as not to waste time with this in the morning. The wonderful teachings of the Sages were still buzzing in his head, but now, with the logic and accents of the Talmud in his mind, he was cogitating on mundane matters. There was the problem where to put the big cask, when it was filled with spirit—on the front of the cart or on the backboard? If it were put on the front, the main weight would press on the front wheels; if on the backboard, it would tilt up this light vehicle. So it would be best to have the big cask filled first, and to place it into the middle of the cart . . . And having thus satisfactorily solved the problem, could he go on being of little faith . . ? Here was the cart, and here were the empty containers, and there in Batiz was Reb Leizer with his huge stocks of spirits. When all these were met together in one place, he'd have this new stock, although he had no money, and it would be "gee-up" for home.

As he was undressing by the moonlight streaming in through the window, a breath of his former doubt returned. He was afraid of Malkeleh's questions. But Malkeleh was sunk in heavy sleep, so that even the loud wailing of the sick baby failed to rouse her. Sholem tiptoed to her bed and carefully lifting the baby, carried it to his own bed.

"Hushaby, baby," he whispered. "Auntie Malkah has been working hard and she is tired out. Let her sleep. Your bellyache is gone, what are you crying for? If you'll be good you'll soon have a little brother. He may be coming along any moment. Then Mother Malkah will give you the same as to him. It tastes very good. In three days . . . two days . . . hushaby . . . perhaps tomorrow morning."

The baby gave a shudder and started to bawl. Sholem thought he had frightened it, whereas he had only tickled the infant's face with his beard. Looking in the moonlight at the infant's skewy little mouth as it gasped for breath, Sholem seemed to hear it talk: "If I go, you'll have to go too. Sroleh Yomtov is master here." He looked round perplexedly. Had Malkeleh spoken? No, she had only sighed and moaned in her sleep. Sholem sat down on the edge of the bed, shaking the swaddled baby and tapping its behind, and humming the song "Fear not, my servant Jacob," half in Hebrew, half in Russian, as he had heard it sung by his father.

Mailech sat up in his bed, gazed across at his father, got down sleepily, lifting his long nightshirt here and there to scratch. Then he joined in with his father:

> *"A star's risen from Jacob,*
> *Tak-tak-tak,*
> *Fear not, my servant Jacob,*
> *Net, net, net. . . ."*

"She is hungry," observed the little boy, "that's why she can't sleep. I'll go to the kitchen and wake Aunt Feiga."

"Don't do that, Mailech. We'll give her some milk."

"She has it with aniseed, Father."

"With aniseed? What we put into the gin?"

"No, no. Mummy makes tea with it."

"She doesn't want that any more. Her stomach is all right now."

There was a jug on the window-sill with a drop of milk left in it. Sholem smelt it and said it was sour. Mailech tasted it and said it wasn't. Sholem opined that the milk ought to be warmed up, but the little boy objected that that was what made milk sour. In any case, you'd have to go out into the kitchen and lay a fire. Mailech fetched a small spoon explaining that if you fed the baby little by little, blowing hot air on each spoonful, that was the same as if the milk had been warmed up. The baby had some difficulty in swallowing, but this was better than letting it cry with hunger. Once it hiccoughed and returned the milk in a curdled form. Sholem gave her some more, and now both he and Mailech began to warm each spoonful with their breath. The baby was sick again and its little face contorted. Still, it must have retained a little of the milk. Sholem placed her into the wooden trough that served as her cradle, rocked it and resumed his crooning. But Mailech said that "Fear not" was not the right song to croon to the baby because it frightened her. So Sholem left the baby to Mailech, who crouched down by the trough, rocking it now and then and crooning the traditional lullaby:

> *"Hushaby, hushaby, baby mine,*
> *Here comes a kid with tid-bits fine,*
> *Almonds and raisins on its back,*
> *Crying, baby, baby, what do you lack?"*

Sholem lay down to rest awhile, mentally preparing for the morrow. Look here, Reb Leizer, I've got five children in the house, including three orphans. By the morning there may be a sixth. Then there's an aged old maid. You know what our sacred books say. He who helps the poor is making a loan to the Lord. Your money will be bearing rich interest. It is forbidden to take interest, but He who forbade it will pay interest a hundredfold. Besides, I'll pay you back too. I suppose you don't know yet who Sholem ben Yoirish is. But you might have heard of the Nikolsburgers. My wife is the daughter of the late Manasseh Nikolsburger of blessed memory. Yes, Malkeleh. . . .

Mailech was beginning to get drowsy and to falter with the lullaby.

"Father," he said, "I'd like to go back to bed. Will you rock the cradle now?"

Sholem sat by the baby till cockcrow. Then Aunt Feiga, who always rose at that hour, came into the room. She picked up the baby, lamenting how green she was in the face. Malkeleh also rose, and with her hand on her stomach hastened after Aunt Feiga into the kitchen.

RICH JEW, POOR JEW

IN THE keen air of the early dawn the numbness went out of his body. His doubts, too, began to evaporate. Kese, the pony, some-how looked confident and cheerful. The mud of the road was frozen hard, and as there were few ruts, the vehicle almost flew along. Lack of sleep had made Sholem somewhat lightheaded and fanciful. He visualized the full casks and seemed to hear the gurgle of the liquids on the way back. If they were empty, or if they contained only the little that he was able to pay for, the gurgle wouldn't sound so nice. Indeed, thought Sholem, the casks would not be enough to hold what he needed and he would have to borrow some more from Reb Leizer. It was a good thing that he saw matters in this hopeful light; at least he could speak with the wealthy Reb Leizer without embarrassment.

"What I want, Reb Leizer, is a big caskful of rye whisky, an-other of potato whisky, a small cask of *shligovica*, a demijohn of rum, a few bottles of *borovichka*, kümmel, and pear brandy, both first and second quality. I also want some vanilla, aniseed, and caraway liqueurs."

"What about wine, Reb Sholem? Surely, you'll have a little Bull's Blood and one or two light varieties, eh?"

Reb Leizer turned out to be a gaunt little man with a coal-black straggly beard and taut parchment skin over his cheekbones. There were six or seven horizontal furrows on his forehead, like so many lines of microscopic script. Sholem could not read that script, and was instead struck by Reb Leizer's great amiability. He knew that Reb Leizer was a Cohanite, a descendant of Aaron, a temperamental type that had evolved through centuries of inter-marriage within the tribe. This was the first amiable Cohanite he had seen. It was this unexpected impression that made Sholem somewhat embarrassed.

"I want some wine as well, Reb Leizer," he said.

"I have some fine bitters. The gentry like it very much. Es-pecially the morning after."

"The morning after what?"

"After they have drunk wine, beer, rye, and plum whisky. The day after the pig-killing banquet, you know."

"I'll have a small cask of that as well, Reb Leizer."

"What did you say? A small demijohn?"

"No, a small cask."

Reb Leizer raised his pitch-black eyes to Sholem's face and gave him such a friendly smile that the pale gums over his yellowing teeth suddenly leapt into evidence.

"Very well, Reb Sholem," he said. "I was beginning to think that you were taking your custom to Rothbart in Karoly. Of course, you can get one or two things there. But you can't compare Karoly with Batiz, nor a Shloimah Rothbart with a Leizer Lazarovich. If you have the time, I'll take you along to the distillery, so you can see the big stills and the huge vats. You'll be amazed, Reb Sholem, at the clean work you'll see there. And if you ever want a drop of wash for your cows, just bring along a few tubs and we'll fill them for you. The customers of Leizer Lazarovich can't complain. Rothbart can't say the same. Fadele, get a chair for Reb Sholem."

Fadele, a hulking lad, brought a heavy wooden chair and deposited it in front of Sholem.

"Take a seat, Reb Sholem," he stuttered, "I'll go and get the keys of the stock-room." The lad's stutter was translated even into his swinging arms and hasty steps as he went up to the office for the keys, for his master and Sholem were still in the courtyard, among the staves, hoops, and gantries. Meanwhile, Reb Leizer told Sholem about the new prices, which were slightly higher that year—a matter of from fifty kreuzers to a florin per forty pints and not worth bothering about. You didn't have to mention the increase to the peasants. You gave them their spirits half a degree weaker to begin with, then a whole degree weaker, so they didn't notice it. In any case, the peasants knew that there had been a drought last year which harmed the grain crops, while the spring was unduly damp, which harmed the potato crop.

Sholem agreed with all Reb Leizer was saying. Reb Leizer, in turn, thought what an intelligent man Sholem was and how likeable. He asked him whether he had attended the *yeshiba* at Sziget, where Reb Leizer had studied when the school was still under Rabbi Yehudah Kahan. No, said Sholem. He had been a disciple of Rabbi Phineas Luria at Homonna, until the Rabbi was driven out of the place for his forthrightness. Then he followed the rabbi to Ujhely, and stayed there until the same happened again. Then for a time Sholem studied under the new holder of the seat, Rabbi Mosheh Teitelbaum. But after that he went to Szentmiklos, studying there under the blind Rabbi Jehuda Leib Kunitz of blessed memory until the latter's death. He was the Rabbi's personal attendant, too.

"Ah!" exclaimed Reb Leizer admiringly. "You are entitled to be proud to have studied under three such famous Sages."

Sholem was entirely inclined to be proud, and in other circumstances Reb Leizer's words would have raised his self-esteem. But just now any talk that strayed from the subject of spirits and business disquieted him. However, Reb Leizer stuck to reminiscence, declaring that his teacher had been a magnificent scholar with a keen brain, and a real *gaon*.

Fadele was shaking the bunch of keys towards his master, but Lazarovich took no notice. Nor did he seem to notice Sholem's impatience. He wanted Sholem to talk to him about the wandering Rabbi Phineas, for he had heard that the Rabbi, who in the course of sixteen years of world wanderings had been everywhere, from Vilna to Salonika and from Jerusalem to Kairuvan, was somewhere in this region. A former disciple had seen and recognized him, but when he addressed him by name, the Rabbi vanished, just like Korah in the Bible. Sholem scarcely listened. It was in a very uncertain voice that he raised a mild objection to any comparison between the great Rabbi and Korah.

"You're right, Reb Sholem," retracted Reb Leizer hastily. "It's far from me to liken the great man to a sinful rebel merely because he said what he meant and was in conflict all his life with the worldly leaders of Jewry. I only tell you what I heard."

"It can't be true that way."

"Why not?" said Reb Leizer with animation. "Those who saw Rabbi Phineas assert that they saw him. I am not judging him. I don't ask why he has become a wanderer and how long he wants to go on being one. I'm sure he's doing it for the sake of our people . . . Are you in a hurry, Reb Sholem? Wait a moment, till we add it all up. Fadele, see how big the casks are . . . Right. And the demijohns? What about wine, Reb Sholem? Three forties or four? Better take five. The roads are still passable, might not be later. And Christmas is coming, you'll sell everything. Five forties? Good. You are a real business man, Reb Sholem. I like you."

Sholem suppressed a sigh. He would soon know whether Reb Leizer really liked him. If he had a few big bank-notes in his pocket, that would no doubt seal the friendship between him and the charming Lazarovich. But as he had no money, the spell might be broken as soon as Lazarovich covered the blackboard hanging on the door of the storeroom with figures. Of course, he, Reb Sholem, might be mistaken. But if so, why didn't Lazarovich order his man to get the casks filled first? He could make out the bill later, couldn't he? As though in reply to Sholem's thought, Reb Leizer put down the chalk and the rag he used to wipe the blackboard and said:

"When the casks are filled we'll work it out again carefully, down to the last copper. This is only a rough calculation. The total is . . . wait a moment, Reb Sholem . . . the total is only a hundred and sixty florins."

"Only," muttered Reb Sholem.

"Too much, Reb Sholem?"

"Oh no, Reb Leizer, no, it's not too much."

"Not for all that liquor, what? I may be five or six florins on the wrong side, but you can pay that later."

Sholem's eyes lighted up. Reb Leizer had brought out the one word he wanted to hear so much: "later." He started fingering his beard and tried to force a smile.

"I'd like to pay for everything later."

"Of course," assented Reb Leizer, "when the casks are filled."

"No, Reb Leizer—when I have the money."

A pause. Sholem's fingers dropped away from his beard, and he looked with glazed eyes at the parchment framed in and mottled with black that was Reb Leizer's face. He felt that the other would now burst into laughter, loud, mocking laughter. The way Shmayeh Kahn, his brother-in-law, used to laugh. Reb Leizer did not laugh. But his manner was even more offensive than if he had laughed.

"If Reb Sholem has no money," he said coldly, "why does Reb Sholem come to Reb Leizer Lazarovich? Why doesn't he go to Rothbart. I leave such customers to Shloimah Rothbart."

Sholem realized that he had spoilt everything. This was the wrong approach. His face was aflame with anxiety and embarrassment, and he felt a dryness about his eyes.

"Reb Leizer Lazarovich doesn't give credit?" he said, trying to sound indifferent. But the hoarseness in his voice gave him away.

"Credit, in the autumn?" exclaimed the other, and there was consternation in his croaky voice.

"Why not in the autumn if it is autumn?" said Sholem in confusion.

"Would Reb Sholem give credit to some one he is seeing for the first time in his life?" countered Reb Leizer, ignoring Sholem's question.

Ah! here was something to hold on to on the slippery slope, something that would at least mitigate the blundering approach and give Sholem, with his experience in Talmudic debate, a chance to continue the argument and perhaps arrive at a compromise, or at least pave the way for an orderly retreat.

"Reb Sholem does give credit to his peasants whom he hasn't known before," he said in a tone of debate.

Reb Leizer was not one to evade a little fencing.

"It's not Reb Sholem that gives credit there, but the business, which always gave them credit."

"Well, Reb Leizer would not be giving credit to Reb Sholem, but to the business, to which he has given credit before."

"Reb Sholem is mistaken. Reb Leizer never gave any credit to the business. The inn of Lapfalva has been buying everything for cash for the past ten years."

Sholem felt squashed. He did not know this. If Lapfalva always bought for cash, then perhaps Reb Leizer was right in demanding cash now. But no! That was the very reason why he should show consideration to such an old customer.

"You've been getting cash from us for ten years," he reproached, "and we don't deserve a little credit this once?"

There was expectancy as well as an impression of superiority in the gaze he turned on Reb Leizer. See, Reb Leizer? Your teacher might have had a keen brain, but I had three real saints for my teachers. Sholem was about to go on: "This once, when in consequence of two deaths and other unfortunate circumstances we have no cash . . ." But the distiller's cold smile and the indecipherable script on his brow warned Sholem that that kind of talk would not appeal to the other man, and he suddenly changed his tactics. The only way to deal with him was by means of sharp debate. Let Reb Leizer see that he, Sholem, was equal to that, too.

"A customer who pays for ten years," he said, almost playfully, "will pay after ten years, and he'll pay even if for once he happens not to pay."

Lazarovich shrugged his shoulders, but did not reply. What did his muteness mean? It meant that Sholem's three saintly masters had scored a victory over the *gaon* of Sziget. Sholem was undeniably on top.

Of course, it was only a theoretical triumph. To ensure completeness, Reb Leizer's capitulation, Sholem would have to have one more argument, the ultimate one: money to the amount of a hundred and sixty odd florins. But without that, and despite his triumph in the argument, he would get no goods.

For the moment, Sholem was content with his theoretical triumph, with his intellectual and moral superiority over his antagonist. On the way to Batiz he had made ready to reprove the wealthy Reb Leizer in case he sent him away empty, recalling a hundred telling sentences from the Talmud and the *Midrash*, from Proverbs and Ecclesiastes, from the stern Amos and from Job, from the sayings of the Sages and the *gaonim*. They were sentences that would stir and crush, elevate and move the rich distiller. Now he was glad he had not produced those sentences. It would have been a pity to waste so much beauty and greatness on such a stonyhearted fellow. His kind only lived to scoop in the shekels. For four thousand years they have been carrying on with the gambol they started in the desert of Horeb round the golden calf. It was for the sins of such as Reb Leizer that Israel had to suffer and do penance.

"Come along, Kese," said Sholem quietly, taking the pony by the bridle.

"Fadele," said Reb Leizer, "take the keys back to the office." Then to Sholem: "A good year to you, Reb Sholem."

Sholem walked past him without replying.

When the cart had rattled out of Lazarovich's yard, Kese made such a spurt that anyone would have thought he would never stop until they reached home. He was in high spirits, because while his master was debating with Reb Leizer, the good Fadele had placed a bucketful of mash before him, brought freshly from the distillery. And by the time Fadele learned that no business would be done and yanked the bucket away, Kese had drunk almost the whole of the contents. He had enjoyed the mash immensely, potato puree, grain porridge, maize husks and all, but what delighted his equine soul was a mysterious fragrant admixture that he had never tasted before. It was that which made him feel light and strong like the flying horse of the fairy tales, and uncovered the beauty of everything. The earth and the sky were beautiful, and so was the man with the keys, and so were the stakes and the gantries and the rusty hoops, and so was the man with the black beard. If Kese had been able to think, he might then have realized what caused the bellringer and the Headman and the other human creatures to sing at the top of their voices when they left the inn of an evening. For what they drank there also contained a little of that mysterious something that Kese had tasted in the wash. It was only a trace, but it was there, thanks to the guardian angel of horses, cattle, and Bileamic donkeys, who must have been standing with sword drawn behind the foreman distiller to prevent him distilling all of it out of the mash, as Reb Leizer would have liked him to do.

Of course, the high spirits of Kese might have been contributed to by something else. On the way from the village to the distillery he suspected that the return journey would not be so easy. If all those casks were filled and Reb Leizer added some more of his own, that would be some load. How fortunate that Reb Leizer had refused Sholem. Now Kese could fly, instead of straining at the shaft. Gee-up, Sholem!

The only addition to the cart's load now was Sholem's humiliation and increased anxiety. Fear of the immediate future lay heavy upon him. What was going to happen now? On the way to Batiz, Sholem's heart had been warmed by the thought that he would go to synagogue for evening prayers and after so many months at last be among a congregation of his brethren. Now he was not even disappointed to have missed the chance. If Lazarovich was the leader—as he must be—the rest of the flock could not be much better, either. How could he talk to any of them, without embarrassment and shame, of his poverty and frustration? His mind was pervaded by the fears that spring from long isolation and detachment, and he now began to believe what he had hitherto with pious faith denied: that people were not good.

But he was annoyed that Kese was in such a hurry. The men in the bar parlor were waiting for their brandy, and Malkeleh was waiting for the good news, and this stupid beast was dashing along with the empty casks. Whoa! Did I tell you that I was not going to synagogue? And even so, I've got something to attend to here. We're not in a hurry to get home. He gave a tug at the rein. Yes, he must call on Simon Mesel and apologize for not bringing his casks along; they were not quite empty yet because they did not drink much wine at the inn. He drove along the endless High Street at a trot, not inquiring, but only sleuthing round for the wine business. Had he met a friendly looking person, he would have paused to ask, but now every one seemed strange and forbidding. Looking over a wicker fence from the driving-seat, he saw a bearded face that did not look strange. It belonged to a potter who sat in the yard whirling his wheel, with rows of clay mugs, saucepans and saucers standing on a board near him. The potter stopped his wheel, came to the gate, and after wiping his hands on his apron, he reached up to Sholem.

"I see from the casks that you are an innkeeper."

"And I feel by your hand that you are a potter."

There was a momentary twinkle in the potter's eyes, but his voice was serious as he said:

"Rabbi Jehuda the Prince said something similar to Rabbi

Yehoshua the blacksmith. It made Rabbi Yehoshua blush, but I
don't see why we should blush on account of our work and our
poverty."

Sholem felt that he had at last met some one he had known for
ages, though he had never seen him. This man too, was a Talmudist, a worker, and poor.

"Brother," he said sadly, "if you were to look into these casks
you might discover that I am no longer an innkeeper." He told
his story briefly. The potter raised his spectacled eyes to him.

"He said he didn't know you, eh? Well, he does. Only you don't
know him. We know all about you here." Then, in response to a
surprise query in Sholem's eyes: "We take an interest in our
brethren."

The potter invited Sholem to come into the house, and as they
entered he said to his wife:

"Gittel, dear heart, Reb Sholem is here," just as if he were an
old friend. The plump little woman, whose smiling face was
framed in a white spotted headkerchief, received him as if he were
a long-lost brother, and overwhelmed him with questions:

"How are the children? Is the little baby any better? And what
about Malkeleh? Has she got over it yet? It's time she had some
rest, the poor dear. Would you like to have some stuffed cabbage?
I've got some left over from the Sabbath. I'll warm it up for you
and lay the table. I shan't be a minute. The oven is always hot at
potter Yossel Yochanan's place."

Yossel Yochanan was only a year or two older than Sholem,
but his spectacles made him look wiser. Perhaps he was, too.

"If you stumble," he said, "you turn round and see what made
you stumble. And every time you stumble, you learn something.
In the end, you learn to walk about without breaking your neck."

When the good Gittel had brought along the warmed-up
stuffed cabbage, he rose to go across to Reb Simon Mesel.

"So that you shouldn't have come for nothing," he said to
Sholem. "You eat your dinner."

"Thank you, Yossel Yochanan."

He had dropped the "Reb"; they were already old friends.
Sholem had a great sense of relief. He was no longer alone. People
were good after all. And he was not going to "break his neck."

He ate with great enjoyment and enjoyed, too, the plump little woman's chatter.

She had seven children, the youngest a girl of five, the eldest a boy of fifteen. The children were now in Reb Lamech's *chaider*, all except the eldest boy, who went to the *yeshiba* at Kallo in the winter. In the summer, when his father had more work to do, the boy stayed at home to help. Yossel Yochanan said that if you sat in front of the potter's wheel for half the year, your head was more receptive for the Talmud during the other half, and that only a *talmid hacham* could be a good potter.

By the time the potter returned Sholem knew at least as much about his family as Yossel Yochanan knew about him. Yossel Yochanan's otherwise serious face now looked rather cheery. He apologized to Sholem for being so long, but Mesel was just leaving to visit a Count who was one of his suppliers. He wouldn't be back till Thursday, but he sent a message to say that he would be pleased to let Sholem have whatever wine he liked on credit, including the very best. But he could not let him have any casks, because there was a shortage of them. The vine harvest had been so rich that year that the coopers could not catch up with the demand. If Sholem came back on Thursday with the casks, Mesel would fill them for him with whatever he wanted.

This was cheering news for Sholem. He was not going home empty-handed after all. . . .

The pre-service confabs in the synagogue yard are an organic part of Jewish life. Inside the synagogue the eyes and heart of Israel are turned towards Heaven; out in the yard, under the open sky, he discusses his earthly affairs. From times immemorial the synagogue yard has been the scene of such gatherings. It was the same from Vilna to Tiberias, and from Buda and Pressburg to small places like Batiz. The agora of Athens and the Forum of Rome might have presented a similar feature. It is in the synagogue yard that Jews discuss world events, public affairs, family and business concerns: it is there that the latest jokes are retold: there that discontent and criticism become vocal; there that vanity seeks the limelight and poverty exhibits its sores. These confabulations, known in Yiddish by a term derived from the word *kahal*—community—which might be rendered as "kahalization," are a regular manifestation of Jewish social life.

Sholem and Yossel Yochanan were not the first arrivals in the yard of the synagogue, which was a thatch-roofed cottage set amid acacias and elder-bushes. Two or three others were already there. They received Sholem with the ancient salutation:

"Peace be with you."

Then there were inquiries and introductions. What was Sholem's name and where did he come from? Oh, he was the innkeeper from Lapfalva, was he? There was a little bent-backed Jew with a bushy red beard in a black caftan who offered his hand to Sholem with a sweeping gesture, addressing him ceremoniously by his full name.

"Peace be with you, Reb Sholem ben Yoirish."

He introduced himself as Nootah *Batlan*. A *Batlan* is usually a man who spends most of his life studying the Law. Nootah *Batlan* drew Sholem aside, leaving Yossel Yochanan in conversation with Tobias the glazier, and Jacob Anshel the candlemaker.

Sholem listened with close attention and no little emotion to Nootah *Batlan's* proposal and for a moment blamed himself for not thinking of the matter before. The *Batlan* offered, on the very next Torah-reading day, Thursday, to recite before the Scrolls of the Law in Malkeleh's name the age-old formula for women about to be confined: "Thou who hast blessed our mothers Sarah, Rebecca, Rachel, and Leah . . ." That was sure to make the delivery easier and the event successful.

"Very well," said the *Batlan*, modestly adding that in view of Sholem's straitened circumstances he would carry out the rite at half-price—nine kreuzers instead of the customary eighteen. "If it's a boy, Reb Sholem ben Yoirish, don't you go and call in anyone but Nootah *Batlan*. My knife was given to me by the Saint of Berdichev himself. I'll show it to you if you like—it's simply perfect."

Sholem had by now completely forgotten his failure with Reb Leizer. Mixing with the other men, he answered and asked questions, showing interest and glad to be the focus of interest.

And being now aware that the others knew all about him, it was meet that he too should learn all about his brethren and about their locality. Fortunately, Batiz was neither a mining town, nor a Royal Free City, otherwise Jews could not have lived there. It was not even a town with an urban council, or a town of any kind. Indeed, if Sholem thought that Batiz was a major village, he was mistaken. It wasn't. But still, it had a name and a fame. Up till now all Sholem knew about Batiz was that this was where Leizer Lazarovich distilled his spirits and Simon Mesel had his wine business. Now he knew more about these two as well. Jacob Anshel, the candlemaker, told him how a certain forthright village innkeeper once said to Lazarovich: "You'll be distilling in the next world." Which might be interpreted as a compliment, meaning that Lazarovich would go on with his trade over there, but was in fact meant as an insult: that his body would be distilling.

This made Sholem laugh. He could do with a little jollity at last. But it would have been tactless for him to laugh at what he heard about Mesel. Simon's father was also a wine merchant, but his name was Mosheh ben Amram. When the Emperor Joseph's officials summoned him to choose a German surname, he said he did not want one, being entirely content to bear the same name as the great leader of Israel, to wit, Moses, the son of Amram. So the officials entered Esel—meaning ass—into his pass. For nearly thirty years thereafter he was known by that name. However, on the signboard of his business and on his notepaper he figured as M. Esel, and by merging the initial with the humiliating surname he created another for his children. Old Mesel was certainly no ass.

"You are right not to buy your wine from Lazarovich," said Doved Troyes, the innkeeper of Batiz. "Reb Simon's wines are better and cheaper."

Sholem liked this Troyes, because he was unassuming. His name was reminiscent of the maternal surnames that were customary in north-eastern Europe, as Sholem Leah's—Sholem the son of Leah. But he somehow looked more western. In fact, his mother's name was not Troy (Faith) but Zissah. Mother Zissah was known far and wide, and if anyone mentioned her name in Batiz it was taken for granted that it referred to Doved Troyes' mother. She always had tears in her eyes, always grieved over something or some one. She helped Doved both in the tavern and at the butcher shop he kept as a sideline, though her help was not to his profit. She seemed to work for the accounts of the after-life rather than for the good of the business. Whenever a substantial amount was missing from the till, Doved knew that Mother Zissah had "lent" it to some one. It was all recorded in the cash book, thus: "To a wandering Jew who was in urgent need of it." Or: "To a sad man with a fox-skin cap." If half of a lamb or calf vanished from the butcher shop, it went into the bellies of the starving serfs. The villagers loved Mother Zissah and the womenfolk of the serfs called her "our lady," like the wife of the Squire of Batiz. Doved Troyes had had a great deal of trouble on account of this, for the Squire had given him notice to quit several times. But the peasants threatened not to frequent the inn if Doved Troyes left. The Jews sometimes referred to him as the "Frenchman," and unassuming as he was, he was proud of this appellation. According to a family tradition, his ancestors had come from no less a place than Troyes, the native town of Rashi. They had left definite notes to the effect that the family was related to the great Rabbi Shlomah Yitzchok.

Another Batiz personage was Reb Lamach Udvari, who had formerly lived in the village of Udvari. Reb Lamach had a beard that concealed most of his waistcoat. He was not a rabbi, only a "rebbeh," and even this modest title was accorded him only by the children who attended his *chaider,* the Hebrew primary school. The grown-ups referred to him as the *Melommed* or teacher. However, as Batiz had no rabbi, and Nootah *Batlan* was only an intruder from the East, tolerated by the community only for his good tenor voice and his sharp circumcising knife, it was to Reb Lamach that the Jewish women of Batiz took the gullet of stuffed geese to obtain his verdict as to whether the birds were *kosher.* Reb Lamach would put on his big spectacles, get the client to inflate the gullet, and examine it for any holes, even the most minute. Being very strict in orthodoxy, he would scratch away at it with the sharp nail of his index finger so long that usually a hole would appear in the end, and the verdict was *trefah.* The women were badly upset and Nootah *Batlan's* chances were rapidly improving.

However, Reb Lamach also enjoyed another distinction. He had a nephew named Shlomah living in Udvari who sometimes came to visit him. These visits were memorable events in Batiz. Shlomah wore only a moustache and side-whiskers, and when he was called up at the Torah reading the text of the appropriate benediction had to be whispered into his ear, because he was scarcely able to read in Hebrew. But everyone thought highly of him, because Shlomah at the age of seventeen—immediately after the Emperor Francis had decreed that Jews should be admitted into his army—became an infantryman and had been promoted corporal within thirteen years. He had fought against Napoleon for nearly eight years—at Aspern, Wagram, in the Tyrol, in Italy and at Waterloo—and had roamed over half Europe, visiting Naples, Rome, Berlin, Corsica, and even Paris. When, six months after Waterloo, he came home on his first leave with a sword-wound on his brow and several shot-wounds in his thigh, the Jews of Batiz received him with the utmost respect. Only his uncle was dissatisfied with him. "Tell me, Shlomah," he said, "are you a colonel now?" "No, Uncle Lamach," replied the soldier. "But you are at least a captain, no?" "No." "A lieutenant?" "No." "Have you spoken with the Emperor?" "No." "With Napoleon, then?" "No." "Have you seen the Tsar?" "No, Uncle." "Then," cried Reb Lamach with consternation, "what use has it all been to you? Was it worth your while, Shlomah, to retire from the world, from Batiz, merely to get two more holes in your behind?"

Reb Lamach must have been right when he said it was not worth while. For Batiz was held to be the center of the Universe not only by its own inhabitants, who were, after all, a numerically insignificant group. The real proof of its importance lay in the fact that all the Jews living there had left bigger and more highly reputed localities to come and live in Batiz. Batiz had no count or baron, no fishpond, no vineyards, nor even a decent wood for a pleasant walk. It was just a dusty lowland village that had never seen even a post-chaise. What, then, attracted the Jews to come to Batiz, which had not a rabbi either, let alone a famous wonder rabbi?

It was Otvar that made Batiz desirable to them. They moved to Batiz so that they might be close to Otvar, the Royal Borough that was barred to Jews. They could not live there at any price, but were allowed to settle in the nearby villages, and that was what they did, moving as close to their "little Jericho" as possible. Why did Leizer Lazarovich buy a house in Otvar if not in order to have at least some of his property "living" in Otvar? They could not expel a house, even a Jewish one.

However, the yearning for Otvar was not due to idealistic motives. Reb Jacob Anshel, not a leading light in Israel, even though he made Sabbath candles for Israel, was telling the absolute truth when he said that the Jews could yearn for and love with a pure love only one town on the face of the earth, and that town was not Otvar, but—some difference!—Jerusalem. That they were trying to settle not around Jerusalem but around Otvar was due to two reasons, a big one and a little one. The big one was that the Messiah had unfortunately not yet saddled his donkey and blown his ram's horn to start the living on their way to the Land of Israel and rouse the dead for the same journey. And the little reason was that the weekly markets and the fairs at Candlemas and on St. Stephen's, St. Jacob's, and St. Philip's Day were held not in Jerusalem, but at Otvar. However, the Jews who had a stall in the market place, or displayed their goods on a board laid across a couple of wooden horses, or only on a rush-mat on the ground, or who vended their wares perambulating or running about the market place blowing a reed or a whistle or a jew's harp or singing, were allowed to stay in the town only from dawn till dusk. If a Jew came from a distance and was late at market, so that he lost the first customers, in a torment of anxiety he packed up and left earlier than the rest, and even so feared for his purse and his goods in the uncertainty and insecurity of the night and the road.

Sholem was beginning to understand why the Jews had Batiz always on their lips. Of course, there were moments during that confabulation in the synagogue yard when he felt that things were not in order. He ceased to chat with the others, shook hands mechanically with new arrivals, answering somewhat absently when they asked him who he was, where he came from and what he was doing in Batiz. Fortunately, the new people did not expect a detailed account. Mermelstein the wholesale tailor,

Filpischer the brushmaker, Reb Hersh the ribbon peddler and Reb Aryeh Leib the linen draper, were all in a hurry. They went up to Nootah *Batlan* and turned on him to hurry up and start the *Mincha* service, then go on to the *Maariv*, the evening service proper. It was Tuesday, and they had to load their carts by torchlight to start for market at dawn. Elephant, the button- and braid-maker, was angry with Yossel Yochanan, saying that he was not going to wait with his cart, and unless the potter's packing-cases were all ready he would leave for Otvar without him. The potter tried to whisper something in his ear, but Elephant was not appeased and left him with a rude remark.

"Don't bother me on a Tuesday," he said. "I'll listen to you on Thursday. The world won't come to an end till then, will it?"

The front part of the synagogue—a plain room with a cross-beam supporting the ceiling—was occupied by a huge pyramid-shaped peasant oven. The roughly constructed ark, with the golden lions of Judah on the curtain, was suspended over the side of the oven. Some one explained to Sholem that the synagogue was too small for the congregation and that on Saturdays and other holy days it was overcrowded. If the oven could be removed there would be more space. But you must not touch an oven, for it was like a mother, giving warmth and bread. Breaking down an oven was like matricide.

Sholem was seized with disquiet. What if Nootah *Batlan* was too late with that Benediction for Malkeleh? He ought himself to raise his voice to Him who had seen the affliction of Leah. Then he saw, by the whitewashed east wall to the right of the oven, in the nook reserved for the more important members of the community, Reb Leizer Lazarovich swaying his body to and fro, and he forgot about the Benediction. He no longer enjoyed being at this *minyan*. He closed his eyes and covered his face with his hands, not, this time, with pious concentration, but to shut out the sight of Lazarovich. The vision of the distiller vanished, but instead, Sholem saw Squire de Sarberek with his untidy chin whiskers coming home from the hunt, tired and thirsty. And there was Mate Bor, the Headman, looking as if he himself were the hunted boar, and also tired and thirsty. Ludpal the bellringer was screeching, Serf Vizhordo was cursing, and Uncle

Galagonya was thumping the table with his fist, because they were all thirsty. And there were all the men of five villages, with hard toil from dawn till dusk behind them, and they were naturally also thirsty. God Almighty, who was going to quench all those thirsts if Reb Leizer was so stony-hearted!

As he left the synagogue he was very discontented with himself. He had so much to pray for, yet he had prayed only for the relief of the drunkards. And whereas there were many decent men in the synagogue who had been friendly to him, he had seen none but Reb Leizer, who stood with his back towards him. Was it a good thing for him to go among people?

"Don't worry, Sholem," said the potter. "I've spoken with the men. But to-morrow is market day in Otvar, so they can't think of anything else. How much is Lazarovich's bill?"

"A hundred and sixty odd florins."

"Less the price of the wine, of course, which you'll get from Mesel. That leaves about a hundred and forty. Wait a moment... Ten and ten and five . . . and three . . . twenty-eight, thirty-four, forty-one . . . We'll get it somehow. Be sure to come over on Thursday."

"If I can," said Sholem uncertainly. Climbing into the driving-seat, he gave a flick with the whip.


All he said to Sroleh Yomtov was that the casks were to stay on the cart overnight, and that he had changed his mind about buying from Lazarovich, and was going to buy from Rothbart. He had learned in Batiz that Rothbart treated his customers better and in any case Karoly was a great deal nearer. Malkeleh he told that he was going to Karoly in the morning and to give him any message she had for her brother.

"We must face things, Malkeleh," he said.

In the bar he gave the peasants strong gin, but entered weak rye on the accounts. Amid the unanimous approval of his customers, he declared that he was going to introduce the tally stick. It had been a great success in the inn of Doved Troyes in Batiz. A stick was split in half, one part for the innkeeper and the other for the customer. The daily consumption was scored into the sticks with a knife—so-and-so deep for a pint, half as deep for half a pint, and so on. There could be no mistakes and no distrust on either side. And the customer, from his part of the tally stick, could always tell how he stood and how much more he could afford to spend on drink.

The peasants were enthusiastic, only Serf Vizhordo had a query to make: What would happen if the Jew mixed up the tally sticks when pairing them together, so that, for instance, the poverty-stricken Serf Gore got the tally of the rich Farmer Galagonya?

Sholem assured him that that could not happen, because the tally sticks would differ both in length and thickness. Besides, he would engrave the customer's name on the stick.

"And how are you going to engrave it?" inquired the bell-ringer. "In Jewish or Hungarian?"

"A Jew writes in Jewish," replied Sholem.

This raised a laugh and the atmosphere was quite happy. For the moment, Sholem was in no trouble about the business. He had no need to worry even about the possibility of a sudden visit from the Squire, having been told that he was three villages away boar hunting, and that if no boar came along he was quite likely to lie in wait for three days and nights. Sholem mentally prayed for a respite for the poor wild beast, at least until he had settled the business with Rothbart.

But from over the house the shadows would not pass. Sholem had sensed disquiet in the air immediately on his return. The children huddled together, whispering. Feiga went about mumbling soundlessly. Sholem became worried, and handing over to Sroleh Yomtov hastened into the house. Malkeleh was dejectedly rocking the baby in her arms.

"I looked after her faithfully, Sholem," she said. "I couldn't have done more if she had been my own."

Sholem was seized with a sense of guilt for giving the baby sour milk the previous night. He stood listening to the baby's labored breathing and looking at its distorted features, then:

"It'll be all right," he said without conviction. "It only has a bellyache, that's all."

"If you say so, Sholem," said Malkeleh, as though clutching

at his words. "If you say it'll be all right . . . I'm so afraid that its little lungs are hurting and that's why it doesn't cry. Our Chayele also kept moaning like this. You remember, don't you?"

"It sounded quite different," said Sholem.

"Do you really think so?"

The night passed quietly enough. The family slept. Sholem kept listening whether the baby was still moaning. It was. That was reassuring. His thoughts went back to his friends in Batiz, and he tried to continue the interrupted confabulation. But Reb Leizer kept sticking his ugly face into the picture and spoiling everything with the words: "In the autumn? Credit in the autumn?" What an unpleasant creature he was, with his pale gums, and his black and yellow teeth. But he was even more unpleasant when he was not showing his face, but turning to the wall, swaying his body and praying. No use pretending to me, Reb Leizer, that you are communing with God. You are not turning to Him, but turning away from me, Sholem ben Yoirish, who has his rabbinical diploma from three great Saints, and who was third attendant to the great Rabbi Judah.

Sholem turned to the wall and gave a laugh. He recalled Lazarovich's disparaging remark about Shloimah Rothbart in Karoly. You yourself gave me the name and address of your competitor.

A man that laughs in bed goes to sleep soon after. When Sholem awoke it was already morning, though no one else was astir yet. He went into the bar parlor. He mumbled the prayers in a low voice. He heard some moans. Then silence. Then a dull, strangled cry. After a brief pause, another. Then a sudden low scream. Sholem dashed into the room and bending his prayer-shawled head over Malkeleh's bed, said:

"You are in pain, Malkeleh."

The woman looked up at him with a tormented smile. There was a brightness in her eyes, as well as pain and laughter and perhaps self-reproach.

"At last, Sholem," she breathed. "The time has come."

Aunt Feiga came in, untidy as usual, with the headkerchief askew on her head. But now she was brisk and aggressive. She roused the whole house, snapping out orders right and left.

"Yiteleh, Mailech, up with you! Out into the kitchen! Don't touch the hot water. You wash with cold this morning. It'll make your faces nice and rosy. Reb Sholem must go back to the bar. No business here. Sroleh Yomtov, out with you! And take your phylacteries. And don't swallow half your prayers. You know little enough as it is, you'll be nothing but an ignorant boor. Yossef, put on your knee-boots and be quick about it. There are some rags on the verandah for socks. But don't go and take a napkin as you did yesterday. Then run across to the Bogyo woman and tell her to come along at once. She knows what for."

Malkeleh gripped the sides of the bed convulsively.

"Don't chase the child out, Feiga. It's still dark and bitter cold in the street."

"You hop it, Yossef," said Feiga, with a finality that brooked no contradiction, "at a time like this there is no darkness or cold."

Yossef smiled sagely. By now he liked Malkeleh much more than the grumbling Aunt Feiga, but this time it was Feiga he had to obey. He moved quickly, and within barely two screams from the bed he was back.

"Madame Bogyo is kneading bread, but she'll be along presently."

"Presently? All right. If she is kneading bread, then the little girl is going to be sound and cheery like crisp new bread."

Both Sholem and Malkeleh wanted a boy, but Feiga was sure it was going to be a girl.

"If it were to be a boy," she had told Malkeleh some weeks earlier, "your stomach would come out to a point. Boys fight themselves forward. The girls are more retiring."

Malkeleh wanted to have the sick baby beside her, but Feiga only showed it to her, then she took it out into the kitchen.

"I'll look after it," she said. "You attend to your own now."

Malkeleh, gripping the sides of the bed, cried out:

"Yiteleh! Yiteleh, come here."

The little girl came in. Malkeleh tried to smile. She felt like screaming but mastered herself.

"Sit down here, on the bed, Yiteleh," she said in a quiet voice.

AN INNKEEPER'S BOY

SROLEH YOMTOV was unusually pale. On other mornings he used
to race through the prayers, scarcely glancing at the old *siddur*
(prayer-book); but now he was reading slowly and carefully,
in a low earnest voice.

Those Hebrew words were not the only mysterious things to
him. There were other mysteries, the kind that terrified him to
the marrow. When he heard the first of those searing screams,
which somehow acquired substance in his imagination, he gave
a start, paused over the Hebrew characters and waited. He knew
that there was going to be another and yet another. And they
would succeed each other more and more rapidly, and would
be more and more piercing. That was what happened four weeks
before. A woman kept screaming, then gave birth to a child.
Then she quietened down and smiled, as though she had never
screamed, and as though she had never known pain. Her pale
face had a brightness, a brightness like that of the Sabbath
candles. And then she just burned away, like the Sabbath candles.
How confusing and incomprehensible it all was!

I ought to ask those bearded Jews, he thought, what this here
means: "Man's life is seventy years." If that is true, why do
people die at the age of thirty-five, or thirty-two, or four weeks?
My father was sick for four years, my mother for four days.
Little Chayah has been sick for four weeks. Aunt Feiga says: "She
brought death to her mother and she was born for death." But
Aunt Feiga doesn't know anything. It is only these Hebrew
words that contain knowledge, and Aunt Feiga cannot even
read them.

The boy closed the *siddur*, folded up his phylacteries, and
raised his eyes to Sholem. Sholem misunderstood the question
that was in them and resumed the sentence he broke off the
previous night. "Rothbart's spirits can't be worse than Lazarovich's, and perhaps they are better," he said. But it seemed that
he would be unable to go to Karoly to-day. Whereupon Sroleh

Yomtov swallowed the question he was about to ask, observing that it all depended on what the peasants were used to. If they were used to the inferior spirits, then for them the inferior was the better. However, now he found his own voice and his own wisdom in matters of business rather foreign. He would have liked to talk about something very different. There was only one vital question, all the rest was only petty chatter. There was a smoldering curiosity in his heart, but when he tried to formulate the question he found that he had forgotten it, forgotten too whether it was only one question, or a hundred merging into one. As he was straining to remember and to bring order into chaotic eddies of thought, he began to wonder why he had intended to turn to Sholem for enlightenment. He did not know either. He was a pious man, a saintly man, but he had only faith, not knowledge.

How did Sroleh Yomtov know this? How was it that his fourteen-year-old intelligence had seized on the great questions of existence, and how was it that though he did not as yet see through things, he was able for a moment now and then to see into them? The recurrent, ever more rapidly recurrent screams illuminated like a flame the dark territories that he had never trodden before.

After his father's death, Menachem, the potash-man from Ombod, came along with his wife. They sat, sometimes silent, sometimes trying to comfort the mourners. When they were silent Sroleh Yomtov had a sense of kinship with them. But when they talked, they began to recede from him. Menachem spoke of the sins of the children of Israel, on account of which the good were taken away young. This explanation did not satisfy the boy. Who were those children of Israel, and how dare they by their actions condemn the good people to death? And what kind of justice was it that punished the good for the sins of the evil? Fancy, letting the sinner flourish and executing the innocent. When his mother died and no one came to see them, he recalled Menachem's talk and began to think about it. With partly justified and partly fabricated penitence he referred those words to himself. The fathers died for the sins of their sons. The sons at one time used to kill their fathers, and they were not entirely

innocent of patricide even to-day. The sons wanted to live, and
the fathers kept them in check. That was why the sons condemned the fathers to death. They did not carry out the sentence,
exercising the prerogative of mercy. Sometimes the reprieve came
from a higher power: at the last moment some one came riding
for dear life flourishing a white cloth. Was it from kindness or
from selfish calculation that the sons refrained from killing those
whose death they desired? Moses built on selfishness. Do not kill
them, so that you may have long life upon earth. If you allow
your fathers to live long, your children will also allow you to live
long. Moses eradicated one custom and introduced another. He
speculated on man's love of life, and his speculation turned out
to be right.

Sroleh Yomtov had never thought so much as he did now. Like
all Jewish children that grow up in loneliness, he was inclined to
brood. But otherwise he was not the introspective type. He was
born to act, to make and execute plans. Even now he had a whole
series of plans as to how to make himself independent and start
a life of his own. But events were compelling him to search and
inquire, to settle matters with himself. Meanwhile, he had to
repress the urge to action within himself.

He found it difficult to reconcile himself to the idea that
Sholem's family should settle down in his heritage. He did not
want a new father and mother, or anyone else who might disturb
him in his grief, in his liberty and in his plans. It was only gradually that he made friends with them and accustomed himself to
their presence. Indeed, in his loneliness he was pleased that they
had not moved on. He needed Sholem to teach him, and even
reprove him. He also needed Yiteleh to have arguments with.
The nine-year-old girl had a keener mind than eleven-year-old
Yossef. She had brought with herself a strange freshness that was
new to him; it made him gape and prick his ears, put all his senses
on the alert. But above all, Sroleh Yomtov felt that he needed
Malkeleh.

How strange he felt with them at the beginning! He had hated
them even before they came. In that Saturday morning the Headman, shortly after he had spoken with Sholem, reported to the
boy that the new Jew had arrived. From then until evening he

waged a bitter struggle with the unknown Sholem family who, he thought, must have heard about the death of the Lapfalva innkeeper, and had come dashing along even before the week of mourning was out to take his place. They did not recoil even from arriving on the Sabbath. And they had started the preliminary negotiations even before they had set eyes on the inn. With what curiosity and fury he had waited for them all that day! Yossef wanted to go to the gypsy camp to see them, but he had threatened to beat him if he set foot outside the house. His emotions were even more violent when he thought of the material aspect of the matter. Sroleh Yomtov had been hoping that the lease would be given to him, just as after his father's death, it had been transferred to his mother. Squire de Denghelegh objected that he was too young. But was it his fault that the Squire was so old? The Squire knew nothing about his abilities, and did not know that during the past four years he had sometimes managed the business singlehanded for months on end. Squire de Denghelegh bought nothing from the inn, because he had his own vineyard and cellar. He did not sell even any of his wines to the inn, but drank them himself with his frequent guests. But the other two Squires and Mate Bor, the Headman, were certainly aware that he was a clever boy.

On the third or fourth day Sroleh Yomtov realized that the Sholem family had strayed to the village by accident, yet he was in no hurry to acquit them. He obstinately stuck to the idea that Sholem was working against him, and had only come to take his living from him. When Sholem offered to give the orphans fifty per cent of the profits, Sroleh Yomtov could not take him seriously, because this meant that the Sholem family, which was bigger and was working, would be getting less than the orphans, who were only eating and scarcely sharing in the work. Sholem was trying to dangle a carrot before their noses. He was going to cheat, so as to conceal the profits, and the orphans, if they were lucky, would get ten per cent instead of fifty. At the same time, Sholem's piety, sincerity, and honesty upset him. You could not carry on like that without making a loss. In the end, neither Sholem nor the orphans would get any profits.

The change of heart in Sroleh Yomtov was brought about not

by Sholem, but by Malkeleh. However, he refused to acknowledge it to himself, refused to see that Malkeleh was a kind-hearted woman, and was so to the orphaned children. Once Malkeleh asked Aunt Feiga what the boys' favorite dish was and hastened to prepare some kreplach for them. Sroleh Yomtov clenched his teeth and did not eat of it, saying that he did not like ravioli. Also, he drank his milk coffee unsweetened, saying that he liked it like that. When Yossef gave him away he threatened to beat him.

He also tried to convert Yossef to his own attitude. That Malkeleh did the cooking and baking and the laundering and mending for them and looked after the baby and was nicer to them than Aunt Feiga—all that was nothing. This strange woman was trying to ingratiate herself. And like Sholem, she too was only out to hoard merits for the after life. She was collecting good deeds—*mizvoth*—for the heavenly account, there being no greater *mizvah* than to succor orphans.

"But what are they paying us for those *mizvoth*? Tell me, Yossef, are they paying us anything for them?"

Yossef stared at his brother with surprise. He had never heard it said, he observed, that you had to pay anyone for doing *mizvoth*. It was a *mizvah* to love your father and mother, to give charity, to say your prayers regularly, not to kill, steal, or cheat, and not to covet that which belongs to your neighbor. It would be funny, said Yossef, if you had to pay every one whom you didn't murder, rob, or cheat for the *mizvoth* you were doing.

"You are a damn fool," cried Sroleh Yomtov. "Have you never been at the synagogue in Karoly or Csenger on a Sabbath or *yomtov*? Didn't you hear the beadle auctioning the *mizvoth* from the dais where they read the Torah? "A hundred for the *mizvoth* . . . a hundred and fifty . . . two hundred . . ." The highest bidder is called up to the Torah."

"Yes," argued Yossef, "but they use the money to build a synagogue and pay poor people's rent and buy them medicine. If you had to pay for being allowed to do a *mizvah* you'd have to give money to *schnorrers* twice over, once as alms, and again because they were kind enough to accept the alms."

This argument was clearly due to Yiteleh's influence, and

Sroleh Yomtov did not like it. Yossef was endeavoring to keep pace with the little girl; he did not want to be less clever than she. But it was clearer still that he was straining his intelligence to fight for the retention of the Sholem family. When Sroleh Yomtov went over to more materialistic arguments, saying that Sholem had brought no money to the business, and if he had he must have hidden it, Yossef said with vehement reproach:

"You didn't hide the money, did you?"

To which the elder brother could reply only with his fists. "And if you don't hold your tongue, you'll get some more," he hissed when the operation was over.

Yossef dried his tears and went back to Malkeleh. He was simply beaming when he was near her. Sroleh Yomtov had none of this childish radiance in him. He was forced by some evil spirit to be surly and pigheaded with Malkeleh, and to give her sullen and rude answers. His ill-humor was unconsciously meant to convey that he was master here, and that the inn with all its equipment belonged to him. He managed matters in such a way that the Sholem family's visit should come to an end one day, and if at times he was beginning to experience a sense of kinship with them, his liberty and his fancies of his new role were dearer to him than any kinship. In any case, even a kinsman must not outstay his welcome.

That morning, hearing the woman's searing screams, he realized to the full, and for the first time, the artificial nature of all his reasoning, and the contrariness that existed between his conduct and his inner self. Those screams stirred him to the depths. He was terrified at the thought that Malkeleh, who had sometimes seemed so weary and worn, might depart in the same way as his mother. He began to identify her with the dead Sarah. As, with his eyes on the *siddur*, his ear strained towards the next room, he had a feeling that his mother was in labor in there on the painted deal bed. His eyes left the *siddur* and gazed into the air, his mind the prey of fancy. His mother had come back, a changed woman. She was younger, prettier, with long delicate fingers and a slender neck, and a pair of eloquent dark eyes behind dark eyelashes. Looking at her eyes, and her arched eyebrows, made you think of a couple of kids holding hands and dancing round and round in the meadow. And her voice, her soft, melodious voice! When she was singing a lullaby to little Chayah, tune and words tripped from her lips in such wonderful unison. Even that morning she had begun the day with a lullaby. But she faltered more and more as she went on. There came the strangled cries, then a piercing scream. The boy's body broke out in hot perspiration, and he dashed into the room. The woman was waving her white fists in the air. The wide sleeves of her bedgown had slipped on to her shoulders and the whiteness of her arms gleamed in the dimness of the room. Sroleh Yomtov had never seen anything like this. It frightened him, yet he was unable to move away. The woman's flushed face ordered itself into a smile, as though to deny that she was in pain . . . Now the screaming had stopped. The boy could hear only whispering from the other room.

JEWISH CHILDREN

HE WENT out into the yard to air his dazed head. He stood under the old rime-covered ash-tree, thinking. He looked at the cart with the casks on it. If Sholem could not go to Karoly, he Sroleh Yomtov, would. It would be a good thing. He would drive the pony hard, and the din and rattle would at least drown his confusion and pain.

He brought the pony out of the stable and harnessed it to the cart. Then he returned to the bar parlor for instructions.

"The most important thing," said Sholem, "is to satisfy the gentry. By to-night they may come back from the hunt and we must have plum whisky for them. I'll give you eight florins. That may be enough for a small caskful. If it isn't, get half a caskful. We'll talk about the rest when you return in the evening."

At this Yiteleh entered, her head covered with a thick headkerchief, her mother's big shawl round her shoulders, and a bundle on her arm.

"Mummy wants me to go with Sroleh Yomtov," she said.

"If Mummy says so, you must go. How long are you to stay?"

"Till evening. We are to come back together."

"You can stay longer," said Sholem. "At a time like this it is better for you to be in Karoly. Aunt Blimeleh knows what it is."

"So do I, Daddy," said Yiteleh.

When the cart was out on the highway, Yiteleh inquired whether Otvar was near Karoly. Sroleh Yomtov shook his head.

"Otvar," he said, "is this side of Batiz, just in the opposite direction."

"Then you must turn back, Sroleh Yomtov."

The boy gave her an uncomprehending look. The little girl went on in a very serious tone:

"Mummy said so. Aunt Feiga told her that there was a famous doctor in Otvar, Dr. Pfirsich, who could cure the worst illness."

"I know him," said the boy. "He couldn't cure my father."

"Nor your mother?"

"We didn't call him to her."

"That was wrong of you, Sroleh Yomtov. She might be still alive."

"What did your mother say?"

"She said to go to the doctor and ask him to come quick. To come back with us if he can. Because God forbid if he is not quick she'll die."

Sroleh Yomtov had just turned round with the cart. He now goaded the pony to greater speed.

"Your mother might die?" he asked in a strangled voice.

"No, the baby, little Chayah. Mummy's all right, thank God."

"But your father wants me to go to Rothbart in Karoly."

"If Karoly were near Otvar we could go to Rothbart," said Yiteleh, "but Batiz is near Otvar, isn't it?"

"Yes."

"Then you'll buy the things from Reb Leizer Lazarovich. We'll buy the things first, then go for the doctor."

"Your father said to get only plum whisky in the small cask."

"But Mummy said to have all the casks filled, because there isn't anything to sell in the bar."

"I know that. But Reb Leizer won't give anything on credit."

"Does Rothbart?"

"No, he doesn't give credit, either. I thought your mother had
written a letter to Mordechai."

"Mummy won't write any letters. Uncle Mordechai has a lot
of worry with the ink factory."

The boy pursed his lips, as though to say that he knew all about
Uncle Mordechai's worries. But looking down at the girl's serious
little face, he decided to stick to the point.

"Your father only gave me enough money for a small cask of
plum."

"He did? That's very good. Mummy gave me enough for all
the rest."

"What?" said the boy. "She gave you money?"

"Not money, only a pledge."

She undid the bundle, revealing a highly polished ebony box.

"This is it," she said, making the lid spring open. "This necklace used to belong to Mummy's grandmother Berenice. Some
of the pearls are missing, but it is still worth something. The
earrings with the red corals we inherited from Granny Chayele.
The gold bracelet belongs to Mummy; she got it when she was
engaged. The gold watch with the key doesn't go, but perhaps
it can be repaired. We had some more, but it was taken by
Eliphaz."

"Who is Eliphaz?" wondered the boy.

"You don't know?" said the little girl, with a gentle luminous
smile. "Eliphaz was Esau's son, a bandit." She looked behind her,
at a cart rattling along in their wake and there was anxiety in her
voice as she said: "Drive faster, Sroleh Yomtov." And as the
noise of the peasant cart receded, she added in a serious tone:
"Jacob is followed by the shadow of Esau."

Another time the boy would have reacted to such talk with an
ironical grimace and the taunt, "*Rebbets'n!*" But now he listened
quietly.

"Daddy says," Yiteleh went on, "that a great Talmudist told
him that Jacob exchanged his shadow with Esau, so that the
good shadow goes behind Esau and the bad shadow behind Jacob."

"And you believe that?"

"I do. Daddy said so."

"How can you exchange two shadows?" argued the boy.

"Jacob and Esau were twins and their shadows were alike."

"How does any one know that they exchanged them?"

"Because Jacob is persecuted, while Esau is all right."

"Why should they have made the exchange?"

"Jacob bought Esau's birthright, and together with it he got his shadow."

"That's nonsense."

"It isn't nonsense. The firstborn already has a shadow when the second one hasn't got one yet. Esau sold for the mess of pottage everything belonging to his birthright."

"You hear this kind of talk only from people who are afraid of their own shadow."

Yiteleh was smiling again. She was not afraid of her own shadow, only of bad men, and then only when she had the box of family heirlooms with her. But having handed it over to Sroleh Yomtov, she felt that it was safe, and she ceased to look behind her. Even a posse of men who came galloping from the direction of the crossroads did not frighten her, though they might have been bandits. The reason she did not speak as they passed was the noise they made.

"These are all the jewels Mummy was able to save," she said. "She always says that they'll be mine when I get engaged to be married. But that won't be for a long time yet."

"Then you ought not to waste them," said the boy.

"When we are in trouble," replied Yiteleh, "we can do anything. Mummy says you are allowed to take the bread even from the holy altar if the children are hungry. Besides, we are not wasting them, only pledging them. The pearls, the earrings, and the bracelet are for Reb Leizer, and the gold watch for the doctor, so he should come back with us."

The pony put on speed. The casks on the cart swayed, reeled, and clashed together like the bodies of drunken men. Sroleh Yomtov was silent, and the little girl did not speak any more, either. It was only when the yellowish-grey meandering body of the River Szamos appeared in the distance, and the white steeple of the Batiz church became visible on the opposite bank, that the boy remarked quietly:

"What your mother says is dead right."

And as they turned into Reb Leizer's street, which was pervaded by the slightly acid smell of the distilling, he asked:

"Doesn't your mother ever wear any jewelry? Not even earrings?"

"She does sometimes," replied Yiteleh, with a flicker of her long lashes. "On holy days, or when she goes on a visit, or when she is feeling happy. I haven't seen them on her for a long time." . . .

Fadele had run across to the distillery to fetch Reb Leizer. Reb Leizer seemed to be in a bad humor.

"You ought to know by now, Sroleh Yomtov," he grumbled, "that Tuesday and Wednesday are distilling days not selling days."

"But if it is urgent, Reb Leizer?"

"Not even if it is urgent. If a thing is urgent, you must attend to it a day sooner."

"But you'll serve an old customer, Reb Leizer, won't you?"

"My old customers can stay at home for all I care—where they've left their money."

Sroleh Yomtov flushed. With an embarrassed look he glanced across to where Yiteleh was standing among giant casks, sniffing at the strange vapors and pungent smells.

"Will you or will you not serve me, Reb Leizer," he said angrily. "I can take my money to Rothbart, you know."

Whereupon Reb Leizer suddenly turned friendly.

"My dear boy," he said, "why shouldn't I serve you? Have you got the money on you? I came down from the distillery, didn't I? If Reb Leizer comes down from the distillery and serves you on a Wednesday, what does that mean? It means that Reb Leizer likes you. And if Reb Leizer likes a person, he'll serve him. And how! With the greatest care and attention."

"I'm in a hurry, Reb Leizer," said the boy impatiently.

"You're in a hurry, Sroleh Yomtov, are you? Why didn't you say so at once? Reb Sholem might have told me yesterday that he was in urgent need of the goods and that you'd be in a hurry. Fadele, spirit into the big cask, potato whisky into the smaller one, and plum whisky into the smallest. Hand the demijohns to me, I'll fill them myself. What about wine, Sroleh Yomtov? I hope you're not taking to Simon Mesel the money you've collected from the peasants this autumn."

"Don't let's talk so much, Reb Leizer. I've got to go to Otvar from here. I don't want any wine."

Reb Leizer thought a great deal of his dignity, and perhaps another time he would not have allowed a young innkeeper's boy to talk to him like this. But now, perhaps because he had already written off the Lapfalva inn as a customer, when Sroleh Yomtov came along with the money he let it pass. Besides, he was enjoying the success of his tactics with Sholem.

"Ah, you're going to Otvar," he said jocularly. "What business have you got there on a market day? I suppose you want to talk with their worships the senators. A clever idea, Sroleh Yomtov, a very clever idea. If you can open an inn there, I'll give you some fine premises, and spirits on credit for a year. Won't you tell me why you're going to Otvar?"

The boy shook his head, but did not reply. As the distiller began to record the items on the blackboard, the boy said to Yiteleh:

"Yiteleh, go and see what the pony is doing."

Yiteleh went along to the cart, but soon returned, reporting to the boy:

"He's all right. He's drinking some wash out of a bucket."

Reb Leizer was just giving him his change.

"You gave me a hundred and fifty and the bill is a hundred and forty-three, so you get seven back."

On the way to Otvar Yiteleh wanted to know whether the distiller had kept the earrings as well.

"No, he didn't," said the boy.

"Was the necklace worth so much?"

"I think it's worth a lot."

"He gave you seven florins change, didn't he?"

"Yes."

"That's lovely. Now we're going to have a little money at home."

At the toll-gate outside the town they were stopped by a moustachioed *haiduk* flourishing a crooked sword above his head. Its glitter scared Yiteleh into drawing closer to the boy. Sroleh

Yomtov merely smiled. He knew that the sword was but the symbol of authority and no active weapon. The *haiduk* was rude, but the boy answered his questions and remarks calmly.

"Huh, little Isaac, you'll have to hitch your pants up properly if you want to get into Otvar on a Wednesday."

"Can't one on a Wednesday?"

"You can't on any day, but Wednesday is market day on top of it."

"What if I want to buy something?"

"Jews don't buy, they only haggle."

"Really, Master Haiduk, I want to buy a cask from the cooper."

"That can't be true. Where are your passes?"

The two children gazed at each other. Passes? Why, they were living in this county. But the *haiduk* said they needed them. Jews had to have them even if they were from Batiz.

"Well, have you got your passes or haven't you?"

The boy fumbled in his pockets, produced a bright coin and pressed it into the *haiduk's* palm.

"There you are, Master Haiduk."

"I'll speak to Master Bagamer," said the *haiduk* gruffly, slipping the coin into his pocket, and turning to enter the toll-house.

"You were wrong not to tell the truth," whispered Yiteleh, nudging the boy.

"Tell the truth to that one?"

"You must tell the truth to every one. It's no crime to be going to the doctor."

"It's no crime," said the boy, "but it is not his business."

The toll-keeper appeared. He had watery blue eyes and a plume in his hat.

"Where do you come from?" he snapped, looking the two children up and down.

"From Lapfalva."

"You've just come from Lapfalva?"

"Yes, sir."

"You've come from Lapfalva by the Batiz road?"

"No, sir—by the Batiz road we came from Batiz."

"Umm. What have you got in the cask—mineral water?"

"No, sir."

"I thought so. Spirits, what?"

"Yes, sir."

"And you want to take them into Otvar?"

"No, sir, we're taking them home to Lapfalva."

"Then get on with it—one-two-three!"

"We want to go to the doctor, sir!"

"Where does he live?" snapped the man suspiciously. The boy mentioned the address.

"What is his name?"

"Dr. Pfirsich."

"You told the *haiduk* you wanted to buy something from the cooper."

"We want to do that too."

"Really? Which of you is ill?"

"Neither."

"Now you have blurted it out all right," said the man triumphantly.

"No, sir—the patient is at home."

"I know you, breed of Israel!" Then turning to the *haiduk*: "They want to trade in the town—sell the drink on the market and come back filled up with water. There's cunning in their very eyes . . . What are you shush-shushing about there? You want to outwit a Bagamer, hey?"

Yiteleh had just suggested to the boy to try and bribe this man as well. The boy said he daren't. Whereupon Yiteleh began to implore:

"Please, sir, let us go in. The baby is sick. If we don't take the doctor with us there's going to be trouble."

"One Jew brat the less," said the official with a gesture.

Yiteleh would not give up, but Bagamer was adamant. Sroleh Yomtov helped the girl up to the driving-seat, followed her, flicked his whip at the pony and turned round with the cart.

"We could go in but for the casks," said Yiteleh.

But Sroleh Yomtov thought otherwise. These men found it suspicious that they had come by the Batiz road, whereas Lapfalva people ordinarily arrived by the Csenger road, entering the town through the toll-gate at the other end. It would therefore be best to attempt entry there, after making a detour. But Yiteleh did not like the idea.

"Then they will think that we are bringing the spirits from Lapfalva to sell in the market. You ought to have told them that we came by the Batiz road because we had just been to Batiz to buy spirits for the inn."

"He wouldn't let me tell him anything, would he?" cried the boy, offended. "No use telling *them* the truth. I'm sorry I didn't say, yes, Master Toll-keper, we have mineral water in the casks."

"That wouldn't have been right."

"That would have been the only right thing to say. I'd have paid the toll for mineral water and we could have gone in to the doctor."

Yiteleh thought this over for a long time before she observed: "I still think it is best to tell the truth."

Sroleh Yomtov kept shrugging his shoulders. He was no longer enthusiastic about attempting entry at the other toll-gate. But what else could he do? The journey was long and tiring. They drove back to Batiz, and thence over mud-tracks to another village, where it took hours before they were ferried across the river. Kese the pony was less spry than the day before; Fadele's wash this time seemed to have depressed rather than elated him. He only just managed to drag the cart along. Of course, there was a heavy load on the cart and the mud-tracks acted like a brake on the wheels.

It was late afternoon when they reached the toll-gate. Sroleh Yomtov pressed a *groschen* into the hand of the lad lounging near the toll-house, so as to give him strength to raise the heavy beam that lay across the road. For the *haiduk* he had a larger coin in readiness. But he had not the time to slip it across to him because the toll-keeper, a thickset man with a round head and hardly any neck, had just come out. He bawled at the two children what they were doing at the town gate at this hour, when they were already beginning to chase the Jews out of the market. Sroleh Yomtov spoke disjointedly because he had to keep dodging with his head the cane which the man was swishing about under his nose to make the official standpoint the better understood.

"You think I've nothing better to do, Jew brat, than to let

you in before sunset, hey! Who will guarantee that you won't stay the night? Or that you won't hide somewhere and stay for weeks? And if there is a scandal who will get into trouble with the Justice of the Peace and the Council? Why, Master Kokass!"

Sroleh Yomtov overcame the menace of the cane by dodging forward. He spoke bravely and intelligently, saying that he was well aware that no Jew might spend the night in the Royal Borough, much less Jewish children. But he and the girl did not intend to stay, for they must get back with the doctor as soon as possible. If his worship the toll-keeper did not believe him, he could have the *haiduk* go with them in the cart.

"Is that all you want, Jew brat!" cried the official. He was flattered by the new mode of address, but it did not soften him. "In the end you'll come to think you're the children of His Excellency the Lord Sheriff. Fancy, two smelly Jew brats driving into town with a *haiduk* sitting beside them on the driving-seat. What do you say to that, Mihaly?"

The *haiduk* gave a full-throated guffaw. The attendant was also holding his sides. This laughter annoyed the boy.

"I want to go in, Master Toll-keeper," he said snappishly; not "your worship" this time.

The official ceased laughing and gave several gasps.

"What? You want . . . to . . . go . . . in?"

"I must get in at all costs."

"The impudence!" bawled the man, his face the color of a beetroot. He began to beat the boy with the cane about the head. "You want to go in, hey . . . at all costs, hey . . ." He struck again and again.

The boy tried to shield his face with his raised arm, but was unable to parry the blows. He felt the blood spurting from his forehead. He touched the spot with his hand and seeing the blood on his fingers he muttered in a strangled voice:

"I'll report this to his worship Squire de Denghelegh."

"Hold your tongue, you!" barked the man, again raising his cane to strike the boy. But the little girl pushed between them, pale, with flashing eyes and shaking her little fists.

"Don't you dare hurt my brother!"

The man lowered the cane.

"Go and complain to your Jehovah," he said contemptuously. "But clear off at once. Or if you want your bottoms tickled . . . Mihaly!"

"Yes, Master Kokass."

The *haiduk* approached the children menacingly. What could they do but turn back?

Yiteleh kept sniffing for a long time. Sroleh Yomtov sat shrunk within himself, wiping the blood off his brow now and then. When they reached the river he alighted and washed it off his face. He wanted to talk but could not. His failure and the humiliation of the beating hurt more than the wounds. He felt like screaming, but suppressed the urge. Only once did he yield to his rage. Looking back at the town against the setting sun, he stood up in the driving-seat, and shook his fist towards the spires of Otvar.

"We're not as good as you, hey?" he hissed.

Yiteleh stared at him, suddenly forgetting to sniff. She was amazed that Sroleh Yomtov could be so angry. She tried to soothe him.

"We'll put a bandage on your wound when we get home. It won't hurt then."

"That's nothing," said the boy, with a wave of the hand. "It doesn't hurt at all."

His right arm felt so heavy from the blows that had fallen on it that he could barely hold the reins. But he held them. He even managed to flick the whip at the pony whenever he wanted to say in a casual tone anything about which he was in fact feeling very deeply.

"Yiteleh . . . don't tell your mother that I was beaten. . . . If she asks about my injury, say I fell over and knocked my forehead against the rim of a cask. You see what I mean, don't you?"

"I see, Sroleh Yomtov."

"I shan't mention it even to Squire de Denghelegh. Why should I? I'll settle this myself. I'll show them."

"What are you going to do?"

The boy did not reply for a long time. He wanted the girl to press him. But Yiteleh kept silent and the boy thought she was sulking. He filled his lungs with fresh air, then he said:

"One day I'll go in and stay in." And it sounded, somehow, as if the words were accompanied by the shaking of a fist.

"Even Uncle Mordechai can't get in," said the little girl, shaking her head. "And Reb Leizer Lazarovich can't get in, although he's got a house there."

"I have no house, but I'll get in. You wait and see." Then, gazing into her eyes: "Don't you believe me?"

"We are strangers here," said Yiteleh earnestly.

"Why strangers? My grandfather was born in Otvar and lived there for thirty years."

"And why did he leave?"

"Because he was forced to."

"You mean they drove him out?"

"Yes, on the Emperor's orders."

"Just as my grandfather was driven out of Nikolsburg," said the girl.

By the time they reached home it was pitch dark. The inn was closed, only the living-rooms showed a light. Sroleh Yomtov alighted to open the gate. There was a tense anxiety within him, hammering at his chest, and higher up too, beneath his injured brow. There was the sound of a baby crying from the house, a queer, crude, jarring sound. This was not his little sister's sickly cry, but a new voice. Dashing up to the verandah, he peered in through the window, listening. He saw and heard everything clearly. There was the peasant midwife, Aunt Feiga, and Sholem. Malkeleh was lying in her bed, with her white hand on her forehead. Aunt Feiga was washing pieces of pitch-black linen in a steaming trough. The midwife was drying and slapping a naked baby, then laying it down beside Malkeleh, who was gazing in front of her with a weary smile. Sholem kept trimming the wick of the candle and shaking his head, as Kese did after a long journey. The baby was no longer crying.

"Where is the other one?" came Malkeleh's voice.

Aunt Feiga looked across through the steam from the trough, saying:

"The other one is all right. I put her beside her mother."

Sroleh Yomtov saw a scared expression on Sholem's face, and

heard a brief cry of pain from Malkeleh. Then he hurried back to the cart and helped the little girl down.

"Come along, Yiteleh! There's some one waiting for you there."

As they were hurrying across the yard, there was a sudden thud on the ground—Malkeleh's jewel-box, which had slipped from the boy's coat pocket. He picked it up and pressed it into Yiteleh's hand.

"Give it back to your mother. It's all there, just as it was. Tell her Reb Leizer didn't want it. And tell her that we got the spirits without that, everything we need in the inn."


### UNDER THE MACCABI LIGHTS


ON THE eve of *Chanukah* there was bloodshed at the inn. Two lads from Gyekenyes, Ferke Por and Pal Bene junior, fought with knives. Ferke was the attacker, but it was he who was carried to his home in a blanket. Pal was somewhat groggy, but he left the inn on his own feet. Sholem received a cut on his left arm while trying to separate the combatants. At noon the following day Squire Gedeon de Gyekeny came along to inquire what exactly had happened. Sholem could tell him but little. He had been sitting behind the screen in the bar, studying, when he heard an altercation. He remembered only one word: "Marika." By the time he went out the knives were already flashing. The gentleman was very angry with him.

"You are the innkeeper, so you must know what goes on in the inn. We didn't bring you here to study the Talmud, but to keep your eyes and ears open. If those two happen to kick the bucket and the pandours come along, what will you say to them?"

"I'll say . . . I'll say," stammered Sholem.

"You'll say nothing, Jew!" roared the other. "You'll send them to me or to Lady Susan. The good-for-nothings! They were due to do their villenage this morning treading cabbage in the pickling vat, and this is how they shirk it."

In the afternoon the peasants came along. Sholem was very

quiet. The big tome was closed and lay on the edge of the counter. Sholem kept his eyes and ears open as instructed, but was badly upset. Things were getting on now, with fresh stock in the cellar, Malkeleh up from her confinement and the new baby bursting with health. The other one had gone, but that had been God's will from the first, and they could not have done anything to prevent it. And now here was a fresh calamity. The customers were talking quietly, only Ludpal the bellringer kept screeching that this was a death inn, where everyone died.

In the evening Sholem lighted the first *Chanukah* light. The Maccabi light, together with the candle used to light it, burned despondently on the window-sill of the living room. The *Maoz Tsoor*, the heroic Maccabean hymn, did not rise triumphantly from the lips of the males of the house, but was hummed in a subdued sing-song.

In the morning Sholem opened the inn early. He was anxiously waiting for the first reports. Vince the carrier came along and said that the priest was calling in the afternoon to administer the last rites to Ferke. Sholem gave a breath of relief—the lad was still alive. At noon Pal Bene senior came in to ask for a drop of strong drink for his own son as well as for Ferke. A good-for-nothing came to no harm, he said; a peasant did not die so easily. He would die either in childhood or when he was too old to work. But so long as he had the strength to do villenage even death could not get him down. The gentry were lucky with the serfs. In the afternoon the news was even more poisoning. The Bene lad had had bacon and onions for dinner, while Ferke had eaten some baked pumpkin prepared by Marika. Marika was sitting by his bed, weeping, and saying that she never even looked at Pal. And Ferke's wound was no longer oozing.

The following day the incident was scarcely mentioned. There was a more important topic: snow was falling in big woolly flakes. There was going to be a frosty Christmas. On the third day there was another scuffle in the inn between two adolescent lads. Fortunately, however, no knives were used.

Towards evening the house was invaded by an unexpected liveliness. There was a visitor, Mistress Golda, wife of Mendel the fisherman from Nameny. The sleigh that brought her was all

a-tinkle and full of music and song and as it glided into the yard
it was followed by swarms of serf children.

"Jewish gypsies!" they cried.

The family hastened out into the yard and the peasants from
the inn also came out to watch. There was a shaggy little man
sitting on the driving-seat, with a fur hat edged with fox-skin,
and a whip in his vastly mittened hand. This was Zisheh, the
feather merchant Jew from Hodasz. Beside him, wrapped in a
big fur-coat, with rugs round her knees, sat rosy-faced Golda.
The Jewish "gypsies," a gaunt man with a goatee and two thin
boys, sat playing and singing in the body of the sleigh. The man
was playing a fiddle, one of the boys another instrument that
looked like a fiddle, while the second boy was beating time with
a flute and singing, accompanied by both Zisheh and Golda. They
were singing some wild Aramaic song, whose words were indistinct, but for two or three that were sung at a rising pitch:

"*Anti—Malkah, Malkah . . . Maylech malkayah. . . .*"

"They are singing this for you, Malkeleh," said Aunt Feiga,
with a toothless grin. "That's Chaim Leib, the fiddler from
Sziget, with his two sons, his *meshorrers*" (choir boys).

Golda was a distant relation of the late Mosheh. She told
Malkeleh that she had come only to see the orphans, having
heard that their mother had also died. She would like to stay
for a day or two. Noting Malkeleh's expectant expression, she
hastened to explain the situation.

"I came with Zisheh, but he is going back home to Hodasz. He
is taking the fiddlers because there is going to be a wedding at his
house to-morrow. His daughter is getting married."

Zisheh went to the inn to have his leather bottle filled with
spirit. He took it to the big room, where the fiddler and his boys
were sitting round the tin stove warming their numb fingers.

"Drink, *marshalik*," he cried gaily, "so you have some life in
you when we get home. You too, Yerucham, and you, Amram
Hersh. Grease your gullets a bit. We're going in a minute, as soon
as I've made *Chanukah*."

The fiddler with the goatee took some generous swigs, then
he cleared his throat. Now that Zisheh had called him *marshalik*,
which meant entertainer and rhymester, he must give him a fore-

taste of the rhymes which he had reserved for the wedding. With a humorous grimace he began to chant:

> *"He's not a man of straw, but a man of feather,*
> *His heart is soft as down, but his face is leather,*
> *He's always jolly and never sore,*
> *May he live a century or more."*

Zisheh laughed and took another drink. Yossef whispered to Yiteleh:

"Uncle Zisheh's face isn't leather, is it?"

"Silly," said the little girl. "It's only for the rhyme."

As Sholem entered he, too, got an impromptu rhyme. He smiled, stepped to the window and lighted the *Chanukah* lights, humming the Maccabean hymn. Zisheh did the same at the other window with wax candles he had brought with him. He waved the "servant"—the candle used for lighting the tiny lamps—towards the fiddler and he and his boys struck up the *Maoz Tsoor*. Zisheh waved his arms and sang with them. He had a coarse voice, but a good musical sense and he sang with gusto and an inner jubilation. His shaggy beard became luminous above the lights. The fiddler had a powerful baritone voice, but was not exerting himself—he had to save it up for the morrow. His sons were less prudent.

The contagion of gaiety spread to the whole family, and all joined in wholeheartedly with a sort of heroic abandon. There were no fighting peasants now, no rude squire, no death and mourning; "we" had triumphed all along the line. The trouble and grief occurred a long, long time ago; but the victory was so recent, only two thousand-odd years old. The Chashmonite Matithyahuh with his strong sons and his gallant *chassidim* ("the righteous") had defeated the armies of the evil Antiochus Epiphanes. The few had mastered the many, the weak had overcome the strong, the good had subdued the evil.

Zisheh too was a *chassid*, though not a gallant Maccabean *chassid*. He knew nothing about the word, but all the more about feathers. For twenty years he had roamed through the villages crying and singing "any feathers to sell." The serf women liked to hear his voice, for it meant a few coppers for them. With the lightest merchandise in the world, feathers, to carry on his back, Zisheh had managed to acquire something of a hump, but now he owned a horse and cart and was supplying feathers to Sachsel's in Pesth, who fifty years before had started in the same way as he. Now he was already marrying off his third daughter. But it was not that which made him gay. He was a follower of the Baal Shem, the saintly leader, who hated nothing so much as sadness. Why be sad and downcast! Man ought to live gaily, bearing the burden, making sacrifices and loving the world with a jolly heart. The Lord prefers a gay dog to a depressed human being.

"Hi!" yelled the nimble little Jew, slapping the sides of his knee-boots as though to sweep something off. Actually, this was the prelude to a Russian-Yiddish dance.

> *"The Rabbi has decreed,*
> *The Rabbi has decreed,*
> *To live gay-gay-lee."*

The song and the dance were very popular and an encore was asked for, but Zisheh glanced at the window-sill and seeing that his candles had burned far down, he shook himself and saying, "Come along, *marshalik*," was already on his way. Within two minutes the sleigh was a-tinkle again, carrying the gaiety off to the wedding.

However, a little of the gaiety was left behind; and so was Goldeleh. She was a gay, feather-brained creature. She was a year or two older than Malkeleh, but dressed "younger." She wore bright-colored silks and varicolored cottons, and sometimes she would tie her red-spotted headkerchief round the nape of her neck, like the peasant women. And she was always humming a tune. Not that of the Maccabi hymn, nor those of the Yiddish songs, but the *goy* songs, such as are sung only by the serf lads and girls.

These songs were not for a respectable Jewish woman, as even Aunt Feiga remarked. But Goldeleh did not bother about Aunt Feiga. She did not bother about the orphans either, although she was supposed to have come for their sake alone. The first quarter-hour after her arrival she talked a little to Yossef, asking him some

ingratiating questions, but he was shy in his replies, so she got tired
of him. They called in Sroleh Yomtov from the bar parlor, and
the woman gave him a smacking kiss full on the lips, making him
flush to the ears.

"What a big boy you've grown, Sroleh Yomtov!" she said.
"Don't you like Auntie Golda any more?"

The boy muttered something and drew away from her.

Goldeleh was not particularly interested in this young savage
either. All she wanted now was to win Malkeleh's friendship.
Malkeleh scrutinized and listened to the strange woman and
took a liking to her, precisely because she was so different.
Though she seemed a shallow-minded woman, she was interesting
because she was by no means secretive, and talked even about
her most intimate concerns. She chattered a lot, often irrelevantly,
laughed a great deal, but also frequently burst into tears, sometimes without any transition. At times she would sit and stare
into nothingness. Malkeleh observed her and was surprised.

"You have no children, have you?" she asked once.

"No."

"Never had any?"

"No."

"Is that why your husband doesn't love you?"

"Mendl?" said Goldeleh, with a pout. "He does love me—
that is just the trouble."

"How's that, Goldeleh?"

"He's so small and so violent."

"He doesn't beat you, does he?"

"Not me. Only the fishermen."

"The fishermen?" said Malkeleh thoughtfully.

"Last Monday night," said Goldeleh, and her face became
clouded, "he rowed out to the lads and threw himself on Berl and
boxed him into the Tisza."

"Who is Berl?"

"Berl? Why, just Berl. Poor, handsome, strong Berl!" Her
eyes filled with tears, and she was shaken with sobs.

"Was he drowned?" asked Malkeleh uneasily.

"He wasn't drowned," sobbed Goldeleh. "He swam across to
the other bank. And he didn't come back." She sobbed a little

longer, then she shook herself. "I'm not going back," she said. "Not ever, Malkeleh. I'd rather kill myself."

Sholem did not look at Goldeleh, and even the sound of her voice roused an aversion in him. Yet the woman did everything to ingratiate herself with him. At table, she would anticipate his wishes and pass him the bread, salt, and anything else. Malkeleh appeared not to notice this, yet soon she began to anticipate the other woman in these little attentions. Goldeleh was a skilful housewife and tried to help in the kitchen with the cooking and baking, bringing to life everything she touched. She had long talks with Yiteleh and was playful with Mailech. There was only one thing she knew nothing about, and that was the baby. Malkeleh would never have allowed her to handle it.

By the fourth day the charming, addle-headed woman seemed to have merged into the household. But towards noon a rattling carriage drew up in front of the inn, and a little Jew with stern features and a trimmed beard entered the bar parlor and demanded to know from Sholem where his wife was.

"You're looking for your wife here?" said Sholem, with surprise.

"I'm looking for Goldeleh!" barked the other.

"Ah, Goldeleh!" said Sholem with a smile. He was smiling not at the funny little man, but at himself. Now he was surprised that he should have been surprised that Mendl, the fisherman, should be seeking his wife in his house. Mendl never forgave him that smile, and in his injured mistrust he included Sholem in the *chassidic* conspiracy that had promoted Golda's flight in the name of the duty of joyousness.

"Come in, Reb Mendl," invited Sholem. "You don't have to get excited. Your wife came to visit the orphans and likes it here."

Sholem knew and saw nothing. He did not even notice that Goldeleh was behaving in a resentful manner, and as they entered, made a movement as if to run away. Only Malkeleh saw this. When husband and wife retired to the guest room to talk, and the talk became rather vehement, besides lasting an inordinately long time, Malkeleh sent Yossef in to them to inquire whether Uncle Mendl was not hungry. The boy came back with the reply that he did not want anything, but would they feed and water his horse, for Goldeleh wanted to go home.

"Aunt Golda is packing and crying," reported Jossef.

When Mendl had taken his wife away, Malkeleh went about the house silently for days. Sholem, realizing that she lacked company, was sorry for her and suggested that she might go over to Golda in Nameny when she had the time and felt so inclined. Golda was somewhat capricious, but she was gay. She was gay when she arrived and just as gay when she left. Malkeleh could do with a little feminine gossip and laughter. Malkeleh nodded affirmation. But she never for a moment contemplated a visit to Golda.

For the rest, life in Sholem's house was not too monotonous. The marsh-side inn lay close to certain business centers, and merchants travelling from north to south to buy, or taking goods from west to east, now and then left the highways to water their horses and rest. There was no other suitable pull-up along the big marsh. Jewish trade and industry, being barred from the big towns, established centers along the highways, often in unimportant villages that, in time, attained importance through the activities of the Jews. In the south, the centuries-old Jewish settlement of Karoly, in the north that of Szalka, and in the east that of the satellite villages of Otvar travelled hither and thither, making deliveries and transacting business, and even if Lapfalva did not lie at the junction of their various routes, the restless folk of the road would nevertheless stray there now and then, especially since it became known that the innkeeper was a pious and learned man.

For example, Zalman the trough-dealer had called for the second time in a fortnight. He had come from up north, across the Tisza, by the same route that Sholem and his family had followed, and was on his way home to Karoly. But Zalman knew the right road, and if he left it it was not by mistake, but because he wanted to be in Sholem's inn before dusk. He alighted from the cart, lifted off what looked like a bundle of blankets, and took it into the inn. There he unwrapped from it a thin, pale, shivering little boy whose general appearance indicated nine or ten years of age, but whose brow and restless eyes made him look a year or two older.

"Well, here we are, Shayeh," said Zalman. 'You'll get warm here. I'll take you into the house in a minute. Madame Sholem will give you a cup of hot milk or whatever you like. Don't be shy, my boy, these people are not strangers."

Zalman told Sholem that the main reason he had made a halt at his place was to light the *Chanukah* lamps, this being the eighth evening, which he would not like to miss, as he might if he reached Karoly too late. But to Malkeleh he said something else. The boy had swallowed a four-kreuzer piece on the way, and Zalman was very worried about him. Heaven only knew how it happened. Shayeh was a clever boy, a grandson of the late Rabbi Oesterreicher, and he was not a baby, either. Yet the accident had happened. Between Szalka and Csaholy the cart had given a jolt, and down the coin went. The boy had been retching and belching ever since, but the big coin had not come up.

"It had better not if it hasn't so far," observed Malkeleh. "It would only hurt his gullet. Sit down over there, boy, among the children."

She hastened out into the kitchen to heat some milk and scald some senna leaves in a small mug. Mixing the senna liquor into the milk, she carried the mixture to the boy, who sat somewhat clumsily at the corner of the table. The children were absorbed in the traditional *Chanukah* game of "put and take," which they played—for money—with a winged lead top. The gamblers were very excited, and the few coppers they had received from Aunt Golda and Uncle Mendl kept traveling to and fro. Sroleh Yomtov spun the top in a way as though he wanted to lose, but somehow it always came to rest with the letter *Gimmel* (meaning "take all") on the upper section.

"Haven't you got any money?" asked Yiteleh of the new boy.

"I've got four kreuzers," replied Shayeh quietly, "but I can't spend that. I'd like to, though."

The other children did not comprehend this, until after Shayeh had left. Then they rolled on the floor with merriment, and Shayeh's hidden fortune became a stock joke for years.

However, Shayeh did not leave that evening. In the course of the next hour or so the children learned that he was going to stay for a few days, and sleep with Uncle Zalman in the guest room. The children did not ask why, but were pleased to have the new boy with them. Gradually they learned some wonderful things about him. Shayeh had come straight from Vienna. It also transpired that he had traveled as far as Szerencs with Yechiel Kranztor, who had been delivering Tokay wine to Vienna. Shayeh had rested at Szerencs for two days, where he was taken over by Zalman, who was on his way home. Now the boy had to have another rest, so that when his mother saw him again he should be looking well. For Shayeh had been away for no less than three years, staying with an uncle in Vienna.

The delicate little boy had suddenly grown in stature. The top lay dead on the table. None of the children was interested in the gambling now, not even Sroleh Yomtov, who went so far as to yield up his winnings to the losers. He wanted to know what kind of Jews lived in Vienna and what their business was. Shayeh was unable to enlighten him. All he could say was that there were poor Jews and rich Jews there, some dealing in cloth, others in corn and timber, while still others lent money. Oh yes, there was a Jew from Frankfort in Vienna, whom Shayeh had seen one Saturday at the old Wertheimer Synagogue when he was called up to the Scrolls of the Law. It was said that he had lent many millions of florins to the Emperor's Chancellor.

"What's his name?" asked Sroleh Yomtov with burning eyes.

"Chancellor Metternich," replied Shayeh.

"I don't mean him. I mean the Jew from Frankfort."

"Solomon Rothschild."

"And how did he get all that money?"

Shayeh Oesterreicher shrugged his shoulders. This was a question he could not answer. Anyhow, he was not yet interested in money matters.

"Did you see the Emperor?" asked Yiteleh.

The boy nodded affirmation.

"What does he look like?"

"He's thin, pale and bald."

This was disappointing news. It seemed that Shayeh was not interested in the Emperor, either.

Sholem came in, unusually brisk, almost excited. With a side-ways nod at Malkeleh he said:

"The guardian of Israel does not sleep, neither does he slumber." He went up to Shayeh, stroked his face and said: "Your grandfather was a great man." Evidently, Zalman had told him something about the recently deceased Rabbi of Karoly that had stirred him. The story of how Shayeh came to be in Vienna was indeed exciting and wonderful.

Rabbi Mosheh Aryeh Oesterreicher, grandson of Mayer Oesterreicher, was Minister of an extensive circuit. Before the principal holidays he used to travel through the three counties belonging to his rabbinate. One Saturday he was preaching at Peer, a village noted for its big fairs. The following day he traveled on to Nyiregyhaza, and thence, four days later, to another town. He had no inkling what trouble had arisen behind him. One Saturday afternoon a peasant girl had been murdered by her jilted lover. At that hour there had been much loud chanting at the house of the Jewish shopkeeper where the rabbi was staying, for they were bidding farewell to the "Queen." The following day there was already a rumor in the village that the murder had taken place at the rabbi's command, so that the Jews could mix the blood of a virgin into the wine used for the Saturday evening ritual. A denunciation was sent to the High Court in Nagyvarad, where the rabbi, in his absence, was sentenced to death by hanging on the statements of his accusers. This was on the eve of the Day of Atonement. The Jews of Nagyvarad were on their way to synagogue when they heard about the sentence. *Yom Kippur* is a great and awesome festival, with a more rigid ban on mundane activity than even on the Sabbath. But could the House of Jacob remain idle in a case like this? After the *Kol Nidreh* they got a young Jew to ride to Karoly on a fast horse. His beard and ear-curls were concealed by a kerchief, so that he should not be recognized as a Jew. Other Jews seeing him riding a horse on the Day of Atonement would have been scandalized, while Gentiles would have sought to discover his errand. The messenger galloped on all that night and the following day, arriving at the synagogue in Karoly towards dusk, when they were reciting the closing prayer, the *Neilah*.

Tearing the kerchief off his face, he dashed into the synagogue and up to the reader's platform and whispered into the rabbi's ear: "For the good name of Israel and your own life, stop."

The rabbi refused to flee and desert his flock and his family. But when the stars had come up, he was put into a carriage, together with Shayeh, who had been standing by him and chanting with him at the synagogue. A week later they were in Vienna. The rabbi's younger brother, Joseph Manasseh, or as the Viennese called him, Dr. Josef Manes Oesterreicher, was a famous man, and a medical attendant of the Imperial Court. Yet it took him more than a year of waiting upon the great of the land to secure a re-trial. For the sentence of the Nagyvarad court was formally valid. At the re-trial the rabbi was acquitted, while the real murderer was convicted. The rabbi returned home and soon after died. Shayeh stayed on with his uncle for a further two years.

### THE STORY OF HAMAN

"NOW IT came to pass in the days of Ahasuerus . . ."

From New Moon in the month of Adar, Sholem began to read to the children from the Book of Esther. There was a ruddy power, a gay curliness in his voice as he chanted the verses. He looked as one would imagine one of those bearded Mede soldiers or one of those Persian nobles who knew Ahasuerus, Queen Vashti and the delicately beautiful Esther, the depraved Haman and the greathearted Mordechai, the Jew who feared for his people as well as for his little niece. The various Books and stories of the Bible require different modes of reading, according to whether they smile and laugh or wail with grief, and according to the climate and the century of their origin. Ahasuerus ruled over a hundred and twenty-seven provinces, from India to Ethiopia, but nowhere did they sing the epics and the royal chronicles and romances with such robust gusto as in the city of Shushan.

That was how the Jews of Shushan chanted the story of

Esther, and that was how their descendants, jubilant over the escape of the Jewish people and the discomfiture of the Jew-hating Haman chanted it. Shushan had sunk into the limbo of history. But Sholem, sitting behind the bar in the inn of Lapfalva, still remembered that melody of Shushan.

"Now it came to pass in the days of Ahasuerus . . . this is Ahasuerus which reigned. . . ."

By then gaiety had returned to the house and to Sholem's heart. He was no longer angry with anyone on earth, not even with Reb Leizer. After all—and no doubt under the influence of his, Sholem's, moral superiority—the man had changed for the better and was giving everything on credit to Sroleh Yomtov, who could talk his language. Mordechai, too, had made amends. One fine winter morning he came over by sleigh with his wife and two daughters and they stayed till evening. They were very pleased with everything—the inn, the land, Malkeleh, the children, and especially the baby. And as they left, Mordechai said to Sholem in a most friendly tone: "And if you need anything, Sholem, I hope you'll know where to come." Sholem was moved.

Of course, anxieties and vexations were not entirely lacking. One early dawn Sholem heard a noise from the direction of the stable. He went out to investigate, but saw no one. Ah! but there was a broken clay-pipe lying on the floor in front of the manger, with the glow of burning tobacco still in the bowl; and there was a man's length depression in the straw, so that some one must have lain there very recently. It must have been some poor tramp seeking refuge from the cold night. Sholem pondered a great deal as to what to do to avert trouble. In the end he stuck a notice, written in Malkeleh's clear hand, on the stable door: "You may sleep here, but please don't smoke in the stable or you may happen to set it on fire." The following morning he found a bayonet stuck into the lintel of the stable door. He took the weapon and hid it under the casks in the cellar. He was still perturbed over the recent search of his house, and guessed that his "lodger" was a deserter.

In any other month this sort of thing would have been far more disturbing, but this was the month of Adar . . . On the eve of the new moon Sholem suspended the traditional drawing

over the doors of the living rooms—silver-scaled fishes swimming
under billowy waves, with a slogan in Hebrew arranged rainbow
fashion over the waves: "From the advent of Adar let joy prevail." Sholem himself was the artist. To make joy prevail Sholem
began by purchasing bright dyes from the peasant women for the
drawings. These women mixed the dyes themselves, and to render
them fast for the thread with which they weaved embroidery
cloth, they added all sorts of things, including even the urine of
the brood mare. Fortunately, Sholem knew nothing about this,
and daubed away with much pleasure and devotion.

Sholem had not learned to draw at the *yeshiba*, but the Chronicle of Esther he knew as well as most learned men of Israel. He
even knew much that was not written in the Chronicle, but could
be read between the lines. Of the heroes of the Maccabean wars
he remembered but little, but his memory was refreshed by
Shayeh Oesterreicher, who told the other children by the
*Chanukah* lamps that Matithyahu's son was called Judah Maccabi,
the latter word meaning "hammer," for Judah beat the enemy
as the smith beats the iron on the anvil. When he had defeated
Apollonius, he took his sword from him, and from then on he
fought with that sword, defeating with it Seron and Nicanor.
And Eleazer, the fourth Maccabi boy, ran under the king's
elephant, stabbing it in the chest. The elephant collapsed, crushing Antiochus Epiphanes, the Assyrian tyrant. The Jews called
him Antiochus Epimanes, for Epiphanes means "the Magnificent,"
while Epimanes means "the Madman." The whole war started
through Jason, the High Priest, building a gymnasium in Jerusalem for the sons of the wealthier Jews.

Sholem listened to Shayeh's lecture with deep suspicion, and
at this point he felt compelled to interrupt.

"Where do you get all this from, my son?" he asked.

"I read it in Polybius, and also in Josephus Flavius."

"Who are they?"

Shayeh glossed over Polybius and spoke only of Josephus, explaining that he was a Jewish historian who wrote a history of
the Jews in the time of the Flaviuses.

"You are mistaken, Shayeh," said Sholem. "The history of the
Jews was written in the Pentateuch and in the Talmud. Matityahu

and his sons are mentioned in the Talmud as the Chashmoneans. Matithyahu, the High Priest, was the son of Yochanan, also a High Priest."

"But," argued Shayeh mildly, "the Chashmonean Matithyahu was not a High Priest. In Antioch's time the High Priest was Jason, and he was followed by Menelaus."

"I don't know about any High Priests of those names."

"Jason is Greek for Joshua," explained the boy. "And Menelaus's Hebrew name was Manasseh. They were two depraved men who bought the High Priesthood for money, bidding against each other before Antioch. All this is written in the Books of the Maccabis."

"Including the gymnasium of Jerusalem?"

"Yes."

"Is that the sort of books your uncle has?"

"Yes."

"They are forbidden books," said Sholem gravely. "We must not read them."

Fortunately—in Sholem's view—Shayeh stayed only a day or two and could not harm the children much with his banned knowledge. Four weeks after Zalman had taken the boy back to Karoly, Sholem was still thinking about him and hoping that he had reformed by then. Sholem had done everything in his power to that end. He had told Zalman to warn the boy's family that though otherwise a clever and talented child, his reading in foreign countries had not been of the kind that could be approved for the grandson of a Rabbi Mayer and a Rabbi Moshe Aryeh. But Sholem still had a remnant of suspicion that Shayeh had after all left behind something of the spirit he had imbibed from the books of Dr. Josef Manes Oesterreicher, Royal and Imperial Court physician in Vienna. For while he, Sholem, was chanting the Chronicle of Esther, the children were now and then exchanging glances and giggling. Sholem acted as though he had not noticed and went on expounding:

"Ahasuerus was not really a good man, otherwise he would have listened to his heart instead of to Haman. When his sly Minister laid before him the decree for the extermination of the Jewish people, he signed it without making any inquiry whether the charge against them was really true, and whether they were really as harmful as their sinister accuser asserted. But there was one nice trait in Ahasuerus; his love for Esther, the lovely Jewish orphan girl. This was all arranged by the Almighty. Vashti was of royal blood, being the granddaughter of the great Nebuchadnezzar, but she had to die when she refused to obey the king's command to come and exhibit herself in the nude before his nobles."

"Ahasuerus must have been drunk," interrupted Sroleh Yomtov with mingled indignation and contempt.

"Of course he was," conceded Sholem. "What do they do at a royal banquet but drink? They must have been drinking better wine than Reb Leizer Lazarovich supplies to his customers." Sholem laughed, accompanied by Yossef. Yiteleh did not even smile. She was watching Sroleh Yomtov, who was in a disputatious mood.

"Ahasuerus was a beast to have Vashti killed for that," he said.

Sholem was pleased to see the boy indignant over an injustice. Had he not himself been teaching him for months to respect truth and justice? But it seemed to Sholem that whenever he was expounding the sacred, traditional—and therefore the only possible—truth, the boy was upholding the exact opposite. That seemed to be the case now, even though on the face of it the boy was right.

"Of course he was a beast," said Sholem. "But you're mistaken just the same. You see, Vashti had to die, so that Esther could take her place. The great *malkah* had to go, because the *malkeleh* had to come."

"That doesn't matter," said the boy with trembling lips. "He might have divorced Vashti."

"But then he might have taken her back," intervened Yiteleh. "Uncle Mendl also wanted to divorce Aunt Golda, but then he came to fetch her."

Sholem was taken aback by this argument. But he was too immersed in the problem of Ahasuerus and Vashti to linger over Mendl and Golda.

"That's true, Sroleh Yomtov," he said mildly. "He might have divorced her—and he might even have forgiven her. But he couldn't. God himself did not want it, so that Israel might be saved."

"Even then it was unjust," retorted the boy. "God could have saved the Jews in some other way."

Sroleh Yomtov was more disputatious than ever, so that Sholem could scarcely go ahead for more than a sentence or two. But he repressed his irritation. After all, this was Adar, the month of Joy.

"And the maiden who found favor in the eyes of my lord," he chanted, raising his voice to a triumphant pitch, "shall reign in place of Vashti. And this counsel pleased the king. And it was so."

Whenever he came upon the name of Esther, who was also known as *Hadassah*, or myrtle twig, Sholem's voice acquired a jubilant, poetic quality. The younger children had learned the chant from him quickly and were chanting with him, but Sroleh Yomtov would not join in. He sat with compressed lips, speaking only when he found cause to take the offensive.

"It was also unjust to hang Haman. What was his crime? That he was in love with Esther?"

"What are you talking about!" snapped Sholem, this time with frank irritation. "Haman wanted to exterminate our entire people, from the Elders down to the women and children, to kill every one of our ancestors living in his hundred and twenty-seven provinces, including Erez Yisroel, and you think it was unjust to hang him—to hang him once! You heathen! I ought to give you a hiding for this."

"Hit me if you like," cried the boy, facing him defiantly, almost pushing his face within close reach of Sholem's hand, the scar on his brow red like a streak of flame. "But it's true just the same that according to the *Meghillah* the reason Ahasuerus had Haman executed was that he discovered that Haman was in love with Esther, and not that he wanted to exterminate the Jews."

"That makes no difference," cried Sholem. "It may be that that was why Ahasuerus hated him, but the wrath of the guardian of Israel was upon him for something else. Besides, you ought to know that a man who loves another man's wife deserves death by burning or drowning, because his sin is as great as if he wanted to exterminate our people."

Sroleh Yomtov ceased to argue. After awhile he left the bar
on some pretext and failed to return.

### THE DOG BAKTER

IN THE afternoons Malkeleh held a class in the big living room,
teaching the children to read and write in German, and arith-
metic. Sroleh Yomtov never attended, and when Malkeleh asked
him why, he answered morosely that he was able to read and
write in Hebrew and to add up the number of pints consumed
by the peasants, and that was enough to enable him to be an innkeeper.

"But," said Malkeleh, "it is not enough to enable you to become
anything better."

"I don't feel like studying Latin and Greek like Shayeh Oesterreicher," shrugged the boy. "I'd rather study the Talmud. Those
people from Frankfort learned nothing else, yet now one of them
has a bank in London and another in Vienna."

"I don't teach Latin and Greek," said Malkeleh, "only German.
Those Frankfurters also speak German. You can go anywhere
in the world with that language."

"Very well," said Sroleh Yomtov, and made off. But he went
on keeping away from Malkeleh's classes, and for the next few
days he dared not meet her gaze when they met at meals.

Why did he not want to be taught by Malkeleh? Was he
ashamed to have to start at the same point as four-year-old
Mailech? No, he could have got over that, for Yossef too had
started like that and was now miles ahead of the little boy. The
reason he did not want it was that he wanted it very much. It
was his evil spirit, his *mehfis tophel*, that prompted him to say
to Malkeleh what he said. And having said it, how could he join
in the classes? Instead, he borrowed the slate from Yossef,
and late in the evening, when Yossef had gone to bed, he
tried to copy out Malkeleh's tall and clear Gothic letters that
were written on it. And during the lessons he would sit in the

next room and strain his ears to hear Malkeleh scanning such
phrases as: "*Sechsmal sechs sind sechsunddreissig. Lernet, Kinder,
immer fleissig. . . . Die Morgenstunde hat Gold im Munde.*"
He felt that the injunction to study was addressed to him, and
that the warmth and radiance of the morning, as well as the
gold, were in the voice that came from the other room. He envied
Yossef, who could sit at the table with Malkeleh. But he envied
him a hundred times more when he was taken ill and Malkeleh
sat on the edge of his bed making him drink hot borsht and
bitter herb juices.

At this time Malkeleh was terrified that Yossef too might go
the way of the majority of his family. After her baby's birth,
Sholem had suddenly realized why it was a girl: to enable him
to propitiate the wrathful heavens by calling her Sarah Chayah,
thus keeping alive the spirits of the departed mother and daughter. Malkeleh's anxiety for the orphans was somewhat assuaged
by this thought, but Yossef's illness brought it back again. It
happened just when she was cooking and baking in preparation
for a joyous Purim festival, receiving and sending out the traditional gifts, from and to Blimeleh, from and to Golda; even the
potter's wife from Batiz, whom she had never met, had sent her
a fine Purim cake in a glazed and flowered pot, and of course this
had to be reciprocated. Malkeleh was looking forward to two
days of gaiety in the house. But the will-o'-the-wisp—as Aunt
Feiga put it—wouldn't have it. This was a special will-o'-the-wisp,
the evil spirit of the vast marsh which floated over the village
and meadows, with wings of fire, hands of marsh thread, and
feet of burning coals. Wherever it passed it left trouble in its
wake, big and small. The big trouble was fire, floods and drought,
the minor trouble, bellyache, toothache, and earache. Fortunately,
Aunt Feiga, who had predicted the death of the baby girl, was
now in a less ominous mood. "The scamp has been chasing the
will-o'-the-wisp," she said, "and it's given him the little trouble."
That it was "little" was also clear from the fact that Yossef had
a sore throat and pains in the ears. Yet Malkeleh was worried,
because Yossef seemed to have the ague when she put him to
bed. His body was hot through the night, and he was raving
about some peasant boys. Later it came out that Yossef had been

skating with them in the marsh, and as they did it in bare feet, he too removed his boots. However, it seemed that he alone had stepped on a spot that had been visited by the evil spirit, for the peasant boys had suffered no ill-effects. Yossef got over it all right, but for five days he had to drink hot lime and hoarhound infusion, so that he was simply bathed in perspiration under the parti-colored down quilt, and to wear a plaster over his ears. At the end of the week he was able to go into the village, though only with several layers of clothes and with his cap pulled down over his ears. "But," warned Aunt Feiga, "if I see you with those brats ever again, I'll tell your stepfather and he'll give you the hiding of your life."

The stepfather did not hear this sort of talk. Just then he was filing away at a rusty saw by the shed, having already sharpened his axe. He was spending three days a week chopping wood because the winter—as the peasants had predicted in the autumn from the behavior of the ice-duck—was very severe. Had he had proper tools, he could have done it all in a single morning, but the fact was he hadn't. He could not even find a grindstone for the axe. However, amid his botherations an apt quotation from Ecclesiastes flashed into his mind: "If the iron be blunted and not whetted, one must strain one's strength." And he was content.

However, his contentment lasted only until he had completed, by straining every effort, the week's ration of logs. Then, with some remorse, he recalled that the wise Koheleth had been thinking not of iron, but of the brain, and that he, Sholem, had omitted to whet *that* for a long time. Since the Squire from Gyekenyes had reproved him, he had not looked at a *Gemarah* during business hours. The month of Adar he had spent drawing and expounding the Book of Esther. But soon it would be Passover, and it was essential to study the complicated laws relating to the sacrifice of the lamb and the preparation of the unleavened bread. The sacrifice had been in abeyance for some eighteen centuries, for both the City and the Temple had been destroyed by Titus, but one had to prepare for it as though it might be resumed next Passover, otherwise the advent of the Messiah might catch one unprepared.

And even if the Passover lamb with its lamb-like patience might

wait—perhaps for another eighteen centuries—the Passover itself
would not wait, and the preparations for it demanded great cir-
cumspection. On the eve of the festival one had to go round the
house with a candle and a feather duster and collect even the
tiniest crumb of leavened bread from every nook and corner.
That was how it had been done by Sholem's ancestors for centuries, and by Sholem himself for decades. But recently he had
come upon a passage in the volume of the Talmud called *Pes-
sachim* which had shaken all his past conviction and assurance.

"Come here, Sroleh Yomtov, and listen to this beautiful piece of
*Gemarah*. This debate is simply breathtaking. Rab Hunah and
Rab Jehuda translate the word *ore*, with which the *Mishnah* begins and ends. What does it mean? Light. And the Lord said,
*Yehih ore*, let there be light. But the two *ores* in this case refer
to two different concepts. The first one means light, the second
only radiance. Well, the *Mishnah* begins by saying that at *ore* on
the fourteenth day of Nissan, that is, in daylight, the remnants
of leavened bread are searched out by *ore*, that is, by candlelight.
Now, the day begins in the evening, but daylight only comes in
the morning. And that is the first day of Passover. If leavened
bread is found in the house on that day, that is a violation of the
festival. Now listen to this. Rab Hunah and Rab Jehuda translate
the word *ore* into Babylonian, the language of their native land.
The former says it means *nigheh* or evening, while the latter says
it means *leleh* or morning. If *nigheh* really means evening, then
the problem is solved, because then we must search for the
leavened bread on the eve of the fourteenth. But if *leleh* means
morning, then we're in a fix. But our Sages say that there are districts where *nigheh* means morning, and *leleh* evening. The only
question is whether both *Tannaim* meant evening or morning,
eh what, Sroleh Yomtov? We're in a trap—caught."

"Ye-es," stammered the boy. "We're caught." He stared at the
door of the bar parlor, which had now quietly opened a crack
and as quietly closed, without causing the bell above it to ring.
Only a small baby could have slipped in like that. But the bottom
of the door was not visible from where the boy sat behind the
bar, only the part above the handle. The boy heard a soft patter
and began to tremble. He was aware that the newcomer was not

a child, not a human being. He gave Sholem a hesitant look, wondering whether he too had noticed. But Sholem was just chewing the mouthpiece of his long-stemmed clay-pipe and muttering, "We're trapped." He did not even realize that the pipe had long gone out. Suddenly the boy jumped up and opened the door of the bar.

"Get out!" he cried angrily. "Get out!"

Sholem looked at his flushed face in which the scar on his brow gleamed whitely, and said with mild reproach:

"It's Bakter again, is it? Why don't you let him be?"

The boy's face was pale again, perhaps a shade more so than usual. But Sholem did not notice the change, nor that the boy's lips were trembling.

"He's no business in the bar parlor!" he said sullenly, trying to conceal his agitation.

The shaggy Bakter slipped behind the bar, and ignoring the boy's antipathy, raised his tousled black head to him, wagging his tail. His big dark eyes seemed to be saying something.

"You're unkind to the dog," observed Sholem. "Yet he loves you."

"I don't want him to love me," snapped the boy angrily.

He hurried out of the room, leaving Sholem to grapple with his problem alone. Sholem took it amiss, as always, but he forgave him, again as always. Indeed, he was secretly glad at the prospect of escaping from the "trap" without aid.

Bakter also went out, loping off after Srolen Yomtov. Why was it that the boy had such a horror of the dog? Bakter had appeared in the late autumn, no one knew whether with Zev, the Jew with the flute, or with Golda, or how. When Mendl took Golda away, the dog did not follow them, nor did he follow Zev, but attached himself to Sroleh Yomtov and followed him like a shadow. Maybe he was only a stray dog, who had temporarily attached himself to Zev, perhaps because he liked the sound of his flute, or perhaps because he was attracted by his personality. Zev was known in the countryside as the "hair-Jew" because he bought hair. He carried two large baskets, one on his chest, the other on his back, the former containing his wares and the latter his receipts. Other peddlers accepted eggs, flour, chickens and walnuts, and rabbit-skins for their ribbons, headkerchiefs, circular combs, and mirrors, but Zev would have none of these things.

"Cash or hair, madam," he used to say.

He would feel the girls' tresses, put his fingers through the hair of young married women, examine it by sunlight or lamplight, and even smell it. He was a comic Jew and the womenfolk used to laugh a great deal while he was examining the "crops." But when he left a village there was much lamentation and quarrelling there, and much cursing of his God for having wheedled the lovely blonde, auburn, and black tresses off the women's heads, in return for a few gaudy rags.

"If he comes here again," threatened the girls' sweethearts and the young husbands, "he'll never get away alive."

But Zev took no notice of the menaces, and within another nine months or so he was back again with his slogan: "Cash or hair, my beauties." The womenfolk hesitated, tried to resist his blandishments, huddled together and giggled, but the "hair-Jew" was never attacked. Of course, by then the tresses were there again, more luxuriant than before. And who would hurt a Jew with such a fascinating way about him?

"A sheared lamb grows a woollier coat," he used to croon. "Besides, if you give your head an airing now and then you get no headaches." And if this failed to produce results, he argued on a more personal level: "Is it better, my beauty, to thin your hair out with the comb, eh? Or is it better if it gets torn out by your husband when he returns from the inn, eh? My scissors are gentle like the nightingale."

He was referring to the sound of the scissors, though he did not say so, nor was he asked. But the womenfolk were willing to believe that the Jew's scissors were gentle, and in the end they obediently bent their heads beneath them. Zev gave them silken headkerchiefs to cover their shame, and bright ribbons with which to tie up the wisps at the back when their hair began to grow again.

In those days Sroleh Yomtov used to brood a great deal. He wanted to do something, start a business of his own with the money he had. There was impatience in his heart and the itch of the road in his feet. Mendl, whose fishery was at the confluence of the Tisz and two of its tributaries, where fish was plentiful, and who supplied the towns of Miskolc and Nyiregyhaza, had been trying to entice him into his business. At first Sroleh Yomtov liked the idea—the silvery scales of the fish were so reminiscent of money—and he thought he might learn the business and eventually start a fishery of his own around the marsh. But one Friday afternoon, as he stood in the kitchen watching Malkeleh cleaning and cutting up the fish for the evening meal, he suddenly, and for no reason that he could tell, lost all taste for the fishery business.

Jacob Anshel of Batiz had also invited Sroleh Yomtov to join him, saying that he would learn the candle- and soap-making business in three or four years, and if he had money, even sooner. He would have liked to go, but Malkeleh prevented him. She herself knew nothing about it, nor did the boy fully realize how it happened, but it was one Friday evening, as Malkeleh was lighting the festive candles, that he decided against Jacob Anshel. And Malkeleh was lighting more and more of them. When she came she began with seven, but soon after she added the three orphans to the candle-family. When little Chayah departed and Sarah Chayah was born, two fresh candles were lighted, the dead baby surviving as a flame. Two more candles were added in memory of the orphans' parents, so that now Malkeleh lighted twelve candles of a Friday evening, the same number as the tribes of Israel. Sroleh Yomtov used to watch Malkeleh bless the candles. She was the same as any other Jewish housewife, yet quite different. As she covered her face with her hands her hands seemed to be luminous. And as she dropped them again, the luminosity was in her face. Would anyone have grasped this as an explanation for the boy's refusal to go to Batiz into the candlemaker's business?

In the evenings he used to listen as Malkeleh crooned the lullaby about the kid that dealt in almonds and raisins brought from distant lands. He had heard it often before, but he had not really noticed it until now. He too ought to go away to distant lands, out into the world, to become something better than an innkeeper, better than Sholem. He used to stand on the dark verandah, looking in through the small window and watching Malkeleh suckling the chubby Sarah Chayah who, even when squalling, was full of vitality. Or he would watch the woman undressing. She used to rub a white ointment into her hands and face. When she removed her headkerchief and her wig to comb her short boyish hair, she was so strange, so different! Reflected on her high forehead and her glinting black hair, even a single tallow candle seemed to have the radiance of a dozen candles.

This was why Sroleh Yomtov was somewhat fascinated by the "hair-Jew." Zev used to talk to him in a gushing way about his business, how he sent the hair to Buda, and Vienna, but particularly to Vienna, to Herr Eduard Hagenmeyer, the court wigmaker. He could never send enough, and if he had a moneyed partner prepared to help with the work, they could both grow rich. Sroleh Yomtov accompanied Zev to the neighboring villages and watched him at work, witnessing the actual shearing scene again and again. When a head of black hair came under the scissors his heart somehow contracted and his breath became short. And when the tresses had fallen, he saw Malkeleh's boyish head before him, and this incomprehensibly stirred him to mingled excitement and grief.

It was on such an occasion that the strange thing happened. Sroleh Yomtov felt a pair of eyes gazing fixedly at him, a pair of mutely searching eyes, and he gave a start. He had a feeling as though some one had surprised his secret. They were only the eyes of a dog, a dog he had known before, but this was the first time that he had noticed his eyes. He left Zev immediately, and started to run back to Lapfalva. When he arrived there, he found that the dog was loping after him. The animal stood swinging his shaggy head at him and gazing into his eyes, as though to say, "I know, Sroleh Yomtov, I know."

The boy tried to chase him away, but it was all in vain. The dog clung to him, following him everywhere, even at night, when he went out to roam in the village. When he stopped in the yard, looking with bated breath towards the kitchen or the living room, the dog stood by him, gazing up at him. Sometimes Sroleh Yomtov was almost pleased with this utter loyalty and watchfulness, but when he saw the animal's eyes there was a surge of anger in him. The children liked the dog, and Yiteleh christened him Bakter ("Watchman")—perhaps because he was guarding the house at night, or perhaps merely because in his shagginess he resembled Uncle Gazsi, the night watchman who, with his horn in his hand, came to the inn at ten o'clock each evening to have his gratis drink. But Sroleh Yomtov thought that even the dog's name meant that every one knew that the dog was watching him and was somehow secretly in league with him.

Sroleh Yomtov was waiting for the spring. After the thaw he would drown the dog in the marsh.

## THE TSADDIK

RABBI PHINEAS LURIA, that aged wanderer, told Sroleh Yomtov that he could settle the matter of the dog in one way only—by settling it within himself. For the dog was really nothing but the *yezer haraa*, his own urge for evil, his own secret unclean thoughts.

How did Rabbi Phineas Luria know this, and how came he to be in contact with the boy? And was it really he, the wandering saint, the legendary Rabbi Luria?

One morning the bell over the door rang and an ancient man with the appearance of a beggar entered. Sholem went to meet him and offer him a glass of brandy. But as he looked into the newcomer's bearded face, he exclaimed:

"Rabbi! Rabbi! *Tsaddik!*"

Seizing the old man's ice-cold hand he bent over it, and reverently kissed it. The old man withdrew his hand with a jerk.

"I am not a rabbi, nor a *tsaddik*," he said.

"But you are. I know you are. You're Rabbi Phineas Luria. I am Sholem. Don't you remember me? Sholem ben Yoirish."

The old man bowed his head and said nothing. Sholem stood gazing at him with the increasing certainty that he was not mistaken. Since Reb Leizer had mentioned that Rabbi Luria was wandering about in this area, he had been anticipating such a reunion. And now the Rabbi was here. There was that bluish swelling on his lower lip . . . how often had he, Sholem, watched it while the Rabbi was lecturing. He thought of Moses, the first teacher of Israel, the impediment in whose speech must have been due to a similar scar. When Moses was a young boy, Pharaoh, fearing for his power, had two pans put before him, one containing gold, the other live coals. He did this to test the soothsayers' warning that Moses would grow up to oppose him. Had the boy reached for the gold, he would have been lost, for that would have proved that he was going to be ambitious for power. But Moses reached for the coals, and carried his hand to his lips with a live coal. Luria had always put his hands into the fire, burning not only his fingers, but also his lips.

Sholem had not seen him for sixteen years. When he left the Rabbi's school, the latter was about sixty. He did not seem older now, except that his back was more bent as though he were carrying on it not a bundle of possessions, but the destiny of his people. Sholem was barely thirteen when he went to Luria's *yeshiba* at Homonna. The Rabbi was then already in sharp conflict with his flock. It was over a divorce case which Sholem did not rightly understand at the time. A rich man named Levy wanted to give his wife a bill of divorcement, and wanted her to be pronounced the guilty party, charging her with extravagance. In this way he would not have had to return the dowry he had received with her some twenty-odd years before. The wife would not accept the bill of divorcement, arguing that Levy merely wanted another woman, and had already established relations with the unmarried daughter of a Lemberg merchant. Rabbi Luria gave judgement for the wife, quoting the words of the Prophet Hosea: "I will not punish your daughters when they commit whoredom, nor your spouses when they commit adultery: for themselves are separated with whores, and they sacrifice with harlots." This judgement caused an outcry in the community, and it was said to be incomprehensible and scandalous that a rabbi should thus brand distinguished men of Israel, and should incite the women against tradition and against acceptance of the superiority of men. The husband had an absolute right to give his wife a bill of divorcement. The wife, on her part, was free to remarry. In the Rabbi's view that freedom was useless when a woman had lost her youth and had had her reputation dragged in the mud. The women were all for the Rabbi, but of course the politics of the congregation was in the hands of the men, and they made the Rabbi's position increasingly difficult. Only the *yeshiba* was wholeheartedly on his side. Whenever he entered the lecture room, the students put added heartiness into the traditional salutation:

"Long live our teacher and master!"

Sholem clearly remembered the Rabbi's unassuming manner as he received the enthusiastic salutation, and how he waited quietly for the noise to subside, so that he might begin his lecture. That was how Sholem had seen the Rabbi shortly before he was exiled from Homonna, and that was how he had seen him last a day or two before. Having tired of the persecution by his enemies, old and new, he took his staff and went away, none knew where, from his second post at Ujhely. And that was how he saw him now: with his head bent, and waiting. Even if he had not seen the scar on his lip, he would have recognized him from his bearing.

"I know," he said stubbornly. "You are Rabbi Luria. I am Sholem."

The old man gave a gentle smile and said:

"Joseph knew his brethren, but they did not know Joseph."

He stayed with Sholem for a few days, but never said a word about himself, nor did Sholem press him. Perhaps he had made a *nehder*—a sacred vow—to cast a veil of silence over his name and his past. Who could fathom the mysteries of a *tsaddik's* soul? The Biblical quotation both reassured Sholem and filled him with certainty. Of course. When Joseph was sold by his brothers he was a girlish-looking youth, while they were bearded men. When they met in the viceroy's palace in Egypt, Joseph too was already a grown man. Rabbi Luria had known him, Sholem, only as a young boy, for he had scarcely any down on his face even when the Rabbi was exiled from Ujhely. He would have liked to revive the past, though, and whenever he was face to face with the old man, the words were burning on his lips.

"You remember, Rabbi," he would have liked to say, "the time when you were examining me in a section of 'Sanhedrin.' You looked at my calloused hands and asked me what I had been doing before I came to the *yeshiba*. I said I had been helping my father to hoe and do navvying. And you said I ought to be sorry not to have stayed in God's peace among the birds, stones, and the sky-ward-straining roots. I was so ashamed of myself. I knew you were saying that only because I was ignorant. Were you? I have been studying a great deal since, studying all the time, yet I am still ignorant."

However, observing his guest's deep reserve, he controlled himself and did not speak of the past. He did not feel worthy to take the initiative in raking up common memories. For the present he was happy to have the *tsaddik* under his roof. On his arrival Sholem hastened to the guest room, laid a fire there, heated some water, and helped to remove the old man's sodden knee-boots and the damp linen rags wrapped round his feet, which he offered to wash. The old man protested that he could do that himself, and Sholem mentally added this manifestation of modesty to the other qualities of his saintly guest.

The only thing Sholem regarded as strange was that the Rabbi told the rest of the household to call him Reb Issur, whereas he allowed him, Sholem, to go on calling him Reb Phineas. He pondered over this for a long time before the explanation came to him. The word *issur* means prohibition. By his new name, the Rabbi had banned the old, and he now called himself Rabbi *Ban* or *Must-Not*. However, Sholem had been so young when he first knew the Rabbi that it was difficult for him to call him anything but Phineas. So for a time he managed to avoid addressing him by name, calling him simply Rabbi, but later he started blurting out both names—Phineas Issur—and the *tsaddik* tacitly accepted this solution.

The Rabbi was not the reserved, unworldly person he appeared to be at a first glance. On the contrary. He used to go out into the kitchen and ask Malkeleh what there would be for dinner, and also discuss next day's dinner with her, once suggesting lentil soup and another time potatoes with pepper sauce. Sometimes he would sit down by Sarah Chayah's cradle, chuck her under the chin and tweet to her. He smacked Mailech on the behind if he was importunate or interrupted the conversation too willfully. Or he would sit down on the ingle-nook and listen to Aunt Feiga's lamentations about her old bones' aches and pains. "But you have no toothache, have you?" once said the Rabbi. "No," she replied, "because I haven't any teeth left." "You see, you are rid of the smallest bones, which ache worst. In time, the big ones will also cease to hurt." Aunt Feiga was comforted, and even grinned at the thought that only the young were tormented by the small bones. This thought helped her to bear the slight pains of her big bones.

Sholem knew that the *tsaddik's* actions had a special meaning even in the most ordinary matters, and that there was a profound significance in everything he said. The *tsaddik* liked the house to be lively, and was pleased if the children laughed at his jokes or hung on his words when he was talking. When Reb Issur talked about that jolly era that was to begin with the advent of the Messiah, Yossef laughed until he cried. There would be much merriment and hilarity upon earth, said the old man, such as had not been seen since Adam and Eve. Mothers and fathers who had died young would hug sons and daughters who had lived to ninety. A father might be thirty, with a little black goatee, and with a sound set of teeth, yet he would say "my son" to a toothless, shrivelled old man. He might even correct him if he was disobedient. Grandmother might be young, younger even than Malkeleh, while her granddaughter was older than Aunt Feiga.

Yiteleh too laughed at this, and Malkeleh's lovely sad eyes also filled with brightness. Mailech asked whether the wolves would participate in the Resurrection. Reb Issur replied that the good ones would, the bad ones wouldn't.

"Are there any good wolves?" asked the little boy.

"Of course there are," explained the Rabbi. "A wolf doesn't always attack a man from malice, but mostly because it is his mission . . . The Baal Shem, when he was still a charcoal burner in the Volhynian forest, was once attacked by a wolf. He didn't defend himself, but simply asked the wolf whether he had instructions to eat him. The wolf shook his head, as if to say no. 'Then I won't taste good to you,' said the Baal Shem. The wolf, being very hungry, wouldn't believe him. Whereupon the Baal Shem cut off a piece of his beard and handed it to the wolf to taste. The wolf swallowed it, then ran away. Now, the hair tickled his stomach and he was obliged to laugh, or perhaps he laughed with pleasure at not having eaten the Baal Shem. In any case, a wolf mustn't laugh, and the pack drove him away, saying that any one that laughed should go and be a man. So the wolf tried to be a man. But the baker was angry with him for eating bread, considering that he was a wolf, and he stuck a knife into the creature's throat."

"Did the wolf die?"

"Yes. But when the Messiah comes, that wolf will be resurrected and he will return the wisp of beard to the Baal Shem. And then both will laugh, because the Baal Shem's beard has grown back in the meantime."

But he could not make Sroleh Yomtov laugh. Perhaps he did not mean to do so. The boy rarely sat with the family, and even then he scarcely spoke. When Malkeleh laughed he smiled, but when she was silent, his face remained immobile. In recent days Malkeleh herself had been rather thoughtful. Perhaps it was on account of Golda, who had visited again, and might have left her unhappiness behind, though she herself did not seem unhappy. Her face was the color of a peach, and she was in such high spirits that she almost twittered. She was not pleased to find that the guest room was engaged, but she did not show it. This time she was only in transit, having been to Karoly on a shopping expedition. She was going on to another town to see her sister-in-law, and had made a detour especially to visit Malkeleh. She brought her a dress length of blue material and a blue-spotted headkerchief.

"I bought it in the market at Karoly from Avrom Kolb. I have been going there for years, he is the most reliable. We'll put a little lace collar and lace cuffs on it, and it'll be just sweet. Don't contradict, Malkeleh. You are pretty again, and nineteen, and you have just had your first baby. I took to you so much when I was last here that I always talk about you to Mendl. You know, we are great friends again. He's stuffing me with money. He'd give me just anything. But now I don't want it."

She flung the cloth over Malkeleh, pinned it up and made bold cuts with the scissors. She was very clever, cutting, basting, and sewing skilfully as she talked. She had so much to say that she did not leave the following day either. She slept with Yiteleh in the children's room, and was especially charming to the little girl.

Yiteleh admired her for her cleverness as a seamstress, but otherwise felt strange with her. Golda drew her to herself in bed and
whispered all sorts of silly things into her ear. The strangeness
changed to repugnance, and when Yiteleh woke up in the morning she felt that she detested "Auntie Golda."

The *tsaddik* talked to Golda as well, and even cracked jokes
with her. Sholem would never have ventured as far as that; he
scarcely looked into her eyes, though she had big, luminous cat's
eyes under arched brown eyebrows that every one, even the
*tsaddik*, found striking. However, Sholem in any case had some
nerve-racking problems, questions relating to the Talmud and
its commentaries that had arisen in the solitude of months, and
which he was unable to solve on his own. Now he was greatly
excited to have the great Rabbi Luria in his very house, who could
help him in everything.

Now it was the fifth day of Rabbi Luria's stay, yet Sholem had
still not managed to place his troubles before him. Usually all
three of them sat behind the bar, but for the sake of Sroleh
Yomtov the *tsaddik* talked about practical matters. If he cited
parables and symbolisms from the heritage of learning, it was
in connection with such matters. He conjured them up from
remote distances or from profound depths, but he did not linger
with them, hastening to return to reality. He said he had
observed that the marsh was desiccating from the south-west
and it would be a good thing for Sholem to purchase a stretch
of it there, which he could still get for a few kreuzers. Sholem
liked the idea, but Sroleh Yomtov was contrary as usual.

"How long will it take to dry out?" he challenged.

"Eight or ten years," replied the *tsaddik*. "Sooner than that if
you work really hard."

"The Messiah might be here by then."

"If he is, so much the better. Then at least you will have
accomplished something meanwhile. But what if he doesn't come?
Just suppose he doesn't come?"

"Then we'll have a fine piece of land," said Sholem.

"Then they'll take it away from us," opined Sroleh Yomtov.

"They can if they like," nodded the *tsaddik*. "The land doesn't
belong to us."

"Then why should we make it fertile?"

The old man looked at the boy and answered with further questions:

"What did we do in Egypt? What did we do in Padan Aram? What did we do in Babylon? We built, we served, we cultivated the land for others." Taking hold of his beard with one hand, he went on: "Moses called his son, who was born in Midian, Gershom. For he said: 'I have been a stranger in a strange land.' What did the stranger Moses do in Midian? He was a shepherd there. Do you think the Midianites didn't have enough shepherds? Of course they had. But there was only one shepherd like Moses, and that was Moses himself." Fingering his lips, and squeezing the purple mark on his lower lip, he continued gravely: "The Jew's real name is Gershom: a stranger in a strange land. What is Gershom doing in Hungary, Russia, Germany, France, or England? What others won't do or don't think of doing. True, he is doing it for others. But meanwhile he is fulfilling the law. And there is a sacred law which says: 'Thou shalt live and make the land fruitful.' "

On another occasion the *tsaddik* said:

"Better pay the Jew tax. Even if the gentry forbid it. Gershom must pay everything the régime demands of him. For have not our great rabbis laid it down, *Dinah demalchutah dinah*—the ruler's law is the law. Where there are two rulers one must satisfy both. Give the gentry what belongs to them, but do not provoke the anger of the Emperor, either. In the end it is the power of the King of Kings that counts."

Sroleh Yomtov had already slunk out. He was not interested in the subject. But the *tsaddik* was already off on another. "Who is wise?" he said. "He who foresees the things to come." And he proceeded to explain that it was not good for Malkeleh to be alone so much. Even if she did occasionally get a visitor who talked to her, she had no one to talk to, for one could never choose one's visitors. It would be advisable for Sholem to send her over to Karoly for a week or two to stay with Mordechai and Blimeleh. After all, she had wanted to go to Karoly to live, and having stayed here for the sake of the orphans, she now deserved a little rest as the guest of some one else. Sholem nodded agreement. The *tsaddik* was right. To-morrow or the day after he would hire a sleigh and send Malkeleh with her baby to Karoly.

It was getting late, and the Talmudic problems had once more been elbowed out of the way by other matters. However, Sholem managed, as a worthy conclusion of the nocturnal talk, to bring up the puzzle of *nigheh* and *leleh*, and was amazed to find how simple it really was once it was submitted to a great rabbi. The question was whether both *tannaim* meant evening or both morning. The Rabbi settled the matter with a gesture:

"They both meant evening." And so, after many brain-racking nights, Sholem could now sleep in peace.

When the old man left the bar, the village was already long asleep. It was a quiet, cold night. Only Malkeleh's window had a dim radiance from the night-light burning there. The old man was shuffling along the verandah towards the guest room, holding a burning candle in one hand, and shielding it with the other. He saw some one standing by the window, but he was not surprised; he knew it was Sroleh Yomtov. As the old man was passing the boy, Bakter gave a bark, startling his master into awareness. The old man held the candle closer to the boy and saw that he looked paler than usual.

"Go to bed, Sroleh Yomtov," he said gently. "You'll catch cold out here."

"I've only just come out," said the boy.

"I say go to bed."

"All right."

The old man hurried into the guest room. The boy heard him fumbling about there, then he went off with the quietly panting Bakter to stand under the snow-laden ash tree in the yard. He stood looking at the small window, which was screened with a white curtain. The old man trudged up to him across the snow, but Sroleh Yomtov was not aware of him until he was startled by the sound of his voice.

"Aren't you going to bed yet, Sroleh Yomtov?"

"Not yet," said the boy resentfully, irritated by the reproachful gentleness of the old man's tone.

"Every one else is in bed already."

"I don't want to go yet."

"You'll be ill, standing here in the snow."

"What of it?"

"That'll be bad."

"It'll be a good thing for me."

"You mean, my son, that they'll put you to bed and nurse you?"

"What do you want with me?" demanded the boy, with an upward jerk of his head.

"I want you to look after yourself," was the reply. "You have more sense than Yossef, haven't you?"

"Yes."

"You don't skate on the ice barefoot. But it is not much wiser to stand here in the dark yard until the cold gets to your bones. Your father was not a strong man. Whom do you expect to nurse you if you take to your bed tomorrow? Old, decrepit Aunt Feiga?"

"No."

"Malkeleh is going away, and only Aunt Feiga will be left."

Sroleh Yomtov was silent for awhile. When he spoke he tried to sound indifferent.

"She is going away, is she? I thought she wasn't. Golda asked her to go to Nameny and she wouldn't."

"She's going to Karoly."

"Karoly?" said the boy, in a scared tone.

"Yes, and she'll stay there for quite a time."

Silence . . . but for a din as of galloping horses in the boy's chest. Did the Rabbi hear it? The boy waited for the din to subside, then he gave a shrug.

"Well, what if she does go away and stays away?" He realized the words were shivering on his lips and was annoyed with himself. He now gave a shudder and said hurriedly:

"You're right, Rabbi, it's getting cold out here." With that he turned on his heels and went up to the verandah. Bakter loped after him, but he kicked out towards the animal with a cry of "Scram!" and hurried into his room.

The old man said, "Come here, doggie, come here, doggie," and took Bakter to his own room.


Early in the morning there was a knock on the Rabbi's door.

"Come in, Sroleh Yomtov," he said.

Sroleh Yomtov entered. There was hesitancy in his bearing and embarrassment in his gaze, as he stepped before the Rabbi, who sat on the bed pulling on his knee-boots.

"How did you know, Rabbi, that it was me?"

"I thought you'd look in, because I brought your dog here."

"He's not my dog; he only comes after me."

"If he goes after you, he belongs to you," said the old man. "Just like your shadow. But you don't kick out at your shadow, nor do you close your door against it, although your shadow wouldn't be cold even on such a cruelly cold night."

"I keep beating him and driving him away," said the boy with a shrug, "but he always comes back."

"Have you ever had a thrashing?" asked the old man, gazing straight into his eyes.

"Yes," said the boy vehemently. "But I hate the one that thrashed me."

"You hate him, so you shadow him—and go back to him like a dog."

"What do you mean, Reb Issur?" demanded the boy. But Reb Issur did not explain.

"Golda is pretty, don't you think?" he asked suddenly and unexpectedly.

"What do I care about Golda!" snapped Sroleh Yomtov.

"She has a nice rosy face, hasn't she?"

"She washes it off at night," said the boy with contempt.

"Yes, yes," muttered the old man, as if talking to himself. "On the other hand, there are some women that are beautiful at night as well."

Sroleh Yomtov listened with a crushed bearing. Then he drew himself up.

"Who told you that Malkeleh was going to Karoly?"

"Sholem."

"Is she staying over the holy days?"

"I don't know. Maybe."

"And why does she want to go away?"

"I don't know."

"You do, Reb Issur. You know everything."

"Everything, Sroleh Yomtov? Then I ought to know why Bakter won't leave you, oughtn't I?"

"You know that, too."

"All I know," said the old man, "is that Bakter clings to you and you hate him. So you ought to understand that the one to whom you are attached—"

"Hates me," whispered the boy.

"I wouldn't say that. No one here hates you. Sholem is like a father to you. Malkeleh—" The boy gave a pronounced pout. Reb Issur ran his fingers through his white beard, wiped the purple "Mosaic" swelling on his lower lip with his hand, then: "You cannot drive the dog away," he said in a tone of admonition, "either with a stick or with a curse, because he is whimperng and barking and howling within you. He is your evil urge, the *yezer haraa*. If you let your urge for good, the *yezer hatob*, grow in your heart, the other will depart of itself." The old man stood up, went out into the yard and washed his hands and face with snow. Returning to the room he started to fumble in his bundle. "Now we're going to pray," he said. "Have you prayed yet? I must be ready earlier this morning."

"Are you going away?"

Reb Issur was already muttering some introductory prayer and would not speak again. Sroleh Yomtov returned to his room, and put on his phylacteries. He stood mumbling the text, pondering and struggling with himself. He lost the place in the prayer-book several times, turned the pages backwards and forwards, then started all over again. Suddenly, he doffed the phylacteries and hurried into the bar. There he served Mendl's coachman, who stood with his sleigh ready in front of the inn, and amused himself by knocking off the icicles from the eaves with his whip and making the snow-laden inn sign of curly wood shavings swing to and fro. Sroleh Yomtov watched him with a smile spreading over his face; the swinging body at the end of the long pole struck him as funny. But this lasted only a moment. Then his face grew serious, his gaze stern, as though he despised himself for smiling. He poured some plum whisky into a slim-necked glass, went into the kitchen, poured some milk into a jug, cut some slices of bread, and put a little salt on the rim of an earthenware plate, then took the whole across to Reb

Issur for his breakfast. He sat down beside the old man and told him the news:

"Golda is leaving."

"She's doing the right thing."

"She's not going to Szalka, but home to Nameny."

"Still better."

"And Malkeleh too is going away."

The old man washed his hands, raised them high while saying the appropriate benediction, dried them carefully, then said another benediction over the bread, which he dipped into the salt.

"I say, Reb Issur," said the boy pleadingly, "couldn't you stay over the holy days? You are needed here. Sholem would feel very lonely if you too went away."

"For the holy days?" said the old man. "That's far ahead. It's only the fourth of Nissan."

"Only ten days to Passover," coaxed the boy.

"I can't stay."

"Is it urgent business?"

"I must go on with my wandering," said the old man.

"Where to?"

"It does not matter."

"Why must you be a wanderer?"

Reb Issur looked at him with his red-rimmed old eyes. There was a momentary glint in them that might have been read by another. But Sroleh Yomtov could not, and he dared not ply the old man with more questions. There is only one thing now that he wants to know.

"Do you want to go to-day?"

"To-day?" repeated the old man, scanning the boy's expectant face. "Perhaps not to-day."

Sroleh Yomtov's eyes expressed contentment. For the rest of that morning he went tramping in the fields, with Bakter constantly at his heels. He not only did not hurt the dog now, but talked to him and stroked his shaggy head. The dog looked up at him with a gleam of gratitude in his eyes, and listened with true doggy attention to his queer mutterings.

"Can't get rid of you by cursing and beating you. But if I'm kind to you you'll leave me. You won't leave me yet—it seems I don't love you yet, or not enough."

Towards noon the boy felt hungry, ran home and asked Aunt Feiga for bread and a bone for the dog. Aunt Feiga scolded him, saying that Bakter was not a fit friend for him, and why did he go roaming all morning, so that he could not be found when wanted. Golda would have liked to say good-bye to him; now she had left. However, Malkeleh gave him a friendly smile, and that made him forget that he was hungry.

They were unusually gay at the table, every one discussing the impending journey. Only Sroleh Yomtov was quiet. Yiteleh asked him whether he would like to go with them, but the boy, with his gaze on the *tsaddik*, shook his head. If the question had been put by his adoptive mother, he would not have looked at the *tsaddik* and would not have shaken his head. But Malkeleh was busy serving. All she asked was whether he wanted any more potato noodles, his favorite dish. He said "Thanks, no." He felt the blood mounting to his head. He would have liked to jump up and run out into the fields. But he could not do that now, otherwise he would be breaking up the minor community of worship, composed of the *tsaddik*, Sholem, and himself. The consciousness that he was a grown-up and could no longer share in childish pleasures had him by the throat. He must live according to the saying of the Fathers: "Who is a man? He who can conquer desire."

It was his turn to-day to lead the minor community at grace after the meal and say: "My masters, let us say grace!" But he had to wait longer than usual, it seemed an eternity. The other children were already playing noisily in the yard, snowballing and rolling lumps of fresh snow to build up the snowman. Malkeleh had also left the table to attend to the children's underwear for the visit, and put the finishing touches to the new dress, which Golda had started so eagerly but which she had left tacked together with huge stitches. Malkeleh had washed some old lace for it and was now ironing it; the smell of the smoothing-iron over cloth was wafted in from the kitchen. Sholem knew that the *tsaddik* was about to leave, and he was exploiting this final opportunity, like an eager student at the *yeshiba*, to discourse theses from *Pesachim*. Reb Issur Phineas was right, the *tannaim* really meant evening by the term *ore*. The sound of the bell in the bar parlor sent Sroleh Yomtov hurrying to serve a stray customer. When he returned, Sholem was still discoursing, while the old man sat humming and nodding, with his mind seemingly far, far away.

Sholem went into deeper points. How wonderful was the transition of the chapter dealing with the Festival of Freedom from *ore*, the two kinds of light, to the tenderness of the spirit and the obligatory refinement of everyday speech. Sroleh Yomtov was sitting on pins. He acted as though he were interested in the subject, yet he was merely forcing himself to listen. To him the old man's name merged into a single reality with his personality, a commanding, reproving, maddening, tender mystery. Who was this Rabbi "Must Not"? Where did he come from and why? Who sent him to make people laugh and cry, to excite and soothe? Sroleh Yomtov would have liked to be alone with him, as with a grandfather to whom a boy could feel attached. He felt that he would like to lay his head on the old man's chest, hide it in his luxuriant white beard and pour out his heart to him. And he also felt he would like to be rude and disobedient with him, as only sons can with their fathers. These two were talking about the purity of the spirit and refinement of expression, whereas he, Sroleh Yomtov, was full to bursting point with ugly, foul curses which he had heard from the toiling, wretched serfs and drunken peasants, and from the giggling women-folk when the "hair Jew" haggled with them over their hair. He had scarcely understood those words at the time, but now every word seemed to be clamoring and straining, bawling and screaming within him. Now they had a body, a hot body, a flushed feminine face and boyish hair. Yes, and round white breasts, with a hungry suckling digging the fingers of both hands into them. When at last Sholem had gone, the boy turned to the old man.

"Tell me, Rabbi," he said urgently, "what is good and what is evil? What you say is good is evil to me, and the only things that are good to me are those that you call evil."

"Sin," said the old man with a shake of his head, "tastes good. No one can say that sin tastes bad."

"Well, then!" cried the boy, with burning eyes. "You see I'm right!"

"But you may die of it," said the old man quietly.

"You are thinking of the life to come. You say we must give up this life to enjoy the next, what is sure for what is not sure. You all think like that when you are old."

"It's true that I am thinking of the life to come," said the old man. "But in the first place, I'm thinking of your life to come here on earth. 'Do not awaken my love till he please'—that's what Solomon said in the Song of Songs. Do you know who doesn't please? The good one of the two spirits that dwell within you. Your good spirit also says that it is not time yet for you to awake. But the evil one, the *yezer haraa*, barks on the threshold in the early dawn and cries, 'Awake, Sroleh Yomtov!' And in the evening it won't let you go to bed. At night it won't let you sleep. The good spirit within you is angry and is urging you to chase away the evil spirit."

"The evil spirit is stronger," said the boy in a low voice.

"The evil spirit is stronger, but the good spirit is wiser—it wants you to live."

"I don't understand."

"There are lots of things you don't understand, my son, but a moment will come when you will. The good spirit not only chases away the evil spirit, but also runs away from it. Is it not so, my son?"

"I think so."

"If the urge for good, which is the root of life, is weak, the urge for evil will drag one into death. You put poisoned meat in the cellar for the rats to eat. But the rat sniffs at it and runs away. It smells the poison first and the poison alone. The rat, too, was created to live. But if it goes back, it is lost. For then it will be struck with the smell of the meat. And the more often it returns, the more often it smells the bait, the less will it perceive the poison, and the more will its palate be tickled by the meat. In the end it will smell only the meat and start to eat. It will guess that it is eating death, but it will eat, for meat is meat even when poisoned."

"Tell me, Rabbi," said the boy, seizing the old man's withered, bony hand, "what must I do to live?"

"Listen to the voice within you, my son. Keep away from the meat that to you is poison. Do not covet that which belongs to your neighbor. Do not covet a strange woman."

The words fell upon Sroleh like so many stones. He stood rigid, staring in front of him, his face bloodless, like that of a dead body.

## A SINNER

MALKELEH WAS surprised and pleased like a child at Sholem's considerateness. She had not believed that he was concerned with her mental processes and would guess a secret wish of hers. Now that Golda had twice been to see her, the urge to go away and have good, long talks was upon her. She had had talks with Golda, but only about externals and about Golda's own affairs. She wanted at last to be among people of her own kind, where she could reveal a little of herself. But she did not agree to Sholem's offer at once, precisely because she was touched by this unusual tenderness. She said the time was not convenient, for she had many tasks to attend to in the house at the approach of the holy days. However, Sholem insisted, partly because the *tsaddik* had advised a holiday for Malkeleh. The children too urged her to agree. So in the end she agreed, but said that she would not stay for more than three or four days.

There was only one snag: starting on Friday. One could pay a visit unasked on a week-day, but to do so for the Sabbath was improper, and Malkeleh could not be guilty of anything like that. She sent for Sroleh Yomtov and very kindly asked him whether he could not go to Karoly the following day.

"I can't," said the boy, more morose than ever, and not looking at her. "I must go to Batiz. To-morrow is Thursday."

"You can say *kaddish* in Karoly."

"I must get some goods from Lazarovich."

"Couldn't you get them from Karoly?"

"No. Rothbart won't give us any credit."

"Then," said Malkeleh after reflection, "go to the bar parlor and if Farmer Galagonya is still there tell him that we're not going till Sunday."

Sroleh Yomtov hurried out, but returned almost immediately after.

"Galagonya is singing," he said.

"What of it?"

"He's already drunk; you can't talk to him."

"Well, we must tell him," said Malkeleh.

"We needn't," snapped the boy. "I'll go to Karoly in the morning."

"What if Rothbart doesn't give you any credit?"

"He might."

He took the message. Yes, he would tell Blimeleh that they were arriving at noon on Friday. Then he hurried back to the inn. The bar parlor was crowded, while Sholem sat behind the bar flagrantly infringing the gentry's orders by poring over the Talmud, having to be jerked out of it again and again to serve the customers. Sroleh Yomtov was both obliging and interested. He asked Sholem whether his reading was interesting. Sholem beamed at him.

"I should think it is," he said. "Reb Nachman ben Yitzchok asks. . . ."

"You get on with it," interrupted the boy, "I'll see to the customers." Then, speaking through the small window in the screen above the bar: "Yes, Uncle Gore—one tot. Have you got the tally stick on you? . . Could you lend me your sleigh for tomorrow? You'll drink it off . . . Very well, I'll come and fetch it in the morning." He went out into the parlor, mixing with the peasants. "Polya," he said to one peasant, "I'll get you some ordinary. Serf Vizhordo, I think you want low-grade. Paul Bene, put that knife away, there's not going to be any more knifing here. Mr. Headman, you like rum. All brainy people do. Farmer Galagonya, why so quiet? Another tot of the green poison? I'll give it to you full to the brim if you'll sing, 'I ferried across the river.' I always liked that song."

He kept popping in and out behind the bar, looking very gay, and even humming accompaniment as Galagonya in his raucous voice intoned the song.

"I'm going to Karoly in the morning," he flung at Sholem between two servings.

"Not to Batiz?"

"No. I can say *kaddish* in Karoly just as well."

"What about stock?"

"I'll go to Rothbart."

"Will he serve you on credit?"

"If Reb Leizer does, why shouldn't Rothbart? . . Yes, Mr. Blacksmith—half a pint of red."

"What if Reb Leizer takes offense?" said Sholem anxiously, pushing the *Gemarah* tome aside.

"Don't worry, Sholem. When he hears that you are buying from Rothbart as well, he'll suddenly take such a liking to you —as if you were his brother. He might even come and see you."

"But is it proper to go to two different people for credit?"

"You can go to ten if you like. If all you worry about is what is proper and not what is good for business, you'll be a poor man all your life. The peasants would like a drop of Karoly stuff for a change."

"Is it better then?"

"It smells different. And if you say it's from Karoly they'll think it's better. And you can ask more for it."

"I wouldn't do that."

Sroleh Yomtov gave a shrug. Sholem could please himself. What was important at the moment was that Blimeleh should know in time that Malkeleh was coming along on the Friday. What would Mordechai say if the guests ate his Sabbath dinner? He was Malkeleh's brother, of course, but he was a rich man. Sholem looked at him admiringly. What a clever boy. And how pleasant he had suddenly become. It was a pleasure to talk with him.

"You can listen to the *tsaddik*," he said suddenly. "He'll put you on the right path, my son."

Early the following morning Sroleh Yomtov took Kese the pony across to Farmer Gore and harnessed him to the sleigh.

Then he drove back to the inn yard to load the casks. He picked
up Bakter, who had been at his heels all the time, and took him to
the smaller cellar which was used only in summer to keep the
beer cool, locking him in and pocketing the key. He then
examined the barred window to see whether it was secure. The
dog whimpered and whined, but Sroleh Yomtov, interpreting
these noises correctly, was adamant. "You stay here, my *yezer
haraa*," he muttered. "I'm taking Aunt Malkah's message to
Karoly." "Aunt Malkah" was different from "Malkeleh"—it
was as if Yossef had been saying it. Sroleh Yomtov now felt like
a little boy, a wise, obedient little boy. Aunt Malkah was sending
him on an errand, and he was going to carry it out. At first
he had said no, because the "evil spirit" made him. But then he
went outdoors, took a deep breath and blew the evil spirit away.
How nice it was to be nice at last. Things would be different
from now on.

He was already driving along the road, but he could still hear
Bakter's wild and embittered bark. He flicked the whip at the
pony's flank and the sleigh streaked along, so that the casks
knocked together, and Bakter's plaint faded out. Not even a rat
could squeeze through those bars, let alone a big dog. Hadn't
Bakter grown since he came! It was awful the way he panted.
Get away, Bakter! Was he still hearing him, or was it merely
his imagination? And why must he think of the dog now? He was
barking so savagely down there that he was bound to wake
Malkeleh. Malkeleh would draw little Sarah Chayah to her, pull
down the nightgown from over her warm, round breast . . . Shut
up, Bakter!

How glad he had been the previous night over to-day's trip.
At last he would be alone from morning till evening. There
would be no one with him, neither Sholem, nor Yiteleh, nor
Yossef, nor the *tsaddik*, nor the dog. Yet the dog was still with
him. No, he wasn't, provided he did not think of him. Nor was
Malkeleh with him. Only the message. The previous night he
had laughed to himself in bed as he visualized Blimeleh, with
eyes lighting up and mouth agape when he told her that Malkeleh
was coming. Even the inky-spirited Mordechai was beaming.
Sroleh Yomtov felt rather embarrassed now. He couldn't say that

"Aunt Malkah" was coming, otherwise they would think he was a silly, immature little boy or sly. He must say Malkeleh and then . . . then they would guess everything.

As the snow-capped turrets of Karoly Castle appeared in the distance Sroleh Yomtov began to feel more composed. He had already solved his problem. He would not go straight to Blimeleh as he had planned, but would first go to synagogue. Mordechai was bound to be there, and he would tell him briefly that his sister and her children were coming. Then he would call on Blimeleh. That would be best; he would be in time for the service and the others would not grumble at him.

However, Mordechai was not at the synagogue, despite the fact that it was Torah-reading day. He must be away on business, thought the boy. Never mind. Carried away by the noise of the other worshippers, he chanted with them, swayed his body, addressing and importuning God in a language that only God himself understood completely. Beyond the communal prayers, the individual members of the congregation each approached the Deity with his own personal prayers. If Sroleh Yomtov could have formulated his own, he would have prayed that his adulthood should not be taken so seriously in Heaven as it was upon earth, where for the past eighteen months the adults had been regarding him as one of themselves. As he was reciting the Aramaic verses of the *kaddish*, a wistful certainty that he was after all still a child, with the sorrows of one, touched his spirit.

A lanky, swarthy-complexioned youth standing beside him was also reciting the prayer for the dead. After the community's final Amen, the youth turned to him:

"Who are you mourning?"

"My father and mother," was the reply.

"That's bad. I lost only my mother, and that's bad enough. What's your name?"

"What's yours?"

"Gaddel—Gaddel Brueder, you know."

"My name is Sroleh Yomtov."

"No German name?"

"No."

"Was your father as poor as that?"

Sroleh Yomtov was offended and looked it, but Gaddel was turning the pages of his *siddur* and did not notice.

"Where do you come from?" he asked. Then: "Did you come to live here?"

"No, I only came for the day."

"I'm leaving Karoly. Where are you going to?"

"Where should I go?"

"If you have no parents you must go somewhere."

"What about you? You still have a father."

"Yes—and he's thrashing me away from home." Bending over his *siddur*, he went on in a low voice, as if reading it there: "He is very religious and very strict. He used to beat me for every trifle before, but my mother was there to protect me. Now he is stricter still. Rosa Purjes wouldn't think of protecting me."

"Who is that?" inquired Sroleh Yomtov.

"The Purjes girl from Somlya, my father's fiancée. He is on a visit to her now. They'll marry when the year of mourning is out. But I shan't wait for that. Next week I'll be saying *kaddish* at Hunfalva." Looking at Sroleh Yomtov from the corner of his eye, he went on persuasively: "The *yeshiba* there is famous. And it's a better place than any other. Every Jewish house gives days. I have three for certain already, Sunday, Tuesday, and Friday. I shan't die of starvation. You might get more days because you're smaller and have neither father nor mother."

"I'm not going to a *yeshiba*," said Sroleh Yomtov.

"No? Then where are you going to? What was your father?"

"An innkeeper."

"Well, even if you want to be the same, you can still go to a *yeshiba*."

"I'm not going to be an innkeeper."

"What, then?"

"I'm going to be more than an innkeeper."

"Who told you that?"

"None of your business."

"Of course," said the other boy. "But if you want to be a business man, like me, then it's best for you to come to Hunfalva. They have just built a big synagogue of stone, much better than this barn here; this used to be the Count's granary. The business men from Cracow come to Hunfalva to find husbands for their daughters. The girls of Cracow are rich and beautiful. They dress in silk and velvet and wear expensive jewels."

He was silenced by the shush-shushing of the other worshippers. A man with a black beard and a caved-in nose came up to Sroleh Yomtov and Gaddel and bade them be ashamed of themselves to be talking instead of praying, especially as they were mourners.

"Aren't you afraid that the dead are looking down upon you?" he said.

Gaddel resumed praying where he had left off, taking no notice of the reproof. Sroleh Yomtov too bent over the *siddur*, but there was a surge of anger within him, as always when his dead and his obligation to them were mentioned. He was thinking of them all right, but these people wanted to prescribe the time. Now he could not have thought of them with due veneration even if he had wanted to. This Gaddel couldn't be much older than himself, yet he was already thinking of marriage. Only a married man could love. The Jewish girls of Cracow were lovely and beautifully dressed. When they married they had their hair shorn and wore a wig, so that no strange man should see their beauty.

The Scrolls of the Law were just being taken out of the ark. Before they were put down on the dais, they were carried round the room, so that the men could touch the gold-embroidered velvet jacket covering the holy parchment with the hem of their prayer-shawls, kissing the latter. Those who had no prayer-shawl, touched the covering with the tip of their fingers, which they then kissed. Gaddel bent down and kissed the velvet direct. Sroleh Yomtov noted this with consternation, and his consternation caused him to observe more vividly the subsequent processes —how the silver crown was removed from the head of the scrolls, then the velvet jacket, then the transparent silk chemise, and finally the silken belt with which the scrolls were tied together. The scrolls were opened and the reader, with a carved "Hand" to guide him, was searching for the passages due to be read. Sroleh Yomtov watched with a sense of fascination. He had seen

all this so often before without thinking of anything, and now
. . . it made him think of a naked woman. . . .

Suddenly, the reader jerked his head back, and his trembling
fingers let the pointer drop on the desk and thence on the floor
of the dais. There was consternation on the faces of the congregation as they stared at Sroleh Yomtov from all directions. What
was the matter? Those piercing looks were stabbing into his
brain as well as measuring him from head to foot. There was a
moment's frozen silence, then the one with the caved-in nose
raised his fist, and after standing rigid for an instant cried with
an awful voice that made Sroleh Yomtov go hot and cold:

"Get out! Get out!"

"Get out!" cried the whole congregation. "A dog near the
Torah!"

Sroleh Yomtov looked down and was horrified to see Bakter
gamboling round him, and at the same time skipping aside to
avoid the kicks aimed at him. Somehow, the dog was chased out
by the others and the door was firmly closed, but as the animal
neared the door he looked back and Sroleh Yomtov felt that
those eyes were saying something. What a disgrace! He had been
caught in the act here. Every one knew everything now.

"Was that your dog?" asked Gaddel.

Sroleh Yomtov nodded, as though making a shameful admission.

"Take no notice of them," said the lanky youth, with a wave of
the hand. "It's not your fault that he came in."

But the black man with the caved-in nose and all the other
prayer-shawled men were staring at him with eyes that were like
live coals. Their gaze was saying: "You have desecrated the house
of God with your evil spirit, you are evil yourself, like Haman."
He hated them because they knew, hated them because they were
right.


He was back home at noon, though he had not been expected
till late evening. But they were all very pleased.

The casks were full: Rothbart had given him everything. And
Blimeleh's message was to come for as long a stay as possible.
Mordechai was on a business tour, buying up goatskins, but would
be back for the Sabbath. Malkeleh expressed her gratitude to

Sroleh Yomtov by seizing his hand and giving it a hard squeeze.

"You are a clever boy, Sroleh Yomtov."

The boy blushed, bent over her hand and kissed it.

"Good-bye, Malkeleh," he said hoarsely.

"Plenty of time to say good-bye," laughed the woman. "We're not leaving till the morning."

Sholem grumbled why he did not stay in Karoly for the evening service as well. The boy explained that Blimeleh had taken him to the best room, where she had glass cases, shiny furniture and upholstered chairs covered with lace, but which was ice-cold. Blimeleh's two little girls were queer. Hannah kept licking her lips and talked mincingly, while Miriam was always in front of the looking-glass beautifying herself. They asked him to stay for dinner, but he preferred to come back home with the goods.

"The goods weren't urgent," said Sholem. "The *kaddish* was more important."

"Today's *kaddish* was not valid, anyhow," snapped the boy irritably.

"Not valid?"

"I locked the dog up before I left, but some one let him out and he followed me to Karoly. He came into the synagogue just as they were unrolling the Torah."

"What a misfortune!" cried Sholem, shaking his head desolately. "It's a bad omen! A bad omen! If I had only known! Go and ask the *tsaddik* would he kindly come here at once."

Sroleh Yomtov regretted having blurted it out; he did not like the prospect of having to recount the incident to the *tsaddik*, though no doubt the *tsaddik* would get to know all about it anyhow. He would hum and smile into his beard, thereby betraying his mystic knowledge of the incident, and perhaps he would also be able to tell why the dog entered the synagogue precisely at the moment when the Scrolls of the Law were being undressed.

But this time the *tsaddik* did not hum or smile, but listened gravely to Sholem, who spoke of the sin he had committed.

The dog had been whining most pitiably in the cellar, so he broke off the padlock and let the animal out. It did not occur to him that Bakter would go as far as Karoly and slink into the synagogue.

"You were right to let him out," said the *tsaddik*. "And if he

followed Sroleh Yomtov it was probably because he too wanted
to be at the synagogue."

Sroleh Yomtov listened in painful agitation: now the *tsaddik*
was going to unmask him. But no. The *tsaddik* went on to say
something that awed and amazed both Sholem and Sroleh Yomtov.

"What if there is a human spirit imprisoned in that animal? I
would not have chased the dog out, but would have let him open
his mouth in the congregation."

Did the *tsaddik* really believe what he was saying, thought the
boy, or was he merely trying to reassure Sholem? Sholem asked
whether he himself ought not to do penance by fasting, recital
of the Psalms, or *Mishnah* reading.

"No," said the *tsaddik*, "there would be no sense in that. God
does not like man to torment himself; He does not want the bread
you leave by fasting. But if you think that the dog took into the
synagogue not a human spirit, but only its own canine spirit—
and you are entitled to this doubt—then come and join me for
midnight prayers."

So the Bakter affair was for the moment settled for Sholem.
But Sroleh Yomtov's inner disquiet had not been allayed. He
would have liked to be alone with the *tsaddik*. He asked him
whether he felt like a walk on the road.

"No," said the old man. "I'll be walking many, many miles in
the snow yet, my son. But have your walk by all means, if you
feel like it, you with your young legs."

The old man went into the kitchen, sat down in the inglenook
and gathered the children round him. One could already hear
Mailech's cry of surprise, Yiteleh's inquiring voice, and Yossef's
laughter. Sroleh Yomtov was of two minds whether he should
not join them. But laughter was not for him just then. He went
out into the yard, walked about for awhile, then stopped by the
ash tree. The dog was at his heel again. Yiteleh came out to the
verandah for a napkin and saw Sroleh Yomtov.

"Why do you stand there all alone?" she shouted across to him.
The voice pleased him, but he was incapable of a friendly reply.

"I'm not alone," he said. "Bakter is here."

"Come in and stay with us."

"I won't. I must go."

"Where to?"

"The *tsaddik* said for me to go out."

And he went out into the snow-covered road. He did not return until dusk—and he was not alone. A strange lad followed behind him, quietly and humbly like a beggar. The boy went into the house, talked with Malkeleh, then came out with a cheery expression on his face. He showed the stranger to the stable, then he hurried into the inn, and sat down beside Sholem behind the bar.

"Listen, Sholem," he said. "I had a look at the marsh where you want to buy land. It is covered with snow, of course, but you can see all the better where the reeds stick out. Where the reeds remain even in winter, the marsh is deep. Don't give more than thirty kreuzer for a chain. The Squire will let you have it with pleasure."

Sholem was surprised. Why was the boy talking about the marshland? Of course, the *tsaddik* had advised him to buy a few chains of land there because in time the marsh would dry out. The *tsaddik* knew that he loved the land. But Sroleh Yomtov had always urged him to stick to the inn and not bother with peasant work. He shrugged his shoulders.

"It'll be a long time before you can put that part under the plough."

"Yes, but it might be all right for the geese in a year or two." The boy looked through the window into the yard, where the snow gleamed in the falling darkness. Then he turned the conversation. "There is a lad here looking for work. He looks strong, though he is very down-at-heel. Malkeleh wants him to look after the pony, chop wood, and help you and Aunt Feiga while she and the children are away."

"What sort of a lad is he?" asked Sholem, raising his eyes from the book.

"He looks all right," said the boy. "He is in the stable; you can go and talk to him."

"I will, later. If Malkeleh wants him. . . ."

"It's snowing again," said the boy, when Sholem had once more returned to the book.

"Yes . . . Saith Rabbi Pappah. . . ."

"The children are going to have a fine sleigh ride."

"Yes . . . Saith Rabbi—"

"You'll have a good harvest this year."

"Perhaps I shall . . . Saith Rabbi Pappah. . . ."

"Your wheat won't get frozen, either."

"If the Above One grant it."

"He has already granted it. There is a yard of snow lying over your wheat. By the time it thaws it'll be spring. The warm winds come from south-east."

Sholem was pleased to be encouraged about his wheat sowing, which the peasants had said would get frozen. In any case, he liked to talk about the land.

"This year," he said, pushing the Talmud tome aside, "I'll plant potatoes and maize in the other half—and hemp. If the land were bigger I'd grow beet—that new, sweet beet. Does that lad know about the land?"

It seemed that Sroleh Yomtov was familiar with the secrets of the soil as well, though he had not betrayed it before. Now he spoke like an expert.

"Don't buy awny wheat for the next year's seed; the awnless is better. You sow it in the spring. And don't buy your maize seeds here, but at Denghelegh, where it is better. Seed potatoes you must buy from the peasants of Sarberek."

"We'll talk about all that later," said Sholem, pulling the well-thumbed tome closer again.

"You don't have to pay, Sholem," pursued the boy. "You'll write it off their debts."

"I know."

"And in the autumn, when the peasants pay up, they pay with grain. You must get it well mixed in the granary, because it's not all alike."

"No, of course not."

"You must take two samples of the mixed corn. Take one to Karoly, to Joshua Brueder, and the other to Batiz, to Leizer Lazarovich. You'll sell to the one that offers more. Reb Leizer buys both maize and potatoes; he needs them for his distillery. And he pays cash."

"Deducting my debt, of course."

"Yes, Sholem, deducting your debt. The peasants of Kacor and Bekato will bring rushes and peat, and also rush-mats and sedge-mats and baskets. You must accept all that; the trough-seller Jew will give you good money for them."

The bar parlor began to fill up and the conversation had to be interrupted. Sroleh Yomtov went off to serve the customers. Later he said:

"Sholem, we must stay on after closing time. I have something important to tell you."

"Something important?"

"You just go on with your reading, Sholem. You might do some of it on my behalf as well. If the noise here disturbs you, you can go to the gentry's room."

"It doesn't disturb me," said Sholem gaily, "so long as I don't have to jump up every minute . . . Saith Rabbi Poppah. . . ."

The reason for Sholem's cheery contentment was the complete change in the boy. Three months ago, nay, even three weeks ago, he was all defiance and resistance. Now, he was simply perfect. No parent could wish for a better son. Not only was he undertaking the solution of the most difficult practical problems, as the obtaining of credit, but he was also approaching spiritually the traditional ideal of the perfect son. Sholem was pleased with this division of labor—the one working, the other studying, and each for the material or spiritual benefit of the other. But just now he had another reason to be pleased: he felt that the boy's behavior reflected penitence for having been involved in the entry of the unclean animal into the house of God. Yet he could not help it that the dog loved him so. Only recently the *tsaddik* had said that there must be a great deal of good in any boy to whom a dog was so attached, and, once more, the *tsaddik* was right.

"HARK, THE COCKERELS, HARK!"

UNCLE GASPAR, the night watchman, drank standing. His office made it improper for him to enjoy comfort from dark to light. He tossed off the drink in one, and in an instant it powered his legs. The reason he did not go at once, but stood there clearing his throat and croaking once or twice, was not that he was making ready for his official vocal effort; no, this was a sort of hint to the peasants that they had done enough carousing for the evening and it was time for them to be off. When Uncle Gaspar at last left the bar parlor, he turned towards it as he bawled:

"Ten o'clock and all's well—all honest folk should go to rest." For of course, the people in the village would scarcely hear the cry. However, the customers at the inn still made no move. It was not until half an hour later, when Sholeh Yomtov had rattled thrice the bunch of keys—the last time with significant vigor—that they rose up, went to the bar to hand their tally sticks to Sholem, and bade a "restful good night." Sroleh Yomtov went behind the bar and sat down beside Sholem.

"Listen, Sholem," he said earnestly.

Sholem raised his head, listening—not to Sroleh Yomtov, but to the growing sound of a sleigh-bell approaching from the Gyekenyes road.

"This can't be Galagonya, can it?" he remarked.

"Of course not, Sholem. He's just left."

The sound of the bells was now quite close, and suddenly it stopped. The windows were illuminated by the light of torches. Deep masculine voices and a hammering at the door.

"Hi, Jew! Hi!"

Sholem jumped up and hastily closed and hid the tome that lay before him.

"The Squire," he whispered with scared awe, and ran to open the door. Yes, it was the Squire—together with the other two Squires, all in fur-coats and sheepskin caps. Squire de Sarberek entered.

"Phew," he breathed, a grimace of distaste on his narrow, stern face. "What a peasant stink! I hope the air is cleaner in the gentry's room, what?"

"Yes, your worship. There's been no one there."

"No fire there, what?"

"I didn't know your worships were coming," said Sholem. "I'll have a fire laid at once."

"Well, here we are," growled Squire de Denghelegh gaily. "To-day is St. Gedeon's Day, and Lady Susan chased us out, saying she wanted some sleep at last. My friend Gedeon knows what that means—no more booze, nor nothing else. Ha—Ha—Ha! What are you grinning about, Moses, hey? Nothing to do with you, see? Get that fire laid at once."

"Yes, your worship. Sroleh Yomtov, light the gentlemen into the parlor and get some candles lit there."

Sholem hurried through the living rooms into the kitchen to get some live coals from the range. As he passed Malkeleh's bed, he seemed to hear a question, though she might merely have been talking in her sleep.

"The gentry," he said in a low voice, yet importantly.

The next instant he was in the gentry's parlor, crouching in front of the big tin stove and blowing at the coals with all his might. The three visitors had already sat down round the table, which was covered with a cloth. Duduy appeared from nowhere—the gentry must have brought him with them—and stood at a corner of the table fumbling with his clarinet.

"Well, Jew," said the grey-haired de Denghelegh, "have you got any good wine? Some Kosher Passover wine—that's what we want."

"I have some Tokay from Mesel," said Sholem, making a gesture with thumb and forefinger joined to express what another would have expressed by smacking his lips. "Some Passover wine," he said to Sroleh Yomtov.

The boy looked depressed, and it was with pursed lips that he took the keys and a stub of candle to go to the cellar.

"Hi! You don't expect us to go thirsty meanwhile, do you?" said de Sarberek with mock irritation. "Get us some plum whisky, Jew, the kind I like."

"Yes, your worship," said Sholem, bowing and scraping, and ran behind the bar to fetch a bottle of plum and glasses. The gentlemen drank and winked at Duduy. "To Lady Susan!" cried de Denghelegh. "Play, gypsy, but be careful you don't wake my lady." The gypsy started to play, gently, so as not to disturb my lady in her first sleep in the next village. The stern de Sarberek, who used to bawl at his serfs, proved a refined gentleman here, humming the tune quietly, almost breathing it.

Old de Denghelegh with his triple chins and the bullnecked, bristle-haired Gedeon Gyekeny joined in just as quietly.

Sroleh Yomtov returned with the wine.

"The devil won't take these away till noon to-morrow," he whispered to Sholem sullenly.

Sholem did not reply, only looked him up and down reprovingly, as though to say: "These are not serfs or strays from the road, but the gentry. No matter how long they carouse, they are still the gentry." He had not yet finished his train of thought when de Sarberek jumped up, stamped with his spurred boot on the floor and after emitting a wild oath started to sing in a vociferous voice, the clarinet rising to a screechy pitch. Soon he was joined by Gedeon, while old de Denghelegh sang hoarsely where he sat. This was bad. Malkeleh had been hard at work all day, washing, ironing, mending, and also suckling the baby, and she was going away early in the morning. Sholem wished the gentry had kept their singing as low as before. However, there was worse to come, for after the next round of drinks all three men began to "raise the roof" with a fresh song, old de Denghelegh leading with his tremulous bass and shaking his forefinger in the air:

> *"Of all the deities up above.*
> *Bacchus is the peer of Jove. . . ."*

Sholem filled the bottle on the table and looked round uncertainly. He wanted Sroleh Yomtov to relieve him, if only for half an hour, so he could join the *tsaddik* at midnight prayers. But the boy had vanished from the edge of the bench along the wall where he had been sitting before. Sholem vaguely remembered that the boy had gone back to the bar parlor. Now he wondered what he might be doing there, since the place was deserted. Besides, he must be tired out, having had that trouble in the synagogue, brought back the goods, and inspected the marsh, quite apart from the fatigue of the journey. He must simply have gone to bed himself rather than listen to such blasphemous songs. All those pagan gods . . . Why, even the night watchman was worth more than they. Just then Uncle Gaspar sounded his horn in the street, giving it a creaky blare in honor of the gentry's presence, and bawling his cry straight at the lighted windows of the gentry's parlor:

> "*Twelve of midnight it has struck,*
> *Pray the Lord for the best of luck.*"

The *tsaddik* was now sitting down on the floor in a corner of the small guest room, sprinkling ashes on his head and reciting the laments born by the waters of Babylon; confessing his sins and taking upon himself the sins of all Israel; mourning the Temple, and the widowed bride, Jerusalem; and waiting for Sholem, to beat their chests in company. But the satisfaction of a shared lament was denied to both. How could Sholem go away now? The gentry were visiting him for the first time, and he must serve them well. In a conflict between heaven and earth, earth was the stronger. Sholem must laugh with the others, whether he understood their coarse jokes or not. Those three were now laughing at everything. "Su-susan's red-letter calendar," mouthed de Denghelegh, and roared with laughter. "The bailiff with the mortar," cried de Sarberek with a guffaw. Even the gypsy was guffawing. However, as Gedeon Gyekeny was silently staring into his glass, de Sarberek turned on the gypsy:

"Hi! Duduy! stop that sly grin or I'll slap your face till it's a bloody steak. How dare you grin when the gentry are talking about Squire Gyekeny's family! Look at the Jew—he doesn't hear anything."

Duduy jerked his head away as though to avoid a blow and made such a penitent face that he looked really funny. The faces of two of the gentry were already beaming like the full moon. Squire Gyekeny's face was flushed, yet he had a dejected air.

"Don't worry, Gedeon," consoled de Sarberek, "next week we'll go over to Debrecen and carouse till dawn in the Bull. Then we'll go and see the bad girls."

For awhile Gyekeny did not respond. Then suddenly he picked up his glass, drained it and flung it at the wall, where it crashed to smithereens. Sholem had enough presence of mind to dodge it and say a silent *mozeltov* (good luck). Of course, there was no good luck about it at all, for now the third squire also jumped into the middle of the room, stamping his feet so hard that it made the whole room shake.

> *"Chase care away,*
> *Hip, hip, hurrah. . . .*

The clarinet screamed, and all three men were stamping about on the floor, bawling with all their might, "Hip, hip hurrah." If it had been by day this might have amused the children, but now it was merely waking them up. Sholem had filled their bottles three times and they were still bawling and dancing. It was surprising the way the old fellow kept it up. True, he was now sitting down, but his spurred knee-boots were still doing overtime. Outside, the night watchman was announcing the passage of another hour. He put his mouth even closer to the window, with the evident intent of inviting an invitation for a glass of wine. However, the gentry failed to take the hint. But they stopped hip-hipping and dancing. For a minute or so they were uncertain what to do next. Fortunately, Uncle Gaspar's receding voice reminded old de Denghelegh of a song from the time of the Turkish occupation, which had in it something of the long-drawn call of the muezzin.

Dawn was breaking and the cocks were crowing. Squire de Sarberek now intoned the song of the Rabbi of Kallo. They were singing it in the right way, slowly, with eyes closed and with reverence in their voices.

> *"Hark, the cockerels, hark!*
> *Dawn breaks through the dark.*
> *Lo! a bird on the verdant lea,*
> *A magic bird I see."*

The Rabbi of Kallo, Isaac Taub of blessed memory, was walking over the lea on the edge of a wood, when he heard a shepherd boy playing his flute, then singing a song about a bird with green feathers on its body and blue ones on its wings, pacing along with golden legs through eons and eons of eons. The holy man paused. It seemed to him that he had heard that song somewhere before— not during the reign of Joseph the Wise, nor under that of the

frigid Maria Theresa, but long before that, two thousand years
or more before that, when it was sung by a chorus of Levites on
Mount Moriah, in the court of the Temple, with the sons of
Asaf and the sons of Yeduthun and the singing masters of Korah
playing their string instruments and their wind instruments. He
gave a copper to the shepherd's boy, to repeat the song. And then
another and another. He gave the boy a hundred and one coppers,
and the boy sang the song a hundred and one times. But he was
unable to repeat it the hundred and second time, however hard
he tried to recall its sounds either to his lips or to his flute. He
had sold the song to the Rabbi, and thenceforward it belonged to
him.

> *"Wait, O bird, wait,*
> *Wait, O bird, wait. . . .*

The gentry were now singing this one line over and over
again, ever more softly, until their voices faded to a whisper.
Had they too forgotten the rest? Or was the next line forbidden
to them, because it was getting close to the sacred line in Hebrew?
Duduy made a spurt, stopped, tried again. "Wait, O bird, wait."
They gave him a tot of plum whisky and told him to play it
all over again. The gypsy drank, wiped his mouth, and the clarinet
seemed to have gained new strength. He managed another line:

> *"Wait, O bird, wait!*
> *Won't it be too late?"*

The door of the room, the one that opened on the verandah,
was flung open, as if it had been blown in by the wind. Framed
in the doorway stood Reb Issur Phineas, the *tsaddik*. His face
was white, only a little less so than his hair and beard, and his
shirt was white too. Had he only just finished his midnight prayers
and was he about to retire, or had he just got out of bed? Sholem
thought he detected a trace of ashes on his temples and on his
beard. The others saw only the ghostly whiteness and the black
skull-cap on the old man's head, and the little prayer-shawl with
the black transverse stripes and the mystic tassels at the corners
that hung from his shoulders over his shirt, and the song froze on
their lips. If the will-o'-the-wisp of the marsh, its thousand-year-

old witch, had suddenly appeared, with tongues of blue flame round her body, it would not have numbed them into immobility so completely as the appearance of the aged Jew in his shirt. Yet there was no reason for terror. Why, Duduy was already quite lively, though the *tsaddik* had barely blinked at him. Jerking the clarinet to his lips, the gypsy started to play again, and lo! it had a triumphant sound. Now he knew the end of the song, for the *tsaddik* himself was leading him:

> *"Wait, O bird, wait,*
> *Won't it be too late?*
> *Yeboneh ha-mikdosh*
> *Eer Zion t'maleh,*
> *That won't be too late."*

The numbness melted into relaxation. The three squires had joined in and were repeating even the Hebrew words off the lips of the aged Jew. Sholem too was singing, and as he saw the out-spread arms of the Christians, and the light in their eyes, he knew that they were singing those words as happily as he and the *tsaddik*. And because the *tsaddik* was enunciating the words in his peculiar way, they understood them. Of course they did. Sholem felt the caress of the warm breeze of the Messianic age as they sang the Hebrew words:

> *"The Holy Place will rise,*
> *Zion will arise,*
> *That won't be too late."*

The warm breeze came and passed. The door crashed open again, and the room was filled with icy wind. Squire de Sarberek bawled: "Shut the door!" Sholem hastened to obey. The *tsaddik* was no longer there. He had vanished as suddenly as he had come. Squire de Denghelegh was white to the lips.

"That was the Wandering Jew," he said with numb lips, his pendent moustaches trembling like frosted twigs.

"Who else?" agreed de Sarberek.

Gedeon Gyekeny looked at Sholem with bleary eyes and said: "They're a ghostly tribe."

Only the gypsy was grinning.

"Another song, your worships?" he said.

Old de Denghelegh gestured that he did not want another song. Gyekeny slipped a coin into the gypsy's pocket. The third squire snapped:

"Get out, gypsy!"

The gentry's coachman came in to drink up the wine left in the glasses.

## "SROLEH YOMTOV, MINOR"

IT WAS still dark when Galagonya's sleigh drew up in front of the inn, Sholem was heavy with sleep, but the rest of the household was already up and about. Malkeleh was washing the children and combing their hair, while Aunt Feiga was preparing breakfast. A stubbly-faced lad brought in some logs on his arms and poked the fire. As he went out he carried with him the luggage that had lain ready in a corner.

"Take this bundle as well, Janos," said Malkeleh in a lively tone. "And this knapsack."

"Yes, madam," said the lad.

Sholem washed and donned the prayer-shawl. The children were making a commotion all around him, and the room was upside down. Malkeleh was busy dressing up the baby. Sholem stood by the window and could see the heavy snow lying on the ground. But his eyes were gazing further than that, into the spring, and what he saw was a bird, a magic bird on the verdant lea.

It was not proper to feel too happy, so long as the Jewish people were living in exile. But perhaps it was permissible to taste the joys of preparation for the journey, to gain a foreknowledge of what it would be like when the Messiah came and blew his horn, ending the long centuries of exile. There had been a period of exile before—seventy years. When the people returned from Babylon "our mouths were full of laughter, and our tongues with jubilation." These children were laughing in the way that the adults did then.

"Sroleh Yomtov!" cried Yiteleh. "Sroleh Yomtov, where are you?" Yossef too repeated the cry.

Sholem was facing the east wall of the room, and for a while he took no notice of these calls. But when he heard it from Malkeleh, whose voice was no longer lively, but anxious and scared, the bird with the green and blue plumage fluttered away like a dream.

"Sholem," said Malkeleh, "did you tell Sroleh Yomtov to go with the *tsaddik*?"

"I didn't tell him anything. Where has the *tsaddik* gone to?"

"I don't know. He just took his bundle and went away."

"You saw him?"

"No, Janos did."

"What Janos?"

"Why," said Malkeleh, "the lad Sroleh Yomtov engaged yesterday."

"And they said nothing to me. What time did the *tsaddik* leave?"

"In the early dawn."

"Why did he go away?"

"I suppose he'd had enough of staying here. But why did Sroleh Yomtov go with him?"

"But didn't you say that he went to see the *tsaddik* off?"

"Janos said they went off together. But if you didn't tell the boy, why should he see the *tsaddik* off? At a time like this, too."

"It's no little honor to see a saint off," said Sholem.

"If I hadn't overslept because the gentry kept bawling till dawn I'd have gone myself. I'm sorry to have missed it."

"Do you think Sroleh Yomtov only went to see him off?"

"What else, Malkeleh? He went with him as far as the next village or a little farther. If you'll wait a little he'll be back."

"Suppose he won't be back—ever?"

"What are you talking about?" cried Sholem.

"I'm worried about him," said Malkeleh.

"You've no reason to be worried."

"The boy's been strange lately."

She sat down to wait, dropping her hands into her lap. The children came in, urging her to come along. "I'm coming, I'm

coming," she said, but she did not move. Then Galagonya came
in to say that his horses would get cold; he had just taken the
rugs off them and put them on the seat. Better get in now while
the rugs are warm. "In a minute," said Malkeleh. As the peasant
left the room, she raised her eyes to Sholem.

"I don't feel like going on a visit any longer," she said.

"Don't be silly, Malkeleh," grumbled Sholem. "Just because the
boy has gone roaming somewhere! He's done it before, just when
he was needed most. I'm sure the *tsaddik* sent him back to be in
time to say good-bye."

"That's just what I'm worried about. He said good-bye to me
yesterday."

"Yesterday!" cried Sholem wide-eyed. But he would not have
the family postpone the visit to Karoly just because Sroleh Yomtov had vanished—perhaps he did not like farewells. Yossef
opined that his brother was envious because he was not coming,
and he hastened to settle down by Mailech on the sleigh.
It was not possible to delay until Sroleh Yomtov turned up, because the peasant was grumbling that his horses had already
worked themselves half to death during the week and that unless
they started at once he could not guarantee to reach Karoly before
sunset. Yiteleh had a suspicion that Blimeleh had invited Sroleh
Yomtov separately and he said nothing about it, lest he be dissuaded because he was needed in the inn. He must have gone
ahead, starting at dawn when every one else was asleep. If they
hurried up, thought Yiteleh, they would catch up with him.
Malkeleh was unconvinced, but acted as though she shared her
daughter's suspicion. And when Sholem promised to send the
boy to Karoly on the Monday for a whole day, she even managed
to smile. And so Sholem too was reassured.

The sound of the sleigh-bells had long died away, and there
was silence in the house. The only noise was the tinkling of the
inn door-bell, though no customers came, only Sholem himself
kept going out now and then to walk into the road and gaze into
the distance. He sat down behind the bar and opened the *Gemarah*. Another time he would have blessed this quiet morning that
gave him an opportunity to gather more knowledge and sharpen
his wits on sacred debate. But now his mind was elsewhere. He

gazed at the text, chanted a few lines, but both the chant and the chanter seemed strange. The characters were mere drawings ranged side by side, without sense or content. Setting aside the millennial problems and happenings, he began to speculate on the petty matters that were going on here, round his own existence.

Why did the *tsaddik* leave unexpectedly on the Sabbath eve? He had liked staying here. Was it because Malkeleh was going away? Of course, with her absent, the Sabbath table was not the same. It was the *tsaddik* himself, though, who advised that she should go to Karoly now, eight days before the Passover. From anyone else, this would have been a silly suggestion, but what the *tsaddik* said always had a profound meaning. The *tsaddik* had a more important mission than to spend his days in the house of Sholem ben Yoirish. But why did he leave unannounced? True, he had waited for Sholem to come to the midnight ritual. Satan himself must have sent those three carousing gentry to prevent the last reunion. The *tsaddik* had come in and had even sung the song of the Rabbi of Kallo with them; he could have said "Peace be with you" then. But he had vanished as though the earth had swallowed him up. Leizer Lazarovich had been wrong to compare the *tsaddik* with Korah and his sons, but it was undeniable that they too had been swallowed up by the earth.

Sholem was not worried about the *tsaddik*. On the contrary, he was glad and proud to know that the holy man who had honored his home was none other than the legendary Rabbi Luria. While he was there, Sholem was more than once in doubt, but now everything went to show that it was indeed Rabbi Luria. Sholem himself had recognized him on arrival by the Moses-scar on his lip, and just before his departure he had been recognized by another—not a biased Jew, either, but a *goy*, the old Squire, who saw Sholem's guest was the Wandering Jew, just as Bileam's ass saw the angel with the sword. For sixteen years Rabbi Luria had been the foremost wanderer of the Jewish people. Jacob's staff could never come to rest, and if a holy man did not now and then take the wanderer's staff, that unhappy people could never rest anywhere.

But what about Sroleh Yomtov? If he had merely gone to see the *tsaddik* off, he would have been back long ago. He might be roaming round the villages, as he had done before, and in that case he would turn up. But what if he didn't? Malkeleh had been anxious about him, and now Sholem too was anxious. However, anxiety was only guesswork, based on fear supported by presumed facts, and a man ought to go by what he knew for certain. What Sholem knew was that Sroleh Yomtov was not there; that he had left with the *tsaddik*; that he had said good-bye to Malkeleh at noon yesterday, so that he must then have decided to depart before Malkeleh had risen in the morning. But he did not know whether the good-bye was not in fact connected with Malkeleh's departure alone. At the same time, with him, Sholem, the boy had talked like one preparing for a long journey, telling him what to sow in the spring and how much to give for the marsh-land. But perhaps the reason he said that was that he had observed the snow-covered marsh and noticed where the reeds were stunted. Yes, but he had also instructed him as to the collection of outstanding accounts in the autumn. In the autumn, thought Sholem. He began to understand why Leizer Lazarovich spoke with such consternation about giving credit in the autumn—that is, at a time when the inn was getting cash for the corn collected from the peasants. What Sholem could not understand was why Reb Leizer gave credit two days later, when Sroleh Yomtov went to Batiz.

However, he did not linger over this question, lest it should deflect his thoughts. But he returned to it again and again, and was glad when Aunt Feiga came in and brought him back to his starting-point.

"That rascal's gone away without a by-your-leave," she grumbled. "Doesn't an old servant like me deserve a good word?"

Sholem tried to comfort her, saying that the boy had not said good-bye to him either, which meant that he had not gone away at all, and would be back before the Sabbath.

"You're a great *talmid hacham*, Sholem," said the old woman. "You sit over your *Gemarah* all the time and you think you know everything. But you don't know nothing. You don't see what's going on in your own house."

Sholem gave a start. There was puzzled inquiry in his gaze. But the old woman did not answer it; she just went on with her own lament:

"Yesterday he brought me his summer knee-boots to clean.

'What for?' I said. He told me not to ask questions, but to get on with it. I said not now when I had such a lot to do, but he said it must be now. And the brat insisted and I had to do them with fish-oil."

"Perhaps there was a hole in his winter boots?" said Sholem hopefully.

"Of course not. It was only the day before yesterday that he brought them back from the cobbler, all mended, soled and heeled, and hobnailed. I thought it was just obstinacy about those summer boots, but just now I looked into the wardrobe, and he took those too."

"Did he?"

"Yes, and his underwear too. I gave it back to him clean yesterday. And he took his Sabbath trousers and his phylacteries and his father's old prayer-book."

"Then it seems he's really gone," said Sholem thoughtfully.

"Yes, the young rascal. But why did he entice away dear old Reb Issur? I made Sabbath for four, and for the handyman besides, and now I've got all that food and no one to eat it. Even the dog's gone."

"Has Bakter gone with them?" asked Sholem in a scared tone. "Did they go towards Karoly?"

"Who knows which way they went," said the old woman, with a shrug that almost brought her shoulder up to her hairy chin.

"Didn't the handyman see them?"

"All he saw was that they went through the gate. But he was just going back to the stable, so he didn't see any more."

"But we must know."

"Why?"

"Bakter is no ordinary dog."

"He's very ordinary, I should think. I have to chase him out of the kitchen with the poker because he has no manners."

"When he's in the kitchen he's a dog. But when he goes to the synagogue. . . ."

He stared into the corner, between a shelf behind the bar and the window, at a knobbly stick standing there. The blind Rabbi Kunitz had bequeathed it to him, and he had succeeded in rescuing it at the last moment before his flight. Here he had thrown the precious relic into the corner and for the past six months he was never aware that it was there at all—perhaps because he wanted to forget about wandering. Now he felt that the old stick with its gnarled head was gazing at him, talking to him: Take me and go out into the road; what you will never learn between four walls, no matter how you rack your brain, may come to you if you follow the track of the departed pair. Aunt Feiga will see to any customers.

"All right," said the old woman, when she heard Sholem's intention. "But don't stay long, because I have a lot to do yet before Sabbath."

A sage's stick emanates wisdom. Sholem wondered which road to take, and suddenly knew which one not to take: the one leading to Karoly. If the boy and the *tsaddik* were on that road, the sleigh would catch up with them and pick them up, so that everything would be cleared up; the dog could always run after the sleigh. Sholem must go along the opposite road, northward, towards the Tisza.

The road, which led across the gypsy camp, was covered with virgin snow, marked by neither wheels nor sleighs. Ah! here were some footprints. A pair of big ones and a pair of small ones, with the marks of a stick to the right of the former, and the tracks of a dog to the left of the latter. Sholem nodded contentedly: the *tsaddik* with his staff and Sroleh Yomtov with the dog. There could be no mistake, for had he not helped the *tsaddik* to remove his boots and was not the iron missing from the heel of one of them? He remembered wanting to send that boot to the blacksmith for a new iron to be put on it, and he regretted having forgotten to do so. Then he met Duduy.

"Yes, sir," said the gypsy, "they went this way, towards Denghelegh, the singing beggar and Sroleh. I played 'Hark, the cockerels, hark!' to them, and the old man gave me a copper. And Sroleh said: 'Good-bye, Duduy!' "

So he said good-bye to the gypsy, thought Sholem, and his heart was heavy. Not a word to Aunt Feiga or to him, Sholem. In what way had he offended the boy? He had been strict with him in the business, compelling him to be honest and give true measure; but then, he could not have dealt otherwise with his own son. Once he had threatened to beat the boy, that time when he tried to defend Haman. None but a Haman could defend a Haman, he thought, but immediately corrected himself: you could not liken the boy to Haman after all.

He followed the footprints, trying to read the mystery in them. Here the big boots and the smaller boots were stepping out close together. This proved that they were in agreement. "Or would they both go together," it said in the Torah, "if they were not agreed?" But a little further it seemed that they were engaged in an argument, the small boots walking in front of the big ones, as though Sroleh Yomtov were leading Rabbi Luria. That was wrong, for it was for the old to lead. Besides, what was the boy hurrying for? If it had been on the road to Karoly, it might have been said that he was hurrying to escape being overtaken by the sleigh and picked up. But as this road led in the opposite direction, one might suppose that he was running away from Malkeleh altogether. Had Malkeleh ever offended him? Had she hated him? Of course not. On the contrary. Had he hated her? No. She was the only one in the house to whom he had said good-bye. . . .

This thought gave him such a sense of astonishment that he cried out and let the stick fall into the snow. As he picked it up he knew that the blind saint's stick refused to go further. In any case, he had to turn back. There were those impenetrable Talmudic questions which, after months and years of debate, baffled even the great *tannaim* so completely that they said *Takah*! This meant: let us adjourn the debate until the advent of the Messiah, when all problems will be solved. This was such a case in Sholem's life. That was the message of the stick. And it was right, for Sholem had to retrace his steps, so that his eyes might be opened in other directions as well, to say nothing of the fact that it was Friday, and that he did not reach home until noon.


The house was empty, strange, deserted. On other days the yard resounded to the noise and laughter of the children; now the only sound was the screechy moan of the saw as Janos worked away on the logs. Sholem had a sense of disquiet. Was it that unpleasant sound, or the mere presence of this stranger? Sholem went up to him, stood watching him for awhile, then asked him whether he had fed the pony. Janos muttered an affirmative without raising his head. Sholem felt that the man was resentful for having to work for him. He had never had a servingman before. In an attempt to be friendly, he asked whether the stable was warm enough of a night. Janos, without changing either his bearing or his voice, replied that he had brought the rugs down from the loft and they kept him warm. Sholem said that he had acted wisely, but hoped that Janos did not make a light or smoke in the stable. Janos shook his head.

Sholem was about to ask at what time the *tsaddik* and Sroleh Yomtov had left, but thought better of it. After all, he already knew more than Janos, knew even the direction they had taken. In any case, why initiate him into the affairs of the family. So, instead, he asked the man what was his name.

"Janos," was the reply.

"Janos what?"

The man raised his stubbled face.

"Janos Nyirhubai," he said in a low, faltering voice.

Sholem gazed into his strange, restless eyes and wondered where he had seen him before.

"Do you belong to this district?" he asked.

"No, sir, I come from the Nyirseg."

Sholem went away, deciding not to bother at a time like this who the man was. He hastened into the inn, where Aunt Feiga tried to give an account of the morning's business. Serf So-and-so had a quarter-pint, Farmer So-and-so half a pint. Before that, some one had had a tot of rye, and another some one a drop of potato whisky, but she could not remember who they were. She would think of it later, no time now to rack her brain when she had so much to do. It was nearly Sabbath and she had to mud-plaster the kitchen floor and it would never dry, and why in heaven was she left in charge of the inn on such a day.

"Janos!" she screeched. "Get me some horse manure for the plaster. Put on a hot foot, you. Were you never in the army?"

Sholem took out his bunch of keys to open the drawer behind the bar, which contained the takings and the tally sticks. He turned the key in the lock hesitantly, his brain completing a thought that had begun in the morning, but broke off in the middle. It was a tormenting thought. He remembered how, the previous evening, the boy had left the gentry's room not by the door leading to the yard, but by the one leading to the bar parlor. Now, as Sholem was slowly pulling the drawer out, the unwelcome suspicion forced itself to the fore that the boy had come here to take away the cash, or what remained of nearly six months' takings. A hundred-odd florins it was, not a great deal, but for a business started without a copper it was an important sum. Of course, the boy, being a partner, had a key of his own. And, reflected Sholem, he was entitled to the money, for everything with which he, Sholem, had started had belonged to the boy. Yet it was a tormenting thought. Sholem's fingers were trembling as he reached into the drawer.

But the hand paused in mid-air. Sholem stared down into the drawer. The money was there in the compartmented tin box in the corner. And beside the box lay a bundle of banknotes, a big bundle. Could he believe his eyes? Why, these red-bellied ones were for a hundred each, these were fifties, twenties, tens, paper florins . . . And here were a few silver thalers. And here was a scrap of paper, covered with spidery Hebrew script. Sholem looked at the signature: "Sroleh Yomtov *hahkatan*"—Sroleh Yomtov, Minor. Of course, this was the boy's handwriting, written here the previous night with the diluted ink. The characters were clumsy and restlessly irregular, now bigger, now smaller, but always slanting upwards. They seemed to be dancing before Sholem's eyes. Or were his hands still trembling as he read?

Sholem, I was not telling the truth. Leizer Lazarovich did not give me credit. Rothbart too wanted cash. The money that came in last autumn was in my hands and there is still seven hundred and eighty-one florins and forty kreuzers left. I leave it all for the business. If it is not enough because the winter might be longer and the peasants drink more, you'll get credit in the summer. Go on buying from Reb Leizer, for his goods are more reliable. If necessary you can ask Mendl of Nameny for the loan of a hundred or two, he will let you have it gladly till next autumn. If you are shy, send Malkeleh to talk with Golda. Don't ask your brother-in-law because he has a lot of money. If he refuses, it will be bad, if he gives, they won't be so nice to Malkeleh. I did not say good-bye to you because you would have said not to go away. Malkeleh is right: if one wants to be something better than an inn-keeper he must see the world and learn things.

Sholem's first reaction was a sense of shame. He had supposed that Sroleh Yomtov had taken the money away, whereas he had done the very opposite, leaving his own money as well, though there was no obligation on him. Sholem had never felt so disgraced in his life, disgraced and humiliated. That immature boy had risen far above him—above him, Sholem ben Yoirish, who held diplomas from three famous and saintly rabbis, certifying that he was not only learned, but also of unimpeachable morality. It hurt, badly. His face was aflame, as though the boy had thrown the money into it. His body felt as if he had been whipped. He strained to think of a verse in the Torah that would serve as balm for his wound, that would mitigate his great humiliation, but could think of nothing.

How fortunate that Malkeleh was not there to witness how small her husband had become. Sroleh Yomtov, "the Minor," had taken the money out of his pocket and had attained greatness. Sholem had received this heap of money and had thereby become poor. He, Sholem, had everything, a house, a business, a secure living and future: the boy had nothing, not even a roof over his head; yet what a difference in the boy's favor!

Feiga kept calling him to his dinner, saying that the potatoes and goose cracklings were getting cold. He sat down and ate mechanically, deaf to the old woman's lamentations. He did not really hear her until she began to talk about "that rascal," who kissed Malkeleh's hand the day before and said good-bye, whereas it was not Malkeleh, but she, Feiga, that raised him from the dirt, not Malkeleh but she, silly old Feiga, that nursed him. Sholem for a moment thought that he ought to defend "that rascal," but he said nothing.

Back behind the bar, he counted the money. In the end he just hid it away at the bottom of the drawer, forgetting the amount.

Then he re-read the letter, mumbling to himself and shaking his head. He was no longer interested in the contents, only in the form of the note, gazing at it with a superior smile. A good boy, but how untutored. His note was full of spelling mistakes. He had written down Malkeleh's name thrice, each time with a different spelling, and always using a *koph*, which looked like the outline of a monkey, instead of a *choph*, which resembled an open hand— a true symbol of Malkeleh's generous nature.

Sholem regretted that Sroleh Yomtov was not there to be told all about his mistakes, to be told, in particular, that whereas if properly spelt Malkeleh's name meant queen, the way he spelt it it resembled the word "flogging." Forty strokes was the punishment, so long as the Temple stood, of the profligate son, and of him who had raised his eyes to another's wife. Of course, you could not charge Sroleh Yomtov with profligacy. Had he not kept last year's takings for the business, down to the last copper? As to women, well, he was angry with Golda for kissing him, although she was a relation. He had kissed Malkeleh's hand the day before, but that was only a mark of respect. Otherwise he used to lower his eyes, as befits a modest Jewish boy, whenever he spoke to Malkeleh. True, at table, the boy would covertly look across at Malkeleh and there was a light in his eyes. But then, Malkeleh was such a sweet woman. That was the way he himself used to look at her when he was eating "days" at Manasseh Nikolsburger's house. Of course, that was different, for Malkeleh was then still unwed, and his, Sholem's, name was already entered beside hers in the heavenly marriage broker's register.

SONG OF SONGS

THE SAW in the yard started to squeal again, and the strange noise startled him out of the thoughts which he ought not to think. He went to the window, a strange heaviness in his chest. His brain too seemed to be simmering. He pressed his brow to the cold pane, staring through the glass, without awareness, at the busy handy-

man. The saw was squealing, moaning, faltering, saying something
inarticulately. What was it saying? Why, it was complaining that
it had lost a dent or two. Sholem was pleased to have thus interpreted the sounds of the old saw. His brain was calming down,
he was thinking of everyday affairs and that was good. He must
buy another saw, and soon, because one must not torment even
an animal with a bad tool, let alone a human being. He would send
Janos to town for the saw. But was he intelligent enough for that
sort of thing? Then he noticed something that he had already seen
before, when he was wondering where he had come across this
man before. His strange eyes . . . The observation hit him right
between the eyes. Why, the man had one dark brown eyebrow
and one blond eyebrow! That was why his gaze looked so strange
and restless—that, and the fact that he was in hiding. Sholem had
never seen the man before, but he had often visualized him, though
Lieutenant Eberle's description of him had been brief as a military
command. This was no Janos, Nyirhubai or other, but . . . what
name did the Lieutenant say? Oh yes! Beni Darazs—deserter.

Sholem raised his fist and struck out into the air. He looked
fierce, without a trace of the gentle Talmudist in his bearing.
So this was the sort of man Sroleh Yomtov brought into the house!
He and Malkeleh had put their heads together and had hired this
shady character. What a calamity! It might bring disaster not only
to the family, but to the whole of Jewry. Sholem was in a fighting
mood. Wrenching the window open with a furious hand, he
cried:

"Janos, come here!"

But his fury had already abated. When he first put his hand on
the latch he meant to say, "Beni Darazs, come here!" But the window was stuck and he had to tug hard to get it open, and some
of his anger evaporated in the process. When at last the handyman
stood before him and he saw how scared and how down-at-heel
he was, there was little of the anger left, though he kept his voice
stern:

"Your name is Janos, what?"

"Yes, sir."

"Janos Nyirhubai?"

"Yes, sir."

"Hum! Janos Nyirhubai . . . Do you know where Otvar is?"

"Yes, sir."

"And you know the Imperial barracks there?"

"Yes, sir."

This was said in a low voice, barely audible. The man's lips were trembling. Sholem had a fleeting vision of the *tsaddik's* lower lip, and the mouth was saying: "What do you want of this unfortunate man?" Sholem's heart softened. He had meant to unmask the deserter, but didn't. Why, the poor fellow might have been very badly treated in the army. Sholem smiled inwardly at the way his anger had passed, and again as he recalled the instructions of Lieutenant Eberle: "You'll bring or send him in to me at Otvar." With the best will in the world, Sholem could not take the deserter in, for he was alone in the inn, and it would be Sabbath soon. On the other hand . . . Sholem reached into the drawer and took out some money.

"Look, my son," he said. "Here are twelve florins. You'll take them to the barracks at Otvar, hand them to Lieutenant Eberle and tell him the money's from the Jew Sholem at Lapfalva, in payment of the tolerance tax on behalf of himself and his family. Do you understand?"

"Yes, sir."

"You'll ask for a receipt and bring it back."

"I'll ask for a receipt and bring it back."

"And here is another florin. You'll buy a new saw, because the old one is useless, isn't it?"

"Yes, sir."

"And here is still another florin for expenses. That is fourteen florins in all. You know what for?"

"Yes, sir. Twelve for tax, one for a saw, and one for expenses."

"Right," approved Sholem. "I can see you're a clever fellow. Now go in to Aunt Feiga and ask for some food—goose cracklings and bread. That's for the journey. If the Lieutenant shouldn't be in Otvar, you can stay for a day and wait for him."

The man was turning to go, but Sholem recalled him. He was thinking of going down into the cellar for the hidden bayonet and sending it to Otvar by Janos. But he remembered in time that his instructions were to take the deserter's weapons away from him, not return them to him.

"It's all right," he said with a gesture of dismissal. "It'll be all right if you return on Monday—Janos Nyirhubai."

As the man turned out of the gate, Sholem looked after him to see whether he was making for Otvar. He would not have been surprised if Janos had taken the Karoly road, but he was in fact walking with long strides towards the Otvar road. Feiga came in grumbling why Sholem must send the handyman away on the Sabbath eve, when she had already told Serf Matolcs, who used to stroke the fire on the Sabbath, that he need not call any more. Now she must go and find that serf or find another Sabbath-*goy*. Sholem took no notice of the old woman's grumbling. He felt that he had done the right thing. He filled his lungs with the cold air that came in through the window and stretched himself. All was well now that the danger had been averted. Beni Darazs had left and Janos Nyirhubai would never return.

Sroleh Yomtov had left him in the lurch and had given him a serving-man to take his place. And Malkeleh too meant him to be looked after in her absence. Well, he did not want to be provided for like a child. He must know of everything that went on in the house, and he must be the first to know. And he wanted no help, either at the inn or in the house. He would even cut all the firewood required for weeks ahead—and with that faulty saw, too. Let Malkeleh see who Sholem ben Yoirish really was.

In an hour it would be Sabbath. There was a humming silence in the house. Sholem found the big leather-bound book and turned up the Song of Songs, which was about love and the joys and sorrows of love. Was it about earthly love? By no means. Nearly two thousand years before, the great *tannai*, Rabbi Akiba, had interpreted the true meaning of this great poem. God himself was the Lover and Israel the Bride. The Song of Songs spoke of God's yearning and wistful love for the People of the Torah. And the Babylonian *Targum* had found other profundities between the flowery lines of the poem.

It was Israel's destiny, from the Exodus to the Conquest, the exile, the advent of the Messiah and the Restoration. "Make haste, my beloved, and be thou like to a roe or to a young hart upon the mountains of spices." Sholem gazed down at the characters on the yellow, frayed pages of the *siddur*, then he closed his eyes and chanted by heart:

> "Let him kiss me with the kisses of his mouth,
> For thy love is better than wine."

But perhaps for the first time in his life, he did not chant with the awareness that this was an obligatory recital for the Sabbath Eve. He was not thinking of Rabbi Akiba and the canonical decisions of the *tannaim*. He was not thinking of God and his beloved people. He was not thinking of the Torah, the essence and content of heavenly love. He was not thinking, either, of the Babylonian *Targum*, or of the roe that had been hasting millennially, to come to rest on the mountains of spices. He was simply not thinking of the allegorical significance of the poem.

He was thinking only of Malkeleh, with whom he had spent every Friday evening for more than ten years, and who had now gone away. How hasty he had been to let her go. Would it not have been better to postpone her journey till Sunday? He saw Malkeleh, more beautiful through the journey, the cold and the dusk. He saw her entry into Karoly, like some Esther-ha-Malkah, to the gay tinkling of the sleigh-bells. And his heart was filled with indignation and resentment, nay, with righteous anger, against the brat who had dared to put that monkey letter into Malkeleh's name thrice over. He was aware of his own superiority, and he went on chanting, and for once understanding, the torments of earthly love.

## THE BOY MAILECH

NO ONE in the house any longer mentioned Reb Issur, the genial, wise, mysterious guest whom Sholem called Rabbi "Must-Not." Only Sholem thought of him sometimes. When there was an accumulation of trouble, or of Talmudic problems that seemed to be beyond him, Sholem hoped that the *tsaddik* would appear

again. But he never did. There were plenty of other visitors:
pilgrims, market venders, soothsayers, knife throwers, chanting
beggars with mutilated bodies, card sharpers, pickpockets, actors,
bear tamers; discharged soldiers and deserters, poachers and
bandits, drovers and itinerant glaziers, Slovak potmenders and
journeyman artisans, blood-letters and purveyors of enlightenment to the serfs; and mingled with this kaleidoscope of humanity,
yet somehow apart, there came the Jews, all sorts and conditions
of them: young and old, well-shod and barefoot, saintly and un-
saintly; rabbis and rabbinical students, *schnorrers*, marriage
brokers, carriers, produce buyers, contractors, and peddlers;
strangers from Russia, the Bukovina and Galicia, and strangers
from other parts of Hungary, for Gershom counted as a stranger
even in his native land; in between Jew and Gentile, yet blending
with the endless procession, were the gypsies, gypsies with hooded
wagons, gypsy tinsmiths, gypsy musicians; and there were Jewish
"gypsies" too, who came playing their fiddles and singing in
Yiddish, Hebrew, Russo-Polish, or a mixture of all three. In the
course of the years all sorts and conditions of people came and
went at such an inn. The more remote it lay from the main routes,
and the more primitive and neglected the tracks leading to it, the
more variegated was its clientele. The memory of the casual
customers of one day, with their foibles, antics, and yarns, was
overlaid by the impressions of those of the next.

But Sroleh Yomtov was not forgotten. They talked about him
and were eloquently silent about him—and always they were
waiting for him to return. This waiting had become a permanent
state, yet it still held a degree of confidence. He had given no
sign of life, yet they were sure that he was alive and well and
would turn up one day. Only old Feiga complained that she
could not wait much longer.

"I buried his father and mother and three of his brothers and
sisters," she would grumble, "but it doesn't enter the young
rascal's head that Aunt Feiga too might want to die at last."

However, Feiga did not die. Perhaps she did not want to. Each
year she shrunk another inch, her spectacles became less and less
translucent, the eye of the needle narrower and narrower, and
the thread more and more tangled. But she did not feel like de-

parting until she had an opportunity to give that naughty boy a thorough scolding, that naughty boy who, since he left without saying good-bye to her, was getting naughtier and naughtier each day.

Sroleh Yomtov's departure became the first important chronological milestone. "It happened before Sroleh Yomtov went away," they used to say. Or: "The dog Bakter vanished at the same time as Sroleh Yomtov." Or: "The peasants made Sholem's brother, Gimpel Zorech, look like a *goy*—that was two years after Sroleh Yomtov ran away." However, now they were talking about a fresh event: the departure of Mailech. That was not so exciting, though, for Mailech only went to the *yeshiba*, and not even to a distant place, as Sholem would have liked, only to Karoly, to study under Rabbi Isaac Frenkel. But there had been some excitement nevertheless, for Malkeleh was vehemently opposed to letting the ten-year-old boy leave home, and now, whenever there was a difference of opinion in the house she began with how pig-headed Sholem had been that time and how rashly he had settled his son's affairs in the strange town.

Mailech's departure marked the beginning of the second chronological era. But there were other, minor milestones, relating to a birth or some more or less exciting happening in the history of the inn or the village. It was at the beginning of the second year that Balazs Patyodi, the pandour sergeant with the big moustache, and three of his men billeted themselves at the inn, they being in pursuit of the bandit Bereg and his band. Bandits—or men supposed to be such—and any suspicious tramps were brought to the inn in chains, and the interrogations took place in the yard, with hazel switches, pummelling, and much bawling. The bawling of the pandours generally almost drowned the screams of their victims. The family withdrew into the house and stayed there in horrified seclusion. The evening, when the pandours jumped into the saddle, brought no relief, for the darkness was often rent by shouting and firing. The bandit Bereg was not caught, but little Manasseh, who was born eight weeks later, was weak and sickly. Aunt Seemah, Golda's mother, said that it had come to her as a revelation, while she was reading the women's Bible one Saturday afternoon, why the boy stuttered: because he had heard the interrogation whilst still in his mother's womb. At seven months the baby was already listening through the wall that separates it from the outside world, and it identified itself with the sufferers. This was a pleasing explanation and it consoled Malkeleh somewhat in her sadness that the child named after the great Manasseh Nikolsburger should be the one that stuttered. By contrast, his daughter's memory made him into a silver-tongued orator.

The memorable events of the third winter were linked with "The Battle of Ecsed." At that time the gentry used to go to Ecsed to gamble at cards with the Baron. One evening old de Denghelegh had a bad run, losing all his ready cash long before midnight. To stop the contest at that early hour was not to be thought of, and in any case the Baron was prepared to go on playing for other stakes. The lands lying between Ecsed and Denghelegh were staked and lost one after another, and even the old man's favorite mount, Borcsa, changed masters. Towards dawn de Denghelegh, who was supported by de Gyekeny, had lost the village of Lapfalva as well, together with all the serfs that dwelt therein. As he made to rise, his host said:

"Have another go—the bank against your Jew."

"Huh," said de Denghelegh, "my Jew's worth a lot of money."

"Well, let's have two goes for him."

"All right, I'll stake the Jew."

Old de Denghelegh lost and lost again. He had to hand over the Jew as well as his favorite mare, and the village, and the serfs. Of course, there was some legal wrangling. The old man was quite willing to pay his debt of honor, but all he could do immediately was to deliver Borcsa to the Baron, for de Sarberek objected that the village, the serfs, and the inn were all the joint property of the gentry. The Baron was not in a hurry about the village and the serfs, it being the slack season for labor, so he let de Sarberek go to law about them. But he was in urgent need of the Jew, because his Jew, Jonas, had gone down with rheumatics and was scarcely able to lift a brandy glass, wherefore the Baron sent his *haiduks* along to collect Sholem for him. They left the family behind for the present, because in the heat of the "battle" the Baron had failed to stipulate that he wanted the Jew together with his family, and there had been no time for a court of honor to give a ruling in the matter. So Malkeleh, who was then nursing little Yoirish, had to manage the inn as best she could. The upset lasted for several weeks, and Sholem was not allowed to return home even for the Sabbath without a special petition. In the end de Sarberek, realizing that he had little chance against his powerful neighbor before the county authorities, challenged him to a *revanche*, staking the manor of Sarberek and the surrounding lands. The Baron accepted the challenge. The battle raged with varying fortune for two days and nights. But the final round (and thereby "The Second Battle of Ecsed") was won by de Sarberek. Brocsa trotted back to Denghelegh, while Sholem was brought back to Lapfalva as a trophy of war. He was not particularly proud of the high value that had been placed upon him at the card table, but (as amid all his other troubles) he saw a silver lining in the incident, for the Jew Jonas had meanwhile sufficiently recovered to resume the management of his business.

When was it that Sroleh Yomtov went away? A long, long time ago. Sarah Chayah was six last winter. She now had three younger brothers. One of them was only just beginning to talk, but the other two were already chanting passages from the Pentateuch and, at the important places, even the small-lettered commentary of Rashi. And when Mailech came home on a visit, his father made him examine the boys, Manasseh, Yosseleh, and Yossel Beilah Yentes, the adopted one, to see whether they had grasped the implacable attitude of Moses to the transgressions of his flock.

Of course, Mailech was not too enthusiastic about playing the examiner, nor was he particularly suitable for the task. The theme used to slip out of his hands, and the other boys used to ply him with irrelevant questions. If they hadn't destroyed the golden calf, would none but golden cattle have been born ever since? What sort of medicine did the High Priest prescribe for a house to drink when it was leprous? And say, Mailech, Aaron's staff was of sunflower stalk, wasn't it? Everyone laughed, including Mailech. Only Sholem shook his head disapprovingly. He expected Mailech to be more serious-minded and strict. He had been studying in Karoly for nearly a year, and soon he would

be praying with phylacteries and count as an adult. How far
ahead he, Sholem, had been at that age, though his father had
been an ignorant small-holding peasant, while Mailech's father
was a man of learning. When Sholem came home on a visit from
the *yeshiba*, he had to help with the digging and hoeing and the
stripping of maize cobs, while Mailech could do at home just
what he did at the *yeshiba*. One would expect that he would be
analyzing the weighty sentences of Maimonides, yet he was more
interested in the market venders' stuffs, red- and green-handled
knives, whetstones and grindstones, than in the polished theses of
the great *Rambam*. He slunk away whenever he could to mix with
the peasants. And for weeks after he had returned to Karoly they
would curse him for having, "with his sly Jewish tricks," enticed
the coppers out of their pockets—for a wretched strop or a
tobacco knife which they were to praise for years to come.

Sholem also grumbled because he had heard that on Tuesdays
and Fridays Mailech did not go near the *yeshiba*. Tuesday was
the weekly market day in Karoly and Mailech spent it helping his
landlord, Avram Kolb, to pack and unpack his piece goods, and
guarding the goods against thieves during the busy hours. Also,
when there were loiterers near by who were merely gazing across
at the treasures in the stall, his small face, greenish-yellow like an
unripe apple in winter, and freckled in summer, would distort
into a smile and he would entice them to come nearer with an
insinuating chant: "Stuff for a lovely skirt, Madam. . . . Fine
spotted Viennese headkerchiefs, Mother . . ." If they took no
notice, Mailech would observe the women's dresses, as well as
their faces, or would strain his ears to catch their low-toned talk
among themselves. He had a keen eye in judging who and what
the prospective customers were. Why, those women over there
had the folds differently arranged on their skirts and the wrinkles
on their faces were different too. Of course, they were Swabians,
old settlers from Gencs, Kaplony, and Fabian, and he must talk
in German to them. So his high-pitched treble rose: *Kimt, kimt!
Feine war, schaine war, billich und gut. Kimt Mudder, kimt schain
datsch Madele!* . . .

On Wednesday and Thursday Mailech was back at the *yeshiba*,
chanting away at the Talmud. "Saith Rabbi Poppah . . . Saith

Rabbi Tarphon . . ." But on Friday he was helping out in Mordechai Nikolsburger's ink factory, secretly learning the mysteries
of ink-making, and what was more important, the tricks of busi-
ness-getting. His uncle gave him no pay, but the first year he
gave him his food on Saturdays, and the second year on Fridays
as well.

Sholem, of course, was secretly hoping that Mailech would
outdo him both in piety and learning. And if at Sabbath dinner
Mailech talked to Yossef about the price of oak-gall, or to his
mother and Yiteleh about the difference between cloths dyed in
Vienna and Breslau respectively, his father would silence him,
not infrequently with irritation. One should talk about higher
things at the festive table: of the Pentateuch and the Books of the
Prophets, of the profound theses of the Talmud, of the lives of
biblical and Talmudic researchers. He who even at one of the
"Three Meals" babbled about business would never taste the
heavenly manna. Such an erring one might develop into a trickster
battening on the peasants, or even into a clever business man, but
from the higher point of view he would for ever remain a boor.

Mailech would smile at this, and being prepared for such crit-
icisms, he would have his defense ready. He always had one or
two striking Talmudic anecdotes, similes, parables, or debating
brilliancies which he had picked up especially for his father's
benefit, not so much in the *yeshiba* itself as among the learned
portion of the market venders. Sometimes he argued so boldly
that it verged on the improper and even on that which was forbidden. Once, when discussing the life of the Patriarch Jacob
(with Malkeleh nodding approval, or perhaps only glinting approval with her eyes), Mailech argued that in the *Haggadah* for
Passover the clever one of the four boys was given first place, and
that this could only mean that piety was not necessarily linked
with helplessness. So long as Jacob was only pious and god-fear-
ing, Laban the Aramite exploited and cheated him. But then
Jacob learned a lesson from the cheat, and thereafter it was he
who took Laban in. If he had not learned to get the better of
others, where would he have got so many hundreds of sheep,
camels, and asses, how could he have provided for his four wives,
thirteen children, and countless servants, and how could he have

bought off Esau and Eliphaz whenever they sought his life? Sholem himself burst into laughter, so the whole table joined in. Mailech, thus encouraged, grew even bolder. Sholem became more reserved, kept shaking his head, hum-hummed once or twice, but said nothing. When he at last opened his mouth, it was to eject a single word: "*Apikores!*"

The term in Maccabean times meant a Jew of Hellenic mentality, a renegade who, in contrast with the faithful *chassidim*, had adopted the hedonistic teachings of Epicurus. In the course of the centuries, the Greek philosopher's name became a term of reproof in the mouths of Jewish fathers, and it struck the sons like a whip, provided, of course, they were not already "epicures" in spirit, and traitors to their people and faith.

Mailech realized that his father did not approve of him, and not being an "epicure" in spirit, he felt that the environment in which he was living, though desirable and even alluring, could not be quite satisfactory. When he smiled or laughed in his father's face, it was not with a sense of superiority, but rather with a timid expectancy. He liked to argue with his father for he was sorely intrigued by his severity when it came to principles, in contrast with his gentleness in practice, and he was burning to get to the bottom of things. But at the end of every argument he was confronted by an overwhelmingly powerful and mysterious will: it is so, and must be so. Sholem used to close the argument with hard, millennial judgments, and they left the boy inarticulate. In the mornings, when the inn was as yet empty, and Sholem held a class behind the bar, the children often grew tired of listening to his recital and explanation of the six hundred and thirteen laws, commandments and prohibitions, but they were not allowed to show it. On one occasion Mailech looked out through the window and said:

"The mulberry tree is blossoming."

"It is not," snapped Sholem.

"But really, Dad," said Mailech. "Have a look."

"The blossoms are here," said Sholem, pointing at the book.

"But there are some on the mulberry tree as well; they are quite big."

"Mailech," said Sholem reproachfully, "you did not read the Ethics of the Fathers last Sabbath."

Mailech was surprised. Surely, he had read the chapter for that week?

"I did," he said vehemently.

"If you had," pursued Sholem, "you ought to know."

"Know what?"

"He who during study," quoted Sholem, "saith: how beautiful is this tree or how beautiful is this meadow, hath sold his salvation."

Mailech remembered the sentence which he had read through mechanically. But he did not understand.

"What does it mean—sold his salvation?" he asked in a scared tone.

"He won't go to heaven."

"How's that?"

"He won't be wakened at the resurrection."

"Mustn't you praise the tree?" Mailech burst out. "Wasn't the tree created by God?"

"You may praise the tree," cried Sholem in consternation, "but not during your sacred reading."


It had happened after Mailech had returned from his first visit to Karoly. This was a great event to the five-year-old boy, not only because it was his first experience of a town, but also because he left it laden with gifts. Aunt Blimeleh gave him a jews' harp, Uncle Mordechai a purse with two compartments, into each of which he put a new kreuzer, thereby laying the foundations of his greatness in Mailech's eyes. For years after, the boy thought of him as of a great lord. However, the boy did not keep the money, but bought licorice-root for one kreuzer, and a pocket-knife with a red handle for the other, so that he could cut up the root into small bits and make it last longer.

The presents created a sensation in the village and the peasant boys competed with each other to acquire them. Janos Galagonya offered half a dozen eggs for the jews' harp, while Bence Topoly bid three for the pocket-knife. But Mailech hesitated to part with his treasures. After all, his mother's hens also laid eggs, but where could he get a pocket-knife that was not only beautiful but sharp as well, so that he could cut himself a popgun and even a flute with it? Nor would he part with the jews' harp, which fitted between his lips so snugly, and on which he was already able to tweet out the tune of the Sabbath-speeding hymn: "A star has risen from Jacob. . . . Fear not, my servant Jacob." Gero Ludpal offered seven eggs for the instrument, and a handful of sunflower seed. He was the most suitable person to have possession of it, his father being the bellringer of three villages, so that when the latter happened to be on the villenage, it was he, Gero, who attended to the bellringing, and it was he who chose the companion to help him tug at the rope in the belfry. However, Mailech shook his head: not for sale. Then the affair began to take a more violent turn. Pista, son of Headman Mate Bor, declared that all Jews were cheats, and the other boys noisily agreed with him. Mailech merely smiled, but the smile froze when the Ludpal boy said that the Jews had crucified Christ and had to be exterminated and their property taken away from them. Mailech retired from the argument, ran home, and did not play the jews' harp that day. At midday he scarcely touched his food. In the afternoon, in class behind the bar, he did not attend, and did not reply to his father's questions. Sholem reproved him, but the boy merely raised his hazel eyes, which somehow seemed tearful.

"Is anything the matter?" asked his father.

"No, Dad. . . . But is it true that the Jews killed the rabbi of the *goyim*?"

"Who told you that?" said Sholem in a startled tone.

"Gero Ludpal."

"Who told him?"

"He knows because he used to ring the bell in the church."

Sholem went into the bar parlor and looked out of the window towards the village. He returned behind the bar and knocked the tobacco out of his pipe. He unwound his tobacco pouch, rewound it again and replaced it in his pocket without filling his pipe.

"No one," he said earnestly, gazing down at the child, "no one can say that he knows. Not even the priest. No, not even the Emperor in Vienna or the Pope in Rome." He turned a few pages in the tome lying on the table, as though searching for something. But he did not look at the pages; perhaps the feel of them between his fingers gave him moral support. "The Gemarah," he said, "had the whole story, the true story, just the way it really happened. But the Government had the pages torn out and burned, so that no one should know anything for certain, and so that we should never be able to defend ourselves." He closed the book with a snap, then went on: "They say what they say so that we should never have any rest upon earth. But we never had the blood of a brother on our hands, either then, or before, or since."

Mailech was staring at his father with childish wonderment. He seemed to be expecting to see the words that fell from his lips. He kept thinking about them all that day, and even after he had gone to bed, though he could not formulate the thought. But by the morning he had forgotten about his mental efforts, though there was still a trace of something vaguely disturbing at the back of his mind. Extracting the jews' harp from his trousers pocket and cleaning it of the breadcrumbs that had stuck to it, he tried to play a tune. But the instrument was not the same as it had been. In vain did he suck in the air the way the market people had done, in vain did he vibrate the little blue steel flap, the jews' harp had lost its sweet twangy sound. It even failed to reproduce the tune of "Fear not, my servant Jacob." Besides, Aunt Feiga was scolding him not to mess about with that grunty thing. It wasn't fit for a Jewish boy, whose mouth should be full with prayer and Psalms, not with a noisy instrument, unless he was a peddler, and even then he should use a plain whistle.

The old woman's grumbling cheered him up. Now he knew what to do. He ran out into the village, mixing with the serf boys and provoking the resumption of the bargaining. He pretended to hesitate, but in the end he sold the knife to Feri Gore for four eggs and a hatful of pumpkin seed, and the jews' harp to Jancsi Galagonya for eight eggs. Gero Ludpal had offered nine eggs, but Mailech would not sell it to him even for ten. The Galagonya boy, to compensate him for the difference, gave him a reed pipe he used when guarding the geese. Mailech sold the eggs the same day to Zalman the ribbon Jew. The three and a half *groschen* he received he kept counting over and over again, until he worked it

out that he could buy two jews' harps and three pocket knives
with the money at Karoly, so one harp, two knives and a hatful of
pumpkin seed was clear profit. The reed pipe was also worth
something. That day he played a tune on it near the Sarberek
mansion. The Squire's boy came out and said contemptuously:
"Jew boy, what's for sale?" This was meant to taunt him, but
Mailech felt flattered. "What's for sale, young master?" he replied.
"Why, a lovely purse with two compartments." The young master was taken aback, but he looked at the new purse and liked it.

The young master paid in cash, with a big four-kreuzer piece.
On one side of it you could still discern the image of the Empress,
with whom great-grandfather David Levi Nikolsburger used to
do such good business. Mailech took the coin home and polished
it up to a bright golden color with ash and stone dust, then, together with the rest of his treasure, he tied it into a corner of his
handkerchief and hid it away in a secret place. Not until six
months later, when his mother took him to Karoly again, did he
go to his hoard. He would have liked to spend at least one kreuzer
on sweets, but restrained himself and invested the whole of his
capital in goods. After his third visit to Karoly he had fifty-seven
kreuzers—three short of a whole florin. Meanwhile, he had been
set upon several times, had had the dogs set on him now and then,
and on one occasion, while trading in the next village, he had been
robbed of his stock. But Zalman the ribbon Jew explained to him
that all this was no more to a Jewish peddler than it was to a
tailor to prick his finger with his needle. Since then Mailech considered these business troubles as natural and did not even complain about them at home. . . .

When the fourth baby to be born at Lapfalva arrived, the house
began to be too small for the family, and Sholem had suggested
that Mailech should be sent to the *yeshiba* in Karoly. Malkeleh
opposed him for a long time, but for once Sholem proved stubborn. He took every opportunity to insist that Mailech's mind was
not on his learning here at home, that he fidgeted during the
lessons, with his ears strained to hear the doorbell and would
bound behind the bar to serve a customer, then skip outdoors to
play with the village boys. They were not the right company for
Mailech, said Sholem. That the boy was not with the serf boys,

but with the "hair Jew," the trough-seller Jew, the whistling Jew, or some other itinerant Jew, was beside the point. All Sholem saw, with increasing anxiety, was that Mailech was inclined to truancy. It was probably because a father could not long maintain his authority, being incapable of the necessary strictness in the long run. Besides, the inn, with wine casks and bottles of spirits all around, was not a suitable setting for study, even where there were no peasants smoking, spitting, and cursing in the bar parlor.

"Also you can't help admitting this, Malkeleh—the boy has no suitable company here. The Gore boys, Serf Vizhordo's brats and the Ludpal brats—why, they'd roast every Jew alive." He was somewhat lonely within the family too, Yiteleh being five years older, Sarah Chayah five years younger, while Yossef was already a young man. Under the eyes of Rabbi Isaac Frenkel, author of *Zeved Tob*, and among scholars of his own age, Mailech would be sure to change.

"Very well, Sholem," said Malkeleh one day, borne down by the weight of her husband's arguments. "Take your ten-year-old son to the *yeshiba*. But when you get to Karoly, you must go and see Mordechai first thing."

"I know what to do." Sholem said.

Karoly was a great disappointment to Sholem. He had taken it for granted that Mordechai and his wife would take Mailech in. He was supposed to be a favorite with them, for apart from the color of his eyes, he was the image of his mother, a real Nikolsburger. However, this time, it was not a matter of a copper's worth of presents, and Mordechai hummed and hawed, doubting whether it was not too early to send the boy to the *yeshiba*. Blimeleh was also less charming now than when the family had come to stay for a day or two.

"You must think it over, Sholem," she advised, "in the interests of the child. He's not too strong yet and it would be a pity to take him away from his mother."

"His mother has agreed," said Sholem timidly. "But, if you don't want him. . . ."

"That isn't what we mean at all," said Blimeleh more kindly. "If you are determined to have him in Karoly, we'll do everything we can for him."

"He can eat with us every Sabbath," put in Mordechai hastily.

Sholem was about to return home, but Mailech insisted on staying in Karoly, so Sholem drove to Rothbart, bought some spirits from him and got him to give the boy a "day." Then he drove to Joshua Brueder, who in the autumns used to come to Lapfalva to buy the corn Sholem collected from the peasants, and he too promised the boy a "day." A third was promised by the wife of the trough-seller, subject to her husband's consent, who was then away on a business tour. Sholem found lodgings for the boy with Avram Kolb, the draper, who always used to pull up at the inn on his way to and from some fairs. Having attended to all this, Sholem took his son along to the Rabbi. Here he had a further vexation, for Mailech did not shape up very well in the brief examination in the Pentateuch, the commentaries, and the Talmud.

"He's rather timid," explained Sholem.

But Mailech did not appear to be timid at all. When the Rabbi asked him about personal matters, he replied quite promptly. The Rabbi wanted to know what he would like to be when he grew up, a rabbi, a ritual slaughterer, teacher, or *dayan* ("judge"). Mailech was ready with the answer: "None of those. I want to be a business man."

"I see," nodded the Rabbi. Sholem felt disgraced. Mailech's answer betrayed a superficial and faulty training.

"That's wrong, Mailech," he essayed. "You want to be a *talmid hacham*."

"I want to be a business man first of all," insisted the boy.

"First of all, Mailech?" said the Rabbi. "And what next?"

"A *talmid hacham*," laughed the boy.

Rabbi Isaac gave an understanding smile. He could easily forgive the boy for mentioning the essential thing secondarily, and only after outside pressure. Grasping his long beard with one hand, he gave several brief nods with his skull-capped head.

"A Jew must live," he said. "The land belongs to the other peoples. All that's left to the Jews is the road. What can you do on the roads? You can beg, rob, or trade. There are no robbers in Israel. But there are plenty of beggars."

The Rabbi rose and paced to and fro, as though debating something with himself. Then he stopped in front of Sholem, fixing him with his soft, strangely distant gaze.

"Do you know what Rabbi Jehuda Hanassih said to Rabbi Joshua the blacksmith?" It was as though he were now trying to examine the father.

Sholem was embarrassed. He had read about this somewhere, but Rabbi Jehuda the Prince had said so many things to Rabbi Joshua that Sholem could not guess which tome of the Talmud and which debate Rabbi Isaac had in mind. However, Rabbi Isaac did not seem to be expecting a reply, for he went on at once:

"Rabbi Jehuda Hanassih once visited Rabbi Joshua. The blacksmith was in his working clothes, but even in those rags he was still Rabbi Joshua, the *tannai*, the great teacher of Israel. Rabbi Jehuda looked round and observed: 'The walls of your home show your trade.' Rabbi Joshua flushed and replied quietly: 'Prince, you cannot imagine how great is the poverty among *talmideh hachamim.*'"

Rabbi Frenkel resumed his seat in front of an open tome, and sat thinking for awhile. Then:

"Train up a child according to his way," he said briskly, quoting from Proverbs, and his hand reached across the table. Of course, if you thought with the mind of King Solomon, you could see ahead, as well as into the past. In a flash, Sholem became aware of his son's petty dealings, which he had seen but not noted before. And he was content that the boy should become a business man— that would not prevent him from becoming a learned man—even if only secondarily. Surely, it would be better if his learning and trading went together, just as Rabbi Joshua was a blacksmith and a great teacher at the same time. Sholem was glad that Mailech had heard that fine story: it would teach him that a man could be learned even though he wielded a hammer.

"Very well, my son," he said to Mailech as they parted. "You'll stay here." He could not think of any other words of farewell.

And he returned to his village with a contented mind. He had trained his son in the right way after all.

THE SCHNORRER

HOWEVER, THE debate at home did not end with Mailech's departure. Already on the way back Sholem felt that Malkeleh would not be satisfied, though he had done his best for the boy's physical and spiritual welfare. Two "days" and a third promised, lodgings and entrance into the *yeshiba*—what more did the boy need? When he, Sholem, set out for the *yeshiba*, his father saw him to the end of the village. There he shook hands, and bade him go in peace. He started with a single "day." He starved a great deal, but it did not kill him, blessed be the Name. And now he had a family and an inn.

Malkeleh, of course, did not consider her boy's position so reassuring. Sholem's assurances that "all will be well," and "the Above One will help the boy," did not satisfy her.

"You might as well have left him in the forest, the big one where the bandits hang out," she said. "What will he eat in Karoly, where there are no berries, or mushrooms to pick, not even roots to chew when he is hungry? Instead of having a serious talk with Mordechai and Blimeleh, you just left the boy with an utter stranger. You need not be so proud, Sholem ben Yoirish, when it is a matter of your own child's fate."

"First of all, Malkeleh," argued Sholem, "Avram Kolb is no utter stranger. He has been pulling up here for years whenever he goes to market. Secondly—"

Much as he liked to talk with Malkeleh, he was averse to argument with her. That "Sholem ben Yoirish" was a cruel cut. Besides, Malkeleh was careful only that the children should not hear the quarrel, but she cared nothing for God, involving Him in the argument in an almost blasphemous manner.

"You leave everything to the Above One," she cried. "The Above One doesn't want to be overwhelmed with so many commissions. You're the boy's father and it's up to you to look after him."

"Yes," countered Sholem mentally, "but He is the Father of

Fathers." He did not say it, in case Malkeleh came out with something even stronger that would be too much even for the Merciful Father. He went back into the inn among his peasants and to his interminable studies.

In the evening, when the inn was closed and the children had all gone to sleep, Sholem sat opposite the silent Malkeleh, supping his hot borsht.

"Secondly, Malkeleh," he blurted unexpectedly, "I'm not proud. What have I got to be proud of? That my father was a peasant? Or that there are schnorrers in my family?"

His voice betrayed agitation. Malkeleh gave a barely perceptible shrug, but did not reply. Sholem lost his appetite. For the argument was in full swing now, even though both were silent for a long while.

Of course, Sholem knew that Malkeleh was right. He was in fact proud. But why? Our Sages said: "Be near the anointed one and thou shalt become anointed thyself." He was near a proud one, so he was proud himself. Had he dared, he would have told Malkeleh how, before he left Mailech, he had enjoined upon him not to go near the Nikolsburger home, and not to take advantage of their gracious offer of Sabbath meals. He would get those when Zalman returned from his business tour. Meanwhile, he must on a Friday evening join the other poor students by the dais and wait for some *baal-bos* (householder) to invite him for the Sabbath. He need not bother if it became known that the rich Nikolsburger, the chief vestryman, was his uncle. Let them see how the son of a Nikolsburger girl stood in the shadow of the dais, shyly and humbly, just like any other starveling. But of course, Sholem dared not tell this to Malkeleh, either then or later.

Strictly speaking, Malkeleh was never rude to Sholem, but rather refined and tactful in her expressions even in an argument. But through his own penetrating Talmudistic analyses of them, Sholem made them intolerably painful for himself. During their sixteen years of marriage Malkeleh had been personal only once, long before Mailech's departure. But Sholem would feel the hurt of it for the rest of his life. Malkeleh was not in good health; she had pains in the kidneys, having had a difficult delivery with little Manasseh, and already—while still full of bother on account of the weakly infant—expecting her seventh. Some stray beggar came along and brought a rumor that Sroleh Yomtov had died in Moravia of the cholera. The rumor was not confirmed, but Malkeleh took it very much to heart. Sholem knew nothing about this, for he knew precious little about Malkeleh's inner life. All he saw was irritability, and he ascribed it to his own inferior origins. The old argument had never ceased, but now Sholem found himself right in the middle of it. Thoughtlessly, and with gentle self-irony rather than hurtful intent, he brought out a remark that he had often repressed, saying that of course the Nikolsburgers did everything much better.

"Perhaps they ought to learn from Borech and Gimpel Zorech," snapped Malkeleh, flushed with anger.

This was a cruel cut. The more often Sholem thought of it, the more humiliated he felt. If he had been anyone else, he could have hated Malkeleh for it. But in his less sensitive moods Sholem told himself that the truth was more important than anything else. One must, in accordance with the ancient injunction, seek the truth and pursue it, run it down. And the truth here was that Borech and Gimpel Zorech were on the debit side with him. Borech, the wandering beggar, was father Yoirish's brother, and the son of Yossel the drover. When he came to Lapfalva with his knobbly staff and his big, empty carpet-bag, Sholem and the children used to kiss his hand. Of course, there was something about the aged beggar that commanded respect, his cleanliness among other things. The children had no idea what Uncle Borech's occupation was, and he always gave them a kreuzer each before he left. Malkeleh liked him for it, for the old man had to walk miles in snow and mud before he collected a few kreuzers in alms.

On the other hand, there was Gimpel Zorech. He was Sholem's youngest brother, the Benjamin of old Yoirish, and the most unfortunate among his children. That he was a beggar was neither misfortune nor humiliation. Sholem himself had done some begging in his student days. At the end of term he would join up with one or two students and they would go begging over seven counties. Of course, a poor student taking alms was far from being a schnorrer. Even the seasonal beggar was not yet that. Among the Jewish proletariat and peasantry of Maramaros begging was a recognized sideline. The begging was to supplement the meagre income of the summer from casual labor, such as log-floating, gravel-carting, landwork, and the like, and from the produce of a patch of semi-barren land, and it was done only before the great holy days and during the winter. This kind of beggar was a *baal-bos* in his own village, and was really God's tax collector, who was doing other people a favor by enabling them, with much toil and trouble on his part, to square their accounts in heaven. The real schnorrer was he who had given up everything and every one, who had no aim, no higher avocation, who did not think either of the past or the future, and who entered into no permanent ties either with God or with man, but begged to live and lived to beg. Gimpel Zorech was a schnorrer in that sense.

Had Gimpel Zorech not been Sholem's brother, he would have been just another of the unknowns who came from nowhere and vanished into nowhere. They were dirty, lousy, and smelly, and one just threw a copper at them, so as not to have to touch them, and bade them "A good year!" with some olfactory discomfort. But Gimpel Zorech was in fact Sholem's brother, and Sholem was married to a Nikolsburger girl, so it was understandable that the wretched little schnorrer should be in the focus of interest. Indeed, it is no exaggeration to say that Gimpel Zorech made history in the lives of the Jews of Otvar and district.

When old Yoirish died, Gimpel Zorech and his brothers Yiddel and Tovyah took possession of what he left. The inheritance consisted of a timber-built cottage with no chimney, only holes in the roof and under the eaves to let the smoke out; three or four chains of stony land; a wretched old pony and a little cow named Leilach, evidently in honor of the memory of the long-dead mother Leile. Or perhaps they called her Leilach only because the animal was white and angular, just like a sheet hung on the fence to dry, and leilach meant sheet in Yiddish. So long as Yoirish was alive, his authority kept the family in good repute in the village of Trebushan. But then the inheritance was divided up between the three boys and there was trouble, especially with Gimpel Zorech. They all kept together for some months, mainly because Yoirish had died on the second night of the *Shevuoth* holiday, when the heavens are supposed to open for the righteous, and that, according to Sholem, was a propitious sign. They kept together, although they were all married, and although the cottage contained only two more or less habitable rooms, the larger one half filled by the oven, and the smaller one, Yoirish's former bedroom, just big enough to turn round in. During the summer and the mild autumn sleeping accommodation was no problem. There was an extra doss made of rush-mats under the eaves, and this was occupied now by Yiddel and his wife, now by Tovyah and his wife. Gimpel Zorech and his wife slept in a bed by the oven, he—the last-born—being the privileged one of the family.

When the nights grew colder, the three couples drew into the house. The Yiddel and Tovyah pairs slept alternately in the small room and on the floor near the oven, Gimpel Zorech retaining the bed. That was where the fighting began. The brothers were unassuming and indulgent; after all, Gimpel Zorech was the youngest. But in the end Gimpel Zorech considered it intolerable that anyone else should sleep in the same room but himself and his Beilah Yenteh. So the three brothers on the one hand, and the three sisters-in-law on the other, were constantly at each other's throats. All the others blamed Beilah Yenteh, who was better looking and more vigorous than the other two women, and judging by appearances, it really seemed as though she had incited her husband against the other two families. Actually, she was innocent. She loved to sleep, and gave Gimpel Zorech clearly to understand that the night was for sleep and naught else. Gimpel Zorech held different views and tried to convert Beilah Yenteh, at first by persuasion, then with increasing excitement and passion and, towards dawn, with fury. Gimpel Zorech did not mind that there were witnesses to his nocturnal debates and frustrations, but thinking that Beilah Yenteh was more modest than other girls of those parts, he demanded with the obstinacy of the spoilt darling that he should be left alone in the room with her.

So the three families parted. Yiddel got a third of the land and the cart and horse, and went carting goods in the neghboring towns and gravel from the river. Tovyah became a bath attendant at the wooden huts built over the mineral-water springs at Danilov, his task being to put into and extract from the fire the big lumps of granite used to heat the water in the wooden tubs for the well-off bathers. That was how Yiddel and Tovyah supplemented the produce of the infertile mountain land. Gimpel Zorech on his part remained a *baal-bose*. He had the cottage, the cow, and the best corner of the land, which was almost out of the shadow cast by the mountain. That was how old Yoirish had ordained it on his deathbed. However, Gimpel Zorech's brothers were not there to work the land. He did not feel like starting anything on his own, nor would he undertake casual labor. Beilah Yenteh, though herself a hard-working woman, always had to go and borrow potatoes, oil, salt, maize flour, and seed from her sisters-in-law, until finally they grew tired of it. Tovyah's wife once told her that she was short of bread whilst in the very act of cutting slices off a huge loaf of maize bread, while Yiddel's wife refused her with the remark that if she had an oven she should bake her own bread. Beilah Yenteh returned home and gave her husband no supper. Otherwise she was not unkind to him that night. But early in the morning she rose before Gimpel Zorech, went into the wood and cut a strong stick. Then she returned to the cot and chased Gimpel Zorech out of bed with it. When he was dressed she set about him again and drove him out of the house. Finally, she pressed the stick into his hand:

"There you are, I cut it for you. Off you go, to beg! If you can make a child, then go and make some money as well, so it should have enough to eat."

"A child?" mouthed Gimpel Zorech with amazement, nursing the bruises on his body.

"If you come back by *Chanukah* with enough money, I'll have the child waiting for you."

"By *Chanukah*?"

"Yes, by *Chanukah*."

Gimpel Zorech would have liked to know more, but his wife locked herself into the house and refused to answer his questions. Only once did she speak. When her husband asked her to cut him a slice of maize bread for the journey, she cried:

"Haven't got any. Go and beg for wheaten bread; that's much better."

Gimpel Zorech went away and returned for *Chanukah*, bring-

ing a bag of money and a bundle of clean baby clothes. Beilah
Yenteh hid the money under the straw mattress, and threw the
baby clothes into a wooden box among a lot of linen and rags.
When Gimpel Zorech demanded to see the child, she shrugged
her shoulders, saying:

"It hadn't enough to eat. . . . It went before it arrived."

Gimpel Zorech stared at her. But there was a glint in Beilah
Yenteh's wide-spaced eyes, the same sort as the cow Leilach had
when she raised her head and was about to moo, and her tousled
red hair smelled like fresh maize cookies, so Gimpel Zorech forgave her for losing his child. She gave him three weeks in which
to have his laze and his time with her, then she again pressed the
stick into his hand:

"If you'll get me some money, the child'll be here by Tabernacles. But you can come back sooner; at least you'll help in the
field."

Gimpel Zorech went off on a great begging tour, but was back
in Trebushan before *Rosh Hashanah*, in the early autumn. He
had brought a bag of money again. But looking at his wife's body,
he thought she was too slim, while her thighs swayed too easily,
as though she were a virgin.

"The child hasn't come," she said with outspread hands. "It was
afraid you mightn't bring enough money."

Gimpel Zorech raised his stick to strike her on the head. The
woman merely laughed at him with her pinkish, cowlike eyes,
and he threw the stick away. But he did not hand the money to
her. Beilah Yenteh took him into the house, talked and giggled
at him, flashing her white teeth. And the following day, on the
eve of the New Year, she had the money in her possession. But
when the two days of the New Year were over, Beilah Yentah
rose at dawn and wakened her husband.

"I'm going to the field," she said, "to gather some maize. You
better go back to your Jews. It would be a pity for you to
spend the other holy days here—this is the time when they give
most."

Gimpel Zorech was aware of that, but he did not go.

"I'm going to wait for the child," he said. "I've paid for it
twice over."

"Come back at Pentecost. You'll have it then for sure."

"And then it'll be 'for sure' some other time, eh?"

"Shut up!"

"You tell me to shut up? A black year upon you, you slut, and eighty-eight Polish curses!"

"Here's your stick—go."

"I'll break your bones with it first."

"You—break my bones?" she sneered. "You blockhead!"

She proved to be the stronger, and it was Gimpel Zorech that got the thrashing. He then stole the money from the straw mattress and went over to Berezna to drink. He returned in the middle of the night, drunk, but Beilah Yenteh locked him out, so he had to go to the dirty little stable. Gimpel Zorech lay down in the manger and complained to Leilach the cow how unkind Beilah Yenteh was. Leilach understood him and licked his ear, nose, and brow with her warm, wet tongue. When he woke up the cow was already grazing in front of the house. Beilah Yenteh must have come in early in the morning to let out and water the cow, yet she took no notice of him. Gimpel Zorech took his stick and went to Berezna again for more drink. That night he did not even knock at his wife's door, but went straight to the stable.

Then one night Beilah Yenteh felt regretful about her shabby treatment of her husband and went out to the stable to call him in. But Gimpel Zorech was no longer there. He had gone back to the road. And he did not return for *Shevuoth* to learn whether he had a child or not. Yet this time Beilah Yenteh had told the truth, and there was a brand new little boy waiting for him at home, Yossel by name, in memory of Yoirish's father, the drover.

Beilah Yenteh waited for money and for her husband all that summer. When the series of autumn holy days had all passed and the weather became chilly, she tied the baby into a bundle and set out in search of Gimpel Zorech. She crossed the Tisza and three other rivers, passed through many villages and two towns, knocking everywhere on doors that had the sacred parchment on the lintel and demanding the coin that they would have given her husband. She found no trace of Gimpel Zorech, but she did find her way to Lapfalva. By then it was winter and freezing cold. She handed little Yossel to Malkeleh, saying that it belonged to

Gimpel Zorech and that he had paid for him. They tried to make
her see reason, but failed to make the least impression. She suckled
the baby once more, then she said:

"He's had enough of the breast."

Then she tied up her possessions and tramped back to Maramaros.

Malkeleh for a time went on suckling the little boy, because
she too had one at the breast, and it so happened that he was also
called Yossel. There was nothing unusual in this, for in a Jewish
family departed mothers, fathers, grandfathers, grandmothers,
great-grandfathers, and great-uncles and aunts are generally re-
vived several times in the names of new offspring. The two
Yossels suckled side by side in peace. There was no danger of
mixing them up, for the newcomer had woolly red hair, while the
other's hair was black and silky. The two babies began to say
"Mummy" simultaneously, though the little stranger said it the
more aggressively. Malkeleh did not mind. After all, he was a first-
born and two months older than her own latest.

It was amusing to have three Yossels in the house, all regarding
Malkeleh as their mother. The outside world, of course, was
more strict and stuck to the facts. In accordance with the
matriarchal precedences ruling in nomadized communities, the
oldest Yossel was known as Yossel Sarah's, Gimpel Zorech's boy
as Yossel Beilah Yenteh's, and Sholem's as Yossel Malkah's. Within
the household the differentiation was far simpler. When Yiteleh
went to the verandah to call the scattered family in to dinner, she
began thus:

"Mailech, Manasseh, Yoirish, Sarah Chayah, Zipporah, Breynah,
Channeleh!" Then, after a breathing space, she would go on:
"Yossef, Yossel, Yosseleh!" And each Yossel knew which ap-
pellation was meant for him.

When, on a hot day in Tammuz, Gimpel Zorech turned up,
his son was already fourteen months old. He was asked whether
he had been at home yet, whereupon he spat out, saying that
he did not feel like going there—it was not home to him.

"Is the road better?" said Malkeleh severely. "Is the ditch
better?"

"Yes it is," said the beggar.

Malkeleh thereupon took him by the hand and led him out into the yard. Pointing out the two babies tumbling about among the mallows and the mint, she said:

"There's your boy, Gimpel Zorech. Which do you think is yours?"

Gimpel Zorech could never have been so drunk that he should not recognize the red-haired, calf-eyed child as his own at a glance, yet he pointed at the olive-skinned Yosseleh:

"That one there."

"You're mistaken, Gimpel Zorech. It's the other one."

"I don't want him."

"Well, you can't have the other," laughed Malkeleh. "He's mine. But the other one is lovely too, and stronger than mine. More wilful too. He always gets what he wants . . . And now, Gimpel Zorech, come and have a wash—wash your hair and beard with soap and comb them out. I'll get you some hot water with a dash of caustic soda. You'll find a clean shirt and drawers in the guest room, and some clean rags for your feet. Sholem has a fairly good pair of knee-boots there, so you can throw away your bast shoes. When you are ready, come back and I'll warm up some borsht for you. Don't dare go into the inn. Sholem is out in the field. I'll tell Yossef not to forget that you are not to be given any spirits even for money. You'll have some drinks on the Sabbath. We've got some fine Sikarlo wine for the *kiddush*. If you need anything, just call out. You still remember my name, don't you?"

"Malkeleh," said the beggar, with a broad grin on his hirsute face.

Gimpel Zorech always felt happy at Lapfalva. He needed Malkeleh's strictness and guidance. More than once, she herself cut and washed his hair and deloused him, and it was always to her that he came "home." He obeyed her too, and even set to work to please her, laundering his own underwear by the well, carrying water, chopping wood, and helping with the milking. And although he was an inveterate drunkard and a beggar by nature, he neither drank nor begged while at Lapfalva. When he sat in the bar parlor talking with the peasants or with passing market venders—who included many of those whom he used to

visit on his tours—he declined all treating and also any alms he
was offered. Sholem, on the whole, was satisfied with him, convinced that the improvement was due to his homilies, whereas in
fact he exerted no influence whatever on Gimpel Zorech. The
latter could not understand either Sholem's piety, or his sobriety,
or his studiousness, or even his ambition to grow things on his
land. He generally answered Sholem in a casual, even perky way
when he called him to account for anything. Sholem's questions
irritated him. Once, when Sholem asked him why he drank, he
replied with consternation:

"Why, didn't Yossel the drover drink? He was known as a
drunkard in three countries, and he was our grandfather. Daddy
Yoirish also drank when he could afford it."

Sholem disliked the family reminiscences. The next time, when
he wanted to talk to Gimpel Zorech about his begging, he
formulated the question more cautiously, lest he should blurt out
in the presence of strangers that Yossel the drover and Daddy
Yoirish also went schnorring occasionally.

"Must you go schnorring?" was the question, delivered in a tone
of reproach.

Gimpel Zorech nodded his head.

"If everything belongs to other people," he said with conviction, "you must either steal or beg."

The only thing Gimpel Zorech envied Sholem for was Malkeleh.
He knew that Sholem deserved her. He went to the same *yeshiba*
for seven years for her sake. Gimpel Zorech would have been incapable of that. But if he, not Sholem, had married Malkeleh! That
thought dwelt only in the darkest recesses of his mind. Physically
Malkeleh had no effect on him; his body was dominated by the
cruel, capricious, greedy Beilah Yenteh. If he but thought of
her, it was enough to make the blood rush to his head. But
Malkeleh was a Jewish woman, a wife and mother, such as he
had dreamed of through the mists of his wretched existence in
Maramaros and of his still more wretched schnorrer existence.

Malkeleh again succeeded in cleansing him, not only of the
filth of his schnorrer tours, but also of his inner filth and con-
fusions. By the third day he ceased to be obstinate about wanting

the dark-haired Yosseleh, and he began to play with his own child.

"*Tateh*," he said to the child. "I am thy *Tateh*. Say *Tateh*, Yosseleh."

And if the child said something similar, Gimpel Zorech flushed with pleasure and summoned every one else to witness the miracle: the little boy had recognized him, had called him *Tateh* without any prompting!

Of an evening it was he who sang the two little boys to sleep. There were two wooden troughs lying on the floor, two primitive cradles. The beggar crouched down between them, rocked them a little and sang the lullaby he had learnt from his mother:

> "*Sleep, sleep, Yossel dear,*
> *The Germans aren't so very near.*
> *Big they are, with sticks so long,*
> *Where they go none sings a song,*
> *But they aren't here, they aren't here,*
> *So sleep, sleep, Yosseleh dear.*"

The two Yosselehs listened with equal interest, while Gimpel Zorech meant the lullaby for both alike. At the same time, he had mentally adopted Yosseleh Malkah's as his son, for the boy's gentle features reflected the sweetness of both Malkeleh and his own mother, Leile. When his face was turned towards this Yosseleh, Gimpel Zorech would make a funny face and illustrate with gestures how big the Germans were and how long their sticks were, and would make a reassuring grimace when saying that they were not near. To his own son he sang more matter-of-factly, as though expecting him to know all about the Swabian Germans, of whom there was reason to be afraid. This Yosseleh was tougher, too, and was not easy to lull to sleep. He went on grabbing and tugging at his father's beard long after the other Yosseleh had fallen aslep. And when at last both babies were asleep, Gimpel Zorech went on humming to himself and swaying his head from side to side:

> "*Where they go, none sings a song,*
> *But they aren't here, they aren't here,*
> *So sleep, sleep, Yosseleh dear.*"

Then Gimpel Zorech would go among the older children and tell them queer stories till late. The stories reminded Yiteleh and Mailech of Reb Issur's tales, though there was a big difference, for after those sessions with the old man they could go to sleep in peace, whereas Gimpel Zorech's tales were ghostly and scary. The *tsaddik* always made the good people come out on top, while Gimpel Zorech always gave best to the bad people. His tales contained the cowardly, hump-backed gnome Luck—*Mozzel*—who was always in hiding and always whimpering because he was afraid of his age-old enemy, the giant Poverty—*Daless*—and the hard-hearted Usurer who picked the last copper out of people's pockets, and dragged even the pillow away from under their heads, together with their clothes, their Sabbath candlesticks, and their bread-knife. The *Daless* laughed and grew and went on growing until his head reached to the sky. The hump-backed gnome Luck one day took pity on the poor people and in the night set fire to the Usurer's house. But the *Daless*, who had a contract with the Usurer to keep the people poor, made rain, pouring buckets of water straight from the clouds on to the burning house, thus putting out the fire and saving the Usurer, who was still alive to this day. As to Luck, the *Daless* gave him such a beating that the poor gnome ran away, with a still bigger hump on his back, and no one has seen him to this day.

The days of his stay at his brother's house were the happiest of Gimpel Zorech's life—a holiday excursion into a normal, prosperous life. But they did not last long, barely a week. Malkeleh and Sholem had worked it out how to save Gimpel Zorech and how to reconcile him with Beilah Yenteh.

"Remember, Gimpel Zorech," Sholem said to him, "remember well what I am saying. As soon as the Sabbath is out you start for home. I don't mean Saturday night, because it is not good to set out at night, in case there are robbers on the road." (The schnorrer guffawed at this. What had he to fear from robbers?) "Malkeleh is preparing some food for your journey and I'll let you have the old leather bottle full of plum whisky. It'll be enough for you if you take a sip or two on the way, so there'll be some left to give to Yiddel and Tovyah for *kiddush*." (The schnorrer nodded his head.) "You'll tell Beilah Yenteh that you are now a different man, and that you'll get five chains of land here on lease. Five chains here is ten times as much as one and half chains there. You won't have to bother about rent; I'll see to that. Let Beilah Yenteh leave everything for Yiddel and Tov-yah. If she is very keen to bring the cow along, she may do so. The cow too will improve here. Trebushan is four days there, four days back. All right, Gimpel Zorech, you can spend two days lazing about there. But remember, I'll expect you both for the Sabbath in a fortnight's time."

Gimpel Zorech left early on the Sunday morning. Sholem gazed with relief at his clean, solemnly sober brother, sure that he would cause him no further heartaches. But Malkeleh's brow was clouded. She could not have told what it was that she did not quite like about Gimpel Zorech. Was it his gait? Or was it the leather bottle slung over his shoulder? She had a feeling that Gimpel Zorech and Beilah Yenteh would never celebrate the Sabbath at Lapfalva in a fortnight's time.

Sholem was not so naïve as not to suspect that the leather bottle-ful of plum whisky might cause trouble. But that precisely was his great idea. It was a test. And if Gimpel Zorech could stand it and resist temptation when his brother's eye was not upon him, then he would have been cured. It was a risky experiment, but if it succeeded it was worth a great deal. He had seen Gimpel Zorech sitting in the bar parlor, with the odor of the drink in his nostrils, and declining drinks, holding himself in check against temptation. He was suffering; he was a hero. For as our Sages said: "Who is a hero? He who conquers his own passions." Sholem had been sorry for his brother and once, when Doved Troyes tried to treat him to a tot, he had almost decided to lift the ban, for it was no little honor to drink with a Doved Troyes. When the latter had gone, Sholem said to Gimpel Zorech:

"Do you know who that was?"

"Reb Moysheh Doved Troyes," replied Gimpel Zorech.

"But do you know who he is?"

"Why, an innkeeper at Batiz."

"Yes, yes, but do you know who he is related to?"

Gimpel Zorech smiled. He was being examined in his own specialty. A country-wide schnorrer had to be well up in such matters, had to know the remotest branches of every family he visited, even if they numbered a thousand. How else could he carry messages or greetings or report in the right places that So-and-so's wife had had a new baby, or that he had moved, or that he had taken a lease of the water-mill? Was he not a substitute for the unreliable mail-coach service and the expensive couriers? Of course he knew about the relations of the Batiz innkeeper. First of all, Reb Mosheh Sopher, the Rabbi of Pressburg. . . .

"The *Ch'tham Sopher*, the great *gaon*!" cried Sholem with an awed, admiring voice, and a gleam in his eyes. "Why didn't you tell me before? And do you know who was Troyes' great-great-grandfather?"

"Who?" asked Gimpel Zorech stupidly. "Some cattle dealer, I suppose, or perhaps some *rosh hakahal* (president of a congregation)." When Sholem mentioned Rashi as Troyes' ancestor, Gimpel Zorech inquired who that was.

"You don't know who Rashi was!" cried Sholem with amazement. It was a disgrace that a twenty-six-year-old Jew should be so ignorant, when any child of five knew that Rashi was Rabbenuh Shlomo Yitzchok, commentator of the Bible and the Talmud, and a man of genius. What a lot this young man had missed in the home of Yoirish the peasant! "Never mind, Gimpel Zorech," Sholem went on more mildly. He was beginning to forgive the neglect of his father, for the task of regeneration he had set himself was present to his mind. "You're no longer the man from Trebushan and the man of the road. After the birth of your Yosseleh you were reborn. A different man, a different life. When you are here I'll see to you. After closing time it is quiet in here and I'll teach you *chumish* (the Pentateuch), Rashi, and even *Gemarah*. No one in Israel shall say that he is ignorant until the day of his death."

Gimpel Zorech himself thought so too, at least in a way. He was now a different man, having succeeded in turning his back upon himself. That was in his mind at the start of his outward journey. Or was it not quite like that? And perhaps it was not his mind that evolved this idea. The odor, the festive odor of Lapfalva was still in his nostrils, and his head was still full of Malkeleh and of Sholem. It was a good thing and very comfortable, you did not have to goad your brain until it panted like a sick horse. You put a sick horse on a cart that is drawn by a couple of strong fellow-horses, and there are no more stones on the road, no rickety bridge, no sticky mud, no snow-drifts. You'll sleep in a proper bed, with a pillow of down. You're not going to drink, but work and feed and bring up your boy, so he shouldn't be like Gimpel Zorech was before his rebirth. And you'll learn *chumish* and Rashi and you'll teach your boy, and your boy will look up to you, what a great Jew you are, a veritable Doved Troyes.

The whisky in the leather bottle gave a glug-glug, and the old Gimpel Zorech reawakened in the schnorrer's head, though at first somewhat hesitantly. After all, even a Doved Troyes had a tot now and then. There was nothing wrong in joining him, was there? Only a sip, a tiny swig, so that there should be enough left for Yiddel and Tovyah to make *kiddush*. He was now out of Lapfalva and on the way to Trebushan, with the road flanked by fine yellow sunflowers. Ah, Beilah Yenteh, you're going to have another eight strong boys, and they'll all be by me. What say, Beilah Yenteh? Have a drop with me. And answer when I speak to you.

He trudged on, pausing now and again to gaze at the yellow heads of the sunflowers. The sunflowers maintained a provocative silence. Gimpel Zorech, with the staff in his hand, and his carpet-bag and the leather bottle over his shoulder, stood staring at them for minutes on end without emitting a sound, waiting for those proud sunflowers to give voice. In the end a big sunflower spoke:

"Have you brought any money, Gimpel Zorech?"

"I haven't."

"Then what did you come home for?"

"Listen, Beilah Yenteh," he began. He went on to defend himself, to complain, to make promises. The sunflower said nothing. Was it because it was listening, or just because it wanted to stay silent? Its head was already slightly turned away, but it seemed as though it was still looking at Gimpel Zorech from the corner of one eye. There was lustful invitation in that look, a kind of voluptuous mockery. Gimpel Zorech did not want to see it—or was it that he had seen it and was now refusing to be held by it any longer?

"You don't know the new Gimpel Zorech, Beilah Yenteh. He's a strong man, proof against temptation."

He shook the leather bottle. It was not quite empty yet, but he did not take a swig this time. He threw it down on the ground, then he sat down on the edge of the road, facing the sunflower.

"Look at this," he said to it, undoing his carpet-bag and producing sundry eatables. "Leg of roast goose, pickled cucumber, and white fancy bread. Did you ever give Gimpel Zorech leg of roast goose, pickled cucumber, and white fancy bread, eh? The hell you did. You didn't even give him a slice of maize bread when he was leaving on a schnorring tour. All you gave him was bloody weals on his back and behind and curses. What's Malkeleh to me? She's Sholem's wife and Yossel Malkah's mother. But she gives me everything, even a bath. She washes the lice and the muck off me, just like off your child, whom you left there without suckling him."

His voice hoarse with anger, he found himself running, the stick in his hand and the empty leather bottle over his shoulder, and the silent sunflower at his heels. Or perhaps he was standing still and the earth was running along? Anyhow, he could not get away from that sunflower. Whenever he looked up, there was a big, haughty, yellow face. It was already turning away from him, yet it was still there.

"You turn away from me, harlot!" raved Gimpel Zorech. "You lock yourself in my stove room, in the house I inherited from my father and mother, eh? You lock me out to sleep in the stable and have Leilach squirt her diarrhoea into my face, eh? Just because you have eyes like a calf and hair like maize? Eighty-eight Polish curses! Take that, Beilah Yenteh, and that, and that! Here are some weals for you for once. Now you can be proud, strumpet!"

The peasants understood nothing about anything. All they saw was a crazy Jew running along by the edge of their fields and smashing the heads of their sunflowers. That he was a schnorrer called Gimpel Zorech they did not know, while his drunkenness, which they could not help observing, was certainly no mitigation. A Jew must keep quiet and behave himself in other people's coun-

try, and must not act like a mad dog. So the peasants seized him
and gave him twenty-five strokes with his own stick, the one that
Beilah Yenteh had cut for him in the beechwood. And so that he
should remember the day when he forgot that he was a Jew and
a stranger, they cut off his long, thick ear-curls and shaved off
his curly chestnut beard which had but recently been combed by
Malkah. What was Gimpel Zorech without ear-curls and a beard?
Certainly not a schnorrer to whom Jews gave coppers. He did not
go home, having already had a deadly quarrel with Beilah Yenteh;
why should she see that she had won once more? He could not
return to Lapfalva, either. With dirt on his body and lice in his
ear-curls and beard, yes, but not without those habitats of the
lice. So Gimpel Zorech kept away from people, sleeping in roadside ditches and under bridges and fighting with dogs for a crust
thrown on the dust-heap. Not until his ear-curls and beard had
blossomed again did he dare to show his face in Jew-inhabited
villages. His first visit was to Batiz, where he made straight for
Moshe Doved Troyes' inn.

"Well, Reb Moshe Doved," he said, his hirsute face distorted
into a smile, "I'll have a drop with you now."

Mother Zissah gave him a scared look out of her ever-lachry-
mose old eyes. She ran out into the kitchen to heat a pot of water
with which to give a wash to Sholem's brother, Malkeleh Nikolsburger's brother-in-law.


A CLEVER LAD


IN SHOLEM's house Gimpel Zorech represented a perpetual load
of care, a cloud that would hang over it for ever. For this one
trouble Sholem could find no remedy in his books, and he con-
sulted in vain itinerant rabbis, some of them seers, who put up
at his inn. Once, when the Saint of Wizhnitz was still alive,
Sholem paid him a special visit. It was on a half-holiday during
*Pesach*. The Saint of blessed memory wanted to hear Gimpel
Zorech's life story. Sholem could only tell him how his brother

was born: that Mother Leah had her labor in the ditch on the edge of her plot of land.

"That's enough," interrupted the Rabbi, raising his trembling hand. "I know all I need to know. A journey begun in the ditch ends in the ditch." Closing his eyes, he went on: "Rachel was delivered of her younger son in the field, and because it was the hour of her death, she called him *Ben-onih*—son of my grief. Gimpel's name is *Ben-onih*." As he opened his eyes he saw Sholem's scared expression, and his voice became more encouraging: "But Zorech means light—and the light is called Joseph." In the end the Rabbi said: "He who traces the paths of man wants it so. The Name—praise be!—does everything with a purpose. He will raise one of his children into the light and plunge another into the darkness of a ditch or a jail. But the ditch and jail are predestination too. And as the case of Joseph proves, they are necessary. On the threshold of the seven lean years they save Israel from calamity."

The words of the Saint boded ill, but Sholem did not grasp their true meaning until long after. Whenever Gimpel Zorech turned up, Sholem recalled with a sense of shock one or another of the great seer's weighty sentences. But his visit to Wizhnitz had been in the spring, and he was aware only of hope and comfort on his return, of his seven lean years that must soon come to an end.

In the spring Sholem was bored with the inn and with his garrulous customers, was impatient when it came to marking the tally sticks and entering outstanding debts, and was neglectful in watching his bottles, demijohns, and the stock in his cellar. Moreover, at ploughing and sowing time he made a break even in his studies. He was a Talmudist to the marrow, and loved to study, loved the insoluble problems that cropped up, and he knew that the briefest pause meant retrogression. "If thou leavest me for a day," said the Law, "I shall leave thee for two days." However, because Sholem loved the land, and because his otherwise passive nature was stirred by the excitement of production, he had in course of time evolved a defence that exempted him from the study of the Law; for if he were studying, he would be sure to say at times, "How beautiful is that ploughed land!" thereby endangering his salvation.

The land was really beautiful, and became more and more so as the years passed. Sholem began with five chains, and in six years it had scarcely doubled, though during the same period the family had increased fourfold. However, there were thirty-odd chains of marsh which Sholem had purchased at a florin a chain on the advice of the mysterious Rabbi Must-Not. At that time the peasants laughed, saying that the Jew had been taken in, and that the stinking toad-puddle wasn't worth so many kreuzers, let alone florins. But after the autumn rains and after the spring thaw Sholem had gone round to watch the current of the water of which Rabbi Must-Not had spoken to him, and he knew what to do. He waited until, during one very hot summer, his toad-puddle dried up. Four years he waited, but it was worth it. Along the bed of the current he, with the aid of serfs whom he engaged when they were free of villenage, dug deeper. This, apart from wages, cost him a further thirty florins, for Squire de Sarberek contended that he had sold a piece of marsh to Sholem, not a piece of arable land, and that the Jew must pay for the arable land now. Besides, the Squire was in need of money, for he had had a letter from his son in Pest by courier to say that he must urgently pay a debt of honor.

Yossef was a great help in the house. He was a big, gentle lad and, in contrast with his restless brother, Sroleh Yomtov, a stay-at-home, so much so that he would not even go to a *yeshiba*, despite Sholem's persuasion. He had long passed the age of thirteen when he at last yielded to pressure and went away to Ujhely, into the *yeshiba* of Rabbi Mosheh Teitelbaum, Sholem's former teacher. But after the first term he returned home, and for good as far as Ujhely was concerned. For it so happened that the boy was needed, it being the busy spring season, and having stayed at home for a month, and then for another week or two, it was not worth while going back for the tail end of the next term. Then Sholem decided that the *chassidic* training of the Saint of Ujhely was not suitable for a village innkeeper's boy, and for the following term he sent Yossef to Pressburg, to the *yeshiba* of the world-famous Mosheh Sopher. But even here, six months was all Yossef could stand. After that, just to satisfy Sholem, he spent another term or two at minor *yeshibas*, Csenger and Hust, but after Ujhely and Pressburg this was of course a come-down. When Sholem sent him to the best places he was moved, on the one hand, by the desire to do his duty as a good step-father, but on the other, he had a secret hope that the boy, with learning derived from those exalted sources, would one day be a great help to him in solving intricate Talmudic problems. In the end, how-ever, he did not profit from Yossef's learning even as much as teachers usually do from the queries and observations of their pupils.

For the rest, Yossef was a clever lad, even though he was not enthusiastic about the *yeshiba*. He knew all about the work at the inn, could talk with the peasants in their own language and attended intelligently to any task entrusted to him. Sholem also liked him because he was so willing to work with him on the land, and if a tool got broken or there were repairs to do in the house, he used to set to with a saw and axe and one or two nails, and made a good job of it. At the same time, he was often pig-headed, undertaking tasks that were beyond his strength and skill, and refusing to be dissuaded; but he did carry them out somehow in the end. A memorable instance was that of the sleigh. Yossef used to watch the carpenters at work, and one day he told Yiteleh that he too could do "it." All it needed was judgment, tools and "swing." He did not rest until he acquired a cross-axe, then he began to make a sleigh out of some worm-eaten beams. For the next eighteen months he kept carving and whittling away, dis-posing of a dozen usable beams. It did not matter, because they were not the right components, and in any case, Aunt Feiga needed the shavings to light fires in the oven. Several times the cross-axe slipped and the boy cut himself in the leg on one occasion, so badly that he limped for months. He even went to *yeshiba* in between, but by then he had arranged matters so that he should be near home. From Csenger he used to come home for a day or two on any pretext, and since he spent the Sabbath there each week, he managed to arrive home early on the Friday morning. On that day he was needed by Malkeleh, Friday being the busiest day in a Jewish household. A Jewish woman divides the year into two periods: when Fridays are long and when they are short. But even the longest Friday is not long enough for all

the work that has to be done, and the Sabbath always arrives
before you expect it.

On Fridays Yossef busied himself only round the kitchen, doing
but little in the inn or in the field. He drew water, cut wood,
dashed across to this or that peasant woman for something, and
if—God forbid—Malkeleh was out of salt, oil, or candles, and it
was not noticed until the Friday, the boy would jump on the
pony and gallop over to Menachem's shop in Ecsed, and on the
way back, and just incidentally, call on Mother Shaindl, the wife
of Naphtali the peddler, in case she had a couple of fatted ducks
or a fatted goose and some barleycorn or mottled beans, or perhaps some split peas, which were even better for the *tsholent* than
beans. If it was a very long Friday, he could also go fishing in the
marsh, and have a Sabbath-eve bath at the same time. Yossef
knew the places frequented by the loach fishers, where the marsh
had a current, as the river Kraszna flowed through it. Loach was
forbidden, but sometimes there were tench and carp to be caught
there, and, if he put good fat worms on the hook and was lucky, he
would take three or four pounds of good fish back to Malkeleh,
who could not praise him enough for his cleverness. Yossef liked
to be praised, but hated the expression "by the way," which his
step-parents used and abused. "And by the way," do this, and do
that, go here, and go there, so that the boy had scarcely a minute
to spare for his sleigh. That was his favorite task. The children
used to stand around, admiring his masterly handling of the cross-
axe. True, Yiteleh was smiling, with a puckish incredulity in her
eyes, but the boy acted as though he did not notice it. Let her
laugh at him if she liked; she won't laugh when the sleigh is
finished.

Indeed, Yiteleh did not laugh when, one cold winter's day,
Yossef hitched the pony to the sleigh and invited her to accompany him to Batiz. It was not Friday, and there was no need to
hurry, nor was it a Wednesday, when Leizer Lazarovich must
not be disturbed, but just an ordinary week-day. An ordinary
week-day? Ah, thought Yossef, then every one will admire his
brand-new sleigh, which was strong as a ship and fast as lightning.
And if anyone should fail to look and admire, his attention would

be bound to be attracted by the shrill bell which he had acquired
for this occasion.

He was not very pleased to see Yiteleh sitting there, wrapped
in rugs, and unsmiling. It caused him to inspect the sleigh and the
iron plates again and again. Surely, she did not think that he had
botched it and that they might get held up or that the vehicle
might simply get broken and they would be stranded there with
all the empty casks. No, there was nothing wrong with the sleigh.
But what was the matter with Yiteleh? At other times she was so
lively, always joking and teasing. Now she did not feel like talking at all, and even when he spoke to her she scarcely gave a nod.

"Are you cold, Yiteleh?"

"No."

"You're not wrapped up properly."

"I am."

"Are you afraid that the sleigh is bad?"

"No."

"But you are."

"If I were I wouldn't be sitting on it."

"That's true," said Yossef, cheering up. Cracking his whip, he
observed: "In half an hour we shall be crossing the river, and
in another hour we shall be in Batiz. Have you ever been to
Batiz?"

"You don't remember?" cried Yiteleh, giving him a surprised
look.

"Remember what?"

"When Sroleh Yomtov took me to Batiz."

"Ah!" said Yossef. He had forgotten about that.

Yiteleh sat looking into the distance for a minute or two, then
she said:

"That time Sroleh Yomtov said he was going to marry me."

"Well?" said the boy, taking a deep breath.

"He'll come back when I grow up. But I am only fourteen."

The girl now became more talkative. She did not talk about
Sroleh Yomtov, but about the big black ravens that were sitting
on the snow like so many black letters. And she was interested in
the frozen river, with the ferry jammed between blocks of ice.
When they were over on the other bank, she pointed right, saying

that Otvar was there, and later she was pleased to have recognized the distillery from the distance. Now it was Yossef's turn to be silent. He finished his buying at the distillery in a hurry, loaded up the casks, then had a bite of the food that Yiteleh had packed for the journey, then geed-up for home. He did not go to Troyes to deliver the message he had for him, nor did he—as he had intended—take Yiteleh along to Jacob Anshel to let her see how the Sabbath candles were made, and how the flat, plaited *havdalah* torches and the colored peasant candles were produced.

"They need the goods at the inn urgently," was all he said, and he did not speak again until they were back home.

Sholem praised him for his cleverness in managing to get back soon after dark. It was a special compliment that he also inspected the sleigh. Of course, that was the explanation of the speed the boy had achieved. The old sleigh was so ramshackle that they could not have been back before midnight with it. Now Malkeleh too began to admire the new structure.

"Our Yossef is a clever boy indeed," she said charmingly.

But Yossef might as well not have heard. He was no longer proud of or pleased with his handiwork.


Sholem had a pet idea. He wanted to build a new shed at the end of the yard. It was to be high, with an open loft for drying maize. The walls were to be wickerwork and rush, plastered with clay, and whitewashed. All sorts of people came and spent the night at the inn. Sholem gave the master a bed in the gentry's parlor, or if he was a man of some distinction, in the guest room, while the driver and servants slept in the yard in the open. It was fortunate for those people if it did not rain, or if there was a hood on the cart. In the shed Sholem proposed to have straw and one or two rush-mats, so that drivers and servants should have pleasant recollections of the inn.

Sholem discussed the plan with Yossef, who had grown in stature a great deal since he had built the sleigh. Yossef himself seemed to be aware of it, for he was no longer gentle and quiescent, no longer said "yes" and "all right" to everything. On the contrary, he usually held the the opposite view. Now he said he would not put the shed at the end of the yard, but in front of the stable, to the right of the gate, where there were four lime-trees. One had been struck by lightning, while another was withered, but they stood in a straight row and would thus serve as pillars for the new structure. It was not a bad idea, but as two of the trees were still alive, Sholem would never agree to kill them, and that was what cutting off their tops and branches would amount to. He could never even look at a shed in which the trees were buried.

Nor did Sholem like the spot, which was right opposite the window at the back of the bar. According to Yossef this was an advantage because anyone who happened to be behind the bar could keep an eye on strangers loitering round the shed. Sholem said this was of no importance, for those that had to be watched did not do things when they were watched. Besides, he could not afford to have it before him when the Sages presented him with a problem requiring deep thought. It was enough that he had the mulberry-tree by that window, a tree full of flowers in the spring, and of fruit and children in the summer, while in the autumn it seemed to be the meeting-place of all the birds of the county, so that it was scarcely possible to close one's ears to their noisy twittering.

"Put it where you like," said Yossef finally. "It's your shed, not mine. Besides, I shan't be here in the spring."

"Are you going back to the *yeshiba*?" asked Sholem, startled. Formerly it was he who kept persuading Yossef to go to the *yeshiba*, but now he would have missed this clever and active boy, whose help he had included in his reckoning with regard to the new building operations.

"Not to the *yeshiba*," said Yossef. "I want to learn a trade."

This made Sholem think. He was convinced in his own mind that Yossef was learning a trade with him. Indeed, he was learning two—innkeeping and agriculture. But perhaps that did not satisfy Yossef, now that he had proved his skill at carpentry.

"Do you want to be a carpenter?"

"I'm not such a fool," shrugged the boy. "The carpenters are all *goyim* and they wouldn't have a Jew for a journeyman, even if he was so clever that he worked with two cross-axes at once.

And if I became a master carpenter sometime, they wouldn't admit me to the guild."

"The Above One wants it so—that we shouldn't mix too much with the *goyim*."

"Well, if the Above One wants it so, then he wants the same things as the *goyim*, because they only let us do the work that stinks in their nostrils."

Sholem gave him a quizzical look. What had happened to the boy? But yesterday he was a child, and to-day he was already an adult with opinions of his own. How old was he? Sixteen? Seventeen? Sholem had to smile: he had only just noticed the down on the boy's chin. He nodded, and there was conviction in his nod. Let the boy go and learn a trade; a father could never oppose that sort of thing. Why? Because our *tannaim* said: "He who does not teach his son a trade, is teaching him to be a robber."

"Does the trade you want to learn stink?" he asked jocularly.

"Rather," laughed the boy. "I'll make soap and candles."

"Not in Reb Jacob Anshel's workshop in Batiz?" asked Sholem.

On the whole, Sholem was content. He himself could not have chosen a better place. He recalled how Reb Jacob Anshel once complained that there was one thing in which God had not been kind to him: he had five children and they were all girls. Even his second wife had not given him a son. If he had a boy like Yossef or Mailech, his business would surely take a different turn. Sholem did not understand the hint then. Apparently the candlemaker had talked more openly with Yossef. Sholem wondered what he could have offered Yossef to reconcile him to the steam and smell of his workshop. Perhaps nothing more than what he could give: board and lodgings, practical training and two days off a week: Friday and Saturday. For Yossef continued to return home on a Friday, as when he was at Csenger, though he did not arrive early in the morning, but on the contrary, he sometimes almost raced the Sabbath to Lapfalva. He could not help in the house, being busy with himself, washing and changing in a hurry. Malkeleh did not take it amiss that he no longer helped her, for after all he was now a young man with a career of his own, and the journey from Batiz was four hours by cart. But when Yossef did not turn up at all, she became depressed. At such

times the house, though not quiet, for the children were making
plenty of noise at any time, lacked an additional voice. Yiteleh
said that the reason for Yossef's absence was Reb Jacob Anshel's
two daughters, Esther and Zireleh, who worked with him in the
workshop. Esther was dark, while Zireleh had red hair.

"On the Sabbath Esther and Zireleh don't work, but sit at the
table like you," said Sholem.

"Yes," said Yiteleh, "they're sitting at the table and listening
to what Yossef is saying."

"No doubt," agreed Sholem, but he felt that this was not to
the point. "Yossef is a clever boy. He has studied under Mosheh
Sopher and Mosheh Teitelbaum."

## "YITELEH IS NO LONGER A CHILD"

THOUGH NEITHER Sholem, nor Malkeleh, nor Yiteleh said anything
about this, all three sensed that something important was happening or was about to happen. Yiteleh was beginning to grow up.
Soon she would be a young woman. Or perhaps she was one
already. Adam de Sarberek, the Squire's firstborn, who was studying in Pest, and was already so learned that he twirled his
mustache with both hands at once, having only a little way to
go to become a lawyer or at least a County clerk, used to stop in
front of the fence and look at Yiteleh. She wore a tight little
bodice and a light cotton skirt, with shoes made by the village
bootmaker on her feet. But the way she walked along the boards
which Sholem had laid across the muddy yard was a joy to behold.
Adam wondered where this little Jew girl had learnt to bear herself so gracefully. He would have liked to ask her, but when she
passed near him all he said was:

"We've grown some, Yiteleh, haven't we?"

On another occasion he already addressed her as Miss Yiteleh.
Yiteleh smiled to herself. The Squire's son was no company for
her, though she was flattered that the boy who had once treated

her in a high and mighty fashion, mocking her as a "Jew-girl," had now mended his manners with her.

Shayeh Oesterreicher also saw her with different eyes. Since the time when he passed through Lapfalva with Zalman the trough-seller and was compelled to stay a week, Shayeh had been visiting the marsh-side inn nearly every year. The previous year he had looked in twice, because he "happened to be passing." To Malkeleh he was welcome, he being one of her "foster-children." Yiteleh would have a lark with him occasionally, but did not take him seriously, though his manhood was already sprouting beneath his nose. Yiteleh could never forget the funny complaint that first brought the boy to Lapfalva, how her mother had treated him with herbs supplied by Mme Bogyo, and what the forthright Aunt Feiga had said when, after a long search, she returned the coin to Shayeh. Shayeh suspected this, for after all, he and Yiteleh had been laughing over it together only a year or two ago. Now they were not laughing, but Shayeh used to look into the girl's face as though he suspected that she was still laughing inwardly. However, Shayeh no longer talked about yesterday, only about to-morrow. The things he said were perhaps not calculated to interest the girl. He said that Israel had a five-thousand-year-old beard, with which they were sweeping the ground before the thresholds of the great and mighty. If at least half of this beard were snitched off, the Jews might also lose the hump on their backs and grow straight and young again. And if they behaved differently and did not kow-tow before the jack-booted gentry, who were intellectual nonentities, they would be held in greater esteem and would receive a more definite place among the nations.

It was evident that Shayeh had not acquired all his education in the *yeshiba*. But he said nothing about that, perhaps fearing that the grandson of the Rabbi of Karoly would not be forgiven for listening to lectures on philosophy at foreign Universities. Recently, when he had been to Jena, he did not mention the fact, but said he had been staying in Vienna with his uncle, who was a famous physician and scientist and even frequented the Imperial Court. However, when Yiteleh rummaged among his books in search of something to read, she found such titles as *Tractatus*

*Theologico Politicus, Kritik der reinen Vernunft, Philosophie der Geschichte*, and saw Shayeh's signature on them.

"Since when do you call yourself Alexander?"

"My professors call me Alexander Isaiah Oesterreicher," said the boy with embarrassment, tilting his head sideways.

Just before the autumn holy days, Shayeh came along with a companion, a lean, bony Talmudist named Wolf, who scarcely spoke when addressed by Yiteleh. Yiteleh liked Wolf's deep-set dark eyes, with which he used to gaze out of the window or follow the flight of a bluebottle zooming overhead. Wolf had long ear-curls, whereas Shayeh's were brief and combed down into his incipient sidewhiskers. Wolf observed with meticulous care all the ritual hand-washings and also kept himself very clean in other ways.

The two young men were in perpetual debate with each other. Shayeh's enthusiasm belonged to the unknown, the eternally new, whereas Wolf passionately defended tradition. Wolf's beard had only just begun to sprout, but Shayeh said it was two thousand years old. Wolf's fiery maturity intrigued and excited him, and he asked his opinion about everything, though he did not agree with him when he heard it. He dubbed Wolf the *Meturgheman*, which is the Hebrew for interpreter or expounder, though what Wolf interpreted was generally a contrary view. However, Shayeh needed contradiction. While making a statement, he could have sworn to its truth, but the next moment he already doubted it and was eager to hear it criticized. If his friend was silent, he would himself urge him with the question, "And what does the *Meturgheman* think of it?" To Shayeh, Wolf Birnbaum was the embodiment of the life of his ancestors, from which he had become somewhat detached, as well as the other half of his own ego, the ever-doubting and ever doubtful half. When they were together with Yiteleh, Wolf was mostly silent. Yiteleh liked to hear Shayeh say that youth must change everything and must build, not on the past, but for the future, its visions and purposes.

"Well, what does the *Meturgheman* think of it?" he said, to break his friend's intolerable silence.

"The building of the young," replied Wolf sagely, with a glance through the window, "is destruction."

Malkeleh liked Shayeh, but Sholem preferred Wolf. Once Sholem asked Wolf whether he was not related to Reb Phineas Birnbaum of Ujhely.

"He's my uncle," said Wolf.

"We were together in the *yeshiba*," observed Sholem. "Now he's a rich man. Does he help you?"

"I don't accept help."

"Is your father supporting you?"

"My father's dead. And so is my mother." His brow contracted as he added: "He who hates gifts retains life."

On their way to Karoly, Shayeh turned to Wolf:

"How do you like Yiteleh?"

"I didn't look at Yiteleh."

"You did, I saw you. She's pretty, isn't she?"

"Prettiness is transitory," said Wolf severely.

"And what isn't?"

"The earth, the spirit, and the Law."

"Really, *Meturgheman*," said Shayeh playfully, "so long as we are here on earth, it is within the spirit of our Law to seek beauty."

"Not beauty—goodness."

"Isn't Yiteleh good? Aren't Malkeleh and Sholem good?"

"I like Mosheh Doved Troyes better."

"And little Rebecca Troyes with her blonde pigtail, eh?"

"I wasn't referring to Rebecca. I was speaking about her father."

"Why not about his great-grandfather?"

"Why not indeed? Do you think it is a small matter to be a descendant of Rashi?"

"But you admit, don't you, that Yiteleh is a hundred times prettier than Rebecca?"

"What do you want with Rebecca? She's a child yet."

"But Yiteleh is no longer a child," said Shayeh, swishing his cane in the air and acting as though he were announcing a great discovery.

Simon Dominus, the travelling watchmender, who had not been to the marsh-side inn for nearly three years, was of the same opinion. Pushing the magnifying glass up to his forehead, he looked at Yiteleh, to whom he appeared as the unicorn of the fairy tales, and even more strange than when he had it in his eye and was fumbling with tiny gear-wheels with his tweezers. The unicorn, who was accustomed to being surrounded by admiring children, was now admiring one of them, and precisely because she was no longer a child. He gazed at her mouth, which was not too small, her teeth, which were whitened with charcoal dust, her hair, her firm little breasts, her eyes. There was an impression of distance about those eyes. Old Dominus had been all over the place in his time, but this was his first experience of that kind of distance.

"Have you got a broken-down watch, Yiteleh?" he asked.

"I haven't even a good one, Uncle Dominus."

"If you keep calling me uncle, I shan't repair your watch."

"You can't if I haven't got one."

"But you have. Your grandma had one."

"Grandma? That's past repairing."

"Nothing is past repairing."

"A watchmaker said so."

"What fool was that?"

"He is not a fool, but a real watchmaker. It was you yourself who said that it was a coffin for cog-wheels."

"Let me see it just the same."

The watch was produced out of Malkeleh's family treasure-box. It was a little gold watch with a key for winding it. Dominus looked at it and shook his head.

"I was almost right," he muttered. Yet he sat down to work on it. He went on till evening, resumed the following morning, but it was not till the third day that he managed to bring the ancient piece to life.

"This is with my compliments," he said, as he handed it back to Malkeleh. "I did it for Yiteleh, because she's so pretty. If I ever made up my mind to settle down it would be only for her." With that he slung his bag over his shoulder and departed.

When Malkeleh reported the incident to Sholem, the latter gave a laugh.

"What fancies the old family destroyer has!"

This sounded like a joke, but in a sense Sholem meant it. Dominus was past thirty and was already beginning to go bald, yet despite all persuasion he would not marry. According to the Tal-

mud bachelorhood was the same sort of crime as the destruction
of a family. Dominus had amassed quite a little fortune, and he
was also highly respected, as witness the fact that he was not
referred to as the Jew Simon, even the county and municipal
officials addressing him as Dominus—Mr.—Simon. Of course, at
first there was a trace of irony in this, but because he was a good
worker and also understood jewelry, the title stuck. Dominus
was certainly not Sholem's idea of a mate for Yiteleh.

THE LOST BOY

THE QUESTION had not yet matured and if Sholem thought of it at
all, it was with an admixture of vague regret to have let Yossef
leave the house, when these two made such a fine pair. Malkeleh
thought otherwise. In her eyes Yossef was not a suitable mate for
her daughter. Yiteleh was more intelligent and had finer instincts
than this docile village lad. She might be his sister, but not his
wife. Malkeleh was thinking as a matter of destiny of the brother,
the wild, restless Sroleh Yomtov.

She had never talked about it in this sense to Yiteleh, but they
did talk a great deal about Sroleh Yomtov, and with the passage
of time he grew in stature. Their memory of him might long have
faded, had he not left all his money for the family when he ran
away. One could forget his aspect, as well as his queer defiant
personality, but not this. For ultimately, the family had been
saved not by the three squires, or as Sholem thought, the three
"angels," but by Sroleh Yomtov.

In Malkeleh's mind a memory of the runaway boy survived in
another sense as well. She had a vague idea that she was the cause
of his disappearance. She could not or would not form a conception of what might have gone on in the mind of the young
adolescent to raise a barrier between him and her, but sometimes
she reproached herself for failing to be more of a mother to him.
By the time she was trying to get closer to Sroleh Yomtov, he
had got tired of waiting and ran away.

Despite the family's relative prosperity, Malkeleh's life was neither easy, nor free from care. Every new baby brought new tones and colors into the house and gave rise to new fancies. But they came one after another, a new baby every eighteen months, and that was too exhausting for her. This was the régime of Trebushan, not of Nikolsburg. The Nikolsburgers also welcomed children, but they came at longer intervals, so that the mother could recover her strength and also devote more attention to the individual child. But she could not approach Sholem in such a matter.

The retention of the lease also involved trouble, nor was the life of the inn free from excitement, and it was Malkeleh's brains and energy that had to be brought to bear on the more intricate problems. Sometimes Sholem put himself in the wrong with his masters, though mostly it was against his will, or in accordance with a higher will. As when the gentry, in a riotously merry mood, offered to clink glasses with him and he refused, blurting out that the wine was not *kosher*. "What?" roared the gentry. "So the wine you serve us with is not *kosher*, hey." "It is, sir, but . . ." How could he explain to the gentry that *kosher* wine ceased to be so as soon as it was touched by the hand of a Gentile who might mentally offer it up to a pagan god? No wonder, then, that the gentry were offended. It was Malkeleh's task to smooth things over, and she did everything in her power to foster and maintain good relations with the gentry. On a Friday afternoon, if her cheese cakes happened to be a success, she would send a small tin of them to Lady Susannah at Gyekenyes, and another to Lady Clementine at Sarberek. If the stuffed goose she killed for the Sabbath happened to have a fine, big liver, she would personally take it over to the manor at Denghelegh, to be effusively blessed by her ladyship there. Before Passover, Malkeleh never omitted to send the gentry a gift of unleavened bread wrapped in a snow-white serviette. The Purim pastry was also very popular with the gentry, though it was prepared in the Jewish way, with plenty of walnuts, raisins, cinnamon, and cloves.

It was Malkeleh's task too to keep up friendly relations with the peasant women. She had a small pharmacy in a wooden box, and also a book of prescriptions for coughs, stomach-ache, and the

like; and of course she knew what to do when the children came
down with the measles. The peasant women came to Malkeleh
with their domestic troubles as well. They considered it quite
natural that their men should drink to drown their sorrows and,
having drunk too much, to be more sorrowful still and to seek
relief in thrashing their wives and children; yet it did them good
to pour out their hearts to some one. They always left Malkeleh
comforted and refreshed. Malkeleh also enabled the women to
earn a little money. She bought from them homespun material,
embroidered towels, and vari-colored rag-mats, partly for the
household and partly for the girls' bottom drawer.

Malkeleh had a small income of her own. Her main source of
revenue was goose feathers, which were stripped by Aunt Feiga
and the children and sold to Zishe in Hodasz. Sometimes Yiteleh
would need a few coppers of which Sholem had better not know,
or Mailech wanted to buy stock, or Yossef was hard up for something. Malkeleh's fund was always there for these purposes. But
she was also generous with it, as with words of comfort and encouragement, when approached by poor wretches, mostly women,
from far and near. In return, these people left their troubles and
agitations behind with her.

Of course, some of the excitements were of the right kind, as
when a schnorrer, a Talmud student, a peregrinating rabbi, a
travelling artisan, or a relative who had been to distant places,
came along and said he had seen or thought he had seen Sroleh
Yomtov. Some even claimed to have spoken with him. Sometimes,
an adventurous schnorrer who did not respect frontiers, either
political or customs, would bring a message from him—from the
northern counties, from the Emperor's western provinces, from
as far afield as Lemberg and Prague, and even from Vienna, from
the bustling, swarming Leopoldstadt. These butterflies of the road
used to take messages to and from so many far-apart places, see
so many people, and hear so many confidences that one could be
satisfied if every twentieth word they said were true. Once
Sholem used to be more credulous, but having learned through his
own brother that the schnorrers were in reality ignorant people,
ignorant even of Rashi, he ceased to take them seriously.

Now it was Malkeleh who was the less skeptical. What she ex-

pected from a schnorrer was not learning, but news. She listened
to all gossip and hearsay, every rumor, every message, genuine
or not, weighing and examining them all. In the course of the five
or six years since Sroleh Yomtov had gone away, she had heard
much false and contradictory news about him, so that the presumed truth of one item belied all the rest, until finally the
presumed truth itself fell to the ground.

Since Sroleh Yomtov's departure, and particularly because he
had expressed a wish to that effect in his last letter, they made up
an account of their business capital at the end of each summer. If
there was an adverse balance, it was Malkeleh's task to secure what
was lacking. Now that Sholem was able to meet his obligations
sooner or later, even Mordechai was prepared to advance a hundred or two until the autumn. But during the first years Malkeleh
used to raise a loan in Nameny. This, too, was in accordance with
Sroleh Yomtov's wish, though at the same time it suited Sholem
better to approach a stranger rather than his rich brother-in-law.
As to Malkeleh, she liked to hear again and again the little that
Golda could tell her about that Sabbath which the boy had spent
in her house.

"I tried to make him stay," Golda would say, "but it was no use.
He said he was in a hurry. I asked if he wanted to go out into the
world and didn't Malkeleh treat him well enough. He was very
morose, but he said you were good to him, but he wouldn't go
back to you because he didn't want to be an innkeeper."

Where the boy went from Nameny, no one knew. He might
have gone east or north. Probably, it was north, towards the
mountain country. A boy from Csenger, who knew Sroleh Yomtov from the time when he used to go there to say *kaddish*, asserted that for a month or two Sroleh Yomtov had been together
with him at the *yeshiba* in Pressburg. But at the same time the
wine merchant Mesel brought news that the boy was employed
in the wine cellar of Yechiel Kranztor in Szerencs. When Sholem
went to Szerencs to inquire, old Kranztor just shrugged and said
that he had no one by that name in his service. He did employ a
lanky youth some time before to accompany his deliveries to
Cracow and Breslau, but on one occasion he failed to return from
the latter city. If that was Sroleh Yomtov, the old man said, he

was sorry to have lost him, because he was an intelligent youth and honest too, having accounted for every copper of the money entrusted to him before he vanished. Was it Sroleh Yomtov?

Market people claimed to have seen him in this or that town, some said he was among the market Jews, others that he was among *yeshiba* pupils. Serf Polya met him on the road to Nyiregyhaza, with a whistle in his mouth and a peddler's pack on his back. Polya, who was carting a load of cabbage, spoke to the boy, thus: "Where are you going to, Sroleh-Anti?" "Just following my nose," replied the boy. "Then you've a long way to go because you've got a long nose." Serf Polya was noted for the fact that he never went carting without a bottle and it was possible that he had got tight on the journey and mistook another peddler boy for Sroleh Yomtov; in any case, Sholem gave him a tot of spirit free for his story. But you could scarcely doubt the word of Aryeh Leib, the rush-mat Jew, who said that he had seen the boy at the synagogue in Szentmiklos. He signalled to the boy that he wanted to speak with him, and the boy signalled back, but by the time Aryeh had repacked his prayer-bag, Sroleh Yomtov had vanished, and inquiries about him failed to elicit any information.

Yes, it must have been Sroleh Yomtov. In the family he had heard a great deal about Szentmiklos, the small mountain town from where Sholem and Malkeleh had set out on their journey together, and which admitted and tolerated Jews within its walls, and it used to excite his imagination. In the course of the years Malkeleh made inquiries in all directions, cross-examining visitors and writing many letters, but never succeeded in securing definite information as to the boy's whereabouts.

When Yossef went to Pressburg, Malkeleh told him to search there for his brother. Sholem did not know, and Yossef did not consider it politic to inform him, that during his brief membership of the Pressburg *yeshiba* he spent more time in the neighboring towns than in the vicinity of the great Rabbi Sopher's college. He did come upon the tracks of his brother now and then, and before his return home from Pressburg he had followed them as far north as Prague. However, just as though Sroleh Yomtov was deliberately playing with his pursuers, he always vanished a day or two before they caught up with him. Of course, the tracks

might have been deceptive and might not have been those of
Sroleh Yomtov at all. In time Yossef became sick of distant
*yeshibas*, as well as of the search for his brother. He may even
have become jealous of him. All Malkeleh was able to learn was
that Sroleh Yomtov was still alive. It was better than nothing, a
great deal better.


### A GOOD BROTHER-IN-LAW


MALKELEH NOW had new troubles, and she ceased her planning in
connection with Yiteleh. Yiteleh was no longer a little girl, but she
was not a grown-up either. She had a great deal to learn about
household management and the care of children. Besides, her
bottom drawer was far from full yet, for all that Malkeleh had
done in that direction for nearly fifteen years. She, Malkeleh, had
tried her best, had indeed tried to do several things at once. But
it was just impossible. The house had been full of trouble most of
the time, so that for the past six years they had had to make a
fresh beginning again and again. Just now she was busy getting
together another layette, and it was far from easy, because few of
the old swaddles, napkins, and baby clothes were in good condition. Only Sholem felt the spur of time, for according to the
Sages a boy was ripe for marriage at the age of eighteen, a girl at
the age of fifteen, and Yiteleh would be sixteen the following
Adar.

"Have you got your first eight hundred florins together?" inquired Malkeleh.

"Money," said Sholem, "is of no importance. A good idea is
much better."

"I seem to have heard that before, Sholem," returned Malkeleh.
"You once had a good idea how to get brandy for the business.
But what use would it have been if Sroleh Yomtov hadn't had
the money?"

"That's true," agreed Sholem. "But don't forget that ideas come
before money."

What his idea was he refused to divulge. But sometimes, sitting

at the dinner table or behind the bar, or pausing in the field, he
would smile to himself, nod his head once or twice or make a
mildly argumentative gesture, just as if he were engaged in
pleasant converse with an invisible someone. To judge by the
paternal expression on his hirsute face, the invisible someone
must have been a young *bocher* of whom Sholem heartily approved. Who he was, no one knew, and indeed, up to a few
months earlier, when he was conversing with him in person,
Sholem himself had been unaware that he was *the bocher*. On that
occasion he had asked the young man what his plans were for the
future, but there was no conscious purpose behind the question.

"After finishing my studies," answered the young man, "I'll sit
down and start learning. Life is short but the Law is endless."

It was only now that Sholem realized that that question of several months ago had not been pointless. As Wolf's ascetic head and
stern eyes rose before his mind's eye, Sholem felt that he was
giving an intimate personal reply to an intimate personal question.
Wolf did not intend to become a teacher or professor like Shayeh,
nor did he want to start a business, or peddle or make candles, or
take the lease of an inn: all he wanted was to study for the rest
of his life. That was the finest thing a man could do. Any man
that supported such learning would have a share in the bliss of the
pious in after life, even though he himself was ignorant. Sholem
was filled with joy as he thought of his own great reward if he
succeeded in settling Wolf in Lapfalva and getting him wedded
not only to his daughter, but also to the *Gemarah*.

He had said nothing to the family yet. When the matter matured, he would come out with his plan, nay, his decision. Sholem
himself could not approach Wolf, nor could he entrust a go-be-
tween with such a task. But he could leave it to Mosheh Doved
Troyes, where Wolf frequently called, and had stayed for several
weeks more than once. For this descendant of Rashi had some
rare books on his shelves, which attracted the young student.
There was no need to worry about Wolf's support: where there
were eleven people sitting down at table, there was room for a
twelfth.

Sholem was already working out the economic side in his own
mind. Soon he would close his accounts for the year and collect

from the peasants a portion of their crop in payment of their
tally debts. Joshua Brueder would pay cash for the corn. With
the money Sholem would carry on till next autumn. But he also
had some nine hundred florins left over, apart from what he had
set aside for the orphans. Then he also had several beams and two
piles of bricks with which he had intended to extend the shed. He
would buy some more building materials and build a couple of
rooms in the garden for the young couple. He would buy them
some furniture and also give Malkeleh one or two hundred florins
for Yiteleh's trousseau. He would need about eighteen hundred
florins, but he already had half, and the other half he could obtain.
He could borrow from relations. Not from Mordechai, even if the
latter were sure to respond readily, but from Azriel, in Szentmiklos. And once he was approaching that other brother-in-law,
it did not matter if he asked for a hundred or two more, say, a
round thousand. After all, there were going to be minor expenses
that one could not foresee.

That year the crops were not satisfactory. The peasants had to
do too much villenage, and when it came to tilling their own land,
they could only scratch it. Besides, it was a lean year, anyhow.
At such a time it was advisable to keep a little cash in reserve,
because part of his outstanding accounts could not be collected till
next autumn. What if he asked Azriel for twelve hundred? In
such a case Azriel wouldn't mind. Sholem mentally patted himself
on the back. The conclusion of the work on the land, his excellent calculation, and the sober logic of his paternal decision,
gave him an easy mind. He kept silent for a little longer, but that
was only a matter of prudence. Mentally, he was already holding
a dress rehearsal of the talk he was going to have with Malkeleh,
and because he had worked out the plan so beautifully he knew
that the final trump card was in his hands. As regards the details
he would not be unyielding. If Malkeleh said to have walnut
furniture and porcelain utensils, let her have her way. A hundred
more there, fifty less here, well, they were not going to quarrel
about that. He would write a nice letter to Azriel and Rachel.
And if it was fifteen hundred that was needed, why, then it'd be
fifteen hundred. It was nothing to them.

A man who is about to marry off his daughter and has more

than fifteen hundred florins in his pocket, can at last afford to engage a servant. Up till now, it had been against his principles. But having become a real *baal-bos*, he could not help acting according to his new status. Besides, the Talmudic debates which he would carry on with his learned son-in-law would in any case leave him little time for the rough work . . . Isaac was a hulking Jew boy of twenty, strong and a good worker, though a real *am-haarez*, and scarcely able to read in the prayer book. He used to gaze at his new employer with only one eye, the other being fixed on his native village and on Varalja, where he had spent six years in the service of the innkeeper Herskovitch. When Sholem ordered him to smoke the mustiness out of the wine casks, Isaac would wrap the sulphur sticks into straw, light them and insert them like that through the bunghole. Sholem would tell him that the straw was superfluous and would only make a litter inside the cask, but Isaac would insist that that was how he had learnt it at Herskovitch's. When milking the cow, Isaac would tie her tail to her horns—another Herskovitch custom. And when Sholem said, gently but firmly, that this or that thing must be done differently here, Isaac used to raise his squinting eyes to his face and declare that he was not going to learn anything twice.

Isaac did not roll the full barrels into the inn, but carried them on his shoulders. And if the peasant lads became unruly, no matter how big or strong they were, Isaac would pick them up like a sack of potatoes and put them out. But he never liked to do today anything that could be left till tomorrow. Sholem used to take an hour or two off even from the harvesting in order to work on the new barn. Let Wolf, when he comes, note the growing prosperity. Isaac was an unwilling assistant.

"Ay, ay, Daddy," he used to say, speaking as though his mouth were full of hot polenta, "what do you want a new barn for? You won't have nothing to put into it."

He was not such a simpleton as he looked. Though boss-eyed, he at least kept his eyes open and knew by now that the harvest was going to be far from good. But Sholem dismissed his objection with a gesture. The toad-puddle wouldn't produce much this year, but after all this was the first time it had been under the plough. But then, the peasants would pay up in the autumn . . .

Anyhow, the old barn was leaky, while the pit made the grain moldy.

Of course, Sholem was not blind either, and he had seen and experienced the troubles that Isaac was referring to. The rust had got into his wheat too, and he too had had to sell his cow to the butcher for next to nothing when she came back from the pasture limping and with a swollen mouth. But at least he could bear the loss. Moreover, the family was anticipating a joyous event, so that it seemed as if the month of Adar had stretched far into the summer. Speaking with Malkeleh that day, he said:

"You'll see, we'll be having a good year." Malkeleh did not understand the cause of his confidence, even when he added: "It's our seventh year in this place, and the seventh year brings a change for the better."

The following day he had reason to feel less cheerful. In the evening he had feasted his eyes thankfully on his sunflowers, which stood sentinel along the edge of his field over his poor crop. He praised the Above One for giving him the finest sunflowers in the area, though his land was still soggy. But by the morning an envious hand had broken them all off, every one of them, depriving him of his store of oil for a whole year. The peasants merely shrugged their shoulders and said that it was the work of Gimpel Zorech. But Gimpel Zorech had not been in the vicinity, and if he had been, he could not have been so drunk as to mistake Sholem's holding for anyone else's. It had become almost a habit with the peasants to blame Gimpel Zorech for everything. Since his memorable exploit, every broken sunflower stalk was blamed on him, even when the peasants knew that it was the result of a storm, or of the activities of some unruly brats.

Whereas Sholem's cheerfulness and confidence were not contagious, the family caught his depression soon enough. Malkeleh expressed the fear that Gimpel Zorech might have got into trouble again. Perhaps he had done damage somewhere in the vicinity, and the peasants ruined Sholem's sunflowers by way of revenge. The last time the unfortunate Gimpel had been to Lapfalva was months before, in the winter, but Malkeleh had not seen him. He came into the inn in filthy rags and broken bast shoes, shivering with cold and faint with hunger and thirst. But

Sholem received him sternly, failing even to offer him a tot of brandy. On the other hand, he held a document written in Hebrew under his nose, declaring that it was a Bill of Divorcement for Beilah Yenteh.

"She wants to get married?" mouthed Gimpel.

"What woman doesn't?" said his brother.

"Ah, she wants another," muttered Gimpel.

"Of course she does," snapped Sholem. "If you don't want to live with her. . . ."

"She wants to put somebody into the bed in the stove room, what?" demanded Gimpel Zorech.

But to Sholem this was unclean talk, so he ignored it.

"Here's the Bill, sign it," he said. "I wrote it myself and it's valid."

"Where shall I sign it?" asked Gimpel.

"Here," said Sholem, pointing.

"I'll be back in a minute," replied Gimpel. "My fingers are numb just now."

"All right," said his brother. "I waited with this Bill for six months, so I can wait another half-hour. Go into the kitchen and get warm."

But Gimpel Zorech did not go into the kitchen to get warm, nor did he even stay to have a look at his son, Yosseleh. Instead, he went back to the road and had not been seen in the house since. Now that he had been mentioned again, the family were wishing that he would turn up. Malkeleh wanted to compensate the beggar for the stern reception Sholem had given him, and she prepared to make him feel happy in the house for at least a week. The children, too, believed that Gimpel would soon be along, together with his hair-raising tales. He was quite sure to appear one day, for had not Aunt Feiga heard the magpie three times in succession?

"If you hear the magpie in summer, you get a visitor from far away," was the old saying.

The visitor arrived towards dusk on Wednesday. He came from far away, too, but he was not Gimpel Zorech. He was a far more fortunate uncle, Azriel Fuerth from Liptoszentmiklos. The children stared at him, then drew away, for this man was a stranger to them.

Azriel gazed at Malkeleh, and Malkeleh gazed at Azriel as they talked. Azriel said it seemed impossible that ten years should have passed since he saw her last. But Malkeleh reminded him that she and Sholem had been living at Ujhely when Azriel and Rachel last came to see them. Since then they had fled from Latorka, where they had lived for two years among savage peasants, shut off from the world. They had been living at Lapfalva for nearly seven years, praise be to the Above One, with many troubles, but without bad shocks.

Azriel smiled gently. The ten years and the six new children had scarcely left a mark on Malkeleh. It struck him that Malkeleh no longer spoke the faultless German she used in her girlhood, saying the Above One instead of *der liebe Gott*, and the Hebrew word *emmes* (true) instead of the German equivalent. And when she spoke about Jews, she did not call them "Juden," but used the Yiddish term, *Yiddelach*. It sounded strange from the lips of Malkeleh, who at the age of sixteen used to read *The Sorrows of Young Werther* and *Faust* and *Peter Schlemihl*.

What struck Malkeleh was a sad expression in Azriel's face that was absent before. He was still well dressed in a light English suit with a high collar, but the clothes seemed to hang on him as on a coat-hanger. His once golden beard, which he wore short, was now a faded yellow, though not yet greying. Malkeleh recalled that her brother-in-law formerly carried an ivory-backed beard brush in his waistcoat pocket, which he used continually. Now she almost missed it. There were a thousand questions in her mind about his and her sister's life at home, yet it was only a childish question that sprang to her lips out of the subconscious accumulations from a jointly spent youth:

"You don't keep brushing your beard any more."

"What difference does it make," shrugged the man, "whether the parting is there on my chin or not? There was a time when I considered it important." He sighed, then added: *Wer nie sein Brot mit Traenen ess. . . .*

Malkeleh nodded her recognition of the quotation. But she did not know whether Azriel was complaining, or whether he was merely showing off his education. She had always been following the family's affairs as far as possible, and she could not imagine that this favorite of fortune could ever have "eaten his bread with tears."

"Really, Azriel," she said with mock severity, "you have little reason for such *Weltschmerz*."

"Perhaps you're right," replied the man. "But do you know, my worst trouble is that I'm not used to trouble. Either trouble or worry. Recently, I have thought a lot about you, who have always had troubles and worries. I envied you for your struggles. You're lucky people."

"You've worries, Azriel?"

"I'm ruined," said the man quietly, almost shyly.

It struck Malkeleh like a blow. She regretted her earlier reproving remark. She wanted to say something, but her tongue was paralyzed. She could only gaze at him, though there was surprise and inquiry in her gaze. It loosened Azriel's tongue.

"I'll tell you all, Malkeleh. But I beg of you not to repeat it, not even to Sholem. Even Rachel doesn't know. And I didn't tell Mordechai, though I was his guest for two days. All I told him was that my business was in temporary difficulties. He advised me to come to you." Malkeleh nodded comprehension. "That upstart from Frankfort is the cause of it all," Azriel went on vehemently. "That adventurer! That thief! That bandit!"

"Who is that?"

"Who? Why, the debating partner of street urchins and foul-mouthed cab-drivers, the domestic Jew of Prince Metternich and the milch cow of Herr von Gentz, the Emperor's latest baron, the laughing-stock and scandal of Vienna, Solomon von Rothschild!"

There was the sound of heavy footsteps from the verandah. Sholem had arrived. Azriel took out his handkerchief and wiped his face.

"When we're alone again, Malkeleh," was all he said.

Sholem's beard and ear-curls were full of chaff. His sun-tanned face was bursting with laughter.

"*Sholem aleichem*, Reb Azriel," he said, hugging and kissing his brother-in-law. "Why didn't you let me know at once?" he

said to the room at large. "Yosseleh said our beloved guest has
been here for an hour."

"Scarcely half an hour," said Malkeleh. She went out into the
kitchen to prepare supper, leaving the two men alone.

They talked about all sorts of things, Sholem mentioned the
reclaimed marsh, the first crop, the inn, Malkeleh, the children,
and particularly Yiteleh, whom he was going to marry off soon.
Sholem was very pleased with the Almighty who had made all
this possible. He quoted a proverb from the Talmud: "Everything
depends on luck."

Azriel seemed tired, and no wonder. It was a long journey from
the north to the County of Szatmar. He had had a rest at Karoly,
but he had been discussing business there, and that too was tiring.

"You know, Sholem," said Azriel suddenly, "if your business
succeeds, it is as though you had just had a bath. But if not, it's
as though you'd climbed a mountain to get something and had to
climb down empty. And if your hands are empty your feet are
heavy."

Sholem looked at him. One of Azriel's eyelids was shorter than
the other—his left eye seemed smaller than the right. Formerly
that left eye flashed irony when they were debating a Talmudic
topic, and he, Sholem, being younger and less learned, had the
worst of it. Now the left eye was only lugubrious.

Azriel's lips began to explain why. He had married off his two
daughters. That cost a great deal of money. The century-old
synagogue had been rebuilt—and who but the Fuerth family were
to provide the wherewithal? They had had a bad, even disastrous
year. Flood water had penetrated the hide warehouse and rotted
the hides. There had been a plague of moths, ruining most of the
cloth. An old customer who owed some thousands had lost all
his money on the Vienna Bourse. The firm's Manchester mills demanded payment in sterling, and it was also hard pressed by a
supplier in Brunn. Unless help came from somewhere, the firm of
Fuerth & Nikolsburger would go on the rocks—after having
weathered so many storms since the reign of Maria Theresa.

Sholem's brow furrowed and a distant look came into his eyes.
"How much money would you need?"

"If I had two thousand florins. . . ."

"Two thousand florins!" cried Sholem with amazement.

He saw by Azriel's scared expression that he ought not to have said that. Whereas he did not mean it the way Azriel interpreted the exclamation. A Fuerth worried about two thousand florins! How badly off he must be! But it would not be the thing to explain that now! Leaning his chin on his fist, Sholem said:

"I've got nine hundred florins. You can have that at once. In three or four weeks, when the peasants pay up, I can let you have another few hundreds."

Azriel gave him a warm look.

"I can't expect you," he said, "to give me all you have."

"You can't expect me!" cried Sholem. "Are you not Rachel's husband and Manasseh Nikolsburger's son-in-law?" He was already opening the cabinet and getting the money out.

"I'm not going to take all of it," said Azriel, shaking his head. "One always needs cash in a business. Give me six hundred and a bill of exchange for fifteen hundred. I can soon get fourteen hundred for it."

Sholem nodded agreement. Azriel produced the blank, while Sholem fetched pen and ink. Then they fell to talking about old times, when, with Shmayeh Kahn, the other brother-in-law, they used to debate on the *Shulchan Aruch* and the *Marshah*. Azriel opined that he and Kahn had been right after all about that debate on the *Marshah*. Sholem gave a superior smile. And by the time Malkeleh returned to announce supper they had warmed to it and were right in the middle of a debate they had interrupted twenty years before.

### A LEAN YEAR

THE AUTUMN was always a time of bustle and excitement. The peasants would gather in the harvest, give a ninth to the squire and a tithe to the priest, pay taxes to the county and the Government, and provide food and fodder for the army. Then they would fill their pits with grain and bring the surplus to the inn to settle the year's tally. They justly suspected that they were being exploited and defrauded by every one, but whereas they were submissive with the squire and displayed due humility towards the priest, the county officials and requisitioning officers, they did not hesitate to speak their minds when they came to the Jew. The brandy had been diluted, the beer stale, the wine green, and the tally wouldn't come right. And even when it did, the peasants would still haggle on for days, because they wanted to have at least a little left for sale, so that for once they might see the color of the Emperor's coin. But this autumn the peasants kept quiet everywhere. They kept quiet when they were rated and browbeaten by the gentry, who blamed the laziness of the serfs for the bad harvest and the plague of foot-and-mouth disease among the cattle, forgetting all about the early frosts, the drought, and the hailstorms. And they were also quiet at the inn, accepting the tally without question. It was a disturbing quietness. Most of the peasants paid nothing, yet went on drinking. Even the more prosperous freemen paid only an instalment, and there was not enough corn in Sholem's granary even to cover purchases for the inn till Christmas.

"It's important that the peasants should have enough corn left to see them through the winter," said Sholem to his wife. "We can't make a living out of the peasants if they starve to death."

"Shall we have enough for the winter?" asked Malkeleh.

"We've got plenty of potatoes from the holding, and some wheat and a little maize from the toad-puddle. No worry about bread till next harvest, Malkeleh."

"Have we enough cash left too?" asked the woman.

"I've managed on less," replied Sholem.

Sholem's carefree explanations failed to reassure his wife. Malkeleh knew all about everything, including the things Sholem had omitted to mention to her. She knew that he had lent money to Azriel, though the latter had not told her either. She had merely noted that whereas he was depressed when he arrived, he was quite cheerful on his departure. How much he had taken Malkeleh did not know, but she suspected that it was more than Sholem could afford. She was quite pleased about it at the time. In the past, her brother-in-law had grudgingly given them a little

out of his abundance, now Sholem was giving him wholeheartedly
a great deal from the little he possessed. But when two months had
passed, and she saw that Azriel was denying them even the usual
courtesy of a letter, while at the same time a load of trouble was
accumulating about the house, Malkeleh began to feel anxious.
She always seemed to be full of disquiet, especially when there
was yet another baby on the way.

"We must be careful with money," she said quietly. "We must
be prepared for anything."

"I know, dear heart," said Sholem. "Yiteleh will be sixteen in
Adar."

"That's not what I mean, Sholem. I'm thinking not only of
Yiteleh, but of the whole family. Our fate is in the balance again."

"What makes you say that?" asked Sholem.

After eighteen years of marriage conversation between husband
and wife had become increasingly rare and laconic. A question
or answer might be delayed for weeks, to be brought out casually
in a talk on a different subject. However, Malkeleh was quick on
the uptake. She even knew what Sholem had been planning for
Yiteleh, though he had not told her. Malkeleh had put two and
two together from stray remarks, a look in Sholem's eyes and
other signs. Sholem had once referred to Doved Troyes' plaint
that the inn and the butcher's shop kept him so busy that he had
no time left to read the Talmud or carry out his plan of marrying
his daughter Rebecca to a Talmudist, who would earn merit for
both himself and Troyes by reading the Talmud all day and half
the night. Malkeleh gathered from this that Sholem had similar
ideas. Then when Sholem had finished the barn he began to pace
out squares in the garden—a large one and, next to it, two smaller
ones. He repeated this so often, at varying distances from the
house, that Malkeleh was able to see in her mind's eye the cottage
with two rooms and kitchen for the Talmudist son-in-law. Besides, one Sabbath at dinner Sholem quoted a saying of Wolf
Birnbaum's, which seemed all the weightier because Wolf himself
had probably quoted it from a sacred book:

"A stupid man who has travelled is wiser than the sage who
always sits at home . . . What do you say to that, Yiteleh?"

"Then," replied the girl, "Sroleh Yomtov is the wisest of all, because he's been travelling for seven years."

"Ah, well," said Sholem, "it isn't good for you to be roving all the time. Wolf travels from one *yeshiba* to another, but in between he sits down to the Book."

So it is Wolf Birnbaum, said Malkeleh to herself. Never, Sholem, never. It is enough if I got stuck here by the marsh, shut off from everything and everybody. Yiteleh shall not have a Talmudist husband whose interest lies with long-dead sages. Let her go out into the world and raise her children in the world. Malkeleh had said this many times and in many different forms, both to herself and to Sholem. But it was only now that her ideas began to take a definite shape. She now had a plan.

"Wolf is out of the question, I want Shayeh," she declared to herself.

She made ready for battle. Sometimes, when Sholem hinted at the subject, she tensed and held her breath. She knew that Sholem would be shocked to the bottom of his heart. A Shayeh Oesterreicher? A young man who went not to *yeshibas* but to Universities, who instead of studying the sacred traditions read forbidden books, who trimmed his beard with a razor! What if he was the scion of a great rabbinical family? An Oesterreicher would have to behave very differently before he could become the husband of Yiteleh and the son-in-law of Sholem ben Yoirish.

However, the clash did not come. They had other troubles. Now and then, Malkeleh had to sit behind the bar for a day or two because Sholem was away carting for the merchants of Karoly or Szalka to earn an extra florin or two. Sholem took nothing but bread and onions with him on these journeys, for one had to be economical in hard times. It reminded Malkeleh of the years they had spent at Latorka. But that was not the only thing that brought back those memories. The peasants were in a ferment, and this time they were noisy not from drink, but from a seething bitterness. As always, they were rebelling against God and the gentry, but whereas in the past they had abused these powers with a certain respectful restraint, now they cursed them with a savage, burning hatred. They generally began by recounting the atrocities of the day, which squire had committed what cruelties against the serfs. They had ample material, for the gentry were in an ugly mood. The Baron of Ecsed had shot his coachman in the belly, allegedly because he had answered back. If he recovered he would go before the court, and his master was the chief judge. He would get a year in jail at the very least.

"The peasants have a stake in the county jail," observed Serf Vizhordo bitterly. "It's they that gave the bricks, as well as the sweat, to build it."

That Lady Susannah at Gyekenyes beat and kicked her female servants, or that Squire de Denghelegh went about among the serfs with a dog-whip, and Squire de Sarberek with a club —all this was mentioned only by the way. But the case of Peter Bonca aroused considerable agitation. Bonca had two pigs. One of them strayed into the marsh and got drowned, whereupon his master, Squire de Gyekeny, confiscated the other pig, declaring that Bonca had secretly killed the first pig and hidden the carcass, so as to escape delivering a tithe of it to the Squire.

"May the hand of God lie heavy on him!" swore one of the serfs at the inn.

"God doesn't carry a club, Andrew," said another.

"Even God only punishes the serf; the gentry are let off."

"If God turns a blind eye, we must keep our eyes skinned."

"And our fists clenched."

Malkeleh listened to the rebellious peasants, looked at their tormented eyes, their mobile adam's apples, and their calloused, toil-deformed hands, and was seized with a great fear. She went out among them, serving them and saying a kind word to them as she did so, but they just went on and on. In the past they used to be nice to her, calling her Mistress Amelia, but now they took no notice of her. Despite herself, Malkeleh kept thinking of Latorka, and feeling that she was eight months pregnant with little Sarah Chayah and that tomorrow they must flee.

"Don't let it worry you, Malkeleh," said Sholem, when she confided her thoughts to him. "The main thing is that they don't mean us any harm. The gentry can take care of themselves. They always curse the gentry, anyhow. They curse them more fiercely now because they've had a poor harvest and the gentry are squeezing out of the serfs what God has omitted to give them."

"And what's going to happen here if there's a famine?" said
Malkeleh. "I tell you, Sholem, we'd better leave here and take
the children among human beings. We can still do it, we still have
a little money to start something with."

"Why go away?" said Sholem. "This happens to be a lean year,
but there are fat years to come."

"You forget about Latorka?"

"I wish you'd forget about it too."

"You didn't want to run away from there either."

"But I did in the end, didn't I?"

"You were afraid then," reproached the woman, "and you
aren't now."

"No," said Sholem. "I give these embittered souls to drink
more than I can afford, and I see no reason to be afraid."

"You don't," said Malkeleh, "because your eyes are always on
the Talmud. You're not afraid because you keep singing, 'Fear
not, my servant Jacob.' I can neither read the Talmud, nor sing,
so I'm afraid."

"That's all wrong," returned Sholem. "A mother who's expecting a baby mustn't live in constant fear."

"She mustn't, but she does. And perhaps it's right that she
should be afraid. My father always used to say that it was fear
that kept the Jewish people alive."

"Reb Manasseh of blessed memory was a wise man. But the
truth is that our people are kept alive by the Guardian of Israel
up above, by Him who does not sleep nor slumber."

"And I think that the Guardian of Israel has implanted fear into
the hearts of our people, as in the hearts of the hare and the gazelle,
so that they should run when they sense danger. If you took fear
away from the hare and the gazelle they'd soon die out."

"And I tell you, Malkeleh," declared Sholem, "that if we were
to run away at the stirring of a leaf, the whole earth wouldn't
be enough for a track. We must stay where the Lord has placed
us."

Malkeleh nodded her head. She accepted her husband's arguments. And she was glad, too, because this was the longest talk
she had had with him for a long time.

THE TAMING OF THE REBELS

SQUIRE DE SARBEREK sent a message to the inn by his servant, Gyurica: The Jew had forgotten to pay his rent and he must come along to the manor at once with a year's rent. Sholem was scared. The rent was not due until three weeks hence, and then only for six months. That was how it was set down in the agreement, and that was how the payments were always made, both by Sholem and his predecessors. One-half on All Saints' Day, and the other in the spring, on St. Philip's and St. Jacob's Day. However, if the Squire says that grass is red and snow is black, then grass is red and snow is black. These were hard times and it was not advisable to upset the gentry.

The Squire was in a stern mood and did not even invite Sholem to sit down, but just crammed the money into his pocket and said in a harsh voice:

"In view of the poor harvest we have decided to raise your rent. It's only for this year, see? We haven't fixed the amount yet; I'll let you know in a day or two. To compensate you, you are directed to reduce the peasants' consumption to one-quarter for the rest of the year. We're determined to tame that rebellious mob and get them accustomed to honest work. You may go, Jew."

Sholem bowed and left.

When he announced to the peasants that by order of the gentry he must reduce credit to a single drink per day, they shrugged their shoulders, exchanged looks with each other, and muttered to themselves, but they said nothing. They had been expecting something like this and comforted themselves with the thought that one drink was better than nothing. Only the bellringer, Ludpal, had something to say:

"Another Jew trick, this is."

The bellringer was never held in any great esteem, but nowadays he was treated with suspicion because he was proclerical and sly. That he refrained from blaspheming was forgivable, but not so his very restrained attitude towards the gentry, he being

as poverty-stricken as the rest, with seven hungry children in his
hut. The bellringer blamed the Jew for everything. Not without
reason, of course, for the other serfs agreed with him in this when
the harvest was plentiful and the gentry were not so hard on them.
But now. . . .

"The gentry guard the Jew's pocket like dragons," observed
Lajos Gore. "That's because they're in need of his money."

"The gentry eat money," said an ancient serf with a spongy,
pock-marked face. "The peasant keeps taking the money to the
county treasury, the gentry keep drawing it out. The peasant
fills the till at the board of guardians, the gentry come and empty
it. Even here at the inn the peasant spends only to enrich the
gentry."

"You didn't spend much this year, Uncle Topoly," remarked
Martin Vizhordo casually.

"If I haven't paid this year, I'll pay next," replied the old man.

"More likely it'll be the worms in the cemetery that'll pay the
Jew. We'll all kick the bucket this year, and even the worms'll
complain that they don't get enough to eat from our carcasses."

The first day of rationed drink passed tolerably well. The
peasants showed no resentment against the Jew. The following
day they were a little more troublesome, trying to get round
Sholem to give them a second drink. But Sholem just kept shaking
his head and saying that orders were orders. The peasants thereupon sat down at the trestle tables and sat smoking their pipes, or
rather sucking at them, for the tobacco harvest had been poor
too. There they sat for hours, expectorating freely and angrily,
for that seemed to be the only thing in which they were not
restricted. They held out until closing time, which was sometimes
near midnight. Then they went up to the bar to collect their tally
sticks, with only a solitary notch added for the day, and left
without a grumble, though also, for the most part, without a
"good night." So there were no noisy farewells, and worse still,
no talking or singing as the peasants gloomily made for home.

The third day the silence lay heavy on the inn. The peasants
sat with their elbows leaning on the tables, while Sholem sat
quietly behind the bar, turning the pages of a large tome. He
could now read undisturbed, for the serving of the few drinks

was a simple matter and soon over, but the silence was more
disturbing than any noise. He could not think of the Sages without the accustomed din. His mind was held down to the problems
of the present, one of which was that he was losing his hard-won
popularity and that the peasants were getting increasingly distrustful. If he had cut credit of his own accord because the peasants
had not paid their debt, his position would have been simpler.
Now they looked upon him as though he were conspiring with
the gentry. Peter Bonca, returning from a day's villenage, turned
on him angrily:

"You didn't cut the ration for the gentry, did you? Hey?"
Then he added, bawling with fury: "My squire stank of rum."

Turning to the others, he reported how Squire de Gyekeny,
reeling drunk, had kept thrashing the men on villenage and shouting: "I'll show you, you swine. You're not going to tipple at our
expense after this. You'll work from dawn till dusk, that's what
you'll do." Ferke stood waiting with the mallet in his hand, to
be told where to drive in some stakes, when the Squire went for
him and slapped his face on both sides.

Similar reports came from the other two manors. Old de
Denghelegh went about scolding the men on villenage for their
drunken abuse of their benefactors. If there were no gentry, he
said, the peasants would die from hunger. And Squire de Sarberek
seemed to know what Serf Topoly had said about the county
treasury and the monies of the board of guardians.

In the past, such reports used to be received with noisy out-
bursts. Now they were listened to in sullen silence. Only the bellringer, Ludpal, would sometimes raise his high-pitched voice in a
remark about the enemies of Christ, but none except Sholem
himself and one or two farm servants would take any notice of
him.

The atmosphere became more and more disturbing. The
peasants just kept looking at each other and saying nothing. They
would arrive as usual in the late afternoon and stay until late at
night, with speech stuck in their throats. When they did talk it
was about their domestic troubles, but that only increased their
bitterness. They came to the inn to drown their sorrow and to hit
back with their tongues at the gentry, who were hitting them with

sticks and fists. But now they found no drink at the inn, only enemies who sneaked on them to the gentry, so they could neither forget, nor relieve their feelings. What was the use of having a Jew if he gave you nothing to drink, and what was the use of having an inn if you couldn't even curse there?

Sholem thought of Malkeleh's misgivings and he no longer thought of deprecating them. The huge, hulking Isaac sat dozing behind the bar, waiting to do his duty. But for days now there had been no drunks to be thrown out and no brawls to be quelled. He no longer trusted his great strength, though he knew he could deal even with the strongest of the serfs. He gave his master a boss-eyed look and there was something like fear in it.

"When the *goy* makes a noise," he said, "he's a good *goy*. But when he's quiet he's just waiting to go home and sharpen his knife."

"What knife?" snapped Sholem in a scared voice.

"The pig-sticking knife," said Isaac.

"Well," said Sholem, "he needs it for pig-sticking."

"He doesn't, not now," argued Isaac, "only in winter."

"Nonsense," waved Sholem. But he was perturbed just the same.

One evening, when the inn was full of grimly sober, silent serfs, Gyurica appeared with a message from Squire de Sarberek.

"His worship says sixty florins—get it ready for him."

"All right," acquiesced Sholem, "I'll take it along."

"No need," said Gyurica. "It's St. Clementine's Day. The gentry are there with my lady: Balthazar and Gedeon and the Baron from Ecsed. They'll be along after their rake's broth."

"After their rake's broth?" wondered Sholem.

"Yes, after supper, when the watchman's given ten toots."

Gyurica talked aloud, so that people should know what an important message he had been entrusted with. A loyal servant is proud of his allegiance. Besides, the message held something for the common herd as well.

"The gentry says," Gyurica went on, "they'll want some plum brandy and rum and rye, as usual, and some Tokay as well. And tell your wife to tidy up the gentry's parlor. And see you have glasses from which no peasant's drunk yet. And have a pack of

cards ready which hasn't been touched by the hand of a peasant."
The lad's eyes swept over the crowd of serfs, then he turned on
his heel and left.

Sholem hurried into the house to talk with his wife. The
gentry would be along in an hour or two—would she attend to
the parlor? However, this was only an excuse, for Sholem could
have got the parlor ready himself. What he wanted was to discuss
with Malkeleh a subject she had raised some weeks before, when
he had pooh-poohed her fears. Perhaps Malkeleh knew more
now that even Isaac was talking about the sharpening of knives.
To his surprise and irritation, Sholem found Mailech in the room,
fumbling with his pack.

"Why aren't you at the *yeshiba*?" snapped Sholem. He was
upset, partly through the atmosphere in general, and partly because he had expected to be alone with his wife.

"I came home for the Sabbath," replied the boy.

"But it's only Thursday today. You can't do any peddling now,
the peasants have no money for ribbons."

"I know, Dad," said the boy. "But I've brought a letter for
Mummy."

Malkeleh had just finished reading a letter, and as she looked
at Sholem her face was radiant.

"Good news, Sholem," she said. "We'll be having visitors. Wolf
will be here tomorrow."

"Wolf Birnbaum?"

"He and Shayeh. They'll stay for the Sabbath."

"Umm," said Sholem, his brow clouding. He had desired Wolf's
visit more than once, but now the news gave him no pleasure. It
was not only because he had long spent Yiteleh's dowry and his
business capital was almost nil. The money would not have
mattered much. But now it was not a question of Yiteleh alone,
but of the fate of the whole family. Had Malkeleh ceased to
realize this?

"Shayeh is a lovely boy," said Malkeleh, and there was music
in her voice. 'I hope you're all well,' he says, 'and that your charming Yiteleh will be at home.' What do you say to that, Sholem?"

"Very good," muttered Sholem.

"Isn't it, Sholem?" said Malkeleh. "Wolf is your favorite, isn't he? You'll get the fisherman of Kocor to send a couple of pike, or better still, a couple of carp. I'll have stuffed fish for Friday evening. You'll kill a couple of ducks in the morning. I'll have the giblets and the legs in the soup, stuff the necks and roast the breasts. I'll have a lot to do in the morning. It's a short Friday and the boys will be along before noon. I'll have to get up early in the morning, so the dough should rise in good time. I'll make some fancy loaves and some egg cake."

Malkeleh had not been so cheerful for a long time. Nay, she was happy, completely happy. Sholem had talked her out of her fears a fortnight before, and she was reassured and confident. She realized that her disquiet had been due to her entry into the ninth month of pregnancy. What could go wrong now? She had brought eight children into the world, and six of them were living; the ninth, too, would arrive without any complications. Her inner conflict with Sholem had also quietened down. After all, what was the use of getting excited in advance. It was not Sholem or she who would decide whether it was to be Wolf or Shayeh, but Yiteleh alone. If she preferred Wolf, then it would be Wolf. But if she preferred Shayeh . . . And anyone who had seen Shayeh larking with the girl could tell at once . . . However, one must be considerate with Sholem and not upset him without cause. Malkeleh was glad to have reached these conclusions. She had been tactful, hadn't she, to mention Wolf first when she told Sholem about the letter.

Malkeleh had changed because she had adopted Sholem's previous attitude. But this had not brought her closer to him because he on his part had adopted hers. Malkeleh was now confident, full of plans for the future and happy in the joys of activity, but Sholem felt slack, disquieted, and even scared. Malkeleh's faith seemed disturbing. He had a hundred things to ask and tell her in conveying his anxieties, but all he could think of in the course of this hurried conversation was Isaac's remark.

"Isaac says that when the peasants are quiet they sharpen their knives."

"He gave me this piece of wisdom as well. But is it so extraordinary if the peasants get their pig-sticking knives ready?"

"It's not pig-sticking time yet," said Sholem.

"Didn't you know, Sholem?" wondered Malkeleh, and there was laughter in her eyes. "The peasants are going to kill their pigs earlier because they've nothing to feed them with. I suppose you don't know, either, that they kill them at night out in the marsh, to avoid giving a share to the gentry. You must have heard the screeching of pigs during the night."

Sholem gazed at her in wonderment. Malkeleh seemed to know everything. Why, of course! That was what Peter Bonca had done—killed one of his pigs in secret, but the squire heard about it and confiscated the other one. A sense of gay confidence flashed through Sholem's heart and on his way back to the bar parlor he was already making a mental calculation. If Azriel repaid the six hundred, he would borrow another hundred from the trough-seller Jew, sell half of his harvest and do some carting besides. . . .

As he reached the bar parlor the figures fled from his brain. The room was almost empty, with only the bellringer and two ancient farm servants sitting in one corner. Sholem found it strange that the peasants should have thus abruptly departed. It was just on nine o'clock, too, more than two hours short of the usual closing time. True, the inn was no fun without any drink, but still, on other evenings the serfs used to stay till close on midnight. Isaac handed him the tally sticks of the departed customers.

"They say you can make as many notches as you like," he rumbled.

"Why didn't they take the sticks away with them?" asked Sholem.

"They don't need them any more," said Isaac.

"Don't need them. . . ."

"That's what they said," explained Isaac.

Sholem was puzzled. He was jerked out of his puzzlement by the bellringer's high-pitched voice.

"At Csenger the innkeeper is an Armenian," he was saying. "He has a notice on the wall: 'Cash down today, free tomorrow.' He's a good Christian, the Armenian is, so he gives no credit. Nothing like this can happen there. At Csenger the priest and the gentry get proper respect."

He never gets tired of running down the Jews, thought Sholem as he hurried into the gentry's room to tidy up. He wiped over the bottles, polished the glasses, spread an embroidered cloth on the table and placed a new pack of cards on the cloth, as well as an envelope with money. He stayed in the room, pottering around, and trying not to think of the peasants. But he had to think of the gentry, who would soon be here to drink and gamble, all three of them, together with the Baron from Ecsed, who would probably soon fleece the others. Then the black squire would demand more money from the Jew, and when the Jew was cleaned out they would start playing for houses, villages, flocks of sheep, and batches of serfs. It had happened before. The Baron of Ecsed was resuming the battle of some years before.

Sholem sat down in a corner and sat gazing in front of him. He tried to think of Wolf and Yiteleh and the Sabbath *scholet*, which Malkeleh was going to prepare with stuffed duck's neck. But these thoughts gave him no pleasure. He racked his brain for an apt quotation, but it just would not come. He tried to hum "Said the Lord to Jacob, Fear not, my servant Jacob," but it just did not sound right. For he *was* afraid, scared. Suddenly, he knew why. He was afraid of his thoughtless, reckless gentry.

A STAR HAS RISEN FROM JACOB

THE NIGHT WATCHMAN had called the hour of midnight. Malkeleh had just dozed off. Suddenly, the little boy who lay beside her dug his elbow into her stomach.

"Mummy, Mummy," he said, "it's morning."

"It isn't, darling," said his mother, startled awake.

"It is," insisted the child.

"Be quiet, Yoirish, and go to sleep."

"Really, Mummy," said Yoirish. "It's morning. Look through the window."

Malkeleh heard a crackling noise and she sat up and looked out through the window.

"That's nothing," she said, yet she jumped out of bed. She woke Yiteleh, Mailech, and Sarah Chayah and ordered them to dress the younger children.

"Is it time to knead the dough?" inquired Yiteleh sleepily.

"No," said her mother.

"The house is on fire!" cried Mailech.

"Don't make such a noise," reproved Malkeleh. "We can all see that the house is on fire."

Malkeleh could be very scared of impending trouble, but when the trouble was there she was calm and brave, though later she might be seized with retrospective alarm at the dire perils her children had been threatened with. Her calmness reassured the children and they obeyed her firm, unhurried orders without hesitation or confusion.

"Help to get the bedclothes out into the yard. Mailech, Sarah Chayah, take the table and the chairs out. Yiteleh, your trousseau. Breathe through your noses, then you won't cough. I'll take the bed to pieces. Manasseh, you can carry the parts. Put them down by the well. Yossel, that shelf is too heavy for you."

Malkeleh hurried outside on the verandah. There she collided with Sholem, whose bearded face looked like an apparition in the glow of the fire.

"The peasants!" he mouthed thickly, his throat full of choking smoke. Then he exploded into a noisy fit of coughing.

"They set the roof on fire over our heads," said Malkeleh.

"The gentry haven't arrived yet," coughed Sholem.

Malkeleh looked at the fire, which seemed to have started on the roof over the gentry's parlor, spreading to the left over the bar parlor, and to the right over the living rooms. Suddenly, she understood.

Sholem ran into the house to get his tomes and to drag out the chest of drawers and the wardrobe. Malkeleh waddled to the fence and stood screaming towards the village.

"Help! Help! Uncle Matolcs! Uncle Vizhordo! Farmer Galagonya! Help! Help!"

But there was not a soul anywhere. The thatch of the roof went on crackling, the wind carried the sparks towards the village, the rows of cottages were outlined blackly in the sulphurous glow. The village seemed to be sunk in sleep.

Isaac was rolling the casks out of the inn and wailing:

"The good people are all dead, the bad ones are hiding. They're our enemies, all of them."

"The storks' nest is on fire," screamed one of the children. "The little storks will be burnt to death."

"Don't worry," soothed Yiteleh. "The storks are already gone."

"You see, Sholem?" said Malkeleh reproachfully. "If we'd gone in time . . ." Sholem raced past her and did not hear the reproach. Malkeleh waddled along to the stable.

"Mailech," she called, "we must harness the horse. The children stood behind her, watching her efforts. Manasseh, wide-eyed, stared at the fire, Yosseleh sniffed, the youngest bawled with fright.

"We're going on a journey, Yoirish," laughed Malkeleh. Then she was off towards the coops to release the fowls in case the coops caught fire.

Mailech helped Aunt Feiga on to the cart, after which he put on his father's old foxskin coat and settled down on the driving-seat. The children and the family's most important possessions were already in the cart. The horse was restlessly pawing the ground amid a rain of sparks.

Malkeleh was crouching in front of a low coop whose door was fastened with string. That was where the ducks were. As she rose she felt a stab of pain. It scared her. She paused, looking down at her loins. Hastily, she waddled back to the cart and heaved herself up. She sat on a bundle, gripping the side of the cart with her left hand, and Yiteleh's arm with her right, her brow suddenly contracting.

"Pull your caps over your ears," she cried in a thick voice. "It's a cold night." Now she was smiling again. "Manasseh, Yosseleh . . . We're driving the same way as the Great Bear."

Yiteleh knew.

"Mummy," she said, "you sit in the middle. I'll put a pillow under you, so you won't get shaken. Leave everything to Mailech and me. We know the way to Karoly. Sarah Chayah, light the lantern."

"Karoly is far away," said Malkeleh. "Perhaps we'd better drive towards Hodasz."

"It's much farther that way," objected Mailech, "at least six hours. The straight way is only five."

"You drive towards Hodasz," ordered Yiteleh. "Do as Mummy tells you. How long will it take to Hodasz?"

"Two hours," replied the boy.

"All right, make a start."

As the cart turned out of the yard, Malkeleh called out to Sholem:

"Sholem, follow on with Isaac . . . No room left on the cart."

"The Lord be with you," replied Sholem, nodding his head. He and Isaac could not go yet. The fire had now reached the granary. The family had been saved, so their bread must be saved too. Isaac was drawing water from the well at a terrific pace. Then Serf Balint Matolcs appeared from nowhere. He was a stocky little man who tended the fires in Sholem's house of a Sabbath.

"I didn't lay this fire," he said shamefacedly. "It isn't Sabbath yet." He took the bucket from Isaac and handed it to Sholem. "The gentry are lucky," he went on. "It's them the people wanted to burn, yet it's you they've roasted." Sholem was not listening. He was toiling like one demented. The sparks flying heavenward from the roof reminded him of the line, "A star has risen from Jacob."

There was an approaching noise of hoof-beats, the rattle of a coach, and hoarse whoops mingled with the sounds of a fiddle and a flute:

> "Hark, the cockerels, hark,
> Dawn breaks through the dark. . . ."

# Book Two

## THE YELLOW HOUSE

*"Now Jericho was straitly
shut up because of the children
of Israel: none went out, and
none came in."*

*Joshua*

A STRANGER to the marsh-side village might easily have mistaken the building with the shingled roof for the residence of some petty noble. It stood apart from the mud-huts of the village and had clean whitewashed walls and a veranda with blue balusters, so what else could it be? It was only on closer inspection that the stranger would observe that the side of the building jutted almost into the roadway and that there was a long pole over the glass door with a mop of curly wood shavings at the end of it. So it was a *csárda* after all, though different from all others. For a *csárda* was not a *csárda* unless it was dilapidated, leaning drunkenly out into the road, with the thatch roof at a rakish angle like the hat of an ancient wine-bibber. That was what the inn of Lapfalva looked like even last autumn, when it seemed to be on the point of collapse, and to be kept up only by the spirits that were stored behind the bar. The old *csárda* had seen more than one Jew measuring out good cheer to the peasants of three Hungarian villages. Sixty years before it was the Jew Abris, then for twenty-odd years the Jew Moses, then for seven years the Jew Sholem. And then the peasants set it alight over his head.

287

The peasants did not hate the Jew. On the contrary, when they saw him toiling and moiling and praying incessantly, they almost began to think that he was human despite his Jewishness. But they did hate their noble masters, who year after year oppressed them with villenage and tithes. The previous autumn the cup of bitterness became full and brimming over. The peasants were made to pay for the bad harvest twice over, once to God, and again to their masters. The wrath of God was already passing, but the wrath of the gentry was only just beginning. It was the peasants that were giving them a headache, because they were lazy and work-shy and because they listened, and had been listening for some time, to itinerant "enlighteners." This, and this alone, was the true cause of the floods, the drought, the hailstorm in the late summer, and even the plague of foot-and-mouth. And when, on the night of St. Clementine's Day, the gentry were about to hold a little celebration, with plenty to drink, a couple of gypsies, and a pack of cards, the peasants threw a bunch of tarred oakum on the roof over the gentry's parlor and set it alight. The gentry were saved by their own waywardness, being late for their celebration as for everything else. So the masters of the three villages came to no harm, though the Jew Sholem groaned under the consequences of the fire for years.

The gentry came by coach, in a merry, singing mood, having begun the celebration at the house of Lady Clementine de Sarberek. The sight of the fire produced a curious effect on each of them. Old Balthazar de Denghelegh, who twenty-odd years before had taken part in the Napoleonic wars, had the gypsies play the Rakoczi March and bawled the battle order to charge. As the coach pulled up, he was the first to alight and he flung himself upon the Jew. Gedeon de Gyekeny belabored Isaac, Sholem's servant, while de Sarberek's guest, the Baron of Ecsed, fired his gun wildly round Serf Matolcs, Sholem's Sabbath servant, the only one of the peasants who had been helping to put out the fire. It was a good thing that the Baron had gone on drinking even in the coach, so that he was seeing double, and the grapeshot only went through the serf's impalpable image.

Only Ferenc de Sarberek—the Black Squire, as they called him in the house—knew what had happened. Standing up in the coach, he saw the part of the roof over the gentry's parlor caving in. He drew himself up and shook his fist towards the village, his small, spare figure the embodiment of menace in the glow of the fire. Did they see him from the village? Perhaps they only heard his arrogant gentry voice, which now rose to a screech like that of a bird of prey.

"Hi! Curse you! Hi!" The peasants came running from all directions. "You watch from behind your windows how your breadgivers' property is being destroyed, what?" screeched de Sarberek. "And you grin because you managed to spoil the gentry's sport, hey? I'll give you something to grin at, you dogs!"

Jumping off the coach, he kicked one peasant in the belly, seized another by the throat and shook him, and crashed his fist into the face of a third. The other serfs, who had all arrived with pitchforks, axes, and staves, understood at once what the gentry desired, and in a trice they produced buckets and ladders and hooks, and in the end even those who had started the fire were helping to put it out.

The following day the Baron of Ecsed sent his haiduks along, and they restored order in Lapfalva and the other villages. One or two serfs were flogged, while the rest were compelled to make good the damage in their own villenage free time. The winter arrived early, so that only temporary repairs were possible, such as closing the gaps in the walls, mending doors and windows, and encasing charred beams with straw. This took about three weeks, during which the family gradually returned. In the end, Malkeleh herself also came back, together with her new baby girl.

Malkeleh's disquiet stayed with her for a long time, and she was always prepared for flight. But Sholem was full of plans. He wanted to complete what he had started, and to rebuild what had been destroyed. He did his best to convince Malkeleh that God did not want them to run away from here, and even the fire was not meant in that sense. The peasants were in despair and they had to do something or burst, that was all. And Malkeleh had to take fright and run away, for she could not have brought the child into the world in a burning house. It was a good thing, too, that she had taken the children with her. It was better for them to live with the Jews of Hodasz than at home, in a cold house without windows and with everything in disorder. But now, of course, it was better for them to be at home.

There were moments when even Sholem was less confident. The morning after the fire he stood in the yard looking at the charred ruins and the charred junk lying about pellmell, and was overcome with despondency. Isaac was sitting on the cattle trough, with his behind in the cold water, collapsed with the sleep of exhaustion. Startled awake, he looked across at Sholem, and his grimy face with its several burns seemed to Sholem like a visible pattern of his own despair.

"If you go after the family," rumbled Isaac, "I'll go back to my old job in Varalja."

Later, he grew more cheerful and tried to comfort his employer. He even managed a laugh now and then, though his scorched eyebrows gave his laugh a strange, vaguely sinister quality.

"But," he said after a long while, "if you'll light the Sabbath candles this evening and sing to me, I'll stay. We've got the table and a couple of chairs, and we can sleep in the stable; the horse isn't here, anyhow."

In the anticipation of a gloomy Sabbath and amid the ominous silence of the peasants, Sholem realized that he could not carry on. He would take his staff and join his family in their flight. His staff . . . It was the seemingly trifling matter of the staff that caused him to change his mind. His walking stick had been consumed in the fire. One could run without a walking stick, but this was more than a walking stick. It had been bequeathed to him by the blind Seer, Rabbi Yehuda Kunitz of Szentmiklos, whose pupil and secretary he had been before his marriage. It was from his death-bed that the holy man said to Sholem:

"My walking stick is in the corner over there. Take it and go hence. Change of domicile, change of fortune."

Had he not been a man of faith, Sholem in later years would often have regretted that he had obeyed the ashes of a burnt stick rather than his instinct. But he saw predestination in everything. The ruins of his house were still smoking on that misty Friday afternoon when his guests arrived: Wolf Birnbaum and

Shayeh Oesterreicher. In the great commotion he had forgotten
that the two young men had been invited for the Sabbath. What
a disgrace if he had obeyed his impulse! Not that he could give
them anything but a poor welcome, without even a little comfort,
though they had come all the way from Karoly on foot and had
been on the road since dawn. But at least his presence saved them
the anxiety for the family which the sight of the ruins would
surely have aroused in them. The sympathy of the two boys and
their indignation that the Jew should be made to pay even for the
feuds between peasant and gentry, was balm to Sholem's soul.
When they left again, he felt sorry that their Sabbath should have
been spoiled; for now, after their long, tiring walk, they would
have to hurry if they were to reach a Jew-inhabited village before
the Sabbath came in. Even so, they would surely miss the gefilte
fish and chicken broth with giblets which Malkeleh would have
given them but for the fire. And they would surely fail to find
in the whole country another Yiteleh, who was not only pretty
and charming, but also clever, and could quote from the Proverbs
and from the Ethics of the Fathers like a learned boy.

Of the two boys, Wolf was Sholem's favorite, the choice of
his paternal heart. Wolf was on his way to Pressburg, to the
rabbinical school of the great Mosheh Sopher. Shayeh was going
to Vienna, or even farther afield, where there were none but
Gentile schools. The two friends were held together by the tie
of contrary outlooks. Even Sholem's trouble and the flight of his
family was made the occasion of a short, sharp debate. Wolf
opined that this was the inevitable Jewish destiny. For was it not
written that the Lord would fill the hearts of the remnant with
cowardice in the land of their enemies, so that the stirring of a
leaf should make them start, and so that they should flee when
none pursues.

"We really ought to liquidate these ancient prophecies," said
Shayeh vehemently. "They blessed Jacob with the promise that
he would have as many descendants as there are stars in heaven.
The very expression is tragic. The stars are isolated by vast
distances from each other, whereas we ought to stick together
when a brother is in trouble."

His tone was irreverent, and he was criticizing traditional

truths, yet Sholem almost approved of the basic idea. Indeed, he might have accepted it without reservations, had he not feared that Shayeh was quoting from forbidden books. What Shayeh said was always suspect in that sense and Sholem kept shaking his head and muttering even when, before parting, the boy tried to console him by saying that "fires are necessary and even desirable sometimes, because they lead to the rebuilding of dilapidated structures."

However, though Sholem was all on the side of Wolf and the truths proclaimed by him, and though he was suspicious of Shayeh's bold ideas, in this period of difficulty and worry it was from Shayeh that he derived guidance. In his imagination he built for and upon Wolf, but he did so in accordance with Shayeh's conceptions. Not long ago, he himself had said to Malkeleh that it was not necessary to run away at the stirring of a leaf, and now the ashes of the blind Seer's staff had confirmed him. He was glad that he did not run away. A day or two after the fire he realized that his old *csárda* had in fact been too dilapidated and decrepit to deserve preservation. The Black Squire told him that the gentry could not give him any money to rebuild, but that if he did so at his own expense, the building would be his property. Sholem had no money either, but he had ideas which, as he used to say, was the chief thing. He was already thinking out a plan, raising the walls, widening the windows, unifying the roof, running a veranda round the house and furnishing a better guest-room. And while extending the bar parlor, he solved the problem of the bar in such a manner that he could read the Talmud undisturbed behind it, amid the hogsheads and demijohns of liquor. The planning itself held a certain satisfaction for Sholem, but this was intensified when he found that despite his many troubles and his few assets he could set about realizing his plans.

First-aid arrived in accordance with Shayeh's idea. The "stars" left their isolation. The Jews of the county were stirred up, partly by the family from Hodasz, and partly by Wolf and Shayeh along the road to Otvar, and they were sending help from all directions. Zishe brought down some bedding, Avrom Kolb linen, the trough-seller Jew rush-seated chairs and some bedsteads, Yossef Yochanan pottery. Bricks came from Aaron Kahan in Csenger, lime from

Menachem in Ombod, beams and boards from Shefteli in Batiz. Everyone brought or sent something to enable the Jew Sholem to rebuild his home. And because the spring arrived early, Sholem and his household were able to start rebuilding in real earnest without much delay. By mid-spring the brand-new Shingled Inn was one of the notable sights of the marsh-side region.

AFTER THE FIRE

DURING THE chaotic days of the winter, Golda, the gay apple-cheeked wife of Mendl the fisher from Nameny, came over to Lapfalva, informing Malkeleh that she wanted to adopt one of her children. Malkeleh stared at her.

"You've got so many," said Golda. "A lot of children means a lot of trouble. We haven't any, and that's still worse. Mendl wants a child at all costs."

Malkeleh shook her head. A lot of children were no trouble to her. The trouble would be if any of them was missing. Golda was not unprepared for resistance.

"I'm not asking for Yiteleh," she explained. "She'll soon get married, anyhow. Besides, she'd make me look older. And I don't want Mailech either, because he already goes to *yeshiba* and is quite a business man. Let me have Sarah Chayah."

"Not Sarah Chayah," said Malkeleh.

"Well, Manasseh, then."

"No."

"What about Yosseleh?"

"No."

"Let me have Yoirish."

"He's only a baby," smiled Malkeleh.

"Then give me Zipporah."

"I'm still nursing her."

"Then," said Golda, in a tone of finality, "I'll take Yossel Beilah Yenteh's, your adopted boy."

"Can't be done."

"What do you want two Yossels for?" said Golda in exasperation.

"Well," replied Malkeleh, "one is my own and the other is in my charge."

"That's the one I want," said Golda. "He'll be better off with me. He'll have good clothes, a good education and he can have Mendl's name. That'll be better for him than to be called after Gimpel Zorech or Beilah Yenteh."

"What if his father comes for him?" argued Malkeleh.

"He'll find him with me," said Golda. "Gimpel Zorech knows the way to Nameny and to Mendl's fishery. We always give him a good tip and I put something in his carpetbag as well. We remember that he is Sholem's brother and that he has made an unfortunate marriage. Mendl does not grudge him a drop of brandy either, not like you. People are what they are and it's no use trying to improve them against their will."

Golda went on arguing until Malkeleh finally agreed to part with the little boy, though only conditionally.

"If he doesn't get on there," she said, "I'll take him back."

However, that was not necessary. After the first week Golda brought the boy back herself.

"This one is no good to us," she said. "Mendl wants another one. I am sure your children are better behaved."

"What's wrong with Yossel?" inquired Malkeleh.

"He's impudent," said Golda. "Whenever we have a visitor he'll pester them for coppers until they give way. No wonder, his father being a beggar."

"He's only a child," objected Malkeleh. "He never did it here."

"That's because your children gave him a good example. I haven't any other children to do that. Besides, Yossel has been terribly naughty. He used to sneak out of the house, cut himself a switch and beat the fishermen's children. He takes after his mother in that. Beilah Yenteh used to beat Gimpel Zorech with a stick."

"All right, Goldeleh," said her hostess with some severity, "we'll have the boy back. He's good enough for me. You can't have another child."

Golda stepped in front of the mirror and extracting from her handbag a piece of rouge paper, started to make up. And before she left she replied to Malkeleh's remarks in honeyed tones:

"I'm afraid he won't turn out well, darling. You haven't been very lucky with your adopted boys, have you? Sroleh Yomtov ran away. He was in such a hurry that he left all his money. Yossef became a candlemaker's apprentice. You'll have trouble with the schnorrer's boy, too. Just wait and see."

Aunt Blimeleh was also moved by the best intentions when, in the late winter, she came over by sleigh to take Yiteleh back with her to Karoly. She said that Yiteleh would be happier in her house than in the patched-up inn, among the coarse peasants. Malkeleh had by then forgotten about Golda's offer, and besides, Blimeleh was not Golda. Blimeleh was Mordechai's wife, and Mordechai himself had sent a message to say that he had important plans with Yiteleh. Malkeleh saw no reason to hesitate and she told Sholem to let the girl go; there was a future for her in the home of her rich uncle.

Sholem agreed with some hesitation, and then only for a limited period, for he too had some plans concerning Yiteleh. He would have mentioned them long ago to Malkeleh, if they had not twice gone up in smoke: once when he had lent his daughter's dowry to brother-in-law Azriel, and again when the house was burnt down. Sholem had not spoken to Wolf Birnbaum either, but the young man must already have guessed what Sholem knew with certainty, for in his great moments of withdrawal from mundane things he had seen the names of Wolf and Yiteleh entered side by side in the heavenly Marriage Register. But how could he broach the subject to Wolf while sitting on the ruins of his home? When everything had been rebuilt, and when he, Sholem, had erected a structure of solid prosperity, then the young scholar might and should be spoken to, he being the only one worthy to become the son-in-law of Sholem ben Yoirish.

Yiteleh's departure, unlike Yossel's brief absence, was no relief. On the contrary, the family missed both her industry and gaiety. Malkeleh thought only of her daughter's future and did not betray that she found life more difficult and colorless. Sholem, on the other hand, had his remoter plans in mind, and could not conceal his fear that Yiteleh might stay at the Nikolsburger home

longer than he had permitted. Sholem could never warm to
Mordechai. He even viewed Mordechai's manifold business activities with strong suspicion, feeling that they might in some way
tend to dictate his own way of life. He liked three things: his
studies, the land, and his family. And he felt happy in his likes,
because he always found some word of wisdom, some occult sign
to justify him. When the house was on fire, his chief care was to
save his books and keep the flames away from the barn where he
kept his grain. And he was satisfied with his lot because the family,
his books, and their bread had been preserved. Since then his faith
had become even more profound and he felt that God must be
praised for misfortune as well. For good fortune tended to make
a man blind, while misfortune served to open his eyes. Even the
previous year's drought had produced a good result, for it had
dried up another stretch of marsh and he was able to wrest another five or six chains of land from the bog which he had
bought from the gentry years ago for a few coppers. If he had not
seen this even through the smoke of the great conflagration, he
would have fled with the family, and might now have to start all
over again, in a strange place and with a larger family, where he
started before when he fled with only two children.

"Don't you remember, Malkeleh," he said, "that when we went
astray on our flight from the North, God showed us where to
stray? Believe me, God is not on the side of the fire-raisers."

Malkeleh was not lacking in faith either, but her conception
was very different. "You must accustom God to the things you
want," she used to say. She had brought this saying from the
paternal home, from which faith was by no means absent. God
may be accustomed to renunciation and poverty. If you want
little, God takes note of it and gives you little. But if you want
to dress your wife and daughters in velvet and to smoke half a
dozen cigars a day, you will get *that*. Whenever Sholem came out
with his ultimate wisdom, that one must wait patiently for better
times and that the good Lord will help in time, Malkeleh used to
say with all the vehemence of conviction:

"It is our business to help the good Lord in his immense task.
God hasn't the time to bother with the petty affairs of everyone."

Sometimes Sholem realized that Malkeleh's more mundane

view was right. After all, God had not sent a downpour of rain
when his house was on fire, but let him, Sholem, carry water in
buckets. Again, while God had sent one or two brothers to help
him, He had also sent some who did the reverse. The schnorrer
Gimpel Zorech would appear now and then, only to carry off the
peace of the home for weeks and months. That could not be
helped, for after all the schnorrer was Sholem's brother and, dirty
and dissipated as he was, the family had to be loyal to him. But
sometimes there came a nice, clean Jew with a carefully trimmed
beard who, when he went away, left a shadow over the house.
His name was Ezekiel Gutfreund, from Karoly, and he usually
began with a lofty Talmudic debate, but ended with a cold
financial demand. He would produce the bill whereby Sholem
had given a guarantee up to fifteen hundred florins on behalf of
his bankrupt brother-in-law, Azriel, and refuse to depart until
he was paid the interest and his expenses, at the very least. But
the debt did not decrease and Sholem was burdened with it for
a long time.

Sholem never discussed this matter with his wife. It was quite
sufficient for Malkeleh to know that her sister Rachel's husband
had taken away six hundred florins in cash before the fire and that
the lack of this money had caused difficulties in the business even
then. After the fire Malkeleh had written to Azriel about the
family's trials. Azriel replied that he too was ruined, having lost
even the remnant of his fortune on the Vienna Bourse. He too was
the victim of evil, Solomon Rothschild, the scoundrelly banker,
having persuaded him to buy certain securities, which Azriel had
then had to re-sell at a tithe of the price he paid. But now he was
wiser and had invested his last money in safer securities, the
Grassalkovich bonds, through a decent banking house. As soon
as he had liquid cash at his disposal, Malkeleh and Sholem would
hear from him. "You need not remind an Azriel Fuerth of his
obligations."

On the other hand, there were instances reflecting a deeper
loyalty within the family. Yossef was going on nineteen and was
in the third year of his apprenticeship in the soap and candle business in Batiz. Yet he still clung to his foster-mother Malkeleh with
true filial affection. If he stayed away one week-end, he would

arrive for the next out of breath, so to speak. Nowadays he never came empty-handed. He would bring a couple of chickens for the Sabbath, a small bag of flour or a pitcher of oil, for Malkeleh was short of everything. Then Yossef would join Sholem behind the bar and discuss with him the rebuilding plans. It had been settled that in the spring, when candlemaking was slack, Yossef would take two months' leave and come home to help with the building operations. The potter's son in Batiz, a friend of his, had promised to come along with him. He, Yossef, would help the carpenters, while the potter's boy would help the masons.

Mailech, too, knew how to spend his painfully hoarded peddling profits. When he returned from the *yeshiba* of a Friday, he always carried in his carpet-bag items of door furniture, window latches, grates and the like, bought cheaply in the junk market at Karoly. He also provided the home with tumblers, cutlery, and cooking utensils. Before the Sabbath came in, he would hand his surplus money to his father. On one occasion he handed over seven florins and thirty kreuzers, and on another, a round ten florins. "This is for you, Dad," said the boy; "you need all the money you can get now." Formerly, Sholem never omitted to ask him what he had learnt during the week; now, he sometimes forgot to ask. Until Rabbi Isaac Frenkel sent him a warning that Mailech was playing truant from the *yeshiba*, Sholem himself acted as if he were unaware that the boy was less interested in Talmudic problems than in the best supply sources of percale, ribbons, and bootlaces, and how he could dispose of the goods quickly and at a good profit. Sholem accepted the moneys with the remark that he would credit them to the boy and return them in one amount when needed. All he was worried about was whether the boy would have enough left for fresh purchases.

"Don't worry about that, Dad," the boy would say, "I can get goods on credit."

If Sholem had been of an envious disposition, he might have envied his son for his assurance on this point. He could get no credit either from Rothbart in Karoly, or from Lazarovich in Batiz, of whom he had been a regular customer for spirits for eight years. Sholem scraped together all the money he could to finance the building operations. He paid the workers regularly and in strict accordance with the Shulchan Aruch, which decrees that laborers must be paid before dusk. More than once, he had no money left for liquor. In his simplicity, he liked to do one thing at a time. The building came first; then the equipment of the house; then one could think about the business.

Malkeleh disagreed. The business came first, because it was not the house that kept the business going, but the other way round. The inn must be either given up or attended to properly. And it had to be attended to even if it was for the time being no more than a few charred beams with a rough thatch. And if Sholem recalled that the peasants had not yet paid him the previous year's accounts, and that the gentry had forbidden him to serve more than one drink per day to any peasant, Malkeleh would argue that the customer must be served, otherwise he would go somewhere else, while as to the gentry, they had long forgotten what they said last autumn. Malkeleh saw that the peasants were sulky and she did all she could to placate them, for without them the family could not stay on in the village. After the bad harvest, the peasants were now doing casual labor in the nearby towns and buying their drink there. That could not be changed by any restrictive measures, but only through friendliness and courtesy.

The Talmudist Sholem loved an argument because it not only sharpened the brain, but also led to a conclusion on the point at issue. He derived particular pleasure from such an argument with his wife, because by the time of the fire they had become accustomed to have long discussions on anything. He knew that Malkeleh was right about serving the customers and cultivating friendship with them. But in this connection there was one thorny problem to be solved:

"Where shall we get the money for everything?"

## MONEY IN A SECRET DRAWER

FORMERLY, MALKELEH used to respond to this worried question, which amounted to an appeal, by going over to someone in a nearby locality and raising a short-term loan of a hundred or two. Sholem was not made for such tasks, for he was by nature shy and would approach only learned men like himself. But in the heat of the Talmudic debate which was the traditional introduction to such a meeting, Sholem usually forgot to state, and the other man to ask, the object of his visit and Sholem would leave with the solution, not of his immediate financial problem, but of a millennial text.

Now Malkeleh felt that their friends could not be approached again, for they had but recently given a great deal unasked. However, if one drawer was empty, why did not Sholem reach into the other?

"You don't think I'm going to touch the orphans' money?" cried Sholem in consternation.

"I'm not thinking of anything wrong," said Malkeleh, "or anything improper. But you shouldn't let the money lie there unused; you should turn it over and carry on the business with it."

This was an old argument, though up till now it had been raised only in the form of veiled hints. But Sholem's view prevailed in the end. For it was based on the Law of Moses and Israel. Eight years ago, when the Lord caused the family to stray to this place and the gentry invited them to take over the lease of the late Jew Mosheh, the house, the bar, and all the goods and chattels contained therein were the property of his orphans, Sroleh Yomtov and Yossef. The gentry held that even Sroleh Yomtov, the elder of the two, was too young to be a party to an agreement, but that was not true. Sroleh Yomtov was then in his fifteenth year, had been praying with phylacteries for eighteen months, and counted as an adult in the synaogue congregation. Sholem had therefore acted rightly in regarding him as a full partner and reserving fifty per cent of the profits for him. Sroleh Yomtov himself had recognized this by implication when, a few months later, he went away for some hitherto unexplained reason without taking any of the business capital with him. So long as Sroleh Yomtov, or at least Yossef, was in the house, it was permissible to do business with their money. But since they left, their share had to be put aside.

All this sounded very noble and was in fact feasible until the fire. But all Sholem had saved from the fire was the peasants' tally sticks, which represented his outstanding accounts, and a very little of his own capital, apart from the entire capital of the orphans. As Malkeleh put it, this was the capital of the two sleeping partners, which ought to work instead of them. The situation now was that Sholem was trying to rebuild the house from scanty or non-existent resources and to carry on the business with no capital, thereby harming instead of benefiting the orphans.

Malkeleh was now formulating her argument more sharply than before because she did not want to comply with Sholem's unspoken wish. He would have liked her to go to her rich brother in Karoly and ask him for money. But how could she go to Mordechai with a petty request now, when he had just assumed the far greater responsibility of Yiteleh's future? She might approach Mendl in Nameny, who was always ready to lend, but Malkeleh felt that after Golda's objectionable behavior she could never go there again. Malkeleh might have forgotten Golda's catty remarks about the drunkenness of Gimpel Zorech and the shrewish Beilah Yenteh who made him into a beggar, because they were, after all, true. But what she had said about Malkeleh's adopted boys was both untrue and hurtful. Malkeleh had always been a good mother to the orphans, and made the sacrifice of staying by the marsh-side for their sake, when she had really intended to settle in the town. No one knew this better than Golda, to whom Malkeleh had confided her secret thoughts. Golda also knew that Sroleh Yomtov had not run away, but had merely gone out to see the world and make a man of himself. He had not forgotten to take his money with him, otherwise he would have come back for it. Malkeleh had shown Golda the boy's farewell letter in which he said quite clearly that he was leaving the money for the business.

It seemed that Sholem, too, was thinking of the vanished boy, for in the course of the argument he remarked:

"And what do we do if one fine day Sroleh Yomtov turns up and demands an account?"

"That would be a fine day indeed," replied Malkeleh wistfully. Then she added: "If Sroleh Yomtov came back he would agree with me."

Sholem shook his head and left the argument unresolved. To show his acquisitive zeal, he now embarked on all kinds of undertakings. He accepted the most strenuous carting jobs over the snowed-up roads. He also attended personally to the marketing, in nearby towns, of the wickerwork goods with which the peasants paid instalments on their debt. He carried grain from the more fortunate regions to the famine areas. Then he went over to Wallachia to bring back the finest seed grain, thereby bolstering up his declining popularity among the gentry, as well as among the peasants. His multifarious activities did not produce a great deal of money, while the peasants could not have been completely placated except by opening the bar for the whole day, instead of only for one hour per day, as had been his rule since the fire. Yet, in a vague, barely perceptible way, Sholem was making progress, though Leizer Lazarovich still refused to supply spirits on credit. Of the hole in the wall which contained plenty of money, Sholem tried not to think.

Then, suddenly, Yiteleh returned from Karoly.

"Have they thrown you out?" asked her mother in a jocular tone, but with anxious inquiry in her eyes.

"No, they didn't," replied Yiteleh. "The trouble was that they wouldn't let me go." There was a trace of defiance in her manner, perhaps because she was afraid that her mother might disapprove of her unannounced return. Of course, she had to explain. Aunt Blimeleh did not treat her badly, nor was she herself lazy or disobedient. Aunt Blimeleh wanted her to learn what she called high-class household management. Yiteleh would have been glad to do so, but she was expected to sew and crochet from noon till late evening for the trousseaux of Hanna and Miriam, while Hanna went out visiting her friends and Miriam played the piano. So she, Yiteleh, said to herself, why were those trousseaux so urgent, considering that Hanna was eighteen months younger than she and Miriam as much as three years younger? It seemed more important to Yiteleh to come home and mend the scorched table-cloths and bedsheets.

"Did you say anything to Blimeleh?" asked her mother.

"No, Mummy, I said it only to myself," was the reply.

"How did Uncle Mordechai treat you?"

"Uncle Mordechai said he was going to open a leather shop in the market square, with Moysheh to run it. Moysheh knew all

about leather, only he was a bit queer, so Uncle did not quite
trust him. He would like me to be in the shop, watching Moysheh
and serving the better-class customers."

"Well?" prompted Malkeleh.

"Well, I thought: why should I serve the cobblers of Karoly?
Why not come home and serve the peasants?"

"Is that what you said to your uncle?"

"No, Mummy, not like that. I said there was a lot to do at
home and there would be more in the spring. Daddy would start
building and he would also have to do the work on the land, and
I couldn't let him break his back."

"What did Mordechai say to that?"

"He said all right, I could come home, but I must come back
in the summer. He promised me a commission on sales."

"That'll be nice."

"Yes, Mummy. Two per cent to start with, and three when
I know the business. Mailech worked it out that in ten years I
could save up four hundred florins, quite a nice dowry. I told him
that all I'd be good for in ten years' time would be for pickling.
I'd be a sour old maid by then."

This made her mother laugh.

"All right," she said. "The main thing is that you behaved
decently and can go back at any time."

Sholem also laughed. He had not had such a good laugh for
months. "My daughter!" he exclaimed with joyous satisfaction.
She had thought rightly and acted rightly. And somehow, perhaps because Malkeleh had spoken about Yiteleh's return to
Karoly, this incident caused Sholem to come to a new decision
concerning the orphans' money.

"You're right about the money, Malkeleh," he said. "It'll only
harm the orphans if I let it lie."

Of course, Sholem was very careful about the formalities.
Before he removed the necessary amount, a round three hundred
florins, from the secret safe, he indited a letter addressed to Sroleh
Yomtov, stating his intention and explaining that he was carrying
it out in the hope of the boy's retrospective consent. He put the
letter into the safe.

Yiteleh took her place behind the bar. The whole place was

still in a mess and both Malkeleh and Sholem were often annoyed
on account of it, but the girl merely laughed. If part of the
floor collapsed under her feet, she laughed. If drops of thawed
snow happened to drip on to her neck from the ceiling, she
laughed. If she got a smut on her nose after unconsciously touching the charred grille of the bar, she looked down at the smut
with a boss-eyed squint and laughed. Her bubbling gaiety did not
leave her in the house, either, while helping her mother or the
morose Aunt Feiga, or sitting at the table with her worried-look-
ing parents. Everything seemed attractive to her in this disordered
house, even the smoke-odored bed in which she slept and the
lame chairs, the use of which involved a balancing act. All this was
nicer and more lovable than Aunt Blimeleh's fine, glossy furniture.
Sometimes, Malkeleh felt that her daughter was laughing too
much.

"What are you laughing about now?" she asked on one occasion.

"I just remembered a letter from Shayeh which was shown to
me by his mother in Karoly," replied the girl. And she laughed
again.

"What was in that letter?"

"Shayeh wrote that he and Wolf came here burning with love
just when the house had got burned down," said the girl.

"That's no laughing matter," said her mother. "You really ought
to be more serious."

But Yiteleh went on laughing, even when she thought of her
having to be more serious. She cheered up not only the house,
but also the otherwise gloomy and irritable serfs, at least when
they were near her.

She used to welcome them with the words, "Lo! the sheep are
thirsty." This was because her father had hung a sheepbell over
the door in place of the small bell, which the fire had melted out
of shape. The peasants liked her gaiety. They looked at her
flashing teeth, her bright eyes, and her dimpled face, and livened
up. The inn had never been so busy as during the few months
when Yiteleh sat behind the bar. The serfs went to the nearby
towns on casual labor, brought the money back and began to pay
off their debt. They also went fishing and fowling in the marsh

and sold the result in the towns. They did not recoil from a little poaching either, if they could procure gaiety on the proceeds. The building operations also tended to improve business at the inn, for most of the wages Sholem paid to the carpenters and masons went back into the till. By the time the Shingled Inn was complete, Sholem was able to repay the loan to the absent Sroleh Yomtov, and even to add a share of new profits. It was a gay, busy spring, and it passed only too quickly. Then came the summer with all its excitements and agitations.


RICH SUMMER


THE SUMMER started well. There were no caterpillars, no drought, no hailstorms. There was rain and sunshine, the crops ripened, the cattle grew fat, the fruit trees groaned under the weight of the fruit. The people sang as they toiled and old Serf Topoly, who had survived the winter again, said that God was behaving in a human way at last.

Sholem had every reason to feel hopeful. He had had his seven lean years here, but even before the end of the leanest of them all he saw that the seven fat years were on the way. "I told you, Malkeleh, didn't I?" he used to say. "It's going to be the way Joseph predicted in Egypt." Malkeleh would nod her head, as if to say: "Wait and see." Or if she felt like humoring him, she would say: "Amen." On the whole, she was satisfied with Sholem, who had helped God a great deal during the past year, even at the expense of his studies.

When the *csárda* had been rebuilt, there was some fear of malice on the part of the peasants. And when Sholem ordered shingles for the roof, Malkeleh thought that it might lead to trouble, because in the villages served by the inn only the vicarage and the manors had shingled roofs. Envy, indeed, did give tongue now and then. But because the harvest was good, envy fell silent. In time, the serfs came to brag about their shingled *csárda*, which

was unique in the whole region. Even the peasants of Csenger had
to drink in a thatch-roofed inn.

People came along from distant villages, just to sit in the
Shingled Inn and see whether Sholem's spirits really had a different taste. Everything was different now, even the land which the
Jew had cultivated by the sweat of his brow. At first the peasants
used to mutter a great deal and they used to mock at him for the
bow-legged way in which he followed the plough and because he
used to scatter the seed with a kow-towing movement, as though
he were praying. Now the peasants saw that he had prayed well,
for the Jew's crops were the finest for seven leagues around. This,
too, was an object of admiration for the strange customers. What
they liked best was that the Jew had wrested the land away from
the marsh, securing it against flooding with ditches and high
banks. The toad-puddle was now twenty-odd chains in extent,
one-half being rich plough-land and the other half grass-land.
The peasants said they ought to learn from the Jew.

Did they? Well, even Isaac was unable to learn everything
from his master. He could be trusted with the ploughing, but
that was all. When it came to sowing, the inadequacy of his work
was exposed by the patchiness of the crop. So now, Sholem
no longer trusted him with this noble task, which to Sholem was
"correspondence with the Lord." It was a profound science, in
which Sholem had to train for a long time. He went to the *yeshiba*
for ten years and, more important still, in the first years of his
marriage he earned his living by copying out the Torah on parchment. It was a poor living, but it taught Sholem a lesson which
was ample compensation to him in later years. When he was
ploughing, he was careful to see that the furrows should be deep
and straight, and when he was sowing he scattered the seed evenly,
the way he used to write the lines of Hebrew characters. Would
Isaac ever learn this, seeing that he could not even read fluently?
And would he ever understand that you must scatter the seed
with a generous hand, for you must learn to give before you can
expect to receive?

Isaac could not be trusted even with a business errand. Once,
Sholem sent him along to Lazarovich with a single cask, telling
him again and again that he wanted ordinary rye whisky. In

the evening Isaac came back with the empty cask and a message from Lazarovich that Sholem should give his order in writing.

"Didn't I tell you," grumbled Sholem, "that I want ordinary rye?"

"I understand," cried Isaac, his big, ruddy face lighting up. He tried to re-mount the cart in order to drive back to Batiz, and Sholem had to pull him off by force and take the money away from him.

"Oy, Daddy," grumbled the lad, "you're a very bad Jew." Later, by way of excuse, he said: "Reb Leizer's man, Faddeleh, gave me such a silly look that I forgot what sort of rye you wanted. Of course it was ordinary."

As to allowing Isaac to serve in the inn even for an hour, Sholem would not hear of it, though Malkeleh would have liked him to relieve Yiteleh sometimes. She believed that with patience, and an addition to his wages, Isaac could be trained to the work. But Sholem remained adamant.

"What are you thinking of, Malkeleh?" he would say. "He'd make such a mix-up that three rabbis couldn't straighten it out."

However, Sholem liked Isaac, and he was aware that the lad was not so stupid as he looked. He spoke with the same kind of drawl as the Jewish peasants of Sholem's native village Trebushan, and this was a special point in his favor. But Sholem wanted to prevent the creation of any pretext that might deprive him of his eldest daughter's presence at home. Of course, he would not let her go into the leather shop in Karoly, and even Malkeleh would not like her to become an apprentice or a shop assistant. Indeed, her relations with Mordechai had become cooler since Yiteleh's return. Sholem was secretly pleased, for he had never liked his brother-in-law. But one could never tell: perhaps tomorrow Mordechai would come along with another, more attractive offer, and Malkeleh might say yes. It was an old delusion with Malkeleh that real happiness could be found only in a town, and she seemed determined that her daughter should live in a town. Sholem himself was convinced that seclusion was good for the soul. He could visualize the son-in-law of his secret hopes sitting in front of a tome of the Talmud from dawn till midnight, while his wife managed the business, either here or, if they liked, anywhere else.

This was the ideal marriage, the ideal division of labor: one spouse absorbed in things of the spirit, the other attending to things of the earth.

And when Malkeleh opined that Yiteleh could not be left for ever among drunken peasants, Sholem merely smiled and replied sententiously:

"A dove is a dove even among swine."

Of course, Sholem was careful not to let Yiteleh sit behind the bar when the peasants were getting very loud. In the evening, when the air grew thicker in the bar parlor, Sholem would relieve his daughter, no matter how heavy a day he had had in the fields or in connection with the building work. If he happened to be away, his place was taken by Malkeleh during the evening hours. Malkeleh knew how to handle the peasants, and she was still pretty enough not to be completely overshadowed by her daughter. However, in course of time, Yiteleh too acquired a certain authority, the authority of the ever-sober possessor of intoxicants over the seeker of intoxication. But Yiteleh also commanded respect in her own right. She could be very determined when necessary, giving orders and making her voice sound like the crack of a whip:

"Uncle Gore, enough for this time, you're drunk . . . Vince Polya, the tally's full up . . . Farmer Perecseny, leave a bit for your kids . . . Serf Vizhordo, stop blaspheming, God hears everything . . . Jancsi Galagonya, better go home to your mummy and help her peel potatoes . . . You too, Ludpal. Go back to your mare and your belfry . . . Uncle Caspar, better go to bed. A night watchman must sleep by day. . ." And so on.

In the forenoon, when the inn was comparatively quiet, Yiteleh sat behind the bar, crocheting. The tablecloth with the basket of fruit in the center and the crumb-picking birds in the corners had been safely completed. Now she was working on the lacy antimacassars whose pattern she had been given by Aunt Blimeleh. She had brought some other things from Karoly as well: one or two German books and one or two desires packed away right at the bottom of her bag, of which she scarcely knew on her return home. At that time she kept laughing for several weeks, happy to have escaped from her rich aunt and to be home again. Since then she had grown serious, as her mother had warned her that she must. And so Yiteleh had begun to think.

Sometimes she would get out the borrowed books and read the *Tales of Hoffmann* and the novels of Wieland. But much reading made her feel dazed, and at such times she became aware that she was missing all kinds of things. She was missing her two finicky cousins, the boys Hanna and Miriam continually chattered about, the visitors who came in the evening, though they were not her visitors, the sound of Miriam playing the scales on the piano, and the lovely Sabbath dresses of Hanna and Blimeleh, which she, Yiteleh, could only look at and admire. She now thought of Aunt Blimeleh's nice, cool drawing-room, with carpets, gobelines, an oval table, a glass cabinet, a turreted shelf and upholstered chairs. Here, all the furniture had been made by the village cabinetmaker in the first place, and now most of it was more or less charred. The new pieces looked even shabbier than the old. There was nothing but a few ragged rugs on the floor of the largest room. They had just built a third room at the end of the house, and her mother had said that when Father had the money he would buy fine furniture for it, table, wardrobe, and chairs. But he had no money yet, at least not for this purpose. What he had was needed for spirits, timber, harness, and a good milch cow. She, Yiteleh, must help her father to get more money. He would have enough next year. And by the time the antimacassars were finished, the chairs too would be finished. Then they could have visitors, and they would not have to receive them behind the bar. They could be sat down in the best room and they could talk about serious matters. She, Yiteleh, would like to have the furniture from the workshop of a town cabinetmaker, and so would her father.

"Of course, Yiteleh," he said. "You will get the best. It is your room."

Of an evening, after closing time, Sholem would take a candle and visit the new room with Yiteleh to see whether the walls were dry yet. He was very satisfied with what he saw. Yiteleh explained that she wanted to distemper the walls in blue, and Sholem nodded approval. Then he said:

"There is a hook up in the ceiling for the lamp. The table is

going to be beneath the lamp. Anyone sitting here will be able to
read undisturbed. The window looks east, so the room gets the
morning sun. The big bookshelf will be over there, by the wall.
And there will be two beds in the corners."

"You want me to share the room with another child?" inquired
Yiteleh. "Perhaps with Sarah Chayah?"

"Not with Sarah Chayah," laughed her father, seizing his beard
with one hand.


### BALLAD OF THE HIGHWAYMAN


THE INN bell gave a shrill tinkle. Yiteleh hurried out from behind
the bar to see who it was. A traveler stood on the threshold: knee-
boots, haircloth trousers, linen blouse and wide leather belt, and
a sheepskin hat on his head. At first sight Yiteleh took him for a
Rumanian peasant from the Avas. Indeed, it was in Rumanian
that he spoke, over his shoulder, to his servant outside, who was
taking two saddle horses to the trough. Yiteleh could hear the
servant's voice too: it was the growling voice of the mountain
Wallach, and it said: "*Da, da, domnule.*" Yiteleh promised herself
that she would now practise her knowledge of Rumanian, which
she had picked up from passing customers, and which she had
extended by a few new words since the arrival of Isaac the
handyman. In an inn you did not need a large vocabulary, for all
that happened was that the customer asked for a drink—and there
was no great variety—and you just had to tell him the price and
reciprocate his greeting: *Noroc bun!* (Good luck), *Sara buna!*
(Good evening), *Senetate buna!* (Good health). However, the
newcomer smiled at the girl and addressed her in Hungarian:

"Well, Yiteleh, have you got any more of that strong brandy?"

Yiteleh gave him a searching look. Who was this man? He had
a strangely stern expression on his brow, and the contrast between
his thick black eyebrows and his smiling blue eyes was rather
striking.

"How do you know my name?" she asked.

"Why, who doesn't know Yiteleh, the beauty of the Shingled Inn? Where's Mother Malkah?"

"In the house."

"And Father Sholem?"

"He's out in the field."

"He's a decent Jew, a very decent Jew. Give him my kind regards."

"Whose kind regards?"

"You don't need to say, Yiteleh. Just say it was me . . . A couple of big'uns, little girl, one in a mug, the other in a bottle."

The man raised the bottle to his lips, tilted his head back and drained the bottle in one swig. As he did so, the fold of his shirt overlapping his belt slipped back, revealing several daggers and a pistol. Yiteleh was a bit scared and repressed a question that was on her lips. She just stood gazing at the man, who was coughing and sneezing and praising the drink with hearty oaths.

"Fit for the hangman! . . Sheer poison, damn it . . ! Another bottle, pretty Jewess. Hi, Yuon, hi!"

Yuon, a sallow-complexioned man with long, greasy hair falling over his shoulders, came in and stopped by the table.

"Yes, *domnule.*"

"Here's the mug," said the other man. "Drink! You rarely get anything as good as this. Distilled by the Jew Sholem. He's a good Jew, don't you ever hurt him."

The man grinned, revealing a set of sharp fangs. It seemed that he too had weapons in his belt. Yiteleh, on second thought, was no longer surprised. It was a great distance to the mountains and the roads were not safe. This Hungaro-Rumanian gentleman probably had much money on him, and nowadays there was a lot of talk about highwaymen. Yiteleh smiled as she saw the stranger extract a big leather wallet from the top of his knee-boot and rummage among the banknotes therein. Her guess seemed to have been correct.

"Can you give me change out of a fifty?"

"In a minute. I'll go and ask Mother."

"Don't. I've got a twenty."

"That's too big, too. We don't get a lot of money here."

"Then give me another couple of drinks."

"Yes, sir."

"Isn't there a gypsy here?"

"Duduy has moved to Otvar. Gebics is asleep at this time."

"Wake him up."

"He lives far away, sir."

"All right, then we're not going to make merry this morning. We're in a hurry, anyhow, aren't we, Yuon?" The second sentence was said in Rumanian.

"Da, da, domnule," affirmed Yuon with a stupid smile. He was still standing, as one about to go. Or was it out of respect for his master? The latter gave another order, drank once again, and burst into song. "Ay-yi, Jew-girl fair. Do you never comb your hair?" Yiteleh was not offended and went on serving him with a smile on her face. But as she was walking back towards the bar, she seemed to show off her pigtails, which were glossy with constant care. The stranger seemed to take the hint and broke off the Jew-girl song, plunging without transition into a kind of heroic howling, his forehead resting on his clenched fist.

*"Benni Darazs, a highwayman was he,*
*Lay down to rest under an oaken tree,*
*They said: Rise up, for here you daren't stay,*
*The pandours are coming, they're on the way.*

*"Let them come, a dozen or a score,*
*If they want to bathe in their own gore.*
*Have a care, Benni, and save your breath,*
*Or they'll take you to the cell of death."*

The stranger raised his head and made a minatory gesture in the air, as though warning the hero of the ballad again to beware. Then he drained his bottle and threw it to the floor with a crash, wiped his mouth with his hand, and flung a banknote for twenty florins on the table.

"Forty-five kreuzers," said Yiteleh, "and one for the bottle. Can you let me have silver and coppers, please?"

"What is it you want?" snapped the stranger.

"If you have no change, can you give me a florin, and I'll give you fourteen kreuzers change. Haven't you a florin?"

"I have, but I won't give it to you. This is all I want to give you. It's a nice, green-bellied note, isn't it?"

The girl knew that it was not advisable to argue with a tipsy man, so:

"Very good, Uncle," she said, "I'll go and get the change."

"Don't get anything, it's all for you."

"Not all, only forty-six kreuzers."

"I said all. It's due to Sholem. More than that, with the interest."

"Why is it due?" asked the girl.

"Don't ask too many questions," said the stranger. "Just tell your father that I've paid my debt."

"But what's your name?"

The stranger smiled.

"I'm me," he said. "Certainly not the miner Yuon."

"I can't accept payment," insisted the girl, "unless I know who the debtor is and can enter it in the book."

"You leave that to your learned father," said the stranger. He bent down to replace the wallet in the side of his knee-boot, and as he did so Yiteleh saw his profile and suddenly felt that she knew him. But why would he not tell his name? He wasn't quite drunk yet.

"I'd rather you told me who you are," said Yiteleh. "I must tell father who brought the money, and he might think me stupid if I don't know."

The man did not reply. Instead, he gave his servant, who stood ogling the determined little girl, a push in the chest.

"Hi, you! Damn you!"

With that he jerked the door open and they went out to take over their horses from Isaac. A moment later they were galloping away. Yiteleh stood watching the clouds of dust they were raising on the road to Csenger.

## THE MARRIAGE BROKER

TOWARDS NOON the heat became sultry, presaging a storm for the afternoon. However, Goldeleh's mother, old Aunt Seemah from Nameny, came first.

She came in a carriage and made a halt by the toad-puddle field, where Sholem and his helpers were building shocks of wheat. By the time she drove on towards the inn, Malkeleh was already awaiting her with a dish of sour milk made nice and cool by being let down into the well in the yard.

"What good wind, Mother Seemah?" she asked.

The old woman removed her headkerchief and adjusted her wig. She sat down, wheezing, took a sip of sour milk and carefully licked the rim of the mug, lest any of the sour milk should drip on the clean table-cloth. Then, looking Malkeleh in the face and wagging her head, she said:

"You don't think it's an ill wind, Malkeleh, do you? It's a good wind, a very good wind." She gave a low laugh, the crow's feet round her eyes making a pattern. Bending close to Malkeleh, she went on mysteriously: "It's good for Yiteleh, though there's a share for you as well."

Malkeleh smiled but did not reply. Seemah did not like her silence.

"But if you don't want it . . ." she said. She gave Malkeleh a searching look, then: "Sholem is not so obstinate," she grumbled.

"Then it's about a young man," said Malkeleh quietly.

"Of course, my darling. And what a young man! A pity I could not bring him with me. Then you could have seen how old Seemah loves you. But how could I bring him? How could I burst into your house without preparing you first? You must whitewash the house, paint the bricks on the veranda steps a lovely red color, buy a few new mugs, make two nice frocks, one for yourself and one for Yiteleh, and of course, scrub the children. When you say the word, I'll speak to the young man and tell him to come along. Then we'll arrange about the dowry and get ready for the wedding. Before the holy days or after? What do you think?" As Malkeleh shrugged, the old woman went on: "I'm not in a hurry. But don't forget, dear heart, that Yiteleh is already a big girl. Would you rather have the wedding for *chanukah?* A cold wedding—a warm nest."

"I think—" began Malkeleh thoughtfully.

"What do you think?" pounced the old woman, "What do you think?" Her mouth was agape with anticipation.

"—we're going to have a storm," completed Malkeleh, gazing out through the window. Then, careful to make her voice sound calm, she said: "Has Sholem agreed?"

"Sholem? Well, he didn't say no."

"Did he say yes?"

"Not yet."

Malkeleh's pale face became suffused with pink, and her voice became somewhat more animated as she said:

"He has objections?"

"He'd like to know a few things."

"Whether the young man earns a living, I suppose?"

"He didn't ask that at all. If God gives a man a wife, He also gives him bread. He gave bread to Sholem, didn't He?"

Aunt Seemah produced her snuff-box and pushed a pinch of snuff up her nose.

"What he wants to know," she resumed, "is what *yeshibas* the young man attended and how many rabbis have given him a diploma."

"Did you tell him?"

"No. But I can tell you," said the old woman.

"Well?"

"He didn't attend any *yeshiba* and has no diploma from any rabbi. But he supplies rags to the paper mills at Hermanec."

"Then everything is all right," said Malkeleh with a sigh of relief.

"You're a clever woman," laughed Aunt Seemah. "I can see that rabbinical diplomas are of no importance to you."

"Of no importance?" said Malkeleh. "Why, if the young man has no rabbinical diplomas he can't have our girl."

"What are you saying, Malkeleh? You don't even know who
it is."

"Of course I know—he is one of the ragmen of the paper mills
at Hermanec." She spoke simply, though with a sense of assurance:
she did not have a decision of Sholem's to contend with.

"Not one of the ragmen," cried the old woman, "but the head
ragman. That's what Shmayeh Susskind is. I'm sure you've heard
about him, he comes this way sometimes. And the smartest of
all his children is Dov—Dov Susskind. They have a fine German
name, haven't they? The Squire of Cseke once called Dov 'Susskind Junior' in my hearing. You know who that is? He is that
one-eyed gentleman who is a Deputy at the Diet and writes
poetry. He's a fine gentleman, though he doesn't like Jews. But
to Dov he said 'Susskind Junior.' And Dov's wife he'll call
Madame Susskind Junior." Aunt Seemah kept stuffing snuff into
her hairy nostrils, tilting her head back to do so, and puckering
her eyelids as she watched the effect of her words on Malkeleh's
face. "Is a Shmayeh Susskind not distinguished enough for you?"
she went on, beginning to get impatient. "He has a name, seven
children, and capital made by hard work and clever speculation.
You think that rag collecting needs only a pair of legs and an
empty sack? Well, that's not enough. You must also have brains
and a full purse. You must know how to buy and you must know
how to sell. And you must be clever enough not to sell when the
mills need the rags most. Just now they need material very badly.
But Shmayeh wouldn't think of letting them have any, though
all his sacks are full. Of course, his purse is empty, because there's
no purse that doesn't empty in the end. So he has decided to increase his business and take in Dov. How much dowry are you
giving Yiteleh?"

"That depends. . . ."

Aunt Seemah took Malkeleh's vague answer as the first sign that
her words were beginning to take effect. She suddenly veered the
conversation to indifferent matters. The air was getting cool, she
said. She hoped there would not be a hailstorm because across the
Tisza the corn was still standing. Thank you, Malkeleh, my
daughter Golda is well and Mendl is doing well in his business.
They're friends again, almost in love, the two old fools.

The small room suddenly grew dark. The children came running in from the yard. They brought relief to their mother, who had grown tired under the continuous assault of the old woman's talk. It was good to bother with the children again.

A streak of lightning caused Aunt Seemah to start. She muttered a benediction, shrinking within herself with fear as she waited for the sound of thunder, though she tried to conceal her fear.

Sholem came in, announcing the great news:

"There's a big storm." He changed his jacket, rejoined the company, accepted a pinch of snuff from the visitor and sneezed. Turning to his wife he said: "I'll go and send Yiteleh in to you. I'll take her place in the inn."

Malkeleh was suspicious again. Sholem wanted Yiteleh to be present here—those two must have arranged something between themselves. True, Dov Susskind had not been to *yeshibas*, but his father had other sons as well, and just now he was in need of money. She determined to fight with all her strength against her daughter being sold behind her back. It promised to be a very violent struggle. Yiteleh entered, humming the lines:

> *"Have a care, Benni, and save your breath,*
> *Or they'll take you to the cell of death."*

"What *goy* song is that?" asked Aunt Seemah disapprovingly.

"It just came to my lips," explained Yiteleh, "I don't know why." She told the story of the strange visitor. Sholem could not think who he was. On inquiry, Isaac said the stranger was a rich man who used to make merry in Herskovitch's inn. He had a mine in Sebespatak, where a few years ago he found lumps of gold the size of a fist. He was said to eat his bacon with a golden clasp-knife.

"He was not a local man, his dress was Rumanian, his behavior that of a Magyar. And his eyebrows were like those of Aunt Golda."

At any other time the story would have been a titbit for Aunt Seemah, who liked rumors and gossip. But now she had had enough of the strange *goy*. She was here on a mission. She must bring together the two young people who did not know each other and perhaps did not wish to. But what did that matter? The old woman was afraid that Malkeleh might give away the plan in connection with Dov Susskind to Yiteleh in an unfavorable form, so she tried to anticipate her. She said nothing definite, only spoke in a general way to draw the girl out and learn her attitude.

"Well, Yiteleh, soon we'll get under the *chupah* and cry. Then when you get out from under it you'll dry your eyes with a nice lace handkerchief and see what sort of a husband the Above One has sent you."

"I'll certainly look at him first," said Yiteleh. "I might not want to go under the *chupah* with him at all."

"You might not want!" cried the old woman with consternation. "What sort of a world are we living in? I went under the *chupah* with my sainted Feivl without knowing whether he was handsome or ugly. He was ugly, but he was a husband. And he gave me five fine children. He'd have given me more if he hadn't died so soon. And if he'd died earlier, I'd have been even less choosy than the first time."

Malkeleh gave a laugh and the children surrounding her joined in. Aunt Seemah looked round sternly.

"What are you laughing at? Let the children go out. The rain has stopped. They shouldn't hear talk like this."

Sarah Chayah ushered the children out into the kitchen, and instantly there was a minor uproar there. Aunt Feiga could be heard grumbling:

"A pack of wolves . . . They won't let you sleep. . . ."

In the room the debate was resumed, though as yet it was one-sided, the old woman holding the stage. But later Yiteleh too put in a word, saying that it was best if the boy and girl loved each other when they went under the *chupah*. The old woman was indignant.

"Where is it written that the young people should love each other?"

"In the Bible, Aunt Seemah," said Yiteleh. "Adam and Eve loved each other."

"What was the use?" snapped the old woman. "They hadn't a shirt to their backs."

Yiteleh gave a full-throated laugh. But she did not retreat.

"Jacob also loved Rachel."

"He had enough trouble with her, too. He served twice seven years for her. And by the time he was able to marry her, poor Rachel could scarcely give him any children. Jacob did not love Leah, yet he lived with her in peace. Leah bore him six sons and a daughter. Where would we all be to-day—the whole Jewish people—if Leah had not produced Judah?" She looked round triumphantly. She was almost sorry that she had chased the younger children out of the room, thus losing most of her audience. She felt that if she kept to this theme it would help her to victory. Malkeleh kept silent and even Yiteleh, though learned in the Bible, could find no answer to the last argument.

"Love," the old woman went on, "is expensive and dangerous and it is not for Jews. Israel is fighting for its existence. If two people who love each other get together, what happens? They fall out of love, but they are still together. But if two people who don't love each other get together, that can only lead to a happy result. Neither the man nor the woman thinks of silly things; they just work and try to get prosperous. And in time they get used to each other and even come to love each other. This slow love doesn't depart in a hurry." She looked out through the window. The sun was out again. She adjusted the wig on her head, tied up her headkerchief and snapped at Yiteleh:

"Tell my man to harness the horses." When Yiteleh had left the room, she raised her pointed chin at Malkeleh:

"You think the rag-picker wouldn't fit into the family?"

Malkeleh did not reply. Suddenly, Aunt Seemah's tone became livelier, assuming a newsy quality.

"I almost forgot," she said. "I met your brother-in-law on the road."

"Which one?" inquired Malkeleh.

"What do you think?" said the old lady. "Which one of your brothers-in-law could one meet on the road of an early morning? Gimpel Zorech, of course. He had heard from another schnorrer, somewhere at the other end of the country, that the peasants had set your house on fire, so he turned back to see how Malkeleh was and how his boy was."

"You told him we were all right?"

"I told him everything. That Sholem had built a lovely house,

just like a *rosh hakahal*. And that Golda had tried to make a man
out of his Yossel, but that by the third day he started to carry
gossip from house to house, so Golda brought him back here.
Gimpel guffawed when he heard this."

"But why didn't you give the poor man a lift?" asked Malkeleh
reproachfully.

"I couldn't have him in my carriage with his bugs, could I?"
said the old woman in consternation. "If I had I could start to
scratch now. I threw him a copper, as much as he gets anywhere
else. Besides, he said he wanted to go along the Kocsord Road."

"How's that?" wondered Malkeleh.

"I don't know," replied the old lady. "He didn't say. But you
can guess. To Gimpel Zorech only the crooked road is straight.
He won't be served in your inn when he gets here, but he can
get drunk at Kocsord."

Malkeleh tried to smile. In a very friendly tone, she said:

"There's no hurry for you to go. Have a good rest and stay
for supper."

"I came and saw you and I am glad to find you all in good
health," said the old woman in an obstinate tone. "If you have
anything to say to me, you'll find me in Nameny." As she was
going out to her carriage, she gave a final warning, her tone quite
frigid:

"But don't think too long about it, my dear. The mill at Hermanec needs the rags."

## MURDER ON THE ROAD

SUMMER VILLENAGE was nearing its end and noisy peasants came
along in the early afternoon, cursing and retailing exciting news.
Robbery and murder again. Ferenc Bor, the under-headman, son
of Mate Bor, who had died the previous autumn, asserted that the
robber band that was now operating round Mateszalka was the
same as that which wrought mischief in another place in the
spring, and in yet another the previous autumn. Yiteleh put down

her crocheting and looked into the bar parlor. An innkeeper must always know what is going on in the vicinity. Of course, it was difficult to get the facts from the confused talk of the peasants, but if you kept your ears open on the Tuesday, you might be the wiser by the Friday.

On the Tuesday one could learn no more than what the under-headman had said. On the Wednesday the peasants also knew that a pig dealer from Otvar had been knocked down and robbed on the road to Szalka. On the Thursday Vince Polya related that the dealer's driver, who fought with the bandits, had been knocked down with an axe. This sounded horrible, but the report was confirmed by Abel Topoly. The driver was still alive, but they gagged him and put the iron-bound bushel over his head and he was suffocated. Jancsi Galagonya, who had been driving the Gyekeny girls to Fehergyarmat, had heard that the County Commissioner had sent three posses of pandours, who were now trying to surround the bandits in the marshes between the Tisza and the Szamos rivers.

Sholem returned from the toad-puddle field late in the evening. After a hasty supper, he would take over behind the bar. He would open a large tome and start to hum quietly: "Saith Rabbi Tarphon . . . Saith Abbayah . . ." He would go on until midnight, oblivious of what the peasants were talking about in the bar parlor. Sometimes he would look in at midday as well, in order to construe a verse or two of the weekly Portion to the children. As he left, he could hear them chanting in the traditional way: "And the Lord spoke to Moses, saying . . ." Then they scattered, leaving only Yiteleh in the inn, for the customers were already beginning to arrive.

On Friday fresh details of the robbery and murder came in. The dealer, Zdenkovich, was on his way from Otvar to the market in Szalka. He was going there to buy, so his wallet was full. He meant to reach Szalka on Sunday evening, but strangely, both his horses lost a shoe from a hind-leg and he was obliged to spend the night at Gyekenyes. Old Gore, who knew Zdenkovich, having more than once acted as drover to his pigs, said that the dealer was fatter than the fattest sow and had a seat with double springs in his carriage. Yet the seat had broken down now. They hit him

on the head proper hard, having first fired two shots at him.
Were he not so fat, he would not be alive now, but they couldn't
pull the bushel over his head.

Yiteleh further learned, from a report of Serf Bene, that the
half-dead Zdenkovich had been dragged to the path leading to the
marsh and abandoned there. Some beggar passing that way heard
his moans. The story was getting more and more exciting, but on
a Friday afternoon the customers must be got rid of, for it would
soon be Sabbath. Yiteleh must hurry into the house to wash and
change and help her mother with the children. Just now there was
some bawling going on. Yossel was refusing to be washed, saying
that he had had a wash, with soap, on the Monday. He did not
want a clean shirt, either, having had one at the same time.

"You tell a lot of lies," he bawled, the freckles agleam on his
little face. "You always say my father is coming and he never
does."

Yiteleh was obliged to employ force, undressing the obstrep-
erous little boy and dragging him before the washbasin.

"If you are naughty," she threatened, "I'll send you back to
Nameny. I hear you were naughty there as well, spreading gossip
in the village."

"I didn't!" protested the boy. "But the black fisherman used to
come when Uncle Mendl was out and Aunt Golda was alone. . . ."

"All right," said Yiteleh, "I don't want to hear any more." But
the boy went on:

"In the evening Uncle Mendl turned on me, and Aunt Golda
cried, then Uncle Mendl gave her some money and they both
laughed and they thrashed me and they called me schnorrer and
they didn't give me any supper."

He was sobbing bitterly as he said this and Malkeleh tried to
comfort him:

"Don't cry, Yossel dear, you're not going to be a schnorrer.
You're going to be a big business man and you'll have a carriage.
Would you like some bread and jam?"

In the evening the family sat round the table under the twelve
Sabbath lights. Sholem, with a kind of contented melancholy,
sang the hymn, "When we returned to Zion." Then he listened to
Mailech, who tried to shine with his little knowledge. The boy

was currying favor with his father because he wanted to stay at home for a few days and do business with the peasants. He spoke not of goods and trade as on other days, but of matters which seemed to indicate a dawning comprehension of the great leaders of Israel, who condemned the mercenary spirit. He concluded his parable with an anecdote from the Talmud.

"Resh Lakish was bathing in the river Jordan. Came Rabbi Bar Bar Chanah, the Babylonian rabbi, and extended his hand. Resh Lakish refused it. He was angry with the Babylonian Jews who did not join Ezra and Nehemiah, and did not return from exile, because they already had established business in Babylonia."

"Where did you read this?" asked Sholem, curious to know whether his son had read the story at the *yeshiba* or had merely picked it up.

"In Yomah," replied the boy promptly.

"That's right," said Sholem. "But do you know why Resh Lakish despised Bar Bar Chanah? Because Bar Bar Chanah was just an ordinary story-teller, who told whoppers in his invented travel talks."

"But," said Mailech, "Bar Bar Chanah also had a reason to despise Resh Lakish, who was the leader of a robber band in his youth."

"True, but he became converted and became a great teacher in Israel . . . You want to ask something, Yiteleh?"

Yiteleh only wanted to speak—not of Resh Lakish's bandit days, but about the bandits of the present who a few days ago had robbed the Otvar pig dealer Zdenkovich. Sarah Chayah had also heard something.

"They killed the driver and drove the horses into the marsh," she reported.

"No," said Yossel. "The bandits took the horses away, they only pushed the carriage into the marsh."

"Y-es," cried Manasseh. "They took a schnorrer t-to Sz-szalka be-because he d-drank the whisky out of the l-leather b-bottle."

"Zdenkovich was taken back to Otvar in a cart with a lot of feather quilts," intervened Yoirish. "But he hadn't got his wallet."

The children seemed to know a great deal, whereas this was the first Sholem had heard of the case. It appeared that a hair-

raising crime had been committed while he was working in the
toad-puddle field. However, interested as he was, he would not
have the matter discussed at the Sabbath board.

"You'll tell me all about it when the Sabbath is out."

"You won't be able to sleep," warned Malkeleh, "if you keep
talking about bandits."

Aunt Feiga swung her head like a horse with a nosebag, and as
she munched with toothless gums, began to talk about demons
and the Prince of Demons, Ashmodai.

"But where there is a *mazuzah* on the lintel," she mumbled,
"Ashmodai can't come in."

"The bandit comes through the window?" cried Yossel Beilah
Yenteh's.

"Is he coming here?" asked Yoirish, wide-eyed.

"No, not here," reassured his mother.

"And what do we do if he does come?" challenged Yossel.

"Then Isaac will chase him away with the prongs."

"And what if the bandit shoots Isaac dead?"

"Y-yes," said Manasseh, "the b-bandit has a p-pistol."

"Did you ever see a bandit?" said Sarah Chayah severely.

"No-no, b-but I saw a p-pistol—a c-customer had it."

Sholem silenced them with an irritable gesture.

"Let us say grace," he said.

The otherwise gay Friday evening scene was overcast by the
shadow of the crime committed in the vicinity. The children got
their prayer-books and for a time there was a hum of low voices,
then silence. There was silence outside too. No one would be
surprised to hear the sound of shots and cries for help.

"What's a bushel?" asked Yosseleh.

"What they measure beans with in the market," replied Sarah
Chayah.

"Then I won't have any more beans," said the boy.

"They also measure millet with it."

"Then I won't have any more millet, either."

"You're a silly boy, Yosseleh. The bushel was taken away by
the pandours."

Sholem felt he had to save the sanctity of the Sabbath, and at

the risk of detriment to the great Resh Lakish's authority, he
began to tell some of Bar Bar Chanah's travel tales.

Once Rabba (as Bar Bar Chanah is shortly called in the Talmud)
saw a frog that was as big as the fortress of Hagronia, which had
sixty barracks. There came a snake and swallowed the frog. Then
a raven swallowed the snake. The raven then flew off and settled
on a tree. How big do you think the tree must have been? Rabbi
Poppah bar Samuel saw it. "If I had not been present," he said,
"when the raven settled on the tree, I should not have believed
it . . ." On another occasion the ship in which Rabba was traveling
was flung by a wave so high that the stars were beginning to
singe the beards of the sailors. . . .

Amazement shooed away terror. The children were already
with the adventurous Rabba. Even Malkeleh and Yiteleh, to say
nothing of the hulking Isaac, followed with increasing interest
the alleged experiences of the Babylonian rabbi. And by the time
the candles were beginning to grow drowsy, and the children's
eyelids grew heavy, no one thought of the murder and the horror
of the recent past. The silence and darkness that descended on
this Jewish island was no longer perturbing. Imaginations were
filled not with gory figures of a real crime, but with the giants,
monsters, witches, and magicians of a despised Talmudic story-
teller, for whom the earth would have been too small, had they
existed.

Reality came the following morning. It was in the manner of
the pandours, who arrived from the direction of Szalka. Sholem
sat chanting over the Portion of the Week and did not hear the
noise in the yard, nor did he notice Malkeleh's entry, until she
touched him on the shoulder. Looking up from the book, he saw
that her face was white as chalk.

"What is the matter, Malkeleh?"

"I don't know, Sholem. Gimpel Zorech is here."

"Gimpel Zorech? On the Sabbath?"

"He came with the pandours."

"He brought the pandours?"

"No, Sholem. The pandours brought him."

They hurried out into the yard, where the stern-faced sergeant
stood waiting for Sholem. Gimpel Zorech stood between two

pandours, hairy, dirty, ragged, with blue-black patches under his swollen eyes. He looked terrifyingly unkempt. Sholem still had the Sabbath in every fiber of his body, and now he was shocked to see that his brother was not wearing even a Sabbath shirt. He wore no shirt at all. One could see his hairy ribs as his ragged jacket parted in front.

The yard soon filled with gaping peasants, curious womenfolk, grinning children. Balazs Patyodi, the sergeant, passed a hand over his mighty moustache and said sternly:

"This your brother, innkeeper?"

"Yes."

"What's his name?"

"Gimpel Zorech."

"And what's your name?"

Sholem tried to smile. Patyodi had known him for years, and had halted at the inn in the course of any inquiry in the neighborhood.

"You know my name, Sergeant."

"Damn your Jewish eyes!" bawled the sergeant. "I don't know anything. I must start at the beginning in every new inquiry. What's your name?"

"Sholem."

"Sholem Zorech?"

"No, only Sholem."

"Why, if Gimpel is your brother and his rear name is Zorech —because you Hebrews start back to front—then you can only be Zorech, like him."

The peasants were exchanging glances and chuckling.

"I can't be Zorech," said Sholem calmly, "because that's my brother's name. He's got two first names."

"Haven't you got a surname?"

"No."

"That's against the law. What do they call you in the synagogue?"

"Sholem ben Yoirish."

"And this lousy fellow here?"

"Gimpel Zorech ben Yoirish."

"Then your surname is Benyoirish."

"Yoirish was our father. We are only the sons of Yoirish."

"Well, didn't your bastard of a father have a surname?"

"His name was Yoirish ben Yossef."

"Enough of the synagogue! Didn't you get a name from the Emperor Joseph?"

"The Emperor's officials didn't come to us."

"Of course. You were then living in darkest Poland."

"My father lived here in Trebushan—in County Maramaros."

"How could you live without a name? Do you pay the tolerance tax?"

"Yes."

"Who do you pay it to?"

"The first year I sent it to Otvar."

"And since then?"

"The congregation of Karoly collects it."

"What name do they put on the receipt?"

"The receipt is in Hebrew."

"But there are no Hebrews in Otvar. That's a free city."

"I didn't get a receipt from Otvar."

"Ah! We'll go into that."

The sergeant pulled out his cane from the side of his knee-boot and flourishing it under Sholem's nose, said:

"Your brother has got himself mixed up in a horrible crime. Robbery and murder. Before we can start investigating the matter we must know his full name. I warn you, in the interests of the accused—we must have your full surname. Without that we can't even hang him."

Sholem gave a shrug.

"There are no robbers in Israel. Nor murderers."

"Better wait, Jew, for the verdict of the court."

"May I ask, Sergeant, what Gimpel Zorech is charged with?" said Malkeleh, stepping in front of the man.

The sergeant spat contemptuously from the side of his mouth.

"We don't advertise that to everybody, my good woman." Swishing his cane towards Sholem again, he bawled: "I warn you for the second time, vagabond, you must tell me your name."

Sholem felt like retorting that the sergeant knew his name:

Vagabond. Since the destruction of the Temple Israel had been tramping all over the earth.

"For the third time, Sholem, I warn you!"

The peasants whispered something among themselves. Then Serf Lajos Gore stepped forth and said:

"I beg your pardon, Sergeant, we call our Jew Csampas (Knock-knee)."

"You see," cried the sergeant with flashing eyes, "he refused to tell. Pandour Pettyen! Note it down. Sholem Csampas, inn-keeper. Gimpel Csampas, dangerous tramp. Done? Attention! Section, about turn!"

Pandour Pettyen, having made the minute, with the sheet of paper laid on the side of the well, replaced the same, together with the ink, the quill pen, and the bottle of sand, in his haversack. Then, nodding his plumed hat at the Sholem family and at the numerous audience, he said, with menace and mystery in his voice: "That's it!" Then he too lined up. Gimpel Zorech was given a push with the rifle-butt, then it was "Quick march!"

Gimpel Zorech, who had been silent throughout, almost indifferent, now tried to speak. He pushed his head forward, so that his big adam's apple could be seen moving up and down in his scraggy throat, but he could not speak, because both the pandours in charge of him were hustling him along. What did he want to say? Perhaps something very important, or perhaps nothing at all, and what he wanted was to take a last look at the red-haired, freckle-faced little boy with the stubborn chin who stood in front of Malkeleh, with hate and challenge in his eyes as he looked at the sergeant and his pandours. But perhaps the schnorrer only wanted to bid farewell to Malkeleh, or he might have brought her a message from somewhere. Sergeant Patyodi struck the prisoner round the back of his neck with the cane, not from anger, but as a matter of habit, and from self-satisfaction over the success of the first part of the inquiry.

"Step out, Gimpel Csampas!" he bawled. As the sergeant reached the gate at the head of his section, he turned his head and shouted at Sholem:

"And don't you forget your name again, Sholem Csampas, in case we summon you to Otvar."

BLACK SABBATH

AUNT FEIGA was squatting on the lowest step of the veranda. She had seen eighty summers and more, but she still loved the summer, and particularly the summer Sabbath, when she could retire from early morning to her favorite squatting point. Her two bare feet stuck to the ground like two withered roots, and her only thought was how nice the Sabbath snooze would be if only the children did not make a noise round her and did not tramp up and down the veranda steps like wild colts. But just now she was content, for apart from the buzzing of a hornet here and there the house was quiet. There had been some noise in the yard, but that was made by strangers, nothing to do with her. That was past, too, and the children were so well behaved, walking silently and talking quietly; even the otherwise over-loud Yossel Beilah Yenteh's could not be heard.

Yes, it was a very quiet Sabbath, so that even the grownups scarcely exchanged a word. Sholem too had lost his fine festive voice. Before Malkeleh had called him he read the Portion in a full-throated chant: "And I prayed to the Lord . . ." Now he was merely whispering the text, as though he had gone hoarse, as though he were reading not the majestic entreaty of Moses on the threshold of the Land of Promise, but his own petty plaints.

Sholem's only consolation was that the disgrace and humiliation did not catch him unawares. About the murder he was the least informed in the family, whereas his children knew even such details as that the pig dealer's leather bottle had been found in the possession of a schnorrer. But there was one thing that none but he knew: that the event happened as it was written, and as the aged Rabbi of Vizhnitz had prophesied long ago. He had had that prophecy in mind for years, and in his heart he was prepared for the hour that held incarceration for Gimpel Zorech after his life in the gutter. The only thing that could allay his anxieties for the future was that both prison and the gutter were pre-destined, and must be in the ultimate interest of Israel in this

case, as it was in the case of Joseph and Daniel. Now he realized
with a sense of terror that he had not been reassured after all.
Israel would survive the trouble, as it had survived all others. But
would Gimpel Zorech get over it? And would he not drag the
whole family with him into disaster?

The attitude of the peasants was also perturbing. Sholem had
one or two friends among them, who would hasten to his aid.
Had not Serf Gore disarmed the sergeant's rage with that alleged
name, perhaps Sholem himself would also have been marching towards jail. But there were few Gores around. The mass of the
serfs counter-balanced their own wretchedness and oppression
by spitting at the Jew or throwing mud at him. The Jew-baiting
Ludpals were already spreading a rumor that Gimpel was a
member of the robber band, which was composed entirely of
Jews. The Jews hated Zdenkovich because he dealt in pigs, goods
that Jews could not touch, and which they hated as the Devil
hated incense. Anyone who refused to believe that Gimpel could
kill a man, was reminded of his old crime, when he got drunk
and smashed up the peasants' sunflower crop. A man who could
kill sunflowers could kill people.

Sholem ought not to think of all this on the Sabbath, but how
could he help it? At table Malkeleh stared in front of her with
tears in her eyes. "If I could only have given him a bite of cold
chicken. No one's eating now." Sholem, who was forcing himself to eat "in honor of the Sabbath," dropped his knife with a
clatter. Almighty God! They would be giving Gimpel Zorech
pig's flesh to eat! He could no longer maintain his severity with
himself in the matter of Sabbath ordinances, and he let the others
talk about the trouble.

Yet he was impatient for evening, when he might go into the
inn and listen to the talk of his peasants. And when evening came
he omitted even to look at a Gemarah.

"Well, neighbor Bene, have you had a good crop?"

"Perhaps I did, and perhaps I didn't," said the peasant with
a shrug. Then he sat down, drank, filled his pipe, sniffed, spat,
but did not speak.

Janos Galagonya came in without a good evening, sat down
and waited to be served. Sholem came out to him.

"The usual Saturday evening brandy, Farmer Galagonya?"

"Rye'll do to-night," growled the peasant.

Serf Perecseny burst in with a curse:

"Damnation! This inn is in pitch darkness!"

"I'll light another candle, Uncle Perecseny," said Sholem mildly.

"Do, do. Don't be careful with my money."

He was eighteen months in arrears with his payments. At other times he was a well-behaved customer, now he was loud and discontented.

"We need another Jew here, not this knock-kneed one," said another serf who was in arrears.

Serf Polya forgot to bring his tally stick. At other times Sholem used to refuse credit to such forgetful customers, but this time he merely said:

"You'll bring it along to-morrow."

He was rewarded with a rude reply:

"But don't go and mark two pints more."

Abel Topoly and his brother Vince said the drink was bad. Abel said it made him belch with a froggy smell, while Vince spat as if with disgust.

"The Jew has cleared the toad-puddle," he said, "and now the frogs are in the casks together with the water."

"No wonder Mate Bor died of the water disease," opined Serf Zacharias. "He drank a lot here."

"Of course," said Bellringer Ludpal, "Gimpel likes something better—rich man's whisky. . . ."

This made the peasants laugh. Even Lajos Gore joined in, though he was rather taciturn that evening.

Teasing and leg-pulling was not unusual at the Shingled Inn. Sholem was equal to it and more than once bested his customers with an apt retort. But that evening he was not in the mood and he took every word to heart. If a peasant made a face or a gesture, if he croaked or spat—and even if he did and said nothing—it was all directed against him. Sholem was prepared to hear the case of his brother discussed, but apart from Ludpal's remark, nothing was said about it. They did not even mention the murder. That was queer. Had they arranged among them-

selves not to talk about it in his presence? Or had they been instructed by the pandours not to blab, lest the suspected family
should learn how matters stood? Sholem's confusion and uncertainty were only intensified when the peasants produced a pack
of cards, and some of them started to play, while the rest gathered
round them to watch. Some mention was made of Serf Vizhordo,
who had been bed-ridden for three weeks, and of Squire de
Denghelegh, who was also in a bad way, and there was also
some talk about the hailstorm, about the heavy villenage redemp-
tions, about the gentry's meanness, about the priest and about
the wise woman. But not a word was said about the murder.

In the summer Sholem used to close the inn towards midnight
on a Saturday evening. He used to wait until night watchman
Gaspar dropped in for his free drink, and by the time the old man
had set out in the silent village street to blow his horn and give
his cry for midnight, Sholem would already be barring the door
from the inside. Uncle Gaspar used to pay for the free drink by
keeping a special eye on the inn, lest there be a burglary, or a
fire again, or lest the livestock should break out. In addition, he
would report the events and the gossip of the day, to which
Sholem would listen more or less attentively. Sholem was not too
interested in such things as that the smith from Gencs was court-
ing Terka Topoly, or that Berci beat his wife, or that Master de
Sarberek no longer called on the Gyekeny girls, but went tippling
with his father to the houses of some other gentry. But to-night
Sholem was waiting for Uncle Gaspar with some impatience. He
was sure that he would learn something from him. The old
watchman arrived earlier than usual, soon after eleven. But he
merely tossed off his drink and turned to go at once. He had
brought no news, only a message:

"Get ready, Sholem, the gentry are coming. They're not going
to Ecsed, because the coachman's been kicked by Barbara." In
the door he turned his head and: "I must hurry and get the
gypsy," he said loudly and importantly.

The message was addressed partly to the peasants. Their
masters were coming, so they had better clear out. But the
peasants did not mean to do that. On Saturday evening they
stayed till twelve, and they would not go away if they sent the

haiduks for them. The fact that the coachman had been kicked by Barbara was one more reason for their disobedience. Sholem saw nothing extraordinary in it, but the watchman's news created agitation among the peasants.

"Barbara!" they cried. "The beast's been at it again . . . It wasn't enough that she crippled Martin. . . The gentry must celebrate this with wine and music. Till dawn. Well, we're not leaving, no matter what."

Sholem had to provide someone to serve them while he was serving the gentry. He knew that they were going to stay till morning, but this time he did not mind. Indeed, he was glad. The Above One must have sent them, like last time, to stand by him in his trouble.

The younger children were already in bed; only Malkeleh, Yiteleh, and Mailech were still awake, sitting round a solitary candle in the house. Malkeleh felt crushed, while Mailech was afraid and shivery, so Yiteleh had to take her father's place. At any other time her parents would not let her go among the peasants at this hour, but there was no other way out now. Yiteleh dried her eyes, tied her hair into a bun, donned a white apron, and the next minute she was busy behind the bar.

"All right, Farmer Galagonya—genuine brandy . . . Rum for you, Vince Topoly . . ? Another tot for Abel . . . Won't it be too strong so late in the evening . . ? Uncle Ludpal, I like you because you ring the bells so beautifully . . . so I'll fill the glass to the brim. Uncle Gore, I can't find the tally stick. Have this on the house, for giving us such a nice name . . . Here's your rye. Farmer Perecseny . . . You wanted ordinary? Well then, I'll charge for ordinary. It's Sunday to-morrow, anyhow . . . Will you have a drop of pear brandy, Uncle Bonca? Is it true that Marika is getting married? If I had such lovely blue eyes. . . ."

Yiteleh was fresh and lively, more charming and more talkative than at other times. None could have told that but a short while ago she had been sitting in the house by a solitary candle, sad and even tearful. The peasants were glad to have her carefree youth among them. They drank differently, and the drink tasted different. The gentry were drinking to the sound of music, but here they had the sound of a young voice, a voice that made them forget about the hailstorm, the oppressive taxes, the mean-ness of the gentry, and the savagery of the mare Barbara. And in the end the girl's presence melted the heavy reserve of the serfs.

Squire de Sarberek was drinking Tokay and lecturing Sholem. He knew nothing about the events that were weighing on Sholem and his family, or if he did, he was scarcely interested just then in Zdenkovich and Gimpel Zorech. He had something very different in mind. He had heard that Sholem had reclaimed the toad-puddle and had grown corn on it. In his view Sholem had no right to do that. Sholem had received a piece of marsh, and if he wanted another he could get it on lease and he could do what he liked with the marsh—catch loach or fish or breed frogs and send pickled frogs' legs to Pest or even Vienna. He could use the reeds and the rushes, and he could cut the long grass with which to feed his livestock and the horses of people pulling up at the inn. But as soon as the marshy parts receded, either naturally or through human intervention, the land belonged to those who had a traditional right to it, in this instance to the speaker's family.

Sholem realized that it never rained but it poured. The good one of the three squires had not come along, and perhaps he would never leave his bed again. There were three of them here again: Squire de Sarberek, Master de Sarberek, and Squire Gyekeny. The first two scarcely needed Gyekeny's support: they were in a majority, and in any case the toad-puddle was theirs. Or it had been. Sholem had bought it and paid for it twice over. Once when it was still marshland, and again when after Sholem's strenuous exertions it had been reclaimed. Sholem explained this in a mild tone whilst filling the gentry's glasses with wine. He did not wish to annoy the gentry. But it was precisely this mildness that angered the Squire. That and the fact that, being a Jew, he insisted on justice. The Squire had just clinked glasses with the other two, but instead of drinking he flung the glass at the wall, where it crashed to smithereens. Gypsy Gebics hopped aside. Sholem, pale and humble of bearing, stood and listened to the Squire's outburst:

"What are you talking about, Judaeus? You say I sold you the toad-puddle? Did you get a contract? Or if you did, did you record it at the *urbarium*? What do you think they'd have said to you there? To get back to Galicia or wherever you came from. To shut your trap and be off. You've no right to own land amid the property of Hungarian gentry. It's by our indulgence that you live, produce more little Jews and hoard the florins. And we, Hungarian gentry, are short of money."

Squire de Sarberek had whipped himself into a rage. Jumping up, he shook a bony finger at Sholem, his bearded chin jutting out, his angular face all anger and cruelty. Now he was about to pronounce what they would have said at the *urbarium* if Sholem had dared to appear there: Back to Galicia, with all your brats!

At that moment Yiteleh entered, smiling, curtsying and saying good evening. She told her father that she had closed the inn— later than usual, but the peasants would not go sooner. She apologized to the gentlemen for interrupting.

Squire de Sarberek's eyes lighted up. Twirling his moustache, he winked at Gyekeny, who was just then pulling together his befrogged jacket over his corporation. Master de Sarberek was expertly at work on his newborn little moustache, his teeth flashing whitely from his open mouth.

"All is forgiven," said the black Squire, whose anger had suddenly evaporated and who was now facing the little Jew girl like a chivalrous old gentleman. "But there's one thing we'll never forgive—that it was not you that came to serve us. You might have sent this acidulated Hebrew father of yours to the bar instead of yourself."

"I must go to bed earlier," explained Yiteleh.

"You want to sleep at night?" laughed the Squire. "Plenty of time to sleep all day to-morrow. What else can you do on a Sunday?"

"I am going to Karoly to-morrow."

"What to do?"

"I shall be helping in the shop of my uncle, Markus Nikolsburger."

"Ah, he's your uncle. Count Karolyi likes him. But we don't like the Count. He keeps a German governess for his daughters. You'll have a farewell glass with us, won't you?"

Sholem was glad that Yiteleh's appearance had softened the Squire's heart, but now he wished she would go.

"She mustn't," he said with embarrassment.

"Why not? Isn't this wine kosher?"

"It is, but . . ." He could not explain to the Squire that the wine was kosher only so long as it had not been touched by a *goy*, who might be thinking of heathen sacrifice at that moment. However, de Sarberek did not wait for an explanation, but raised his glass:

"Gedeon! Adam! To Yiteleh!"

The three gentlemen drank a toast to Yiteleh, and the girl's face dimpled.

"What are you gaping at?" snapped de Sarberek at the gypsy. "We're saying farewell to Yiteleh . . . Strike up, strike up!"

The gypsy struck up, with Squire Gyekeny beating time on the floor with his spurred knee-boots and jerking his fat body right and left to the fast, clipped rhythm. Master de Sarberek sprang to his feet, went up to Yiteleh and clicked his heels together.

"May I?" And he put his hands round her waist.

Sholem was taken aback. He stood tense, with fascinated eyes, waiting for Yiteleh to do what a Jewish girl ought to do when a *goy* boy touched her—push him away . . . kick him . . . slap his face. . . .

But Yiteleh did nothing of the kind. Her big brown eyes smiled. Her full lips, her flashing teeth also smiled. The flounces of her blue-spotted Sabbath frock gave a flutter as she started to dance, spinning round and round and tapping her foot on the floor. Her palms were pressed under her bun, her tender white arms with pointed elbows seeming to fly round her head like a pair of white doves round a dovecot. Had she ever done this before? Or had she merely seen the peasant girls who of a Sunday used to dance in front of the church? Gedeon Gyekeny clapped his fat hands rhythmically, and de Sarberek senior was following suit, while the gypsy gave a whoop and flashed the bow like lightning. Master de Sarberek was putting little extra tricks and refinements into his performance, as though he was dancing this *csárdás* in a Pest ballroom amid general applause.

Sholem was scandalized to the marrow of his bones. His daughter dancing with a *goy*! That Yiteleh herself finally came to her senses and, scarlet with confusion and a sense of guilt, suddenly ran out of the room, was no mitigation. Nor was it any comfort to Sholem that the gentlemen went on talking about his daughter until dawn. Squire de Sarberek was already hiccoughing and talking half in Latin:

"Well, Gedeon! You're the *nobilis senior* now, but in this case I'd reserve the *jus primae noctis* for myself."

Gyekeny, red like an angry turkey-cock, chuckled wheezily. Master de Sarberek hurled his glass at the wall above the gypsy's head, just as his father had done before.

## "FOR OUR SINS"

MALKELEH DID not consider it such a mortal sin that Yiteleh should have danced with the Squire's son. It would have been different had she yielded to the invitation of a serf boy. There she would have had the choice of refusing. But how could she refuse the son of a man on whom the family's whole future depended? Why did not Sholem try to resist the pandours? He might have told the sergeant that he was not going, on the Sabbath, to answer such questions as whether he had paid the tolerance tax and received a receipt, because it was forbidden to talk about business on the Sabbath. Or he might have used force when he saw Gimpel Zorech being beaten. Yet he held his tongue throughout.

"How could I have done anything?" cried Sholem, flinging his arms into the air.

"I don't say you could have," said his wife. "I don't say it was cowardice, either. What I say is that you had a good reason. But so did Yiteleh."

Very well, thought Sholem. Yiteleh had not done anything rash, had not pushed away the young man who had taken her hand and touched her waist, although she ought to have done it regardless of the consequences. But why did she smile? And whirl? And tap? And press her palm to the back of her neck? Sholem dared not say what he felt about all this, though there was a storm raging within him ready to burst: let no one touch Yiteleh with unclean hands, or approach her with an unclean thought. She was not like other girls, she was—Yiteleh. Yiteleh would become engaged to Wolf Birnbaum, but even that pious Jewish lad would not touch her before he was her husband. Even at the wedding feast she would dance with him only from the other end of a handkerchief, not to the music of a pockmarked gypsy, but to the tunes of Jewish fiddlers and singers. What they did to Yiteleh might have been a kind of force, but what she herself did could not be overlooked or explained away. His modesty forbade expression of his thought. Later, when he thought of this second humiliation on his Black Sabbath, he scarcely formulated his daughter's name in his mind. If now and then he quoted an ancient phrase, it was in a general way, with the sternness of a Jewish father guarding the traditions and morals of his family:

"For our sins we have been exiled from our land."

"And it is for our sins that they keep us in strange lands," Malkeleh would say.

It gave Sholem a start. It was not good if she was silent, but it was not good when she was not silent, either. What was she thinking of? He had told her that the Squire had been at him on account of the toad-puddle. But he had not mentioned that he was just about to be kicked out of the lease when Yiteleh, who must have heard de Sarberek's bawling from the parlor, entered and with a single smile disarmed his fury. But it seemed that Malkeleh knew that, too. Perhaps it was no sin for Yiteleh to smile. The lovely Esther had also smiled at Ahasuerus, thereby saving the life of the whole people. But Yiteleh had done more than smile. . . If the price of tolerance was that our wives and daughters should amuse the strange masters, then it would be better that we take up the staff again and go away in search of an uninhabited island or return to the wilderness where our ancestors roamed for forty years. . . . .

Malkeleh, of course, was not thinking of Esther and Ahasuerus, but perhaps of her own brother Mordechai, or still more of Leizer Lazarovich who distilled spirits and lent money at usurious interest. Recently, she had used the expression about Jews whose only pleasure was to dance round the Golden Calf, which Sholem himself had used about Lazarovich, so she must mean him. "One Jew is not all Jews," Sholem had replied. To which Malkeleh retorted, "But there are some that live on the vices of the people, who exist in a state of wretchedness and oppression."

This was getting too personal, and Sholem thought it best not to pursue the subject. Malkeleh's reproach went back to that Saturday when they got stuck on the road before Lapfalva. It was not good to go back so far, for it was apt to deepen the rift between them. Malkeleh had resented innkeeping ever since. To her Lapfalva had never been anything but an extension of the muddy road. Yiteleh's departure for Karoly had not given her the satisfaction she had expected from it. It was not she that had sent her, but events. What choice was there? The house was now branded, and no suitor or best man could come to it, and not even a marriage broker. One would have to talk quietly and humbly, just as if the would-be bride was suffering from some visible defect or deficiency. There was no urgency, no urgency at all. Let the child sit in the leather shop until the atmosphere cleared. For six months, a year, or even longer. Let her argue there with the tanners and the grimy bootmakers. At least she would be buying and selling honest goods, instead of doling out intoxication to serfs living in filth and misery.

Sholem on his part saw nothing shameful in innkeeping. The inn gave him and his family bread, and that was the chief thing. It brought a lot of trouble, but it also brought a measure of peace, and you could study and teach the young in the shadow of the wine casks. The important thing was that the measures should be honest and the blending correct. Otherwise selling spirits was no more disgraceful than making ropes or mixing ink. There were those who hanged themselves and there were those that were hanged innocently, and there were those that were blackened with ink, especially by malicious officials. Yet no one said that ropes and ink were not useful and necessary things. It was the same with drink. If anyone wanted drink, you had to give it to

him, for if the Jew did not give it the Armenian and the Serb
would. Of course, it would be better to give happiness. But you
know what King Lemuel, who learned to prophesy from his
mother, said? "Give intoxicating drink to him that is lost and
wine to him whose heart is bitter, so that he may forget his
poverty and not remember his wretchedness."

To till the soil and write letters to God in furrowed lines,
was a finer occupation. But you see, Malkeleh, they won't let us
do that. I reclaimed the toad-puddle, grew flax, maize, and corn
on it, and now they have told me off. I must let the marsh come
back, else there will be trouble. What can we, strangers in a
strange land, do? We can sit down on the land that belongs to
all—the road. Lapfalva is still the road for us, but so is Karoly.

About one thing Sholem agreed with his wife: that it was a
good thing that Yiteleh was in Karoly. Though he had opposed
it at first, now he thought it was sheer luck that Mordechai had
sent that invitation long before the disgrace had come upon them.
He hoped that they would not hear about it in Karoly, and that
Yiteleh would say nothing. He was not thinking of Gimpel
Zorech's arrest, which could not be kept secret anyhow. In any
case, that was no disgrace, only a misfortune.

"Quite right, Malkeleh, let her stay in Karoly as long as possible.
The young master, it seems, does not feel like going back to his
yeshiba."

Malkeleh was getting sick of the veiled references to Yiteleh's
sin and her own similarly veiled defence, so she changed the
subject.

"Tell me, Sholem, what are we going to do about Gimpel
Zorech?"

"Is there anything we can do?"

"We must do something. We can't leave a brother of yours
involved in a case of robbery and murder."

"Well, they'll find out that he's innocent."

"What if they don't? And what if they do, but only after a
long time? Is the poor wretch to rot in prison meanwhile?"

"If it is fated like that . . ." Sholem was thinking of the
prophecy of the Saint of Vizhnic.

"If everything is fated," she said, "why do anything at all?

Why not wait until the pandours come along again and take you as well? The pandour sergeant is not such a gentleman as the Imperial officer."

Sholem was scared. It had already happened once, just after they had come to Lapfalva, that he was about to be arrested, when a section of soldiers had come from Otvar, in search of a deserter. Sholem was then saved because the lieutenant who led the section was impressed with Malkeleh's refinement. But it was only now that she heard from Sholem that the deserter had in fact been hiding about the house and had later taken service with him, though Sholem had kept him for only one day. That was when Malkeleh had gone on a visit to Karoly. Sholem kept the story from her in order to save her worry.

"Do you think," he now said, "we'll get into trouble on account of the Jew tax? I sent twelve florins to Otvar by that lad, who called himself Janos. But he never came back and I got no receipt, so I am sure he did not pay the tax."

"How did you know that he was the deserter?" inquired Malkeleh.

"It was easy to recognize him from the description they gave me. One of his eyebrows was blond, the other brown."

This was no time for a detailed explanation why Sholem should have sent the Jew tax by a deserter, and Malkeleh was not too inquisitive.

"The Jew tax," she said, "is an old story which they may or may not remember. But there are some older matters which never fall into abeyance, but are repeated again and again. Have you forgotten Latorka? What crime did you commit there? Did you kill the Christian child and did you hide his body under the hemp? All you did was to let the peasants steal from you the hemp you had bought from them. Yet it was not the thieves that had to run, but we. Do you think we are safer now? Do they love you more? You've got enemies here as well. And even if they know that your brother is innocent, the fact is that he is in prison, and that is held against him. You can't trust the gentry. The old one is sick, the other one doesn't count. The Black Squire does count, but he is angry with you."

"On account of the toad-puddle?"

"No, not on account of anything, but simply because he needs money."

"You think de Sarberek wants money from me?"

"What else?"

"Then why didn't he say so?"

"A noble never says it to a Jew. He just rages at him—about something or other. The Jew understands and hastens to offer him money. And the sooner he does that the sooner he gets over it."

"You're right. I'll go and see him to-morrow and take fifty or sixty florins with me."

"At least a hundred, Sholem. We're in it up to the neck and the Squire knows it. Reconciliation costs more at a time like this."

"I'll take a hundred," said Sholem after a swift mental calculation. "It's all the same . . . You're a very clever woman, Malkeleh."

"I'm not very clever, Sholem. Only I don't bury myself in thousand-year-old books. You can't see the world for the texts."

She had touched a sensitive spot.

"I can see things too," he said in an injured tone, "precisely through the texts."

Malkeleh gave a shrug.

"And when you've paid what's due to him because he's angry about the toad-puddle, don't you talk about the toad-puddle. That's of no importance till the spring. Talk about Gimpel Zorech and ask him to say a word to the Commissioner at Otvar who has the Zdenkovich case in hand."

"All right, Malkeleh."

MALKELEH'S MISSION

WHEN SHOLEM returned from the Squire, Malkeleh saw at once that he had not achieved much. The Squire was glad to see him, had in fact been about to send for him, because the young master was going back to Pest. He let Sholem have the peaty stretch next to the toad-puddle, though he did not give it in writing.

That part was not worth much and Sholem was not pleased about it. He had not asked for the addition, nor did he want to talk about land at all. However, Malkeleh was very understanding and said it did not matter, for after all the Squire needed an excuse to accept the money. His wife's understanding relaxed Sholem's tension somewhat. He told her about his attempt to obtain help concerning Gimpel Zorech. The Squire did not believe that Gimpel Zorech was guilty. But he had made one mistake: he had allowed himself to be caught. Real bandits were never caught. Sergeant Patyodi was just cattle, as the Commissioner himself well knew. But until the culprit was caught, they had to have someone to take it out of.

"The Jew, of course. Didn't the Squire promise to do anything?"

"He said one had to know who committed the murder, and that Gimpel Zorech had no share in it. When he knew the facts he would be pleased to get in touch with Andras Erdy, the Commissioner, who is a pal of his. He said that we must do something ourselves. But what can we do?"

Malkeleh nodded. Then:

"Tell Isaac to get the cart ready," she said quietly. "I'm going over to Batiz."

"Batiz?"

"If you need some stock I'll get it at the same time."

"I don't need anything just now."

"The people at Batiz are only at a stone's throw from Otvar. They may have friends there who can do something."

"But what?"

"Not much, perhaps. But if they deliver to Gimpel Zorech this mended underwear they'll have done something. The poor wretch can't sit in jail without a shirt. If he's decently dressed his jailers'll treat him more decently. I've mended two, one for weekdays and one for the Sabbath."

"You're right, Malkeleh," said Sholem with wetly shining eyes. "But it would be more important than anything that he shouldn't eat *trefah* food. How could we settle that?"

"We must go there, Sholem, that's all."

Malkeleh was sitting on the cart, wearing the blue dress with the white lace collar and a lace headkerchief. The dress looked glossy with much brushing. She smiled at Sholem and the children, who were now better behaved than ever before; even the youngest did not squall to be taken with her. She looked very confident.

When she had gone Sholem blamed himself for having allowed her to go in such a hurry. Now he realized how important it would have been to send at least a small order by Malkeleh, so that she should not tire herself with vain calls, but go straight to the one man who could do something. True, Malkeleh disliked Lazarovich, but he, Sholem, could have made her understand that he was the only Jew with influence in Otvar.

Of course, Malkeleh saw all that without being told. She set aside her own prejudices and made her first call at the right place. As her cart turned into the yard of the distillery Leizer Lazarovich stared.

"You came to buy, Malkeleh?" he greeted her. "Why, you haven't any casks. Where's my learned friend, Reb Sholem? He's not sick, God forbid?"

"No, Reb Leizer. And I'm not here to buy. I came on another matter."

"What an honor, Malkeleh. Come into the office and tell me all about it."

Lazarovich's amiability did not dispel Malkeleh's prejudice and distrust, but rather intensified them. Embarrassed at first, she soon got into her stride, and spoke warmly and intimately, as to an old friend.

Here was a man, an unfortunate Jew, lying in the county jail at Otvar. Everything humanly possible must be done for him. Gimpel Zorech was not an evil man, only unfortunate, the victim of an unhappy marriage. He was a good-hearted, well-intentioned man, but having nothing to live on and having no real home, he went on the road and stayed there. He had suffered a great deal, more than anyone, that she knew, because he had opened his heart to her. She and her husband had tried to raise him, save him, but fate wanted it otherwise. He was a young man burning with passion and loving Beilah Yenteh for all her badness. Or perhaps she was not bad, only not the right woman for him. Gimpel Zorech had run away from her, and from his own passion. And

he had run straight into another vice—drink. That was his only
crime. That he might have had something to do with the murder?
Or that he might be an accomplice of the highwaymen? Nonsense. They had found him standing by the half-dead pig dealer,
with the latter's leather bottle in his hand. He was probably
passing there, and seeing the leather bottle slung over the unconscious man's shoulder, took a swig of it—perhaps because the
sight had given him a turn. That did not make him into a bandit
or an accomplice of bandits. The worst that could be said was
that he could not resist the temptation of drink.

"That's quite enough," said the distiller with an impatient
pursing of his lips. "And what can I do for Sholem's lady?"

"I want you to help. You're the only Jew here who can do
something. You have a house in Otvar. You are friendly with
Burgomaster Lam and the councillors. And they know Commissioner Erdy."

"Who told you that I had a house in Otvar?"

"Everybody knows that. The Yellow House in the market
square is yours."

"They know it wrong. I have money invested in the Yellow
House, nearly as many florins as there are bricks in it. If a Jew
could have a house there, he could also live in it. That house
doesn't belong to me. And as to my friends in Otvar, surely you
don't think I can bother Burgomaster Lam or any of the councillors with such stories as that Beilah Yenteh has grown tired
of Gimpel Zorech!"

"You don't have to tell them that, Reb Leizer. That was only
for you, so you should know who the man was. Though all that
you need to know is that a Jew has been flung into jail innocently."

"How do I know that he is innocent?"

"You ought to know it, Reb Leizer. A Jew does not rob or
murder. And if that is not enough, your own heart must tell you
that Gimpel Zorech cannot be guilty."

Reb Leizer tugged at his straggly beard and shook his head.

"My heart doesn't tell me anything. I listen to my own common
sense. And my common sense tells me: Reb Leizer, keep away
from these drunken sots and their affairs."

Malkeleh looked at him and, strangely, all she saw was the

cobwebby red pattern covering the whites of his eyes. She never knew that white could contain so much black. She felt like answering him sharply that he was not keeping away from the other drunken sots, but was on the contrary relying on them for his affluence. But she repressed the urge and said:

"Of course, you don't have to know that Gimpel Zorech is innocent. There are papers about it, and you can ask those gentlemen to show them to you or at least tell you what is in them. And you can ask them to interrogate him in your presence. If we are to defend Gimpel Zorech, we must know what he is charged with."

"Did I say a single word about wanting to defend Gimpel Zorech? I wouldn't think of it. Let him defend himself as best he can. Was I tramping on the Szalka road or he? Did I drink the pig dealer's plum whisky or he? It's no use your telling me that a Jew doesn't murder or rob. An inveterate drunkard is capable of committing murder to get drink. And a man who takes the leather bottle of an unconscious person away from him is a robber in law. Whether he is connected with the highwaymen or not, he has committed a crime for which neither I, nor you, nor Sholem, but he alone must answer."

The distiller's argument depressed Malkeleh. If a Jew thought like that about the matter, what could one expect from non-Jews? She would have liked to get up and say:

"You're right, Reb Leizer. You cannot risk your business connections, your outstanding high-interest loans, and your good name for the sake of a beggar who has not even a decent shirt. Anyone who has committed robbery and murder should be in jail, and anyone that is in jail has committed robbery and murder. You're right, Reb Leizer, in wanting to keep away from your guilty brother."

But for all the bitterness that was in her heart, she controlled herself and said nothing that might irritate this rich man. There was still an aspect of his character left where he could be approached: his piety and his strict observance of the food laws.

"Look here, Reb Leizer," she said. "You're a Cohanite. It's your task to bless the congregation and watch over cleanliness. Besides, as far as I know, you are the President of the congregation. There is a Jew sitting in jail. Whether he is guilty or not guilty will come out in the end. But meanwhile, one must see to it that he shouldn't turn heathen. What does he get to eat there? Bacon or food cooked with lard . . . Would it not be possible. . . ."

"Who should give him kosher food," interrupted Reb Leizer, "when there are no Jews in the town? If I were living there, I'd send him goose-liver and roast duck from my own kitchen. But I can't send any from here: that would be an expensive and bothersome luxury." Taking hold of his straggly beard, he went on: "We must do everything for our Jewish brother. But he also must do everything for us and himself. Whether Gimpel Zorech eats *trefah* or not depends entirely on him. Let him live on bread and water. Bread and water are not *trefah*."

"What if they keep him for two months or more?"

"Suppose they keep him for two years? What then?" Reb Leizer's eyes lighted up as a quotation that might end this annoying debate flashed into his mind. "Chananyah, Mishael, and Azaryah had roast meats brought to them from the kitchens of Nebuchadnezzar and wine from his royal cellars. But they did not touch them. They ate only vegetables and drank water. Yet their faces stayed nice and rosy. And because they had observed the Law, an angel of the Lord freed them from the fiery furnace."

Malkeleh looked through Reb Leizer with a wry smile at the corner of her mouth. She was not unaccustomed to have vital issues settled with a fine Biblical quotation. She sat silent, waiting for Reb Leizer to go on. But he had nothing further to say.

"It doesn't matter about casks," he said, suddenly turning amiable. "I can lend you some. What can I get you?"

Malkeleh passed a pale hand over her brow and said.

"Nothing, thank you. I haven't been told to buy anything."

"A pity," shrugged the distiller. "I'd do anything for you, you know."

## THE WISE SLAVE OF JERUSALEM

MALKELEH SENT Isaac back with the cart and wrote Sholem a letter reassuring him that all was going well, though it was a more protracted affair than she had expected. Reb Leizer had recommended a very simple way for Gimpel Zorech to observe the dietary laws in prison, but she had another idea, which with God's help she would carry out. If he should be in need of stock, would he send the cart back on Thursday morning; she would then return with it in the afternoon. But if the order could wait, would he not send Isaac to Batiz, but let him stay with the children, who obeyed him more than Sarah Chayah. If he should get a reliable traveller putting up at the inn, would he send at least twenty florins by him to the innkeeper David Troyes or to his mother, Zissah. "If the cart won't go, you have to grease the wheels. And the front wheels need more grease than the rear wheels . . ." But Sholem should not send the money if he had no suitable person to entrust it to. She would borrow from Mother Zissah, and Yossef would take it back to her on the Sunday. If Isaac should not come on Thursday, Jacob Anshel, the candlemaker, would take her, Malkeleh, back at dawn on Friday. She was very well and Zissah and the others were very nice to her.

If Malkeleh wants Sholem not to worry, it is not right that he should. True, the village was more unfriendly than ever. The peasants were saying that the Jew had a guilty conscience and was preparing to run away again, was already sending his family all over the place. What could he do about it? He could not accost everyone and tell them that it was all an invention, just as the charges with which they were trying to blacken him and his family were libels. The one thing that would help was the truth. Truth penetrates into every house and cot, just like the sun.

If Malkeleh had ideas of which Sholem was ignorant, he in turn also had one that was unknown to her. Sholem's big idea was to seek out the truth in its hiding place. The rest could be left to truth itself. This idea illuminated his mind like a revelation, all the more because it was linked with a compelling urge to act. Malkeleh wanted it like that. She had left her children, and tired and ill as she was—for on Saturday she had complained about pains in the kidneys—she set out to mitigate Gimpel Zorech's misery. Malkeleh had performed an important task over there, he must perform a no less important one at home. She was saving Gimpel Zorech's body from filth and his soul from damnation; Sholem must find the tracks leading to the discovery of Gimpel Zorech's innocence and the acquittal of Israel from blame.

Where to start the search? On his bookshelves, of course. There was a fine story somewhere in the Midrash: "Our Sages relate: An Athenian Greek bought a slave in Jerusalem. On the way towards Athens, the slave turned to his master and said: 'If we hurry we shall overtake those traveling ahead of us.' The Greek gazed into the distance and said: 'I cannot see anyone on the road.' 'We cannot see them,' said the Jewish lad, 'because they are four miles ahead. They have a pack camel, a female, and she is blind in the left eye. She carries on her back two old, cracked leather gourds, one containing oil, the other vinegar. The camel is followed by two young camels. The drover is not a Jew.' 'How do you know all this?' asked the Athenian. 'Look, Master,' replied the man from Jerusalem, pointing at the tracks on the road, 'as you can see, the grass has been grazed off only on one side of the road, the right side. This shows that the animal cannot see with its left eye. That it is heavy laden and that it is a female can be seen in the sand, in which its dragging udder has made marks. The four large hooves are followed by eight small ones: those of the two young camels. The two leather gourds are worn and dripping. The marks made by oil are different from those made by vinegar, and the flies gathering on them are also of different types.' The Greek was amazed. 'But how do you know that they are four miles away?' 'Because their tracks are only just visible. And after four miles the tracks of a laden camel start to get faint.' 'And from what sign do you see that the drover is not a Jew?' 'At the same spot. You saw, Master, that big puddle in the middle of the road that we had to avoid. That was the urine of the camel. A Jewish drover will not allow that sort of thing, but will lead the animal to the ditch alongside the road.' The Athenian hurried forward

and saw that everything was exactly as his wise slave had predicted."

"You see, Malkeleh," said Sholem, raising his bearded face from
over the tome, "this is what we learn out of our books. To search,
draw conclusions, and see the truth from miles away."

Of course, Malkeleh did not hear him, for she was in Batiz, and
that was fortunate for Sholem. Because had she been there, she
would have replied:

"Well, Sholem, then go ahead: search, conclude, find the
truth."

However, for the present Sholem could see nothing but the
printed page. He left the book open and sat down in front of it
again and again to study this prototype of detective work. In the
case in hand he had not yet noticed any special clues. There were
plenty of reports and rumors, for the inn was visited by all sorts
of people who have heard this or that or the other, the inn being
the first stop for news, hearsay, beliefs, and opinions. But if you
kept your ears open from morning till night, it was as well before
bedtime to tilt your head to the right, then to the left, and shake
out all that flood of words, as the swimmer shakes out the water,
because it will only impede you in your reasoning. Even a brainy
fellow like Szimchah Roth, a timber merchant who had spent the
evening before the attack with Zdenkovich in the Armenian inn
in Csenger, recounted, under the retrospective effect of events,
so loquaciously what he had seen and heard that one could not
decide for a long time what to forget and what to retain of his
story. Zdenkovich wore a heavy gold chain over his waistcoat
and was not afraid of bandits because he carried a pistol, while
his coachman was as strong as a bear. However, Zdenkovich liked
to play cards and his coachman liked to drink. Zdenkovich had
gambled till late Sunday afternoon with the rich Florian, who lost
more than a hundred florins to him. The bandits had taken that
too. It was said that Zdenkovich had more than three thousand
florins on him. He wanted to leave at noon, and would then have
reached Szalka before dark, but his coachman was lying dead
drunk in the stable with Florian's man and two other Rumanians,
who had brought cartloads of apples. So what could he do but
return to the card table? He lost about thirty florins that time. The

Rumanians were taking the apples to the market at Szalka, but while they were in their drunken stupor anyone could steal their apples. That day the whole of Csenger seemed to be munching apples.

Then there was Tamas Csuvasz, a beater of Count Karolyi's, who also did some poaching on the side. He sold many a fox, badger, and otter skin to Jonah Zicherman, the furrier from Hodasz, who was now spending a day at the inn while collecting skins in the neighborhood. Csuvasz must have known something, for at the time of the murder he happened to be lying in wait in that part of the marsh, but he had said nothing even to Zicherman, though he dropped a remark now and then about such matters as that the pandours had arrested two men in the market square at Gyarmat and they had hatchets and knives in their kneeboots. Yet the real bandit took fish to market or sweet pumpkin and was never armed.

All this is very interesting, Sholem said to himself, but Monday is gone and Tuesday is gone and I am none the wiser. On the Wednesday he made up a small order running to fifty-odd florins. He could have done with more stock, but at least Malkeleh would now travel more comfortably on her way home. Why should she stay away till Friday if she could return on Thursday? Sholem tightened the hoops of the casks, poured water into them and rolled them about to see if they were leaking. They were leaking, some badly. In recent weeks he had had little time to look after his vessels, and the staves had got dry. He filled the casks with water and left them in the yard. By morning there was a puddle round them. Sholem fancied that the big cask was the mother camel and the two small ones her young ones, and that they had all lain down in the mud, refusing to go to Batiz. He read over Malkeleh's letter again: she did not seem too keen on it either. He racked his brain to think of the simple method Lazarovich had recommended to enable Zorech to eat kosher food in prison.

"Hi, Isaac! Do you know what Reb Leizer said?"

"He said if we didn't buy any spirits not to water the horse in his yard."

Sholem looked at the coarse features of his servant, as if reading there what a bad man Lazarovich was, grudging water from his well to a tired horse. A suppressed anger rose up in Sholem. He now agreed with Malkeleh that Lazarovich was a bad man.

"Then you're not going to Batiz to-day," he said to Isaac.

"I couldn't, anyhow. The horse has lost a shoe from its front leg and the smith of Gyekenyes is at Szalka to-day."

"What is he doing there?"

"The pandours have summoned him."

"What for?"

"They found the pig dealer's horses, which he had shoed a week ago last Sunday. They called him in to see if he recognized them."

"Why didn't they bring the horses here?"

"The sergeant ordered the pandours to stay at Szalka," replied Isaac, grinning and blinking with his boss-eye. "That's where the highwaymen are hiding."

"Well, if they found the horses at Szalka the sergeant may be right."

"Long live Pharaoh if they are there."

"But perhaps they have gone that way."

"Those were only the bottom ones."

"What bottom ones?"

"Those of the highwaymen who find the mug, then sell the horses in the market."

"What's a mug?"

"The fellow with the fat wad. The top highwaymen take the money. If the bottom ones went that way, then the top ones came this way."

"How do you know?"

"I just think so."

"But if they catch the bottom ones they'll catch the top ones as well."

"Where there are pandours," giggled Isaac, "there are no highwaymen. And where there are highwaymen there are no pandours."

Isaac refused to say more, no matter how hard his master pressed him. He was no Jerusalem slave. He came from the darkest Avas mountains. Yet he was not such a blockhead as he seemed, for he could reason and keep his counsel.

Sholem went down into the cellar, pushing the casks about on the sleepers. These casks were not leaking, having stood in a damp spot. Not that he needed any casks now, having decided after all not to send for stock. But something had drawn him to the cellar, where it was dark and quiet and one could think undisturbed. Besides, a siphonful of wine could do no harm to the innkeeper for once. Sholem thought that he had learned something of importance from Isaac. The bottom ones went that way, the top ones came this way. But where could they get to from here? What a fine bouquet this *shel pessach* from Mesel had! Queer that the whole of Csenger should have been munching apples on the eve of the murder. Sholem would not have believed it if it had been told by anyone but Szimchah Roth. Those apple-carting Rumanians did not sleep in the stable, but on their carts. No matter how sleepy or drunk, they would crack a whip at anyone at the back of the cart trying to steal. But what have the Wallach's apples to do with us? We are searching for clues. Or at least for some casks that don't leak. For we shall have to replenish sooner or later.

There was a long knife stuck in the ground somewhere about, one with which Sholem used to scrape the mold off the sides of the casks. Not really a knife, but a two-edged dagger, a bayonet. It was left by that lad—what was his name? Janos. Sholem looked at the bayonet and sat down on the cellar step with it in his hands to think. It was an old story, and he ought not to think of it now, it would only upset him. It would be more important for him to find the key to the latest events. As Malkeleh said, the tolerance tax of eight years ago was a thing of the past . . . But perhaps it wasn't after all. He had told Sergeant Patyodi that he had sent the tax in. If he, Sholem, was summoned before the Commissioner, they would probe that too. If he failed to prove what he knew, how would he prove what he didn't? But how was he to prove anything at all, when he had sent the tax by someone who was not going to Otvar? The messenger was the deserter with the odd eyebrows.

"We are getting away from the subject," said Sholem to himself. As a disciplined Talmudist, he knew that that was a grave error. He stuck the bayonet back into the ground, thereby putting

a full stop to the old story. Then he returned behind the bar and
to the matter of the murder. He did not know where to start, saw
no clue anywhere. Even the text before him was the same—the
story of the slave from Jerusalem. Fortunately, Serf Gerencser
came in and started him off.

"The pandours have been following the tracks of three horses
as far as Telek. There the marsh is dried up, so the tracks go no
farther. But it's only a stone's throw from there to Szalka, so it
is clear that the three highwaymen were making for Szalka."

"How can you tell there were three?" asked Sholem with the
logic of the Talmud.

"Three horses, three highwaymen."

"Suppose there was only one, leading the pig dealer's two
horses by the halter?"

"The pandours are looking for three."

"Perhaps they are looking for the top ones, who didn't go to
Szalka."

"That's possible."

"But if the pandours are looking for them at Szalka, where they
didn't go, then it isn't certain that there were three top ones."

"How many, then?"

"Maybe two, maybe four. Maybe three—but one can't be sure."

"But, Sholem, you said there was only one."

"The one that led the horses, I mean. But perhaps even that was
done by more than one. If they were bottom ones, there were at
least two, and if they were top ones they were at least two again."

"The pandours say there were three."

"But two and two are more than three."

"If you say so, Sholem. You can reckon better than me."

The peasant finished his drink and left. He did not feel like
participating in Sholem's brain-racking reasoning. Sholem returned to the clever Jerusalem slave. It would be a good thing if
he could discuss the Szalka crime with such a one.

Under the corner of the tome lay a banknote. Sholem had
got it out the previous evening to send to Malkeleh by Isaac, for
palm grease. It seemed as though this banknote had been waiting
for just such a destination. It was the one left by the mysterious
stranger, and Sholem still did not know to whom it belonged.

Sholem had thought of putting it into Reb Meir the Miracle Worker's box, in which one accumulated the donations to the rabbis and students reading the Law in Palestine. Then he thought of adding it to the orphans' money, which he kept separate, for the stranger might have owed it to the old innkeeper. But he changed his mind about that too, for had not the stranger said to Yiteleh, "Tell Sholem it's due to him?"

Before replacing the banknote, which now had a destination (Yossef would take it to Zissah on Sunday), into the drawer, Sholem took a good look at it. There was a mark in one corner written with diluted ink. Or was it a letter? It certainly looked like a Hebrew *daleth*. *Daleth* meant door, and its numerical value was four. If it was a *daleth* then it signified a secret. If it was not a *daleth* it was more mysterious still.

### DEATH OF A SERF

THE BELL above the door gave an intermittent tinkle, Serf Martin Vizhordo entered with dragging steps and with his neck rigidly tilted. Sholem would have preferred to be alone with his speculations. Here and there a clue bobbed up, to vanish again like a will-o'-the-wisp, but it might be captured. Even the children, who were playing beneath the window of the bar, annoyed Sholem now. Sarah Chayah's high-pitched childish voice could be heard singing some horrid song, such as the market people used to chant: "Have a care, Benni, and save your breath, or they'll take you to the cell of death."

"Well, how are we, Serf Martin? We've been ill, what? How many weeks were you laid up? But it'll be better now."

"Maybe and maybe not," said the peasant with a wave of the hand. He had brought a pungent smell with him, a mixture of rotten onions and of the byre. Dragging himself to the big table he sat down at a corner of it, and indicated only with his gnarled forefinger that he wanted a mug of his usual.

Sholem deposited the drink before him and returned behind

the bar. Fortunately, the serf was not in a talkative mood. Where were we? Sholem mechanically bent over the tome and began to murmur: " 'An Athenian hired a servant in Jerusalem . . .' " He pushed the book away and picked up the mysterious banknote again. Queer . . . the person who wrote the *daleth* had drawn the top bar in a rectangle, as one who had plenty of time, but had abbreviated the "lintel," as though in a hurry. Did that indicate anything? No, nothing at all. If it had not been Saturday when the sergeant came, he would have shown him the receipts for the tolerance tax he had paid to the Karoly congregation. But that *goy* could not have read them, anyhow, for they were in Hebrew. But there the *daleth* was written properly, with two clear strokes. Daniel Enten, the Honorary Treasurer, who wrote those receipts, was never in a hurry, though he never had much time either. This was the "woolly" Enten who last spring had been held up by masked bandits on his way home from market.

"What's the matter, Serf Martin?"

"Nothing, Sholem, nothing at all."

"Then it's all right."

No one would believe Enten, least of all the Commissioner, that the bandits were masked. The Jew must have said that only because he was afraid of the bandits' revenge. For though they had taken his money, they had not hurt him. The perpetrators of the more recent crime probably wore no masks, otherwise they would only have bound Zdenkovich and his coachman, as they had Enten. True, Zdenkovich carried a pistol, whereas a Jew did not carry firearms, lest they should go off . . . What was that? That noise out there . . . Manasseh crying. Sholem jerked the window open.

"Sarah Chayah! Why is Manasseh crying?"

"Because Yossel Beilah Yenteh's is teasing him. He says Yu-yu is a bandit."

"Yes," cried Yossel, "because he's teasing me. He says shno-shno."

"It isn't true," stuttered Manasseh. "He's teasing me with Yu-yu is a bandit."

"What does that mean?" asked Sholem.

"Manasseh," laughed Yossel, "says Yu-yu-on is a bandit."

"Who is Yuyuon?"

"Yuon is Black Cap's servant," cried the children in chorus.

"What Black Cap?"

"Black Cap is the Golden Dagger."

"The Golden Dagger?"

"That's the leader," chorused the children.

Sholem frowned.

"I don't like you playing bandits," he said sternly. "Get your books and rehearse."

It occurred to Sholem that he too was "playing bandits." Just now he was a pandour and a Commissioner. He felt that it was all so childish, but he could not tear himself away from his detecting. Even his books had lost their power over him.

"It's not a game," explained Yossel, flailing his arms. "Isaac says the Golden Dagger is the leader, and Manasseh says the Black Cap and Yuyuon—"

"He's t-teasing again," squalled Manasseh.

"Why did you say shno-shno?" asked Sholem, trying to be impartial.

"Because Yossel is a shno . . . shnorrer."

"You mustn't tease anyone, just because his father is a poor man. And you, Yossel . . . If I ever hear you teasing Manasseh because he stammers, there's going to be trouble. Moses also had an impediment in his speech, but no one teased him for that."

Now Yossel too was crying, so all was well. Sholem withdrew, mentally patting himself on the back for comparing Manasseh with Moses. The boy might grow into a great rabbi for all his stammer. The parallel, by association, reminded him of something else. Moses hesitated, saying "how then shall Pharaoh hear me, who am of uncircumcised lips?" And so the Lord made Aaron his mouthpiece, for he was eloquent. Israel was always in need of advocates to represent them before the mighty.

Sholem looked out through the grille in case the customer wanted anything more. But no. The serf sat numbly, with his head drawn into his shoulders, just like a wet jackdaw. Sholem was struck with his attitude and with the fact that he was not drinking, and went out to him.

"No use telling me there's nothing the matter," he said, touching the serf's ragged coat. "I can see you're in trouble."

The serf gave a barely perceptible shrug, and his lips and eyes twitched with pain.

"There always is trouble, Sholem. But it passes, so long as you have cowdung."

"Cowdung?"

"And you always have that. Even a poor man gets it for nothing. He can always trudge after the cow and wait till it comes out. Fresh and warm—that's best."

"Fresh and warm," repeated Sholem mechanically. He did not understand what the serf was talking about, nor had he the patience to listen to him. His brain was going on with the work of detection. But he could not help noticing that the serf's right eyebrow was darkened with some dirt, probably cow-dung, contrasting with the sandy-colored left eyebrow. Once more he had clutched at a thread that was floating in the air like gossamer. It broke in his grasp, yet it reminded him of something that was of no importance, but which was good to know because it had vaguely bothered him. That Janos whose real name was not Janos used to look at him just like this serf: one eye fierce, the other gentle.

"The wise woman recommended cow-dung. It was good for swellings and for the ague."

Ah, thought Sholem, so the wise woman was treating the sick peasants with warm cow-dung. He looked at the other's pale face and twitching blue lips.

"Are you in pain, Martin?"

The man compressed his lips, emitting a moan or two only through his nose. Which of course meant that he was in very great pain. But all he said was:

"It's got to be. My father perished in the same way. He too was only thirty-eight. He too was kicked by a horse."

"Well, well, Martin," consoled the innkeeper. "You don't die of that. How many times have I been kicked by Kese? Yet in the end it was Kese that died."

"Kese was a Jewish horse. A Jewish horse is more decent. Peasant horses don't murder, either. But the gentry horse does."

He gave an upward tug to his untidy mustache as he spoke, revealing withered gums and blackened teeth. "It aims at just the right place. As if to order. One serf less, what's it matter? Plenty of brats get born, God's curse they are."

"That's wrong, Martin. Children are God's blessing. They'll have a better life."

"It depends who they are. The serf's children will have a worse life. That multitude of serf brats is the bane of God."

His eyes were the same again: one rebellious, the other humble. Looking at them, Sholem suddenly remembered the name of the lad with the odd eyebrows: Benni Darazs. A childish voice rang into his brain; he pricked his ears, listening into the past. But the voice came from the yard: "Benni Darazs, a highwayman was he . . ." Strange, thought Sholem. Where did his children get that from? He would have liked to go outside and ask them, but looking at the serf's pain-distorted face, it struck him that it would be futile to search for the origin of a market or tavern song. In any case, he could not go out now. Here was a human being in torment who needed someone to cling to.

"Where did it kick you?" he asked sympathetically.

"Just the right place. Under my left armpit, over the heart. My shoulder's like a pumpkin. The wise woman's medicine won't get it down. My bed stinks, and is sticky with the dung. Is this what God made me for?"

"You ought to go and see Dr. Gabel in Karoly or Dr. Pfirsich in Otvar."

"That costs money," waved the serf dispiritedly.

"I'll give you some. You'll pay it back sometime."

"Where from, Sholem? I owe you enough as it is, and if I kick the bucket I'll take this with me as well. It isn't my family that drank all that spirit. They'll do villenage for my coffin. They must do that . . . can't let me rot and stink in the house. I stank enough in my lifetime."

Sholem vainly tried to persuade him to accept a florin or two from him for the doctor and the apothecary. The serf said he would take it any other time, but now that he was "on the brink. . . ."

"No, Sholem. You're a Jew—keep your money. You want it

for your family. The serf is born here and has his grave here.
But if you don't pay the rent, you'll have to go on again. And if
the peasants have a bad year or if villenage and tithes are too hard
on them, like last year, they'll say you'd done murder and robbery
and fire the inn over your head. Then you'll have to go again.
Just let me expire . . . Damn that horse and its bastard of a
master. I can't even lift the half-empty mug for pain."

Martin Vizhordo was a stubborn man. The gentry said he was
bad and quarrelsome, because he was never satisfied and would
like to change the immutable law that the gentry are the gentry
and the serfs—serfs. He was always grumbling and inciting the
other serfs, who would otherwise be contented with God's
ordinance, or at least resigned to the inevitable. Now it seemed
that he was moved at Sholem's offer of money. But he took a
hold on himself and hardened his heart against himself and the
world.

"Of course, the gentry are not so nasty to you as to us. But
that's only because you're their other tax collector. What the
serf has left after he's been fleeced, he brings to you. And you
give a cut to the gentry. It's all right, Sholem, you can't help it
that you are a Jew. For a Jew, you're one of the best. To hell
with all the damned braggarts who ride to county assembly on a
Spanish or Arab steed with a furred dolman on their backs, though
they borrow both the horse and the dolman."

Sholem drew his head down between his shoulders. His sympathy was profound, but his common sense made him reserved.
This peasant was alternately blaspheming and cursing the gentry.
He, Sholem, ought to have nothing to do with that. God might
forgive him, but what if the gentry hear about it? It would not
do him any good.

"I think, Martin, you'll be better off in bed. Stay there for
another day or two, then you'll get over your trouble."

"You're sending me home, Sholem?" said the serf with reproach in his voice. "I thought you were my friend. I shan't lie
down again more than once in this life." He went on, bitterly,
as before:

"Of course, the mansion is falling to pieces. Everything is eaten
away by worms, rust, and debt. But for the autumn county

assembly they get even the pomade for their whiskers from Vienna. They curse Vienna and the Emperor, just because he wants to do well by the peasants. He has given a freedom charter for the serfs many a time, but the county has always done away with it." He drained the mug and dropped it on to the table. Then he raised his fist to wipe off the dribble from his mouth. "Hell and damnation!" he went on. "The many teams they get from the peasants for nothing are not good enough for them. They must have an Arab steed for a hundred and fifty. Can't go to Karoly in the autumn without that. Here in Dengheleg they show off their rags. A squire is a squire to his serfs even if he's in rags. It's true that the whole county is laughing at them over Borcsa, for that mare is older even than her master. That was why the Squire sent a message to Ecsed to say that he could not go to the county assembly this year because Borcsa was not well. But the Squire of Ecsed sent back to say that a de Denghelegh could not stick by his wife's skirts when they had such important matters to deliberate on, as how to oppress the serfs more and how to let the Governing Council in Buda and even the Emperor in Vienna know that they were not going to give way. So he sent an Arab horse from his own stables. Young Barbara instead of old Borcsa. And who but Serf Martin Vishordo was to feed her and brush her coat glossy? The old man rode her for an hour and felt rejuvenated. Now he's in his bed. She has a free spirit, that mare has, not like the serfs. She did give me a proper kick. If it had been a bit higher, she'd have blinded me, so at least I'd never have seen this rotten world again. It would have been better."

The serf's anger and despair had communicated themselves to Sholem. He had heard such talk before, having kept the inn for four villages these eight years. But what he heard from behind the bar sounded only like grumbling, the usual complaints of peasant folk. It was a discontented moaning and groaning, rather than live and tormented despair. He would have promised the serf to take him in to the doctor not later than on the following Monday. But looking at his chalk-white face, at the sweat on his brow and at his burning eyes, he lost all faith in medical science. None but King Lemuel's medicine could do any good here.

"I've got a drop of old gin here, extra strong," he said. "It'll do you good." He ran behind the bar, took a wicker-covered bottle off the shelf and filled a measure with it. Then he took it back to the serf, depositing it in front of him. The man was breathing in quick, short gasps. Sholem opened the door to let in some fresh air. He paused to think. There was something else he needed. What was it? He had known but a moment ago. Returning behind the bar in search of recollection, his eye fell on the open tome. That was it. He took the book out into the parlor and sat down with it opposite the serf. Then, in the usual chant, he began to read:

"Our Sages relate: 'An Athenian noble purchased a slave in Jerusalem. On the way towards Athens, the slave said to his master. . . .' "

Serf Martin Vizhordo stretched his neck in an effort to hear, his eyes like burning spheres, his nostrils trembling and distended like those of a horse halted in a gallop, his open mouth a black cavern. He could not understand the Talmudic story about the clever slave. Evidently it was only Sholem's chanting voice that fascinated him. His pale face was suffused with pink and in the corner of his mouth there appeared a rapt expression. The fine gin stood before him, but he never touched it. And when Sholem had finished his chanting, the serf raised his heavy eyelids to wink at two serfs who were now standing in the open door, Lajos Gore and Bellringer Ludpal.

"Beautiful!" he breathed.

With that he pitched forward and crashed to the floor.

## THE CANDLEMAKER'S APPRENTICE

MALKELEH HAD a pain in her back and allowed herself to be pampered. Mother Zissah had made french beans and cream cheese pancakes with raisins for dinner, after which she served coffee made from freshly roasted beans in porcelain cups. Malkeleh smiled, but scarcely ate. She felt very happy in the Troyes home;

she felt at home and yet a guest, for they would not let her help in the kitchen. Old Zissah was as kind to her as if she had been her own daughter. She kept searching Malkeleh's face, as if trying to guess her trouble. Realizing that Malkeleh was tired, Zissah made her lie down on the sofa in the cool living-room, covering her with a big vari-colored woolen blanket, lest she should catch cold if she fell asleep. Malkeleh submitted to her gentle compulsion. But for these kindly people, she would have been embittered for her error in going to Lazarovich, despite her own instincts, and letting him humiliate her.

Only an hour ago, when she sent Isaac back and wrote to Sholem that all was well, the matter seemed almost hopeless, and she had not the faintest idea whether anything could be done at all, and how. And when she wrote that she was well, thank God, she was in fact feverish and depressed, with shooting pains in her kidneys, of which she had been free for more than six years, since the weaning of little Manasseh. She wanted to get up, but the sofa drew her down, and the thought that she might have to stay here sick terrified her. But when old Zissah and Brachah came in she was already smiling. She was almost glad of her indisposition, somewhat like a child who was relieved of homework and school.

Yet this was the very time for her to attend to her task. Since Lazarovich had said No, Otvar had become even more inaccessible. She could not even enter the town. But now that her shooting pains became more and more frequent she had an excuse. She was going to see Dr. Pfirsich. The doctor was a kindly man and in addition had a special liking for Malkeleh because he could converse in German with her. Perhaps he could do or advise something in the case of Gimpel Zorech.

"If you don't mind, Mother Zissah, I'll laze away another quarter of an hour here, then I'll go over to Jacob Anshel."

"My dear, you're not going anywhere to-day. Anyone that wants to see you must come here. You're not an everyday sight in Batiz. The candlemaker and his family will be here in the evening. The potter, Yossef Yochanan, and his wife are also coming. You will see, Malkeleh, Reb Leizer is not the only Jew here."

There was a mild debate about this, but in the end it was agreed that Malkeleh would not go to Otvar until morning. On the other hand, she would get up in an hour's time and tidy herself, for she could really not receive the visitors calling in her honor lying in bed.

Yossef was different. He was her foster-son. The boy's eyes were bright, his face radiant, and he kissed Malkeleh's hand with passionate joy as though he had not seen her for years. He fidgeted and tugged at his downy beard and could scarcely wait for old Zissah and the stern Mme Troyes to leave the room. Malkeleh had asked him before how he was and how he was getting on with his work, and he had replied with the casualness he had learned from adults that all was well. Now he was able to tell her that he was very happy here. If Malkeleh would come to the workshop she would see that candlemaking was tremendously interesting work. It was called candle-dipping too, when the wicks were tied to a lath and dipped into the fluid tallow. But he had improved on that by means of a small but useful invention. Instead of tying the wicks to a lath, he screwed some tiny hooks into the bottom of the lath and hung the wicks on those, so that the intervals were more uniform and you could use up the whole of the wick. The results were still better if you made the candles on a board or on a drum. And you had to know how to pack too. There were packings of one pound, half, three-quarters, and three-eighths of a pound.

Guessing that Malkeleh had had enough of candlemaking, he hastened to inquire after Yiteleh.

"She has gone into the leather shop in Karoly," replied Malkeleh, her face clouding.

"Has she, after all?"

"There was nothing else she could do," said Malkeleh.

"It'll be all right," said the boy. "Mordechai will make a fine business woman out of her. Jacob Anshel's daughters work in the business too. Esther is not so clever as Yiteleh, but she already helps her father to do the costing. She prefers the workshop to being in the kitchen with her stepmother. Yiteleh too will be better off in the shop than in Blimeleh's kitchen."

Malkeleh was cheered by Yossef's point of view.

"What about Zireleh?" she smiled.

"Zireleh?" repeated Yossef in a livelier tone. "She's different from Esther. She doesn't speculate or calculate, she works. If you could only see her, Malkeleh. Like a witch she is, simply scorching along . . . When she works with a lath, she does a gross of candles easily between noon and evening, and more on the drum. She sings while she works and when she runs through the workshop you'd think she was dancing. Her red hair is sometimes tousled. Sometimes it is full of candle grease, but she doesn't mind, it suits her. And when she laughs, her teeth are also like drops of candle. Don't laugh at me, Malkeleh, but I really think Zireleh is the cleverest girl not only in Batiz, but in the whole county. I have learnt a lot from her; Jacob Anshel scarcely showed me anything. I didn't tell you that Zireleh is the best mangler too."

"She does the linen?"

"No, I mean the big church candles. You have to mangle those, so they are evenly round all over, and you have to polish them as well. If you saw how she can paint, and what patterns she has!"

Yossef had a vague feeling that he had been gushing too much about Zireleh and this might not be welcome to Yiteleh's mother, so he began to talk about Yiteleh again. As though revealing a jealously guarded secret, he said:

"There was a time when I liked Yiteleh best. But then she told me something."

"Did she?"

"She said that Sroleh Yomtov had promised her that when they grew up he would marry her. So I left home and got myself apprenticed."

"When Yiteleh last spoke with Sroleh Yomtov," said Malkeleh with a smile, "she was barely nine years old. You can't take the talk of a couple of children seriously."

"You could take Sroleh Yomtov seriously, Malkeleh. He was then nearly fifteen. Only he never promised anything to anybody, not even to me, his own brother. If he had made that promise he would have come back. Seven years is a long time. And he knows where to find us, though we don't know where to find him."

"That's true," agreed Malkeleh.

"Anyhow, Yiteleh admitted to me that she had invented the whole story, just to brag and pull my leg."

"Never mind, Yossef. It seems that it was ordained that you should have Zireleh."

"I think so too, Mother," said the boy.


A JEW IN JAIL


IN THE evening Malkeleh was pretty and smiling again, and sat enthroned at the head of the table. Old Zissah gave her some furtive looks. Was this the woman who had borne nine children and gone through all those troubles? Her eyes were bright and the fine wrinkles in the corners of her eyes were ironed out. No one would say that she was not a young woman, who had stood under the *chupah* only a year or two ago.

"Yet," explained Zissah to Reb Yossef Yochanan's wife, "she has a grown-up daughter."

"Yes," said Malkeleh, having overheard the flattering remark, "Yiteleh is nearly seventeen."

"Seventeen!" cried Mme Troyes in a tone of consternation. "I thought she was not fifteen yet. Why, she ought to be married by now."

"I'm not in such a hurry to become a grandmother." This made the company laugh. Jacob Anshel whispered to Brachah: "She wants to bear a few more children."

Yossef Yochanan had had enough of feminine chatter and came to the point. Ten men, meeting in the synagogue yard between *minchah* and *maariv*, had each offered to provide a day's food for Gimpel Zorech. As that was too many, they weeded out three. They also excluded a fourth: Lazarovich. This did not come off smoothly. Tobias the glazier had said to the distiller angrily: "It'll do if you give the drinking water. The county will provide the bread." Reb Leizer withdrew, offended, and then they had to draw lots for Friday-Saturday because there were three offers: from Mechl the dyer, Jacob Anshel the candle-maker, and Mosheh Doved Troyes. Troyes was the lucky one. Now there were only two matters to settle. First, how to get the food into Otvar. There was only one man who sent a cart there daily and that was Lazarovich. Fadeleh, who took the distillery wash to the municipal stables, would attend to this on his own account.

"We can't make use of Reb Leizer's cart," cried Tobias, a bony man with a black goatee.

"The glazier is right," said Troyes. "Reb Leizer will discover it and one fine day he'll forbid it."

"We don't want him to permit it either," said the glazier. "Let this too be put to his account in the Beyond."

The potter searched Malkeleh's features with the eyes of one practised in reading the faces of the women looking at his goods. He judged that Malkeleh was pleased with the glazier's attitude.

"All right." he said, "we'll drop the plan with Fadeleh. But what else can we do? Who else has a cart to spare? Wednesday is the easiest."

Yes, on Wednesday the people going to market could take Gimpel Zorech's rations along with their own. But what about the other days? According to old Zissah, Friday-Saturday rations were also a simple matter. Her son, Troyes, could take in rations for the two days on the Friday. Troyes smilingly agreed.

Then Jacob Anshel said that having failed to win the right to supply Friday-Saturday's food, which counted most where good deeds were recorded, he would like to do Tuesdays, but only on condition that delivery was left to him on the other three days as well.

"Otvar is only seven miles," he said, turning to his wife. "An hour there, an hour back. Yossef will go with the candle-cart and take in the food."

"That'll be very good," said Yossef gaily. "Which day will you come with me, Zireleh?"

"There is only one other thing now," said Yossef Yochanan the potter. "How do we get the county to allow us to get into the prison?"

"That's easy," observed Troyes. "They'd gladly let every Jew in."

"Yes," laughed the candlemaker, "but how do we get out?"

Tobias and the women also laughed.

"A brother of ours is in prison," reproved the potter. "He's either starving or eating *trefah*—and we're laughing."

Malkeleh's eyes were now almost as bright as old Zissah's, which so easily filled with tears. She had no doubts any longer; everything would come right, sooner than she had expected.

The others were not so optimistic. They shrugged, gesticulated, went into a huddle and were full of doubt. They were racking their brains for a way to approach the county. Tobias agreed with the potter that this was the hardest nut to crack. The county was even more exclusive than the town, and also more anti-Jew. Yet the town had a century-old charter, which it had got from the Emperor Charles, entitling it to keep the Jews out for ever. But while the town was in fact exercising that right, Bagamer the turnpike attendant, Bekas the toll-keeper, Renyi the market inspector, and Kontos the stall fee collector, could be indulgent, and if their palms were greased they would even crack a joke with the Jews. They could go in not only on market days, provided they put the right banknote in the right place. But the county hall was occupied by gentry, not burghers. The Lord Sheriff was like a haughty viceroy, and the Under-Sheriff was also a bad man and would not accept anything. At the county hall even the haiduks were forbidding and menacing, like so many bulls, to say nothing of the pandours, whom it was best for a Jew to avoid.

Whether all this was true, or whether it was only a sort of horror story, Malkeleh could not tell. She had heard this kind of talk before, but now she was beginning to understand the situation. It seemed that the Jews of Batiz and other localities round Otvar were more afraid of the county hall than of the Imperial Burg. True, the Burg was in Vienna, whereas the county hall was the county hall and was there in the market square. There they could always think of something to make the position of the Jews more difficult. The candlemaker recalled with deep distrust in his tone, the county's repeated call to "patriotic Jews" to stop paying the tolerance tax and in general anything, whether designated as tolerance or chamber tax, that sent money direct into the Imperial Treasury. They asserted that the Emperor had no right to collect a Jew tax, for the Diet of nobles had never agreed to it. What were the Jews to do? Were they to refuse the demand of the gentry or the demand of the Emperor? Whether the pitcher fell on the stone, or whether the stone fell on the pitcher, it was the pitcher that got smashed. The best one could do was to say to the county that one had refused to pay the tax, and at the same time pay it in secret.

What the candlemaker was saying was very wise, and what the others were saying also sounded very well. But, like all public affairs, the case of Gimpel Zorech was reaching a stage when people were making clever remarks about it. Just now Malkeleh's presence was a special inducement in that direction. But it was past midnight and she was getting tired, so she wanted to return to the question how to get Gimpel Zorech's rations into the prison. There was another long discussion, and fresh candles had to be lighted, because the old ones were already guttering. The situation was saved by Yossef, who saw that Zireleh too was getting sleepy.

"Who will do the Tuesday?" he asked.

"Tuesday is mine," said the potter.

"Then I'll call on you to-morrow morning, and you'll hand me the packet of food. I'll hand it over to the prison warder."

Everybody approved, especially Malkeleh. Why deliberate so long? All you had to do was to cook the food, wrap it up in a bundle, and send it along. If these experienced men dared not talk with the gentlemen of the county, the inexperienced Yossef would. He did not think of calling on the Lord Sheriff or even the Commissioner, but only on the prison warder.

"All right, Yossef," said Malkeleh. "Call for me before you go—I'll come with you."

The others were more confident too. If Malkeleh went in, it was sure to come off. Gimpel Zorech would be eating kosher food to-morrow. The Jews of Batiz would go to bed that night with a clear conscience.

WARDER KOCZOR

IN THE Otvar market square people turned their heads to look at them. Why, here was an ear-curled Jewish youth and a Jewess with a lace headkerchief, and it wasn't market day, either. It was only Tuesday. Now they were alighting from their cart outside the Zoldfa Hotel, each carrying a bundle of something. What might be their business? Ah, they were making for the old county hall. Would they be admitted?

A mighty haiduk with drawn sabre stood guard at the gate of the county hall. The Jews of Batiz considered that he was dour and inaccessible. But Yossef was not aware of this. So he went up to him and did approach him. The haiduk was human, after all, and far more intelligent than his reputation. He did not kick or even strike out with his big curved sword. He just held it upright in his strong right fist, like a living barrier. But his left hand closed on the tip.

"Pass in," he bawled. "At the far end, on the right, just below the steeple, is a green door. That's the clink."

"Clink" sounded humorous, almost intimate, and robbed the idea of prison of its terrifying aspect. Still, when Yossef, brave, enterprising Yossef, stood facing the green door, with its heavy iron clamps and bolts all over, he was scared.

Malkeleh raised the knocker that hung on the door and gave a rap. There was the sound of footsteps inside, then the creaking of a key in the lock. A giant with martial mustachios appeared. His face was hard, his eyes penetrating, but his voice was less coarse than one would have expected from his appearance.

"Well, what is it?" he demanded. "What are you doing here?"

Yossef relaxed. He had a silver florin ready in his hand and he slipped it into the man's free hand. Feeling that the coin was welcome he spoke without embarrassment.

"We came to see Gimpel Zorech, Master Warder."

"Who?"

"The Jew, Gimpel Zorech," explained Malkeleh.

"Ah, the Jew! I was sure it wasn't the murderer Mureshan you came to see." He said this with a broad smile—a good sign. Malkeleh too took courage and, swinging the bundle containing the mended shirts, she said:

"Can we see him, Master Warder?"

"Hm. What is he to you?"

"My brother-in-law."

"What about this Moysheh here?"

"He's his uncle."

"Have you got a permit?"

"I got one from Master Bagamer."

"Bagamer's permit is no good here. Besides, you can't see Gimpel."

"Why not?"

"Why not? Because he's not in the prison."

"Have they let him out?" beamed Malkeleh.

"No, we haven't. It's not so easy as all that. We've sent him out to work, to help on the dam."

There were people coming and going in the yard of the county hall. They kept looking in the direction of the jail, wondering who the visitors were and what they wanted. This was obviously not to the liking of the warder, and his voice began to sound more in keeping with his appearance and office.

"Peddling, loitering, and importuning," he declared, "is prohibited in the yard."

With that he pushed the other two inside and locked the door. The vaulted, brick-floored corridor was dimly lit and silent. One could hear the echo of one's own footsteps and that was strange. The smell of whitewash, carbolic, and a yeasty something mingled into a heavy odor that caused Yossef to sneeze. The warder gave him a look as though to say that sneezing was prohibited here. He opened a door leading to a big, bleak room. It had a strongly barred gable window, and all its furniture consisted of a table, a chair, a wooden bench with a crucifix above it. Yossef looked round timidly. Malkeleh too was hesitant. But the warder's voice was friendly again:

"Sit down, pretty Jewess. You too, Moysheh, there on the bench. I'll let you out, so you can come again. Just ask for Peter Koczor

when you come. Peter Koczor is not a man-eater. To a murderer
he is murderous. But to a man who's only had a sip of whisky . . .
Peter Koczor likes that too." He was laughing and revealing his
yellow fangs. Then he suddenly grew grave: "But it's no child's
play by any means. Peter Koczor is not the law. The law is the
law. Anyone they bring here is guilty. And anyone that's punished
deserves it. So there."

The last couple of words meant that Malkeleh now had his
leave to speak. She said that she had brought some shirts and
underwear for the prisoner, and also some food, and that Yossef
and the other Jews in Batiz wanted to bring him Jewish food
daily, because if he was guilty it would be set against all the Jews,
while if he was innocent, let him know that he was not deserted.
This was something new to Peter Koczor. He had not heard in
Otvar about any special Jewish diet. It was true that Gimpel was
his first Jew. He was a funny little man, only he was terrified of
slaps in the face. He was rather neglected, that was why he had
sent him to help on the embankment, where he was up to the
neck in water from morning till night, so if he liked he could wash
his face as well in the nice yellow water of the Szamos.

The warder grinned to himself.

"There's only one thing Gimpel can get from me," he said,
raising a sledgehammer fist. "The rest is for Master Erdy the
Commissioner to decide. What you've brought now I'll hand to
Gimpel to-night. But what you bring tomorrow and later, you
must ask a permit for in competent quarters."

Malkeleh opined that the Commissioner could not object to
getting the county relieved of the necessity of feeding a prisoner,
but the warder said that none but the Commissioner himself knew
what he objected to. Malkeleh thanked him for the information
and observed that, of course, she could not expect his help for
nothing. Besides, at home in the inn she had some old plum
whisky, and also rye and gin and rum, and she would like to
send Master Koczor a bottle now and then, but there was one
condition: that Gimpel Zorech should not be given any of the
drink. She realized that Master Koczor meant well by Gimpel
Zorech and the reason he had sent him to the embankment was
that he should keep clean and have plenty of fresh air. But if he

wanted to go on treating him decently, he should not treat him
to strong drink. It was better for him to get used to drinking
water. At the same time, too much water was not good for him
either, and while just now, in the heat of summer, a little bathing
in the course of his work only refreshed him, autumn was already
on the way, and that unfortunate fellow was so sickly that perhaps he would be unable to bear navvying and carrying stones in
the cold current of the river.

Peter Koczor wished to absorb only the flattering part of
Malkeleh's words.

"I sent him to the embankment," he said, "because he's such
a runt. He'll get stronger there."

"It won't do him good just now to get stronger. The judges
will say it was he that knocked down Zdenkovich and his coachman."

"What the judges are going to say—" He was interrupted by
a knocking at the window. He went across, and speaking through
it said: "That you, Joska? What is it?"

"Madame Erdy says," came the invisible Joska's high-pitched
voice, "that she'll have a big wash-day on Thursday, and she
wants four men to carry water from the river. The butts and
troughs under the eaves are all empty, with no rain for a
fortnight past."

"All right," said the warder, and came back to Malkeleh. He
looked at her, trying to remember where he had left off and
also beginning to lose his patience. Malkeleh noted this, so she
rose to her feet and said she did not want to waste his precious
time or disturb him in his work. She only wanted to know one
more thing: When and where could she speak with Gimpel
Zorech?

"You don't think," the warder replied with consternation,
"that you can speak with him on the embankment, just along the
gentlemen's lawns? What would become of us if one could just
call the prisoners aside from their work for a little family chat?"

"Then perhaps I could see him here?"

"No. No stranger is allowed to talk to the prisoners."

Malkeleh bowed her head to convey that she understood. She

motioned to Yossef and turned to go. The warder looked at them
obliquely and said:

"And what would you be wanting to say to him?"

Malkeleh gazed at him with wonderment, as though to say:
How can I tell you now? But Master Koczor wanted an oral
reply, and after a pause Yossef came out with it:

"We must tell him that Reb Yossef Yochanan sent two earthenware plates to keep. The yellow one is for milk, the brown one
for meat. Then we have two spoons here, one for milky things,
one for meaty things."

"What nonsense is this?" growled the warder. He shook the
keys in his hand: the audience was over.

In the street Yossef chattered gaily. He was glad to be in the
open air again, and also pleased with the result of the visit to the
jail. Malkeleh was dazed and unable to share his pleasure. She felt
as though she had achieved nothing. She must do something, for
things were even worse than she had expected.

In the afternoon she went along to Dr. Pfirsich and sat there
for a good hour and a half, at the end of which time she also
mentioned her shooting pains. The doctor ordered her a day or
two's rest in bed and also gave her a prescription: *Folia uvae ursi*.
At the apothecary's they told her to boil a pinch of the bear's
breech and drink the juice hot. She returned to the hotel, and
sitting down on the cart, stared in front of her. Yossef wanted
to go, fearing that he was being missed at the workshop. But
Malkeleh wanted to stay a little longer, though she did not say—
and perhaps did not know—why. Yossef asked whether she was
in pain. She shook her head. But there were shadows under her
eyes and her face looked tired. Yossef was already thinking of
taking a room for her at the hotel and asking the doctor for a
certificate, or better still, pressing a round coin on Master Bagamer's eyes at the toll-gate, so he should not notice that Malkeleh
was not on the cart. He himself must unfortunately go back
home, because they needed the cart to bring candles and soap to
market the following dawn. But Malkeleh did not wish to spend
the night in the town. She was coming along presently, she assured
the boy.

When the sun was already low in the west, she suddenly pulled herself together and said:

"Let's go."

Going up the castle hill the cart trundled along heavily, as though sensing Malkeleh's heavy cares. But downhill it went more briskly. At the end of the road they could see the gleam of the meandering river. Malkeleh felt a stab of pain in her heart.

"Slow down!" she cried in a scared tone.

Yossef did not know what had happened, but slowed down. A tired yellow-grey procession was approaching from the direction of the river. They were trudging along in the dust mechanically and clumsily, yet in some sort of military rhythm. Some twenty-odd convicts in haircloth garb, with a briskly stepping pandour with fixed bayonet marching in front, behind, and on both sides. They could see the last ranks, and in them a scraggy little figure dragging itself along, his bearded, ear-curled face contrasting sharply with the shaven or stubbly faces round him. They were quite close now. The Jewish prisoner looked up at the cart and there was bafflement in his eyes. He stumbled, lagged behind, staring; the pandour went up to him and kicked him, cursing. Gimpel Zorech took no notice of the kick, but went on gazing into Malkeleh's face and laughed. It was a loud, free laugh that sounded like the whinny of a colt whose nostrils are assailed by the fragrance of a lush meadow on its emergence from a barren road. He got another kick, but did not care. He quietened down only when the cart had passed. He took hold of his beard as though to smooth it out, drew himself up and fell smartly into step. Where was the crushed little Jew of a moment ago? Malkeleh turned her head, but could no longer see whether Gimpel Zorech was looking back too. Her face burned in the setting sun and heavy tears were falling from her eyes.

ODD EYEBROWS

MALKELEH WAS talking, Sholem and the children sat tensely listening. The Sabbath candles were already guttering, and she was still talking. It was as wonderful and exciting as the stories of the exodus from Egypt. Yossef kept nodding his head in affirmation, until he got sleepy. However, she knew a great deal more than Yossef, for she had also had a discussion with Dr. Pfirsich.

About this she reported to Sholem when they were alone, though not quite fully. She mentioned just by the way that her kidneys had been troublesome, that was why she rested on Wednesday and Thursday. The doctor had ordered bear's breech, which intensified the pain the first day, but allayed it by the second. She must go on drinking the juice at home as well. Pfirsich had promised to talk with the gentlemen of the county, and when Zdenkovich, who was under his care, got better, he would find out from him about the robbery. Perhaps the information could be used in favor of Gimpel Zorech at the trial.

Had Zdenkovich already talked about the matter? Malkeleh could only say that he had scarcely recovered consciousness. The doctor said he might even lose his memory. When he raved, he kept shouting Rumanian names—Pintea, Yuon, Vasilie—though he was a Serb himself. Pfirsich thought the names might refer to childhood memories. Sholem, who was cheered by this information, asserted it might be later memories. Malkeleh agreed that that was possible. She knew nothing about such matters, and in any case the doctor had supposed rather than asserted. If Malkeleh had wanted to tell all, she would have observed that the doctor paid little attention while she was talking about her brother-in-law's trouble and that his promises were also made in a casual way. The chief discussion between them had been of a very different character, the doctor saying that apart from the poet Ferenc Kolcsey there was scarcely anyone in that rustic town with whom one could discuss higher things.

Malkeleh realized that it was a mistake of her own that turned the conversation from the essential point to another plane. As she started to tell the doctor the case of Gimpel Zorech, about which he had already heard a little, he raised his side-whiskered face to her and said affectedly, lightly scanning the words:

"Zwar weiss ich viel, doch möcht ich alles wissen."

Malkeleh knew that he was quoting from *Faust*, so she capped it with another quotation:

"Wenn Ihr's nicht fühlt, Ihr werdet's nicht erjagen."

The doctor smiled and adjusted his white bow-tie under his tall collar. On his desk, by his grey top-hat, lay a small flagon. Picking it up, he unscrewed its top, sniffed at it, then handed it to Malkeleh. Gazing out of the window, and above the low roofs opposite into the distance, he forgot about the Jewish prisoner, the gentry of the county, the sick Zdenkovich, and even what interest he had in Malkeleh's complaint, and he began to talk about music, books, and poets, and above all about the author of *Faust* and *Hermann and Dorothea*, whom he had visited the previous year in Weimar. They had had a long, friendly talk, chiefly about scientific questions relating to comparative anatomy and plant biology and the new theory of simple and composite colors, in which matter the poet challenged the theories of Isaac Newton, the great English physicist. He had strange eyes, and one had the impression that they had been looking at things ever since Creation, though if one looked closer one saw the eyes of a young man of twenty-five— and the poet was nearly eighty. His brow was cool, but his eyes were alight. It was said that he was in love again, with a very young lady, to whom he had recently written a beautiful elegy.

The doctor also praised the new generation of poets. He showed Malkeleh a book of poems he had brought from Germany. It was *Buch der Lieder*. It had created feverish excitement among German youth. The book had only just been published, yet the doctor could only get a copy of the second edition. Not a day passed but that he read over this or that poem, and he knew most of them by heart. They were light as gossamer and had a radiance about them. "Du bist wie eine Blume, So hold und schön und rein . . . Ich weiss nicht, was soll es bedeuten, Dass ich so traurig bin . . . Und mein Stamm sind jene Azra . . ." It was difficult to think that these were written by someone and had not just grown.

The poet was the son of a Jew from Dusseldorf, but he had ceased to be a Jew three years ago. It was wise of him, a genius ought to leave the ghetto . . . The doctor had visited the theater at Stettin and saw an eighteen-year-old boy, a small, fragile lad with long hair, conducting a composition of his own, "Prelude to a Midsummer Night's Dream." It was a great success. They said he started composing at the age of ten. He, too, was a Hebrew. His father's name was Abraham, his grandfather's Moses. But his name was Felix. He had reason to be happy, too. His clever mother had brought him into the Lutheran Church, so the world was open to him.

Malkeleh could not talk to Sholem about all this. In her own mind she was ashamed for having listened to the doctor so quietly, and for failing to contradict him even when he said that of the talented peoples only the Chinese and the Jews continued to wear a pigtail, adding that the Chinese were at least wearing their own, while pretty Jewish women wore wigs of strange hair. He also said that it was silly for Gimpel Zorech to have to eat kosher because the Christian food was unclean. If the Jews had to suffer only because they were Jews, it was best to eliminate the cause of the suffering and the next generation could be free of the disease. Malkeleh left the doctor with the impression that he liked the Jews only if they entered the family of peoples according to his ideas, but that, like all Christians, he hated them so long as they remained in their own family.

Sholem, too, had many important things to report. So many things had happened between Monday and Friday that he could not tell it all in a hurry and had to wait until the children had gone to sleep. Sholem also omitted a few things, but Malkeleh had already heard about some of them. She knew that Martin Vizhordo died at the inn and that Sholem had been reading from the Talmud to the dying serf, and she had heard that Bellringer Ludpal was charging him with sorcery. Of course, no one in the village believed that the mortally sick serf had been read to his death by Sholem, for the serf's wife had ordered a coffin from the carpenter four days earlier. But even the priest was furious because Sholem had not sent for him, and Martin died not like a good Christian, who returned to the Lord, but like a no-account

Hebrew who returned to the bosom of Abraham. He had to con-
secrate the body twice over, charging a double fee and saying
that it should be collected from the Jew.

Of all this Sholem scarcely said a word, but instead told her
with gusto about a visit by Herskovitch, the innkeeper from
Varalja. Malkeleh was then already in bed, with her arms folded
under her head, gazing at the night-light above her. The visitor
was the same Herskovitch who in the first years did everything to
acquire the Lapfalva lease, raising the rent in his offer to the
gentry. This time he did not go to Gyekeny, his patron, but came
straight to Sholem with his offer. He had a very prosperous inn
at Varalja, which was a populous mountain township, with enough
Jews for four *minyanim* and even a Mishna Society. He wanted
to exchange his inn for the one at Lapfalva without any extra payment. The house contained three rooms, apart from the kitchen,
and there was a stable and a shed and a big vegetable garden and
several acres of land suitable for maize and potatoes. Herskovitch
arrived towards noon on Thursday, an hour after the peasants had
taken away the body of Martin Vizhordo, and in the afternoon
he left for Bator, where he was spending the Sabbath with his
brother-in-law. But he would be back on Sunday for the answer.

"There must be something very wrong with his lease," said
Malkeleh without removing her eyes from the shadows trembling
on the ceiling.

"I suspected that, too," said Sholem. "But Herskovitch explained
what is the trouble. There is nearby a rich mine-owner who goes
carousing to his inn because his mistress lives in that town. Recently he came in with five banknotes for a hundred each, asking
for change with which to pay his workmen. Herskovitch handed
the money on the same day to Mesel the wine merchant. But
three days later Mesel came bursting in and demanded what sort
of money he had given him, for Mesel had paid one of the notes
to his cooper, and straight away the other four were confiscated
by the pandours. Herskovitch went out to the mine, but the man
there was a big bully and he said to hold his tongue if he wanted
to go on living. It seems the money was counterfeit. What was
he to do now? If he did not tell the truth they would lock him
up."

Malkeleh was silent for awhile, then, suppressing a sigh, she said:

"There's trouble everywhere."

"But," said Sholem. "I think that if two troubles change places, they cease to be troubles."

Malkeleh thought this over at length. Was Sholem right? Was she already beginning to consider the offer, which according to Sholem had come just at the right moment? Malkeleh had said more than once that she would like to live where there were more Jews, and where the children could get a better education. Sholem's school behind the bar and her own in the living-room were not exactly adequate. And now, as she talked about the days she spent in Batiz, she still seemed to long for such a familiar environment. The old instinct to flee, the suppressed desire to live among brethren, live a communal life and let Sholem experience the joys of synagogue and common Mishna readings, were at work within her. The prospect of a change could never have been more alluring to her than just now.

However, in the end Malkeleh said No. They could not go away now that Yiteleh too was in Karoly. They could not move farther away from the children. From here Karoly was a stone's throw, but from Varalja it was a day's ride. And they could also not go away, lest it should be said that they were running away.

"He who runs away is guilty. But we're not guilty, neither you, nor I, nor Gimpel Zorech."

This in turn made Sholem think. There was something in what Malkeleh was saying. They must stay and prove their innocence—by staying as well as with the facts. He had not yet mentioned to his wife that while she was away he had started the work of detection. How could he talk about it? Malkeleh had done a proper job, saving Gimpel Zorech from physical and spiritual damnation. What he had been building up here by day, collapsed by evening, and what he had put together during the night was blown away by the morning breeze. Many clues had proved false, and even the one or two that seemed right lacked consistency. The trouble was that he had interrupted a task of detection eight years ago, the case of the deserter Janos, and this was avenging itself now. One must never interrupt anything. Before one began a new thing, one had to finish the old. The old puzzle was disturbing, but he had to take it up. He felt somehow that if that was solved the new puzzle would also solve itself though at times it seemed that the one only made the other more confused.

He had started wrong, no doubt about that. The slave from Jerusalem followed real clues, left by humans and animals in the road. In recent days he had been going over to this, the only correct method, but Martin Vizhordo's eyebrows had deflected him. However, when the serf had died and Lajos Gore covered his eyes and scraped off the dung from his eyebrow, Sholem recalled Joshua ben Perachyah's injunction: "Make friends and judge every man on the favorable scale." What if that Janos had also merely dirtied one eyebrow with dung-liquor? After all, he was working in the stable. In that case he was not the deserter, not Benni Darazs, but the person he said he was, a decent, honest young man. A Janos. And if he was a Janos, then he must have taken the tolerance tax to Otvar. He had brought no receipt of course. But he may have met with an accident on the way back. So that matter was settled and he could return to the real clues.

The tracks of three mounted highwaymen led to Szalka. The pandours swore that there were three. But three horses of three highwaymen and Zdenkovich's two horses made a total of five horses. The original assumption that the two horses were led by one highwayman had not yet been upset. But the old poacher, Peter Csuvasz, had said that the highwayman took fish and pumpkin to Szalka. Yes, but you did not use a bushel for that. Nor was the bushel taken on horseback, but in a cart, with the goods. What if there were cart tracks as well along the tracks of the horses? There might have been beans or millet in the cart—or apples. But they had not seen any cart tracks. Or perhaps they had seen them and took no notice. In their view, highwaymen went by horse so they could flee from the scene of the bloody deed.

According to Isaac the two top highwaymen came this way. Isaac did not invent that, but must have heard it somewhere. He was not saying anything more, being afraid for his own skin. Aunt Seemah was coming from the direction of Szalka that morning, so she might have seen two escaping highwaymen on the road. A pity that she talked about nothing but the ragman's son and left so quickly. If she had stayed at least another day, she would have talked about the highwaymen as well, for she never kept quiet about anything she had seen or heard. He thought that Isaac knew something about the stranger as well, but Isaac had been talking nonsense. He said that Golden Dagger found gold watches and gold rings in his mine, but did not take them to the Royal Mint office to be changed, like the gold he mined, only sold them to Herskovitch. The children, who invented the game about Yuon the bandit, said they learned the song about Benni Darazs from Yiteleh, and Yiteleh had heard it from the stranger. Careful, Sholem, don't be rash in your judgements, remember what Rabbi Joshua ben Perachyah said. Suppose he did not dirty his eyebrow with dung, and suppose he was Benni Darazs himself. Then he did not take the tolerance tax to Otvar but used it himself . . . But now he has repaid it with interest. One could not suspect a man who acted like that. A song was no proof. That customer may have heard it from someone else, just as Yiteleh had heard it from him. What did Yiteleh say about his eyebrows? That they were like Aunt Golda's. He, Sholem, had never had a good look at Golda, but he could swear that she did not have odd eyebrows. He would have noticed that at a mere glance, and they would have talked about it in the house besides.

Sholem turned over in his bed and tried to pierce the darkness with his eyes to see if Malkeleh was asleep yet. She was tired when she arrived, and had got things ready for the Sabbath and had stayed up late. Before going to bed she drank that bear-breech tea. She said it was nothing, only she had to drink that nasty liquor to prevent recurrence of her complaint. But it was good to stretch out in her own bed, and to-morrow there would be no cooking to be done, as it was Sabbath, so she would sleep till late. Sholem called her name in a low voice.

"Do you want anything, Sholem?" came in a faint, mumbly voice.

"No, nothing, Malkeleh. I only wanted to know what sort of eyebrows Golda has."

Malkeleh was silent for a while. She was not asleep yet, he could tell that by her breathing. When she spoke again her voice was not indistinct. It was a strange voice, almost sharp.

"Goldeleh's eyebrows are dyed."

This was exciting information for Sholem. It did not let him go to sleep.

In the next bed Malkeleh tossed sleepless till morning.

THE LAST EVIDENCE

ON SUNDAY Malkeleh began to scold her children in the early morning. They were sitting in front of their milk mugs and their mother felt that they had got rather neglectful during her absence. Looking at Little Yoirish's hand she turned on him:

"Did you wash your hands before you sat down to breakfast?"

"Yes, Mummy."

"Put your bread down at once and go into the kitchen to wash your hands. You mustn't touch God's bread with such filthy hands. That goes for you, too, Yossel."

"But I did wash my hands, really. Sarah Chayah saw me."

"Then wash them again. Neither of you'll get anything to eat till you do." As the boys were sidling out, Malkeleh called after them: "You have to wash with water, not with the towel. One can't do enough laundering after them." She looked at Sarah Chayah, who was quietly sipping her hot milk. "Did you feed the chickens?"

"Not yet. I'll feed them presently."

"Not presently—now."

"But I'm having my breakfast."

"What do you mean, Sarah Chayah?" said Malkeleh severely. "How many times haven't I told you that the chickens in the coop come first. They can't help themselves. Put down your mug and do as I told you."

The little girl went out, on the verge of tears. The other children went on eating in scared attitudes.

Only Yossef made a remark now and then. He would have liked to cheer Malkeleh up and racked his brain for something amusing to say, perhaps about the candlemaker's shop, or the synagogue, or Nootah Batlan's wisecracks, or, in particular, about Shloimah's experiences on the battlefield. However, Malkeleh was not very interested in any of that. She only pricked up her ears when Yossef came to talk about the far from amusing county jail.

"Sholem thinks that the warder distributes Gimpel Zorech's leavings to the other prisoners. But Peter Koczor is no saint. He just steals them. That is why he doesn't mind if we don't go to the Commissioner. They say Koczor has the fattest pigs. He fattens them on the prisoners' bread."

That morning Malkeleh started her cooking earlier, because Yossef was going back immediately after dinner and taking Gimpel Zorech's food with him. This was the candlemaker's day, but Malkeleh had arranged with his wife to do it instead of her because the other woman would have no one to send the food by, whereas Yossef could go to Otvar on his way back to Batiz. She was preparing french beans with vinegar, which Gimpel Zorech could have cold. She also baked some maize cookies, which Gimpel Zorech liked. She sat down for a while, dropping her hands into her lap. Yossef noted how drawn and pale her face looked.

"Didn't the doctor tell you to stay in bed for a day or two?"

Malkeleh raised her eyes.

"A woman mustn't be sick," she said in a low voice, almost in a sigh. "If she's sick, there are so many other women that aren't."

Yossef did not understand this, but Malkeleh did not intend that he should.

When Yossef had gone with the food—and with the borrowed money for old Zissah—Malkeleh relaxed a little. But her body was heavy with fatigue. She would have liked to lie down, but could not. Herskovitch had come back to discuss the exchange of inns. He could not talk with Sholem because the bar parlor was crowded, so the task fell to Malkeleh. Herskovitch preferred this, for women had a flair for such things, and in any case he had heard that Malkeleh was the brains of the business here.

Malkeleh did not feel inclined to change her decision, and knew the essentials of the offer, yet she listened to her visitor. He said the inn of Varalja was an excellent business, better than the one of Lapfalva. The environs were also more beautiful, with mountains and valleys. Everyone else would be happy there, but he, Herskovitch, had already married off his daughters and had only two children at home, and in addition, there was trouble with Florian, who had got involved in a suspicious affair and had probably got into the clutches of a counterfeiting gang. Being reckless and extravagant, he was capable of anything if he got hard up. His mistress in Varalja was insatiable for money. He had bought her a house and a vineyard, and she would load on herself all the silk and velvet there was. Even a gold mine must give out sometime.

Herskovitch was a scraggy little old man, with a big wry nose and an upward crinkle in his chin. His trimmed goatee was an extension of the crinkle, so that it almost met with the tip of his nose. The expression in his piggy eyes held entreaty, and Malkeleh was sorry for him. But she could not suppress the suspicion that Herskovitch had something to do with Florian's affairs. What made her think of that? Herskovitch's reputation was never good, and in this house he was always mentioned as a rival who was not very scrupulous as to the means he employed. It seemed to Malkeleh that the man was suppressing a great many things—and not merely to make his offer more attractive. Herskovitch was talking about seemingly irrelevant matters, as that they had formerly never mined gold in Sebespatak, only miles to the east and south-east, but that this lucky fellow, this Florian, had found a rich vein in some abandoned workings six or seven years ago, and had been lucky ever since. He was working on a small scale, with only five or six picked men, whom he paid well, and also gave a share, so they stuck to him through thick and thin. Malkeleh was tired of it all, and feeling that she had heard enough about Florian's past, she brought the conversation back to the present.

"You think that now his vein has given out and he is making counterfeit money?"

"I didn't say that, Malkeleh," said Herskovitch, looking around with a scared expression. "I didn't say he made bad money. He wouldn't know how. He was born a peasant and he can't even read and write. All I think is that he knew what sort of money he was giving me. He always knows what he is selling to me, but how can I know? It's none of my business anyhow. When I went out to see him he pointed a pistol at me and said he'd shoot me like a dog if I blabbed. I haven't said anything to you and I haven't said anything to Sholem."

"How do you know that the money was counterfeit?"

"Mesel said so. The pandours confiscated four hundred florin notes from him."

"Did he tell them they were from you?"

"No. He said he could not remember. They gave him a week to jog his memory."

"You too can say that you can't remember who gave you the money."

"I can't. Mesel is a big wine merchant and he gets big sums of money. I am a small innkeeper in Varalja and my customers bring me only coppers."

Malkeleh thought for a while, then she said:

"Invent something. Say that one night a stranger came along and bought several casks of drink for some carousal or for a wedding."

"Not a bad idea," said Herskovitch, his eyes lighting up. "But you know, Malkeleh, I am afraid, more than I've ever been these twenty years. You'll say I'm afraid for my old hide and creaking bones. But it isn't me. That desperate gang are capable of exterminating my whole family with me."

Malkeleh gave the frightened old man a sideways glance. She would have liked to ask who that "desperate gang" were. But Herskovitch came back to the proposed exchange.

"You could live there safely," he said; "you've had no business with Florian."

"We haven't much peace even here," replied Malkeleh. "But the Above One has sent us here, so we'll stay here." And as Herskovitch would not take even this as final, she added: "In danger it is best to behave calmly. Plenty of time to get frightened when the danger is over. If you were to come here, they'd find you just the same. And if we run away from here, we shall be branded."

In the evening Malkeleh reported to Sholem. Sholem seized his beard with one hand and began to chew the end of it, as when he was pondering a Talmudic problem. After a long while he said:

"I'll go to Rothbart for some stock in the morning."

When Sholem returned from Karoly there was laughter in his eyes as well as on his lips. Malkeleh had not seen him so gay for a long time. He talked about his meeting with Yiteleh as though it was his first meeting with her after several years. The ultimate reason for his gladness, though he did not confess it even to himself, was that he had succeeded in repressing his inhibitions sufficiently to look in at the leather shop in the market square even before he went to Rothbart. The reason he did so was that he had to find out some important things. However, Yiteleh knew nothing about this. She flung her arms around his neck, covered him with kisses and even gave a few pulls at his beard, chattering and laughing the while. Her eyes were clear, her brow serene and what she said was like the dew on the grass, the way Moses used that word in his call to heaven and earth.

Sholem had a great deal to talk about. He did not mention what Yiteleh had heard from the peasants when she was in charge of the inn, and what she said about the customer with the black sheepskin cap who sang "Benni Darazs" and paid with a twenty-florin note, though that too was important. But it would not interest Malkeleh now, especially as she knew nothing about that matter. What did interest her was to hear that Yiteleh was liked by everyone and that she in turn liked to be there. Mordechai praised her for her attentiveness and industry and the refined yet firm manner with which she handled suppliers and customers alike. He said he was genuinely sorry she was not his daughter, for though she had only just started, it was already clear that she would become an excellent business woman. The man that married her would be a lucky fellow.

"You ought to see, Malkeleh," said Sholem, "how strict she is in the shop. Gadli Brueder, the son of Joshua, came in. He is a fine young man, with his moustache sprouting, and he has laughing eyes, like his father. She just showed him the door. Not rudely, not at all. She told him quite sweetly that she had no time to talk during business hours. 'Just go home, Gadli dear, or you'll be smelling of leather. Come along to Aunt Blimeleh's in the evening, then we can talk.'" Shayeh Oesterreicher had also looked in, but she did not send him away. True, he was very quiet, just sat in a corner while Yiteleh was serving. He was reading a book which was not what the grandson of the Rabbi of Karoly ought to have read.

"I like that boy," said Malkeleh with smiling eyes.

Sholem's face grew grave. He was no longer thinking of Shayeh, who had been reading the poems of the poet from Dusseldorf, and had then handed the book to Yiteleh, but of Master Adam de Sarberek, whom he saw loitering round the shop as he came away. He was not at all pleased to find the young man there, though he had been quite amiable with him, Sholem, shaking hands with him and asking for the loan of ten florins. He had even confided his secrets to Sholem—that he would take a post either at the county or at the manor court, in which latter case he would stay in Karoly. That was not good news. However, Sholem did not talk about this. He talked about Mailech instead. He was looking well and said that he was studying hard. And yes, at the synagogue Sholem had met Simon Mesel, who had been talking with his squire, the Count of Erdod, about Herskovitch's notes. The count had said: "Simon, you'll remember only the things that won't get you into trouble. Herskovitch will make up for your loss and that's that. I'd like to see anyone lay a finger on my Jew." So Mesel was not afraid. A man with such a patron. . . .

The next few days passed quietly, without any major excitement or trouble. Sholem was less distrustful and also less reserved than he had been before. He stopped to talk with a few of his customers, so the peasants too grew more friendly. Malkeleh also calmed down. Whether it was the bear's breech or the few days of comparative rest, she was beginning to get color into her cheeks. The fortunate event at the Shingled Inn was that there was a pause in events. All that happened was the manifestation of ill-humor up above: the autumn rains had started earlier than usual. Bad weather was once more a topic of conversation, together with the quagmire of the county roads.

On the Sabbath the house was quieter than usual. Mailech had not come home, so there was no report about the *yeshiba* or the boy's little trading excursions, nor had Yossef turned up to gush about the secrets of candlemaking. One could not take their absence amiss, seeing that carts which might give them a lift did not pass this way just now, and they could not walk the distance in the quagmire. Malkeleh missed her adopted son more than Mailech, because Yossef might have seen Gimpel Zorech when taking food to him in prison, and he might even have spoken with him. However, Yossef would surely come along for the following Sabbath.

He came long before then. He came by the candlemaker's delivery cart on the Monday evening. There were no goods to deliver in the cart, neither candles nor tallow, nor soap, nor potash. It carried only Yossef himself, yet it was drawn by two strong horses. Yossef was soaked to the skin, though it had not rained, nor was it so hot as to cause one to sweat.

"What's the matter, Yossef?" asked Malkeleh.

"Call Sholem," panted Yossef.

"Why? What's up?"

"I'll tell you when he's here."

Malkeleh ran into the inn and returned with Sholem.

"The money . . . the money . . ." said Yossef, stammering with agitation.

"What money?" asked Sholem.

"The twenty you sent to Aunt Zissah."

"What about that twenty?" prompted Malkeleh.

Yossef tried to pull himself together. But he must have driven desperately hard to get here in time, and he was so overwrought that he could not explain clearly why he was sent.

"Aunt Zissah gave it to the butcher. The butcher gave it to the cattle dealer. The cattle dealer paid the peasant for the bullock. . . ."

"Well?" said Sholem impatiently.

"Well," said Yossef. He looked round to see if there was anyone else present. Then, low and quick, he said: "The pandours took it away from the peasant. . . ."

"Why did they take it away?"

"It was Zdenkovich's money."

"Good God!" Malkeleh moaned.

Sholem did not catch the agitation of the other two. There was a stern expression on his face.

"And what did Aunt Zissah say?" he asked, as though cross-examining the boy.

"She told the pandours that she got the money from a stranger passing through the village, whom she had never seen before. But she said to tell you to do something because you probably got the money from Gimpel Zorech."

"How do the pandours know that it is stolen money?" said Sholem with a deep frown.

"Zdenkovich's sign was on it."

"There was a *daleth* on it."

"It wasn't a *daleth*."

"What else?"

"It was a Cyrillic z—Zdenkovich's initial."

"Still more trouble!" moaned Malkeleh. She sat down on a chair, swaying her head, staring in wide-eyed terror into nothingness. She saw the disaster that had descended on her home.

Sholem was very calm. He was no longer stern. The wrinkles had disappeared from his brow.

"Tell Aunt Zissah," he said to Yossef, "not to worry. There's no blood on Gimpel Zorech's hand. He did not touch the money. He is quite innocent."

Malkeleh raised her tear-stained face to her husband. Sholem went up to her and placed a hand on her shoulder. And like an attorney who had the threads of an inquiry in his hands, but kept silent until he had all the evidence in his possession, he announced in ringing tones:

"We've got the murderer, Malkeleh."

### IN THE VIENNA SYNAGOGUE

SHAYEH OESTERREICHER bumped his head against that of a strange young man. The two had suddenly bent down at the same moment. The stranger raised his bearded face and said in a strangled tone:

"Damn!"

"Hush!" came from Shayeh. "Don't you know where we are?"

They were in Vienna, in the New Synagogue built by Kornhäuser in the Seitenstetten Gasse. Many a thing was permitted here that was forbidden in strictly orthodox synagogues. Here they were praying on the basis of Moses Mendelssohn's reformist ideas. The foundation of religion was no longer the fanatical "I believe" but the more elevated conception of "I realize." But swearing was forbidden even here, and even in Hungarian, though Shayeh was not the man to be shocked for long by a little impropriety. In an instant he realized the humorous side of the situation.

"I beg your pardon," he said with a smile. "My fault."

It was the last day of Passover. They were performing a rite of the morning service which was confined to one or two members of the congregation. Up on the dais they were raising and dressing up the Scrolls of the Law. Cantor Sulzer was racing through the blessing of the participants. His beautiful but just now somewhat sleepy tenor rang out only as he mentioned a biggish sum among the offerings he was reciting. Round the richly gilt, baroque-carved seats by the eastern wall the elect of the congregation were chatting. Joseph Manes Oesterreicher, the aged court physician, snapped open his snuff-box, offering a pinch of perfumed Levant snuff to his neighbors, extending it first to the left, then to the right. The strange young man loitering round the stalls considered that the aged physician ought to have begun on the right. For that was where the most noted Jew of the Imperial City, Baron Solomon Rothschild, was sitting. The man on the left was only an old mummy with a swarthy, wrinkled face, and he kept nodding his head somberly and dispiritedly like a superannuated cab-horse. It was old Eschkeles, head of the banking firm of Arnstein & Eschkeles, who had been made a back number by the Baron enthroned on the right.

However, Joseph Manes was himself a self-made notable, and he was of a somewhat rebellious character. He did not depend on the financiers, having made his fortune and his fame with his medical research, his chemical discoveries, and his balneological knowledge. He did not forget that the man from Frankfurt had been living in Vienna for barely a decade, and that although for years he had been the leading financial authority of the Monarchy, he was a mere newcomer as compared with the other man's half-century in the financial world. So, with a subtle touch, he honored

the outmoded past before the celebrated present. He knew that
Baron Solomon was piqued about it. To pacify him, or perhaps to
increase his pique, the physician also paid attention to the future,
represented by the gleaming white collar, silken bow-tie, and
silver-lamé prayer shawl on the Baron's right. This was Baron
Anselm Rothschild. Anselm, either from curiosity or mere
courtesy, asked to see the famous snuff-box, which the physician
had received as a gift from the Emperor himself. He looked at the
lid, with the two-headed eagle on it and an obliquely placed F
underneath. His father made an impatient gesture to snatch the
box from him. The golden box fell to the floor and rolled away.
Two eager young men bent down for it and bumped their heads
together.

That was the beginning of friendship between the two young
men. Shayeh, having handed the box back to his uncle, turned to
the stranger.

"You come from Hungary?"

"Yes."

"What part?"

"Beyond the Tisza."

"County Szatmar, isn't it?"

"How do you know?"

"You have the Szatmar accent."

"What is that like?"

"You drawl. I come from there myself."

"Csenger or Szalka?"

"No, Karoly."

"I used to know Rothbart there."

The two young men looked at each other searchingly. Shayeh
was not handsome. He had a long, horsy face, a bumpy, somewhat
slanting nose, a big soft mouth, and projecting teeth. He wore a
little rusty moustache and muttonchops that made his face look
longer. He had a high forehead and angular temples. The only
really beautiful feature in this complex of irregularity was his
eyes. Anyone talking with him for a minute or two would see
nothing but his eyes, which were large and brown, with a restless
flame in them that made them luminous. Perhaps it was this that
made his sallow complexion look sallower still.

The other young man had a darker skin and broader shoulders, though he was lean. He had bony hands and mobile muscles and a jutting chin above a pronounced adam's apple. His pointed beard served to accentuate the impression of aggressiveness. He had a sharp, hooked nose and greenish-grey eyes. The prominence of his cheekbones was but slightly mitigated by the downy edges of beard brushed over them. There was a slanting white scar across his brow. Shayeh looked at him thoughtfully: he had seen this boorish border country type before. Had he seen this fellow as well?

"My name is Shayeh Oesterreicher," he said.

"Mine is Israel Yomtov."

The Cantor's voice rang out, intoning the Hallelujah, accompanied by a choir of boys, and the conversation had to be interrupted. Shayeh withdrew into the box along the wall, while Israel Yomtov resumed his seat in a row lower down. After the service Shayeh joined his uncle, while Yomtov went with Baron Anselm.

That afternoon they met again in the synagogue yard. Shayeh gazed into Yomtov's eyes and said:

"I know you, but I don't know where from."

Israel Yomtov compressed his lips and did not reply. Shayeh was about to say something, but was prevented by the advent of Anselm, who with a tilt of his grey top-hat gave them the traditional greeting:

"Gut Yomtov, Shayeh. Gut Yomtov, Herr Yomtov."

"Anselm," said Shayeh teasingly, "you must get some money from your papa. You've broken the snuff-box."

"Is it broken?" giggled Anselm. "How funny!"

"Very funny. The lid is caved in and it can't be opened. It has to go to the goldsmith."

"Send the bill along. If possible at dinner-time. Then at least we'll have a row at table."

"A row at Solomon Rothschild's on account of a florin or two?"

"Only on account of a florin or two. Papa is very cheerful when he has to spend thousands."

Shayeh looked at the fat, clean-shaven face of the younger Rothschild. It was the face of a naughty boy. There was a boyish glint in Yomtov's eye too, and for an instant Shayeh saw his face hairless. It recalled a half-forgotten childhood memory. He was traveling home for the holidays. On the road to Karoly there was an accident: he had swallowed a large coin. They took him into a roadside inn for first aid. That was his first visit to Malkeleh's house. A big, lanky boy with a scar across his brow was sitting among a group of children, manipulating the Chanukah spinning top and smiling to himself because he was always winning.

"I know who you are," he said suddenly. "Sroleh Yomtov from Lapfalva."

The other raised his face—a bearded face. Shayeh seized him by the hand.

"The lost boy. Mother Malkah and Yiteleh talked such a lot about you. They'll be happy to hear that I've found you."

Yomtov's face clouded and the scar on his brow became scarlet. He tried to sound casual, but there was embarrassment in his voice as he said:

"And you are Shayeh, the Shayeh who—"

"Who used to eat money in his childhood," completed Shayeh with a laugh. "But since then I have come to my senses. I have realized that money is tasteless. I leave it to the Frankforters to stuff themselves with it."

This was a dig at Anselm. But Anselm was not offended. He knew nothing about the incident of Shayeh's childhood, but he knew Shayeh.

"One man stuffs himself with money," he retorted, "another with print. But you can leave your money for your son, whereas the print you take with you into the grave."

This might have developed into an interesting discussion, but just then a white-faced man with a round yellow beard and deep furrows in his brow came up to them. Placing a hand on Anselm's shoulder he said:

"I've spoken to the old man."

"What did he say, Herr Levy?"

"He won't hear of it."

Anselm looked at Yomtov. The latter shrugged.

"If Solomon Rothschild doesn't want it. . . ."

Anselm drew aside with Herr Levy and they became immersed in a long discussion. When he came back he looked dejected.

"I put the cabbage in charge of a goat," he said. "Our manager is against anything new and anything that he did not think of himself. Instead of supporting our plan, he talked about it in such a way that the old man said no without investigating the matter. And if a Frankforter once says no . . . They are a stubborn lot."

Shayeh listened without interest, for this was business. But even Yomtov did not seem to be particularly interested. The young Rothschild looked at their faces searchingly, then his own changed to gaiety. With the glint of a naughty boy in his eyes he said:

"I have an idea, Yomtov. You'll come along and have dinner with us. My father welcomes any guest of mine, and when there is a stranger at the table, he's charming and generous with me, because he likes to be regarded as a kind father. I will broach the subject at the right moment, and you'll join in. We'll enfilade the old boy and soften him. Good idea, what?"

"I'm spending the evening with Yeshayeh," said Yomtov simply after a moment's thought.

"If," said the other with a trace of annoyance, "you attach more importance to his Jacobin ideas than to a big deal where you might make thousands. . . ."

"We're childhood friends," replied Yomtov.

The young Rothschild gave his hat a tilt and turned away.

TWO FRIENDS

ISRAEL YOMTOV sat beneath the packed bookshelves in Dr. Manes' small study. Half an hour before he had been listening to the aged court physician's wry philosophy, but now the latter had retired and Shayeh was talking. Speaking with youthful vehemence and somewhat rhapsodically, he reverted to the conversation interrupted in the synagogue yard, and spoke as though Anselm were still present, fulminating against the commercial-minded Jews, who still thought that money was the main pillar

of society, whereas there were more important pillars. The peoples
of the world now placed a higher value on liberty and equality
than on profit. If tyranny were overthrown everywhere, as there
was every reason to expect, everyone would benefit, even ancient,
yet mentally ever youthful Jewry. Israel Yomtov said neither yea
nor nay, but just nodded his head now and then. And when at
last he spoke, it was to veer the conversation to a more personal
sphere.

"You know a lot, Shayeh," he said with respect in his tone.
"Where did you learn it all?"

"I have two degrees," replied Shayeh modestly.

"Are you a physician too?"

"Not yet. Only a doctor of Theology and Philosophy."

"Why both?"

"A wise question. It's just to have something to rack my brains
over: shall I go as assistant rabbi to Arad, or shall I accept the
invitation of the congregation of Buda. They want me there as
a teacher at their school."

"Which is better?"

"The question is, which is worse? I wouldn't like to go for a
rabbi, though I come from a rabbinical family. It would be all
right if I could go the way my great-grandfather went to Karoly,
taking the congregation with him: he was a Joshua and Ezra
rolled into one. It's worth while like that. But to play second
fiddle, is not so good."

"What of Buda?"

"The people there are stubborn and backward. The school has
an old-fashioned head. I can't expect to be the head myself: my
beard is not yet moldy enough for that. The pay is low too, can't
marry on it. I should be a master only in name, but in reality only
a *melommed*. That is the lowest post in Israel. Do you know why
the *melommed* beats the children? He is angry that he hasn't made
more of his life. That's what we call education!"

"What are your plans?"

"If my good old uncle doesn't get tired of it meanwhile, I'll
get a medical diploma. I'm already studying for it."

With a quizzical eye on Yomtov's sharp features, he said:

"I see you go about with Anselm. Has he got an undertaking of some kind?"

"Yes, he does this and that and the other. I bring him ideas. But his father is very stingy. He's jealous and treats him like a young brat, though Anselm is twenty-five."

"Just a big boy."

"He's brainier than you'd think, though. But he can't talk about brainy things at home. It upsets him. He says the old man has lived long enough."

"I don't envy a crown prince," laughed Shayeh. "The heads of a dynasty never die soon enough. Our rulers have created a precedent, though. Marie Theresa made Joseph her companion. Frances did the same with Ferdinand."

"Solomon Rothschild won't learn from anyone. He won't hear of his son being his partner. Yet we would bring a new spirit into the business."

"What for? He's making millions with the old spirit. Don't forget that his mighty patron, Metternich, hates nothing so much as a new spirit. Solomon knows what he is doing."

"I should say so!" said Yomtov with genuine admiration.

They went on talking, inquiring. Israel Yomtov became more communicative and began to tell the other about his own life. After the death of his parents he had stayed for a while with the new innkeeper's family. One day he got tired of them and ran away to become something more than a village innkeeper. He had roamed about a great deal, had seen many lean days and had engaged in a great many pursuits. He had tried to settle in some places, but was too restless. He had tried a few trades, including watchmaking, but his interest had lasted only until he had learned to understand the mechanism of springs and cogwheels. He had been a peddler, agent, merchant. Sometimes he had much money, sometimes little. He was not very interested in money, what attracted him was enterprise itself and the ideas on which it was founded. He made money only to be able to do something with it. Once he had been told that everything depended on luck and that luck went to fools. But it was not so in reality. Everything depended on keen observation: one must see what was lacking and where and when and supply the deficiency before anyone else thought of it. A stupid person might be lucky once or twice, but if one wanted to be permanently successful one had to be on the alert always. Shortly after his arrival in Vienna three years before, he had managed to get into an old banking firm, Geymueller & Steiner. They put him to office work there, but he did not like it and went over to Arnstein & Eschkeles as a customer's man and inquiry agent. His task was, on the one hand, to persuade rich citizens to invest their money wisely, and on the other, to discover the financial status and character of prospects. He had been head of the inquiry department and thought he had learned a great deal there. Old Eschkeles was irritable and did not like reports to be read to him; they had to be recited from memory. And the old man would be teaching you the while:

"Beware of the excessively amiable person, my boy. Don't worry about a rude one. Choleric people pay up in time. Where a man abuses everyone else and praises you, tighten the terms. If a man offers you the highest interest, demand a guarantor and triple security. To the idler give the loan he wants by instalments. Demand services of him and enter the loan among the doubtful items."

The customer's man, explained Yomtov, had a difficult task. When a Hungarian, Czech, Polish, or Austrian noble had squandered his revenues and became hard up, he applied to the bank for a loan and the bank went to the public for the money. There were unfamiliar names and names of ill-repute which no one trusted. When it was a matter of a Prince Schwarzenberg or Windischgratz, or Count Hadik, out came the stockings from the recesses of the wardrobe. With a Prince Grassalkovich they were simply delighted. Everyone remembered the founder of the family, how he became a favorite of Marie Theresa and how he acquired untold wealth. Arnstein & Eschkeles had lent several hundred thousand florins on that name twice. One could not lend on the estates because they were entailed. The interest came in smoothly, and the price of the bonds rose. But when Prince Grassalkovich wanted two million florins at one time, Eschkeles dared not do it alone. Rothschild was not attracted by the business, but Stametz & Company came in.

"Jew Solomon," said Yomtov, getting into his stride, "does not lend on the past. He gives money to Metternich, the Eszterhazys, and in view of the Chancellor's impending marriage, to the Zichys. But he would not give any for the Grassalkovich loan. He had a good nose. Barely six months after the issue the business began to look doubtful, for the Prince was not paying the interest. Then came the smash. The bonds fell to half and even lower. To-day they are worth less than fifteen per cent. There's been a scandal, as you may have heard."

"I have, a little," said Shayeh. "I don't pay much attention to the Bourse."

"At that time Arnstein and Eschkeles ceased to grant loans. It was understandable, of course, but there were certain things that puzzled me. Solomon was giving loans freely, perhaps only to confuse the old firms and push them further into a decline. But Eschkeles was distrustful even when there was no good reason for it. They sent me to Hungary to inquire into the financial status and the affairs of a certain Count Istvan Szechenyi. The Count had asked for a small loan of ten thousand florins. My report was rather favorable. The Count is somewhat eccentric, likes to carouse and gamble and spends a great deal on women and horses. But what count doesn't? He is reckless in other directions as well. Once, in company, he offered a year's revenue of his estates, sixty thousand florins, to found an academy and support bookworms. Of course, he has not actually handed over the money to this day. But a man with an annual income of sixty thousand was in my opinion good for a loan of ten thousand. But Eschkeles refused the loan, precisely on my report. He would not have the Hungarian nobles being generous with his money. I didn't worry about the Hungarian nobles, but I was offended to find they did not trust my judgement and I left the firm."

"What did you do next?"

"I went to Herr Levy, the manager of the Rothschild firm, and offered him my services, submitting my references. Herr Levy laughed at me. He said he'd pay me a salary to stay with the rival firm. I was to go on giving my work and ideas to the Geymuellers, the Arnsteins, and the Stametzes and help them farther down the slope, and when these old gentlemen had at last expired, I could come to him again. This impertinence made me furious, I joined hands with Anselm, though up till now we have only put through some trifling transactions, with the money of his uncle in Frankfort rather than with that of the Vienna firm."

Shayeh tilted his head in an attitude of attention and Yomtov went on:

"In barely a year we built nine windmills in the valley of the Upper Inn. Once, when I was traveling that way, the people with water mills complained that they could run their mills only for one or two months, because there was too little water in summer and the frosts came early. Well, it was true that there was little water, but once, when I had to run after my hat, I realized that there was plenty of wind. That was the foundation of my plan. The capital was provided by Anselm. Now the windmills are working summer and winter, not only milling flour, but also cutting chaff, raising water from wells, irrigating, and three of them are even making boards with a circular saw. On this idea we have now worked out a much bigger plan, by which the debts of the Hungarian nobles could be secured. For even though the soil is entailed, the forests can be cut down. But now everything depends on whether Anselm has succeeded in persuading his father. If he fails. . . ."

Shayeh trimmed the candle and looked at Yomtov's somewhat resentful face. Then, without transition, he remarked:

"Yiteleh has grown into a very pretty girl, my friend."

There was animation in Yomtov's features.

He waited for Shayeh to talk about the family in Lapfalva. That was really why he had come. In the synagogue yard Shayeh had begun to say something, but did not get far. At any other time Yomtov would have jumped at Anselm's invitation, for being a guest at Rothschild's table might have been the prelude to great advancement. The reason he had been loitering near the upper boxes in the synagogue was also in the hope that he might get an opportunity to do a service to the great banker. And when he used that expletive it was not on account of the blow he had received, but because Shayeh had been more nimble and had robbed him of the honor of handing the snuff-box to Solomon Rothschild. He knew the latter's suspicions and prejudices and that he regarded all his son's associates as thoughtless and extravagant people, and

Yomtov wanted to prove the contrary as regards himself. But he had refused Anselm's invitation without hesitation because he felt a need to spend some time with Shayeh. The cold and calculating Israel Yomtov had been pushed aside by Sroleh Yomtov, in whom the memories of his puberty were aglow.

Yet he had long abandoned that Sroleh Yomtov. He had tried to discard this name, because it recalled the village and back-wardness. But when Shayeh had said it with that friendly spontaneity, he heard the old voices calling him: "Sroleh Yomtov! Sroleh Yomtov!" The world from which he had fled, and which he had already buried in his own mind, had followed him and was demanding him back. Malkeleh wanted to be his mother and he protested against this. You can't love a mother the way he loved Malkeleh. She was the first woman to arouse desire in him. But he could not love her in any case, because she was a strange woman and the wife of another. That was why he behaved as though he hated her. Had the woman ever guessed why he was so rebellious and disobedient that time? Had she guessed that his sinful desire, which attracted him to her, at the same time drove him away from her, and that it was on account of her alone that he had left the house, as he thought, for ever? Malkeleh had not forgotten him, little Yiteleh had not forgotten him. They were still talking about him "at home." For the first time in eight years he had met a friend with whom he could talk about his own eventful, ambitious life. Was Shayeh's naturalness the key that unlocked the door of his reserve? Not quite. Behind Shayeh there was Malkeleh, and to some extent it was to her that he was rendering an account. He had struggled hard, making several new beginnings, to become something more than a village innkeeper. The reason Shayeh listened to him so attentively was probably that he wanted to report everything at home, and per-haps to write about the runaway boy.

Shayeh watched his eyes and the scar on his forehead and asked whether he was married yet, or whether he had found someone he wanted to marry. Yomtov answered in the negative. He had not found anyone, though there had been girls who had found him. In any case, he first wanted to have his affairs in order before he would think of marriage. Shayeh did not seem partic-

ularly interested, and perhaps his question was only a pretext to
bring the conversation back to Yiteleh. He spoke of the girl with
greater ardor and enthusiasm than he had spoken about the destiny
of the Jews before. On this subject he was more colorful, and his
enthusiasm lent a loftiness to his talk. He even quoted poetry to
make himself better understood. One thing was certain: Shayeh
was not optimistic concerning his implied intentions. He admired
Yiteleh's beauty, but was conscious of his own ugliness. He could
not help blurting out his unhappy, hopeless love.

Israel Yomtov was a good listener and his interest did not flag
even by cockcrow.

"I can quite imagine," he observed with a casual air, "that
Yiteleh is now a young lady. She must be pretty, too; her mother
was a pretty woman."

"She still is," said the other with animation. "No one would
say that she is the mother of eight living children. Sometimes,
she looks as if she were Yiteleh's sister. Wait a moment, I've got
a drawing of them side by side."

He searched on his shelves and produced his sketch-books.

"I am no great artist," he explained as he showed his sketches,
"and couldn't be, either. Since Abraham smashed the idols in his
sculptor father's workshop, and Moses expressly forbade us to
make images, we have not developed much in this sphere. But I
could draw a likeness of Yiteleh with my eyes shut. This is the
drawing where they are together. It is not very good, but Malkeleh is interesting here. Those deepset eyes! I beg your pardon?
I thought you were saying something. That little Jewish girl with
the tousled hair and the shawl round her neck is Yiteleh. She has a
bottle in her hand—coming out from behind the bar to serve
the peasants. This was after the fire in the new inn, the Shingled
Csárda. Here you see her in the leather shop, serving the bootmakers and quarrelling with the tanners. What leather shop?
Why, her uncle's in Karoly. This frock with the lace collar she
wears on Saturday, not at home in the village but at her aunt's
house. In this drawing she is crocheting a table-runner; here she is
knitting a sock. Clever, what? The needles flash in her hands like
lightning. Here she is reading, her head tilted sideways. The book
is Heine. Here she is staring into the air with her bright eyes,

thinking. Isn't she sweet? Here she is leaning against the piano at the Thursday salon of Madame Adel Rooz. This jackass paying court to her is Gadli Brueder. Here she is dancing the *csárdas* with the Sarberek lad in the gentry's parlor. I drew it out of my own head as Yiteleh was telling me about the incident. She liked this one best and I made her a copy of it. Here she is showing her lovely teeth, laughing at a young man named Shayeh Oesterreicher who has two degrees. Here Yiteleh is sad. She's all the sweeter like this, isn't she?"

"What is she sad about?"

"Bad news from home. They won't let Gimpel Zorech, Sholem's brother, out of prison. They arrested him in the summer in connection with a murder. They know he never killed even a mayfly, but until the murderer is caught he is the culprit. Sholem had a lot of trouble both with the authorities and his squires. The time this sad drawing was made they had just given Sholem notice to quit. He was overbid by another Jew. There you have our mercenary race."

"It's morning, Shayeh," said Yomtov, rising. "Sorry to have stayed so long. You must be sleepy."

"Not in the least." Shayeh was really not sleepy. He would have gone on talking about Karoly, Malkeleh, and above all Yiteleh. But Yomtov already knew all he wanted to know.

THE HOUSE OF TROUBLE

THE ICE had thawed in the marsh, the ice-duck was already hatching, and the drake with its bright plumes was somersaulting as he fished in the water. There was but a memory of the snow left, but it was a substantial memory, for the roads were such a quagmire that it needed great enterprise for anyone to go to the Shingled Inn. The mud was drowning any incipient event, good or bad. However there was little good in prospect and it was all the better if the bad failed to happen. They were expecting the Otvar Commissioner to come and visit the family of the accused, who were generally believed to be implicated. But he did not come, evidently delaying until the roads became passable.

The spring was always oppressive in these parts, but this year the unrest was even worse than at other times. The peasants were putting their heads together and each day at the *csárda* began with whisperings and ended with savage cursing. Even the milder serfs were abusing the system and the Estates as though possessed by the disputatiousness of the late Martin Vizhordo, though he had been followed into the grave by the favorite subject of his abuses. But that too only brought trouble. Old de Denghelegh had died at the beginning of the previous autumn, yet his heir, Ferenc Jeky, had not yet shown up. He had sent only his steward with a clerk to go over the serf homesteads belonging to his father-in-law's estate and take a look at the inn as well. That sort of thing had happened before, but somehow it was more burdensome now. The peasants had heard that the feudal services and payments would shortly be abolished, so that the serfs could redeem their homesteads and freedom. The burdens of the county and the country would thenceforth be borne jointly by the gentry and the people. It was the will of the aged Emperor Francis, who was already being assisted in his rule by his first-born son in the name of Ferdinand. But there was treachery in the wind again. The gentry, as so often in the past, were opposing the royal will. What better proof was needed than the fact that the new Squire no longer considered it necessary to show his face to his serfs, but sent his steward to register working cattle, homesteads, and the serfs living in them?

The examination of the lease agreement for the inn and the new arrangements arising therefrom only served to intensify the agitation of the villages. Squire Jeky knew that the agreement, like all other similar agreements, stipulated above all that the Jew should sell the Squire's wines. It was only as a side-line, and when he had sold that wine to the last drop, that he was allowed to sell home or factory distilled spirits and beers and wines from other sources. Up till now this was not taken very strictly, for the estates of de Denghelegh and de Sarberek, being on marsh-side land, grew but little wine, and that little was usually consumed by their guests. If now and then they sold a caskful or two

to Sholem at a good price, it was only to maintain the legal con-
tinuity of the lease agreement. Now, during Squire de Denghelegh's illness there were few guests at his manor, so much of his
wine was left over. Squire Jeky himself had a separate cellar, and
being in need of money, he quickly came to an understanding
with de Sarberek, who had little wine but was also in great need
of money, and they went for the Jew, there being a rumor current that he had made a fortune and was sitting on his money.
They had even nicknamed him "Broody."

So there was this, too, to add to Sholem's many troubles. His
peasants, who in the course of the years had got used to spirits
and drank wine but rarely, now had the gentry's wines forced
upon them, and they saw more in it than a mere change over
from one drink to another. They saw in this, that the gentry,
whose power was fast waning, were determined to regain their old
privileges at all costs and were even coming out with fresh demands. The serf laws only imposed villeinage, tithe, military
service, taxes, and tolls, but did not prescribe that the serfs must
spend what little money was left to them on the gentry's wine.
Formerly the serfs had a free choice here and if they fancied
spirits or a drop of home-distilled stuff they could have it. But
wine they did not drink for decades, if only out of defiance, and
if the innkeeper wanted to observe his agreement he sold the
wine to passing travelers and what was left he allowed to get
old in the cellar.

More than ever, Sholem's life was being ground up between
the millstones of gentry and serf. The peasant wanted to drink,
so as to forget his misery and those that were the cause of it. But
if there were no spirits that one could drink, only wine that one
had to consume, then a visit to the inn did not bring forgetful-
ness. One had to think of Squire Jeky, who had seized with a
firm hand the whip that had fallen out of the hands of the aged
de Denghelegh, and they had to think of de Sarberek, who was
always the cruelest of the gentry and who still boxed the ears
of the serfs if they worked without enthusiasm. Sholem excused
himself by saying that even four horses could not drag the cart
with full casks from Karoly or Batiz through the muddy roads,
that was why he had no spirits, and he acted as though he did

not hear the curses of his customers or their offers to help with the carting. However, transport was not Sholem's worst trouble; he had no money and his credit had deteriorated. At Christmas he had paid a biggish debt to Mesel; a week or two later Squire Jeky demanded seven hundred florins for his wine, and de Sarberek nearly five hundred. Sholem could only take delivery of part of the wine, for he had not enough casks or cellar space, yet the gentry were already advancing new demands.

Then, a week before the Jewish Passover, Ezekiel Gutfreund from Karoly turned up, produced Azriel's bill, saying that the entire amount was now due. The amount had grown to seventeen hundred and forty-six florins and twenty-three kreuzers. Execution could be levied for it, but Ezekiel advised that Sholem had better redeem it as it stood, because the charges alone would amount to twenty or thirty florins, and perhaps several times that sum. Sholem suggested that Ezekiel might perhaps approach Azriel first, but Ezekiel informed him that Azriel had failed to reply to three letters and had, in reply to a fourth and more stern demand, replied that Sholem would attend to the matter. Sholem's heart grew heavy, partly on account of Azriel, who was doing so badly that he could not settle a small bill like this, whereas in the past he used to pay tens of thousands to his manufacturers; and partly—and mainly—that for a part of the bill he had to touch the capital of the orphans.

In the early autumn Herskovitch had gone along to Gyekeny and had over-bid the rent of the inn. He must also have given an advance to Lady Susannah, who needed a great deal of money because her daughter Antonia was engaged and her trousseau was absorbing considerable sums. At all events Gyekeny was now endeavoring with unusual energy to persuade his fellow Squires to change the lessee of the inn, and he did not recoil even from identifying Sholem with his brother's affair, saying that this was bad for the reputation of the manorial villages. At that time Malkeleh went along to see her ladyship, laden with gifts. But just then her ladyship was "indisposed" and did not receive the innkeeper's wife. Thereupon Malkeleh, herself ill, went over by cart to Varalja to see Herskovitch. Herskovitch came back with her to Lapfalva and apologized to Sholem with tears in his eyes;

then he went along to Gyekeny to inform him that he was with-drawing his offer. He agreed to forfeit his deposit, so Gyekeny did not mind. But from then on Sholem and Malkeleh talked about certain matters only in whispers, and also expressly en-joined Yossef not to mention Gimpel Zorech's affair in Batiz. The fact that Sholem knew who committed the murder on the Szalka road might bring mortal peril to a highly respected Jewish family.

Those were months of trouble and painful perplexity, and even though the recent weeks had been on the whole uneventful, this quietness was by no means reassuring. The menace still hung over the family's head. It was in Sholem's blood to wait patiently for better times, but this time even he was discontented. When, by straining his faculties, he had discovered who the murderer was, he experienced a great relief. He felt as though his thought was almost an act, and it required only one or two practical steps to make it so. Once that was done, Gimpel Zorech, the family, and the whole of despised, slandered Jewry would stand before the world in all its pristine purity. But he neglected to take those practical steps. He had saved the lease, which had brought more excitement in these days than ever before, he had saved Hersko-vitch, who was no longer afraid of the highwaymen's revenge, but of the law (though he said that he was not aware that he was acting as a receiver); but he had failed in the real task, the saving of his brother and Israel.

The only consolation was that Malkeleh could not reproach him for inactivity, for they had made this decision jointly. But Malkeleh too must be regretting that nothing had happened. She did not say so, but Sholem could see that she was worried. She was irritated by every trifle, kept scolding the children, and also objected to Sholem's smoking in the house. However, so long as she was scolding it was all right, it was worse when she was silent. At such times she would sit over her mending or knitting, worrying and brooding; she was feeling the futility of the strug-gle, and how the family was getting isolated from the world.

Even Yossef came less frequently. The bad roads were no explanation. There had been spring thaws before, and there had been rainstorms in summer and blizzards in winter, yet Yossef used to come home every Friday or at least every other Friday,

eagerly recounting to Malkeleh all that had happened. Nowadays
it was well if he came once in six weeks. And he was more
reserved too, refusing to say what was the matter with him.
"There's nothing the matter with me, Malkeleh," he would say,
"and Zireleh is all right too. He would talk perfunctorily about
remote matters, as that the Candlemakers' Guild in Otvar wanted
to stop Jacob Anshel selling candles in Otvar. This was a heavy
loss to him and Jacob Anshel was presenting petition after petition,
at great expense. Yossef did not mention to Malkeleh that he
wanted to become a partner in the business and that his marriage
depended on it. He made no direct demand to Sholem, either,
but Sholem guessed that he was in need of money. This was a
big worry to Sholem, but until Yossef came with an express request, he would not see the urgency of the matter. He kept postponing it until the Good God should send succor from somewhere. Malkeleh had other suspicions. She knew that old Zissah
had become involved in the affair of the crime and she was afraid
that the Batiz people had also grown cooler. They were still sending rations to the prisoner, but their interest had flagged and
there were some who sent only bread and onions, saying that
that was their own supper for that day.

There had also been a minor scare about Mailech. At the beginning of the autumn it was noted that he was giving no sign
of himself. He had missed coming home for a Sabbath or two
before, but he had written frequently enough. He knew which
market vender from Karoly was passing by the Shingled Inn and
when, and he used to send his notes, scribbled on market leaflets
or wrapping paper, by them. There was not much news in these
notes, but Malkeleh saw filial love in the fact that he sent them.
His mode of address—Dear Father and Mother, may you live an
hundred and twenty years—was touching. She liked to read
again and again that Mailech was well, thank God, and was
hoping his note found them the same, and that he had had his
boots soled and the mud was not getting into them, and that the
cookies he had received were very good and had gone fast.
Sholem too received a line or two in these notes as to what book
of the Talmud was being studied at the *yeshiba*. Sholem used to
comment with mock severity on that "being studied." That

meant by the others, not Mailech. Yet Sholem was glad that Mailech thought of him too.

Now, there were not even notes from Mailech. Strangely, even Yiteleh did not mention him in her letters. Just when Malkeleh began to worry that Mailech might be lying ill at Avram Kolb's house, Kolb himself pulled up at the inn on his way to market and reported that the boy had joined a traveling watchmaker who had been doing business in the town for a time, and was obviously a bad influence on him.

Fortunately, however, the Mailech mystery was soon cleared up. A fortnight before Passover he came home. He was somewhat dirty, but sun-tanned and stronger than before. He submitted to the inevitable scolding quietly, then with the charming smile with which he used to win the confidence even of the suspicious Swabian peasant women in the market, he began to talk about his first big business tour. It was a pity for the family to worry about him, he said. He would not have joined just anybody. His partner had been Simon Dominus, the watchmaker, who was a great respecter of the family. If anyone had to be careful, it was a watchmaker, who carried gold and silver and precious stones in his bag. Dominus wanted someone to go with him because a Swiss manufacturer had sent him nine dozen watches to sell on commission. Simon was a very kind man and this time it was sheer luck for Mailech to be with him. They scarcely had to tramp and traveled mostly by carriage and post-chaise and slept at inns. They traveled through several counties and did good business. There was a lot of paper money about, for the gentry got more for the wheat and the sheep and they were more ready to spend. The whole nine dozen watches were sold in three months. They could have sold them sooner, but Dominus had also done some repairs at the better houses. He, Mailech, received five per cent on every watch sold, and ten per cent on every chain. He had traded in his own wares as well, replenishing his stock in the large towns. He had made a total net profit of sixty-eight florins. He had brought his mother a fine headkerchief and his father an old silver watch that was wound with a key. Dominus had also made a bracelet for Yiteleh out of an old piece of jewelry.

"Shall I give it to her when she gets engaged?" said Mailech. "I think I can give it to her now, can't I?"

"Not yet," said Sholem, his brow clouding. Once upon a time he had money and a lovely idea. The money went, but the idea was left. Now, that too was gone. A few days earlier he had been making tentative inquiries of David Troyes the innkeeper of Batiz, observing, obliquely, that he would like to know Troyes' opinion of Wolf Birnbaum and that he, Sholem, thought that it would be best for Wolf not to interrupt his studies, but continue them in his father-in-law's house. Troyes gave him a look and laughed. If he had not been a descendant of the great Rashi, Sholem would have been disgusted with him for that laugh.

"I agree, Sholem," said Troyes. "I have already seen to it that it should be so. I'm having two rooms built for them in the garden."

"For whom, Reb Moshe Doved?"

"For my daughter Rebecca and her future husband, Wolf."

Sholem did not mention this defeat to Malkeleh, much less to Mailech. However, the boy was not satisfied with his father's curt reply and kept nagging his mother to let him go to Karoly and hand the trinket to his sister. Malkeleh's brow was cloudier still.

"No, my son," she said simply. "Yiteleh can wait."

"But mother, I heard that she and Gadli Brueder—"

"He's not her kind."

THE SCHNORRER'S WIFE

MAILECH WAS struck by his mother's depressed manner, but even more so by the unusual quietness in the house. He soon learned the reason of this: the noisiest child, Yossel Beilah Yenteh's, was gone. The children said he had been taken away by his mother. She came along and quarrelled with mother and father, saying that Yossel belonged to her and that she needed him to help with her work.

"What work?" asked Mailech. "Yossel is barely seven."

The children did not reply, not even Sarah Chayah, who probably knew more than the others.

Mailech returned to Karoly, partly to the *yeshiba*, his father having enjoined upon him to mend his ways, but partly also into Avram Kolb's shop and Mordechai's ink factory. In the Nikolsburger home he was received with mutterings; they thought he would never return. Even the Kolb woman mingled irony with her amiability.

"I was telling Avram that you'd stay with Dominus and learn his trade. Drapery is not high class enough for you."

But Yiteleh, in the shop, fell on his neck. She sat him down beside her, and her teeth kept flashing as she listened to him. Stroking his apparently chillblained hands, she asked:

"How often did you get a beating?"

"Only three times," said Mailech with a wave of the hand. "At Szollos they cried 'Hep! Hep!' But that was nothing. At Ujlak I went into a house. The gentleman was quarrelling with his wife, and he kicked me and spat at me, and shouted: 'Dirty Jew-brat, get out!' Another time a peasant woman attacked me with a stick. She screamed so that people came running along. Fortunately, Dominus was not far away, so I didn't have to run a long time."

"Why did she scream?"

"She said she'd bought a headkerchief last year and it was already going to pieces on her head."

"Did she buy it from you?"

"No, but the person she bought it from was also Jewish." Mailech considered it quite natural to be beaten because he was a Jew, and to be beaten for the fault of another Jew. But noting the scared expression on his sister's face, he added:

"Don't worry, I sell honest goods. They won't beat anyone on account of me."

"I'm not afraid for you," said the girl. "You can stand on your own feet—and you can run as well."

Mailech was glad of the opportunity of having a talk with his sister. He could tell her everything, even what he had to suppress at home. He was flattered, too, that Yiteleh should admire his cleverness.

"If you need money," he said grandly, "I can let you have some."

Yiteleh's face dimpled.

"How much would you give me?"

"Is ten florins enough?"

Yiteleh shook her head.

"I've got that much myself. You think I don't earn? We've enlarged the shop. Now we sell ink and paper as well. I get a commission. You see that freshly planed shelf? That's where the new goods are."

"I can give you more if you need it."

"What do I want money for?"

"If you get engaged."

"I don't want to be engaged," she said earnestly, almost dryly, the smile vanishing from her face.

She sent Mailech away and went behind the counter to relieve Moysheh.

Mailech was already a big boy, over thirteen and independent, but he was still too much of a child to be told everything. He would soon learn about things, for he kept his eyes and ears open. On the Tuesday, when he turned up again at the house of Joshua Brueder for his meals, the beautiful Aunt Roza, who, being Joshua's second wife, was twenty years younger than he, extended her hand reluctantly to be kissed. By then Mailech had got accustomed to being scolded for his unannounced absences and returns, but this lady said nothing, only compressed her lips and that was worse. The host had also lost his old cheeriness. At other times he used to ask where Mailech had been and what he had been doing and how much he made, and the boy had to tell him everything in detail. Now he observed morosely that he had offered a day's meals to a *yeshiba* pupil, but not to a peddler boy. Mailech replied penitently that now he was going to study again. But this did not help and the atmosphere at table remained chilly. Even the younger children did not chatter. In the evening they put his supper out in the kitchen: bread and left-over cabbage. Old Bruche was more talkative than the family.

"Mailech, is that beggar woman who came here with her little boy your aunt?"

"What beggar woman?"

"She showed us her little boy and cried, saying this was the Yossel whose father was in prison."

Mailech now realized why he had not enjoyed his dinner and why the stuffed cabbage, though warmed up, tasted even worse than it did at midday. He learned a thing or two more from old Bruche. The lady of the house was a genuine Purjes girl and she had to be careful about whom the other members of the family married. And it would harm Joshua Brueder as well if his son Gadli made an unwise choice.

Before Mailech had gone away with Dominus the situation was very different. Frau Joshua Brueder, Aunt Blimeleh, and Frau Philip Rooz had discussed everything concerning trousseau and the dowry that Uncle Mordechai was giving out of the profits that Yiteleh had helped him earn. They had even fixed the date of the wedding: the thirty-third day of the vernal *omer* count, two weeks before the Jewish Pentecost. The standing of the bridegroom-to-be had been raised by the fact that his father had taken him into his corn business, the style of the firm being changed to "Joshua Brueder & his Son Gedeon." The charming, light-hearted and deeply enamored Gadli seemed to realize what he owed to Gedeon Brueder, and underwent a great change, becoming more serious and self-respecting. That was evident on the very first Thursday evening after his elevation when, at the usual weekly meeting of young people in the *salon* of Mme Rooz, Gadli appeared in a brand new suit. He had an idea that Yiteleh was looking at him with different eyes now, whereas up till then she treated him merely as a pal, sometimes with a trace of superiority; and he was aware that other girls of good family in the town were beginning to envy Yiteleh on his account.

All these calculations and plans had quickly withered away. Beilah Yenteh passed through Karoly with her boy, called at every house in the Jewish quarter, told a pathetic story about her husband's misfortune, and extended her bony hand for alms, taking a good look at the amount. That she herself had started the calamity with the knobby stick that she had cut for Gimpel

Zorech, of that she said not a word. Nor was this necessary. The people thought of the brother who lay in the filth of the county jail, and being unable to help him, they relieved their consciences by helping his family. Every one of them gave the woman alms, from Mechl the bootmaker up to the rich and prominent Lebl, and down again to the poverty-stricken synagogue beadle. The pious Abraham Roth went so far as to offer Gimpel Zorech's wife a room and kitchen in his house, which he held on lease from the Counts Karolyi, while Mme Rooz, on behalf of the women of the congregation, offered her full board until her husband was released. But by the following morning Beilah Yenteh had vanished from the hospitable house of Abraham Roth. It suited her better to be on the road, besides which she was in a hurry in case the people managed to get Gimpel Zorech released soon. She was now roaming round all the neighboring counties and spreading the family's shame everywhere. People again became conscious that Yiteleh on the paternal side was descended from tramps and schnorrers.

Yiteleh held herself heroically, endeavoring to console herself with the thought that Gadli Brueder was nearer to the hearts of her Aunt Blimeleh and Mme Rooz than to her own. She had been reluctant to enter into the engagement, saying that she could wait until she found someone she really loved. But in the end she had yielded to persuasion, which was of the same kind in the *salon* of Mme Rooz as in the house of old Seemah: that a marriage where the parties came to love each other gradually was better than one that is started with love, love being liable to cool. Gadli's admiration of her was of no great value when there were boys of greater worth swarming round her, as Shayeh and Wolf. But Shayeh had gone back to Vienna, and shortly after, Wolf had also returned to Pressburg to be near his debating partner. Wolf never wrote to Yiteleh, only Shayeh kept writing her droll yet melancholy letters.

She needed those letters; they kept her spirits up in the time of her humiliation. But as the letters came at intervals of four or five weeks, and as in any case she was not of a passive temperament, she sought comfort and compensation in other directions as well. There were one or two busy days in the leather shop, but otherwise the week passed rather somnolently. She tried needle-work, but that was no solution, for she only brooded and fretted the while. With the aid of Moysheh, she rearranged the stock and also carried out a fresh stock-taking. But that was soon over. She next suggested to her uncle, who spent most of his time on buying tours, to reserve a corner of the shop for ink; and once there was ink, it was necessary to have paper as well. Ordinary paper was easy to obtain from the new mills in a nearby locality, while the finer writing-paper to which the gentry were accustomed was obtained from farther afield. The shop also stocked pounce boxes in all the colors of the rainbow and also quills and pencils. The servants and haiduks of the county hall, the guardians, the manor court, the customs office and the salt-tax office soon got used to the shop in the market square, and sometimes an official would also look in. One morning de Kölcsey, the worshipful County Deputy himself, came in to buy something and had a long talk with Yiteleh. He liked this alert Jew girl and even remarked, in the presence of her uncle, that if all Jews were like him and his niece it would be all right. Unfortunately, however, there was a great influx from Galicia. The Galicians engaged in usury, distilled spirits, and were stultifying and debasing the peasantry with drink. Markus Nikolsburger was very flattered by this august praise, but Yiteleh thought of her father in Lapfalva and began to feel ashamed of his business.

Yiteleh was backed up by her uncle throughout, though he too had suffered through her family's disgrace. He was about to be elected President of the congregation, an honor to which he was entitled by birth and status, when Beilah Yenteh turned up. And as the elections took place soon after, he lost this honor to Jacob Lebl and had difficulty in retaining even the Vice-Presidency. But he never made Yiteleh feel this. He went on talking about her as "my daughter" and viewed her with the same affection as before. Perhaps because she was as active as only the male Nikolsburgers used to be and he had no son, Mordechai loved Yiteleh even better than his own daughters—or perhaps he only loved her in a different way. His own daughters he continually reproved and criticized, but in Yiteleh he found nothing to reprove. It was true that his own daughters were only spending his money, whereas Yiteleh was helping to increase his prosperity. But that did not appear to be the only reason. Yiteleh was Malkeleh's daughter, and Malkeleh had been the youngest and most beautiful of his sisters.

Gadli Brueder fell away, but he was soon replaced by other boys, including Zelig Adler, whom his friends called Felix, and Isaac Hoenig, who called himself Ignats. Felix and Ignats were bosom friends, and always paid court to the same girl, and this time it was Yiteleh. The two boys had read a little, and they brought her books. One day Felix brought along the poems of Uhland, but Yiteleh returned it, saying that she was already reading Heine. Whereupon the more modest Ignats recommended to her a certain Hungarian book he had at home, and Felix shut him up, saying that she was not old enough for that sort of book. One of their usual quarrels ensued, which were perhaps only stage-managed for her amusement when their witticisms gave out. The two boys reminded her of Shayeh and Wolf. But how puny they were by comparison.

One thing that reflected on Yiteleh—and it was discussed more than once in Mme Rooz's *salon*—was the fact that she was the recipient of attentions from non-Jewish young men as well. The most persistent was Adam de Sarberek, who had a small clerkship at the county hall. When he grew tired of pen-pushing, he looked into the Nikolsburger shop. More than once, he chucked Yiteleh under the chin, only to get his hand slapped. Once, when the shop was empty of customers, he put his arms round her and bent over her. Yiteleh pushed him away and slapped his face resoundingly. Moysheh, who was sitting in a dark corner fingering his beard, was petrified to see a Jewish girl strike a gentry boy. But Yiteleh did not seem to care about the consequences.

"And now get out, young man," she snapped. "And don't come again."

Nothing happened. The young man was not even offended. Three days later he came again, but behaved very correctly. He bought a pounce box and a few sheets of paper, said a few amiable words, and raised his hat as he left.

This incident could be mentioned only in whispers, but it was mentioned in the Rooz *salon*. This was something to restore

Yiteleh's standing somewhat. Even Gadli began to smile at her again, anticipating a response; but Yiteleh did not smile back. She was angry with him for his cowardice. He had failed to stand by her and had, a day or two before the date of the official engagement, deserted her, though he was allegedly in love with her. In all probability, Gadli was really in love with Yiteleh and stayed love-sick for a long time. Whereas he dared not resist his parents and public opinion, he was little use in the business now, despite his partnership. He used to loiter for hours near the shop waiting for Yiteleh to close it, then he would follow her from afar like a remote shadow. In his more courageous moments he would pace up and down in front of the shop, struggling with himself whether he should not go in. He waited for a look or a word from Yiteleh. That one word would have kindled his revolutionary spirit and made him shake his fist at the world. But Yiteleh did not say it, did not even leave the shop door open. She would have liked the young man to come in of his own accord and do his fist-shaking spontaneously. She missed Gadli and sometimes she thought she was in love with him. But when she knew that he was loitering outside she did not go near the glass door, but either attended to the customers, or when there were none, she counted the expensive bits of morocco over and over again with the aid of Moysheh. Moysheh seemed to have got tired of the continual stock-taking, or perhaps he was upset to see Yiteleh grieve over the fickle Gadli. Whatever it was, Moysheh one spring morning jerked the door open and barked out at Gadli, who was again loitering nearby:

"This is no promenade, young fellow. If you want to take the air, go where your uncle Leibish keeps his pigs."

Gadli winced. At first he thought Moysheh was acting on instructions, but his rage and his rudeness argued against that.

"I am not taking the air here," he stammered, unable to think of anything else to say.

"No," cried Moysheh, "only measuring the side-walk."

"None of your business what I do," said Gadli, recovering his wits somewhat. "I do as I like."

"You don't, young man, you don't. You do what your papa

likes. And your papa does what your proud step-mamma likes.
Your mother was a good woman, God rest her soul."

Gadli did not reply to this, but reverted to his uncle's pigs.

"Uncle Leibish hasn't got any pigs."

"No?" laughed Moysheh, "I suppose Leibish deals only in
kosher cattle, what? Why, everyone knows that he's fattening
seven hundred pigs down-town, even if they're in the Armenian's
name. It's good business, of course. And your father supplies the
wheat for the Passover flour. A fine family, I don't think!"

"What's my family got to do with you?" cried Gadli in consternation. "You . . . you gutter-snipe."

"What business, eh?" cried Moysheh. "Well, I, the gutter-
snipe Moysheh, say that there's more of the gutter about your
family than me. Just because you have more money? And because
your papa is leasing a flour mill? Money and the flour business
are not everything. A poor Jew's been put in jail and so Yiteleh's
not good enough for you? You'd be damn lucky if we let her
marry you. But we won't. You'll tear your hair yet, fathead!"
As Gadli was sidling away, Moysheh called after him. "And next
time you come this way, just come in and get yourself some ink
and paper to write to your rich fiancée, that Fischbein girl in
Szalka."

Yiteleh had heard it all and she was shaking all over. When
Moysheh had closed the door she turned on him vehemently:

"How could you say such things! How could you!"

"I had to tell him," muttered Moysheh. "If everyone hold their
tongues, someone must speak out. There's such a thing as honor."

He saw that Yiteleh was angry with him, so he returned to
his corner, sat down and hung his head. Then Yiteleh was in
front of him, giving a caress to his beard and saying:

"Moysheh, you're a dear."

The man's mouth opened wide, revealing his broken teeth, and
there were tears and laughter in his eyes.

### THE TWO FIDDLERS

ON THE second Saturday of Passover week the two sons of the fiddler from Sziget sang in the synagogue at Karoly. This was a trial. The community's reader had grown too old and the younger element in the vestry wanted a cantor to take his place. Being more than a century old, and comprising six hundred souls, the community could afford to keep a cantor, yet it was only after impassioned debate that the plan was agreed to. The older people were so accustomed to the voice of Reader Chunah that they scarcely noticed its progressive deterioration, but the more active members of the younger generation, who had travelled on business all over the country, and had heard even the famous Sulzer in Vienna and Denhof in Pest, found the old man's croakings and groanings and toothless mumbling intolerable. There was quite a row concerning the financial aspect, the Treasurer though in sympathy with the younger set, opposing the dismissal of old Chunah on the score of an unbalanced budget. The old man was also the ritual slaughterer, and as he had no more young children, he was content with a small salary. But in the end the younger generation prevailed, and while the question of funds for a cantor's salary was not settled, sufficient money was provided to invite one or two candidates for the cantorship.

The appearance of the two fiddler boys was an event in Karoly. On the Friday evening the synagogue, which had been converted from a granary of the Count's, was crowded to the doors. Even the women's gallery was full, though at other times the women-folk did not attend the Friday evening service, but awaited the return of the menfolk by the festive table. There were as many candles burning in the wooden candelabra hanging from the ceiling as on the big autumn holy days. As the two slim young men in their rustling caftans, with silken prayer shawls on their shoulders, and black skull-caps on their heads, mounted the dais, the candles dipped their blue-red flames, not under a mystic force, but under the breeze of a mass sigh from the women's gallery.

The elder fiddler boy wore a small dark beard, the younger's face was almost bare, but for a pair of downy side-whiskers beneath smoothly pendent ear fringes. How different was this "Come, let us sing to the Lord!" And how much life and color and nuptial emotion there was in the welcome to Sabbath the Bride!

"*Come, my friend, let us welcome*
*The lovely Bride. . . .*"

The day service on the morrow only intensified the enchantment, though the weather was unpleasant, with sleet drumming on the windows, and with only the three candles over the reader's desk to relieve the dimness of the interior. On Sunday the community were only debating which of the two young men was to be engaged. The object of having them on the same day was to simplify matters, but now it was found that it had only complicated them. Jerucham's bass-baritone and his little beard raised him to a more solid plane, but Amram Hersh's tenor was the more seductive. They went on debating on Monday and Tuesday. Then Lebl, the President, called an urgent vestry meeting for Thursday. They debated the matter till late at night, but failed to reach a decision, except to hear both candidates again the following Saturday. Both Jerucham and Amram Hersh came out with brand-new tunes, singing Aramaic songs with a rhythm of abandon, the kind they sang in Polish *chassidic* synagogues, thereby converting to their side even the extreme Right. On Saturday morning, and with a view to this same extreme Right, they settled on the little beard and the bass-baritone. But the service was still going on, so no formal decision was made.

The final word was said by Rabbi Isaac Frenkel who, after the Scrolls were taken from the tabernacle, and contrary to any pre-determined program, mounted the dais. He began quietly, but went on with increasing warmth, expressing his pleasure that the women and even the young girls were now attending the House of God, and even on Friday evening, whereas formerly only one or two pious old ladies used to come on Fridays. It was gratifying to see that the young daughters of Israel were attracted not only by the spinets and pianos of the drawing-room, but also by the ancient melodies of the synagogue. However, one could not overlook the fact that a murmur of approval had been heard from the gallery, and once even something like applause. The synagogue was not a theatre, but the House of Jacob. Here one had to behave differently both in the auditorium and on the dais. No doubt, there were attractive young men with pale hands and long fingers that looked striking when they were playing the violin. But the violin, even an imaginary one, had no part in the singing of synagogue hymns and other portions of the liturgy. Perhaps it would have a part when the Temple was rebuilt and we would take up the fiddle of King David again. But at present we were in the *galuth*. The singers of the exiled people must not finger their beards, or their ear fringes, must not let their hands float in the air, but must think only of the sacred text and of the saying of Koheleth: "All is vanity." Our women must think of that, too. It was shocking—and the more pious women-folk had in fact been shocked—to see girls laughing in the gallery and some women arrive at the synagogue as if at a wedding banquet. He had also heard, though it was scarcely credible to him, that women who called themselves Jewish came, not with a headkerchief or a lace bonnet, but with a hat on their heads. One hat even had a plume torn from the tail of some African bird.

The speech had a crushing effect. The *mussaph*, the concluding part of the service, was read by old Chunah, in a toothless, colorless chant, with the croaky triumph of a senile general who, thanks to adventitious aid, had remained master of the battlefield. Old Chunah behaved decorously, not letting his hands float in the air, lest the gallery should look. But the gallery did not look. Instead, it emptied itself in a rush. The ground floor also emptied, though more slowly, until only a few determined old people were left. This was not a demonstration against the Rabbi, but how could anyone bear the impact of old Chunah's bawlings and croakings after the beautiful voices of the fiddler boys!

On Sunday the two young men packed their bags, but could not obtain a cart to take them away. On Monday they missed the mail-coach for Tokay. It was said that they had missed it deliberately because in the meantime they had received invitations to three other localities and negotiations were still going on as

to whether they should go singly, as they desired on the basis
of their experience in Karoly. They had also been invited to Mme
Rooz's at home for the Thursday. It turned out that the repertoire
of the *marshalik's* sons was not confined to sacred music, and it
further came out that the younger one had certain ambitions and
would only become a cantor temporarily, for financial reasons.
The invitation was a challenge to the Rabbi on the part of Mme
Rooz, but she could venture such a challenge, for the Roozes
and the Oesterreichers (she being née Oesterreicher) were among
the first Jews to come to Karoly a century before, whereas the
Rabbi had been in the town barely a decade. Besides, the challenge
had really come from the Rabbi, for everyone knew that the
woman who had gone to synagogue with an ostrich-plumed hat
was none other than Mme Rooz, Jr., the silk and velvet merchant's wife.

If the appearance of the two young men at the synagogue was
an event, their forthcoming appearance at the Rooz *salon* promised
to be something of a sensation and roused excited anticipation.
On the intervening afternoons, Mme Rooz herself sat at the piano,
rehearsing with Amram Hersh, whose name had been modernized
to Amram Hirsch. Mme Rooz was close on forty, but looked no
older than thirty. She was no beauty, but having had no children,
she had been able to keep her figure. The older generation called
her Edeleh, but she hated this ghetto name and preferred to be
called Adèle. She felt that the French version of the name would
give her a certain distinction. However, the Jews of Karoly were
unable to say it without embarrassment and if they dropped
Edeleh, they did not take to Adèle either, and Mme Rooz had
to be content with the Hungarian version—Adel.

Mme Rooz always had one or two adopted children in the
house. She had already married off two adopted daughters, one
to Pest, the other to Kismarton. She was a passionate matchmaker
and if she came across two young people who were attracted to
each other she would not rest until she had brought them together. Her Thursday at home was only a means to that end.
She had other hobbies too, which her husband's family called
eccentricities, while the Rabbi and the conservative portion of the
community regarded them as sins: she was endeavoring, by her

example, as well as by persuasion and material inducements to deflect the young people from the path of tradition. It was attributed to her influence that Shayeh, her nephew, and a descendant of an old rabbinical dynasty, did not go to the *yeshiba*, but to Grammar School and thence to foreign Universities, from which he could no longer escape. Even more serious were the cases where Mme Rooz had taken young men right out of the *yeshiba* by attracting their attention to the possibilities of a secular education. Zelig Adler and Ignats Hoenig were two shocking examples. With Mme Rooz's encouragement and financial support, they bought books and sat for examinations at the Roman Catholic Grammar School. For a time it could be kept secret, but now it was known that the Adler boy was qualifying at the Roman Catholic teachers' college, while the Hoenig boy, who had also started as a pious *bocher*, was preparing to enter the Medical Faculty at Pest University.

No gossip or intrigue could deflect this little brunette from the task she had set herself. Her husband sometimes took her with him on his business tours to Pest, Prague, Brunn and Vienna, thinking that this would satisfy her craving for movement and activity. But all it did was to enable her to learn about the latest fashion, and pick up a few new books and musical scores, and inject fresh life into the somnolent little town through her own at homes. She liked to sing and was gratified by applause, but it pleased her even more if she discovered a goodish voice among her "children." Yiteleh had brought with her from the Shingled Inn a pleasing voice and a fair musical sense, though it took some time before she got over the influence of the peasant songs and ballads and was able to sing with the right grasp such songs as "Oh selig ein Kind noch zu sein!" from Weber's opera, *Zar und Zimmermann*.

However, the impending event surpassed everything that had been done before. Amram Hersh sang, not synagogue hymns but songs by Mozart and Beethoven and above all by Schubert, who had just then, two years after his death, come into vogue. Rehearsing with him, Mme Adèle Rooz pulled down the venetian blinds on her windows, lest the sounds of the phenomenal tenor should dart out into the streets and the people should learn prematurely what was in store. She thought with happy excitement of her discovery—she, Mme Adèle Rooz, in her little drawing-room, was launching a young man with a God-given talent. She rehearsed with the singer from afternoon till late at night, and also strained every nerve to make sure that the arrangements for the *soirée* should be just so. She had to see that there should be room for more than the usual number of visitors, for she intended to invite the music-loving ladies and gentlemen of the county, the Lord Sheriff, the Under Sheriff, the Deputy and, above all, the patron of the Karoly Jews, the Count and his family.

Jerucham, the elder brother, had scarcely any part in the program. He had rehearsed with Hersh a duet from Kreutzer's *Night Camp in Granada*, but this was only to be held in reserve as an encore. Jerucham was glad that he did not have to participate in the exhausting rehearsals, for the foreign texts and melodies did not accord with his mentality and musical interest. Jerucham had no concert or stage ambitions; his ambition lay in tradition, in a cantorship with some prominent community. This was the haven of his dreams where he would settle and found a family. It was here in Karoly that the dream had become a conscious wish. In view of the community's hesitancy after the first Saturday he had been in a hurry to leave, feeling that this was not the right sphere for him. But now he was glad he had stayed. He had met Yiteleh, and now he knew why and on whose account he had stayed, and why he must find a haven as soon as possible.

He knew from the first that he had seen Yiteleh somewhere before. True, this feeling is characteristic of all great and decisive encounters. But Jerucham had indeed seen the girl, even though only for a brief hour, and when she was barely ten years old. He had long forgotten the incident, but Yiteleh recalled the time when the feather merchant from Hodasz came along with Goldah and the Sziget *marshalik* and his sons, whom the peasant boys called "Jewish gypsies."

"It was very nice," she said to Jerucham. "It was a day of gaiety in Lapfalva. The sleigh ran into the yard with bells tinkling and you people were playing and singing.

"I remember you also sang our family song."

Jerucham gazed at her dimpled face and her bright eyes and tried to remember.

"Sorry, but I can't recall. What was the song? How did it go?"

Yiteleh smiled and hummed the opening words of the song: 'Yah ribbohn olam.'

"Ah!" cried Jerucham, his face lighting up. "I remember now. My father is a great funster. He struck up the tune when he found out that your mother's name was Malkah and your little brother's, Mailech."

Yiteleh laughed teasingly: "We called it our family song because it has even the name of Sroleh Yomtov in it."

Jerucham seemed puzzled: "Where does Sroleh Yomtov come in?"

"You see, Sroleh Yomtov's name is Anti in Hungarian, that's how the peasants called him," explained the girl.

"And who is Sroleh Yomtov?"

"My stepbrother."

"Ah! That sulky boy. He looked a big blockhead."

"You're mistaken," said the girl. "Sroleh Yomtov was no blockhead. On the contrary."

"The whole family was singing by the *Chanukah* lights, but he just kept pursing his lips and was silent."

"A boy isn't a blockhead just because he is silent. He didn't sing because his voice was not so good as yours or your brother's. He preferred to enjoy your singing, and not to spoil other people's enjoyment by his own singing."

Jerucham gave in. He looked round in the leather shop, then, quietly, he began to hum the Aramaic song:

"*Yah ribbohn olam vah-olmah-yah
Ant-he, malkah, mailech malkah-ya. . . .*"

"That was it!" cried Yiteleh, clapping her hands.

"Let me translate it for you," said the young man.

"No need, Jerucham. If you say the words distinctly, I understand them myself. 'Oh Lord of the world of worlds, Thou art majesty, King of Kings. . . .'"

"You understand Aramaic?"

"Why not? When my father taught me the Pentateuch, we used to read the *Targum* Onkelos besides the Rashi."

"You know who *Targum* was, too?"

"No one knows that. They say Onkelos was the nephew of the Emperor Titus, who was converted to Judaism and translated the Bible into Aramaic."

"Well, I never!" marvelled the young man.

Yiteleh had no notion that she was starting trouble. The *soirée* on Thursday was a brilliant success from the first item as far as the last. But the last constituted a flaw in the production. Amram Hersh, his somewhat abbreviated ear fringes combed into his incipient side-whiskers, stood by the piano, looking even slimmer in a befrogged jacket (Heaven only knew where he had borrowed it!) than he did in a caftan. He sang the Heiderösslein, the Loreley the Wanderer, and Schubert's Serenade. The audience in the two rooms (the door of the dining-room having been removed) applauded with rapture. The crowd in the street also applauded, but they did not count. Indeed, even the usual visitors of the at home, who occupied the dining-room, did not count. The important people sat in the first two rows. There was Fräulein van der Huden, piano teacher of the Karolyi girls, then Ambrus Muzsaly, the Burgomaster, then Nyeky, a clerk at the Under Sheriff's office representing his chief, then Miss Antonia Kölcsey, the pale and refined niece of the Deputy, whose applause reflected both refinement and admiration.

The second part of the program was received with undiminished interest and no one left after the refreshments. On the contrary, there were some newcomers, including Cili Rothbart, who apologized for being late and said they had had a visitor, a dear friend, by the mail-coach from Tokay. The success of the evening seemed to mount. Amram Hersh sang Mozart "like an angel." Miriam Nikolsburger said this to Master Adam de Sarberek, who had attached himself to her during the interval and had been paying court to her since. Before the interval she stood by the piano turning the pages of the music. In her apple-green silk frock, and flushed with the warmth of the candles and with artistic enjoyment, she was quite pretty. Later her place at the piano was occupied for a time by Yiteleh. Miriam had an understanding for music, having studied the piano for seven years. But Yiteleh, too, was already able to read music. And although she was wearing only a blue cloth frock with a lace collar, she looked very attractive.

If only the last item had been omitted! Mme Adèle Rooz was not to blame for anything. A moment before it started she was radiantly acknowledging the applause, and when she sat down to the piano again she took it for granted that the next item was the duet of the two brothers. If she had guessed that the duet was not to be the one from *Night Camp in Granada* . . . As she raised her hands, and with them her fashionable leg-of-mutton sleeves, to strike the keys, and Jerucham stopped her with an impatient gesture, Adèle sensed that there was something wrong. But it was already too late. Jerucham began to sing with the wildest abandon, skipping in front of Yiteleh and clapping his hands with an alternating rhythm, and Amram Hersh, too, was carried away, so that his combed-down ear fringes came loose from his mutton-chops and began to fly in the air. Yiteleh had been busy trimming the candles, but now she dropped the trimmer into the brass bottom of the candlestick and stood listening wide-eyed and with slightly parted lips to her mother's song, which the two young men now appeared to be singing in her honor.

> *"Yah ribbohn olam vah-olmah-yah*
> *Ant-he, malkah, mailech malkah-ya. . . ."*

A scared frown appeared over Mme Rooz's otherwise smiling eyes. It was a disgrace, almost a scandal, that these two should treat the Christian notabilities, contrary to the program and without notice, to this Lithuanian-Russian-Yiddish song, whereas the earlier parts of the program pointed to the conclusion that the younger generation of Karoly Jews was receptive to a higher musical culture. It was fortunate, though, that discipline was not relaxed and no one left their seats amid the *chassidic* abandon, nor did any of the usual visitors signify their disapproval by hissing or in any other way. This must have been due to the frown on the hostess's brow. At all events, the audience was quiet, almost stunned.

There was a murmur that might have been interpreted as a

murmur of approval. But it originated not in the room where the singers were, nor yet in the second room with its second-class audience, but in the street. The pious students of the *yeshiba*, whom Mme Adèle had forgotten to invite, were walking there, and the community's ultra-orthodox members, including some Galicians, were loitering there, just as if they had business at that late hour in front of Mme Rooz's house. They had already got over their indignation that the voices that belonged to "Come, my friend, let us welcome the Bride" and "Come, let us sing to the Lord," were being used to sing "Liebchen, komm zu mir" and "Dein ist mein Herz, dein ist mein Herz." The only reason they had not gone away was that they wanted to enjoy their indignation to the limit. They would not forget or forgive anything they had heard, but while listening to "Yah ribbohn olam," they set their anger aside and enjoyed the two divine voices. Some even accompanied the singing with rhythmic clapping and the stamping of their feet.

One need take no notice of the street. The crowd was composed of market vendors, touts, peddlers, bootmakers, glaziers, ragmen, *batlanim*, and *bochers*, who never had any manners. What was strange and at first even alarming was the fact that the Christian notables were also applauding the performance. What was this but irony cloaked in courtesy? It was both painful and offensive. It was even more painful when Fräulein van der Huden said that this "thoroughly Eastern song" was most intriguing. Miss Antonia Kölcsey nodded agreement, while the Burgomaster observed that those bitter-sweet Hebrew whoops would go well on the bagpipes and the clarinet. The opinion of the Under Sheriff's clerk was even more crushing. He confessed that he had enjoyed the incomprehensible song far more than the German songs. Mme Rooz blushed and thought of Amram Hersh's Yiddish pronunciation of German, which she had not had the time to correct. Yet that was not what Master Nyeky meant. He was a sworn partisan of the national tongue, and the German language, together with everything else that came from Vienna, even the music of Beethoven, Mozart, or Schubert, offended his patriotic sensibilities.

However, strangest of all was the observation of Master Adam

de Sarberek. He thought that the performers had been singing in
Hungarian, and it was only owing to the stamping and clapping
and whooping that he could not comprehend the words. Felix
Adler, with his tongue in his cheek, explained that the Aramaic
language was a dialect of the Magyar language, spoken in Asia
Minor, or to be precise, along the Euphrates. Master Adam was
pleased with this explanation and ordered an encore, just as if
he were in the Shingled Inn, ordering the gypsy to replay a Magyar tune.

"Encore, boys!" he cried. And the cry was taken up by the
whole front row, spreading throughout both rooms. The frown
disappeared from Adèle's brow and there was an uncertain smile
playing round her narrow lips. She nodded to Jerucham per-
missively.

The two young men burst forth again, accompanied by a hundred voices outside. But soon the visible chorus also joined in.
Master Adam clapped his hands in the Jewish way, alternately
downward and upward, over his head, as he had seen from the
singers, while Master Nyeky was stamping his feet and His Worship the Burgomaster kept whoopee-ing, and even Fräulein van
der Huden and Miss de Kölcsey were clapping their delicate
hands. In view of all this, what could one expect from the casual
visitors of the backroom? They too joined in with gusto, whoopee-
ing, clapping their hands, stamping their feet, and singing with a
vociferous abandon which showed that none but the wall divided
them from the street, and that they were not yet ripe for higher
musical enjoyment.

The whole house was an almost palpable mass of thunderous
sound, a frenzied vociferation of a crowd of people carried away
by the *chassidic* abandon of the *marshalik's* boys. Even Mme
Adèle's lips seemed to be moving.

The only one that took no part in this orgy of gaiety was
Yiteleh. There were strong emotions at work within her, but her
lips did not even quiver. She seemed rooted to the spot, her arms
hung limply, heavily. As she looked at Jerucham's glittering eyes
and Amram's fluttering ear fringes, she felt as though she were
being moved far, far away from this strange world. She saw the
droll face of the *marshalik* with his goatee, saw him playing the

violin and singing, while his two young boys were singing and clapping their hands, and Zisseh the feather merchant was singing and dancing, and all the rest, her father, mother, Goldeleh, Aunt Feigah, Yossef, and Mailech, stood round the *Chanukah* lights, singing in chorus. Only one of those present did not sing, but stood with compressed lips, uttering no sound. Why was he silent? Because he—Sroleh Yomtov—had been silent since the beginning of time.

The thought startled her out of her reverie and frightened her a little. What made her think of that scene of long ago and of that sulky boy? She looked across to the next room, at the singing, swaying, vociferous crowd. There was one there, too, that was not singing: a strange young man with a brown beard standing by the door with a coat over his arm and his hat in his hand. He was gazing into the drawing-room with a keen eye, perhaps straight at Yiteleh. Yiteleh saw his mouth, his hooked nose, his high forehead with a scar on it. Bounding away from the piano, she burst through the crowd of singing people, knocking against Miss Antonia and tilting Fräulein van der Huden's hat with her shoulder without even thinking of an apology. She was already at the door, panting, as though she had run a long way.

"Sroleh Yomtov!" she cried in a strangled voice.

The strange young man smiled and extended his hand.

The others went on singing and clapping their hands. None noticed that something had happened.

### YITELEH AND SROLEH YOMTOV

THE GIRL talked, the young man sat listening in front of the counter. It was Friday, a weekly market day, and the bootmakers were at their stalls in the market square and there were scarcely any customers in the leather shop, but for one or two that came for stationery, and they could be served by Moysheh. It was eight years and more since Sroleh Yomtov had run away, and so many things had happened in the meantime, that one day was not long enough to recount it all. Besides, one did not remember every detail, though Sroleh Yomtov was interested even in apparently insignificant trifles.

"Go on, Yiteleh," he would prompt.

Yiteleh went on telling him. About the little boys and the big sorrows, about her father's worries, her mother's anxieties and griefs, about what happened to the family and to the inn, about the fire and the flight with the seven children and the return with eight, about the rebuilding of the house, the new hopes and the new disappointments. She felt that she must not suppress anything, nor understate or overstate anything, but must tell Sroleh Yomtov everything that had happened the way she herself had seen or heard it. She was pleased to have the opportunity to go over her own and the family's past. Gathering together the scattered happenings, seizing on elusive memories, passing over points of time, then retracing her steps, she felt, at first vaguely, then with the certitude of discovery, that there was a pattern, a destiny about it all. Sometimes she talked as though she was giving an account to herself alone, trying to fit things into a pattern. And as her mind worked on the material, sometimes with a febrile agitation, she was amazed to realize that nothing had happened without cause and that there was a logical thread throughout, so that even the presumed accidents emerged from solid causes and happened because they had to happen. The Good God wanted it so, Sholem would have said. But Yiteleh, though she had her faith, now felt that events had been determined, to an extent, by human intentions, volitions, and actions.

There was, for example, Gimpel Zorech, who had already caused so much trouble to the family. He had been unhappy, having been driven from home by an unloving wife, so he became a schnorrer and went to seed. He tramped the roads, drank, and behaved crazily. The family had to look after him when he turned up, but Malkeleh had been worried about him when he did not. It was only now that Yiteleh began to understand this. The rest of the world was not concerned where Gimpel Zorech was heading for. Well, he had been heading for jail. No one believed that the unfortunate wretch was guilty, but he was in jail and that was quite enough. Beilah Yenteh called on Malkeleh and demanded her

son back. Malkeleh would not part with him, because she wanted
to bring Yossel up to be a decent man. She had an idea what sort
of "work" Beilah Yenteh wanted him for. But the woman cried
and screamed until the whole village came running along. Yossel
was her son, not Malkah's. Malkah had eight children, what did
she want a ninth for? In the end, Malkeleh had to let her have her
son. It was a sad thing that Yossel was pleased to go with her.
Blood was thicker than water.

Yiteleh felt it was queer to see a Sroleh Yomtov with broad
shoulders and a beard, when but yesterday he was a lanky youth
with a smooth face. But she soon got used to him. She applied his
dimensions to herself, realizing at last the meaning of other
people's surprise that she had grown up. She now felt it in her
own voice and in her manner of speaking. And the things that
came into her mind!

"If anyone had told me a year ago that Gimpel Zorech's drinking would give me a headache, or that if Beilah Yenteh went begging in seven counties I'd have to pay for it, I should have
laughed in their faces. It would have seemed so unreasonable and
unjust. Today I'm not laughing. It was not unreasonable because
it has happened, and it's not so unjust either. I can't stand aside
and say that my uncle and aunt and their child are nothing to me,
that I don't care if they live like gypsies because I'm a respectable
Jewish girl. I've had friends here too, including Aunt Adel. She
did everything she could, trying to explain to people that Sholem
was not Gimpel Zorech, and that my mother was after all a Nikolsburger. They were beginning to realize that she was right. But I
wouldn't. I can't detach myself from my father because Gimpel
Zorech is his brother. And I couldn't disown Gimpel Zorech himself either, just because he was unfortunate and in trouble. We are
one family and if any member is in trouble the rest must take
their share. It is not possible for any of them to stand aside and be
happy while any other is in tears. A member that brings disgrace
on the family is like one that gets recklessly into debt: the family
must work harder to pay the debts."

The young man listened to the girl's earnest voice, gazed at her
lips and eyes, then, suddenly, he asked:

"Were you in love with Gadli?"

The girl gave him an interrogative glance.

"I think I was fond of him," she said hesitantly.

"What about him?"

"He said he loved me. He's still saying it to others. He's waiting for me to say a word."

"Well?"

"I'm not going to. If he really loved me, he would understand. But all he says is that the Brueder family are so-and-so, and the Adler family—his mother was an Adler—are such-and-such. That's nothing to me. My father is Sholem the innkeeper. He sits behind the bar studying the Talmud and manages his business badly. He doesn't know how to handle people, and he doesn't know how to make money. He's always full of worry, but he leaves his worries to God, with whom he debates when he goes into a corner to pray, or when he sits humming to himself of a Saturday afternoon. Father's uncle is Borech, an old *oirech* with a bent back. An *oirech* is a more respectable kind of beggar than a schnorrer, but he's a beggar just the same. And my father's brothers, Yiddel and Tovyah, also go on a begging tour as far as Pressburg and Pest in the autumn, especially when the crops are bad in Trebushan, and there is no navvying, nor gravel-carting, nor timber-floating to be done. When the son of a Joshua Brueder falls in love with a girl, all this comes out. But I refuse to repudiate them, Sroleh Yomtov." She felt that there was undue agitation in her voice and she tried to repress it. Quietly, but stubbornly, she repeated: "I refuse to repudiate any of them, including Yosseleh with his mendicant parents."

She fell silent, watching Sroleh Yomtov's face. His eyes were the same as before, yet somehow different. The former defiance and restlessness were no longer there, and there was no sulkiness about the full lips that peeped forth from his whiskers. But there was a certain reserve about his features, which reflected receptiveness, but no communicativeness. Indeed, Sroleh Yomtov had scarcely said anything about himself. Yiteleh felt she must give him a lead.

"And what have you been doing all these years?"

"All sorts of things, but nothing notable."

"Did you study?"

"A little."

"In a *yeshiba?*"

"Partly."

"Did you go to work?"

"I made a living."

"Are you a business man?"

"I do business, but I'm not a business man."

"An artisan, then?"

"No."

"Are you a purveyor?"

"Not that, either."

"Then what are you?"

"An enterpriser."

"What does that mean? What do you do?"

"The things that other people don't think of."

"Does it pay?"

"It's just like anything else. You lose on one thing and make a profit on another."

"But have you anything to lose from?"

"If I haven't, other people have."

All this was too general for Yiteleh to learn anything. But she did not press him. With some embarrassment, she asked one more question:

"And how do you like it here after that beautiful big city?"

"Shayeh Oesterreicher is right," shrugged the young man. "All he sees here when he comes home is mud and darkness."

"Shayeh is a clever boy," said the girl. "I miss him."

"You don't have to be so clever to notice such things," smiled the young man. "In Vienna there are flagged pavements and they use gas for lighting." He rose and extended his hand: "See you again tomorrow."

Yiteleh stood by the glass door looking after him as he crossed the square. Then she returned to her shelves and stood thinking what to do next. She was confronted by Moysheh who, nodding his shaggy head, and clicking his tongue, observed:

"Some difference!"

Yiteleh acted as though she had not heard. Assuming her businesslike manner she said severely:

"Bootmaker Gabok has returned two pieces of Russia leather. Better see whether he hasn't cut any off."

"I have already done that."

"Russia leather is expensive. They can't make it even in Debrecen."

"I know that."

Yiteleh went to the writing-desk and opened a ledger. She tried to add up yesterday's items. Her pencil moved up and down mechanically, but she really did not see the figures. She was trying to see Sroleh Yomtov, who had sat opposite her for two hours, but she could not conjure up a vision of him. She also tried to recall the few words he had said about himself, but all she remembered clearly was the word tomorrow. So he was not coming again today. She wondered what he could have to do. He was staying at the Rothbarts' and when Mordechai invited him to his house he said Rothbart was an old friend and he wouldn't change. True, Sroleh Yomtov never liked Mordechai, but he seemed glad to have a business talk with him the previous evening and had also accepted his invitation to dinner on Sabbath. Mordechai admired Sroleh Yomtov and recalled that he had always said the boy would go a long way. Had he stayed at home, he would have become an innkeeper, a butcher, or at the most an ink mixer. But having run away, he had developed, had seen the world and had vision.

Tomorrow is Sabbath, the leather shop will be closed. What a pity. They will talk to him, Miriam, Hannah, Blimeleh, Mordechai, and even Moysheh. They will ask him questions. The young man from Vienna will answer them all. She, the poor relation, will lay the table and serve the dinner. She will be silent. And she had so many things to ask and so many more to tell him that she had recalled since he left the shop.

### FERDL AND HIS MASTER

THE PEASANTS in the village street paused to stare at the strange horse that frisked past them like a high-bred hunter. The rider was only one of those Hebrews, yet he moved his bottom in the saddle just as if he owned several villages. They were like that, the whole tribe of them. They had been cheating the world for thousands of years. When they first come along, they bend double with humility, but once they have feathered their nest they draw themselves up and look just as impressive as the gentry.

Isaac, standing outside the gate, also stared, though differently from the peasants, because he was boss-eyed. His grumbling was also different. He knew that a man who rode such a horse was entitled to give orders. But not any kind of orders. To take the horse into the stable, put a rug on him and feed him? Yes, sir. But to take a pack from behind the saddle and carry it into the house? No, not that. Into the bar parlor, yes; into the house, no. A customer's pack belonged to the bar parlor. He was pleased with himself for being clever enough to work this out, and it was with a satisfied grin that he reported to Sholem who, as usual of a morning, was swaying his body to and fro in front of the Talmud:

"A horse has come, Sholem. Oy mamma, what a horse. A real Ferdl!"

"A Ferdl?" asked Sholem. "Alone?"

"No, it was brought by another horse."

"What are you talking about, Isaac?"

"Really, Sholem. The other one sat on his back. A big young Jew."

"A big Jew?"

"As a Jew he's not very big—he's very small fringes."

"Bah!" said Sholem and returned to his reading.

The visitor was standing in the yard, looking round and sniffing. The smoke of the chimney was billowing down, and it had such a familiar smell. The old mulberry tree in the middle of the yard was already sprouting leaves. Farther on was the ash tree, scarcely sprouting yet, but the heavy odor of last year's blister flies still hung about it. Or was Sroleh Yomtov only imagining it? It was the odor of fourteen years of childhood, nothing else. He did not want to grow sentimental. He stood immobile, gazing round with a stern eye. The yard had become smaller, although it had been extended towards the garden. The shed was also bigger, the stable longer, the house reached farther down. What a mix-up! Instead of the charming little guest-room there was an extension, with a veranda and big blue-washed wooden pillars. The warm reed-thatch of the roof had also vanished and there were shingles instead. Where was the stork's nest? The stork too had gone.

A cock crowed shrilly into the bright daylight. Sroleh Yomtov looked up. He was now surrounded by a crowd of barefooted children, raising their familiarly unfamiliar faces to him. Suddenly he caught sight of yet another child, an infant in arms. The child had a plump, pink face, contrasting with the pale, oval face of the woman carrying it. Sroleh Yomtov felt as though he had seen the same picture but yesterday. He hastened up to the woman and, seizing her free hand, he kissed it.

"I've come back, Aunt Malkah," he said.

Malkeleh's face was suffused with pink. For a fleeting instant the beauty that eight years before had been so overpowering flared up. But then she was paler still. There were deep wrinkles round her eyes, and two fine lines on each side of her mouth.

"Sroleh . . . Sroleh . . . Sroleh Yomtov!" she cried in a voice thick with emotion. "It's good to see you again . . . very good. . . Manasseh, Yosseleh . . . call your father at once. . . Come in, my son. What a pity, Yossef is not here. Yiteleh is in Karoly."

"I have seen her there—talked with her."

"Oh, you did? She's grown, hasn't she?"

"Grown up, Aunt Malkah."

"Don't call me Aunt Malkah . . . You've grown up too. You're a man now."

"Yes, Mother Malkah."

"A big girl she is," said Malkeleh, her brow clouding, "and a big worry. Has she sent any message?"

"She didn't know I was coming here."

"Didn't you tell her?"

"I didn't know myself last night. The roads are very muddy, I couldn't get a carriage. I bought the horse this morning."

Malkeleh deposited the baby on the floor. She adjusted the table-cloth on the table and the kerchief on her head. Then she sat down opposite Sroleh Yomtov.

"She's very lonely there," she sighed.

"I don't think so, Malkeleh. They like Yiteleh there. Everyone is praising her for her cleverness."

"I think she's fretting. She doesn't show it, because she is so clever. She doesn't tell anybody what's troubling her. Her letters are always cheerful, yet I feel that she is fretting."

"She's not. She's working."

"It's not suitable work for a young girl."

"Why not? Yiteleh likes it."

"As a sick person likes medicine."

"No, Malkeleh. Yiteleh was born to it."

The boys came back to report that Sholem could not leave the inn. Serf Gore had gone, but another serf had just come in and had to be served.

"Did you tell your father who is here?" asked Malkeleh.

"Y-yes," stammered Manasseh. "I said the uncle who took Bakter away."

"What Bakter?"

"The dog."

"How do you know about that?"

"Sarah Chayah told me."

"And who told her?"

"Mailech."

Malkeleh's eyes were smiling as she turned to Sroleh Yomtov:

"They talked a lot about you in this house."

Aunt Feiga came shuffling in from the kitchen. She seized him by the lapels of his jacket with gnarled, withered fingers, then felt him all over, bending her half-blind eyes close to his face.

"You dirty dog," she croaked. "You naughty, naughty brat. You *goy*, you heathen. Couldn't you come when Aunt Feiga was still able to see? You waited until she was half blind, hey? Never mind, my little lamb, I can still see you. My left eye is quite good yet. How big you are! I can't reach the fringes by your ear. You haven't cut them off altogether yet. I can still pull them for you. He's got a beard, the rascal. His father had one, too. Where have you been since you ran away, eh? You tramp! Bless you, darling."

Sroleh Yomtov had been determined not to grow sentimental. But he could not help giving the old woman's hairy face a caress.

"Your right eye is bad, what? Well," he comforted, "we'll have it made better, so you'll see with it better than ever. I have an eye-doctor friend in Varad, I'll take you to him."

"You see, Malkah," said the old woman. "I always told you that everything would be all right when Sroleh Yomtov came back. I used to wash the rheum out of his eyes, so he won't let me go blind. When your father got married he was so handsome that the girls used to cry after him, even I, though I was an old maid even then. I want to see if you too are as handsome."

"I'll look into the inn," said the visitor, on the verge of sentimentality.

Walking on the boards across the yard he met a little girl. She was carrying a mug of milk in each hand and walked slowly and carefully, not to step into the mud and not to spill the milk. Sroleh Yomtov looked at her smooth hair and the glossy pigtails swaying as she walked, and was taken aback. Why, this was Yiteleh! You're a fool, he reproved himself mentally. Yiteleh is a big girl and she is in Karoly. This little girl had rustier hair and her eyes were hazel. He even remembered her name.

"What have you got there, Sarah Chayah?" he asked superfluously.

"Milk, Uncle," she said with surprise in her tone.

"Haven't you got a cow?"

"We did have one, but we sold it."

"Didn't she give any milk?"

"She did. She had just calved and gave a lot of milk. Mailech said you had to sell a cow when she gave a lot of milk."

"Where is he?"

"He's gone again with Dominus to sell watches. But first he gave the money to Daddy."

"Doesn't he go to *yeshiba* any more?"

"He had to leave Karoly because he had too few guest days."

"I suppose they stopped them because he wasn't studious enough?"

"I don't know. He gave up one himself, the one he had with Joshua Brueder. He called and said he was not coming again be-

cause he'd heard that Joshua's brother dealt in pigs. Such a family
was not good enough for him."

The inn was empty. Sholem, long-stemmed pipe in his mouth,
sat swaying his body and chanting an Aramaic text. Sroleh Yomtov went up to him and said quietly:

"Still at it, Sholem?"

Sholem's bushy beard jerked up and his red-rimmed eyes distended. His hand extended involuntarily.

"It's you, Sroleh . . . Reb Sroleh Yomtov!"

"Yes . . . but without the Reb, Sholem."

"That blockhead Isaac and those silly children babbled such a
lot, I didn't understand them. I thought it was some passing
stranger and so I wasn't in a hurry. He was sure to come in here
sooner or later. But I had just been thinking of you. I had a lot
of vexation with you . . . no, only debates . . . over this passage:
'It's better for two to live together' . . . You're not Reb? Why,
you've got a beard. What *yeshiba* did you qualify at? Still at
this volume? Oh no—it's again. I've gone through the Babylonian
Talmud twice since then, and once through the Jerusalem one.
The more you learn the less you know. The text is old, the meaning new. If I remember aright, we had this passage that time in
'Marriage Laws.' Now I'm reading it in 'Sisters-in-Law.' That
lovely verse occurs twice in the *Gemarah*. What they quote twice
is important."

"No other troubles, Sholem?"

"Why should there be any trouble. Rabbi Yehudah Kunitz,
the blind seer, once said to me: 'Change of domicile, change of
luck!' There was a time when I wanted to move away from here,
but then it occurred to me that it was enough to paraphrase: I
sell my wheat and maize at Bator instead of Karoly. Solomon
Mandel is a good man, better than Brueder in Karoly. He has not
yet had delivery of anything, but has already paid for half of the
autumn crop."

"And if the crop fails?"

"Why should it? The Above One will see to it that the people
should not be left without bread. I see now that the inspiration to
change buyers came just at the right moment."

Taking the old ledger out of the drawer, he sat close to the visitor and started turning the pages.

"Listen, Sroleh Yomtov. Up to last autumn, that is, in eight years, net profits were two thousand four hundred and sixty florins. You can check the items afterwards. I deduct one tenth for the Mosaic tithe, which I have paid out to the poor of Karoly, Csenger, Batiz, and Szalka. Here are the receipts. Then, in addition, there is the six hundred and eighty-one florins and forty kreuzers which you left when you went away. Then there is the bill you paid to Lazarovich, a hundred and forty-three florins, and what you paid Rothbart, eighty-six florins and twenty kreuzers. Twenty and forty is sixty, that is, one florin. One and six is seven and three and seven . . . That makes two thousand and eighteen florins. All this is yours, yours and Yossef's. It is all there, to the last copper."

Sroleh Yomtov seemed to be thinking, as though reckoning up in his head.

"There's something that doesn't tally," he said, shaking his head.

"What?" asked Sholem, paling. "Is the money too little?"

"Not too little—too much."

"I'm not giving you more than's due," said Sholem with relief.

"I'm not so sure. I think you're wanting to give more. Is the profit from the land included?"

"Yes."

"And it's still five chains you have?"

"No, eighteen."

"You see. The land's nothing to do with us. You worked it alone. And I have no right to the revenue from the inn, either. I helped you for barely six months in the last eight years."

"But Yossef did help. And the money you left was also working for me."

"You want to pay interest on my money?"

"No, that's forbidden. But I want to stick to the agreement. Look here, my son, I wrote it in in Hebrew: According to the law of Moses and Israel and according to the law of Hungary."

"The gentry who signed it did not understand that."

"But I explained it to them. You don't think I would keep the money of orphans? It was bad enough that I could not settle with

Yossef because I had no authority from you. A lot of other things were lacking besides. There are many unexpected needs in a business and one thoughtlessly touches the capital. I'm burning to get rid of this money at last. I'm glad you're here and we can settle."

Sroleh Yomtov examined the shelves, sniffed, tapped at the hollow casks, then returned to Sholem.

"You haven't any stock, Sholem."

"No, not much."

"You've no money to buy any."

"Where there is two thousand and eighteen, there's a florin or two more."

"You've sold the next crop, you've sold the cow, and you've scraped together our money. But what have you done with your own?"

Sholem stared. How did this new arrival know about all this?"

"I made a bad speculation," he said shrinkingly, with apology in his tone. "I scraped together your money, because Yossef wants to get married and needs his share."

"But I don't want to get married."

"No-o? How could I know that? I had to be ready for you to turn up any moment—and you have."

"What do you give the peasants to drink if you have no spirits?"

"Wine."

"But they don't drink wine."

"They must. The new Squire has ordered it so."

"That never happened before."

"It was always like that, Sroleh Yomtov. It's in the agreement. Squire Jeky, Squire de Denghelegh's heir, showed it to me. And he showed me the royal decree of fifteen hundred and fifty. Section thirty-six says that the peasants must buy the Squire's wine on pain of flogging and imprisonment. And if they gave it in tithe to the Squire, they must buy it back with money."

"Those are antiquated laws."

"You're mistaken, Sroleh Yomtov. So long as there is a power that holds a stick and the keys of a jail, every law is valid. 'The law of the power is the law' according to our Sages."

"There's a more sacred law than that."

"What is it?" asked Sholem in a scared voice.

The young man folded his arms across his chest and said: "One must live, Sholem."

INTERVENTION

SROLEH YOMTOV sent Sholem to Batiz to buy stock from Lazarovich. Sholem no longer had a horse, and he had also sold his cart. He had to hire a cart from Serf Bonca. In the evening, when Sholem returned with the stock, Sroleh Yomtov said to him:

"Tomorrow is market day in Otvar. You'll go there and buy a strong cart."

"In Otvar?" said Sholem reluctantly.

"Yes. Otvar carts are best. Besides, you'll go to the horse market and get two strong draught-horses."

"A good horse is at least sixty florins."

"You can give seventy apiece if necessary."

"That's a hundred and forty—and the cart will also come to forty-five."

"Quite. And you'll buy harness too. The old one is very ragged."

"It can be mended."

"Not worth while. It's better to spend the time repairing your casks or clearing the caterpillars off your fruit trees."

Sholem hummed and hawed.

"Isn't one horse enough? I had only one before."

"That was a mistake. Two horses will bring you back from Batiz in four hours. One will take eight or nine hours, that is, if you don't get stuck."

"That's true. But two horses eat twice as much."

"They eat twice as much but produce six times more."

Sholem was at the end of his arguments. He had to go to Otvar. Before he left, his "partner" impressed on him that he must not bother about an extra florin or two, so long as he got the right things. An innkeeper and farmer could not exist without horse and cart of his own. Besides, a Jew was judged by his cart and horses. His credit rose and fell accordingly.

Sroleh Yomtov also intervened in family affairs. Two of the children, Manasseh and Yosseleh, were coughing and he thought they were suffering from whooping cough; they ought not to go barefoot. Sholem smiled, for it was precisely those children that had boots that also had coughs, while those that went barefoot in mud and slush were as right as rain, and he said so. But Sroleh Yomtov said that that made no difference, and that in any case April was a treacherous month; besides, Jewish children should be properly shod. He sent Isaac and Sarah Chayah to Dengheleg to order boots for the little ones from the bootmaker. There was great joy and excitement in the house.

Sroleh Yomtov took charge of the inn, and this was a great event in all the villages the inn catered for. Sroleh Anti gave the thirsty peasants the right kinds of drink: home distilled, and rye and ordinary. Even the ordinary was a hundred times better than Squire Jeky's wines. Sroleh Yomtov did not even touch the wine.

"We'll sell the wine to Mesel, if necessary at a loss. In the inn the customer is master, not the Squire."

Sholem hemmed and hawed and put up a mild resistance. But he had to admit that Sroleh Yomtov was right. It's always the result that tells, and the result was that the peasants gradually stopped the agitation against the Sholem family. From one day to another open hostilities ceased, and from there it was but a short step to the old friendly relations. The peasants must know, explained the guest, that the Jews were also only a despised and exploited class and that in some respects they were squeezed even harder than the serfs who, after all, can go slow if they don't feel like hard work, can scratch the soil instead of plowing it if it is too hard, and can steal back half the tithe they pay in if they consider it too much.

"That's true," said the peasants, and Sroleh Anti's prestige began to rise. He had gained some when he arrived on that fine horse. But even if, being a Jew, he did not seem to fit into that saddle then, he was now retrospectively held to have fitted into it more and more. Serf Vince Polya grinned so broadly that his mouth looked like a dark cavern. He kept squinting at the bar and expressing his amazement to the others so that the innkeeper could hear.

"When he came I thought it was some foreign merchant come to the Count of Erdoed and the Baron of Meggyes to bring them coffee, saffron, and raisins. I went all groggy when I heard as how he was Sroleh, the son of good old Moses."

It came out that Sroleh had come from abroad, straight from Vienna. Lajos Gore cleared his throat.

"And did you see the Emperor, Sroleh?" he asked respectfully.

"I saw him riding in his carriage."

"What sort of a man is he?"

"Just a weakly old man."

"But at least he's got the money for the doctor and the apothecary, not like us."

The peasants giggled at that. But Gaspar Galagonya, at the head of the table, scratched the graying hair on the back of his neck and said:

"Don't grumble, Lajos. Must everyone know that your children have consumption?" Giving his mustache a twirl, he turned to Sroleh Yomtov: "Who's headman in Vienna, now? For I'm that here."

Sroleh Yomtov smiled and was friendly. He listened to the older men and watched the younger. The former treated him to accounts of the past. Mate Bor, the old headman, had died of the "water disease": from the spirits Sholem had sold him. Serf Martin Vizhordo had collapsed. Old de Denghelegh had been scared to death by his old mare Borcsa. The wise woman, Mme Bogyo, had also carried her secrets to the grave. She had helped many people into the world, but more out of it. Now the wife of Gypsy Duduy was the wise woman. She could do magic too.

This was more or less jocular talk and the older men laughed, but the younger did not. There was Jancsi Galagonya, Bence Gore, Samuel Vizhordo, and the rest, who in Sroleh Yomtov's time were but young lads. Now they too were beasts of burden, so they too were in the inn. They were drinking and arguing so fiercely that it made their eyes bulge. It was about Vienna and the Emperor, but they spoke differently about them from the older generation. Bence Gore, tugging at his baby mustache, was shouting that the Emperor too was on the side of the gentry, while the gentry curried favor with him by pampering his Germans.

"That's because the Germans are Papists," cried Matthew Hacsak, purple with rage, "and we are Calvinists and Magyars."

"The Swabians have already pushed the Magyars out of two towns. Now they're continuing the push as far as Erdoed and Otvar, where their brother-in-law is master."

"It's easy for the Swabians," said Jancsi Galagonya, "they do only twenty-six days villenage a year, and even that they do just anyhow. Our Squire demands fifty-two days if we've got draught animals and a hundred and four and more if we haven't."

Vince Polya transferred among the younger men and said:

"It's against the Emperor's will."

Serf Vizhordo junior spat contemptuously:

"The Emperor and the gentry are birds of a feather."

"But really," said Uncle Polya, "Joseph too was a good Emperor, but the gentry did away with him because he was on the side of the poor."

"And we'll do away with the gentry," said Vizhordo vehemently.

"Careful, Samuel," warned Headman Galagonya, "or you might have to join your brother Andris." Turning to Sroleh Yomtov he explained: "He's in the same place as Sholem's brother, Gimpel. Martin Vizhordo left little for his sons, but he left them his sharp tongue."

Sroleh Yomtov felt that the case of Gimpel Zorech had to be gone into too. That was at the back of all the stench around here. Sholem did not feel inclined to talk about the matter, and all he said was that his brother was innocent.

"How do you know?" asked Sroleh Yomtov.

"It's come out as clear as daylight."

"Then why do they keep him inside?"

"They don't know yet."

"But you do?"

"Yes."

"Then you must tell them."

"I can't."

"What if the house crashes on you?"

"If it's God's will it's not going to crash."

"You can't let an innocent man stay in jail and your entire family suffer."

"They are suffering for Israel!"

"But you'll at least tell me what you know?"

"I can't. Please, Sroleh Yomtov, stop asking questions."

Sroleh Yomtov considered it wise to stand aside to some extent from Sholem and his affairs. He had scarcely spoken with Malkeleh yet, and he must not neglect her. Malkeleh was working in the house and, with the aid of her children, revivifying the little flower garden which the guest had not noticed on his arrival, perhaps because there was nothing to notice. Now, however, it was bright with yellow cowslip, beds of daisies and pansies. The knobby geraniums were weeded out, and while they had no flowers yet, they had a fragrance and the leaves were sprouting, and the ivy was already creeping up on the strings tied up on the veranda.

The interior of the house also looked fresh, with bright colored table-cloths and new crockery, some of it porcelain, and there were even one or two forks and knives with proper handles. Part of this consisted of Passover utensils, which were not used during the rest of the year, but this time Malkeleh thought that with God's help she could replace them by next Passover. Malkeleh herself had also changed. She moved more briskly and there was more color in her cheeks, and when she smiled one saw not the wrinkles round her mouth, but the dimples on her chin and in her cheek. She smiled a great deal, as though bragging, through the resemblance which this accentuated, that she was Yiteleh's mother. Only her eyes contained something that was absent from her daughter's bright orbs: the sorrow of the years, which could not be smiled away in a hurry. Yet her sorrow was attractive rather than forbidding and Sroleh Yomtov felt as though it were calling to him.

Malkeleh was not secretive, and she told Sroleh Yomtov frankly that Sholem had found the murderer. True, they, she and Sholem, had vowed not to talk about it to anyone, and had not told even Yiteleh, but she felt she could confide in Sroleh Yomtov. The situation was that the Jew Herskovitch was involved in the matter, and if Sholem said anything, the man would either get into the hands of the law, or the highwaymen would avenge themselves on him and his family. Herskovitch had been a receiver for years, though he asserted that he was not aware that the goods were stolen. Unfortunately, Sholem's silence had not helped much, for instead of Sholem's hope that the Above One would show them a way out being realized, they had only got more involved, and now in addition to Gimpel Zorech's case appearing to be hopeless, the whole family was in it.

Sroleh Yomtov listened with keen attention, endeavoring to make a note of every detail. He put a question here and there, and Malkeleh answered as best she could. Then he asked how Sholem had found out. Had he gone to the scene of the crime for clues? Or had he visited the bandits' lair at Sebespatak?

"He didn't go anywhere," replied the woman. "He just sat in front of the *Gemarah*, thinking. And by the time the pandours returned to Otvar and the Commissioner pigeonholed the file of the case, deciding that Gimpel Zorech alone would be enough to justify a trial, Sholem had found the murderers."

The young man was silent for a while, then he said:

"And you consider it right that a man who's entirely innocent should stay in jail, so that one who is not entirely innocent should escape punishment?"

"We don't consider it right. But what can we do? There was a saying in my father's house: 'When a Jew tells the truth he gets beaten all the worse.' My father said: 'You must tell the truth just the same.' But how can we, when others might get beaten for it?"

"Perhaps we can," said Sroleh Yomtov quietly.


A HAPPY BOY


YOSSEF WAS full of bitterness and grievances because his career in Batiz did not proceed as he had expected. The accumulated resentment of the years had burst to the surface and he intended to overwhelm his brother with reproaches for having left the whole

house in a torment of anxiety about himself, but not having
thought for a moment of him, Yossef, his only blood relation,
whom he had abandoned to his own devices. But when he arrived
in Sholem's house on a Friday afternoon and was face to face with
Sroleh Yomtov, all he could remember of his reproaches was:

"How could you do it, Sroleh Yomtov?"

"What? Coming home?"

"No, running away."

"That was long ago."

"We searched for you everywhere."

"The world is a big place, Yossef. No use trying to find a grain
of millet in a hayrick."

"You might have dropped us a line to say you were alive."

"Perhaps I wasn't alive the way I meant to be."

"You were always restless. Are you still the same?"

"Wait and see," laughed Sroleh Yomtov. "You'll know in another eight years."

Yossef had always looked up to his brother, and it was more so
now. He admired his social ease and self-assurance; it was clear
that Sroleh Yomtov knew what he wanted. For example, now he
wanted to hear about Yossef's life, whereas Yossef had taken it for
granted that Sroleh Yomtov, having come from afar, would be
the one to render an account. However, the way his brother was
listening to him made Yossef believe that his story, too, was important. At night, when they were lying in the two beds of the
guest-room, Yossef interrupted himself to ask, "Are you asleep,
Sroleh Yomtov?" "No, I am listening," was the reply. Yossef
was surprised that he had so much to say, and that his brother
was so interested. He told how he had apprenticed himself to
Jacob Anshel, how he had taken to the trade and also to Zireleh.
The parents would have let him marry her, and Jacob Anshel
would have taken him in as a partner if he had had four hundred
florins capital. But he had not. Now there were other suitors
coming along. There was Zebulon, the potash man's son, who
was offering six hundred, but he, Yossef, had overheard Zireleh
herself say that Yossef was worth more with only three hundred
than Zebulon with a thousand. For while Zebulon understood
about potash, he had no idea how to make candles either with a

lathe, or with a wheel, or with a drum. He also knew nothing about making fine soap and was also ignorant of other secrets of the trade.

"How much money do you need?" asked Sroleh Yomtov.

"I think three hundred would do now," replied his brother.

"You shall have it."

Yossef was thrown into a ferment of excitement by this brief sentence. He wanted to hear more, but Sroleh Yomtov said he would like to sleep now. Yossef himself could not sleep. He always knew that he was not alone in the world after all, for he had a brother who would not leave him in the lurch. Now he was here and he had said the word. "You shall have it." And he would, he would.

By morning Yossef was overtaken by a breath of doubt. His brother asked him why he had not approached Sholem. Sholem would have let him have some money. After all, it was due, as Yossef's share in the business.

"I mentioned the matter to Sholem," said Yossef, "but I didn't ask straight out. I couldn't. The house is full of worry and poverty. And there's nothing due to me. They kept me for six years like their own child."

"I don't think this house is full of worry and poverty," said Sroleh Yomtov with smiling eyes. "Just have a look round."

Yossef did so. The children were wearing brand-new boots. There was a brand-new cart in the shed. New harness, too. In the stable there were two young colts. Isaac seemed to be very proud of them. He pointed out their strong hindquarters, and referring to the way they swished their tails towards each other, he said:

"Like two rabbis talking, isn't it?"

There was also a fine saddle horse in the stable, but Isaac was not very enthusiastic about him.

"That's Ferdl," he said. "Not worth much. It's got a short tail and won't be harnessed to a cart. He don't belong to us."

At the mouth of the cellar there were two big casks and three small ones, all full. There was more stock on every shelf behind the bar. The whole house had changed. There was fancy bread on the table, and wine, and fish and roast duck. Malkeleh was beaming. Sholem was contentedly chanting the psalm of homecoming.

Yossef had not spent such a gay Sabbath in the house for a long time. He could not resist putting a question to his brother:

"Did you give Sholem money?"

"Me, Yossef? Not a copper."

Yossef was at sea. And more so when, after the Sabbath, Sholem called him behind the bar and counted out five hundred florins on the counter for him.

"Sroleh Yomtov said I was not to give you more, but if you want more just let me know."

"I don't want more," said Yossef timidly. "But I thought . . . four hundred would be quite enough."

"If four hundred is enough," smiled Sholem, "five hundred is not too much."

It was all a mystery to Yossef. He knew that the brother-in-law's bill had cost Sholem nearly two thousand florins. He also knew that the gentry had been squeezing him dry. And now, suddenly, he had money—such a lot of money. And Sroleh Yomtov had not given him a copper . . . But something must have happened. If Sroleh Yomtov had not given any money, the change was nevertheless due to his advent.

He would have liked to discuss the matter with his brother, but his brother was taken up with Malkeleh and the family. When they went to bed, it was again Sroleh Yomtov that asked the questions. He wanted to know whether it was still so difficult for a Jew to get into Otvar. Yossef told him what he, and everyone else, knew. One could get into Otvar any day, except Saturday— because a Jew did not carry any money on that day. But you had to clear out in the evening, no matter how much money you had.

"And has it not occurred to you that this must come to an end?"

"It has occurred to everybody. But there's nothing that can be done. Otvar is a royal borough."

"Vienna is an Imperial city. Pressburg is a coronation town. Buda is a royal seat. If Jews can live in all those places, then they can live in Otvar."

"That's what you say, Sroleh Yomtov. But Burgomaster Lam and the Council think otherwise."

"Do they?" said Sroleh Yomtov. Yossef expected him to go on.

But he just turned to the wall and said abruptly: "Good night, Yossef."

In the morning Yossef woke very gaily. He talked about Zireleh, how very pretty and charming she was. Yiteleh was also pretty and charming and some people thought she was prettier than Zireleh, because Zireleh had red hair. But she was just right like that, and no hair of another color would suit her so well. Sholem and his wife would have liked him to marry Yiteleh, and he had in fact thought of doing so for a time. But Yiteleh was so clever, and it wasn't a good thing for a girl to be cleverer than a man. Yiteleh was reading German books, though she knew the Pentateuch, the Prophets, and Rashi like a rabbi's daughter. Zireleh was more modest and read only the Women's Bible in Yiddish.

"And what do you know about Gimpel Zorech?" asked his brother; he was standing in front of the washstand, splashing his somewhat bony chest with water.

Yossef would have liked to go on talking about Zireleh and he turned to the subject of the schnorrer, who had caused him nothing but trouble, reluctantly. He explained that he, Yossef, took Gimpel Zorech's rations to Otvar three times a week. The prisoner was generally out of the jail, and Yossef got a great deal of abuse from the warder, who was never satisfied with the money and drink one brought him.

"Couldn't you link your visits with some business?" asked Sroleh Yomtov. "You could take in candles and soap and sell other things as well to the townspeople."

"Can't be done. We must sell only on the weekly market day. The Council has forbidden us to trade in the town on other days."

"Have you tried to petition the Council to lift the ban?"

"There would be no sense in that. The Candlemakers' Guild would upset everything. Guild Master Haitayer has a long arm."

Sroleh Yomtov rested his gaze on his brother for a long time, as though he were going to put an important question. But then:

"We'll talk about these things another time," he said curtly. "I'll go over one day this week."

"You will?" said Yossef, beaming. "You'll come and see Zireleh?"

"Zireleh and the business," replied Sroleh Yomtov. "I'm interested to know what you're doing and how."

THE BLACK SQUIRE

IN THE afternoon Sroleh Yomtov mounted his horse and rode over to the Sarberek mansion.

Sholem was impressed, for the pace at which the young man was going was somewhat staggering. At dinner Sholem had muttered something to the effect that Sroleh Yomtov ought to pay his respects at the two mansions some time. Some time—not today. It was not urgent—because it was very urgent. Very urgent matters must be important, and important matters require time. Sholem did not wish to tell Sroleh Yomtov about it yet. Why should he see that there was trouble closing in on all sides? Of the three Squires Jeky was far away, and Gyekeny had been pushed aside by the Black Squire, but the Black Squire was there and was making Sholem feel his spleen. Even the strongest plum whisky was now too weak for him, lacking the former bouquet. The Jew that distilled it must be mixing it with turnip juice. The rental kept growing higher and higher, yet he still thought it was too low. The Squire was also raising the price of his inferior wine again and again, until it was more expensive than Mesel's Tokay. He placed the blame at Sholem's door for the disobedience of the serfs and the rebellious spirit of the younger generation. Sholem, he said, was teaching them disobedience out of the Talmud. That was proved beyond a shadow of doubt when Andris, son of the late Martin Vizhordo, had dared to tell de Sarberek and Gyekeny to their faces that the gentry were only usurping the land, which belonged to the peasants, and that soon there would be a change. De Sarberek had him soundly flogged and sent to jail in Otvar. But then he went and swished his cane under Sholem's nose, warning him to beware: he, the Squire, knew that Sholem had been preaching to Martin each evening about the revolt of the sons of Korah.

Late at night the sound of galloping hooves could be heard from the Sarberek road. The inn was full, but Sholem was standing in the door, waiting for his stepson.

The young man looked at his worried face and asked:

"What's up, Sholem?"

"That's what I want to know."

"Nothing as far as I am concerned."

"Did he quarrel with you?"

"Who?"

"The Black Squire."

"Why, he was most friendly."

"He complained about me, I suppose?"

"Not at all. He praised you."

"He never did that to my face. All he ever said was that he needed money, and more money, and still more money. And that I was to blame for everything. If the serfs drank too much or too little. If that blockhead Master Adam failed to get a post as Chief Magistrate and got only a small clerkship. Yet it is I who pay the difference."

Sroleh Yomtov gave him a searching look.

"You're not to blame for anything, Sholem. And that young man is not such a blockhead as you think. He is one of the most learned lawyers."

"How do you know?"

"I talked with him in Karoly."

Sroleh Yomtov was an established authority in the house and everyone recognized his worldly experience. But in the case of Master Adam, Sholem firmly disagreed with him. That young fellow had never gone near the University in Pest, but spent his time carousing, gambling, and making debts, just as if he were the son of a magnate and not of a sixth-rate petty noble.

The late de Denghelegh, shortly before his death, had examined Master Adam in the Tripartitum. The young man could only croak. Squire Gyekeny had remarked laughingly: "Well, my boy, you sure know more about skirts and corset cords than about the Corpus Juris." And the new Squire, Jeky, had been around to all the county offices on his behalf, and then he said that a young fellow with an empty head who was not a count ought to be grateful to get any little job. If he had a patient behind, he would in time shift farther, from the common table of the clerks to a smaller one, then to a still smaller one. The smaller the desk the bigger the income, with a big salary and freedom to steal. But it was a hundred to one that Master Adam would be a gray old donkey by the time he managed to climb the ladder.

Sroleh Yomtov just shrugged his shoulders and they did not discuss Master Adam any more.

On Monday morning Sroleh Yomtov saddled his horse to ride to Batiz and, on the way, call at the Gyekeny mansion. Malkeleh came out of the house and said:

"Don't say anything to Squire Gyekeny, he tells his wife everything."

It struck the young man that she looked very pale.

"I was not thinking of telling him anything. But having called at Sarberek, I must call on them too."

"I don't know," said Malkeleh, "whether it is wise for you to go and see Commissioner Erdy."

"We must know how matters stand."

"You must be very careful, Sroleh Yomtov."

She seized him by the hand and said with unexpected vehemence:

"My dear boy, I don't know why, but I'm afraid. I had a premonition all night. I can't get rid of the idea that there's some big trouble ahead. Whenever I have been happy for a day or two it was followed by some disaster. I can never be quite carefree."

Her restlessness communicated itself to the young man, and while his gaze remained steady, his voice became deeper as he said:

"Just what are you afraid of, Mother Malkah?"

"I don't know. But I'm afraid. It's in my throat and in my legs. I'd like to run away from here, take the whole family away, take Yiteleh away from Karoly, up to the mountains in the north, up to Pressburg, or still farther."

"No reason for that, Malkeleh."

"I wish you were right. I've been like this several times before. I sensed in advance what was coming."

"Perhaps you're only exhausted, run down."

"Perhaps. There's been too much all at once. When one has rested a little, one's knees begin to tremble."

Sroleh Yomtov kissed her hand. She tried to smile. This reassured him a little. He led the horse out of the yard.

Sholem had just concluded his morning reading behind the
bar. He was very pleased with Rabbi Akiba and Rabbi Tarphon.
He was all ruddy gaiety as he stepped out of the door.

"Well, Reb Sroleh Yomtov? Going to Batiz?"

"Batiz and Otvar, Sholem."

"What will you be doing at Otvar?"

"Just looking round."

"Very good. May you start in a happy hour."

They were very pleased at the Gyekeny mansion. They had
already heard that old Moses's son had returned and had already
called on Sarberek. It was nice of him to call here as well. And it
was nicer still that he had not come empty-handed. For Squire
Gyekeny he had a hand-carved Viennese meerschaum pipe, for
Lady Susannah, an ivory brooch set in gold. It was so lovely that
she had to put it back into its case and present it to her daughter
Antonia, who would be married soon. Lady Susannah opined that
Sroleh Yomtov had grown into a fine young man, what a pity
that he was a Jew. The Squire, however, said that there were
decent people among the Jews as well. They had already been
saying at the county that they would send a submission to the
Diet in Pressburg that the better type of Hebrews be given dog-
skins (patents of nobility), with the right to carry swords, like
real nobles. They would have liked to talk at length with the
visitor about the great big world. But he was in a hurry, and said
that he would pay his respects again some other day.

How empty was the chatter of her ladyship and her Antonia
and Ludmilla! How different was the deep human note in
Malkeleh's talk, the sincerity in Yiteleh's! He pressed his legs to
the horse's flanks. He was in a hurry. He had told Malkah that
he'd be away till the end of the week, and if he did not return
by Friday noon not to expect him for the Sabbath, only for the
beginning of the following week. He had a plan and it required
time. He would finish with the Commissioner quickly, but once
he was in Otvar there were other tasks for him there . . . He
realized that his sole mission now was to clear up the matter of
Gimpel Zorech. Everything else could wait. He might be back

by Wednesday, and perhaps by tomorrow evening. Malkeleh was worried and this fact dictated a faster pace.

A gray-green troop came galloping from the direction of Otvar. They were pandours, seven or eight, led by an officer with a fluttering plume on his hat. They galloped past him. Who or what were they after? Sroleh Yotmov looked behind him: they were making for Lapfalva. He turned round, trotting after them. He kept his distance, but he could still see them. They had turned into the village street and were now dismounting rapidly in front of the inn. The young man knew. This was the trouble Malkeleh had sensed. He had thought he could anticipate it. But Commissioner Erdy's pandours were quicker than Justice.

Cutting across the fields at a gallop, Sroleh Yomtov plunged into a maze of footpaths, urging his horse to a faster pace. The animal, as though conscious of the desperate urgency, went all out over the sticky ground.

Commissioner Erdy bawled in a different way from Sergeant Patyodi. His mustache was clipped, so he did not twirl it, and his hair over his low forehead was *en brosse*. And his steel-gray eyes held such menace that he would have made a terrifying figure even if he had not been beating at the table with the hilt of his sword. Sholem did not lose his presence of mind. He used to worry a great deal about this possibility, and he used to think of it with terror in his heart. But now that the Commissioner was here, surrounded by pandours whose eyes were as sharp as their bayonets, the warning of Akabyah ben Mahalalel came into his mind like an inspiration: "Reflect where thou comest from and where thou goest and before whom thou wilt stand to give an account." He would not tremble even before the Judge of Judges because he would be telling the truth. Of course, his calmness and truthfulness now only served to enrage the Commissioner, who had come with the set determination not to believe the Jew.

"On Tuesday you were at the distillery of Lazar Lazarovich."

"Yes, sir."

"You bought two big casks of spirit, hey?"

"No, sir."

"Then what did you buy?"

"Three big casks of spirit."

"I can see you daren't deny anything. We know everything, you see. You bought liqueur, rum, plum whisky, and gin in four small casks."

"Yes, sir."

"You bought kummel, pear brandy, and vanilla in bottles and demijohns."

"That's right, sir."

"You paid a hundred and ninety-three florins twenty kreuzers."

"Quite right."

"Then you went to the Jew Mesel. What did you buy there?"

"Nothing. I paid an installment of fifty florins on my debt."

"You did, did you. You had money, what?"

"Yes, sir."

"Very well. On Wednesday you went to Otvar and bought two horses. One for sixty-florins, the other for sixty-five."

"Correct."

"I'll bash your face in if you don't answer properly, damned Jew. Who do you think you're talking to? Your drunken peasants? Or a dirty Jewish dealer?"

"Yes, sir."

"How dare you! Patyodi, you'll give him ten for this when we have finished."

"Ten strokes. Make a note, Corporal."

"Yes, sir . . . Ten for the Jew for impertinence."

Master Erdy banged the table with his sword and went on with the interrogation. Sholem answered. He had bought a cart, new harness, and a spring seat in addition to the ordinary driving-seat.

"What do you want a spring seat for, Jew?"

"For my wife."

"Isn't your wife a Jewess?"

"She is."

"The ordinary seat is too hard for her, what?"

"Yes, when I take her to see the doctor in Otvar."

"What doctor?"

"Doctor Pfirsich."

"Ah! Make a note, Corporal Pettyen. The Jewess goes to Pfirsich."

The chief pandour knew everything in detail. About the four pairs of boots made in Dengheleg for the children. About Sholem's negotiations for a cow. And about the five hundred florins Sholem had given to Yossef, who was an apprentice with Jacob Anshel, the candlemaker, the money to be hidden, of course.

For the first time Sholem lost his patience.

"Did you take it away from him?"

"Of course we did. We'll confiscate the fine new boots as well. And the horses and the spring seat and the cart and the spirits."

"Why?"

"Because you bought everything with stolen money, Jew."

"I have not bought anything with stolen money. There's no blood on my hands."

"Of course not. You think I don't know who sent the first marked banknote to the butcher in Batiz? We know everything, Master Innkeeper."

Sholem had been prepared for this revelation—but differently and in different circumstances. Now he was taken aback. For the first time, he dared not tell the truth. Was he to reply at all? He looked at Malkeleh's pale face, then he said quietly:

"We get all sorts of people coming to the inn. I don't look at the money they give me."

"You didn't look at the money your brother Gimpel Zorech gave you either, what?"

Sholem jerked his head back.

"I saw my brother only when he was brought here by the pandours. They say he was arrested on the scene of the crime."

"Having gone back there from here."

"Why should he have gone back?"

"Because every criminal goes back at least once. In case he can find something more on his victim, that is. But he didn't, except for a bottle of plum whisky. But he liked it, and that was his undoing."

Malkeleh gripped the wooden grille of the bar, the blood draining away from her face. Sholem, to hearten Malkeleh, and because in the consciousness of his innocence he knew something that would settle the matter in his favor in the end, defended himself with even greater firmness and tenacity, behaving as though the Commissioner were not the representative of power, but a debating partner who might be convinced of a point.

"But if I am a robber," he said, "why didn't you put me in jail as well?"

The Commissioner waved his sword under Sholem's nose, as though this was his reply to the Jew's argument. But then he replied in words as well:

"Because we were watching you to see when you'd be spending the rest of the money. You kept it hidden, apart from giving four hundred to the Jew Mesel. You acted the poverty-stricken creature. The peasants might have their tongues hanging out with thirst, but you hadn't the money for whisky. Now, thinking that the eyes of the law were not on you, you came out with all that money."

"What money I had left belonged to the orphans. The new money is my son Mailech's money, Isaac's money, the money I got for my cow. . . ."

"The cow you're haggling to buy now?"

"No, the one I sold."

"Because it wasn't good enough?"

"No, it was better than this new one."

"I see. You sold the better cow for forty florins, to buy a worse one for fifty, eh? A Jewish custom! And where else did you get money from?"

"I sold my horse and cart. I got most for my crop."

"What crop did you have in the spring?"

"I sold the next crop."

"The one you haven't got yet, what? What fool has given you money for that?"

"Solomon Mandel from Nyirbator."

"The Jew Mandel—a fine witness!"

Commissioner Erdy raised his sword.

"The inquiry is concluded. Corporal, search his pockets and the drawers. Sergeant Patyodi, bracelets on him."

Malkeleh gripped the grille convulsively, afraid that she would collapse. She stared at Sholem, who held his hands extended, with a humble bearing, ready for the handcuffs. Israel had sinned against Jehovah, and it seemed that the sufferings of Gimpel Zorech were not enough to atone. The pandours had already produced the handcuffs and chains. Malkeleh averted her eyes. She was not so indulgent with the Jewish God, who had thus deserted them. Everyone had deserted them, even Sroleh Yomtov.

Suddenly her head jerked up, her eyes distending. The sound of horse's hooves in the distance, coming closer and closer. This was his horse! He had turned back, sensing the trouble. She could imagine him bending forward in the saddle and spurring his horse all out. She did not ask herself what Sroleh Yomtov could do against all these bayonets, so long as he was here at this moment of peril.

The horse stopped outside the inn and one could see it through the glass door jerking its head up and down and shaking its mane. It was Ferdl! There was a noise outside, the voices of the peasants whom the pandours were keeping away from the inn. Someone had jumped off the horse. The noise quietened to a murmur. The bell shrilled. There in the doorway stood the Black Squire, tall, scraggy, with tousled hair and a threadbare jacket in which he might have lounged at home. Swishing his riding-crop in the air he said, quietly but incisively:

"Who dares to touch my Jew without my knowledge and consent?"

The pandours dropped the shackles. The corporal shut the drawer in which he was rummaging. Commissioner Erdy stood on his hind legs and set his shoulders.

"I'm the man, Squire Francis de Sarberek."

"Who're you?"

The Commissioner's face grew a shade more purple. This de Sarberek would not know who he was!

"Andras Erdy, Pandour Commissioner of the County. In the name of the law."

"Don't bawl, young man. I don't bawl, though I'm at home here. And don't flourish that sword, I carry only this crop. I knew your father. He too was a great hero. He participated in the battle of Gyor and made Napoleon's troops flee—after him. The Emperor just let Thomas Erdy run along in his ragged dolman and with his bare-backed hag as far as County Ung. You're one of the Ung petties, aren't you?"

"That's got nothing to do with this matter," said Erdy darkly. I'm here on official business."

"Where's your authority?"

"That's not necessary in this case."

"It's very necessary, young man."

"The Jew has committed a crime."

"You'll have to prove that first."

"It has been proved in the course of the inquiry."

"I want to see the evidence."

"I can't show it to just anybody."

"That'll do now!" snapped de Sarberek. "On the basis of the *jus gladii*, which I have the honor to exercise here on behalf of my lords of Karoly and Ecsed, I call upon you to get out of here, and at once."

Commissioner Erdy was very quiet. He motioned to Sergeant Patyodi. The bristles on his head seemed to rear up.

"Right about—turn!" commanded the sergeant.

As he reached the door, Erdy turned his head, gazing with bleary eyes at the Black Squire.

"We'll be back."

"Not here, young man. You can come to the manor at Sarberek. You'll knock politely, and ask: "Please, is His Honor Squire Francis de Sarberek and de Portelek in?""

### THE PARABLE OF JERICHO

THE SCARE in Batiz started on the Sunday morning, when Yossef was stopped by the pandours on the outskirts of the village on his arrival from Lapfalva, and had the five hundred florins confiscated from him. With the arrival of Sroleh Yomtov, on Monday, the scare abated somewhat. Sroleh Yomtov assured his brother that he would have no trouble whatever in connection with Gimpel Zorech's case and that his money would be restored to him to the last copper. He informed Jacob Anshel that if the money was not returned within a fortnight, he himself would provide the partnership capital, and if necessary, a hundred or two more.

Sroleh Yomtov spent barely an hour with Jacob Anshel's family, after which he went over to Lazarovich, then to the wine merchant Mesel, and later to Shefteli the timber merchant. It was late night by the time he returned to the house. In the early morning he inspected the candlemaker's workshop and stockroom, then he again went over to the distiller's office, where the wine merchant and the timber merchant were already waiting for him.

What Sroleh Yomtov had to discuss with the notabilities of Batiz, no one knew, but on the Tuesday morning (and for many days after that) the talk in the synagogue yard centered on him. Yossef Yochanan the potter, who was known as the sage of Batiz, and who was in fact a man of intelligence and experience, for he used to take his pottery to many distant markets, had examined Sroleh Yomtov's horse, and had immediately stated that it came from the stables of Count Karolyi. For the Count's groom used to brush a chessboard pattern on the Count's saddle horses, and there were traces of the squares on Ferdl's back. Chaim the buttonmaker claimed to know that the late innkeeper's son, who in Vienna frequented the homes of Hungarian nobles, had been commissioned by Count Karolyi himself to come to Batiz. The guessing game went on and on. Filpischer the brushmaker was flushed with excitement (or as the malicious Nootah Batlan had it, from the spirits he had imbibed at his work) as he blundered on the great truth that the Count's family, which had brought prosperity to Karoly by allowing the Jews to settle there, had decided to buy Batiz and develop it into a center of trade and industry as a rival to the Jew-hating Otvar.

However, the brushmaker's prestige was not very high, and the others merely laughed at the things he invented among his bundles of horsehair and pig's bristle. Troyes, on the other hand, was a more serious and reliable man, and in his view the Count Karolyi had no need of Batiz. And if he had, he would send, not a young Jew to negotiate for him, but his haiduks to occupy the place. Feivel the tailor wondered how anyone could talk such nonsense, but Troyes, without taking offense, cited actual facts to support his theory. The old Count once went hunting round the Ecsed marsh and he took a fancy to the area. Returning home, he armed three hundred haiduks and sent them out to conquer the marsh. Who was there to resist him? One or two petty nobles tried to kick against it, threatening legal proceedings. But the Count merely laughed at them. The rest gave in and became his vassals. To the serfs it was all one who was squeezing them, the Count or the gentry. Indeed, the Count was better, because he demanded no villenage, only double tithes to be delivered to his stewards.

Once they were arguing about a thing it was no longer a matter for ridicule. What the brushmaker had said sounded incredible, yet it was true. It was truer still, that they all wanted to believe it. At the bottom of their hearts the Jews of Batiz had always dreamt of a time when their synagogue would be as populous as those of Karoly, Kallo, or Mad. And they also cherished a secret and fierce hope that they might one day show the stubborn Council of Otvar what the Jews could do if they got a little help and support from outside. Between the two extreme factions stood Tobias the glazier. He held the scales between them, and did so most happily, because being cross-eyed he could look at both parties as he talked. In his view the Count would think twice before starting an armed war, for though that might involve no risk for him, it was very expensive. Instead, he had sent a clever young Jew with some money for an advance. The balance of the money would perhaps be provided not by the Count, but by the rich Jews, who wanted to promote the advancement of Israel in the *galuth* by these means.

This was received with general approval, and Reb Lamach *Melommed* considered it necessary to confirm the glazier's theory with a parable. True, he was only a *melommed*, but he was an old Talmudist. Just now, his parable was from the sphere of military strategy, but after all, he was the uncle of Shlomah the ex-service sergeant who had fought through the Napoleonic wars and had ended up in the paymaster's department.

"When they lay siege to a fortress," said Reb Lamach, "they

send the strongest army to the weakest gate, and this army is
led by the cleverest general. To the strongest gate they send a
weak force, with a donkey at the head of it. On the back of the
donkey is a sack of gold. As the donkey approaches, the chinking
of the gold causes the strong gate to shake on its hinges, and by
the time the donkey gets there, it caves in."

The men liked Reb Lamach's parable. The story itself was
attractive, but even more attractive was the fact that an old dream
was shaping into reality behind it. A thing to which such poetical
parables were applied almost reflected the prose of accomplished
fact. Only one man pursed his lips: the swarthy, bent-backed
Galician, Nootah Batlan. Nootah used to score easily in debate
even with the most noted itinerant rabbis, and when he engaged
in debate with the rich Reb Leizer or the learned Reb Simon
Mesel, he denied himself the satisfaction of final victory only as a
matter of obligatory courtesy. The old *melommed* was not
worthy of his steel, and Nootah envied him only for his flowing
white beard. But this time Nootah could not avoid crossing
swords with the old man. He, Nootah, wanted to be the first rabbi
of the big synagogue of which the men were dreaming and it was
an open secret that his only serious rival was Reb Lamach.

"That's a strange parable, Reb Lamach," he said challengingly.
"Batiz is no fortress. It has neither walls nor gates, and any Jew
can come in without having to prepare for an attack."

The *melommed* passed his hand over his beard and replied in
a superior tone:

"If a learned man tells a parable about a fortress, every sensible
hearer imagines the walls and gates for himself."

"But why talk about imaginary walls when we are standing
before a real fortress?"

"Where is the fortress, Batlan?" inquired the *melommed*.

"Here in front of us," snapped Nootah.

"You mean Otvar?"

"What else? Jericho, perhaps? Every sensible person here
knows that Otvar has strong gates and everyone is longing for
the time when those gates will be flung open at last."

"That's true," said the men.

Reb Lamach felt that his authority was in danger.

"You want to open the gates of Otvar?" he said in a tone of ironical contempt. "Where will you find an ass big enough to carry such a big bag of gold on his back?"

This made the men laugh. However, Nootah was not the man to retreat before a cheap child-beater like Reb Lamach.

"You don't mean to say," he exclaimed, in a tone of indignation accompanied by an argumentative gesture, "that Reb Sroleh Yomtov is an ass!"

Reb Lamach, noticing that Jacob Anshel and Yossef were present, considered it necessary to keep on the right side of the future notables of the synagogue, so he hastened to explain:

"It wouldn't occur to me, Nootah. Sroleh Yomtov is one of the appointed leaders of Israel and I have no reason to doubt the keenness of his brain. But if you are acquainted with the cabbalistic traditions, you ought to know that our holy ancestors considered the donkey as one of the most useful, and indeed as one of the most intelligent animals. And even if the donkey were nothing but a donkey, remember, Nootah, it's he who'll bring the Messiah."

Nootah Batlan withdrew sulkily, and the others now began to bombard the candlemaker and his companion with their questions. For during the past twenty-four hours it had come out that Yossef was now a partner in the candle and soap-making business. However, Jacob Anshel was unable to answer any questions, and Yossef, too, merely kept shrugging his shoulders; which only served to confirm public opinion in the belief that there was something brewing.

Then Sroleh Yomtov himself appeared, flanked by Simon Mesel and the rich timber merchant, Shefteli. So no one could get near him. However, he broke away for a moment and went up to Yossef. Yossef told him what he had heard, and asked whether there was any truth in it.

"There's no truth in it," smiled Sroleh Yomtov, "though it's well invented."

Nootah Batlan, loitering nearby, retied the girdle round his ragged caftan and stepped up to Sroleh Yomtov.

"Something important, Reb Sroleh Yomtov," he said, "something very important."

The young man allowed himself to be drawn aside by the Batlan, and to be told, exclusively, really exclusively, the Batlan's own special parable, which was not so commonplace as the *melommed's* parable about the donkey laden with gold.

"Listen, Reb Sroleh Yomtov. In the time of Joshua our ancestors laid siege to Jericho. They walked round the walls seven times, blowing their horns and trumpets, and the walls collapsed. That's what we are doing today. We are living around our little Jericho we so much desire to enter, and walking around its walls with our whistles and flutes, aren't we? There's some difference between the trumpets of Joshua and the instruments of our peddling brethren. On the other hand, we have walked round Otvar not seven times, but seventy times seven times. Then why won't the walls collapse?"

"Why indeed, Nootah?"

"Because," said the Batlan, tugging at his scraggly beard, "because our wooden whistles and our tin whistles are understood only by the common people—and the common people don't count. It's the guards who count, the guards on the walls and at the gates. Their ears are used to the sound of a brass trumpet, so you can only get at them with a silver flute. But the Captain, who is sitting up there in the citadel, won't hear the silver flute, either. One must play a tune to him on a paper flute—English paper for preference. But if that's scarce, the red and blue bellied Austrian paper will do."

Sroleh Yomtov reached into his pocket and gave him a tip.

THE INTRUDER

WHEN, EARLY in the afternoon, Sroleh Yomtov left for Otvar, people asked each other: "What has he gone to Otvar for?" The excitement became more intense when, on the Wednesday, the market people returned from Otvar and reported that Sroleh Yomtov was still in the town and staying in the White House Inn in the market square. The oldest Jews, including Reb Lamach, said on their oath that such a thing had not happened for a hundred years. Since the Jews were expelled from Otvar on the basis of a charter from the Emperor Charles, no Jew had been allowed to spend a night in the Royal Borough.

There was a scare on Wednesday too. Two haiduks entered the inn yard, where the market people had left their vehicles, and asked the proprietor about Sroleh Yomtov. The proprietor vanished, then returned to say that the gentleman was busy and had a visitor. The haiduks said they were not going to wait, having been sent by Police Captain Kokass. They went up to the first floor and tried to enter room No. 13. But the door was locked from the inside. The haiduks started to bang on it, whereupon the door opened and a young Hungarian gentleman with an aggressive little mustache and a bunch of bristles in his hat came out and told them off sharply. Could they not wait, once Master Sroleh had sent a message to say he was busy! The haiduks muttered something about their orders from Captain Kokass, whereupon the young gentleman made a threatening gesture and bawled:

"Get out of here! I'm from the county. A mere municipal official can wait."

The two haiduks withdrew and stood waiting by the gate. They waited half an hour or more. Finally, Sroleh Yomtov came down—arm in arm with his visitor. In the yard he had his horse fetched from the stable, but he did not mount it; it was his visitor that mounted the splendid Ferdl. The gentleman from the county shook hands with him and said:

"So long, old man."

"A pleasant journey, Adam. When do I see you again?"

"A week to-day in Karoly, at the latest."

This was what the market people had seen and heard with their own eyes and ears. And not only those from Batiz, but also those from half a dozen other villages of the environs of Otvar, all of whom had come to sell their goods, so that in the evening they could clear out in a hurry, producing market vouchers to be stamped as proof that they had left the town in accordance with the regulations. However, the market people had seen more: they had seen Sroleh Yomtov shaking hands with the two haiduks and had heard him tell them just to go ahead, he knew his way to the town hall. And the two haiduks had made friendly faces, saluted and went away. Sroleh Yomtov strolled across the square and knocked at the door of Captain Kokass. The Jewish market people were tremendously excited, and none believed that they would see him again soon. Kokass was a beastly fellow, and anyone summoned by him was sure to be the worse for it. Fifteen days in the town jail would be the least. How was it that towards dusk Sroleh Yomtov was in fact seen at Jacob Anshel's stall, talking gaily with him, Yossef, and Zireleh, who this time was enchantingly sweet, addressing Sroleh Yomtov as brother-in-law? The Jews were overwhelmed with puzzlement, but Sroleh Yomtov said not a word of what had happened. However, it was enough to hear him say that he was sorry he could not return to Batiz because he had business in Karoly, though he would spend the night at the White House Inn. So, though the Jews knew nothing about certain matters, they sensed that this was the beginning of a new era. Here was a Jew who had dared to stay a night in Otvar, nay, two nights, and he was not flogged, nor even put into prison.

Captain Kokass could not be reproached with undue indulgence in the face of such a challenge. He was quite ready with the flogging and a term in jail for the impudent intruder, nor would it have been anything unusual if, in the heat of the interrogation, he had employed his special personal arguments, boxing the accused's ear right and left, and when he saw the blood streaming from his nose, bawling out in a proclamatory voice, so that the whole market, and more important still, the whole town hall could hear: "And now go to your synagogue and denounce me to your Jehova, so that all your kin should know what they may and may not do within the gates of the Royal Borough of Otvar." Master Kokass had not changed at all since he was a plain toll-inspector. On the contrary, his hostility and his personal vengefulness towards the foreign race had only become intensified with the growth of his official authority.

He was not scared by Captain Kokass's bawling. He spoke deliberately, with few gestures. If there was any trace of feeling, it was the pink of the scar on his forehead. The scar was re-

membering the past. Once, its color deepened to purple. That
was when the young man said:

"Master Kokass, I'm not a boy any longer."

"What're you babbling there, Jew!"

"I repeat, Master Kokass, I'm no longer a child."

Kokass's big round head, right down to his fat neck, was
suffused with red.

"Are you not a Jew?" he barked.

"I've grown up, Master Kokass. I'm a man."

Kokass felt impelled to employ his usual forcible arguments,
because he could not think of anything to say on the spur of the
moment, but looking at the well-dressed, well-groomed young
man before him, he thought better of it just in time. Besides, he
had heard from the haiduks that the accused had been visited by
a gentleman from the county with whom he had had a long discussion and who parted from him in a very friendly way. This
had only just penetrated into Master Kokass's intelligence, he
being only a burgher, and not a noble like that gentleman. He
growled and sputtered for awhile, as though in disapproval that
the highest and lowest stratum should thus get together, ignoring
the in-betweens. But his practical sense warned him to control
himself. This was no scared village Jew; there was something
behind this. Picking up a document he began to read, as though
dictating something to his clerk:

"Master Bagamer from the toll-gate reported yesterday that
Israel Yomtov or Yomtov Israel . . . which is the right name?"

"Both," replied Sroleh Yomtov. "In Vienna I am Israel Yomtov.
At home, in Hungary, I am Yomtov Israel."

"Hum. In Vienna . . . Well, Master Bagamer reported that
Yomtov Israel entered the town at half-past two yesterday afternoon. But neither he nor any of the other keepers have reported
that he had left in the evening. It has been found that the afore-
said Jew spent the night at the White House Inn. I impose on the
Jew Yomtov a fine of two florins, or thirty days in prison."

Sroleh Yomtov reached into his pocket and deposited four
florins on the table. Kokass looked at his clerk. With some embarrassment and more or less indignantly, he said:

"I said two florins, not four."

Sroleh Yomtov nodded.

"I'm paying one night in advance."

"What!"

"I'm staying tonight as well."

"Really!" cried Master Kokass, scarcely able to control his rage. "How dare you . . . We shall not tolerate it that a Jew should treat an Otvar authority with contempt."

"I didn't come to treat the authority with contempt, but to negotiate with it," was the calm reply.

"Negotiate with whom?" snapped Kokass.

"With Burgomaster Ambro Lam."

"What negotiations are they?"

"The Burgomaster has not authorized me to divulge them."

Master Kokass subsided. After this he was very polite.

"Then you've already started negotiations with the Burgomaster?"

"I've had talks with him. My appointment for the negotiations is now. Unfortunately, you're preventing me from being punctual."

"I couldn't know that," said Master Kokass apologetically. "In that case, of course, I shall remit the fine."

"I can't accept that," said Sroleh Yomtov, "having been fined."

"Please . . ."

Israel Yomtov could have laughed. It was good to see the brutal former toll-keeper, whom his ruthlessness and family connections had since promoted to be the first policeman of the town, becoming so tame at this second meeting. However, Sroleh Yomtov had rigid self-discipline and he did not laugh. He merely smiled, in a most friendly way. But he considered it necessary to define his attitude:

"My dear Captain, if the fine is due, I shall pay it. But please let me have a receipt, to add to my expense account. But I shall accept a refund when it is established that a Jew may also lie down to rest where he happens to be if he's delayed till night by important business. A Jew is a human being too, nothing more. When he is tired and sleepy, he wants to sleep."

"The brazen breed!" grumbled Master Kokass, slamming a document down on the table. "He has the face to say that a Jew is no more—no more!—than a human being. One ought to wring their necks before they grow up."

But Israel Yomtov heard none of this. He was already sitting face to face with Burgomaster Ambro Lam, in the latter's office.

## BURGOMASTER LAM

ISRAEL YOMTOV had learned one thing abroad: how to deal with notabilities. It was best to say little and let them talk, at least at the outset. Yomtov was economical with words and no matter how great the accumulation of things he wanted to say, he repressed them, waiting his turn patiently, rather than interrupt his partner. He just sat listening attentively, and answered briefly when a question was put to him, then went on listening, well aware that what he heard might be of greater value than what he might say himself. And the things he intended saying varied according to his reception.

Ambro Lam did not give him a very friendly reception. He was mistrustful and rude. But how different was his rudeness from the rage of Captain Kokass! Lam was not a handsome man, and at first glance he might even have seemed deformed. He had a pale, pumpkin face, with a projecting forehead and a narrow nose with wide nostrils, while his chin was as straight as if it had been cut with a chisel. He had thin hair, deep shadows under his eyes, and an untidy greying moustache over mobile lips. He was probably past fifty and looked a sickly old man. But his voice was deep and virile, with vigor and conviction in it. And as he warmed to his talk his pale grey eyes acquired a glitter and the projections on his brow somehow came alive. What a handsome ugly man, thought Israel Yomtov. This rough, forthright Ambro Lam exerted a strange attraction on him.

"I like people who come from far away," said Lam morosely, rather than with a note of welcome. "But those that come from Vienna I don't like." He gave the young Jew a searching look, then he drawled on: "They send all sorts of queer people here, accountants, inspectors, taxhounds, and the like. I'm glad to see the back of them." His bushy eyebrows contracted. "But these are not so bad," he went on. "There are those that come with sundry pretexts, and when they're gone at last, I discover that they were spies. They came to find out whether we have secret designs against the august Imperial House, whether we have imported any 'secret goods' from France or England and hidden them in the dark recesses of our minds."

He looked at Yomtov's attentive features. And as this mute attention irritated him, he blurted out:

"It'll be better, my boy, if you tell me yourself, instead of my finding out about you afterwards."

"What do you wish me to tell you, Burgomaster?"

"That you've been sent by the Black Cabinet."

Israel Yomtov went red in the face.

"I can't tell you what is not true."

"Isn't it, then?"

"All that I have to do with the Black Cabinet is that they're watching me too and are opening my letters."

"Really?" said the Burgomaster, and his tone became a shade friendlier. "What have they got against you? You're not a Jacobin, are you?"

"No. But my friends—"

"Subversive, are they?"

"No, neither Jacobins, nor subversive. Only they're discontented and speak out."

"Criticizing the Emperor, what?"

"Not so much the Emperor as the Prince Chancellor."

Ambro Lam hummed.

"I'm surprised they don't like him. The Prince Chancellor wants everything to stay as it is for ever. You Jews have been wanting the same for four thousand years."

Israel Yomtov responded only with a flicker of his eyelids. Perhaps it meant "You're mistaken." Ambro Lam did not notice it. Or perhaps he did, because he went on:

"You reverence the Emperor because he was appointed by God, and the noble landowner because he's protected by the Emperor. And you pray that nothing should ever change."

"If I prayed for that, I shouldn't be here now." Sroleh Yomtov said this very quietly. Ambro Lam gave him a sideways look; he was beginning to feel friendly towards him. He took out his snuff-box, took a pinch of snuff, then held it out:

"Have a pinch, my boy."

Yomtov was no snuff addict, but he could not repel this amiable gesture. He sniffed, sneezed, and laughed inwardly. Contrary to his rule, he did not wait for the Burgomaster to speak. Suddenly, his say had become urgent.

"I lived in Vienna, but have never been either to the Imperial court or the Chancellor's. I was in the service of another power there."

"Is there another power?"

"Yes."

"Who?"

"Rothschild."

"Huh!" cried the Burgomaster. "I never thought of that. But how could I—the Burgomaster of such a poor, backward town? We can't think of the mighty Viennese banker, no matter in what straits we are. They lend money to Buda, Pressburg, Pest. But Otvar. . . ."

"They might lend to Otvar as well if they had security."

"What security?"

"First, Otvar must endeavor to get out of its poverty and backwardness."

"Without money?"

"The Jew'll give you some if he'll get something in return. The Jew wants to live too."

"I let them live."

"You let them make a living as best they can by coming in and trading once a week. But that's not enough. The Jews want to live here in Otvar."

"I should think they do."

Israel Yomtov was no great debater, but this time he had prepared for it. It was not in accordance with the facts that the Jews were satisfied with everything as it was, and did not desire a change with all their hearts. The Jews wanted anything but to stay excommunicated and despised. They would like the host peoples to know, or rather to wish to know how useful and important is the work the Jews are doing. True, Otvar had a century-old right to keep the Jews out, having received its charter from the Emperor Charles for being less rebellious than the other *kuruc* towns. But Otvar too was rebellious to some degree. Yomtov knew that from his father, whose grandfather had lived in the town, until they expelled him under the Imperial charter. If the people of Otvar had not given up thinking, they would have realized that the Emperor was punishing rather than rewarding them. He took the Jews away from the town—the leaven from the bread. The town was not developing and was instead going backwards. It was all mud and darkness, without a single properly paved street. It was the heart of the county, the center of its communications, and the town was on the banks of the navigable river Szamos, too. Karoly was a small out-of-the-way township, but because the Count wanted it so, it was now the center of the region. The Count had brains. There were no Jews in Karoly, so he had some imported from distant parts. He gave them protection, a living, and rights. He even brought them a rabbi from Pressburg just to please them. Otvar, on the other hand. . . .

"That's the truth, Master Burgomaster, and it has to be told even if it sounds unpleasant. I don't think you take it amiss, because from what I can see you're not a friend of immutability, either."

Ambro Lam kept smoothing his thick moustache and blinking his eyes. That meant that he was far from displeased. He liked frankness, even from a Jew, he said. He knew very well that mistakes had been made. He himself was not very enthusiastic about seeing the town relegated to the background. They had taken the county seat away, leaving only the jail and the gallows. They had expelled the Serbs, Armenians, Greeks, and Jews, all under the charter of freedom. He knew that this was not freedom. He also knew that times had changed and a new era was dawning in Europe. He had done what he could, so that the town should not be caught unprepared by future events. He had admitted the Serbs. Zdenkovich even made a fortune here. Fortunately, the robbery and violence of which he was the victim did not take place in the town. He had also admitted the Armenian traders, and now there are also two Greeks in the town. One could not do everything at once. In due course one or two Jews would also be admitted.

The Jew Yomtov would have liked to reply, but this time Ambro Lam did not give him a chance. He felt like revealing himself. He said he was a liberal, and would like to educate the citizens to the new ideas. He had had some luck, but also a great deal of trouble when, four or five years earlier, Otvar received some refugees of the Greek War of Liberation. There were two brothers, Theodor and Gregory Nicopolis. They knew but a word or two of Hungarian then. Even today people laugh when they recall the malapropisms they used to make. Well, the citizens behaved well and subscribed to a fund to help the two unfortunate men. In those days the town was flooded with *agents provocateur*, Metternich having laid a ban on talk about any war of liberation. One could only refer to the Nicopolis brothers as "the victims of Ibrahim Pasha," and they had to be kept in hiding for a time too. Now they were burghers of the town. Theodor had the lease of the White House, while Gregory was an undertaker. They've become good Hungarians.

"I've already thought of admitting one or two patriotic Jews," the Burgomaster went on. "But I'm afraid that if there are one or two, another eight will want to come along, so as to form a prayer quorum. And there'd be an influx of Galician Jews. The Deputy is right—the danger comes from Galicia: illicit distillers, traffickers, rabbis, and schnorrers. I don't want them to come here. Let them go to Munkacs, Sziget, and Hust. Let Jehovah make their beards grow there. And if their sons get born with shorter beards, they can come a town nearer. We shall only admit Hungarian-Jewish gentlemen to Otvar."

"It doesn't depend on beards, Burgomaster, whether a man is a useful and honest burgher."

"We can't spoil the look of the town," said the Burgomaster with a shake of his head. "Besides, it would not be advisable to talk about the admission of Jews just now. We've got a Jew here who's been enjoying our hospitality for nine months. The pandour Commissioner tells me he's the only known member of the gang that committed the Zdenkovich robbery and murder. It doesn't help to popularize his race, to say nothing of what might happen if he's hanged."

"That can't happen, Burgomaster."

"Why not?"

"The man's innocent."

"What?"

"It'll come out shortly."

"I don't believe it. That he's innocent, perhaps; but that it'll come out, no. . . ."

"And if I prove to be right?"

Ambro Lam rose to his feet and gave a full-throated laugh.

"In that case, my dear lad, come and see me again, and I'll make room for one or two decent Jews. For you first of all, Israel Yomtov, seeing that your great-grandfather lived here."

Yomtov left in high spirits. He shook hands—slipping over a florin—with the haiduk who was, on the instructions of Captain Kokass, outside the Burgomaster's door to see how long the Jew was staying. In return, the haiduk handed him the receipts for the twice two florins fine. Thus that matter was settled, and Sroleh Yomtov might have left, for he had it in writing that he had spent two nights in Otvar. But he did not wish to leave. He went to have a look round in the town. He stayed in the streets long after nightfall, although it was raining and it was muddy underfoot, and the darkness was pierced only here and there by a lantern. Pedestrians swung them in front of them, so as to avoid the worst puddles. Some failed to avoid them and cursed profanely. The Jew Yomtov was amused.

In the morning he called on Dr. Pfirsich and had a good half-hour's talk with him. Then he returned to the White House, packed his bag and took the noon mail-coach for Karoly.

He went straight to the leather shop. Yiteleh was reserved, seemed even sulky. Was there anything the matter? No, nothing, only. . . .

"Only?"

The girl looked into the young man's smiling eyes and said with some embarrassment:

"I've received two letters. One is from Shayeh."

"That's interesting. What does he write?"

"He writes that he's found the Prodigal Son—then lost him again. I was worried."

"What about?"

"That Shayeh will find you again, while we . . . we'd lose you again."

"You think I'd go away without telling you?"

"You've done it once."

"That was different."

"You said you'd be back in one or two days. You were away for more than two weeks."

"For less than two weeks. For eleven days exactly."

"You said yourself that there was nothing but mud and darkness here. You don't like it here at home. Of course, Vienna is more beautiful."

"Just because I don't like the place I'm not going to leave it. On the contrary. I'll find a place that is even less satisfactory."

"Less satisfactory?"

"That's right. Where everything is just so, there's nothing much one can do."

The girl gave him an inquiring look.

"And the second letter?" asked the young man.

"Can I tell you?"

"Of course."

"It's from Jerucham, the singer. He's very happy. He was engaged as cantor at Hunfalva after a single trial. He writes that he's getting a good salary and there are prospects of extra earnings. There is a brick-built synagogue and there are many substantial Jews in the town. He would like me to marry him."

"You can't do that," said the young man with a decisive gesture.

"Why not?"

"Because you're going to marry me."

There was a new brightness in the girl's eyes. Her finely chiselled nostrils gave a quiver. But she controlled the twitching of her lips.

"Marry you?" she said belligerently. "Did you ask me whether I want to?"

"Not yet. I had to attend to a few things first. And I also had a talk with your mother."

"You did? What did she say?"

"She said you were a grown girl."

"Did you talk with my father as well?"

"Your father said: 'It's better to sit together than to squat alone.'"

The girl waved her arms.

"My father!" she cried delightedly. "He's the wisest man on earth!"

A PHENOMENAL CAREER

THE GREAT event of the county, which was the subject of discussion for weeks, and would, no doubt remain so for months to come, was the phenomenal career of Master Adam de Sarberek. Not within living memory had a barely twenty-two-year-old young man risen in such extraordinary circumstances from a small clerkship to one of the highest posts in the county. He was an unknown name, indeed, scarcely a name, but rather a cipher in the lowest stratum of the nobility, yet suddenly it became a household word. His coevals envied and admired him, the old generation considered that his daring was unexampled. But no one had any doubts as to his merit and aptitude. On the contrary, it was unanimously agreed that at last energy, ability, and youthful brilliance had prevailed without the rotten methods of patronage.

Only the inner circle of the county office knew that Adam de Sarberek's surprising emergence had been preceded by a special row between his and the Erdy family. Few bothered about that sort of thing, for every gentry family had an antagonist, with whom they carried on a petty feud all their lives. What happened, it was said, was that Commissioner Erdy had, in the name of the law, laid hands on the Jewish innkeeper of the Sarberek estate. But de Sarberek had only one Jew, indeed only a part of one, for he had to share him with two other Squires, so no wonder that he stood up for him. Master Erdy went to the Under Sheriff to obtain authority overriding the *jus gladii* exercised by de

Sarberek in a doubtful manner. But Francis de Sarberek appealed
to the Lord Sheriff. It seemed that Erdy would come out on top,
when Adam de Sarberek plunged into the dispute by jumping
into the saddle and riding through the length and breadth of the
county. In a single week he gathered sufficient material to unmask Erdy's gross errors and ineptitudes of the past eight years.
So Master Erdy was in disgrace and Adam de Sarberek swung
into a high position before the eyes of the whole world.

The most important feature of the affair was that these processes
were to the public benefit. For nearly nine years a gang of highwaymen had been menacing the roads in the county without a
single one of them being rendered harmless by Erdy's pandours.
The pandours arrived everywhere just too late, and Erdy was
always following the wrong clues. To maintain the prestige of his
office he arrested innocent people, filling the jails with them. That
was at an end now. Public safety in the county was now in
capable hands. The roads were free from the menace of decades,
trade and communications were gaining fresh vigor, and the
citizens of the county could sleep in peace.

It was an extraordinary story. When Adam de Sarberek returned from his quest, having spent most of the time of his absence
in the Avas mountains in the eastern part of the county, he did
not even look in at his office, from where he had been granted
only one week's leave, but went straight to the Lord Sheriff, with
whom he was closeted for several hours. At one point the Under
Sheriff was also called in. Everyone was surprised that this young
lad with the perky moustache should be holding the attention of
the highest officials of the county to this extent, but no one knew
what was behind it all. Indeed, it would not have been advisable
that anyone should learn about the matter, for secrecy was essential. Adam de Sarberek, having convinced the gentlemen of the
county that his inquiries were along the right lines, was given
special authority and fifty pandours to smoke the bandits out of
their lair. The pandours were sent ahead, while de Sarberek himself left Karoly alone, so as not to attract attention. It was many
miles away from Karoly that he was joined by Corporal Peter
Ardelan, a Rumanian lad from the Avas area, who knew every
corner of the mountains. Ardelan proved to be a most useful

companion in any case, for he was a clever lad and a keen observer. After the conclusion of the inquiry he was promoted to pandour sergeant over the heads of other men. This was the second career that was built on the rounding up of the bandits, though there was little mention of it among the gentry, this being the sensation of the lower strata.

The bandits' lair was surrounded in accordance with Adam de Sarberek's plan, which he prepared on the basis of his own inquiries in the area. The fifty pandours advanced in small groups from the direction of Varalja, Erdoszada, Sikarlo, and Laposbanya. They met near Sebespatak on a pitch-dark night. There they dismounted and laid siege to the house of Florian, the local nabob. Fortunately for the young commander, the night, in addition to being dark, was also stormy, and the bandits were asleep. It was only at dawn, when they heard a volley of musketry fire, that they jumped out of their beds. Florian himself dashed out into the yard, swearing in Rumanian. He was caught and shackled. His men, Yuon, Pintea, Vasile, and Dimitri surrendered without resistance. The whole thing went off without bloodshed.

However, the rest did not proceed so smoothly. The pandours searched the house but found nothing that could have been regarded as accumulated loot. True, they found small-arms, and daggers, but Florian asserted that they were to arm his men when he was transporting gold to the Royal Mint office in Nagybanya. What about the two barrels of gunpowder he had in a cave, sufficient for a score of muskets for twenty years? Florian smiled: he needed it for blasting in the mine. Master Adam was already beginning to think that he had blundered after all, and that Florian and his men were respectable miners, not bandits. But Peter Ardelan walked round the four shackled men, sniffing at them, then came back to say that they were not miners.

"How do you know?" asked Master Adam.

"They don't smell like miners."

This was a smart observation. Master Adam had been in the area barely a week before and as he trotted through the streets of the mining towns he was unpleasantly struck by the pungent smell that emanated from the bodies of the people. It was a mixture of withered onions and moldy vinegar, and Master Adam could scarcely enjoy the lovely mountain scenery on account of it. He stepped up to the four "miners" without saying anything to them, but only sniffing at them. They stank, but it was a different kind of stench; Corporal Ardelan was right.

Ardelan saw other things as well. There were some picks in the house. While there was nothing extraordinary about that, Ardelan said that they had not been used for years. Not because the picks were rusty—that could happen after a day or two, especially if the tools were left in a damp place. But the handles showed that they had not been used. They lacked the gloss of constant contact with the human hand.

Master Adam was now sure he had made no mistake. Leaving a section of pandours at Sebespatak, he took the captives back to Karoly.

The trouble was that the bandits knew nothing about anything. Also, Florian steadfastly refused to understand Hungarian, though he often made his captors smile by the way he Rumanized Hungarian words when he could not think of the right Rumanian word. What made things more difficult still was the fact that all the documents were in the possession of Commissioner Erdy—that is, if he did keep a file of the robberies of the past eight years. Even so, however, it might take months to hack one's way through such a file, and there was no time. Adam must either perform a swift operation and prove that he was right, or he would have failed. If the bandits held out on him, the loss of time would serve the interests of his rival and would promote his intrigues.

There was only one affair that the temporary Commissioner had studied thoroughly: the robbery and murder on the Szalka road. The two old clerks at the county office were amazed at the young lawyer's thorough grasp of the details, though he had only carried out a brief inquiry some ten months after the event, as an amateur, too. He had a partial success, though. One day he summoned Pintea before him and charged him with having removed the shoes from the hooves of Zdenkovich's horses in the stable of the Armenian inn at Csenger. Pintea listened numbly and said nothing. Then Master Adam turned on him:

"And it was you that knocked down the coachman!"

"Not me," blurted the man with a start, "but Yuon."

Yuon was brought in and made to face Pintea. Each accused the other. Then the other two men were brought in.

"Well, Vasile and Dimitri, how much did you get for the apples in Szalka?"

The two men exchanged glances, but said nothing.

"You didn't get anything," went on Adam, "because there were no apples left on the cart. You didn't even go to Szalka; you went to Kocsord to lie in wait. You'd left the bushel on the coachman's head."

"We did go to Szalka," said Dimitri darkly.

"Yes—to sell the horses. They were fine horses. You got a hundred and fifty florins for them."

"Only a hundred and twenty," muttered Vasile.

"Of course, you asked a hundred and fifty but didn't get that much. Perhaps because you'd removed the horseshoes from the horses' hind legs."

"Pintea did that."

Now Florian was taken in hand. He was confronted with his men and Adam said:

"This one took the money, didn't he?"

Florian gazed at his men; and they knew nothing, were scarcely able to talk now. They even forgot that they had confessed one or two things a minute ago.

Adam stopped the interrogation for a while. He had progressed half-way, but had not yet got over the difficult stretch. He still lacked decisive evidence. He summoned witnesses who, he thought, might know about other cases in addition to the Zdenkovich case. He summoned people of whom Erdy had not even thought, including the Armenian innkeeper, at whose place Florian had been carousing and gambling the day before the attack on Zdenkovich; and David Enten, the Jewish wool merchant, the victim of an earlier masked robbery; Mesel the wine merchant, Aunt Seemah from Nameny, and Herskovitch, the innkeeper from Varalja. However, before all these witnesses arrived, the zealous young lawyer listened to Yiteleh's story, and also spent a great deal of time, in his own private office taking evidence from Israel Yomtov. This seemed strange, since Yomtov had been away for more than eight years. Yet it seemed that he knew something about the inception of the robberies in the county. Master Adam's energy and brilliance were beyond doubt. And if he kept the young Jew with him till late at night, he must have a good reason.

It was late at night now, and Master Adam de Sarberek was very gay and whistling a tune. He sent for his clerks and for Corporal Ardelan. They lighted the big candles and brought Florian up from his cell. He looked lankier and older than before. Master Adam stepped up to him:

"Well, Florian, I want you to tell me, in Hungarian, your real name."

Florian shook his head and said in broken Hungarian that he did not understand.

"You understand all right," said Adam. "A cut-throat from County Nyir ought to."

Florian gave a barely perceptible start and now said that he understood a little.

"A little, eh? Wait a moment. Suppose I whistle a Magyar tune, will you understand that?"

"I don't know."

"You don't? Well, listen." Adam screwed up his lips and whistled the tune of the highwayman's song. Then, quietly, he began to sing the song:

> *"Have a care, Benni, and save your breath,*
> *Or they'll take you to the cell of death."*

Picking up a candle in each hand he went up to Florian, who sat between two pandours with fixed bayonets. The man paled visibly.

"A fine song," Adam said. "I made merry to it once or twice."

He held the candles close to Florian's face, searching his eyes. Then he held the flames a little higher, to illuminate his eyebrows. Taking a pocket mirror from his jacket, he handed it to Florian.

"Take a look at yourself, perhaps it'll remind you who you are."

The accused handed the mirror back without looking into it.

"Why, my friend, you won't even look at yourself? You're quite a handsome cuss, too. The pretty lady in Varalja is going to cry for you. It's a pity one can't get brown hair-dye in jail. The color of your left eyebrow is already beginning to fade. In a fortnight it'll be flaxen blonde. Then I'll let you have the mirror again, so you can see the highwayman who nine years ago began by deserting from the barracks in Otvar. . . ."

Florian jumped to his feet. His lips were twitching.

"You're going to talk, Benni Darazs?"

"Yes, sir."

### IN THE SHADOW OF THE GALLOWS

GIMPEL ZORECH sat in the jail counting the seasons. It was summer when the pandours had brought him to Otvar, and since then an autumn, a winter, and a spring had passed and it was summer again. He had set out with the intention of visiting Malkeleh and having a talk with his son, who was getting bigger and more handsome and impudent each year. And cleverer, too, for he was already learning Rashi in Sholem's school. He knew already more than his father, who was nothing but a steer and a blockhead, and who was a man with a beard before he first heard that there had been a Rashi in the world. All Gimpel Zorech had learned—and that he had learned thoroughly—was that you had to beware of a bad woman. A bad woman was worse than death, because death took your life only once, a bad woman a hundred times. That was what Gimpel Zorech wanted to tell his Yosseleh, who had turned six and was learning Rashi. Rashi was very important, but so was this lesson. There had been men, great Talmudists who had great learning, but because they had not learned this one lesson, they perished.

What a calamity it was that he kept roaming about that time instead of making straight for the Shingled Inn. He had set out from Szalka, intending to take one road, then he said to himself that a short cut would be better. Well, it had not been a short

cut. It was the guardian angel of pig dealers that made him go that
way. Zdenkovich was lying in his own blood on the edge of the
swamp and would surely have died if he had not been passing.
Did Gimpel Zorech regret what he had done? No. But he often
cursed and shook his bony fists because they were thinking only
of the pig dealer and it didn't occur to them how badly the
schnorrer's boy was in need of paternal instruction.

When he was standing in the yard of the Shingled Inn, ragged
and lousy, and with shackles on his hands and feet, looking at the
freckled face of his Yossel, that and that alone was the message of
his eyes: "Look at your father, my son, take a good look at him.
All this is the work of a bad woman." He was a little pleased to
be able to present a living example. But had Yossel understood? A
bad woman gets you into jail, but jail was better. There you lay
on your filthy couch, bitten by bugs and with rats running over
you, but you could sleep and dream. You could not sleep by a
bad woman, only suffer.

Jail is not so bad, Yossel. It's a relief. Hard work is not so bad
either, it's an escape. And if you are lucky you can escape from
the hard labor as well. Gimpel Zorech laughed to himself at the
thought of how he was going to expound all this to his son, who
was living in a nice, clean house, with Malkeleh combing his unruly red hair, laundering his shirts and mending his trousers. Your
father was lucky, Yossel. For two months he helped to build the
embankment, but in the third month he was already washing
sheep's wool in the river in big baskets, then he worked with hides,
then he carried water for Master Erdy. And in the end he made
friends with the cow in the byre.

Ah, Yossel, it sounds simple like this, but it isn't. I'll have to
tell you everything in detail. Gimpel Zorech would still be standing in the river, up to the neck in it, if he hadn't started to
cough. He coughed as you do after drinking rum, or after smoking green tobacco. But there's neither rum, nor green tobacco in
jail. If you have a pipe-stem you have to hide it in your mattress.
There are only bandits and serfs in the jail, who thrash you if you
cough at night. How fortunate are such fights. The warder can't
sleep from them, and so next day Gimpel Zorech can go to the

wool-washing. Gimpel is too weak for the embankment; that's for Andras Vizhordo and other hefty lads.

Wool-washing isn't easy either, and you have to learn it. If it stayed filthy and greasy, then Master Erdy gets no money from the Guild of Mantle Makers. Master Erdy is a kind man, a very kind man. He comes out to the river and says: "Hi, men, I'll put aside a florin or two for the one that does the washing best, so he can start something with the money." Gimpel worked well and Master Erdy probably has a good bit laid by for him. He has also done the drying of the hides uniformly. That's paid for by the tanners' and the bootmakers' guilds. Some convicts had no faith. They don't believe they'll ever get out, or if they do, they don't believe that Commissioner Erdy will give them anything.

But the luckiest thing is the cow. She is a little one with crooked horns and she's boss-eyed, but she's a good milker. In the spring they drove her out to a damp meadow, and she got blown, so she nearly died. But Gimpel was there and he understood about cows. What a fine farmer he would have become with a good woman at his side, like for instance Malkeleh. Like this he became a tramp, a schnorrer of twenty-seven counties. But he still understood about cows. He pushed his arm into her behind, scraped out what had to be scraped out, and he did it for three days. The fourth day you could already have a talk with the cow. No one else but Gimpel Zorech and the little cow understood, because he was talking to her in Yiddish. He told her that there was a great lord in the world, even mightier than God. His name was *Daless*. Daless had more children than Jacob, not only Jewish children, but also Hungarians, Ruthenians, Russians, Rumanians and Poles. When *Daless* ordered you, you had to take the cow out of the byre and sell her to the butcher, who would strike her between the horns with a big axe. The little cow looked at Gimpel Zorech with scared eyes, for she had understood his story.

Master Erdy could not understand Gimpel Zorech, and did not listen to him. He too is a great lord, like *Daless*, and when he gives orders to Peter Koczor not to bring Gimpel Zorech before him because his lingo was not for decent ears, Peter Koczor obeys. Throughout the whole year they have not interrogated Gimpel even once. But Master Erdy knows everything. It was only recently that the warder had mentioned to Gimpel that the judges would soon get together to try him.

"You must pull up your socks, Gimpel," the warder had said, "or they'll pull you up by the neck."

Gimpel merely smiled. Master Erdy was a kind man; he was saving up money for him for the time when they let him out. And Erdy was the little cow's master and would not forget what Gimpel had done to save her.

Still, Gimpel Zorech was a little scared. He implored Yossef, when he came with his rations, to bring along his little son, so he could talk with him. Yossef just shook his head, saying he ought to have asked before, and it was too late now.

"Why too late?" asked Gimpel Zorech, and his eyes were like the little cow's when he mentioned the butcher.

"Yossel is no longer with Malkeleh. Beilah Yenteh has taken him away."

This information was more devastating than the news of the arrival of the hangman could have been. For days he took no interest in anything, neither wool, nor hides, nor even the little cow. Even the kosher food from Batiz had no taste for him. He did not care now, and he thought he would not even defend himself before the judges.

However, when he was standing before the judges he realized that they were real judges and that the trial was real too. At the head of the table, with a crucifix above him on the wall, sat a great gentleman with a big black moustache. He was the chief judge. On his right was a bald-headed gentleman with a huge double chin; on his left, a lean man with a deep furrow running from the base of his nose right down to his chin. There was also a clerk. Master Erdy was there too, and also Sergeant Patyodi. Then there was a fine gentleman with side-whiskers and a pair of gloves and a grey top-hat in his hand. The situation made Gimpel Zorech's heart contract: yes, he would fight for his skin. Perhaps they'd let him out and then he would find Beilah Yenteh and take his son away from her.

The three judges were now talking with each other. If they were talking in Hungarian, Gimpel Zorech might catch a word or two, but they were talking in another language. The chief judge said something, whereupon the bald one said in a deep voice:

"Jurium regni non capaces."

"I beg your pardon," said the gentleman of the grey top-hat. "If I understand the Latin sentence aright, it means that these people have no share in the rights of the country."

"That is so," replied the chief judge. "You, Dr. Pfirsich, are here only as a witness and medical expert, but I will gladly explain. According to the decree of our King Ferdinand the Third, issued in sixteen-forty-seven, the Jews have no share in the rights of the country."

"I think, your Honor, that that principle cannot be applied to criminal cases. There it is purely a matter of guilt or innocence."

"What does Judge Szudy say to that?" asked the chief judge.

The stern-faced judge scratched the back of his head. There were bits of chaff in his hair, and it seemed that he had been called into the seat of judgment straight from hay-making or threshing.

"I think that whereas Dr. Pfirsich may know about the pancreas and the water-disease, he has no idea about the Corpus Juris."

"That is possible," said the doctor politely. "I'm therefore not quoting from the Corpus Juris, only calling attention to the spirit of the times."

The chief judge turned to his right.

"Judge Tokody. . . ."

The judge gave the doctor an embarrassed look. He was his patient and was being treated for some ailment just then.

"Dr. Pfirsich is well versed in literature."

"Literature and the prevailing order are two different things," burst out the chief judge. "The order is eternal and inviolable. All talk about equal rights and freedom is nothing but the fancy of idling, good-for-nothing scribes."

Dr. Pfirsich bowed and sat down.

"Jew Gimpel," said the chief judge, "the charge against you is that you knocked down and robbed the pig dealer Zdenkovich."

Dr. Pfirsich jumped up.

"I beg the indulgence of the court. Perhaps the court had better

summon Zdenkovich, who was my patient. He described his
attackers to me very differently."

"There's no need for that," cried Erdy. "His evidence is on the
file."

"But Zdenkovich told me that he owed his life to this Jew."

"Really, really."

"It is so. And later I established it myself."

"I ask the court to eject this witness," said Erdy angrily. "He's
only teaching the accused what lies to tell."

"I think," said Pfirsich, "the accused does not understand what
I'm saying." Turning to Gimpel Zorech, he asked, in German:
"Did you understand anything that was said?"

Gimpel Zorech shook his shaggy head and said, in Yiddish: "A
little."

The judges exchanged glances. The chief judge turned to
Pfirsich:

"You understand this gibberish?"

"Yes, Your Honor. It's medieval South German—the language
of the *Minnesaengers*."

"Then will you kindly interpret the question: What was the
accused doing around Zdenkovich?"

The doctor put the question in German. Gimpel replied in
Yiddish:

"I worked on the *goy*."

"How?"

"I rubbed his heart with whisky. The *goy* was dying."

Dr. Pfirsich faced the court:

"What he says agrees with what Zdenkovich told me. This
poor beggar was passing that way and found Zdenkovich lying
in a pool of blood. He took the leather bottle and poured some
whisky into his mouth. Then he rubbed his chest with whisky
in the region of the heart. Zdenkovich recovered consciousness for
a moment and saw the Jew's face above him."

"Hum," said the chief judge. "But the Jew drank some of
Zdenkovich's whisky."

"He really deserved a drop of whisky."

"Judge Szudy, what do you say to that?"

The lean judge shrugged his shoulders and said:

"You don't muzzle a working ox."

"And you, Judge Tokody?"

Judge Tokody had been snoozing. Now, startled awake, he barked:

"Ego sum pro morte!"

"That's the only correct judgement," said Erdy. "I'll have the gallows erected."

The chief judge rose.

"I adjourn the trial. We must hear Zdenkovich."

Dr. Pfirsich performed a courtly bow.

## THE THREE NOTABLES

THERE WAS great rejoicing in the villages round Otvar, and particularly in Batiz, when it became known that Burgomaster Ambro Lam had promised to admit, or rather re-admit, the Jews into the town. What was most important was that Sroleh Yomtov had also got round Councillor Csanyi, who had also given in, though only after long hesitation and many objections. Csanyi was not only a councillor, but also the keeper of the archives, and was reputed to be a fierce nationalist. He worked, or rather spent his time drinking wine, smoking his pipe and driving the flies away from his bald pate, in the turret-room of the town hall. When Sroleh Yomtov knocked at his door, he barked out irritably, "Come in!" But after an hour or two of conversation he parted from him most amiably, saying: "Come again, my young Israelitic friend."

It was understandable that Master Csanyi should be irritated with those who disturbed him in his solitude and that he should have looked askance at the young stranger, even though he had been sent by the Burgomaster himself.

"For a hundred years," he growled, "it was not important for you to find out what forebears you had living here, and now it has become urgent all at once? Who's in a hurry?"

"I am, Master Councillor. I'm about to marry and want to settle down."

"Why here, where you can't? The world's big enough."

"Otvar is part of it."

"Hum. It's part of the Jewless world."

"It was not always so. You know that best. I came to ask you to find out from the old files how long my great-grandfather lived here. He dealt in linen and percale and moved out of the town not entirely of his own accord."

"What was his name?"

"Same as mine—Yisroel Yomtov."

"What is Yisroel?"

"Israel."

"And what is Yomtov."

"It means a good day."

"Then he was called Israel Daygood, what?"

"No, just Yisroel Yomtov."

"How do you know he lived here?"

"From my father and grandfather. Besides, we have a family prayer-book and it's all noted down on the inside of the cover. The year five thousand four hundred and ninety-odd. That's according to our calendar. It corresponds to seventeen hundred and thirty-odd."

"And you want me to dig it all up, eh? But how the devil can I do that when the papers are all in a heap?"

"I'll look through them myself. Then I'll tidy it all up. I'm used to this sort of work. I worked at a bank in Vienna for years."

"There's a difference between bonds and the files of the municipality. We don't deal in money here."

"But you can't carry on without money, can you? You have accounts, surely. You have tax ledgers?"

Councillor Csanyi gave a tug at his thick black moustache and said:

"That's a good idea, my boy. The tax ledgers are over there on that shelf. Have a look at them, you may find something there. I won't let you disarrange my files, because then I'll have people coming to me all the time to find this or that or the other." With that he sat down at his desk and tossed down a glass of wine,

letting the young man look through the ledgers. But he was upset when, only a minute or two later it seemed, the Jew startled
him out of his reverie. Or was it a reverie?

"I've got it, Master Councillor. In the year seventeen hundred
and thirty-five seventeen Jews lived and paid taxes in Otvar.
Their names were Abraham, Moses, Solomon, David, Yossef
Yochanan, Jacob, Yisroel Yomtov. . . ."

Councillor Csanyi grumbled and growled and even tried to
quarrel with the Jew. But when the latter, smiling amiably all the
time, extracted something from his pocket and suggested that no
one could indite the necessary petition to the Worshipful Council
better than Councillor Csanyi, the latter gave in. It came out that
Master Csanyi personally did not hate the Jews, and that he was
far more hostile to the Serb butchers, the Armenian tripe dealers
and the two females who ran eating stalls in the market square
and sent an intolerable stench up to him through the window, to
say nothing of flies. But Master Csanyi insisted on one thing: he
would write the Magyar version of the petitioners' names or not
at all.

"Anyhow," he said, "I have a kinsman in Pest, Professor Hor-
vath's the name, and he says that the Jews and the Magyars are
close relations and that God wrote the Bible in Hungarian." And
he proceeded to cite several Hebrew names that could be twisted,
by their sound, into association with Hungarian words, somewhat on the lines of Adam—don't care a dam.

Sroleh Yomtov smiled. It made no difference what was put into
the petitions. He would still be Israel Yomtov among the Jews,
and Sroleh Yomtov among his intimates.

However, his contentment turned out to be premature. Sroleh
Yomtov had learned a great deal abroad, but he had also forgotten
a great deal. He had forgotten that Batiz was Batiz, a world of its
own. The gentle Jacob Anshel, who had been so eager to move
into Otvar, was now very doubtful, saying that he did not feel
at all like settling there. No matter how good the trade prospects
might be in the town, he did not want to change the fine name he
had inherited from his father and had borne honorably for forty-
two years. True, the peasants always called him Jacob Antal, but

he would not have that nickname on his shop sign. He would much rather withdraw the petition.

Jacob Anshel's change of heart remained in the family for the present. The Jews of Batiz were also ignorant of the subject of discussion between Sroleh Yomtov on the one hand, and the three notabilities—Lazarovich, Mesel, and Shefteli—on the other. But it gradually came out that Leizer Lazarovich did not wish to become known as Lazar Lazarfi, that Mesel would not at any price give up the name that took his father years of manipulation to change from Esel (donkey) to its present form, and that Shefteli, too, though he would not have to change his name, would for the present be satisfied if the Council permitted him to establish a timber depot in the timber market, thus enabling him to save cartage by leaving his planks there, instead of having to cart it to and from Batiz every time.

However, the real objection in the eyes of the three notables was not the change of name. After all that was only a bee in Councillor Csanyi's bonnet, and he would listen to reason. Leizer Lazarovich said that everyone listened to reason; he was convinced that he would be a rich man to-day if he still had all the money it cost him to get the Town Council to listen. That, indeed, was the real trouble. They never got tired of listening. Israel Yomtov heard Lazarovich with a polite smile. Lazarovich was enraged by that smile, which to him was not polite, but impudent. He knew Sroleh Yomtov too well as a brat to doubt that. However, Lazarovich just scratched his straggly beard and smiled back, revealing his withered gums with a yellow tooth here and there. Lazarovich never exploded when he was angry, but on the contrary, behaved more amiably than ever.

"I'll tell you something, Sroleh Yomtov, my boy," he said. "You believe in their promise. Very well. I don't want to shake your faith. I always respected those who regarded the great with filial trust. After all, the young may also do something useful sometimes. True, our Sages say that the building of the young is destruction, and the destruction of the old is building. But to err is human, and our Sages too were human. So that you should see that I take your plan seriously, I shall not withdraw from the financial side of the matter. But I want to look after you as well—you know I always took a paternal interest in you in the past. I am prepared to let you have my house in Otvar for six months free of rent. And if you succeed in living there for six months, you can have the house for another year for a rent of only one florin. I promise this before reliable witnesses: my friends Mesel and Shefteli. It is the finest house in Otvar, a corner house in the market square and three floors high. There are one or two doors that open into the street, so it's suitable for a shop."

Israel Yomtov extended his hand in acceptance of the offer.

Simon Mesel was just a plain man, and he explained quite frankly that his reason for changing his mind about moving into the town was that he was no longer young and aggressive enough to be among the first to enter a town that was full of enemies. There were the Hungarian and German wine merchants there, who were doing everything to annoy him even now that he was living outside the town. The latest thing was a summons to appear before the Special Commissioner in Karoly. Though Sroleh Yomtov reassured him that it was in the matter of Zdenkovich's marked banknotes, and that the affair was well on the way towards a just conclusion, Mesel was afraid that it might be something else. He had bought a large quantity of Tokay wine from some prominent Hungarian nobles and had forwarded it to Vienna in all good faith, and now it had turned out that it was a mixture of raisin juice and cheap wines.

Shefteli considered that Israel Yomtov had undertaken a worthy task, and must be supported. But he too held that the struggle could be waged only by those who had nothing to lose. The older men ought to stay behind and provide the advancing troop with counsel—and if necessary with "gunpowder." He himself could not desert the community of which he was President, lest it be said that he had deserted the flag. If his stocks were in the town, he would go there frequently in any case. And when the position was consolidated and there was a goodly congregation in Otvar, he would not recoil from personal sacrifice and would accept the Presidency, though it involved a great deal of trouble.

Gradually, it became known that the three notables did not desire to move into the town. However, Yossef and Zireleh kept going in together, and sometimes they were accompanied by

Esther and the girls' stepmother, and there was a great deal of floor-scrubbing and window-cleaning in the big house in the market square. Sroleh Yomtov himself had brought masons and carpenters to the house to attend to necessary repairs. Once, Yiteleh came over with Moysheh by the Karoly mail-coach to inspect the premises. They decided to start the leather and stationery shop on the side looking away from the market square, where the goods would have been exposed to too much sun. Malkeleh brought along some bedclothes.

They were so sure of themselves that they were already bringing furniture into the house. But the Jews of Batiz were increasingly doubtful. Yet how enthusiastic they had been at first! The artisans, traders, market venders, stallholders, peddlers, drapers, potters, and button-makers had been talking about a new dawn. They would no longer have to pack at night, hurry to drive into the town by dawn, scramble to secure a good spot, then, in the late afternoon, re-pack in breathless haste and leave the town whatever the weather and whatever dangers awaited them on the road. Instead, they would just stroll along to the market square from their homes in the town, and in the evening stroll back comfortably, perhaps pulling a hand-cart with their goods on it. It would be a very heaven as compared with the present rush and bustle. There were those who planned to build themselves a permanent booth in the market square, so they would not even have to carry poles and canvas sheets. The bolder spirits dreamt of their own shops, so that the customers would come to them, instead of them having to go to the customers. It was going to be just fine.

How was it that all these hopes and dreams were now beginning to fade? Yossef Yochanan said he did not mind if his customers called him Master Potter or that he was entered in the town's records as Jozsef Janos Fazekas. After all, one of our great rabbis had been known as Antigonos when Greek was in vogue. We also had High Priests and Kings with Greek names. And we had scholars with Arab, Spanish, Portuguese, Italian, Dutch, and Russian names. "But," he said, "the important thing is that we should be able to curb our desires with common sense. A young child wants to go out into the street, but its mother won't allow it.

Why won't she allow it? Because she is wise; because she knows that there are horses and buffaloes racing along the street. Common sense is the brake on desire. We want to go to Otvar and we will. But we must not do anything in haste. First we must look round thoroughly, a thing we have not done so far. I, gentlemen, am a potter. It is important for me to know whether there is any suitable clay near there and precisely where. I must also look around to see who are going to be my neighbors. They may be amiable outwardly and malicious at heart; or they may be malicious both ways. Maybe there are too many bootmakers' apprentices and other unruly brats who would throw stones at my pottery when I put it out to dry."

These words were more in keeping with the general anxiety. No doubt, however, this anxiety arose from the vacillation of the three notables. If they were making no move, if Lazarovich, Mesel, and Shefteli were not in a hurry, then the others ought to exercise prudence too. Elephant, the button-maker, had discussed the matter with Bagamer, the market inspector, who was known as an official of inexpensive courtesy. Bagamer merely laughed. He said there was no question of admitting any Jews. The guilds would make such a to-do that even those Jews who stayed out of the town would feel it. He, Elephant, had every reason not to incur the displeasure of the button-makers' guild. The same applied to the tailor, who would be provoking the ire of the tailors' guild. It was best to look after what one had got, and to wait and see where the recklessness of the young people would lead them. Perhaps it would turn out for the best. But supposing it didn't? Then Nootah Batlan spoke, sticking to his parable about Jericho, and hitting the nail right on the head:

"It'll be enough if two people move in to begin with. Joshua sent only two men into the Land of Promise. The people waited patiently for the report of the spies. They did not run with their heads against the wall. They waited until the walls collapsed." Then, turning to Yossef: "Don't be discouraged, you two. Just go ahead, you and Sroleh Yomtov. And if you want a third to say grace at table, just send for Nootah Batlan. Nootah Batlan has no pots like Yossef Yochanan and no sheets of glass like Tobias

the glazier. He needn't be afraid of the guilds, either. Nootah is
ready to sit down with the brave and sing hymns over a good
dinner."

### THE THREE WHO SPREAD THE LIGHT

HERE AND there, a more violent note was struck in the synagogue
yard. Tobias the glazier turned on Nootah Batlan just as the
latter was calling the congregation to prayer with the cessation
of the sing-song in Reb Lamach's school.

"You talk too much, Batlan. You tell people I'm afraid for my
glass."

"Who told you that, Tobias?"

"I heard it from several people. You say I hesitate to move in
because Lazarovich and Mesel are still thinking it over."

"What if I did say that Reb Leizer Lazarovich and Reb Simon
Mesel are thinking? Is there anything wrong about a man with
brains making use of them?"

"There's nothing wrong about that. But it's wrong for us to
think with other people's brains."

"You may be right there, Reb Tobias."

"May be right! I am right. I'm not going to think with the
head of either the distiller or the wine merchant. I'll go my own
way and not think at all."

Nootah Batlan laughed. Avrom the brushmaker said:

"Tobias is right. Why think about it?"

"I don't think," repeated Tobias aloud. "If Jacob Anshel moves
in, or if he has part of his business moved in by Yossef, I'm not
going to stay in Batiz. I don't chatter and I don't deal in intoxication. Like Jacob Anshel I spread the light."

Nootah Batlan was no longer laughing. He went into the
synagogue with the congregation and standing before the reading
desk intoned, in a somewhat husky voice, the beginning of the
service. "Blessed are they who live in thy house and praise thy
name, Selah."

Nootah Batlan was no fool. He knew that one had to praise the powers that be, both heavenly and earthly. Reb Leizer Lazarovich was the richest Jew in the whole county. A man who acquired a fortune with his brains usually looked after his brains, so as to keep his fortune. If Reb Leizer held that it was necessary to reflect, one had to reflect. Nothing had been settled as yet, and everything was uncertain. Despite the flowery petition Councillor Csanyi had indited, the Council of Otvar did not seem to be taking any notice. Reb Leizer had good sources of information, as he owned a house there. Reb Leizer was not a happy man. By acquiring wealth, he had lost his courage. But those who were going to live in his house were happy because they had dared to start something.

Tobias was always a reckless man: his poverty had made him so. He was temperamental by nature, being a descendant of Aaron. Lazarovich was also a Cohanite, but he knew how to curb his temperament because he had something to lose by rashness. Tobias was rebellious and sometimes rude, and he always paid for it. Only recently Lazarovich had had his windows mended by an itinerant Slovak glazier. Now Tobias was saying that he and Jacob Anshel were spreading the light. Yet he was in rivalry with Jacob Anshel as well. He was trying to persuade the peasants who were building new houses to have larger windows, arguing that they would get back the cost of the extra glass many times over by what they would save on candles.

However, thinking of all this with his Talmud-trained brain, Nootah Batlan realized that for once Tobias was right in yielding to his temperament. Why should he stay in Batiz, where it happens but rarely that a peasant builds a house, while the poor serfs go on using pig's bladder instead of glass for their windows? Otvar was the right place for him. There were twelve thousand burghers living there, mostly in brick-built houses, and in one part of the town the Hungarians and Germans were in constant conflict with each other and whenever there was a row they broke each other's windows. Tobias had two sons who already counted as adults in the synagogue, and both had adopted their father's trade. When autumn came with its cold winds, they went round the neighboring villages with the sheet glass on their backs and

the tools and lead in their carpet-bag to repair the broken windows. They visited Otvar as well, though the distance made it
exhausting. It was understandable, therefore, that Tobias was now
getting his sheet glass delivered in Otvar, where he kept a stock
in Lazarovich's house. Tobias was going to live there, among the
happy younger generation.

It was rather intriguing that Tobias, who always used to speak
out before, had now turned secretive. He would go aside for
hours with Yossef or Sroleh Yomtov, when the latter was in
Batiz, yet he said nothing about their discussions. Sroleh Yomtov
had taken him into his confidence precisely because he was such
a frank, forthright man. But there may have been another reason
why Sroleh Yomtov had chosen Tobias. At first the idea was that
seventeen families would be permitted to settle in Otvar, exactly
the same number as had lived there in seventeen hundred and
thirty-five. Sroleh Yomtov had been looking for big families, but
he had been warned from Otvar about this. Seventeen families
may mean two hundred or more persons, and such an invasion
might provoke the burghers, who had never seen anything like
such a crowd of Jews except on market days, when they had to
clear out in the evening. Burgomaster Lam himself must have been
warned by other leading members of the Council, Councillor
Gindel and Revenue Inspector Jeney, who were all in favor of the
*status quo*, not to fall for Jewish intrigue, the Jew being the kind
of dog that would snap at one's whole hand if one showed him a
finger. Councillor Csanyi also interpreted the list of taxpayers of a
century before in the sense that there were seventeen souls, not
seventeen families. Abraham, Jacob, Moses, Solomon, and Yisroel
Yomtov and the rest only lived in the town to pay taxes, and the
tax ledgers did not show that any of them had even thought of
founding a family. "All right," agreed Sroleh Yomtov, "let it be
seventeen souls. Perhaps there'll be even fewer of us for the present as the notables don't want to move in." But he insisted on
having Tobias and Jacob Anshel.

These preparations intrigued not only Nootah Batlan, but the
whole of Batiz. Nootah might have been intrigued more intensely,
but that was only because he was idle and had plenty of time to
observe what was going on. He did the thinking for those that

were working. Ah, thought the Batlan, for years Lazarovich, Shefteli, and Mesel kept declaring that they wanted to move into Otvar, but never could. Now they were suddenly reluctant to move in, therefore they must be preparing to do so. If the project failed, they would disclaim responsibility and assert that they never said a single word about it. But neither did Sroleh Yomtov. He didn't say a hundredth part as much as the three notables used to talk all those years. "Whoso is profuse of words causes error," says Rabban Simeon ben Gamaliel. Sroleh Yomtov had not committed a single error so far, so he would surely succeed in moving into Otvar. The Big Three were cautious, and would for the present stay where they were, though they might transfer their businesses. The candlemaker and the glazier were less cautious; they would go in themselves. It could not be otherwise, for if Israel, that is, Israel Yomtov, wanted to penetrate into the dark town, he would need them to carry the light. But he must know that the real torchbearers are those who study the Law and think. A Nootah Batlan cannot stay away. He has no goods and no business, only similes and parables and colorful, burning words that are so many torches to the soul.

For the present, he carried the light so that it illuminated his own path. The chances were definitely favorable. If seventeen souls moved into the town, the half of that would be eight and a half—eight and a half men and eight and a half women. But as they were not going to cut anyone in half, the proportions would probably be nine men and eight women. But where there were nine men, they would need a tenth to make a *minyan*. Well, they would either have to make the Otvar Council understand that seventeen was a figure of no significance, while eighteen had an age-old significance, partly because it was associated with the Eighteen Blessings, and partly because the alphabetic equivalents added up to *chai*, the root of the word *life*; or they could not make them understand and then the *minyan* would have to be found among the seventeen. All this required courage, thought Nootah. However, he was now determined not merely to sit down at table with the brave ones, but also to lead them at prayer. Reb Lamach would stay in Batiz with his children's school, while he, Nootah, would set out, unencumbered with a rival, on his urban career, beginning with ritual slaughtering, the examination of goose gizzards, Torah reading and unofficial preaching on Sabbath afternoons, and ending in a comfortable rabbinical chair.

The excitement reached a climax when Batiz learned that Sroleh Yomtov was recruiting immigrants in other villages as well. News came from Udvari that Judah the tinsmith was getting ready to transfer his family and his workshop. Solely on Sroleh Yomtov's encouragement, and without waiting for the Town Council's final decision, he had already despatched his stock of sheet iron to Otvar, storing it in the rear part of Lazarovich's house, which was also to serve as his workshop.

But the Council's decision was still to come. It was summer and the weather was so hot that a Council meeting before the harvest was quite out of the question. Burgomaster Lam himself had gone away for six weeks' holiday. But the other sensational event had already taken place: Commissioner Erdy had been dismissed, his place being taken by Master Adam de Sarberek. Gimpel Zorech had been released, and for weeks thereafter he was the most celebrated person in the county. The Jews would have paid for the privilege of shaking hands with him. After all, his acquittal meant the rehabilitation of Jewry. But the schnorrer vanished from Otvar, without saying good-bye even to the little cow. Picking up his knobby beechwood stick, which the pandours had confiscated on his arrest, he made for the highway in the middle of the night. He went to search for Beilah Yenteh, to take his son away from her and to teach him how to be a man and lead a decent life.

JEWFORT

LAZAROVICH WAS a careful business man who studied his self-interest even when he gave a copper to a beggar. It was said that once, when he had given a schnorrer a two-kreuzer piece instead of the usual kreuzer, the schnorrer asked suspiciously:

"Say, Reb Leizer, what do you want me to do for this extra kreuzer?"

It was the same with his seeming generosity as regards his house, which, in the public interest, he had let free of rent for six months and for a nominal rent for a further year. He made a tidy bit on it because Sroleh Yomtov spent a small fortune on repairs. The house had once been the town hall, and had later been leased by the bootmakers' guild. But when the guild transferred to its own new building, they left it in a very neglected state and Lazarovich could get no tenant for it. In course of time even the doors and windows had been stolen, while the paint and plaster were peeling, the chimney-pots were collapsing and the shingles on the roof had begun to rot. In those days the market square was not exactly impressive, but it did have a few substantial buildings, as the former county hall with its turret, the town hall, the White House Inn, the new building of the bootmakers' guild and, on the same side as the Lazarovich house, the "Kuruc Death Cell." This last was so called because it was there that, a hundred and twenty years earlier, the peace between the defeated insurgents of Prince Rakoczi II and the Austrian Emperor was concluded, giving the town an historic name and the right to expel the Jews. The "Death Cell," which was the town house of the Barons of Ecsed, had turrets green with age, Gothic windows, and a heavy barred gate, and was one of the finest buildings in the town. By contrast, Lazarovich's house for years had been in such a deplorable state, that it was dubbed the Tearful Jew. The guttering hung down limply, like damp ear-curls, on both sides and in a high wind there was an eerie whistling through the house, as though it were full of peddling Jews.

All this suddenly changed. Sroleh Yomtov's carpenters and shingle layers worked throughout the summer, putting the building in order inside as well as outside. They repaired or replaced doors and windows, re-floored the rooms, raised the chimney-pots with new bricks. Judah the tinsmith covered the roof facing the square with tin which was painted red, while Tobias glazed all the windows with unpatched panes. For nearly three weeks Avrom Filpischer's long-handled whitewash brushes were at work on the outside of the house, while a host of women and painters scrubbed and daubed within. In the end the Tearful Jew was no more, giving place to an almost new bright yellow building. Now it deserved to be called the Yellow House. It was known as such for decades, and even when it had long become a dirty grey.

The house also had another name given to it: Jewfort. This too stuck. It was the expression of suspicion, vexation, and envy. Of course, things did not proceed smoothly either at the beginning or later. The burghers of the town always looked askance at the intruders. True, the market square had become more attractive with a fine new building, but there was little pleasure in that. The Tearful Jew had gone, but there were now all those gay, enterprising Jews, and what might not become of the town if they were not got rid of in time! The people of the town were proud of the fact that the site of the town had for centuries been occupied by five forts (which is the meaning of the name Otvar). There was a Greek Fort, a Tatar Fort, a Turkish Fort, a German Fort, and a Magyar Fort. True, objective historians held that it was only one fort, renamed according to the holders. The fine Calvary Church now stood on the site of that one fort, looking down on the river. But the local patriots disbelieved both the objectivity of the historians and their facts, considering that the town was still dominated by five forts: the Magyar Fort in the Hungarian district, the Swabian in the German part, then the rebel fort at the old county hall, the imperialist fort at the town hall, and the gypsy fort down in the section called Gehenna across the river.

The Greeks, Armenians, and Serbs, whom the town had admitted despite the Royal Charter, did not constitute separate forts, but adhered to one or other of the existing forts as the spirit moved them. But the town could tolerate these and still exercise its right under the Charter to keep Jews and gypsies out of its area. Of course, the gypsies had come in without even bothering to present a petition to the Worshipful Council. They had pitched their camp in Gehenna Town and could not be expelled. Besides, the town had to have a dog catcher, someone to clear the cesspools, and also a tinsmith and a fortune teller, to say nothing of a Mari and a Rozi to entertain the soldiers, and musicians to play to the gentry of the town. But what was the use of the Jews?

What they made and sold was made and sold without them. Without them and without trouble. The Jews were only introducing new fashions and spoiling the market for the guilds and traders.

Now Otvar is going to change into Hatvar (six forts) said the burghers with foreboding. These Jews had not yet received their permit, yet they had already moved into the Yellow House. Tobias and his sons had already glazed the last window of the last room and could return to Batiz, but they were still there. From morning till night they were working in the yard, on a big table with their rulers and diamond cutters. They were cutting rectangular panes, with one end narrower than the other. At the bottom of the yard Judah and his sons were cutting out sheet iron and hammering away at it. Shefteli's planks, poles, and beams were being stacked along the ditch running towards the Calvary, though the house was far away from the timber market. The saw and cross-axe did not rest for a moment in the hands of the carpenters, and when Israel Yomtov-Daygood came to see them, the foreman, with his flat pencil, went to meet him and listened to his instructions, and wrote figures on a planed plank.

Of course, Jewfort was as yet sparsely populated. Tobias and Judah stayed there only on week-days and on Friday they swept their working place, packed up their tools and returned with their sons to their home villages, returning only when the Sabbath was over. In the part of the Yellow House looking away from the market square there were already curtains in the first-floor windows and of an evening a light could be seen through them. Someone was already living there. Of course, it was Israel Yomtov, the stubborn young Jew, who had the impudence to sleep in the White House Inn, though Captain Kokass was tearing his hair with rage. That time Captain Kokass had sent two haiduks for him and had fined him. But now he was turning a blind eye, although the Jew had settled in for good, and had brought his young wife with all her possessions.

His younger brother at least had the decency to wait for the Council's decision and was not getting married or moving in meanwhile. At the same time, Yossef's conduct also provoked the suspicion of the burghers. He came and went as often as three times a day with his cart, arriving from the direction of the German fort, that is, from Batiz. What was he bringing in his cart? What else but candles and soap? Just as though there were no candlemakers' guild in the town, and just as though the master of the guild and his brother-in-law, Councillor Poncikter, had no say at the town hall. Why, Jacob Antal's future son-in-law was accumulating enough candles in the Yellow House to last the winter for half the town. Something must be done about this, and at once.

Burgomaster Lam had long returned from his holiday, yet the Council had not met. At first it was he that urged the Council to sit, and it was the Council that resisted. Now the Council was urging him to call a meeting, but he was waiting. What for? He was waiting for the burghers to get accustomed to the new faces. The word Jew was heard too often among the burghers. "We can wait till Judgement Day before they get used to the Jews," observed Councillor Gindel to Revenue Inspector Jeney. The latter did not reply. What had happened? Jeney had always fought for the preservation of the old order, and now he had not a word to say even when Dr. Pfirsich declared in company that the Jews were also human, as proved by the case of Gimpel Zorech. True, Gimpel's acquittal had created something of a stir in favor of the Jews, but thank heaven it did not last long. The schnorrer had vanished as if he had been swallowed up by the earth. If he was innocent why did he vanish like that? Now that Benni Darazs and his gang had been brought to Otvar, it turned out that public opinion was favorable to the highwaymen. Vast crowds had gone out to the Karoly road to meet them, so that the pandours could scarcely clear a path for them. What a fine, handsome man, said the women. He had tears in one eye and laughter in the other. It would be a pity to hang him. Much rather hang that bandy-legged little Jew. A Jew deserved the rope even if he hadn't done anything.

Burgomaster Lam was waiting until the trial was over and the excitement abated. Fortunately, the court passed only two death sentences and the bandit chief himself escaped the rope. What saved him from being put into "a cell of death"? The fact that during the trial he was referred to as Darazs de Nyirhuba, so he must be a petty noble. Of course, they found no dog-skin patent on him, but that was understandable. A highwayman would naturally hide or destroy any document relating to his identity. For nine years he figured as Nabob Florian. You could not subject a member of the gentry to the disgrace of the rope, for that would have repercussions on the entire class. He had confessed his crimes and it would be sufficient to give him a life sentence and take him to a distant jail.

The cases of Yuon and Pintea were quite simple. It was proved that they committed several murders, and being only Wallach peasants, there was no objection to having them hanged. Thus the court, by adopting the golden mean, were able to satisfy both the avenging and the forgiving spirit of public opinion. Above all, the burghers had something to talk about and less was heard about the Jews.

There was a little to-do, though. Peter Koczor went to market on the Wednesday to buy the candles for the death cell. He went to Jacob Anshel, probably with the idea of giving him some slight return for all the tips he had received from him and Yossef during Gimpel Zorech's year in jail. But Jacob Anshel told the warder that he had no candles for people about to be hanged, and would he go to Hajtajer. The latter made a row, saying that it was just like a Jew to grudge the last respects to two poor fellows sentenced to death. Jacob Anshel explained that the light of his candles was to work and study and pray by, and what his rival called the last respects was merely torture. He wouldn't have poor erring people see horrible visions by the light of his candles.

However, the incident passed and was forgotten.

## SPIES

"I CAN scarcely keep pace with you, Sroleh Yomtov," said Yiteleh. "Do they take such big steps in Vienna?"

"No. Yiteleh. They take small steps and big jumps."

Husband and wife looked at each other. There was laughter in their eyes.

"You think if you hurry the town will follow you?"

"I don't, Yiteleh."

"Well, I'll follow you, anyhow. They can't say that I'm back-ward." They laughed at that.

"I learned to walk like this in Otvar," said the man. "There is so much mud that you can avoid it only by taking big steps."

"In the mud you sometimes take big steps, sometimes little ones, and sometimes you jump. But there's no mud now. There hasn't been a drop of rain for three weeks. There's nothing but dust."

"You have to avoid the dust as well."

"You won't avoid it here, not ever."

"Not ever? I don't think so. You can protect yourself against dust as well."

"By taking big steps?"

"No—by paving and sprinkling the roadway."

Yiteleh smiled inwardly. Sroleh Yomtov was taking big steps not on account of mud or dust, but to measure the length of the street. He would never admit it to Yiteleh, not because he was secretive with her, but because he was not in the habit of com-municating his plans to anyone unless he was sure that they were feasible. Yiteleh did not press him. She was glad to have a laugh and a talk with her husband. The gaiety and banter of such talks always led to a serious sentence or two, and while Sroleh Yomtov did not communicate his plans, he did communicate his thoughts and that was enough for Yiteleh.

In the beginning she used to fret about him. She used to wait with dinner for him and he was never on time. If he returned half an hour earlier than he had promised, he was still late. What was going to happen when there was a synagogue in the town? He was not the talkative type, of course. On the contrary, his strength lay in his ability to listen, and while doing so he would think and put his plans in order. But while it was right that he should not talk about his plans to everyone, he might at least confide in his wife.

"When things are more settled," he told her once. "Just now everything is uncertain."

"I want to have a share in your plans and struggles," she said. "Even if everything is uncertain."

"You are sharing in them by being with me," he said. "Even when we were not together I did everything together with you—even in Vienna."

He said this so charmingly that he could be permitted to be uncommunicative for the next three days. It was sufficient if he gave a nod or a blink while Yiteleh was talking. Yiteleh was not loquacious either, but she had so much to say. It had accumulated in her since that day when Sroleh Yomtov made her talk in Karoly, then suddenly went away, and indeed ever since Sroleh Yomtov ran away. If he had not run away she could not have loved him so much, just as she did not love Yossef. But Sroleh Yomtov had run away and had been silent for eight years.

Once, caressing the scar on his brow, she said:

"I love this scar. We got it together, and it hurt both of us."

"I never liked it," said the man. "Whenever I saw it in the mirror or touched it, I was seized with anger."

"Then I love it all the more. Because it was that anger that brought you back to me."

Now it was Saturday and they were walking round the town. They were in the German part, among the small houses. Sroleh Yomtov looked at the clean little dwellings and the tall swapes. Suddenly he bounded away. He had not visited this part yet and it seemed that he was measuring the ground. Yiteleh hurried after him, and, seizing him by the hand, said:

"We don't work on Saturday. We're out for a walk."

"You're right, Yiteleh. It's Saturday."

"My father never took my mother for a walk," said Yiteleh with mingled laughter and tears in her voice. "He just used to walk beside her, piously and modestly, as if he were not her husband at all. They were like two stars, two worlds. They were not moving away from each other, but they were not moving closer to each other, either. I was so afraid that you too might follow the traditional path. But you lived for years in the West, didn't you?"

Sroleh Yomtov gave her hand a squeeze and smiled into her

face. They turned back and strolled towards the Yellow House. He enjoyed the rhythm as they stepped in unison.

"Listen, Yiteleh," he said at length. And he began to talk about his plans. Yiteleh listened attentively. It was only when her husband asked her what she thought of them that she said, with the excitement of admiration in her voice:

"It'll be splendid!"

The town was beginning to talk about them. The girl in her small pointed shoes was stepping along perkily, with her white cotton stockings gleaming forth from under her frock. It was a blue, white-spotted sateen frock, with puffed sleeves and a lace collar and cuffs. She wore lace mittens and a lace kerchief on her head. Her earrings were pearls set in silver, and she wore them only because they went so well with her eyes. She laughed a great deal, perhaps only to show her white teeth and her dimples. She had a cunning little nose and her nostrils kept quivering, as though she were sniffing at everything.

Her husband too was sniffing, but in a different way. With his hooked nose and keen gaze, an attitude of attention made him look like a bird of prey. That was how the German shopkeepers, the master artisans, and other burghers saw him. Their women said he looked so haughty that if he were not a Jew he might be a count. Many regarded it as sheer audacity on his part that he wore apple-green pantaloons, a grey jacket, and a brown hat. Why, his grandfather wore a caftan, while his father must have gone rag-picking or walking the streets with a bundle on his back and chanting "Bones, rabbit-skins, scrap-iron!" Once the Jew got out of the filth he behaved as if he were as good as anyone else.

If they only did not keep talking in whispers! True, other lovers talked like that too. But other lovers talked only nonsense, whereas it was clear from their manner that this couple were saying other things than darling and light-of-my-eyes. Yes, their whispering was highly suspicious. Even when they raised their voices one could not understand a word they were saying. The citizen sitting on the bench outside his house, the womenfolk standing in the gateways and pedestrians who happened to be walking behind the couple, strained their ears in vain to catch an intelligible word. In the Hungarian part of the town they talked in German, in the

German part, in Hungarian. Of course, they might as well have talked in German in the German part too, for the Swabians could not understand their refined city talk in any case. But Dr. Pfirsich did understand them. There he was, coming along in his carriage and waving to them from afar. He wore a wide-brimmed straw hat and his greying side-whiskers gave a silvery gleam now and then against his sun-tanned face. There was the light of summer in his eyes and his voice was soft and caressing as he spoke to Yiteleh.

"Du bist wie eine Blume . . ." he quoted, stroking her little face.

"So hold und schön und rein," continued Yiteleh.

She curtsied baby-fashion, like a little girl who had just finished reciting a much-rehearsed poem of Heine.

"Her mother's daughter," said the doctor to her husband. "Mother is still a pretty woman, and she had brains too. A pity she has to spend her life by the marsh." He gestured towards his carriage. "I've brought some fruit from the hill: pears, peaches, plums, and apples. I'd be pleased if you'd take a basketful of each."

"Many thanks, Doctor," said Sroleh Yomtov. "We don't work on the Sabbath. Perhaps some other time."

The pedestrains in the street stared. And the news spread through the town like wildfire that Dr. Pfirsich had alighted from his carriage and spoken very amiably with the Jew and his Jewess.

However, Dr. Pfirsich did not matter much. After all, everyone knew that he was eccentric. He was pally with tipsy painters and traveling actors, but gave a wide berth to the burghers, even those that belonged to the gentry. He did not even visit the renovated Casino, though they had already decided to order a newspaper. It was far more sensational when the new Pandour Commissioner, riding along at the head of a section of pandours across the square, "presented arms" to the Jew and his wife, then stopped his horse, dismounted and went up to them, shaking the Jew by the hand and calling him "old man" and kissing the hand of his Jewess. The sun was high up in a clear sky, without a wisp of cloud to hide its face behind. There was a commotion in the square as groups formed to discuss the incident. After all, Adam de Sarberek was the most celebrated person in town at the moment.

After this it was not at all surprising that Councillor Csanyi, the fiercely nationalistic keeper of the town's archives, should greet the young Jew like an old friend as he came out of his office.

"Hullo, my dear Daygood. Is this lovely lady your wife? I'm really pleased to meet you."

What next? said the people. It was only necessary for the Burgomaster himself to come along and talk to these Jews! But that was precisely what happened. The Burgomaster had just come out of the town hall and while his acknowledgement of other salutations was hasty and perfunctory, he not only reciprocated the Jew's greeting with great courtesy and friendliness, but also paused for a moment to exchange a few words with them.


AN ANT HEAP


ISRAEL DAYGOOD was a great disappointment to the people of Otvar. He was not like their idea of a Jew at all. He did not kow-tow, did not slink, did not rush, did not play horrible Jewish tunes on a tin whistle, did not shake his fists, did not curse, and was not afraid either of dogs or the brats in the street. He walked upright, with unhurried steps. If stared at, he was serious; when spoken to, he was courteous. He anticipated the greeting of those he knew and raised his hat to anyone that greeted him first. The people expected that he would start trading in the town, but he was only buying instead. Moreover, when he accompanied his wife to market he never haggled with the venders, while in the shops he displayed no mistrust either as regards the quality or the price of the goods. There were some Gentile artisans and workmen working on his house; these he paid regularly. Indeed, he kept the carpenters on even when the repairs of the Yellow House had been completed, and also went on employing the navvies to get sand and gravel from the river, saying that the summer was the best time for such work, because the bed of the river was narrower and it cost less both in trouble and money to dredge. He was not in a hurry to have the material carted away, but just left it to accumulate off the river-bank.

The members of the guilds, particularly the traders, were depressed. The leading burghers had forebodings. The Council was almost entirely anti-Jewish. They had a superstitious horror of the race that had such mysterious prayers and such low prices. They thought that this Daygood in sheep's skin was even more dangerous than the ever amiable Lazarovich. It was known of the latter that he was a usurer and had got possession of the Yellow House through a legal swindle. In all the contracts he had made with the municipality the town had had the worst of it. That was the case with the distillery wash he supplied to the municipal stables, and also with the liquor he supplied to the Otvar inns . . . It was most fortunate that Lazarovich had outwitted the town for this at least gave it an excuse to defend itself. In vain did he present eloquent petitions, and in vain did he intrigue with one or two of the more influential councillors, the Council had kept him out. And with the rich Lazarovich they had also kept out the rest of his synagogue.

What a pity that they had not taken the house away from Lazarovich at the same time! But in those days it was so dilapidated that they did not consider it necessary, and left Lazarovich to pay the house tax. The town had so many repairs to see to without that. If there was a hole in the road they had to fill it in, and had to dig a bigger hole for the purpose next to it. Now there was the Jew house, fresh and bright, completely repaired, and there were the Jews, too. Not the Lazaroviches, but the Israels and the Jacobs, which was perhaps far worse.

Evidently, those who said to keep the Jews out had been right. But Councillors Gindel, Poncikter, and Bakoc only laughed and said to leave the Jews alone and just let them go on repairing the house: it would be for our benefit in the end. Indeed, one might lodge a complaint against the Burgomaster himself for letting the Daygoods and their fellows stay in the town before their petition had been settled. Now it was they that had settled. And the audacity of the tribe! The shop doors were still closed, but they were already arranging things inside, putting the stock on the shelves. There were big bundles of hides, reams of paper, and big bottles of ink. It was said that the stationery would be in a separate shop, to the left of the corner shop, and would be run by the girl. Next door would be the candle shop and next to that the tinsmith's shop. Anyone that said that they were to be only store-rooms was wrong. Just look at the two signboards that were set out to dry in the yard. One of them bore the legend: "Jacob Antal and Son-in-Law, Candles—Soap," and the other: "J. Einhorn, Tinsmith—Repairs Undertaken." What right had he to call himself a tinsmith, just like that? Anyone would think he was a master tinsmith, whereas he had not passed an examination before the guild, which he could never do, being a Jew, and so he would always be a botcher who could at any time be sued for unfair competition. That he knew his trade as well as anyone else was beside the point.

Yossef, realizing how easy it was to get into trouble, was very careful. He was bringing into the shop stock that was being made at the Batiz factory at a tremendous rate, just as if they were preparing for the biggest fair ever. True, St. Stephen's Day, the most famous pilgrim's day in Otvar, was approaching. St. Stephen was the patron saint of the Catholic Germans living in and around the town, having been settled in that area by the royal saint and his Bavarian wife in the year one thousand and something. But this stock was not made for St. Stephen's Day. A customer came in now and then to buy some candles. Yossef just shook his head, saying that those candles were not for sale.

"Then why are they here?" the customer would demand.

"Just to be here. These are not for the house—you can see by the sizes." He well knew that these impatient customers were all spies sent by Hajtajer, of the guild, and if he sold a single pound of candles before the Council's permission came through, there would be trouble. He had already said too much as it was, and he did not mention these incidents to his father-in-law. For some time past Jacob Anshel's candles had been acquiring a special reputation. Sroleh Yomtov had brought a new process from Vienna which made manufacture quicker, the candles better and nicer, yet cheaper. Hajtajer and the other Otvar candlemakers were still using nothing but tallow. Jacob Antal was mixing the tallow with some white substance that looked like quicklime, though that too was ninety-five per cent tallow. But how different were his candles! They were hard, straight, and glossy.

And they stayed like that down to the last stub. The wick was different, too. It was spun and woven flax and scarcely needed trimming. Hajtajer's candles were yellow and soft and were liable to collapse. They gave a blinking yellow light which was rather depressing, especially to those who had already tried Jacob Antal's candles. His candles gave a bluish-red flame, and the grease that dripped on the table-cloth or on one's clothes was pearly white and left no stain; you only had to scrape it off.

Tobias and his sons were not careful at all. They just dashed through the town with sheet glass under their arms and the cutter and the small hammer in their pockets. They were now working with putty; that, too, was something new. Putty was cheaper and easier to work with than lead, and when it was dry it could be painted the same color as the window-frame. It was still warm and it was not yet the window-mending season, but the more prudent burghers had theirs mended now, because in the autumn one had to wait for the glazier. It was good to have the panes whole, anyhow, to prevent the flies coming in. The town soon got used to a certain speeding up in this matter. When Tobias or one of his boys measured a window and said they would be back with the glass in an hour, you could rely on it. Formerly you could only wait; the glazier would promise to return in a month, but usually it took even longer than that.

There was no mistaking it: The Yellow House and its Jews were seeping into the public consciousness. Even before the Council had given its decision, the people had accepted them, or at least took due note of them. They might even miss the Jews if they should be expelled. The general view was that this was now out of the question, though the guilds and the shopkeepers were moving heaven and earth to secure such an outcome. What upset them in particular was that Councillors Gindel and Bakoc, who used to be unyielding opponents of the admission of Jews, were no longer so unyielding. It was the same when Zdenkovich's petition was under discussion. Those two banged their fists on the table, saying that they would not allow the rights of the town to be infringed, and that Serbians should stay in Serbia, together with their pigs. They did in fact frustrate the dealer's admission at the first meeting. But at the second meeting they were quieter.

It was said that the Serbian pigs in the sties of Gindel and Bakoc
were all the noisier.

The street was noticing something similar now. The blonde
Amalie Gindel came to the evening promenade between the
county hall and the town hall in a velvet frock. The Councillor
had bought the material in Varad, from Ullmann in the ghetto.
Councillor Bakoc, on the other hand, had just brought a new
carriage and a couple of nifty ponies from the same town for
his children. At that time Israel Daygood was also away from
Otvar. However, there were even more serious rumors going the
rounds. A reliable German burgher whose neighbor was acquainted with Councillor Gindel's bosom friend had heard, with
his own ears—but this was in strict confidence!—that the Jew
Daygood had brought a letter from Vienna which he had shown
to Burgomaster Lam alone. The letter contained a warning from
high quarters that Otvar must now drop its opposition to the admission of the Jews. And unless they received the Jews kindly,
immediate arrangements would be made to deprive the town of
its privileges. So any number of Jews that felt like it could now
invade the town. The letter was said to be—mind, this is in confidence!—by Chancellor Metternich and perhaps—you won't
blab, will you?—from an even higher personage. It was a fact
that it had been handed by Metternich to the Jew Daygood's influential co-religionists.

The Yellow House itself appeared to be getting impatient.
There, they did not understand Burgomaster Lam's indecision.
For he was postponing the important council meeting from one
week to another. Yossef was the most impatient, for his wedding
could not take place until after the council's decision, and Zireleh
was eager to join him in Otvar. Yiteleh too was restless. There
were days when Sroleh Yomtov brooded but said nothing, and
sometimes she thought he was cross with her. True, nice old
gentleman that Pfirsich was, it was not seemly that he should
chuck her under the chin. She could neither snub him, nor tell
her husband about it. She had already told him earlier that she had
danced a *csardas* with Master Adam, and that her father had not
looked at her for weeks on account of it. But could she have done

anything else just then? Sroleh Yomtov merely laughed when she told him. Nowadays he did not laugh much. Perhaps he did not like Master Adam kissing her hand in the street. True, they were the younger generation here, but she was just a plain Jewish woman for all that. Or perhaps Sroleh Yomtov had other problems and worries, and that was why he was silent. Yiteleh did not know how to broach the subject. In the evening, when she cleared the table, she sat down by him.

"Do you like living here, Sroleh Yomtov?" she asked.

Her husband raised his face to her.

"Don't you?"

"I don't know. The town is like an ant heap. Sometimes I feel it would be better to go away."

"An ant's place is in an ant heap," laughed the man. "Where would you go?"

"To some safe place."

"Where is there a safe place for us? We must create one."

"Perhaps. But perhaps it would be easier elsewhere. We can't leave now, but I often think it might have been better to start in some other place, where we could have been alone and could have lived for ourselves."

"For ourselves?" he repeated earnestly. "You know, Yiteleh, I have been out in the world a lot. I have been to *yeshibas* too. But I haven't retained much of the teachings of our Sages. I learned most from your father behind the bar. One Saturday afternoon he expounded the Ethics of the Fathers. In those days I used to think and brood a lot, more than ever since. I remembered how stirred I was by a saying of Hillel's. I kept reciting it to myself. It was my own idea really, only Hillel thought of it first. Do you know what saying I'm referring to?"

Yiteleh reflected.

"Wait a moment," she said. "One moment. You see, Hillel said so many fine things." Then her eyes lighted up: "I know. 'If I'm not for myself, who is for me? And if I'm for myself alone, what am I? And if not at once, then when?'"

The man took her face between his hands.

"My learned Rebbets'n. You know everything."

"You're right, Sroleh Yomtov," she said with quiet conviction. "We can't live for ourselves alone."

Then she gave a relieved laugh.

COUNCIL MEETING IN OTVAR

BURGOMASTER LAM gave a violent tug at the cord of the table-bell.

"I warn the audience again that this Council meeting is not public. If I have nevertheless invited a few prominent burghers, and have not barred the gallery to the general public, I have done so solely on account of the importance of the subject under discussion. I want the town to learn through reliable witnesses what happens in the town hall on this historic matter, and not be misled by rumors and gossip. But the audience are to listen only, not to talk. Councillor Bakoc. . . ."

The noise subsided and Councillor Bakoc, standing at one end of the table, continued, with violent gestures and turning now towards the auditorium, now towards his colleagues, where he had left off.

"I protest against unworthy insinuations against any member of the worshipful Council."

From somewhere at the back of the room, despite the Burgomaster's recent warning, came a voice:

"What price was the carriage from Varad?"

The Burgomaster raised his heavy eyelids and gazed reproachfully into the body of the room, but said nothing. Councillor Bakoc banged his fist on the table.

"I consider it an insult that the domestic affairs of councillors working for the public good should be aired at this place. Farmer Bakoc took his melons to Varad to sell and bought a carriage there. It is well known that the coach-builders of Varad are the best in the country."

The disrespectful voice, or perhaps another disrespectful voice, rang out again:

"A couple of melons are three groschen. What's the price of a couple of ponies?"

"I consider it beneath my dignity," barked Bakoc, going purple, "to answer such an irrelevant question. We are not here to discuss carriages and ponies, but something a hundred times more important. The question is, shall the town surrender the rights granted to it by our august ruler as a reward of its patriotic loyalty, or shall we defend them? I am going to defend them to my last breath."

The gallery applauded. The people at the back of the room gazed up with consternation. Councillor Bakoc had started on a very different note. He had spoken about reasonableness, tolerance, and Christian charity. This was surely a bold about turn after such a beginning, and after what the Councillor had told his friends privately. He had said he did not mind if a dozen or two Jews did move into the town; it could only benefit the town.

"No one can say," he went on, "that I am prejudiced against the Jews. Without the least prejudice, I hate them all. I grow melons and fruit, which I take to Varad, Debreczen, and other places. I don't need any Jews for that. And in my humble opinion the town does not need any Jews either. The Jews cheat, steal, and bribe. That's how they try to worm their way in among decent citizens. But we're not going to let them!"

Councillor Bakoc wiped the sweat off his brow and sat down. The next speaker was Councillor Gindel, a man with yellow hair, yellow whiskers, and yellow teeth. He spoke very cautiously. He agreed with the previous speaker in all respects. The town and its rights came first. For a hundred years Otvar had lived in peace and brotherly amity without Jews. The different nationalities had come closer to each other. The stream that had been flowing between the Hungarian and German parts of the town had changed its course and now there was nothing to divide the two peoples. It was the responsibility of those who had met here today to decide the fate of the town for the next hundred years to see that everything should go on as before.

The Burgomaster smiled into his whiskers.

"But this does not mean," went on Gindel, slightly raising his voice, "that we must rigidly bar innovations of any kind. Innovation does not necessarily mean the giving up of rights. Innovation is neither destructive, nor constructive, neither a pulling down, nor a building up, but simply renovation and repair, like the renovation of a dilapidated building. One can see what industrious hands could accomplish. What others abandon or throw on the dustheap, is salvaged by these industrious people, patched and repaired and raised to a new glory. And new glory, new light, new brightness is always needed. Gentlemen, with regard to the preservation of our ancient rights, my attitude is inflexible. And I say that in going in for innovations we must take care not to throw aside everything that is old. Let's rather sell it to the Jews."

It was a fine speech, but it had one great fault. It was not quite clear from it whether Councillor Gindel was or was not in favor of the admission of the Jews. However, the way he sat down suggested that he had not yet said all he wished to say, so one had to wait and see. The artisans and traders sitting in the body of the room were satisfied about one thing: Councillor Gindel was an inflexible adherent of the preservation of the Royal Charter rights. The next speaker was Councillor Poncikter, who spoke angrily, and was therefore cheered by the audience.

"They got out an old tax ledger and discovered from it that the Jews paid taxes here in the year seventeen hundred and thirty-five. In the ledger of the following year they do not appear. But the conclusion to be drawn from this is not that they were no longer living here, but that they were living here and evaded the payment of taxes. Who knows for how many years they carried on this swindle. I see Councillor Csanyi is incredulous. Very well. Let us say that what Councillor Csanyi wrote in the petition represents the true position. In seventeen hundred and thirty-six the Jews were no longer in Otvar. But the guilds were here. These honest Christians did not run away, but have been doing their duty as taxpayers ever since. Now Councillor Csanyi and some other so-called reformers want to reward the Jews for having paid no taxes for ninety-five years. And they want to punish the members of the guilds because they did pay taxes."

"What punishment are you talking about, Councillor?" inquired Csanyi.

"Foisting the Jews on them."

"We'll shake them off!" cried Hajtajer, the head of the candle-makers' guild, from the first row in the auditorium.

Many more speeches were delivered pro and con—or rather mostly con. This was the best attended Council meeting for years. Even the councillors of the outlying districts were present, including the Reverend Gulyacs. His Reverence advanced arguments of a religious character. Heavenly justice had condemned the Jews to be wanderers because they had crucified the Savior. An earthly corporation like the Council of Otvar could not change the heavenly judgment by giving the Jews the right of permanent settlement in the town. Another councillor, amid general applause, said that whereas the Jews had a horror of swine, they did not recoil from any swinish act. Their corkscrew ear-curls were only a symbol of their tortuous minds.

Then Burgomaster Lam rang the bell and announced that he himself wished to speak. There were cries of "Hear! Hear!" What did these people want to hear? They wanted to hear that in view of the general opposition he had revised his attitude and was going to drop the Jews. But the Burgomaster did not begin with the Jews and did not even refer to them for some time. He talked about his summer holiday and how he had visited the towns of Northern and Western Hungary, including Pest and Pressburg. He had not been out of Otvar for ten years and had learned a great deal during his tour. He was pleased to see how much a town could develop in ten years if the burghers were of a progressive turn of mind, and were not dominated by the mania that their town was a fixed star in the centre of the Universe and was there for the planets to travel around it.

The burghers in the body of the room, as well as the smaller fry in the gallery, listened with strained attention. But at this point the Burgomaster was interrupted by His Reverence.

"When you talk of travel, are you referring to the wandering race?"

"No, Your Reverence," replied the Burgomaster. "I'm referring to stars that have gone cold and give no light any longer."

His Reverence pursed his lips and sat down. The Burgomaster hastened to abandon the similes from the Universe, deciding to descend to the level of his audience.

"My pleasure was not unalloyed," he resumed. "Whenever I saw a nice clean town, I could not help thinking of the filth of Otvar, to which I would have to return. I have returned to it and found it worse than ever. For Ambro Lam being away, the brooms and shovels had a long rest. When I saw a nicely paved street, I thought of the mud, dust, and puddles in our streets. In the evenings I had a special sorrow when, walking along beautifully lighted streets, I thought of my beloved Otvar, where we leave illumination to the moon and the stars, and where on moonless and starless nights only the lanterns of one or two more prudent citizens bring a little light into the pitch darkness."

"We'll light the town if we get paid for it," cried Hajtajer.

"I quite believe you, Master Hajtajer," replied the Burgomaster. "Ten years ago the town had two hundred and fifty street lamps. In the course of time, fifty of them went out of commission. Another fifty are without panes. Recently I looked the matter up in the records of the town and found that we are still paying the candlemakers' guild for two hundred and fifty lamps, although at least a hundred have been out of commission for years."

There was a commotion; the councillors exchanged glances. Hajtajer said to his neighbor, Gyapjas the soapmaker, in an agitated whisper:

"Didn't I tell you: they send spies round the town."

The Burgomaster rang the bell.

"I do not want to talk about what was, but about what is going to be. From now on everything will be different. I have decided to increase the existing hundred and fifty lamps by another six hundred as soon as possible. (Murmur of amazement.) I am not content to have street lighting only in front of the town hall, my own house, the councillors' houses, the county hall, and the bishop's house. Every street and every citizen of the town deserves to have the new light."

The gallery clapped and cheered. The Burgomaster raised his voice.

"But the reason I want more lighting is not so that you should see even at night the mud, dust, and filth. What I want is that you should not see them even by day. We have decided to pave the streets. Unfortunately, we are not in the same position as the mountain towns, which get cheap paving from nearby quarries. But we've got the river. The cobblestones will make good paving. They call them 'potatoes' in Varad and Kassa, but if they can walk on them, so can we. The gravel will do to bank up the market square, so that people will not be trudging about with the mud up to their knees."

Henrik Wallon, the head of the Chamber of Trade, interrupted:

"You want to make it easier for the Jewish market venders, Burgomaster, what?"

"For the Christian buyers, Master Wallon," replied the Burgomaster coolly. This did not satisfy Wallon and the shopkeepers grouped round him. The Burgomaster went on:

"In the side streets and alleys, for which we shan't have any 'potatoes,' we shall put down some planks for paving. The Avas forests will provide good hard beech timber, and there'll be work for our carpenters for several years. For we propose to have other repairs done in the town as well."

The program was getting more and more attractive. The gallery was getting enthusiatic, though the stalls were considerably cooler. The burghers were gazing at each other with overcast faces. Gradually, these important people realized the menacing nature of the Burgomaster's program. All this was very fine, but where would the money come from? Was it to come from the pockets of the burghers? Wasn't the special tax big enough already? The Burgomaster read the faces of the audience, and before anyone could ask he dispelled their doubts:

"The cost of the proposed works will be covered from a municipal loan."

This was received with great relief. Now the body of the hall was also beginning to get enthusiastic. Even the councillors who had known about the plans applauded. In all its history the town of Otvar had never been able to secure a loan. Ambro Lam had accomplished that too. He was a great man, he was.

There were cheers. Master Wallon waited for the noise to subside, then:

"Who is giving the loan?" he asked.

"Who but the Jews?"

"And who'll repay it?" came another voice.

"The Jews, of course." The Burgomaster laughed and the audience laughed with him. This was good. The Burgomaster was getting the better of the Jews. Only the Wallon group kept on with their importunities.

"The Jews don't give anything for nothing," said Francis Contra, the leather merchant.

"Of course not," cried His Reverence. "They made thirty pieces of silver on our Lord."

In his reply the Burgomaster came to the point at issue, which at the beginning of the meeting had given rise to such passionate exchanges. Well, yes, the Jews wanted to settle in the town. And he, the Burgomaster, was saying to them: Step in. But it was not as simple as that. Anyone that wanted to come to Otvar had to pay for his ticket.

"Hear, hear!"

"I said to the Jew Daygood: You want to come and live here? All right. But this is a very backward town, with darkness and mud, and without a single properly paved street. We know that this is the natural center of the county, its heart, yet its blood circulation has been transferred to Karoly. Karoly was an out-of-the-way township, but because the Count wanted it so, it is now the capital of the county. He had some sense: when Otvar was expelling the Jews he brought them in, admitting those that were expelled from here. They did him good services against us. It came out that the Royal Charter we had was not so much a reward as a punishment, because Otvar continued to be suspected of rebel sympathies. Of course, the Count has not only brains, but also money, and if we want to compete with him, if we want better and safer communications, which is also in the interests of the trading people that want to settle here, we must have money. The Jew Daygood had a look at my plans, took out a pencil and made some calculations, then he said: 'You need at least twenty thousand florins for this.' 'That's the exact figure, Israel Daygood,' I said. So he said, 'I'll let you have the money if we get the contracts for the work and the materials.' "

"What work?" demanded Master Wallon aggressively.

"And what materials?" demanded Master Hajtajer, no less aggressively.

The Burgomaster explained that the Jew Daygood would pave certain streets with timber supplied by the Jews, but with the labor of the carpenters and blacksmiths of Otvar. He would also pave the better roads and bank up the market square with cobblestones and gravel navvied from the river. He would further repair the dilapidated lamps of the candlemakers' guild, which would continue to be supplied with candles by the guild itself. In addition, however, the Jew would provide six hundred new lamps at his own expense, but on condition that the candles for those would be supplied by Jacob Antal.

This was received in deathly silence. The guild members, carriers, timber men, and shopkeepers exchanged looks, as though to say: We applauded too soon, now we are caught. Master Hajtajer looked at his brother-in-law, Councillor Poncikter. The latter gave him an encouraging wink, whereupon Hajtajer raised his voice.

"That won't do," he said hoarsely. "The candlemakers' guild has a contract with the town for street lighting."

"For two hundred and fifty lamps, Master Hajtajer," said the Burgomaster. "Up till now you supplied candles for only a hundred and fifty, but we shall raise it to two hundred and fifty, so that the contract should be observed on both sides. The rest will be done by the Jews. However, I am prepared to give all to the guild, provided the guild undertakes to provide the six hundred new lamps. I would add that the Jew Daygood proposes to have the poles bored through, in case we go over to gas lighting at some later date. We must keep pace with progress."

Hajtajer did not reply. The Burgomaster faced the burghers in the body of the hall and went on:

"I am prepared to leave the whole plan to you, gentlemen, if you in turn are prepared to provide the twenty thousand florins, so that I can return to the Jew Daygood the bond he has deposited with me for security. I must call your attention to the fact, however, that the Jew wants neither interest, nor redemption for five years."

"And after five years?" came an uncertain voice from the back of the hall.

"After five years the town will be able to pay even the whole amount with the greatest ease, because the improvements in trade, industry, and communications will also add very considerably to our revenues."

Jeney, the Revenue Inspector and Town Treasurer, who had so far said nothing, now said briefly but emphatically: "That's correct."

At the back of the hall a moon-faced man rose to his feet and stabbed the air with a thick finger to indicate that he wanted to speak. He was a member of the bootmakers' guild.

"I beg your pardon, Master Burgomaster, but if there are planks on the sidewalk people will need fewer boots."

"But if we have cobblestones, people will need more boots," replied the Burgomaster. Then he went on, with decision in his voice: "Well, gentlemen, is there anyone here who'll overbid the Jews? I'm waiting, gentlemen. No one? Why, it's a matter of only twenty thousand florins. I'll give you five minutes."

There was profound depression among the men in the auditorium. The men in the gallery crowded to the railings to enjoy the confusion of the big pots. The gallery represented the common people; carpenters, masons, blacksmiths, navvies, and carters. They trusted the Burgomaster and they were also more or less acquainted with the Jews. The Jew Daygood gave them work and paid them well. The five minutes were up—the Burgomaster had won. And so had the Jew Daygood. The Burgomaster rose to conclude his speech.

"Gentlemen, this meeting started rather stormily, but passion has given way to a more sober attitude. There were moments when I had to be strict with our invited guests, but then I realized that it was best to let them speak out, so that the pros and cons should be put fairly on both sides. At the beginning I myself was accused of having brought spies into the town. I did not defend myself, but I shall take the responsibility for what I have done. Spies are usually hidden, but my spies have done their spying before the eyes of the whole town. I wonder for whom Israel Daygood might have been spying in this open town, the Sultan of Turkey or the Russian Tsar? I admit that he went all over the town with a notebook in his hand, measuring the streets with his feet. He did that in his own and in the town's interest. There

are some old burghers here who have been living in the town
for sixty or seventy years. Can a single one among them tell how
many streets the town has, or the length of any street, or the
points where the planks on the sidewalk are rotten and dangerous
at night? Israel Daygood has only been here a month. We must
wait and see what is going to happen when he and his brethren
will have been living here for a long time. You say that the Jews
cheat. Well, everyone with goods and weights and measures is
inclined to cheat. But you don't need a policeman to spot a cheat:
the customer will spot him at once, and he won't go to such a
one again. The trader who has to run away will cheat. The trader
who is staying is obliged to deal honestly with his customers."

The Burgomaster paused. He raised his eyes to the body of the
hall, but his gaze was remote, as though he was looking not at
the burghers, but beyond them, and through the wall, into the
distance.

"Fellow citizens," he said with a new note in his voice. "We
are on the threshold of a new era, we of this town, as well as the
whole country and the whole world. Those who do not know it
yet will be made to know it soon. The mills of time may appear
to be stagnant. But they never are. Just now they have begun
to revolve fast. Those who realize this will gain new life. Those
who do not or don't want to realize it, and above all those who
would like to stop the millstones, will be ground to dust between
them. I have known this for a long time. You remember what I
said when the two Greeks sought refuge here from Ibrahim
Pasha's Spahis. The Spahis were sent after them not by Ibrahim
Pasha, but by those who watch that the mill should not start.
But across the seas, in the country of the noble Washington and
the learned Franklin, new sails are being rigged, and new winds
are rising in Europe, new winds, generated by the storms of the
past. Ten years ago I knew that the new era could not be stopped
by mortars and bayonets. That summer there was a revolution
in Naples, and the carabinieri rose against the régime that tried
to hold up the new era. Since then Greek freedom has triumphed
and now, at the beginning of July, the people of Paris have risen
and driven out their oppressors the Bourbons. In our own country

the spirit of the new era is being fanned into flame by Szechenyi, Wesselenyi, Kossuth, and our great poets. We here must fight for our rights, the rights of our town. But they are not the so-called rights granted to us by the Royal Charter, which permits us to stay backward and live in poverty. We demand the right of progress and development. But he who wants rights for himself, must not deny rights to others. Those that accept a share of the risks, the toil, and the duties, must also be given a share in the rights that are the due portion of all beings created in the image of God. If we have received the freedom to forbid, let us exercise the freedom to permit."

The speech acted on the audience like whiffs of opium, dazing, animating, raising visions before their eyes. The people were stirred, moved, stimulated. Jeney stood up, then Gindel, then the whole of the Council in a body, cheering the Burgomaster. The gallery was raving. The chairs in the body of the hall also began to move and the burghers were swept away by the emotion of the moment. Only Hajtajer's face remained clouded, only Wallon's features reflected no enthusiasm. However, Wallon behaved cleverly. He went up to the Burgomaster to shake hands with him and congratulate him on his speech. Nevertheless, he did not forget to ask him how many Jews would be permitted to settle in the town.

The Burgomaster gazed at him absently and was already shaking hands with someone else. But Councillor Csanyi replied instead of him:

"Seventeen Jews altogether, Master Wallon."

"That's all right, then."

His Reverence folded his arms over his stomach. His clean-shaven fat face beamed with satisfaction.

"Pax et prudentia," he said in a deep voice, as though this were a revelation.

### THE PROPHET'S LETTER

SHOLEM WAS working at the back of the house, planting fruit trees. The sky was overcast and there was a drizzle, but Sholem was in high good spirits. He dug the pits, banked up the earth around the trees, careful to leave a trench around each. He was humming the song about a bird on the verdant lea, the song of the late Rabbi of Kallo. What made him do that? And why was he not thinking of the mystic sense of the words, of the time when the Messiah would appear in the mountain passes and blow his horn of liberation? That might be in a hundred years' time, or it might be in a month or two, or even to-morrow. Sholem was planting year-old saplings: apples, pears, plums, cherries, Spanish cherries, and walnuts. When would they come into bearing? For three years one must not touch the first fruits, and in the case of a walnut tree, for seven years. Apparently Sholem did not expect the Messiah to come within three or even seven years. Indeed, he did not expect the Savior of his hunted and persecuted people. He was thinking of his grandchildren, who were sure to be born, and he was planting fruit trees for them. In seven years' time even the walnut trees would be free and one or two little boys might be climbing them around the Feast of Tabernacles.

On the Sabbath the children—Yiteleh and Sroleh Yomtov and Yossef and his wife—had been here, and the festive taste was still in Sholem's mouth. For the first time Sroleh Yomtov listened with interest, at table, to the teachings of Israel, and it was he who silenced Mailech, telling him not to chatter about flannelette, percale, and linen, when his father was citing the wise sayings of Rabbi Teitelbaum and the letters of the Prophet Jeremiah. Reb Sroleh Yomtov! A taciturn and modest man who had a great deal to be modest about. This was his son-in-law. Sholem smiled to himself as he planted the three walnut saplings in the middle of the garden. A man who planted walnut trees at the age of forty would be long-lived upon the earth. Not on the part of the

earth that God had given to our fathers, but on the part of it that
we had fought to acquire. Sholem had been away from home for
a day or two and had obtained a new perspective as to the future.
Thank God, the children who were still at home were well and
had got over their whooping cough. Only Manasseh had grown
thinner. And he also had a queer new habit: dancing. He would
get up from breakfast and dance; leave the dinner table and
dance; dance in the house, in the yard, in the street. Warnings
and persuasion were useless and Malkeleh was worried that he
would dance himself even thinner than he already was. Malkeleh
thought it would be best to take the boy to Dr. Pfirsich. Now
she could stay there with him for a week. She was at home in
Otvar, more so than in Karoly. But Sholem merely waved his
hand. Dancing was not a matter for a doctor. Now that other
troubles had gone, the *shadim*, those restless demons, were still
loitering round the house. They had entered the feeble body
and were making it dance.

Sholem knew where to take the boy: to the saintly Rabbi
Moses Teitelbaum in Ujhely. How reassuring it was when the
*tsaddik* looked into the boy's eyes and said that the boy was
surely not possessed by *shadim*. The boy would grow into a
great *chassid*, that was why he danced. King David also danced,
and so did the Baal Shem. They must let the boy go on dancing.
It was the spirit that was dancing within him and that was the
same as if he were reciting a Psalm or praying. But if one day
he should leave off dancing, they must not press him to resume
it. He blessed the boy and gave him a *kamea*. The *kamea* was a
piece of parchment on which the Rabbi had written, with holy
ink, "Shaddai, exorcize Satan." *Shaddai* is the most secret name
of the Almighty; it was those letters that kept evil away from a
house on whose lintel there was a *mezuzah*. The *kamea* was sewn
into a linen bag and worn round the neck.

Rabbi Teitelbaum had also discussed earthly matters with
Sholem.

"The soil is very important, Sholem," he said. "That's what
we stand and dance on."

"It's not our soil," replied Sholem humbly. "We are in exile
here."

"Haven't you read the letter of Jeremiah?" asked the aged Rabbi with surprise.

"What letter?"

"The one Jeremiah wrote to the people in the Babylonian exile. 'Build houses and live in them. Plant orchards and eat the fruits thereof. Work for the prosperity of the land in which you live. Its prosperity is your prosperity.'"

"I've read it, of course."

"But not in the right way, my son. This was written by Jeremiah not three thousand years ago, but yesterday. And it was addressed not to the Babylonian exiles, but to you and your brethren who are living in exile here. You must talk about this to your family, report it to your neighbors. It's no common occurrence for anyone to receive a letter from a prophet in Jerusalem."

Just then Sholem had no time to marvel at the profound meaning of those words. He felt that what his former teacher was saying was exactly what he wanted to hear. But the Rabbi was already talking about practical matters, and giving him advice, and also a recommendation.

"I have a member of my flock living in Kotaj. His name is Michael Zicherman and he is a landowner. For the past month or two we've been relations, his son, Emanuel, having married the daughter of my brother Abraham, who is a farmer in Mad. Just go along to him and say I sent you."

Sholem went along to Kotaj and did not regret it. The Zichermans were hospitable people and they kept him and Manasseh for three days. They showed him over the farm. He saw the dairy, the sheep fold, the clean stables, the new tools and ploughs. They taught him how to handle manure, how to rotate the crops, how to grow tobacco, and how to breed silkworms. They explained how he could refresh a piece of exhausted land by sowing starwort and ploughing it in. That was as if the soil was given oil to drink. They also gave him saplings, together with all instructions on planting, trimming, and pest destruction. The visit to Kotaj gave Sholem matter to ponder over for years. Fortunately, Manasseh was there and scarcely danced. He just kept his eyes and ears open and now at times he would talk about things that his father had forgotten. Manasseh was beginning to take an interest in the soil and was helping with the planting.

The song "Hark, the cockerels, hark!" Sholem had picked up in Kallo. He had known it before, of course, but now that he had actually visited its place of origin, the words and the tune assumed a new significance. What could one do in Kallo from morning till noon? One went to the synagogue, then to the Jewish cemetery. The singing *tsaddik* lay there beneath a big, round, red-colored gravestone. At the base of the gravestone was a small letter-box with a shute going down into the grave. Sholem murmured a prayer and inserted the scrap of paper containing his petition into the letter-box. "O Advocate before the Lord, pray that my family should be free from sickness and that there should be peace in Israel and upon all the earth." He gave some coppers to the beggars loitering round the cemetery, then it was "Gee-up!" for home. Beside him on the driving-seat sat his son, in the cart were the saplings. And in his ear was a song. It accompanied him right home, and there, on the lush, verdant lea, stepping along with dignified steps, was a bird.

"Every trouble is a blessing in disguise," he had said to Malkeleh when he reached home, and she gave an understanding smile.

Malkeleh did not always smile like that and she was not pleased when, in the midst of trouble, Sholem came out with the ancient sayings. It was nearly two thousand years ago that Rabbi Nahum, the compiler of the Talmud, had said, "It is for the best." He was nicknamed Rabbi Forthebest. Nahum held that evil was also transitory, and once evil has passed none but good can follow. He who was too critical was lost. But Israel was trustful and optimistic. When trials came, Israel received them with the words of Rabbi Nahum—"Gam zoo le'tobah"—"This too is for the best." Israel having had many occasions to say this, it had become a proverb.

"I told you, Malkeleh—and I was told by no less a man than the *tsaddik* from Vizhnits—that the calamity that came on Gimpel Zorech would come to an end one day and Israel would come out of it fortified. This little disturbance that we are having now is nothing as compared with the old troubles. Zireleh is timid because she is a village girl, and Yossef too is of the anxious kind,

that's all. Yiteleh has never complained has she, that there was
anything wrong in Otvar? Sroleh Yomtov merely smiled. Erdy
is a Jew baiter. He always was, but now he has more time for it."

Malkeleh sat resting her face on her fist.

"I'm not afraid of Erdy. He's used to bawling, so now he bawls
in the street. He's a back number and has no power. But Wallon,
Hajtajer, the tanners' and the bootmakers' guilds and the Chamber
of Trade, are intriguing against us."

"They'll get tired of it in time. They'll realize that God and
the Burgomaster are on our side."

It was again difficult to reassure Malkeleh. She was not so
forgetful as Sholem, who remembered the sayings of the rabbis
of two thousand years ago, the wisdom of the saint of Batyu
and the prophecies of the *tsaddik* of Vizhnitz, but no longer remembered the words of Rabbi Luria, the wandering *tsaddik*, that
the name of the Jews was Gershom: stranger—everywhere.
Sholem did not see that the family's continual crises were part of
the destiny of his isolated people. Malkeleh could scarcely enjoy
the good things, because she knew from experience that they
were only a very brief interlude.

However, she was glad that Sholem was what he was. She
needed this opposite pole, this trustful attitude of Jewish existence.
It was, after all, necessary to have someone at hand who before
or during a calamity should cite the eternal benevolence of the
heavenly power. Malkeleh used to argue and wait for Sholem's
contradictions. When he failed to contradict, she knew that they
were in real trouble. For there were times when even Sholem no
longer said, "This, too, is for the best," but went about with a
clouded brow, either silent, or saying that one must praise the
Lord for everything, even for misfortune. At such times they
were very much at one. It was not Sholem that drew closer to
his wife, but the other way round. Malkeleh often thought of
her father, who in the evening of his life had found the truth
and an inner peace. And though she herself did not know the
Cabbalistic secrets of her father or the basis of Sholem's deep
faith, she was filled with a deep faith and was strong in adversity,
comforting the grief-stricken, raising the despondent, and smil-

ingly promising a better to-morrow. At such times it was she who contradicted doubt, she who was the prop of the weak and the timid.

### THE WAR OF THE CANDLES

AT THE moment the disquieting thing was that now, after the enthusiasm over the triumph in Otvar, the Jews of the surrounding villages were again viewing the matter with a certain reserve. The quota of seventeen was still not in the town, though it was three months since that successful attack. Nootah Batlan was among the braver spirits and kept impressing on Yossef that seventeen was not a propitious figure anyhow. The numerological value of seventeen was eight. The number eight was most important because a newborn boy entered the Covenant of Abraham at the age of eight days. But that always involved loss of blood. And if the operation was not carried out by a reliable expert, it also meant grave complications. ("Don't forget to come to Nootah if it's a boy, Yossef.") On the other hand, eighteen was a propitious figure, because it was the same as that of the fee paid for a blessing at the synagogue. Besides, eighteen was one and eight, that is, nine, and that was the figure of maturity in the womb.

Reb Lamach was more cautious.

"It is a fine and laudable thing to break into a besieged fortress," he explained to the Jews of Batiz, "but to hold the fortress is even finer and more laudable."

In Reb Lamach's eyes even eighteen was not a figure of any account. Even if one or two families did move into the town, he himself would have to stay in Batiz for a long time yet. In course of time Reb Lamach expressed his views concerning the siege of Otvar even more clearly.

"If you conquer a city," said Reb Lamach, "you throw the enemy out and put your own soldiers in. If you fail to drive the enemy out, then the battle continues within the walls of the town."

Reb Lamach was not saying this with the intention of discouraging people from moving into Otvar. He was merely prophesying in retrospect, interpreting facts that were already generally known. Unfortunately, it was true that Sroleh Yomtov had only won the first battle and the war was still going on. Those who had followed events were aware that the war between the burghers and the Jews, or as they called it, the war of the candles, was continuing with changing fortunes but with unchanging violence, and had now gone on for a year. And though the war ended or seemed to end with the flight of one side, it was known through what tragic events the victors were able to remain in possession of the battlefield.

Those who said that there had been actual street fighting from the outset were exaggerating. The inhabitants of Otvar were far too chivalrous to make a physical attack on a handful of Jews. They jeered at Jews, but also raised their hats to Jews. The boys in the street shot pebbles at Tobias and his sons with catapults and sang mildly abusive verses right into his face. But Tobias merely laughed. He did not get angry even when a sheet of glass was smashed in his hand. One of his sons ran after the culprit and took the catapult away from him, but Tobias returned it to the boy and even stroked his grubby face.

"You just go and tell your mother that I live in the Yellow House and that I glaze windows and frame pictures and mirrors."

Tobias could be very angry with the hard-hearted rich, but he liked naughty boys. Besides, they were useful to him through their activities with the catapult.

One could talk about street fighting only in the figurative sense. Israel Daygood's workmen went from one street to another with spades, shovels, and picks on their shoulders and dug holes in the ground at equal intervals. Then the carpenters came along with wooden posts, laid them down, painted them over with tar, and left them to dry. The town was filled with a smell of tar. But it was not an unpleasant smell, and there was an eventfulness as well as anticipation about it. Then the first lamp-posts were set in the holes and the workmen went away. They were followed by Judah the tinsmith who put on the lamps, then Tobias and his sons came along with panes of glass ready cut, so that they had only to be fitted in. Everything happened with the rapidity of wizardry.

Yossef drove along the streets with his candle cart and the very first moonless autumn night the lamps were alight in twelve streets.

Then soon they shone in sixteen, twenty, and more streets. The lamps of the candlemakers' guild were also repaired, the posts re-set and tarred and glazed. A big H was painted on these lamps, to indicate that the candles for these lamps were to be supplied by Hajtajer's guild. The rest of the lamps bore the letter J, which according to some stood for Jacob, and according to others Jomtov. The Germans held that it stood simply for "Jew." Still, what did that matter? The Jewish candle was thick and white, perhaps half an inch shorter than that of the guild, but it was firmer, did not bend, gave a nicer flame and lasted longer.

It was impossible not to notice the difference. The people did notice it and were divided into two camps, the H camp and the J camp. At first the H camp was far bigger than the other. This was quite natural, for the H candle was a native Christian candle, while the J was just an intruding Jewish candle. The popularity of Hajtajer and his group in the first weeks increased further because they speeded up the lighting in their own area and had the glass on the lamps cleaned more often than before. There were those who claimed to know the reason, but the majority did not look for the reason and admired the old guild for showing the Jews that they too could do things.

But as the J lamps increased in numbers and were erected in street after street, the adherents of the H lamps shrunk to a minority. In course of time all defensive talk ceased and gave way to grumbling admiration. But the admiration was for the J lamps, which burned brightly and cockily, whereas the H's gave a yellow flame and blinked sleepily like old women. There were streets that were illuminated partly by the J's and partly by the H's. These were the old, exclusive streets, and their exclusive in-habitants soon began to murmur. Why did they get the worst lighting, while the newer and more plebeian houses in the same street had bright lights burning in front of them? Besides, the candles of the guild said good night long before midnight, while the Jew lamps often had the candles still blinking in them a quar-ter-past midnight. In the streets lighted by the Jews, the citizens could stay much longer in the taverns. This fact again brought about a division: the women cursed the Jews and veered public opinion in favor of the H lamps. However, it was only feminine public opinion and the men, who after all were the directors of the town's policy, were pleased.

Sometimes, even in daylight, there were groups moving from one lamp-post to another, pointing out the difference. The J lamps dropped nice white blobs of grease into the dust beneath them, or on to the newly made plank pavement, whereas the H lamps had shapeless chunks of tallow hanging at the base. Besides, the glass of the J lamps stayed clean, whereas that of the H lamps was covered with soot after a night or two. In the circumstances it was understandable that the initial anti-Jewish attitude should have become modified. The Jew had won, and had won without striking a blow, so to speak. Thus Israel Daygood, Jacob Antal, and the rest had impressed themselves on the burghers, even though they had not yet gained their affection. At all events, they were now at least mentioned with a degree of admiration.

The candlemakers began defending themselves by accusing the Jews. The rascally Jews had bored a hole from end to end into the H lamp-posts, so that the guild's candles got a draught from below and therefore burned badly, got bent, and went out prematurely. Israel Daygood mobilized the carpenters and they, in their own rather than in the Jews' defence, informed the burghers that they had bored holes only in the new lamp-posts, which were all Jewish. Of course, then said the guild, that was the real secret. The Jewish candle burned more uniformly because it got air from the ground. Whereupon the carpenters confessed that, by error, they had in fact bored holes into fifty H lamp-posts. There they stood in the Capucine Street and its neighborhood. The hole made no difference, and the guild's candles were deplorably second-rate.

The next accusation was that the Jews mixed something into the tallow that was harmful. The guild could do the same, but they were not so unscrupulous as to endanger the health of the citizens. This accusation was not taken seriously by anyone. The Jewish candles stood firm like a pillar, and their flame was bright and even, so that there could be nothing the matter with them.

And if the candle was sound it could not harm those that walked under it.

Then the guild tried to make people's flesh creep by warning them of financial consequences. The Jews were trying to wrest for themselves the whole of the street lighting, and when they had done so they would increase prices. Rates would have to be increased to enable the Jews to grow rich at the cost of impoverishing the burghers. This aroused a certain militancy on the part of some burghers. Let the Jews try! they said. But that was about all. In any case, they said nothing very alarming. The guild people gnashed their teeth. They also racked their brains to discover why the Jewish candles had become so popular.

Of course, for the present only the street candles were at stake, which was annoying, but by no means dangerous. Nor did the Jews cause any loss to the guild, for they were doing only the new lighting, for which the guild had not even been prepared. Indeed, they would be badly embarrassed if they were suddenly given the additional six hundred lamps. Then they could either not do the street lighting or let their private customers go short. And the twelve thousand citizens of Otvar were still burning guild candles in their homes.

Then a man entered the grocery shop of Henrik Wallon & Sons, at the far end of the market square and asked for J candles.

"What candles?" asked Wallon Junior.

"J candles."

The young man pretended to be puzzled. Then he acted as though he had suddenly realized what it was all about, and with an ironical smile in the corner of his mouth he said:

"Ah, you mean synagogue candles!"

The customer shook his head. That was not what he meant, but those new Jew candles that gave such a nice light. One could get them on market day from the candlemaker of Batiz, but the customer would not like to wait till then.

"You had better wait till market day," said the young shopkeeper's father, "we don't keep Jewish goods here."

However, old Wallon was a shrewd business man and he kept telling Hajtajer that it was not enough to squeal and spread rumors. If they wanted to avoid a calamity they must act. Wallon himself was the first to act. He ordered six cases of J candles, pound, half-pound, and quarter-pound ones. He hastened to introduce the J candles in his shop before his customers learned that they were obtainable at Jacob Antal's stall on market days. Indeed, he used them to light his shop. His little old eyes were sound enough for distance, but he wanted to watch his assistants from close by to see whether they did not tip the scales in the customer's favor when weighing out the more expensive goods. He comforted the head of the candlemakers' guild by saying that he was selling the J candles at a higher price, so that customers should give them up. But the customers refused to be discouraged.

However, Hajtajer and his friends must not think that old Wallon had given up the struggle. Why, if he did that he would only be surrendering his own interests and those of the traders represented by him. It was *Hodie mihi, cras tibi*. The Chamber of Trade had already learned that other Jews were coming into the Yellow House and a signboard bearing the legend, "Ezekiel Nadler, Linen Draper," was in preparation. Wallon was on the alert. It was really the business of Hajtajer and his friends, but if they were idle, he'd have to do something himself.

One day old Wallon sent for Hajtajer. He had made a discovery. Sitting in his cubicle in the shop he whittled down J candle after J candle with a penknife. He lighted a bit, smelled it, put a bit on his tongue and tasted it. He was familiar with many smells and tastes. His discovery was that the Jews mixed the tallow with quicklime. He did not know in what proportion, but that was for the candlemakers to find out. Hajtajer was happy and dashed back home to make a start. It took him four weeks and all his stock of tallow, so that he had to cut into the fats required for soap, but he would not give in. He divulged the secret to another candlemaker, Master Gyapjas, and the latter also started to experiment with quicklime with even more stubborn determination, but with the same result. And the Jew seemed to know all about it. He either had spies in his rivals' establishments or he had the cunning to take a peep at their stalls on market day, where there was scarcely any stock just then, either of candles or of soap. The following week Jacob Antal came to market with a new kind of soap: J soap. It was available in a better quality too, and that was called J-J soap. It was a toilet soap and prevented rashes, pimples, and any sort of skin complaint. True, it had a tarry smell, but that made it just like the finest goods of the apothecary. It was obtainable throughout the week, except on Saturday, in Jacob Antal's shop in the Yellow House, where the popular J candles were also in stock.

But this was too much. Hajtajer called a meeting of his guild. They indited a petition for Councillor Poncikter personally to hand to the Burgomaster. The tone of the petition was rather peppery. It said that the Burgomaster had talked about a certain mill, which had started. It was quite evident that he meant the mill of the Jews. And, of course, if the authorities sent grist to that mill it was bound to go. But this caused the mill of the guilds to go slower and that could not go on. The Jews were taking away the guild's customers by cunning and fraud. But the Jews had no right to do any cheating here. The guild insisted on its ancient rights. The town might surrender its rights, but the guild certainly would not.

The petition was supported by the other guilds. The tanners were angry with Israel Daygood because he imported the leather for his wife's shop from Debreczen, whose tanners were the best in the country, and the Otvar tanners could not hope to compete with them. The bootmakers' guild, in turn, had realized that the plank pavement did in fact reduce the demand for boots, for those that walked on the planks instead of in the mud required fewer boots and repairs. The button- and cord-makers and tailors were afraid that their trade would also be swamped by invading cheapjacks, and the other guilds shared their anxiety. Even the haircloth coatmakers were worried, though there were no Jewish artisans in their trade not only in the whole county, but even in the whole country. Their trouble was that since Commissioner Erdy had been removed from office there was no cheap woolwashing in the river by convicts. The new Commissioner would not hear of any such abuse of authority, and the guild had to pay high wages.

JEW BAITERS

THERE WAS a party in the town that one heard little about so long as the town was Jewless, but now it was getting more and more noticed. This was the Anti-Jew Party, who, in contrast with the guilds, who acted from self-interest, carried on their campaign for pleasure. This disinterested party was headed by Erdy himself and it was an open secret that one or two leading town and county officials were among the members. There were Captain Kokass, ex-Sergeant Patyodi, and ex-Warder Peter Koczor. They all frequented a tavern in the chicken market, which was adjacent to the main market and near the Yellow House. These gentlemen on their way home had to pass the Jewfort, and what was more natural than that, in their anxiety for the Fatherland, they should give vocal expression to their anti-Jewish attitude. When prose proved ineffective, they resorted to the gems of the national folk poetry. "Judah, Judah, cunning Judah," they used to sing with conviction. Or, with the odors of the chicken market still in their nostrils:

> *"A Jew he went and bought two geese,*
> *A black'un and white'un he did seize,*
> *Two white'uns or two black'uns wouldn't do,*
> *The Jew was choosey, a plague on the Jew!"*

They also had more personal rhymes. "Hi, hook-nosed Israel. They'll soon take you down to hell." Captain Kokass himself, who was usually with the anti-Jew group at their carousals, refrained from any open vocal expression of his hatred. But he liked to listen to the serenades outside the Yellow House. One could see by the bright light of the Jewish candles the contented expression on his puffed cheeks.

The Jewish question was also constantly on the agenda at the gentlemen's Casino. The Reverend Gulyacs quoted Homer and talked about the Trojan horse. That was how the Jews were preparing to occupy the town. Councillor Filep in turn had seen through the diabolical plot whereby the Jews were trying to enslave the burghers. They made the pavements from unplaned planks, so as to make the burghers tread them smooth. Then they just scattered the cobbles in the sand in the roadway, so that the pedestrians should stamp them in as they walked over them. Thus twelve thousand citizens were toiling for a dozen Jews. Decent people must avoid this treadmill labor and walk in the mud. Councillor Filep was doing so himself.

The Yellow House seemed not to take any notice of all this, or if they did, they kept to Israel Daygood's dictum: "Our task is to go on working." The Jews worked with redoubled energy —for their daily bread and for the future, especially for the future. A constant hammering could be heard from the tinsmith's shop. Orders were coming in from the nearby streets. Judah and his sons were determined to give first-class craftsmanship. There was also a small candlemaking shop in the back premises where Yossef worked with two assistants. This was only a branch, the main factory having remained in Batiz. They brought the candles for the street lamps from Batiz direct each day, and mostly they were not even unloaded, but taken along to the lamps immediately. The lamp-lighter was a little thickset Magyar peasant named Matthew Matolcs whose father used to be Sabbath *goy* to Sroleh Yomtov's father and also to Sholem. Small as he was, he looked impressive with the ladder on his shoulder and the torch in his hand. His wife Erzsi helped him with the lighting and cleaning of the lamps.

In the Yellow House the days passed in work and the usual daily worries and vexations. The nights passed too. In the evening, an hour or two after dark, they closed the shops, which for the moment had but few customers. The women then retired to the kitchen. After supper the company gathered in the tinsmith's shop, where there was plenty of space and plenty of seating and where there was a fire in the tin stove. The nights were already chilly and a fire was welcome.

They usually stayed up till midnight or a little later. They deliberated, argued, discussed, or just talked. In company it was easier to bear the vociferous jeering of the drunks from the anti-Jew tavern. Israel Daygood made it clear that he did not care a rap about them. Yiteleh entertained the company by singing one of the anti-Jew songs. The others were not quite satisfied, and as antidote they sang an anti-*goy* song, Judah and his sons leading.

> *"Drunken is the goy:*
> *Drunkard is he,*
> *Guzzle must he,*
> *'Cause he is a goy."*

Their eyes were laughing, but their voices were low, lest even a snatch of their song should seep through to the street. The antidote was only for domestic consumption, not to incite the Jew baiters further.

Strangely, at these gatherings stories of scuffles, street fights, resistance against heavy odds, and clever escapes were a frequent topic. The tinsmith knew a hundred interesting details of a great fight in another locality, where they let some drunken cattlemen loose on the Jews on a Friday afternoon, when they were about to leave for synagogue. Zebulon, the Jewish butcher's son, charged the enemy with an axe. His father used only his fists, but some of the cattlemen had cause to remember him nevertheless. Judah himself had received a blow on the head that he did not even feel at the time, though his head hurt for years after. He fought his way through sticks and hatchets with his mallet.

Tobias related, amid full-throated laughter, how he once out-witted some peasants who had attacked him on the road. Throwing his sheet glass into the ditch, he crawled on all fours through a maize field, then forded a stream and walked into a village, where the Jews gave him some dry clothes. He coughed for six months, but was right as rain after that.

The gate was bolted and barred, yet Zireleh was very jumpy and anxious. Once she said that she had heard a banging on the gate and that someone must have got into the house.

Yossef said he had heard nothing, but as Zireleh was pale with fright he and Tobias's elder son went out into the yard with a lantern to look round. They came back smiling. There was a high wind and there was no other sound in the street. Zireleh drew her shawl closer round her shoulders and went into the house with Yossef.

"You're a baby, Zireleh," he said. "What are you afraid of? At our inn they used to tell stories about robbers all winter, yet I'm still alive."

"I don't know why I'm afraid, but I am. This big town and this big empty house . . . And people here are so bad."

"They aren't good anywhere."

"They are in Batiz."

"No better than here. There was a lot of quarrelling and fighting there before we got used to the place and the people got used to us. You heard what Judah said. We can't run away, because wherever we run to there'll be enemies waiting for us. Why exchange enemies? Let's stay in one place and try to make friends. That's what Sroleh Yomtov is doing, and he's right."

"He's been very quiet lately."

"Sroleh Yomtov was never very talkative. When he's quiet he's merely thinking. And I'm sure he's thinking in the correct way. Look at his eyes, his smile. And Yiteleh too is brave and cheerful. I admit we have enemies here, but what have they achieved against us? The guilds have demanded that the town should withdraw its permission for us to settle here. One or two of the councillors have again behaved in a sneaky sort of way, but the Burgomaster just waved his hand. The Jews were useful people and their expulsion was out of the question. And that was that."

"That's true," said Zireleh, somewhat reassured.

"You see, Zireleh. We Jews are lucky to have such powerful friends."

### A LIBERAL IN PRISON

SROLEH YOMTOV was really very quiet. It made Yiteleh wonder. He came home for dinner, scarcely spoke during the meal, and hurried off again immediately after. He had been like this before, and just now he had many botherations. It was autumn, with a chill in the air, and the carpenters and navvies were complaining of lack of work, and were making all sorts of demands. However, Sroleh Yomtov was not the man to be upset by anything like this, and he always handled the workers calmly. There must be something else on his mind.

Then one Monday morning he left, saying that he was going to see the Burgomaster and would not be back till two in the afternoon. But he returned at eleven with a set face.

"Pack my big bag, Yiteleh," he said. "I shall want linen for two or three weeks. I am leaving for Pest by the one o'clock mail-coach."

"What are you doing in Pest?"

"I must see someone there. A man called Pal Ribary."

"Who's that?"

"A former schoolmate of Csanyi's. He's a government official."

"Is it very urgent?"

"I also have a message for Mendel Kanicz, Shefteli's brother-in-law. And I must also call on Goldberger the dye-maker in Buda."

"Are you buying or selling anything?"

"Neither, Yiteleh."

Yiteleh was used to her husband's taciturnity and she knew that he resented being bombarded with questions. She went to the wardrobe to get his linen. Sroleh Yomtov went up to her.

"They've arrested the Burgomaster," he said quietly.

They sat down and he gazed into her scared eyes. He knew that she had grasped the significance of the news and there was no need for further explanation. But for once he could not keep things to himself. After all, everything was now at stake, and it was for Yiteleh to hold the fort while he was away.

"Our enemies are ruthless," he said. "They could not get at us because that strong, honest man was in the way, so they had to get rid of him. They could not attack him for any corrupt action, but they could attack him through his ideals. He believes in a better future, in liberty and human rights. They sent an anonymous denunciation to the Governing Council in Buda to say that he had made a subversive speech before the Council in August. Last Thursday night he was fetched by secret agents from his house. They gave him just enough time to dress and took him away, no one knows where."

While the girl was packing, Sroleh Yomtov went on:

"In time, our people will learn that the Burgomaster has been arrested, but I don't want them to hear it from you. Jeney tells everybody that he is on sick leave; that he has an ulcer on his leg and had suddenly to be taken to Pest, into the Rokus Hospital. I gather from this that he is held in the ill-famed Ujepulet prison. Don't tell anyone where I have gone or why, either. Just to re-assure our people, say I'm having important financial conferences somewhere. The work for this season is coming to a close and what little is left will be attended to by Yossef. Don't let anyone negotiate with the Council. Shefteli promised to see to things at the town hall while I am away. He now comes to his timber yard daily and stays till evening. Jeney is the Deputy Burgo-master. For the present he is still on the side of Lam, but I know he'd like to take his place. The only really honest man here is that eccentric Csanyi."

As he kissed his wife farewell, Sroleh Yomtov impressed on her the need to keep cheerful.

"Worrying will ruin your looks," he said. "Besides, the knowl-edge that you're not upsetting yourself will enable me to work better."

"I'll be all right," assured Yiteleh.

The roads, amid the autumn rains, were barely passable, espe-cially through the Plain, and Israel Daygood did not reach Pest until late on Friday morning. He went straight to Buda to the offices of the Governing Council, and conveyed Csanyi's greetings to Pal Ribary. He had also brought a small package for the Burgo-master. It contained some pills from Dr. Pfirsich, the same that the Burgomaster had been taking for years for his liver trouble. "Would you kindly hand this to Master Lam," said Israel Day-good. "He's in the Ujepulet prison. And tell him it was brought by the Jew Daygood."

Master Ribary stared.

"Who told you that Ambro Lam is in the Ujepulet?"

"Councillor Csanyi."

"He ought not to know that. And the same applies to you. Ujepulet is a secret prison for political offenders."

"It is a big building, everybody can see it."

"But they mustn't see what's in it."

"I don't know anything, Master Ribary. I'm only acting as messenger. I'm a business man passing through Pest. I shall stay here for Saturday and go on on Sunday."

The official grumbled for awhile, but then he cooled down and had a friendly talk with Daygood. Did Csanyi still run after women? And was he still addicted to the cup? Daygood replied that Csanyi was now a good husband and father, with three children, but that he still took a glass of wine now and then in his office. Ribary was pleased to hear this. The following day Israel Daygood came again to inquire whether the Burgomaster wanted anything further from home, for the Jew Shefteli would also be coming to the capital in a week or two.

"He doesn't want anything," said Ribary. "He thanks you for the medicine and wishes you good luck at the Vienna Fair."

Israel Daygood understood the message. Mendel Kanicz and the dye-maker, Goldberger, had also advised him to go on to Vienna. The Governing Council were only acting on the instructions of the Chancellery and could do nothing on their own account. This being Saturday, Israel Daygood went to the synagogue and did his best to make new contacts and obtain useful information. At dawn on Sunday he left for Vienna.

On Monday evening he was knocking at the door of Baron Anselm. As Anselm was out, he left a message for him and went on to Dr. Manes Oesterreicher. Shayeh was delighted to see him and embraced and kissed him.

"You ran away from me, what?" he reproached jocularly. "Was it fair to treat an old pal like that? I suppose you were in a hurry to carry out my idea of a Jewish Conquest and to snatch away from me that clever, lovely little girl. You didn't hesitate like me. And of course, you're a much handsomer lad, Israel Yomtov."

"Daygood's the name now."

The two young men sat down to talk. Daygood explained why he had come to Vienna, and Shayeh, pushing his books aside, listened with tense interest and growing excitement.

"So that's the sort of man Ambro Lam is!" he cried. "Wonderful. He must be saved. Even if he were dead he'd have to be resurrected. He's a rare specimen in this corrupt world. He has a part to play in the future. The day is not far distant, my friend Israel, the day of liberation."

Israel Daygood liked his friend's enthusiasm, but was not carried away by it. The freedom of the peoples was a most important matter, and perhaps this time even the Jews would not be left out. But for the present the release of Burgomaster Lam was more urgent. One had to attend to the tasks of to-day, regardless of any hope that everything would be put right to-morrow. For to-day passed quickly, while to-morrow was slow in coming. And meanwhile one had to live. He explained all this to Shayeh and Shayeh agreed.

"You're a more practical person," he said. "Well, what do you think we'd better do?"

"We must get to someone at whose word the prison gates will open."

"The Emperor?"

"No, Metternich."

Shayeh gave a bitter laugh.

"Might as well go to the Devil and ask him to open the gates of Hell because you have a friend there. Don't you know that Ambro Lam and others like him are the personal captives of Metternich?"

"Perhaps that's so. But they told me in Pest that the lovely Countess Zichy has great influence with him."

"Then," said Shayeh, "we must find someone who has influence with Countess Zichy."

"I know of someone—Solomon Rothschild."

"It's like that, is it? Of course, the old fellow is a year or two younger than Metternich."

"I'm thinking of him in his capacity as a banker. The Countess acts as agent in negotiating loans for the aristocracy. Solomon is not stingy with commission."

"If you like," offered Shayeh, "I'll ask my uncle to speak with Solomon."

"We'd better try Anselm first."

"Right," said Shayeh. "Let's go across to him at once."

"Not at once. I left a message to say I'd be calling to-morrow. Anselm is not an enthusiast like you. He and his father go about with money in their pockets and a pencil in their brains. If we talk to them now, that would give them too much time to work out the pros and cons."

In the morning they called on Anselm, prepared to make a concerted attack on him. But it was not necessary, for Anselm grasped the problem at once and hurried across to his father. Half an hour later he returned.

"We must leave my father out of it," he said, the words tumbling from his lips rapidly. "The Chancellor is after a loan again. We can't talk with his fiancée, either—it would worsen the terms. My father is leaving it to me, and he'll bear all expenses."

He donned his cloak, picked up his walking-stick and went out with his friends. In the street he hailed a cab.

"To Herr von Gentz," he said, partly to the cabby and partly to the other two. It was clear from his manner that he had confidence in the success of his mission. It made Shayeh very cheerful.

"A sly old man, Solomon," he said. "He washes his hands of the matter because he's negotiating a State loan. But he's given the right address to his son."

Israel Daygood was less confident. He knew that Anselm did not let the grass grow under his feet, and even admired him for this quality and had in the past tried to emulate him. But this was a delicate matter requiring deliberation, where a hasty move might spell failure. He tried to recall what he knew about Gentz. His file at Arnstein and Eschkeles was not favorable. "Politician, diplomat, scribe," it said. "Runs after women, gambles, drinks, squanders other people's money." On the other hand, the Rothschilds counted it in his favor that he was easy-going and frivolous.

"Do you think Gentz is reliable, Shayeh?" he asked.

"Depends who relies on him. You must have heard about the affair of my grandfather, the Chief Rabbi of Karoly. The court at Varad sentenced him to death for alleged ritual murder. He fled to Vienna. My uncle kept having audiences for eighteen months, while my grandfather himself sent petition after petition to the Chancellor. The Emperor couldn't do anything and the

Chancellor wouldn't. Then Gentz settled the matter in twenty-four hours."

"You don't mean to say that von Gentz is more powerful than the Chancellor?"

"Not more powerful, but more flexible," said Shayeh. "And he has a bigger brain. My grandfather concluded his petitions to the Emperor with the Hebrew sentence: '*Tittahn emmes l'Jacob.*' It's from the last verse of 'Fear not, my servant Jacob' as you know. Well, they asked Rabbi Aaron Chorin of Arad, who was then a candidate for the rabbinate in Vienna, what the quotation meant. Chorin translated it as: 'Grant rights to Jacob.' Metternich got angry and said that he would not move a finger for the Jacobin Rabbi Oesterreicher even if the Emperor wanted it. This was all behind the scenes, but of course Gentz knew about it. And when the affair passed to him he went to another rabbi for the translation. It was Rabbi Mannerheim, and he said that the phrase meant 'Deal justly with Jacob,' which of course, was quite correct. The Chancellor was mollified and ordered a re-trial."

"*Emmes* really means truth," said Israel.

"Yes, but it also means right or rights. I like this interpretation —it fits in with modern ideas. But Chorin paid a heavy price for his version. The Chancellery vetoed his appointment as Rabbi of Vienna, saying that he translated things too freely. They preferred Mannerheim's literal translation and so the appointment went to him. Chorin returned to Arad and was very careful ever after, because he was being watched. He had the reforming spirit."

"It's the same with Ambro Lam," said Israel, his face clouding. "And he's more than a reformer."

"He's a rebel," said Shayeh. "I know—and so does Gentz."

"That's bad."

"It all depends on interpretation."

### HERR VON GENTZ

ISRAEL'S FEAR that Anselm might have been acting rashly proved to be groundless. Nothing could be done for several days. Gentz could not be found at the Chancellery and he did not receive anyone at his house. He was too busy with a little dancer with whom he was just then enamored. He was having her portrait painted by the famous miniature painter Daffinger. Israel listened eagerly to Anselm's stories about Gentz. He was interested in every trifle, even smutty gossip. According to Anselm, Gentz's latest love affair was a most serious matter. Up till now it was he who had always fooled the women, but now, when he was nearly seventy, he had become enamored of this female. And he, the leading diplomat of Europe since the Congress of Vienna, who had made the foxiest diplomats of other countries dance to his tune, was now dancing attendance on a little actress.

"Don't run away with the idea that you can approach him through this Fanny Elssler," said Anselm. "You can't buy her enough things to compete with Gentz—and your bills can't be sent to my father like his. However, there are two other women who have influence with Gentz. They are renegade Jewesses, Rachel von Varnhagen, and Henrietta Herz. They are both in Berlin at the moment, and you can't write to them because your letters would be on Metternich's desk as soon as you posted them. But if the worst comes to the worst, you'll travel to Berlin and see them."

Israel Daygood did not feel like going to Berlin or visiting the allegedly famous *salons* of those two women, though he would go if there was no other way. However, there was another way. One day von Gentz sent for Solomon Rothschild. Solomon sent his son, and von Gentz, after a brief conversation with Anselm, handed him a note for Solomon and said that he would be pleased to receive the deputation from Otvar at the Chancellery the following afternoon. In the meantime, he would go through the file of the Burgomaster's affair.

No one knew whose idea the deputation was, and Israel Day-good was not particularly interested.

"You'd better come along too," said Anselm to Shayeh. "Von Gentz likes to talk and he's pleased when there's someone who understands him. He talks about Hegel, Aristotle, Machiavelli, politics, philosophy, and literature. You know better than I or Yomtov where to nod your head. But mind you don't say anything. Von Gentz is not a rabbi, a *bocher*, or a student with whom you can argue. What he says goes."

Shayeh felt excited and uneasy as, in his Sabbath best, he stood before Metternich's right-hand man as a member of the deputation. He kept biting his lips, perhaps by way of practice to check any urge to speak. The leader of the deputation was neither excited, nor even embarrassed. He was pleased to be here at last and he was sure that no mistakes would be made so long as he was present. He now had a clear picture of von Gentz. He knew that von Gentz was not bound by any office or rank. He was not a Minister, or a General, or an Ambassador, but just an author, or as Shayeh put it, a statesman-author, and was feared as such. He was paid heavily for every line he wrote, and even more heavily for every line he refrained from writing. He had not written anything recently, so he must now be having a considerable income. However, despite his lack of office or rank his influence was so enormous that kings were afraid of him. Israel was not a king, so he had no reason to be afraid. He listened calmly, modestly, waiting for the moment when he himself would be allowed to speak. That must come, now that he was here. Would he succeed? Well, everything was all right so far.

Herr von Gentz sat at his desk, with some documents before him. He kept passing his fingers through his tousled hair. It was greying fast, but that was all that betrayed his age. His finely chiselled nose, his large, hard mouth, his jutting cleft chin, and his clean-shaven, freshly powdered face, all had a youthful color. (Anselm said he used makeup.) His brow was furrowed, but any wrinkles on his face were hidden by his high collar, whose upper edge went from beneath the lobe of his ears to the corner of his mouth. A gold cross was pinned to his high white waistcoat beneath a flowing bow tie. There was a fresh yellow rose in the lapel of his frock-coat.

Israel Daygood looked at his eyes, speculating what manner to adopt when it was his turn to speak. Gentz's eyes were steel-grey, keen and somehow bleak. But there was a kind of smile in the depths of them, puckish rather than ironical, and this relieved the bleakness. He gave Israel only a brief glance, then he turned to Anselm:

"I see that your protégé is an enemy of the prevailing order." His voice was precise, almost forbidding.

"Only of the order that wants to drive the Jews out of the world, Your Excellency," said Anselm calmly.

"Is that all?" asked von Gentz sharply.

"As far as I know, Your Excellency is also an enemy of that order. Your Excellency once said that no government has yet increased the prosperity of its country by oppressing the Jews."

"Frederick the Great said that," smiled von Gentz. "I only paraphrased it: No government has been impoverished through Jewish prosperity."

"It's even better like that, Your Excellency," flattered Anselm. Herr von Gentz began to thaw.

"If this Ambro Lam is only friendly to the Jews . . . So am I. And so is the Prince-Chancellor. The other day we summoned the burgomaster of a Styrian town. The complaint against him was that he refused to admit some tightrope walkers into his town. He excused himself by saying that he wanted to save his burghers from a double alarm: the breathtaking performance itself, and when the tight-rope walker went around with his plate. He was reprimanded for advancing an unskilful excuse. The second alarm could not arise because by the time the tight-rope walker came to earth the spectators would have scattered."

There was a glint of fun in his eyes. The other three exchanged glances. Did this anecdote mean anything? Von Gentz's voice became deeper as he went on:

"Both the Chancellor and I are of the opinion that the citizens must not be deprived of diversion. There must be people who do dangerous things. We need both aerial acrobats and Jews, so that the people should not turn their attention to forbidden

things. The Jews are even greater artists at balancing themselves
than the tight-rope walkers. If anyone's found the Archimedean
point, it's the Jews. All they got of the earth was what stuck to
the soles of their feet as they fled, yet they were always able to
stand on that soil. Indeed, while balancing themselves they help
to maintain the balance of those that have all the rest of the
earth, including kings and governments."

He looked round, as though about to ask a question. But then
he went on:

"It was lucky for us during the last quarter-century that the
Jews were on our side. The Corsican had better soldiers and more
talented generals. But he had no Jews, or if he had, he didn't know
what to do with them. The fool settled them on the land, instead
of leaving them suspended in the air. He gave them rights, common human rights . . . whereas the Jews are not human."

Shayeh had a strong urge to interrupt, but Anselm gave him
a stern look, so he suppressed the urge. Von Gentz, with a vibrant
smile in the corners of his mouth, went on:

"Some think they're devils. I disagree. I wouldn't say they were
angels, but since the angels departed from the earth, their tasks
have been taken over by the Jews. Whenever my own financial
balance was upset, I had an unexpected heavenly messenger to restore it. On my first visit to London—Napoleon was then still
small fry—I was about to throw up the sponge and return to
Breslau as tutor. Then there was a knock on my door and a
bearded Elder from Whitechapel came in. He said his name was
Hirsch and he planked fifty thalers on the table, telling me not
to worry because there was going to be more money for me
shortly. The Jew Hirsch didn't come to my inn again, but his
prediction came true. A few days later Baron Kruedener, the
Tsar's Ambassador, presented me with a gift from the Tsar, then
Lord Grenville sent me five hundred pounds with a most charming covering letter."

Anselm smiled at his friends. To Shayeh his smile meant: "Don't
you dare to open your mouth!" To Israel Daygood it meant:
"All's well; the old chap is in a talkative mood." Von Gentz
seemed to be glad to have such an appreciative audience, and he
went on:

"I like the Jews because they are different. They buy and sell everything, predict everything and prove everything. There is only one thing I don't like about them. Their Jehovah created them in his own image, and they are trying to recreate the rest of the world in their image. What Saul the Jew failed to accomplish, was accomplished by Paul the Christian. The nephew of the Hamburg banker Solomon Heine, the charming and talented Harry, who received the name of Henrik in holy baptism, is feeling lonely in his new environment, so he wants to change the whole world. He wants to prescribe, à la Jehovah, what everything should be like. This has always been the mania of the Jews. The overwhelming majority of the world was always opposed to continual change. On the basis of what the masses want, we can only pursue one policy: the policy of what not to do. But the son of another banker, this time from Frankfort, writes that we are backward and reactionary. You may have heard about the fellow: his father is Jacob Baruch, but he—a friend of mine, by the way—calls himself Börne. If he had not entered the Christian flock, the Jewish world would today be admiring his fine Hebrew style and his keen Talmudic commentaries. But he's exchanged his Hebrew pen for a German one, and now he is a wild Jacobin in Paris."

"Our people has always fought for ideals," burst from Shayeh at last.

Von Gentz's eyebrows shot up. His tone was peppery as he said:

"What ideals are Solomon Heine, Jacob Baruch, Arnstein and Eschkeles, Nathaniel Rothschild, and Anselm Rothschild fighting for?"

"Not all Jews are money-changers, Your Excellency," replied Shayeh quietly.

"Yes—the father is a money-changer, the son a savior. But whom does he want to save and why? The world does not want to be saved. Why don't the Jews attend to their own internal troubles?"

"The world is one and indivisible, Your Excellency," said Shayeh. "Our prophets were concerned not only about our own troubles, but also about the troubles of the whole world. We were a small country and we suffered a great deal from wars, because every conqueror had to march through us. Thereupon one of my ancestors, whose name I bear, preached that a time would come when the sword would be beaten into a ploughshare and the lance into a pruning hook and no one would pursue the trade of war."

"What has that fool of a prophet achieved with it? He merely called attention to the fact that the ploughshare and the pruning hook could also be made into swords." Von Gentz made a gesture. The debate was concluded. He glanced at the documents that lay before him, then he said coldly:

"It is clear from the reports before me that this Ambro Lam is a common rebel. He spoke at a council meeting about certain mills that were about to grind up those in power."

"May I explain, Your Excellency?" said Israel Daygood with due humility.

Von Gentz gave permission with an abrupt gesture. Israel did his best to be brief, because His Excellency now appeared to be impatient. He explained that the Burgomaster had not been referring to the powers of the State at all, but to the activities of the Jews, whom for the first time in a century the town had just permitted to settle there. The Burgomaster shared His Excellency's and the Chancellor's view that there was need for the Jews. The guilds held the contrary view. Thereupon the Burgomaster said that the Jewish mills ground finer than the antiquated guild mills. And if there was a threat against any power, it was only against the power of the guilds. Ambro Lam was a man with clean hands.

The diplomat gave a contemptuous smile.

"He's clean hands, therefore he's a rebel."

"But no—"

"But yes, young man. The guild masters are reliable men."

Israel Daygood was sure at last that, as he had guessed, the denunciation had come from the guilds. Von Gentz began to stack the documents. The audience was at an end. Anselm kept tugging at Israel's coat to stop talking, but Israel was determined to go on, even if he was thrown out or locked up for it.

"Yes, Your Excellency," he said, "I agree that they are reliable, but if they were asked they would only confirm what I say."

Von Gentz's brow contracted. At that moment he was just a stern old gentleman.

"We're not in the habit of asking questions," he snapped.

"That's not necessary, Your Excellency. The petition of the candlemakers' guild, which was supported by all the other guilds, lies in the archives of the town hall in Otvar. It bears the signatures of all the guild masters and it states quite clearly that the Burgomaster had talked about Jewish mills at the council meeting."

"Can you prove that?"

"It can be ascertained by any Chancellery official who can read Hungarian. All he need do is to read the document in Otvar."

Von Gentz rose to his feet.

"Very well," he snapped. Then he went up to Anselm and put a hand on his shoulder. "Have you seen Fanny dance?" His look, his voice, his bearing were all different now—those of a senile lover.

"Yes, Your Excellency," said Anselm.

"What do you think of her?"

"She's very beautiful."

"Very beautiful? Why, she's phenomenal. She's unique, the one and only since women have gone on the stage. Vienna ought to be proud and happy to have her."

Down in the street Anselm turned on Shayeh.

"I told you not to argue with him! You almost spoiled everything."

"I was patient enough," said Shayeh indignantly. "What could I do? Ought I to have flattered the old cynic, as you did? The Jew is not human. He must not feel human and must not intervene in human affairs where his own skin is at stake. You know what they mean by it."

"I do. But it's no use arguing with them. They always have the last word. Fortunately, Israel was wiser. He understood what Gentz meant when he said that the Jews bought and sold everything and proved everything." Then turning to Israel: "You too made one mistake. You ought not to've talked about clean hands. He doesn't like that. He's thoroughly corrupt himself. You've no idea what this Fanny is costing my father. And he gets nothing out of it. He's never even seen her dance."

Anselm had reverted to his gay-dog manner. He invited both the others to supper. Shayeh refused, saying that he had lost too much time already, but Israel accepted. When he returned to the Oesterreicher home late at night, Shayeh was still up. He was reading a newspaper and as Israel entered he raised his head and said in a very serious tone:

"I'm worried about you all."

"I'm not," said Israel.

"There's trouble moving down from Russia. It's already reached the Bukovina and Galicia. I'm afraid that it'll come to your place soon."

"What kind of trouble?"

"Asiatic cholera."

"That's an act of God," shrugged Israel. "You can't do anything about it."

"But you can take precautions," said Shayeh. "If it doesn't get to you by the spring you'll be lucky. Because then you'll have a new doctor. Have you got one or two good rooms for a surgery? I want you to get a signboard painted. 'Dr. Alexander Oesterreicher Surgeon.' "

Israel was scarcely listening. He was packing his bag, ready to leave in the early morning. By way of farewell, Shayeh said to him:

"If there's trouble, write me an express letter."

Israel smiled. He had settled everything in the best possible way. There could be no further trouble.

He traveled by the northern mail-coaches, where the roads were better, and five days later he was back home. He went straight to Councillor Csanyi, conveyed Ribary's greetings, then sat down to have a talk.

As he was about to leave, there was a knock on the door. A gentleman with a ruddy complexion, a stiff hat, and a big stick in his hand entered. Had he the honor of addressing Councillor Csanyi? he asked in German.

"Nix daytch," barked Csanyi.

Whereupon the stranger said in excellent Hungarian:

"I'd like to see you alone, sir."

Israel Daygood withdrew. As he reached the door he winked back at Csanyi, as though to say, "This is it."

Csanyi winked back at him.

### LIGHT AGAIN

NOW THAT Sroleh Yomtov was back, everything was different, and the Yellow House became more hopeful again. Shefteli had tried in vain to make the Deputy Burgomaster understand the nature of the town's agreement with the Jews. One day Jeney sent for Yossef and Mme Daygood, showed them an old agreement, and said that on the basis of it the candlemakers' guild was entitled to claim the exclusive right to light the town. Though for the present he did not wish to use compulsion, he strongly advised the Jews to stand aside. Yossef was very scared, but Yiteleh told the Deputy Burgomaster that they could do nothing until her husband returned from his buying tour, but that she would send him along immediately on his return.

However, Israel Daygood was not in a hurry. He spent a day or two resting and discussing things with his workers. On the Wednesday he went to the market square, visited the stalls of the Gentile candlemakers and had friendly talks with Hajtajer and others. Then he went to see Jeney. Jeney produced an agreement dated 1809. Israel produced his own and pointed to a clause under which the Jews were to pay a fine of a hundred florins for every week when they failed to provide the lighting, while if the agreement was broken by the town, the loan of twenty thousand florins became due immediately.

"If we now stop lighting the streets," said Israel, "the town can sue us for breach of contract and get heavy damages."

Jeney scratched the back of his head and said that something ought to be done just the same. Israel Daygood was very amenable.

"We made the agreement with the Burgomaster and the Council. We are prepared to make certain changes if the other party to the agreement desires it. I understand that Burgomaster Lam is on sick leave. He may be back in a week or two."

"What if he isn't?"

"Then I'll come along with my offer."

Israel went home and called his men together.

"For the next fortnight," he said, "there's not going to be any work of any kind here, either in tin, or glass, or leather. Judah, you go to Szalka and Samson and buy up all the tallow you can get in the markets—you'll have all the money you need. Tobias, you'll do the same at Varalja and nearby places. Moysheh, you go to the butchers in Karoly. Yossef, you go and tell your father-in-law. We'll buy up all the tallow in the county. We shall store it in Batiz, not here. We must work quickly and quietly."

The Yellow House was empty for the next fortnight, but for the women and Israel himself. There was a rumor going round that the Jews were preparing to leave the town. There was only one thing to cast a doubt on its truth: Israel made an agreement with the butchers of the town to take all their tallow for two years. It seemed that the Jews were expecting to go on with the lighting after all.

Ambro Lam was still sick, but there had been "a substantial improvement in his condition." Councillor Csanyi said so on the basis of an express letter he had received, no one knew from whom or from where. Daygood called on Jeney again, as promised.

"Burgomaster," he said, "we are prepared to get out of the agreement, provided the guild will take over all our obligations, including the indemnity clause."

Hajtajer was sent for and he came with two other members of the guild. They praised the Burgomaster for his skill, and the Jews for their reasonableness. They had made peace. The following day the lighting of the entire town was already in the hands of the guild. Now that the whole town would have none but guild candles there would be no grumbling about any difference in the quality of the candles.

The change was rather unexpected. Of the eight hundred and fifty lamps barely four hundred were alight. However, one had to allow for initial difficulties. The following day five hundred lamps were burning, on the fifth day, five hundred and fifty. But on Saturday night only three hundred and fifty were burning, and on Sunday night less than two hundred. Never mind, said Hajtajer, there was a temporary shortage with raw material, but it would not last long.

However, the shortage seemed to be permanent. There was no tallow. At the beginning of Christmas week there was only an odd candle burning here and there, while on Christmas Eve the town was plunged into complete darkness. Even lanterns were scarce. The citizens began to grumble and sigh for Ambro Lam and the Jews. Then one fine day Ambro Lam arrived. There was a proposal to illuminate the town that night, but there were no candles: the Jews did not have any, and the guild did not have any. There was little tallow to be had, and what there was was needed for soap. Jacob Antal had brought out a new soap, which he called Health Soap. There was an epidemic in the neighboring countries and one had to prepare against it.

In the first week of the New Year the town was in the grip of a new excitement. On two successive nights, in two different districts, people had been knocked down in the pitch-dark streets. The citizens dared not go out at night. Commissioner Adam de Sarberek sent a stern note to the Council saying that this state of affairs was intolerable. Ambro Lam, who had gone away to convalesce after his "operation" in Pest, was urgently recalled, and under the pressure of public opinion approached the Jews again. For two days the Jews refused to resume lighting the lamps, then they yielded. That evening the streets were bright again, with eight hundred and fifty white candles burning in eight hundred and fifty lamps. The guild gave up the struggle, and they were even glad to escape the contractual fine.

Israel Daygood had won again. The period of disquiet that had cast a shadow over the Yellow House had passed like an evil dream. Yiteleh and Zireleh stood in front of the window gazing out at the lights shining in the square and in the adjacent streets, with silver snowflakes glittering in the new radiance, and they thought with new hope of the spring. To Yiteleh the town now appeared like a huge flower-garden. Zireleh burst into sobs of relief.

"Everything will be all right now, Zireleh," said Yiteleh. "You don't have to be afraid any longer. Our time has come at last."

"If you say so, Yiteleh . . . And if Sroleh Yomtov says so . . . You're so brave."

The evening gathering in the tinsmith's shop was all happiness and gaiety. The talk was no longer about defeats and escapes, but about Jewish successes and victories. If there was not enough material in the recent past, there was plenty in the distant past. There was the heroic Bar Kochba, there were the Maccabis, Samson Haggibor, and King David, who had fought the Philistines for a lifetime and had besieged and taken the fortress of Zion.

"We too are fighting against the Philistines," said Tobias with a roguish light in his squinting eyes. "Only they have no Goliath."

Judah the tinsmith, who had for years lived in a village near Debreczen, which was also a privileged Jewless town, talked about the good Hungarians who liked the Jews because they too were oppressed. The Protestant peasants used to sing about Zion just like the Jews themselves. When there was a drought, or when the gentry had been particularly vicious with them, they used to gather in the open and sing, "Do not despair, O Zion."

"It's a fine song," said Judah. "We sing it as a hymn at table on the Sabbath."

The Friday evening was strangely festive. For once, Israel sang the hymns at table instead of merely humming them, as he had always done. His fine, resonant voice was something of a revelation to Yiteleh, and she joined in with gusto. It was not "Despair not, O Zion" they sang—Judah and his sons were doing that in the next flat—but David's triumphal Psalms and "When we returned to Zion we were like dreamers."

In the morning Yiteleh rubbed her eyes and smiled.

"Sroleh Yomtov," she called quietly.

"Yes, Yiteleh?"

"I was met by two kings."

"What?"

"David and Solomon. I was walking in the royal gardens in Jerusalem. Two kings were coming towards me from the cedar palace with crowns on their heads. I recognized them at once. David had a sword in his hand, Solomon a scepter. They nodded to me and said something that sounded very important, but I couldn't make out what it was."

"You're going to have a baby—a boy," cried Sroleh Yomtov, sitting up in bed.

"You know everything," laughed the girl. "If it's a boy we'll call him David Solomon."

"David Solomon Daygood . . . a fine name. And what if it's twins?"

"Then," said the girl thoughtfully, "we'll call one David and the other Solomon."

Her husband laughed.

All that day Yiteleh went about the house in silence. She thought of her mother, who also behaved like that sometimes. And she thought of her husband's laugh. It was a queer laugh, such as she had not heard from him before. At dinner Sroleh Yomtov looked at her slender neck and the silvery light in her eyes and wondered why she was silent. He tried to make cheerful conversation, but Yiteleh remained monosyllabic for a long time. It was only towards dusk, when the shadows had descended on the house, that she spoke. Her voice was thick, as though she was about to burst into tears.

"You'll hate me, Sroleh Yomtov."

"Hate you? Why on earth—"

"If it's twins."

"Nonsense," said the man, taking hold of her hand. "How could I hate you for trying so hard?"

The girl heaved a sigh and snuggled close to him.


### THE AUSPICIOUS TWELFTH


THERE WERE nine men in the house: Tobias and his two sons, Judah and his two sons, Sroleh Yomtov, Moysheh, and Yossef. So they had a table quorum thrice over, but there was one man lacking to make a prayer quorum.

"Nootah Batlan is only waiting for a word from you," said Tobias to Sroleh Yomtov. "He'd come like a shot."

Israel shook his head. He would not have Nootah, though he did not say why. But in his own mind he had long decided that Nootah with his dirty, patched caftan and his Galician habits would only spoil the ensemble of the Yellow House. And he— Israel—had to consider the Burgomaster more than ever, for the Burgomaster was more prudent and circumspect than ever.

Tobias could not understand Sroleh Yomtov's attitude. After all, this was not a matter of some petty wish or childish caprice, but of the essence of Jewish solidarity and indeed of Jewish survival. They were together in the Yellow House, and working and struggling together for their daily bread. That was important. But was it not even more important that they should also pray together? And they were only one man short.

Tobias's impatience in this vital matter was understandable, and there were excited discussions in the Yellow House about it. But though the excitement soon passed, Simon Dominus and Mailech having unexpectedly turned up and more than filled the gap, the men were not easy in their minds. It seemed to them that Sroleh Yomtov was no longer so sure of himself. He had become cautious and reserved, one might almost say afraid. If Sroleh Yomtov was afraid everyone had cause to be afraid. There were moments when they were almost terrified. Small occurrences which they had not even noticed while they were in the midst of the real struggle now began to loom large, and the Jews were alarming each other with rumors and hearsay.

Ezekiel, the linen draper from Madarasz, had taken a lease of some premises in the Yellow House and had already had discussions with Councillor Csanyi. It was expected that he would not take his stock back to Madarasz at the end of the previous market day. But he had done so and nothing had been heard of him since. What could Ezekiel have learned at the town hall to make him forfeit his deposit? There must be something in the air. The Jew baiters of the chicken market were more vociferous than ever, and there was more anti-Jew talk in the Casino as well. The guilds must be preparing for the decisive attack.

And Nootah Batlan had sent an ominous message. Eleven was

not a propitious number. Eleven meant the stars: the stars signified destiny; and—*cholilah!* (heaven forbid!)—it might be a bad
destiny. Nootah was prepared to complete the congregation to
a round dozen. Twelve meant the twelve Tribes and was the
lucky number of the Jewish conquest of the Promised Land. The
community began to turn superstitious. Yes, they must have a
twelfth man.

On some days, of course, there were twelve at prayer. Jacob
Antal would come in to have a look round at the town branch
of his business; or Elephant the button-maker, or Filpischer the
brushmaker, or Marmelstein the tailor would come in to sniff
around whether they might not start something in the town in
the spring. Lazarovich too came driving in to see what they had
made of his house. He was not very pleased with the yellow
palace and tried to find fault. He said they had no right to use
the old floor-boards for firewood because they were his property.
Also, there used to be a back gate through which he used to bring
in such goods as could not be brought in in the sight of everybody
through the front gate. What did they mean by boarding it up
without his permission? Israel Daygood merely smiled and observed that there had been no gate or anything else there, and he
had therefore considered it advisable to raise a fence. Lazarovich
insisted that there had been a gate, and if there was not, then the
opening itself constituted an entrance. In any case, he said that
the year would soon be up, and according to his recollection, the
rent for the further period was to be two florins per month per
head.

"If that is your recollection," said Israel Yomtov, "then it's
sure to be so."

Sometimes they even had visitors who stayed a night or two.
At the back of the yard in the Yellow House there was a small
guest-room, with a bed, a table, a chair, and a shelf. On the shelf
there was leaf tobacco, some flint, and one or two battered
Hebrew books. If a wandering *bocher* wanted to stay over Sabbath he had to answer only one question: Are you lousy? If the
answer was in the affirmative, he was enabled to de-louse himself,
otherwise he slept in the hay in the loft. Tobias's or Judah's wife

did not launder the sheets and pillow-cases to have them filthied with vermin by any beggar.

Of course, the classic question could not be put to every visitor. For example, Yankel Maggid, the old preacher who spent his life traveling over three empires was received with great reverence, as though he were a great rabbi. He was not a rabbi, nor did he possess qualifying diplomas, and he was familiarly known to the Jews from Vilna to Sarajevo as Yankel Maggid (Yankel the Preacher) or Yankel Bocher (Yankel the Bachelor). But he had one great merit: he had been secretary to the great Preacher of Dubnow. Since the latter's death some twenty years before, Yankel Maggid had carried on on his own account. With his anecdotes, parables, true and fictitious stories, he could make exiled Israel laugh or cry at will. Like his great master he took his parables and similes from real life, resorting to Biblical stories only when he felt that present reality would be too much for his brethren. Yankel Maggid had been to many places, seen and noted many things, and sometimes his preaching seemed to be like the shadow of coming events.

"So long as Jacob is struggling with the angel," he said on that memorable Saturday when he preached in the glazier's workshop, which was the temporary synagogue, "he need not be afraid. Jacob triumphs because truth is with him, and the angel himself realizes it towards dawn. There is only one truth, and it is bound to prevail when both protagonists believe in truth. However, Jacob has to wrestle not only with the angel, but also with Ashmodai, and Ashmodai is more dangerous because he is out to crush truth. When Jacob triumphs, his name is Israel. But when Israel is defeated, his name is Exile. None will believe Exile that truth is with him."

This too was ominous talk. The Maggid had long gone, and his anecdotes and witticisms were scarcely remembered, but the above words stuck. Did the Maggid mean anything special? He must have. The Sons of Jacob must stick together. And there must be twelve of them. Until that figure was reached, they lacked that something that a fighting army must have: unquenchable faith in final victory.

However, this too came to pass in the end. One fine day the

twelfth permanent resident and congregant arrived at the Yellow House, the lucky twelfth. It was not Nootah Batlan, but someone whom none expected, whom none had mentioned, and whom all had been trying to forget: the schnorrer Gimpel Zorech.

He had not come to the Yellow House, did not even know of its existence. Nor did he go to Councillor Csanyi for a permit to live in the town. He had a right to be here, being the first Jew to have lived in Otvar for a whole year without the Council being in the position to say him nay. Gimpel Zorech made straight for his former lodgings, the county jail. He asked for Master Peter Koczor, the warder. He was upset to hear that Koczor had been retired, for he had something to say that could be said to none but Koczor. Then he met Sergeant Ardelan, through whose skill he had been released from prison.

"Well, Gimpel," said the Sergeant. "I suppose you've come for your wool-washing money?"

"No."

"Have you had it?"

"No."

"I thought so. Well, then what have you come for?"

"To be locked up."

"What for?"

"I killed a woman."

"You're drunk, Gimpel."

"I'm not."

"Who was the woman?"

"Beilah Yenteh."

"Who was she?"

"My wife."

"Is she really dead?"

"I'm not sure."

"Then you just gave her a hiding?"

"Yes."

"That's nothing, Gimpel. Everybody beats his wife now and then."

"What if she is dead?"

"Go and see if she is."

"Let the pandours do that."

"Where did it happen?"

"In Trebushan."

"That isn't in this county, is it?"

"No, in Maramoros."

"Then your case belongs to Sziget. Go to the Commissioner there and give yourself up."

Gimpel Zorech could not understand this. They had kept him locked up here for a year because someone else had knocked down a man. Now he himself had knocked down a woman, with this knobby stick that he had in his hand, and they would not lock him up. He went along to find Peter Koczor, who knew more about such matters. He had had many a kick and many a resounding slap in the face from Koczor. However, the ex-warder was more enraged at the sight of his former prisoner than he had ever been in the old days and would gladly have answered him with his fists.

"Damned Jew!" he barked. "You come to jeer at me, hey? Get to hell out of here!"

"But, Master Warder—"

"Get out, I say! Go back to the synagogue that sent you. We've enough trouble with the Jews without you bothering us."

For some time Gimpel Zorech loitered in the street. He was depressed and ravenously hungry. He no longer had any idea to whom to turn. There was a time when they tried to frighten him here with the gallows. He was afraid then, because he had not done anything wrong. But now he had left Beilah Yenteh lying in a pool of her own blood, and she must be dead. She was a bad woman, but she was a woman just the same, and he had no other. It would be best if he were hanged, so that his Yossel, who had seen it all, should take warning and should be different. Gimpel Zorech had been on the road for four days, trudging along determinedly towards the gallows. And he had not eaten at all during those four days, and little on the day of the great conflict. In the end he saw not so much the gallows as the prison with its strict rules—and the kosher food that Yossef and others would bring him from Batiz. This time they'd bring him even more, because they'd learn that he was guilty and wretched, with unspeakable things to face.

Then he caught sight of Yossef in the street and stood staring and rubbing his eyes, thinking that it was not Yossef at all, only the *Daless* playing a cruel joke on him. However, when he saw the figure vanish in a side-street, he ran after it. He no longer cared if they did not put him in prison so long as Yossef took him along somewhere and gave him food.

Yiteleh placed a dish before him and he ate ravenously. He intended to tell her afterwards why he had come to Otvar, but she did not give him a chance. She was very strict with him and he obeyed, just as he had obeyed her mother.

"I'll give you a bucket of hot water with soda," she said. "You'll go into that shed and have a thorough wash. I'll get you some underwear and a pair of boots. You'll stay here and work. You'll get paid, but there's going to be no drink for you either here or at the tavern. Understand?"

"Yes, Yiteleh."

They got a bed ready for him in the guest-room, with pillows and a down quilt and all. But in the morning, when Yossef looked into the room, Gimpel Zorech was not there. He found him in the stable, lying on the floor between the legs of the horses.

"Are you crazy, man?" cried Yossef. "There's a proper bed for you and you come and sleep here?"

"It's better here."

"What if the horses kick you in the eye or smash your head in?"

"That'll be very wise of them," said Gimpel.

Gimpel was stubborn and it was impossible to get him to change his habits. But the main thing was that he did not drink. Also, he was making himself useful round the house, fetching water, chopping wood, feeding the horses. He did not respect the horses because although he lay between their legs they would not kick him, but just raised their hooves, then let them down gently. Gimpel did not converse with the horses the way he had done with Erdy's cow. That cow was different; she understood him. Horses were strange to him; they understood none but *goy* talk.

Gimpel was prepared to do anything that he was asked to do, including participation at prayers as the tenth man when there happened to be only nine available. But he was very quiet and did not talk to anyone, making neither friends nor enemies. He did not even curse, though cursing had been a favorite pastime with him before. In time he was entrusted with more responsible work: the lighting of the lamps on the river-bank, for the work was too much for Matthew and his wife. Gimpel Zorech loved his candles and used to talk to them. Sometimes the boys in the street would follow him about, trying to overhear what he was muttering as he lighted the candles. But they could not catch or understand anything, because his mutterings were in Yiddish.

"I put out one, I light one . . . I put out one, I light a hundred . . . So that Yossel should see what it is to be a man. . . ."

The people in the Yellow House were beginning to regain their peace of mind.

True, there had been a row in the chicken market recently, apart from the nightly ones. On a Friday morning the wives of Tobias and Judah went out to buy some birds for the Sabbath. Being unable to find what they wanted, either as to quality or as to price, they walked on. Whereupon a big market woman with a pockmarked face started to abuse them, so that the whole place resounded to her screechy voice. What did these Jew-women mean, fingering and squeezing every chicken and duck in the market, then going off without buying! If they didn't like it here, let them go to Jewland! Tobias's wife, being a timid little woman, tried to slink away, but Judah's wife was not one to run away from a sharp exchange, and she gave as good as she got, saying that she took her money where she liked and was entitled not to buy goods that were not up to her requirements. Thereafter the peasant women refused to sell her anything. "Look at them," they cried. "You let the Jews in and they bite your head off." Yiteleh had to go down herself, with Moysheh, otherwise there would have been no fowls for the Sabbath.

However, this was a trifling affair and was soon forgotten. There were some important things afoot. Elias, the dyer from Hodasz, came along, selected a workshop for himself in the yard, and agreed with Israel on the rent. He would have liked to move in at once, but he was not satisfied with the water, saying that the water of the well in the yard was too hard for his purposes. Israel said he would try and find soft water, and the winter was not yet over when he started to dig. At a depth of fifteen ells his men struck water. Israel tasted the water, then had the hole filled in and started digging at another spot. Twenty ells down, under a layer of sand, they found sweet water seeping through from the river. That was a great event in the town, which had scarcely any drinking water in the built-up part. They fenced the well round and fitted it with a wheel. The other well with the swape was kept on to water the horses.

In the corner shop the carpenters were hard at work, getting it ready for the grocery and general store of Jonas Ellenbogen, which was to open in the late spring. The cheery din of the saws and hammers remained cheery despite the continual sneezing of Henrik Wallon, which could be heard from the far end of the market square (seven hundred paces away). "His nose is made for sneezing," said Yossef. "It's just like a red capsicum." The men laughed, just as if the remark had been made by Israel himself, or at least by Yiteleh.

What matter if Ezekiel did hesitate? Mailech wished he would give up the lease altogether. The shop was long and narrow, but there was ample space for a counter and for many, many customers. One could not dream of anything better. True, Mailech was only fourteen, but he could go into partnership with Mendel, Avram Kolb's son, who was already nineteen. They both knew all about linen goods and headkerchiefs, and Mailech already had a capital of nearly a hundred and sixty florins. It made Yiteleh laugh to look at her lanky young brother and to think that he had already tramped all over the country with a pack of ribbons, headkerchiefs, and combs on his back. She remembered the time when Mailech had a capital of only fifty-seven kreuzers, made by trading.

Simon Dominus was a gay bachelor. Despite his restless nature, he now decided to settle down. There was a tiny shop in the Yellow House, no bigger than a shop window. That was what it really was. Dominus put himself on display there, with his tools and eyepiece, and pedestrians used to pause and gaze at him as he fumbled with the delicate mechanisms. He needed no signboard. The townpeople soon got to know where the watchmakers' shop was.

However, there were far bigger propositions afoot. During the thaw the river Szamos had overstepped its banks and part of the town was still flooded. Israel Daygood had made an offer to the Burgomaster to build a protective embankment, and negotiations were now proceeding. It would cost a great deal of money and would take five or six years. The Jews were prepared to provide the money; it was up to the town to let them have the years in which to complete the work. If they succeeded with this project, new avenues of enterprise would open up for the Jews. And why shouldn't they succeed? When Israel Daygood took a thing in hand. . . .

The Jews now relied on Israel without any reservations. They had realized that he had been right as regards Nootah Batlan too. True, Nootah Batlan was the first to see the real aim, the conquest of Jericho, with a prophetic vision, but wasn't it an old truth, that prophets never enter the Promised Land? Besides, Tobias was a better reader at the synagogue than the unpractical Nootah. On busy days, as on market days, and whenever there was much to do in any direction, he speeded up the services, making up for it on quiet days, when he led the congregation more slowly, compensating his deficiencies as a vocalist by greater fervor. Moreover, Tobias had now cooled down and had acquired a certain balance. Intent on the loftier considerations, and forthright to the point of rudeness, now that the *minyan* was there, together with the auspicious twelfth, Tobias was the first to realize the purposiveness of Israel's plans.

"The House of Jacob cannot live in darkness," he once said to a group gathered outside his workshop, which was used as a temporary synagogue, "just because it is surrounded by a ring of enemies. We can only have peace of mind if there's light. On the other hand, better roads are good for trade, and the more agile get ahead in the race. Of course, this does not mean that we should press forward everywhere. If you always win you make more and more enemies, and we need friends. So we must think not only of our own prosperity, but also of the interests of the others. Then gradually they'll come to like us."

On another occasion the glazier said:

"Sroleh Yomtov has seen to three things: To give us light,

to create good communications, and to show that our people are useful to the rest of the world. His purpose is mutuality, security, friendship."

It sounded like a codification, the first law of the Yellow House.

PERIL FROM THE NORTH

THE PERIL came towards the end of spring. It came from the North, like all perils, as the prophet Jeremiah described in his great vision of the seething pot. It came from Galicia. It was not the invasion of Jews, against which the county's Deputy had so often warned the people, but the Asiatic scourge against which no one had warned or prepared the people.

Death stalked the roads. And once he had set foot in a region he stayed. The country was filled with terror and wailing. All who could manage it fled to the South or in any other direction; those who could not, tried to find someone to blame. The peasants in the villages said that their masters had poisoned the wells before they themselves had fled to safety, so that people should be weakened and not have the strength left to fight for their rights. The people of the towns blamed the dairy produce and the vegetables supplied by the peasants from the villages.

In Otvar it began in the River Street. One Monday Mme Sule told a neighbor woman, Mme Kiss, that her husband had got severe indigestion from Sunday's stuffed cabbage, though she had put cream into it, and he simply loved it that way. The beef she put into the stuffing must have been off, and perhaps the cream hadn't been quite right, either, and she had said so to her milkman. Four days later Martin Sule was buried. A week later the neighbor woman's husband also died, although she had taken no risks with meat or cream and had given him boiled beans with vinegar sauce on that Monday. However, she made the mistake of telling him the cause of the neighbor's illness, and as he was eating the beans he kept thinking of bad stuffed cabbage and was so nauseated that he was taken sick himself. Mme Kiss was so upset that she followed her husband into the grave within three days.

Other tragic cases occurred in all parts of the town. People would complain of stomach-ache and intestinal trouble, and a few days later they were dead. In the area near the inlet they buried five people in one day and the citizens were getting scared. Dr. Pfirsich blamed the criminal negligence of the Council. He had for years been calling attention to foul ditches, gutters, and cesspools, and to the danger of swampy inlets, pointing out that it was a matter of factual observation that epidemics usually occurred in the vicinity of stagnant and foul water.

It seemed that the Council was beginning to realize its sins of omission. A special meeting was called, and there was a violent debate between Burgomaster Lam and his small group on the one hand, and the majority of the Council on the other. The leader of the majority, Councillor Bakoc, said that if the Jews had really wanted to serve the interests of the town, they ought to have applied for admission much earlier, at least eight or ten years before. Now their services were no longer required. Lam contended that it was precisely the calamity that had come upon the town that had demonstrated the usefulness of Israel Daygood's offer of two months ago to drain the dead inlet of the river and fix the course of the river by means of embankments.

Councillor Gindel was also with the Opposition. He too was of the opinion that the Burgomaster was too late with his Jews. He posed the question what was going to happen if the Jewish artisans worked under more favorable conditions than the Christian artisans. For example, the dyers belonging to the guild were working with hard water from their wells, and had water fetched from the river only for the finest work, because it was difficult and expensive. Now Israel Daygood had got soft water for the Jewish dyer. Should not the Jew Daygood be compelled to bore suitable wells in the yard of each Christian dyer before the Jewish dyer was allowed to settle in the town?

This proposal was supported by Councillor Poncikter. He had heard that a Jewish weaver was also intending to come to Otvar, and he was already working with machinery. It might happen

that while the worthy Christian weavers and their journeymen
worked eighteen hours a day over their handlooms, the Jew
would be sitting about smoking his pipe and slave-driving his
Christian workers.

"The law of the land," said Councillor Poncikter with a rising
inflection, "makes it possible for us to defend ourselves against
the Jews. The Synod of Szabolcs, which sat during the reign
of King St. Ladislaus, forbade a Jewish employer to employ
Christian labor. Similarly, the Golden Bull—"

Burgomaster Lam interrupted to remind the speaker that the
special meeting was called not to discuss the Jewish question,
but to find ways and means of combating the epidemic that was
taking an increasing toll.

"The Jewish epidemic is no less dangerous," cried Councillor
Poncikter. "It's got a certain strong Burgomaster before this."

Ambro Lam made a contemptuous gesture and returned to
the matter in hand. He read a memorandum from Dr. Pfirsich,
stating that the most urgent task was to isolate the sick in special
huts, that being in accordance with the best practice in foreign
countries. The big shed in the haymarket could be converted
and a hut could also be erected on the Promenade. Jacob Shefteli
was prepared to provide timber free of charge. This offer was
received by the Opposition with some suspicion.

The Reverend Gulyacs, amidst the consternation of the majority, reported that while administering the last rites to one of
his parishioners, he noticed a framed blessing hanging on the wall
and it was made by the Jew Tobias. What right had the Jew
to deal in blessings and icons and fill the homes of our suffering
brethren with them in these grave days?

"I must add," said the reverend gentleman in a voice trembling
with indignation, "that the text of the blessing was printed by
the Jewish printer in Karoly!"

This gave rise to an impassioned debate, which did not end
until late in the evening. The grocer Jonas Ellenbogen, the linen
draper Nadler, the watchmaker Dominus, and the peddler Mailech, were all dragged in. They also talked about the way the
candlemakers' guild had been outwitted, about the grievances of
Henrik Wallon and other shopkeepers, and generally about the

discontent prevailing among the citizens. The epidemic was not mentioned again until the end of the meeting, when Councillor Rekettye proposed that when the epidemic had passed (for it would pass whether they did anything about it or not), the Council should order a census in order to find out to what extent the number of Jews had increased while that of the native population had decreased.

The prominent citizenry in general adopted a similar attitude. The Casino was already taking a newspaper, and they knew that the epidemic came from Galicia. But that was where the rabbis with their big beards came from, bringing the terrible disease with them on the heels of their kneeboots. Amid all the confusion there was no one to supervise their comings and goings. It was only on the threshold of the Yellow House that they wiped the mud and filth off their boots. Besides, was it not intolerable that the Jews should keep a doctor all to themselves—a doctor for eighteen persons, when there were only eight doctors in the whole town?

Who were the Galician rabbis with the big beards? Nootah Batlan came along to the Yellow House with *kameas*—little triangular linen bags smelling of ginger, aniseed, myrtle, camilla, mint, and centaury, and containing a section of garlic and a piece of parchment bearing a mystic inscription in Hebrew. Such amulets might have been offered by a wandering rabbi or two as well, but by then every inhabitant of the Yellow House had one, even Matthew the lamplighter and his wife Erzsi. They wore it day and night on their bare chests, because it did not act otherwise.

Sholem, with his flowing beard, had also come in now and then, always bringing something towards the children's domestic equipment. The last time he unloaded from the cart a lovely blue-painted cradle, a little masterpiece carved from a single block of wood which was much admired by passersby. It was painted with white and mauve flowers on the sides, and a kid with goggly eyes at the head. Yiteleh received it with cries of delight, while Zireleh laughed and cried, saying that she too would like to have one. Sholem assured her that he was already seasoning a block for it. It would be carved by the peasants of Gyekenyes and painted mauve, to distinguish it from the other cradle. It would be ready for Zireleh by the autumn.

How were things at home and was the epidemic raging there as well? Sholem replied somewhat thoughtfully that all was well. There were occasional deaths in the villages, but then, that was nothing unusual. The bacon was already rancid at this time of the year, and the peasants got indigestion, that was all. But things were better than before. The sick peasants did not come to the inn, and it did not happen that a customer collapsed there.

"You're well off there," said Zireleh and her eyes filled with tears.

"You're all right here too," said Sholem, "and it'll get better. The Above One looks after his flock." He looked round in the house and said to his daughter: "Be careful of *kashruth*. Be careful when salting and soaking the meat. Keep the salting board well scrubbed, and keep the shelves of milky and meaty utensils clean. And never forget, when baking bread, to make the burnt offering by throwing a lump of dough into the fire. Since the destruction of the Temple you women have been our priests. Do everything as your mothers have done, then everything will be all right."

He promised that Malkeleh would come and see Yiteleh soon, and that he himself would of course be present at the *brith* when Yiteleh's son was born. Then he mounted the cart and drove with his empty casks to Batiz.

Among other visitors there were two young rabbis, but they did not wear caftans and had scarcely any hair on their faces. They were visiting the Jewish communities on the instructions of the Chief Rabbi Isaac Frenkel to impress on the Jews the need for extreme cleanliness. Wolf Birnbaum and the grave-faced Meir Perles inspected all the kitchens, and also examined the hands of all the children and asked them whether they washed their hands before taking food according to law. If a child had long nails, the young rabbis pared them with their sharp pen-knives, carefully collecting the parings, wrapping them with a few wood splinters in paper, and throwing them on the fire. Woe to him who lost even the tiniest bit, for he would be sent

back from the Beyond to look for it . . . But there was great
relief once the parings were safely in the fire.

"That's how our sins get burned," explained Meir to the
children.

Wolf found it strange that there should be two wells in the
yard. Yossef explained that the bad water was for the horses.
Wolf said that there was no reason why the horses too should
not drink sweet water. They must move the trough to the other
well, that was all. The hard-water well was not too deep and if
extended and covered over it would serve as a ritual bath. It was
vital that both men and women should take baths in accordance
with the law, especially as the Yellow House was the center of a
community that was likely to grow. Israel Yomtov examined the
terrain to discover how the used bath water could be drained
away and found that the ditch running along the rear of the
house debouched into the river. He decided to start on the ritual
bath as soon as the workmen had finished the hut for the sick.

Meir Perles looked into the cow byre. He stood watching for
a while as Erzsi milked the cow, then he went into the house.

"A Jewish woman must not be lazy," he said sternly. "You must
not leave the cow to a servant. And when you are about to milk
the cow, see that you clean your hands thoroughly with bran
and water, in case you touched meat, fat, or a candle. It's not for
nothing that the Holy Torah says in three different places: 'Do
not boil a kid in its mother's milk.' We must keep milky and
meaty things rigidly apart."

The young doctor who had come from Vienna could say no
more than the two rabbis. Cleanliness, cleanliness! However,
Alexander Oesterreicher was even stricter than they. He was not
content to let the people rinse their hands before taking food,
then dry them with the towel, but insisted that they should use
soap—the carbolic soap produced by Yossef. He was not against
the ritual bath, provided it was kept clean. The washing-up must
be done with boiling water, and even the drinking water must be
boiled first. The water from the new well was all right, for it
came up through a layer of sand and was far enough away from
the stable and the dust heap. But it was best to boil the water,
nevertheless, best to exaggerate cleanliness. No exaggeration was

superfluous, and no precaution was an exaggeration. Meir Perles asserted that the carbolic soap was not kosher. Very well, said the doctor, let the women use bran and water after using the soap.

"We cannot cure," he said. "Only God can do that. But we can try to avert the trouble." And now that Wolf and Meir were arguing with him jointly, he cited Maimonides. "Read what he says. He was court physician to the Sultan of Cairo. He held that prevention was better than cure, and that the organism must be strengthened with water, sunshine, fresh air, exercise, and a proper diet."

"And with fasting and prayer, Shayeh," said Wolf.

"I'm not against occasional fasting, when a person can bear it. And in so far as prayer gives confidence, that too may be a factor in prevention. You can pray as much as you like, but see that you pray well—so that there is no fear left in you. Fear promotes disease."

"We're in the hands of God," said Wolf.

"If God wants to punish Israel," said Meir, "He puts fear into their hearts."

"We're not concerned with Israel," said the doctor vehemently, "at least not with Israel alone, but with everyone else. We either save the world or we don't. If we don't, we'll all perish."

"Don't you believe it, Shayeh," said Wolf. "The world'll survive and we alone'll perish."

"For the multitude of our sins," added Meir darkly.

"And for our stupidity," snapped the doctor.

"Their stupidity," said Wolf.

### THE ANCIENT CURSE

THE YELLOW HOUSE did not know with whom to agree. The doctor was a very important person in these troubled days, but God's messengers were no less so. In any case, the debate did not go on, for Dr. Oesterreicher was too busy with patients, and soon the two young rabbis also departed. However, shortly after, they returned, bringing with them the decisive argument: The aged Rabbi Isaac Frenkel.

It was Thursday, a Torah reading day. Judah's workshop was crowded, the Jews of the surrounding villages, including Batiz, also being present. The Rabbi had ordered a fast and he wore his shroud, as on the Day of Atonement. He led the congregation at prayers and also read the portion of the Torah himself. When he had finished he hurriedly unrolled a considerable part of the scrolls, then he suddenly paused and pointing down at the parchment began to read:

"And it shall be, when thou art come in unto the land which the Lord God giveth thee for an inheritance, and possess it, and dwellest therein . . . And thou shalt go unto the priest that shall be in those days and say unto him, I profess this day unto the Lord thy God, that I am come unto the country which the Lord sware unto our fathers for to give us."

He raised his head from the parchment and stabbed the air with a trembling finger.

"This," he said in a voice hoarse with age, gazing at the community with fierce eyes, "is not the land which the Lord swore unto our fathers. This is the land of Nimrod, the land of Hagar. But you have come here and are living here. And you did not go to the priest to profess unto the Lord God, and did not ask him how to live that your actions should be welcome to the Lord. The Lord made a covenant with you and you have not kept it. You have been foolish and self-opinionated, and vain and conceited. You have despised the teacher and mocked at his teaching. You have counted money in the holy congregation and talked about business. Your daughters have smiled at the sons of Nimrod and your sons have gone after the daughters of Hagar. Thus every word of this *sidrah* that I am reading from applies to you. It speaks of Mount Garizim, where the blessings come from, and of Mount Ebal, which sends curses. Foolish and perverse people, you have chosen Ebal."

There was a shocked silence. All eyes were glued to the aged Rabbi who stood in front of the tinsmith's table, white and impassioned, waving his fists like an angry prophet. He might accuse and condemn like this in general and biblical terms, any-where else, and particularly in his home congregation at Karoly, where for more than a decade indignation against the mockers and the perverse had been accumulating within him. But here the people were thinking of their own sins, of the evil they had done or had been intending to do, and of the good they omitted or neg-lected to do. They had broken the Commandments, infringed the prohibitions. They had committed all the transgressions and sins against society enumerated in the two "Confessions." God's avenging wrath as reflected in the calamity that had come upon the world, meant one thing: that Israel had sinned. It was woe to the world when Israel was sinning. And it was a hundred times woe to Israel, who could never drain the cup of bitterness, be-cause it became filled again and again.

The Rabbi bent over the scrolls again, then he drew himself up, chanting:

"Stand forth, ye who will . . . Stand forth, ye who won't . . . Let the whole congregation stand forth!"

The form of the call was unusual, and the voice reminiscent of the Festival of Grief. Ordinarily, it is an honor to a Jew to be called up before the scrolls of the Law, by his Hebrew name, his titles and, sometimes, the name of his tribe; and he stands reverently while the reader reads aloud a passage from the Portion of the Week. Only twice a year is he reluctant to accept this honor: when the terrible warning of the Mount of Curses is read. At such times the reader makes a general call: "Let him who will stand forth." Usually, it is some miserable wretch of a beggar or some unlearned casual laborer who comes on to the dais for the sake of a small fee; and the reader races through the curses, in order not to offend the ears of the congregation. Now Rabbi Frenkel had broken with this tactful tradition, summon-ing before the Torah the entire congregation, including the reluctant ones; And he read with vehement emphasis, his voice breaking with grief:

"Then the Lord will make thy plagues wonderful, and the plagues of thy seed, even evil diseases of long continuance.

"Moreover he will bring upon thee all the diseases of Egypt, which thou wast afraid of. . . .

"And the Lord shall scatter thee among all people, from one end of the earth even unto the other. . . .

"And among these nations shalt thou find no ease, neither shall the sole of thy foot have rest. . . .

"And thy life shall hang in doubt before these: and thou shalt fear day and night. . . ."

There was probably only one man in the whole assembly who listened to the Rabbi's hard sentences without fear or any other emotion. Gimpel Zorech the beggar, had heard and used so many curses in his life that they produced no effect; the four-thousand-year-old message could make no difference to him. Indeed, it made him grin, because the general call was familiar to him. He had heard it often enough during his years as a wretched wanderer, and had made good money out of it. He had a right to hold up his head as he took the cash and the drinks, for it required courage to have the curses of Mount Ebal read over oneself.

## HEBREW PLAGUE

THE RABBI had gone, but his shadow lingered. There he stood at the back of the tinsmith's shop, his bushy eyebrows, his grey beard, and his shroud gleaming like a white light. The days were full of disquiet, the nights were oppressive. No one in the house had as yet been taken sick, but at the bottom of their hearts the Jews were prepared for everything, to mourn or be mourned. At the conclusion of the gathering on Thursday, Rabbi Isaac had made them recite the *Vidduy*, the death-bed Confession. This brought a certain relief, for now they need not fear that if and when their time came they would lack the strength or the opportunity to make the last confession. But there were graver fears than the fear of death. Rabbi Isaac's Hebrew sentences sounded like bells of doom that rang from the distant past into the future.

Tobias, the most learned man in this company, who was otherwise intolerant in religious matters, was now trying to distract the attention of the others from their inner terror by means of jokes and witticisms. He talked about Lazarovich, who during the reading of the *Vidduy* beat his chest with the greatest penitence, and who, Tobias said, had the lion's share of such sins as inveigling, cheating, stealing, usury. He was the first to kiss the Rabbi's hand. For the Rabbi had not concluded his speech without a crumb of comfort. "Penitence, prayer, and good deeds will avert judgement," he had said. "Reb Leizer," said Tobias, "chose the first two, leaving the third to others. Shefteli has offered a fresh gift of timber, and Mesel put five hundred florins on the Burgomaster's table and gave six casks of wine for the poor among the sick."

However, the effect of jocularity did not last. The atmosphere in the house remained oppressive, and even Dr. Oesterreicher went about with a clouded brow.

"What are you thinking about, Shayeh?" asked Israel Yomtov.

"About the Rabbi's words."

"You too?"

"He quoted the expression 'evil diseases.' In Hebrew that is *cholahim rahim*, isn't it?"

"Yes."

"What's the singular?"

"You know that better than I."

"Well," said Shayeh, "it's *choleh rah*—cholera."

Israel did not understand the little flame that sprang into Shayeh's eyes.

"Look, Shayeh," he said. "I think this is no time for us to brood. Let the sinners repent, and let anyone that has the time pray. We must work."

"I quite agree, Sroleh Yomtov," said the doctor.

The hut in the timber market stood ready, Tobias having finished the windows. Israel sent his people to the villages for bedding. There were plenty of beds, but not enough sheets, pillows, and mattresses. The Jewish women everywhere gave up their surplus, while Yossef Yochanan sent a whole cartload of pottery for the improvised hospital.

Dr. Oesterreicher was rarely seen in the Yellow House now. He did not even come back to sleep there, but furnished a cubicle for himself in the hut and lived there. In the mornings Dr. Pfirsich was in attendance, while Dr. Oesterreicher visited patients round the town. There were so many of them that even eighty-year-old Dr. Goda was on his feet all day. Dr. Oesterreicher drove round in the candle cart, Gimpel Zorech being his driver. Originally, Yossef himself acted as driver, but Zireleh was afraid for him. There was no one to be afraid for Gimpel Zorech, and he himself was certainly not afraid either of the patients or of the disease.

"Gimpel Zorech is a great help," Shayeh would say. "A veritable blessing in these bitter times."

The schnorrer did not realize that he was a blessing. He just went on driving the cart, popping in to the patients, and helping to carry them to the ambulance when they were being taken to the hospital hut. There he sat by the patients, rubbing their feet if they felt numb and cold, and giving them doses of medicine from a big brown bottle which seemed to soothe them. The doctors called it tinctura and sometimes also laudanum, but Gimpel Zorech did not care what the medicine was called. All he knew was that the brown fluid was a help, and sometimes helped the patient out of this earthly wretchedness.

Gimpel Zorech no longer slept in the stable at the Yellow House. At night, when the hut was quiet for an hour or two, he went into the Jewish doctor's cubicle and lay down on the bare floor. It was summer, and the weather was mild. Gimpel Zorech had slept in worse places in his time, including cold ditches by the roadside and that room in Trebushan with that evil woman.

If a patient burst into tears, Gimpel sat by him and tried to comfort him, and if he was afraid he tried to give him courage. He now knew enough Hungarian to say:

"Don't be afraid, brother. If you fall asleep I'll wake you up. So long as Gimpel is alive you're not going to die."

However, Gimpel Zorech insisted on going on with one part of his former work: lamp-lighting. Towards dusk he always grew restless and hastened away to the Yellow House as soon as possible to sling the basket of candles over his back, pick up the ladder and go off to light candles along the river. He kept talking to the candles as he lighted them.

"Nine've gone out . . . I'll light nine . . . Thirty-four are out . . . I'll light thirty-four. A hundred and seventeen are out . . .

I swore they'll live as long as I'm alive . . . Burn brightly, little candles. . . ."

Children in the street put out their tongues at him and threw mud at him. Grown-up pedestrians drew away from him. Gimpel took no notice. Having finished his round, he hastened back to his patients, who were already waiting for him. The way the patients looked at him—just like Erdy's cow—compensated him for everything. Of course, he could cure the cow, but he couldn't cure these people. Why, even Shayeh, who had come straight from Vienna, kept racking his brains and poring over big books. But no matter how hard he thought or studied, he could not find any other medicine but that brown liquid with the pungent smell that made people sleep. And the old doctors did not know of anything better, either.

Gimpel Zorech used to crouch down in a corner and listen agape when the doctors were talking among themselves. He did not understand what they were saying, but he knew that it was something important. The nuns with the white bonnets who were pouring the medicine into bottles probably understood their talk, and so did Master Arvay and Master Csermak, they being barbers, who bled people or put leeches on them when people were not sick in the mass. Just now they only helped to heat the tiles and waited for the doctors to say something clever.

The three doctors, Pfirsich, Goda, and Oesterreicher could only talk about the increasing virulence of the trouble. Goda opined that the disease began with the gall, for *chole*, the first half of cholera, was the Greek for gall. Pfirsich said that the Greek physicians might have been mistaken in their assumption. For whereas at the later stages of the disease the gall also became affected, the primary seat of the disease was in the intestine. Oesterreicher held that the *materia peccans* arrived from the upper digestive passages. What it was no one knew, unfortunately. All that was known was that the course of the disease resembled that of fungus poisoning and that it originated in damp weather and in a damp place. One might draw certain conclusions from this fact, because fungus throve in a damp environment. It was beyond doubt, however, that the Greek word *chole* had no relevance to the disease. Cholera was a Hebrew term, which occurred in the

Old Testament in the plural, showing that it was infectious. The Greek physicians already knew that cholera was contracted via the mouth and the alimentary canal.

Pfirsich liked this explanation. Dr. Goda merely h'mmed and while wiping the sweat off the back of his neck with a large checkered handkerchief, he observed:

"In ancient times the chief seat of the infection must have been in the swampy regions of India. It was from there that it must have got into the land of the Jews."

The medical discussion continued the following day in the hairdressing shops of Arvay and Csermak, the former's shop being near the town hall, and the latter's near the Casino. In the course of lathering and shaving, Master Arvay reported to Councillor's Gindel and Bakoc and to Revenue Inspector Jeney that it had been discovered at last where the dread disease came from. "From the land of the Jews, Master Councillor. Yes, sir. The little Jew doctor blurted out that even the name of the disease was Hebrew." Jeney smiled, or performed what went for a smile in those bitter times, and observed that the Jews had not had a land of their own for a very long time. But Councillor Bakoc asserted that the place was still there, somewhere in Asia.

Master Csermak's customers had it in greater detail. Asiatic cholera was a Jewish disease, which had been taken by mysterious rabbis from Palestine to Russia, Poland, and Galicia, the rabbis having gone there ostensibly to collect money from the Jews. The old suspicion of the gentlemen of the Casino that the Jews had something to do with the epidemic seemed to be proved. For the present this was no more than the gossip of depressed people. Thanks to the counter-action of Drs. Pfirsich and Goda, and to the work of enlightenment of the group of members in the entourage of the poet Kolcsey, who read foreign as well as Hungarian papers, the rumor survived only in the card-room. When a man was losing, as often happened, he would exclaim, "the Jewish plague again!" or, "The curse of the rabbis!"

All this scarcely affected the epidemic, which was still spreading. The Shefteli group was already offering the Council timber for the third hospital hut, which was for a badly hit area along the river. The Burgomaster praised the Jews at a Council meeting for their generosity and for toiling and making gifts of money, timber, and bedding regardless of the faith of the sufferers. Even a poor beggar like Gimpel was doing everything in the public service. The Yellow House was happy to hear about this recognition of Jewish devotion, which was both useful and necessary in those agitated times. They told Gimpel Zorech that the Burgomaster had praised him. He pursed his lips and shrugged. He said he was only doing what he was told. He could not explain by whom. "What *they* tell me," was how he put it. "They" were mysterious powers which the schnorrer himself probably did not understand.

For the rest, the Burgomaster's fine speech aroused no echo. None was interested in the merits of the Jews, and none could have been persuaded to like them or even respect them. The people refused to believe even their own priests, especially when they were told that they had to die because they had sinned. It was not they that were guilty but someone else. It would come out one day who that someone was. Truth will come out.

"Do you know where the trouble comes from?" a burgher would say to another.

"From the North, from Galicia," the other would say.

"And who brings it here?"

"The Galicians."

"Who are they?"

"Why, who do you think they are?"

In the evening neighbors were talking over the fence:

"Do you know where it comes from?"

"From the North."

"The river lies north."

"Well, that's where it comes from."

"Then you've heard?"

The ladies were talking in the chicken market:

"It comes from the river, my dear, from the river."

"I know, Mistress Kontros. That was where it started."

"Do you know when?"

"About six weeks ago."

"And do you know who brought it?"

"Do you, Mistress Kontros?"

"Well, who could have brought the Jewish plague but the Jewish candlemaker?"

"You don't say, Mistress Kontros!"

"I'm only telling you what I know!"

A woman poultry dealer said to another:

"The Jewish lamp-lighter has put an enchantment on the candles."

"I heard something like that myself."

"That hairy beggar whispers a blasphemous curse while he's lighting the candles."

"How awful! How awfully awful!"

"They send him from the Yellow House to curse the town."

"The devils!"

There were those who knew even more. They said the curse against the Gentiles was from the most secret of Talmud books which was guarded by the rabbis in Palestine. And if the epidemic abated, messengers of that secret council would bring another still stronger and more effective formula of the ancient curse. Until now no one knew what Gimpel was muttering. But one evening the Reverend Gulyacs stood under the lamps and heard it—every word. The Reverend Gulyacs understood Hebrew. He had found a copy of the secret book in the Bishop's library and had found the curse that brought the plague.

What an incredible horror! Soon it was just a horror, and not at all incredible. Who would have believed that Master Gyapjas the candlemaker, who was such a fine upstanding man, would collapse in the street and die? Who would have thought that Adolf Wallon, the sober and thrifty brother of Henrik Wallon, would go to bed on his return from the shop in the evening and be found dead in his bed in the morning? But none of the Jews had died so far! The Jews wanted to exterminate every able-bodied person, so that they should be undisputed masters of the town. They were already bringing along their brethren from all over the place.

The people began to recall the warning of the candlemaker's guild. There was something wrong with the Jewish candles after all. They had mixed something into the tallow that was harmful and injurious to the health of the citizens. That was why they were white as chalk and that was why they burned with such a bluish ashen light. At that time the citizens had smiled at the warning because the Jewish light had mesmerized them. They smiled too soon. They ought to have listened to Master Hajtajer, Poncikter, Henrik Wallon, and the other selfless Magyars. And they ought to have listened to the very reliable men of the Poultry Market Inn. Ex-Warder Peter Koczor told his version of the story of the death-cell candles. The Jewish candlemaker sold them and took them back half burned. He had melted down the murderers' candles and mixed them with the others. The evil eyes of the two Rumanian bandits were looking down on the burghers from the Jewish lamps. Now the burghers could see for themselves. The grease that dropped into the dust and on to the pavement planks were plague drops, the excrement of the murderous candles. Anyone stepping on them was lost, together with his entire family. And anyone that even happened to glance at them had better recite a Paternoster in a hurry. "Deliver us from the evil Jew-candles." The old women all knew the changed line. As they recited it they crossed themselves and stepped off the pavement planks. It was safer to walk in the mud and in the gutter, for the mud and the gutter were free from the plague. Even the children had heard about this and they were pleased to be free to paddle in the filthy water. But their pleasure was not complete, because they had to avoid the spots of grease that lay at the base of the lampposts, continually chanting, in a scared tone, the anti-enchantment couplet:

> *Evil spell, evil spell,*
> *Get thee back to the devil's hell.*

However, all the chanting in the world could not get rid of the evil, which continued to claim more and more victims. The citizens of Otvar were in extreme terror.

THE LAST BATTLE

IT BEGAN on the Thursday morning in the poultry market.

Judah's wife returned from market with her shopping basket empty, her headkerchief awry.

"I had enough of this in Samson," she cried angrily. Samson was the village where she and her husband had experienced the fight with the cattlemen. She had a brief argument with her husband, at the end of which he said:

"Very well, we'll go to Batiz for the Sabbath."

"This minute, Judah," said the woman. "I'm not going to stay in this place another day."

Dominus called Mailech into his tiny shop and said:

"Look here, I've got watches, rings, and precious stones. If you like you can come with me to Kallo. The people there are more decent, and they're used to Jews."

Mailech did not feel like exchanging certainty for uncertainty. He had already worked it out that he was going to peddle J soap and flannel body-belts. There was a demand for both. He helped Dominus to pack and saw him off on the noon mail-coach. On his way back he suddenly realized how unfriendly the street was. People shook their fists at him, called him names, and one young man standing outside a bootmaker's stall even spat at him. Mailech tried to convince himself that these people were the same as before, and that it was he that was upset. Yet the thought that he was without his old friend filled him with alarm.

In the evening there was a great commotion in the town. Matthew and Erzsi went round lighting the lamps in their part of the town. There was comparative quiet there. But in the vicinity of the river, which was Gimpel Zorech's beat, crowds of people were gathering round every lamp-post, waiting for him. Now they knew what he was going to say. They must stand still and be very quiet and strain their ears. It was enough if they caught some such word as Jehovah or Zeboath.

The sky was overcast and darkness was falling fast, yet the Jew

did not come. On other evenings he had finished by this time, now
he had not even begun. Perhaps he got wind of the trouble awaiting him and would not come at all. Actually, there was no reason
why he should, seeing that he had already performed the task
with which his brethren had entrusted him. It was not necessary
for him to come again. For six weeks he had been climbing his
ladder just like an executioner, he having lived in the shadow
of the gallows for such a long time. And each evening he had
been sending words of death out of the secret Book of Curses
towards all parts of the town, with a demoniacal grin on his face
in the light of the diabolical candles. It was an intolerable thought.
The crowd would wait no longer.

"To the Jewfort!" cried someone.

The cry was taken up by others and the crowd began to move.
They started slowly, then quickened their pace, then they ran.
They ran across the dyers' market, across the poultry market,
over the planks and cobbles of the big market square, and as they
ran they were joined by groups of people suddenly emerging
from the side-streets.

They approached the Jewish citadel of Otvar from several
directions, and soon the big corner house was attacked by howling
mobs on both sides.

The gate was locked and barred, as the mob had expected.
Conscious of their guilt, the Jews had barricaded themselves.
The gate would not yield either to the strongest shoulders to be
found among the mob or to the cudgels which some of them had
brought with them.

So they loosened the pavement planks for battering-rams and
also the cobbles of the roadway. The cobbles were not set yet and
yielded to the fingers of the enraged mob. Somewhere, the crash
of glass could be heard.

"Hi, Jew! Hi, Daygood! This is your last day on earth . . . Hi,
Jacob! . . Hi, Judah . . . Rabbis! . . Robbers! . . Grafters! . .
Poisoners! . . ."

The Jew Daygood stood in a window, watching them pry loose
the pavement planks and the heavy beams underneath. Then the
gates of the journeymen bootmakers' hostel opposite burst open
and the journeymen charged howling into the fray.

"Prise it up! . . Wait, I'll get an axe! . . The Jew-sluts must have planks to walk on!"

Israel gazed across the square. It was high time the haiduks of the town or the pandours of the county came along. But they were not coming. Only howling men and women were coming from all directions.

"Murderers!" they cried. "Thieves! . . Go back to Palestine! . . Go back to Galicia! . . Plague spreaders! . . ."

Israel spoke over his shoulder:

"Yiteleh, wrap up the baby, and take the big shawl . . . Zireleh, get ready. Go down to the tinsmith's shop. Tell Judah to try to slip out at the back and run along to the Burgomaster. And tell Tobias to go to the Pandour Commissioner."

"Judah left the town this morning," came the reply.

"What of his sons?"

"The whole family went."

"Where's Tobias?"

"He was here a minute ago. He ran down to his wife . . . Zireleh says that Tobias has sent his wife away with his boys. She was crying and the boys helped her over the fence at the back."

A stone crashed through the window and came down among the glass and porcelain on the sideboard.

"Yossef," said Sroleh Yomtov urgently, "harness the two horses. Tell Matthew to pull down the rear fence a couple of planks wide, so that the cart can get through. Mailech, don't mess about with your stock now. Go and help Matthew."

He put new candles into the candlestick illuminating the room. Then he walked to and fro past the window to draw the mob's fire and cover the retreat. The tumult increased and there was now an admixture of shrill female voices:

"They want light, the dirty Jews! . . They made us pay for the candles with which they cursed us! . . They bring a cradle for the Jewess and a coffin for us! . . Give it to them! . . Hit them on the head! . . ."

Tobias came into the room, his face so white that it was almost luminous.

"If you stay, I stay," he said vehemently.

"Go after your family!" cried Sroleh Yomtov, seizing him by the hand. "We'll meet later. Peace be with you!"

He hustled him out of the room. As the glazier looked back there was a brightness in his squinting eyes. Perhaps it was only the flame of anger, because they were already battering at the gate with the beams from the pavement.

Matthew had already picked off part of the fence and Tobias could climb over easily. He ran across the gardens towards the timber market. If he could shout, his sons might still hear him. But could he? They were already beginning to move round to the back of the house. And they were still coming along from all directions. Those who were crowded out by the attackers at the house were going round to the street lamps with sticks and cudgels, smashing the lamps. The cudgels were stronger than the light. The town grew darker and darker. The mob were dashing along and howling:

"Down with the lamp-posts! . . Spit on the light! . . Trample it into the mud! . . We don't want any death-cell candles! . . Stones, stones! . . Smash it! . . The Jews made us pay for the plague! . . ."

The crash of glass, at other times such a pleasant sound to the ears of a glazier, now sounded like the demented music of Ashmodai. Everything that he had helped to build up was now collapsing. These people did not want any light.

Bounding across a ditch, Tobias stumbled over a body. He bent down to have a look at it and gave a cry of pain:

"Praise be to the just Judge!"

It was Gimpel Zorech, still convulsively gripping the ladder. He was doubled up. He must have died a painful death. What to do with the body? Tobias asked himself. He could not take it back to the Yellow House now. He would send a cart for it from Batiz before the night was out and Gimpel would be buried according to the laws and customs of Israel. At the edge of the grave Reb Lamach would beg his pardon for any insult or offense that the House of Jacob might have committed against him, and Nootah Batlan would recite the *Kaddish* over him.

Tobias changed his direction, bounding along towards the German part of the town and pausing now and then to listen. The sound of an approaching cart!

"They've got out!" muttered Tobias joyfully. And with a great relief in his heart he ran on.

There were five adults and one baby in the body of the cart, and Matthew was driving. Yiteleh was nursing the baby, and hush-hushing to it. Then she turned to Sroleh Yomtov:

"We must find Shayeh and Gimpel Zorech. We can't leave them here."

Sroleh Yomtov shook his head.

"They must stay, Yiteleh. They're doing vital work." He had a grave look and there was determination in his voice. "I'll come back too as soon as I've put you down somewhere. I've already started to build the third hospital hut."

"They hate you worst of all," said his wife quietly. "Because you're so strong."

Zireleh leaned over the side of the wagon and began to tremble all over.

"There's someone lying in the ditch. There's a dead man lying in the ditch."

"There's no one there," said Yossef, drawing her to himself. "You must be careful, Zireleh, very careful. You mustn't get ideas when you see a log of wood in a ditch."

"What if they come after us?" wailed Zireleh. "What if they come after us? Batiz is not far away."

"They won't."

Mailech did his best to introduce a note of gaiety. He played the tune of "Fear not, my servant Jacob" on his flute. When he saw that this produced no effect, he pocketed his flute and began to talk.

"This is nothing to us, Yiteleh, what?" he bragged. "We had to flee before, didn't we? We slept in the cart for a week and stayed a night on Gypsy Field. And when the peasants set fire to the house, we fled into the night, scarcely knowing where we were going."

Yiteleh pressed her baby close to her bosom and said:

"But this time we have somewhere to go."

The tumult was now far behind and almost inaudible, and the cart was already rolling along on the road.

"Drive to the Shingled Inn at Lapfalva," said Sroleh Yomtov to Matthew.